THE
50 GREATEST
MYSTERIES
OF ALL TIME

compiled by
Otto Penzler

PHOENIX
BOOKS

ISBN: 1-59777-550-9
Library of Congress Cataloging-In-Publication Data Available

Printed in the United States of America

Phoenix New Millennium Inc.
9465 Wilshire Boulevard, Suite 315
Beverly Hills, CA 90212

10 9 8 7 6 5 4 3 2

For Elizabeth,
whose smile brightens my life

CONTENTS

INTRODUCTION

OTTO PENZLER

TTEMPTING TO COMPILE ANY list of the best of anything is inevitably an exercise doomed to failure. Quite naturally, and properly, the immediate response on seeing the phrase "the best of" is, "Oh, really? Says who?"

Well, in this instance, says me, although I will immediately begin to provide a list of cop-outs and qualifiers. And I'll also concede that, next week or next year, the list might be a little different.

Having put forward the notion that this is not a mathematical exercise but a subjective one, I'll also say that I've been reading mystery short stories for more than four decades and really like the form, which in many ways is, as John Dickson Carr once noted, the natural form of the mystery story. I've read thousands of ordinary stories, and thousands of bad ones, and also many good ones. Some have stayed in the mind for years (always a strong indication that it is something special), just as great novels and motion pictures have.

Among the stories I've picked for this volume is "The Red-Headed League," which was my introduction to Sherlock Holmes. I was about ten years old at the time, and I thought it was the best thing I'd ever read, which to a voracious reader is saying something. I'm not sure it's a better story than a half-dozen other Sherlock Holmes

stories, but it had to be included because of the magical moments it gave me. The story was in an anthology and picked off the shelf pretty much at random as I was attempting to read the entire library at the time. It was begun in school during a 45-minute class known as "library," in which the entire class left its classroom and walked down to the school library. In this class, we were taught how to open a book, how to take care of a book, how to find the proper section of the library so that we could find what we wanted on our own, without having to ask the teacher or librarian for help. Then we were allowed to read whatever we wanted to for the remainder of the period. I remember being instantly drawn into the gaslit era and being entirely baffled by what was going on, but totally convinced that this strange genius, Sherlock Holmes, was up to the job. I was horrified when the class came to an end before I could finish the story and find out what happened. I had to wait until the next day and my excitement at pulling the book from its shelf was barely containable. The solution was so brilliant and so perfect that I glowed in its memory for a long time. Is it any wonder, as I look back at it now, that I became a member of the Baker Street Irregulars some years later and still maintain a great interest in and affection for the greatest of all detectives?

I admit I'm a sucker for surprise endings and brilliant little twists that cause that satisfying moment when one realizes what transpired, or who did it, or how they were caught—or how they managed to get away with it. As a result, there is a greater number of stories here than one might expect with that wonderful "gotcha" moment, when all becomes clear in the last sentence or two.

It is likely that my favorite story in the book is one of the least known. Barry Perowne's "The Blind Spot" is a perfect crime story and a perfect locked room mystery all in one, as well as a riddle story that tops Frank Stockton's "The Lady or the Tiger?" While we never learn in the Stockton tale whether a crime has been or will be committed (and it remains the most famous riddle story of all time) we know it in Perowne's masterful puzzler.

There are some excellent stories that did not make it into this volume and, like unhappy families, there is a different story to explain each.

First, I decided for this volume to restrict an author to a single appearance. It would have been easy to have used five or six stories by Stanley Ellin, for instance, arguably the best American mystery writer of short stories in the twentieth century. I finally picked his most famous story, but there are several others equally compelling. And who could argue that there should be more Sherlock Holmes stories, or others by Ruth Rendell and Patricia Highsmith? It would have been a no-brainer to include Harlan Ellison's other Edgar-winning story, "The Whimper of Whipped Dogs," and Melville Davisson Post should have been represented by Uncle Abner but I just love this Randolph Mason adventure so much that I couldn't leave it out.

Second, some stories didn't get into the collection because the authors' agents were simply too greedy. Hence, no stories by Agatha Christie, John Dickson Carr, Cornell Woolrich, or Damon Runyon, all of whom are among my favorite authors of short fiction. The agents apparently thought they were dealing for the next big-budget movie instead of an anthology with a limited budget. Go and read "Witness for the Prosecution" by Christie, "The House in Goblin Wood" by Carr, "Rear Window" by Woolrich, and anything from *Guys and Dolls* by Runyon, as they should have been included here and you're sure to enjoy them.

Finally, there are wonderful stories not included here because of technical difficulties, such as publishers refusing to allow stories to be reprinted or recorded on audiotape because they prefer to have exclusivity, or agents being unable to clear rights in time for this book's deadlines.

Watch for the second volume of *Greatest Mysteries* and many of these terrific stories will be collected there.

But listing those stories that are not present should in no way diminish the pleasure to be found on these pages. The only criterion for inclusion was excellence and every one of the following fifty stories easily met it. The time spectrum covers everything from the first genuine detective story, Poe's "The Purloined Letter" (1844), to the very contemporary crime tale by Elmore Leonard, "Karen Makes Out" (1996).

It is expected that you will disagree with some of these selections. Inevitably, you will prefer a favorite story to one selected for this anthology. And that is as it should be. But I nonetheless guarantee that you'll enjoy this anthology as much as any short story collection you're ever likely to read. These are the greatest stories by the greatest writers in the history of mystery fiction. If you fail to enjoy *that,* take a nap and come back later!

THE PURLOINED LETTER

EDGAR ALLAN POE
(1809–1849)

One of the greatest, most influential, and enduring poets and writers of the nineteenth century, Poe is credited, correctly, with inventing the detective story as we know it. His three tales about C. Auguste Dupin provided all the essential elements of the classic mystery: brilliant and eccentric detective, baffled sidekick, blundering police officials, clues, red herrings, alibis, even the least likely suspect. He is the father of it all.

T PARIS, JUST AFTER DARK ONE gusty evening in the autumn of 18—, I was enjoying the twofold luxury of meditation and a meerschaum, in company with my friend C. Auguste Dupin, in his little back library, or bookcloset, *au troisième*, No. 33 Rue Dunôt, Faubourg Saint-Germain. For one hour at least we had maintained a profound silence; while each, to any casual observer, might have seemed intently and exclusively occupied with the curling eddies of smoke that oppressed the atmosphere of the chamber. For myself, however, I was mentally discussing certain topics which had formed matter for conversation between us at an earlier period of the evening; I mean the affair of the Rue Morgue, and the mystery attending the murder of Marie Rogêt. I looked upon it, therefore, as something of a coincidence, when the door of our apartment was thrown open and admitted our old acquaintance, Monsieur G——, the prefect of the Parisian police.

We gave him a hearty welcome; for there was nearly half as much of the entertaining as of the contemptible about the man, and we had not seen him for several years. We had been sitting in the dark, and Dupin now arose for the purpose of lighting a lamp, but sat down again, without doing so, upon G——'s saying that he had called to consult us, or rather to ask the opinion of my friend, about some official business which had occasioned a great deal of trouble.

"If it is any point requiring reflection," observed Dupin, as he forbore to enkindle the wick, "we shall examine it to better purpose in the dark."

"That is another of your odd notions," said the prefect, who had the fashion of calling everything "odd" that was beyond his comprehension, and thus lived amid an absolute legion of "oddities."

"Very true," said Dupin, as he supplied his visitor with a pipe, and rolled toward him a comfortable chair.

"And what is the difficulty now?" I asked. "Nothing more in the assassination way, I hope."

"Oh, no; nothing of that nature. The fact is, the business is *very* simple indeed, and I make no doubt that we

1

can manage it sufficiently well ourselves; but then I thought Dupin would like to hear the details of it, because it is so excessively *odd*."

"Simple and odd," said Dupin.

"Why, yes; and not exactly that either. The fact is, we have all been a good deal puzzled because the affair *is* so simple, and yet baffles us altogether."

"Perhaps it is the very simplicity of the thing which puts you at fault," said my friend.

"What nonsense you *do* talk!" replied the prefect, laughing heartily.

"Perhaps the mystery is a little *too* plain," said Dupin.

"Oh, good heavens! Who ever heard of such an idea?"

"A little *too* self-evident."

"Ha! ha! ha!—ha! ha! ha!—ho! ho! ho!" roared our visitor, profoundly amused, "oh, Dupin, you will be the death of me yet!"

"And what, after all, *is* the matter on hand?" I asked.

"Why, I will tell you," replied the prefect, as he gave a long, steady, and contemplative puff, and settled himself in his chair. "I will tell you in a few words; but, before I begin, let me caution you that this is an affair demanding the greatest secrecy, and that I should most probably lose the position I now hold, were it known that I confided it to anyone."

"Proceed," said I.

"Or not," said Dupin.

"Well, then; I have received personal information, from a very high quarter, that a certain document of the last importance has been purloined from the royal apartments. The individual who purloined it is known; this beyond a doubt; he was seen to take it. It is known, also, that it still remains in his possession."

"How is this known?" asked Dupin.

"It is clearly inferred," replied the prefect, "from the nature of the document, and from the nonappearance of certain results which would at once arise from its passing *out* of the robber's possession—that is to say, from his employing it as he must design in the end to employ it."

"Be a little more explicit," I said.

"Well, I may venture so far as to say that the paper gives its holder a certain power in a certain quarter where such power is immensely valuable." The prefect was fond of the cant of diplomacy.

"Still I do not quite understand," said Dupin.

"No? Well; the disclosure of the document to a third person, who shall be nameless, would bring in question the honor of a personage of most exalted station; and this fact gives the holder of the document an ascendancy over the illustrious personage whose honor and peace are so jeopardized."

"But this ascendancy," I interposed, "would depend upon the robber's knowledge of the loser's knowledge of the robber. Who would dare—"

"The thief," said G——, "is the minister D——, who dares all things, those unbecoming as well as those becoming a man. The method of the theft was not less ingenious than bold. The document in question—a letter, to be frank—had been received by the personage robbed while alone in the royal boudoir. During its perusal she was suddenly interrupted by the entrance of the other exalted personage from whom especially it was her wish to conceal it. After a hurried and vain endeavor to thrust it in a drawer, she was forced to place it, open as it was, upon a table. The address, however, was uppermost, and, the contents thus unexposed, the letter escaped notice. At this juncture enters the minister D——. His lynx eye immediately perceives the paper, recognizes the handwriting of the address, observes the confusion of the personage addressed, and fathoms her secret. After some business transactions, hurried through in his ordinary manner, he produces a letter somewhat similar to the one in question, opens it, pretends to read it, and then places it in close juxtaposition to the other. Again he converses, for some fifteen minutes, upon the public affairs. At length, in taking leave, he takes also from the table the letter to which he had no claim. Its rightful owner saw but, of course, dared not call attention to the act, in the presence of the third personage who stood at her elbow. The minister decamped, leaving his own letter—one of no importance—upon the table."

"Here, then," said Dupin to me, "you have precisely what you demand to make the ascendancy complete—the robber's knowledge of the loser's knowledge of the robber."

"Yes," replied the prefect; "and the power thus attained has, for some months past, been wielded, for political purposes, to a very dangerous extent. The personage robbed is more thoroughly convinced, every day, of the necessity of reclaiming her letter. But this, of course, cannot be done openly. In fine, driven to despair, she has committed the matter to me."

"Than whom," said Dupin, amid a perfect whirlwind of smoke, "no more sagacious agent could, I suppose, be desired, or even imagined."

"You flatter me," replied the prefect; "but it is possible that some such opinion may have been entertained."

"It is clear," said I, "as you observe, that the letter is still in the possession of the minister; since it is this possession, and not any employment of the letter, which bestows the power. With the employment the power departs."

"True," said G——; "and upon this conviction I proceeded. My first care was to make thorough search of the minister's hotel; and here my chief embarrassment lay in the necessity of searching without his knowledge. Beyond all things, I have been warned of the danger which would result from giving him reason to suspect our design."

"But," said I, "you are quite *au fait* in these investigations. The Parisian police have done this thing often before."

"Oh, yes; and for this reason I did not despair. The habits of the minister gave me, too, a great advantage. He is frequently absent from home all night. His servants are by no means numerous. They sleep at a distance from their master's apartment, and, being chiefly Neapolitans, are readily made drunk. I have keys, as you know, with which I can open any chamber or cabinet in Paris. For three months a night has not passed during the greater part of which I have not been engaged, personally, in ransacking the D—— Hotel. My honor is interested, and, to mention a great secret, the reward is enormous. So I did not abandon the search until I had become fully satisfied that the thief is a more astute man than myself. I fancy that I have investigated every nook and corner of the premises in which it is possible that the paper can be concealed."

"But is it not possible," I suggested, "that although the letter may be in possession of the minister, as it unquestionably is, he may have concealed it elsewhere than upon his own premises?"

"This is barely possible," said Dupin. "The present peculiar condition of affairs at court, and especially of those intrigues in which D—— is known to be involved, would render the instant availability of the document—its susceptibility of being produced at a moment's notice—a point of nearly equal importance with its possession."

"Its susceptibility of being produced?" said I.

"That is to say, of being *destroyed*," said Dupin.

"True," I observed; "the paper is clearly then upon the premises. As for its being upon the person of the minister, we may consider that as out of the question."

"Entirely," said the prefect. "He has been twice waylaid, as if by footpads, and his person rigidly searched under my own inspection."

"You might have spared yourself this trouble," said Dupin. "D——, I presume, is not altogether a fool, and, if not, must have anticipated these waylayings, as a matter of course."

"Not *altogether* a fool," said G——, "but then he is a poet, which I take to be only one remove from a fool."

"True," said Dupin, after a long and thoughtful whiff from his meerschaum, "although I have been guilty of certain doggerel myself."

"Suppose you detail," said I, "the particulars of your search."

"Why, the fact is, we took our time, and we searched *everywhere*. I have had long experience in these affairs. I took the entire building, room by room, devoting the nights of a whole week to each. We examined, first, the furniture of each apartment. We opened every possible drawer; and I presume you know that, to a properly trained police agent, such a thing as a *'secret'* drawer is impossible. Any man is a dolt who permits a 'secret' drawer to escape him in a search of this kind. The thing is *so* plain. There is a certain amount of bulk—of space—to be accounted for in every cabinet. Then we have accurate rules. The fiftieth part of a line could not escape us. After the cabinets we took the chairs. The cushions we probed with the fine long needles you have seen me employ. From the tables we removed the tops."

"Why so?"

"Sometimes the top of a table, or other similarly arranged piece of furniture, is removed by the person wishing to conceal an article; then the leg is excavated, the article deposited within the cavity, and the top replaced. The bottoms and tops of bedposts are employed in the same way."

"But could not the cavity be detected by sounding?" I asked.

"By no means, if, when the article is deposited, a sufficient wadding of cotton be placed around it. Besides, in our case, we were obliged to proceed without noise."

"But you could not have removed—you could not have taken to pieces *all* articles of furniture in which it would have been possible to make a deposit in the manner you mention. A letter may be compressed into a thin spiral roll, not differing much in shape or bulk from a large knitting needle, and in this form it might be inserted into the rung of a chair, for example. You did not take to pieces all the chairs?"

"Certainly not; but we did better—we examined the rungs of every chair in the hotel, and, indeed, the jointings of every description of furniture, by the aid of a most powerful microscope. Had there been any traces of recent disturbance we should not have failed to detect it instantly. A single grain of gimlet dust, for example, would have been as obvious as an apple. Any disorder in the gluing—any unusual gaping in the joints—would have sufficed to ensure detection."

"I presume you looked to the mirrors, between the boards and the plates, and you probed the beds and the bedclothes, as well as the curtains and carpets."

"That of course; and when we had absolutely completed every particle of the furniture in this way, then we examined the house itself. We divided its entire surface into compartments, which we numbered, so that none might be missed; then we scrutinized each individual square inch throughout the premises, including the two houses immediately adjoining, with the microscope, as before."

"The two houses adjoining!" I exclaimed; "you must have had a great deal of trouble."

"We had; but the reward offered is prodigious."

"You include the *grounds* about the houses?"

"All the grounds are paved with brick. They gave us comparatively little trouble. We examined the moss between the bricks, and found it undisturbed."

"You looked among D——'s papers, of course, and into the books of the library?"

"Certainly; we opened every package and parcel; we not only opened every book, but we turned over every leaf in each volume, not contenting ourselves with a mere shake, according to the fashion of some of our police officers. We also measured the thickness of every book *cover,* with the most accurate admeasurement, and applied to each the most jealous scrutiny of the microscope. Had any of the bindings been recently meddled with, it would have been utterly impossible that the fact should have escaped observation. Some five or six volumes, just from the hands of the binder, we carefully probed, longitudinally, with the needles."

"You explored the floors beneath the carpets?"

"Beyond doubt. We removed every carpet, and examined the boards with the microscope."

"And the paper on the walls?"

"Yes."

"You looked into the cellars?"

"We did."

"Then," I said, "you have been making a miscalculation, and the letter is *not* upon the premises as you suppose."

"I fear you are right there," said the prefect. "And now, Dupin, what would you advise me to do?"

"To make a thorough research of the premises."

"That is absolutely needless," replied G——. "I am not more sure that I breathe than I am that the letter is not at the hotel."

"I have no better advice to give you," said Dupin.

"You have, of course, an accurate description of the letter?"

"Oh, yes!"—and here the prefect, producing a memorandum book, proceeded to read aloud a minute account of the internal, and especially of the external, appearance of the missing document. Soon after finishing the perusal of this description, he took his departure, more entirely depressed in spirits than I had ever known the good gentleman before.

In about a month afterward he paid us another visit, and found us occupied very nearly as before. He took a pipe and a chair and entered into some ordinary conversation. At length I said:

"Well, but G——, what of the purloined letter? I presume you have at last made up your mind that there is no such thing as overreaching the minister?"

"Confound him, say I—yes; I made the reexamination, however, as Dupin suggested—but it was all labor lost, as I knew it would be."

"How much was the reward offered, did you say?" asked Dupin.

"Why, a very great deal—a *very* liberal reward —I don't like to say how much, precisely; but one thing I *will* say, that I wouldn't mind giving my individual check for fifty thousand francs to any one who could obtain me that letter. The fact is, it is becoming of more and more importance every day; and the reward has been lately doubled. If it were trebled, however, I could do no more than I have done."

"Why, yes," said Dupin, drawlingly, between the whiffs of his meerschaum, "I really—think, G——, you have not exerted yourself—to the utmost in this matter. You might—do a little more, I think, eh?"

"How?—in what way?"

"Why—*puff, puff*—you might—*puff, puff*—employ counsel in the matter, eh?—*puff, puff, puff.* Do you remember the story they tell of Abernethy?"

"No; hang Abernethy!"

"To be sure! hang him and welcome. But, once upon a time, a certain rich miser conceived the design of sponging upon this Abernethy for a medical opinion. Getting up, for this purpose, an ordinary conversation in a private company, he insinuated his case to the physician, as that of an imaginary individual.

"'We will suppose,' said the miser, 'that his symptoms are such and such; now, doctor, what would *you* have directed him to take?'

"'Take!' said the Abernethy, 'why, take *advice,* to be sure.'"

"But," said the prefect, a little discomposed, "*I* am *perfectly* willing to take advice, and to pay for it. I would *really* give fifty thousand francs to anyone who would aid me in the matter."

"In that case," replied Dupin, opening a drawer, and producing a checkbook, "you may as well fill me up a check for the amount mentioned. When you have signed it, I will hand you the letter."

I was astounded. The prefect appeared absolutely thunderstricken. For some minutes he remained speechless and motionless, looking incredulously at my friend with open mouth, and eyes that seemed starting from their sockets; then apparently recovering himself in some measure, he seized a pen, and after several pauses and vacant stares, finally filled up and signed a check for fifty thousand francs, and handed it across the table to Dupin. The latter examined it carefully and deposited it in his pocketbook; then, unlocking an escritoire, took thence a letter and gave it to the prefect. This functionary grasped it in a perfect agony of joy, opened it with a trembling hand, cast a rapid glance at its contents, and then, scrambling and struggling to the door rushed at length unceremoniously from the room and from the house, without having uttered a syllable since Dupin had requested him to fill up the check.

When he had gone, my friend entered into some explanations.

"The Parisian police," he said, "are exceedingly able in their way. They are persevering, ingenious, cunning, and thoroughly versed in the knowledge which their duties seem chiefly to demand. Thus, when G—— detailed to us his mode of searching the premises at the Hotel D——, I felt entire confidence in his having made a satisfactory investigation—so far as his labors extended."

"So far as his labors extended?" said I.

"Yes," said Dupin. "The measures adopted were not only the best of their kind, but carried out to absolute perfection. Had the letter been deposited within the range of their search, these fellows would, beyond question, have found it."

I merely laughed—but he seemed quite serious in all that he said.

"The measures, then," he continued, "were good in their kind, and well executed; their defect lay in their being inapplicable to the case and to the man. A certain set of highly ingenious resources are, with the prefect, a sort of Procrustean bed, to which he forcibly adapts his designs. But he perpetually errs by being too deep or too shallow for the matter in hand; and many a schoolboy is a better reasoner than he. I knew one about eight years of age, whose success at guessing in the game of even and odd attracted universal admiration. This game is simple, and is played with marbles. One player holds in his hand a number of these toys, and demands of another whether that number is even or odd. If the guess is right, the guesser wins one; if wrong he loses one. The boy to whom I allude won all the marbles of the school. Of course he had some principle of guessing; and this lay in mere observation and admeasurement of the astuteness of his opponents. For example, an arrant simpleton is his opponent, and, holding up his closed hand, asks, 'Are they even or odd?' Our schoolboy replies, 'Odd,' and loses; but upon the second trial he wins, for he then says to himself: 'The simpleton had them even upon the first trial, and his amount of cunning is just sufficient to make him have them odd upon the second; I will therefore guess odd'; he guesses odd, and wins. Now, with a simpleton a degree above the first, he would have reasoned thus: 'This fellow finds that in the first instance I guessed odd, and, in the second, he will propose to himself, upon the first impulse, a simple variation from even to odd, as did the first simpleton; but then a second thought will suggest that this is too simple a variation and finally he will decide upon putting it even as before. I will therefore guess even'; he guesses even, and wins. Now this mode of reasoning in the schoolboy, whom his fellows termed 'lucky'—what, in its last analysis, is it?"

"It is merely," I said, "an identification of the reasoner's intellect with that of his opponent."

"It is," said Dupin; "and, upon inquiring of the boy by what means he effected the *thorough* identification in which his success consisted, I received answer as follows: 'When I wish to find out how wise, or how stupid, or how good, or how wicked is anyone, or what are his thoughts at the moment, I fashion the expression of my face, as accurately as possible, in accordance with the expression of his, and then wait to see what thoughts or sentiments arise in my mind or heart, as if to match or correspond with the expression.' This response of the schoolboy lies at the bottom of all the spurious profundity which has been attributed to Rochefoucauld, to La Bougive, to Machiavelli, and to Campanella."

"And the identification," I said, "of the reasoner's intellect with that of his opponent, depends, if I understand you aright, upon the accuracy with which the opponent's intellect is admeasured."

"For its practical value it depends upon this," replied Dupin; "and the prefect and his cohort fail so frequently, first, by default of this identification, and, secondly, by ill admeasurement, or rather through nonadmeasurement, of the intellect with which they are engaged. They consider only their *own* ideas of ingenuity; and, in searching for anything hidden, advert only to the modes in which *they* would have hidden it. They are right in this much—that their own ingenuity is a faithful representative of that of the *mass*; but when the cunning of the individual felon is diverse in character from their own, the felon foils them of course. This always happens when it is above their own, and very usually when it is below. They have no variation of principle in their investigations; at best, when urged by some unusual emergency—by some extraordinary reward—they extend or exaggerate their old modes of *practice*, without touching their principles. What, for example, in this case of D— —, has been done to vary the principle of action? What is all this boring, and probing, and sounding, and scrutinizing with the microscope, and dividing the surface of the building into registered square inches—what is it all but an exaggeration of the *application* of the one principle or set of principles of search, which are based upon the one set of notions regarding human ingenuity, to which the prefect, in the long routine of his duty, has been accustomed? Do you not see he has taken it for granted that *all* men proceed to conceal a letter, not exactly in a gimlet hole bored in a chair leg, but, at least, in *some* out-of-the-way hole or corner suggested by the same tenor of thought which would urge a man to secrete a letter in a gimlet hole bored in a chair leg? And do you not see, also, that such *recherchés* nooks for concealment are adapted only for ordinary occasions, and would be adopted only by ordinary intellects; for, in all cases of concealment, a disposal of the article concealed—a disposal of it in this *recherché* manner—is, in the very first instance, presumable and presumed; and thus its discovery depends, not at all upon the acumen, but altogether upon the mere care, patience, and determination of the seekers; and where the case is of importance—or, what amounts to the same thing in the policial eyes, when the reward is of magnitude—the qualities in question have *never* been known to fail. You will now understand what I meant in suggesting that, had the purloined letter been hidden anywhere within the limits of the prefect's examination—in other words, had the principle of its concealment been comprehended within the principles of the prefect—its discovery would have been a matter altogether beyond question. This functionary, however, has been thoroughly mystified; and the remote source of his defeat lies in the supposition that the minister is a fool, because he has acquired renown as a poet. All fools are poets; this the prefect *feels*; and he is merely guilty of a *non distributio medii* in thence inferring that all poets are fools."

"But is this really the poet?" I asked. "There are two brothers, I know; and both have attained reputation in letter. The minister I believe has written learnedly on the differential calculus. He is a mathematician, and no poet."

"You are mistaken; I know him well; he is both. As poet *and* mathematician, he would reason well; as mere mathematician, he could not have reasoned at all, and thus would have been at the mercy of the prefect."

"You surprise me," I said, "by these opinions, which have been contradicted by the voice of the world. You do not mean to set at naught the well-digested idea of centuries? The mathematical reason has long been regarded as *the* reason *par excellence*."

"'*Il y a à parier*,'" replied Dupin, quoting from Chamfort, "'*que toute idée publique, toute convention reçue, est une sottise, car elle a convenue au plus grand nombre*.' The mathematicians, I grant you, have done their best to promulgate the popular error to which you allude, and which is none the less an error for its promulgation as truth. With an art worthy a better cause, for example, they have insinuated the term 'analysis' into application to algebra. The French are the originators of this particular deception; but if a term is of any importance—if words derive any value from applicability—then 'analysis' conveys 'algebra' about as much as, in Latin, *ambitus* implies 'ambition,' *religio* 'religion,' or *homines honesti* a set of *honorable* men."

"You have a quarrel on hand, I see," said I, "with some of the algebraists of Paris; but proceed."

"I dispute the availability, and thus the value, of that reason which is cultivated in any especial form other than the abstractly logical. I dispute, in particular, the reason educed by mathematical study. The mathematics are the science of form and quantity; mathematical reasoning is merely logic applied to observation upon form and quantity. The great error lies in supposing that even the truths of what is called *pure* algebra are abstract or general truths. And this error is so egregious that I am confounded at the universality with which it has been received. Mathematical axioms are *not* axioms of general truth. What is true of *relation*—of form and quantity—is often grossly false in regard to morals, for example. In this latter science it is very usually *un*true that the aggregated parts are equal to the whole. In chemistry also the axiom fails. In the consideration of motive it fails; for two motives, each of a given value, have not, necessarily, a value when united equal to the sum of their values apart. There are numerous other mathematical truths which are only truths within the limits of *relation*. But the mathematician argues from his *finite truths,* through habit, as if they were of an absolutely general applicability—as the world indeed imagines them to be. Bryant, in his very learned *Mythology,* mentions an analogous source of error, when he says that 'although the pagan fables are not believed, yet we forget ourselves continually, and make inferences from them as existing realities.' With the algebraists, however, who are pagans themselves, the 'pagan fables' *are* believed, and the inferences are made, not so much through lapse of memory as through an unaccountable addling of the brains. In short, I never yet encountered the mere mathematician who could be trusted out of equal roots, or one who did not clandestinely hold it as a point of his faith that $x^2 + px$ was absolutely and unconditionally equal to q. Say to one of these gentlemen, by way of experiment, if you please, that you believe occasions may occur where $x^2 + px$ is *not* altogether equal to q, and, having made him understand what you mean, get out of his reach as speedily as convenient, for, beyond doubt, he will endeavor to knock you down.

"I mean to say," continued Dupin, while I merely laughed at his last observations, "that if the minister had been no more than a mathematician, the prefect would have been under no necessity of giving me this check. I knew him, however, as both mathematician and poet, and my measures were adapted to his capacity, with reference to the circumstances by which he was surrounded. I knew him as a courtier, too, and as a bold *intrigant*. Such a man, I considered, could not fail to be aware of the ordinary policial modes of action. He could not have failed to anticipate—and events have proved that he did not fail to anticipate—the waylayings to which he was subjected. He must have foreseen, I reflected, the secret investigations of his premises. His frequent absences from home at night, which were hailed by the prefect as certain aids to his success, I regarded only as *ruses,* to afford opportunity for thorough search to the police, and thus the sooner to impress them with the conviction to which G——, in fact, did finally arrive—the conviction that the letter was not upon the premises. I felt, also, that the whole train of thought, which I was at some pains in detailing to you just now, concerning the invariable principle of policial action in searches for articles concealed—I felt that this whole train of thought would necessarily pass through the mind of the minister. It would imperatively lead him to despise all the ordinary *nooks* of concealment. *He* could not, I reflected, be so weak as not to see that the most intricate and remote recess of his hotel would be as open as his commonest closets to the eyes, to the probes, to the gimlets, and to the microscopes of the prefect. I saw, in fine, that he would be driven, as a matter of course, to *simplicity,* if not deliberately induced to it as a matter of choice. You will remember, perhaps, how desperately the prefect laughed when I suggested, upon our first interview, that it was just possible this mystery troubled him so much on account of its being so *very* self-evident."

"Yes," said I, "I remember his merriment well. I really thought he would have fallen into convulsions."

"The material world," continued Dupin, "abounds with very strict analogies to the immaterial; and thus some color of truth has been given to the rhetorical dogma, that metaphor, or simile, may be made to strengthen an argument as well as to embellish a description. The principle of the *vis inertiae,* for example, seems to be identical in physics and metaphysics. It is not more true in the former, that a large body is with more difficulty set in motion than a smaller one, and that its subsequent *momentum* is commensurate with this difficulty, than it is, in the latter, that intellects of the vaster capacity, while more forcible, more constant, and more eventful in their movements than those of inferior grade, are yet the less readily moved, and more embarrassed, and full of hesitation in the first few steps of their progress. Again: have you ever noticed which of the street signs over the shop doors are the most attractive of attention?"

"I have never given the matter a thought," I said.

"There is a game of puzzles," he resumed, "which is played upon a map. One party playing requires another to find a given word—the name of town, river, state, or empire—any word, in short, upon the motley and perplexed surface of the chart. A novice in the game generally seeks to embarrass his opponents by giving them the most minutely lettered names; but the adept selects such words as stretch, in large characters, from one end of the chart to the other. These, like the overlargely lettered signs and placards of the street, escape observation by dint of being excessively obvious; and here the physical oversight is precisely analogous with the moral inapprehension by which the intellect suffers to pass unnoticed those considerations which are too obtrusively and too palpably self-evident. But this is a point, it appears, somewhat above or beneath the understanding of the prefect. He never once thought it probable, or possible, that the minister had deposited the letter immediately beneath the nose of the whole world, by way of best preventing any portion of that world from perceiving it.

"But the more I reflected upon the daring, dashing, and discriminating ingenuity of D——; upon the fact that the document must always have been *at hand,* if he intended to use it to good purpose; and upon the decisive evidence, obtained by the prefect, that it was not hidden within the limits of that dignitary's ordinary search—the more satisfied I became that, to conceal this letter, the minister had resorted to the comprehensive and sagacious expedient of not attempting to conceal it at all.

"Full of these ideas, I prepared myself with a pair of green spectacles, and called one fine morning, quite by accident, at the ministerial hotel. I found D—— at home, yawning, lounging, and dawdling, as usual, and pretending to be in the last extremity of ennui. He is, perhaps, the most really energetic human being now alive—but that is only when nobody sees him.

"To be even with him, I complained of my weak eyes, and lamented the necessity of spectacles, under cover of which I cautiously and thoroughly surveyed the whole apartment, while seemingly intent only upon the conversation of my host.

"I paid special attention to a large writing table near which he sat, and upon which lay confusedly some miscellaneous letters and other papers, with one or two musical instruments and a few books. Here, however, after a long and very deliberate scrutiny, I saw nothing to excite particular suspicion.

"At length my eyes, in going the circuit of the room, fell upon a trumpery filigree card rack of pasteboard that hung dangling by a dirty blue ribbon, from a little brass knob just beneath the middle of the mantelpiece. In this rack, which had three or four compartments, were five or six visiting cards and a solitary letter. This last was much soiled and crumpled. It was torn nearly in two, across the middle—as if a design, in the first instance, to tear it entirely up as worthless had been altered, or stayed, in the second. It had a large black seal, bearing the D—— cipher *very* conspicuously, and was addressed, in a diminutive female hand, to D—— the minister, himself. It was thrust carelessly, and even, as it seemed, contemptuously, into one of the uppermost divisions of the rack.

"No sooner had I glanced at this letter than I concluded it to be that of which I was in search. To be sure, it was, to all appearance, radically different from the one of which the prefect had read us so minute a description. Here the seal was large and black, with the D—— cipher; there it was small and red, with the ducal arms of the S—— family. Here, the address, to the minister, was diminutive and feminine; there, the superscription, to a certain royal personage, was markedly bold and decided; the size alone formed a point of correspondence. But, then, the *radicalness* of these differences, which was excessive; the dirt; the soiled and torn condition of the paper, so inconsistent with the *true* methodical habits of D——, and so suggestive of a design to delude the beholder into an idea of the worthlessness of the document—these things, together with the hyperobtrusive situation of this document, full in the view of every visitor, and thus exactly in accordance with the conclusions to which I had previously arrived; these things, I say, were strongly corroborative of suspicion, in one who came with the intention to suspect.

"I protracted my visit as long as possible, and, while I maintained a most animated discussion with the minister, upon a topic which I knew well had never failed to interest and excite him, I kept my attention really riveted upon the letter. In this examination, I committed to memory its external appearance and arrangement in the rack—and also fell, at length, upon a discovery which set at rest whatever trivial doubt I might have entertained. In scrutinizing the edges of the paper, I observed them to be more *chafed* than seemed necessary. They presented the *broken* appearance which is manifested when a stiff paper, having been once folded and pressed with a folder, is refolded in a reversed direction, in the same creases or edges which had formed the original fold. This discovery was sufficient. It was clear to me that the letter had been turned, as a glove, inside out, redirected, and resealed. I bade the minister good morning, and took my departure at once, leaving a gold snuffbox upon the table.

"The next morning I called for the snuffbox, when we resumed, quite eagerly, the conversation of the preceding day. While thus engaged, however, a loud report, as if of a pistol, was heard immediately beneath the windows of the hotel, and was succeeded by a series of fearful screams, and the shoutings of a terrified mob. D—— rushed to a casement, threw it open, and looked out. In the meantime I stepped to the card rack, took the letter, put it in my pocket, and replaced it by a facsimile (so far as regards externals) which I had carefully prepared at my lodgings—imitating the D—— cipher, very readily, by means of a seal formed of bread.

"The disturbance in the street had been occasioned by the frantic behavior of a man with a musket. He had fired it among a crowd of women and children. It proved, however, to have been without ball, and the fellow was suffered to go his way as a lunatic or a drunkard. When he had gone, D—— came from the window, whither I had followed him immediately upon securing the object in view. Soon afterward I bade him farewell. The pretended lunatic was a man in my own pay."

"But what purpose had you," I asked, "in replacing the letter by a facsimile? Would it not have been better, at the first visit, to have seized it openly, and departed?"

"D——," replied Dupin, "is a desperate man, and a man of nerve. His hotel, too, is not without attendants devoted to his interests. Had I made the wild attempt you suggest, I might never have left the ministerial presence alive. The good people of Paris might have heard of me no more. But I had an object apart from these considerations. You know my political prepossessions. In this matter, I act as a partisan of the lady concerned. For eighteen months the minister has had her in his power. She has now him in hers—since, being unaware that the letter is not in his possession, he will proceed with his exactions as if it was. Thus will he inevitably commit himself, at once, to his political destruction. His downfall, too, will not be more precipitate than awkward. It is all very well to talk about the *facilis descensus Averni*; but in all kinds of climbing, as Catalani said of singing, it is far more easy to get up than to come down. In the present instance I have no sympathy—at least no pity—for him who descends. He is that *monstrum horrendum,* an unprincipled man of genius. I confess, however, that I should like very well to know the precise character of his thoughts when, being defied by her whom the prefect terms 'a certain personage,' he is reduced to opening the letter which I left for him in the card rack."

"How? Did you put anything particular in it?"

"Why, it did not seem altogether right to leave the interior blank—that would have been insulting. D——, at Vienna once, did me an evil turn, which I told him, quite good-humoredly, that I should remember. So, as I knew he would feel some curiosity in regard to the identity of the person who had outwitted him, I thought it a pity not to give him a clue. He is well acquainted with my MS., and I just copied into the middle of the blank sheet the words:

> *Un dessein si funeste,*
> *S'il n'est digne d'Atrée, est digne de Thyeste.*

They are to be found in Crébillon's *Atrée.*"

A TERRIBLY STRANGE BED

WILKIE COLLINS
(1824–1889)

Just as Edgar Allan Poe was the father of the short detective story, Collins may lay claim to being the inventor of the detective novel with The Woman in White, *one of the greatest and most popular novels of the nineteenth century. His most famous short story, collected here, first appeared in book form in* After Dark *(1856) shortly after he had met Charles Dickens, with whom he collaborated frequently, sometimes acknowledged and often not.*

HORTLY AFTER MY EDUCATION at college was finished, I happened to be staying at Paris with an English friend. We were both young men then, and lived, I am afraid, rather a wild life, in the delightful city of our sojourn. One night we were idling about the neighborhood of the Palais Royal, doubtful to what amusement we should next betake ourselves. My friend proposed a visit to Frascati's; but his suggestion was not to my taste. I knew Frascati's, as the French saying is, by heart; had lost and won plenty of five-franc pieces there, merely for amusement's sake, until it was amusement no longer, and was thoroughly tired, in fact, of all the ghastly respectabilities of such a social anomaly as a respectable gambling-house. 'For Heaven's sake,' said I to my friend, 'let us go somewhere where we can see a little genuine, blackguard, poverty-stricken gaming, with no false gingerbread glitter thrown over it at all. Let us get away from fashionable Frascati's, to a house where they don't mind letting in a man with a ragged

coat, or a man with no coat, ragged or otherwise.'—'Very well,' said my friend, 'we needn't go out of the Palais Royal to find the sort of company you want. Here's the place just before us; as blackguard a place, by all report, as you could possibly wish to see.' In another minute we arrived at the door, and entered the house, the back of which you have drawn in your sketch.

When we got up stairs, and had left our hats and sticks with the door-keeper, we were admitted into the chief gambling-room. We did not find many people assembled there. But, few as the men were who looked up at us on our entrance, they were all types—lamentably true types—of their respective classes.

We had come to see blackguards; but these men were something worse. There is a comic side, more or less appreciable, in all blackguardism— here there was nothing but tragedy— mute, weird tragedy. The quiet in the room was horrible. The thin, haggard, long-haired young man, whose sunken eyes fiercely watched the turning up of the cards, never spoke; the flabby, fat-faced, pimply player, who pricked his piece of pasteboard perseveringly, to register how often black won, and how often red—never spoke; the dirty, wrinkled old man, with the vulture eyes and the darned greatcoat, who had lost his last *sou,* and still looked on desperately, after he could play no longer—never spoke. Even the voice of the croupier sounded as if it were strangely dulled and thickened in the atmosphere of the room. I had entered the place to laugh; but the spectacle before me was something to weep over. I soon found it necessary to take refuge in excitement from the depression of spirits which was fast stealing on me. Unfortunately I sought the nearest excitement, by going to the table, and beginning to play. Still more unfortunately, as the event will show, I won—won prodigiously; won incredibly; won at such a rate, that the regular players at the table crowded round me; and staring at my stakes with hungry, superstitious eyes, whispered to one another, that the English stranger was going to break the bank.

The game was *Rouge et Noir.* I had played at it in every city in Europe, without, however, the care or the wish to study the Theory of Chances—that philosopher's stone of all gamblers! And a gambler, in the strict sense of the word, I had never been. I was heart-whole from the corroding passion for play. My gaming was a mere idle amusement. I never resorted to it by necessity, because I never knew what it was to want money. I never practised it so incessantly as to lose more than I could afford, or to gain more than I could coolly pocket without being thrown off my balance by my good luck. In short, I had hitherto frequented gambling-tables—just as I frequented ball-rooms and opera-houses—because they amused me, and because I had nothing better to do with my leisure hours.

But on this occasion it was very different—now, for the first time in my life, I felt what the passion for play really was. My success first bewildered, and then, in the most literal meaning of the word, intoxicated me. Incredible as it may appear, it is nevertheless true, that I only lost when I attempted to estimate chances, and played according to previous calculation. If I left everything to luck, and staked without any care or consideration, I was sure to win—to win in the face of every recognized probability in favour of the bank. At first, some of the men present ventured their money safely enough on my colour but I speedily increased my stakes to sums which they dared not risk. One after another they left off playing, and breathlessly looked on at my game.

Still, time after time, I staked higher and higher, and still won. The excitement in the room rose to fever pitch. The silence was interrupted by a deep, muttered chorus of oaths and exclamations in different languages, every time the gold was shoveled across to my side of the table—even the imperturbable croupier dashed his rake on the floor in a (French) fury of astonishment at my success. But one man present preserved his self-possession; and that man was my friend. He came to my side, and whispering in English, begged me to leave the place satisfied with what I had already gained. I must do him the justice to say, that he repeated his warnings and entreaties several times; and only left me and went away, after I had rejected his advice (I was to all intents and purposes gambling-drunk) in terms which rendered it impossible for him to address me again that night.

Shortly after he had gone, a hoarse voice behind me cried: 'Permit me, my dear sir!—permit me to restore to their proper place two Napoleons which you have dropped. Wonderful luck, sir! I pledge you my word of honor as an old soldier, in the course of my long experience in this sort of thing, I never saw such luck as yours!—never! Go on, sir—*Sacré mille bombes!* Go on boldly, and break the bank!'

I turned round and saw, nodding and smiling at me with inveterate civility, a tall man, dressed in a frogged and braided surtout.

If I had been in my senses, I should have considered him, personally, as being rather a suspicious specimen of an old soldier. He had goggling blood-shot eyes, mangy mustachios, and a broken nose. His voice betrayed a barrack-room intonation of the worst order, and he had the dirtiest pair of hands I ever saw—even in France. These little personal peculiarities exercised, however, no repelling influence on me. In the mad excitement, the reckless triumph of that moment, I was ready to 'fraternize' with anybody who encouraged me in my game. I accepted the old soldier's offered pinch of snuff; clapped him on the back, and swore he was the honestest fellow in the world—the most glorious relic of the Grand Army that I had ever met with. 'Go on!' cried my military friend, snapping his fingers in ecstasy— 'Go on, and win! Break the bank—*Mille tonnerres!* my gallant English comrade, break the bank!'

And I *did* go on—went on at such a rate, that in another quarter of an hour the croupier called out: 'Gentlemen! the bank has discontinued for tonight.' All the notes, and all the gold in that 'bank,' now lay in a heap under my hands; the whole floating capital of the gambling-house was waiting to pour into my pockets!

'Tie up the money in your pocket-handkerchief, my worthy sir,' said the old soldier, as I wildly plunged my hands into my heap of gold. 'Tie it up, as we used to tie up a bit of dinner in the Grand Army; your winnings are too heavy for any breeches pockets that ever were sewed. There! that's it!—shovel them in, notes and all! *Credié!* what luck!—Stop! another Napoleon on the floor! *Ah! sacré petit polisson de Napoleon!* have I found thee at last? Now then, sir—two tight double knots each way with your honourable permission, and the money's safe. Feel it! feel it, fortunate sir! hard and round as a cannon ball—*Ah, bah!* if they had only fired such cannon balls at us at Austerlitz—*nom d'une pipe!* if they only had! And now, as an ancient grenadier, as an ex-brave of the French army, what remains for me to do? I ask what? Simply this: to entreat my valued English friend to drink a bottle of champagne with me, and toast the goddess Fortune in foaming goblets before we part!'

"Excellent ex-brave! Convivial ancient grenadier! Champagne by all means! An English cheer for an old soldier! Hurrah! hurrah! Another English cheer for the goddess Fortune! Hurrah! hurrah! hurrah!"

'Bravo! the Englishman; the amiable, gracious Englishman, in whose veins circulates the vivacious blood of France! Another glass? *Ah, bah!*—the bottle is empty! Never mind! *Vive le vin!* I, the old soldier, order another bottle, and half-a-pound of *bon-bons* with it!'

'No, no, ex-brave; never—ancient grenadier! *Your* bottle last time; *my* bottle this. Behold it! Toast away! The French Army!—the great Napoleon!—the present company! the croupier! the honest croupier's wife and daughters—if he has any! the Ladies generally! Everybody in the world!'

By the time the second bottle of champagne was emptied, I felt as if I had been drinking liquid fire—my brain seemed all a-flame. No excess in wine had ever had this effect on me before in my life. Was it the result of a stimulant acting upon my system when I was in a highly excited state? Was my stomach in a particularly disordered condition? Or was the champagne amazingly strong?

'Ex-brave of the French Army!' cried I, in a mad state of exhilaration, '*I* am on fire! how are *you*? You have set me on fire! Do you hear; my hero of Austerlitz? Let us have a third bottle of champagne to put the flame out!'

The old soldier wagged his head, rolled his goggle eyes, until I expected to see them slip out of their sockets; placed his dirty forefinger by the side of his broken nose; solemnly ejaculated 'Coffee!' and immediately ran off into an inner room.

The word pronounced by the eccentric veteran seemed to have a magical effect on the rest of the company present. With one accord they all rose to depart. Probably they had expected to profit by my intoxication; but finding that my new friend was benevolently bent on preventing me from getting dead drunk, had now abandoned all hope of thriving pleasantly on my winnings. Whatever their motive might be, at any rate they went away in a body. When the old soldier returned, and sat down again opposite to me at the table, we had the room to ourselves. I could see the croupier, in a sort of vestibule which opened out of it, eating his supper in solitude. The silence was now deeper than ever.

A sudden change, too, had come over the 'ex-brave.' He assumed a portentously solemn look; and when he spoke to me again, his speech was ornamented by no oaths, enforced by no finger-snapping, enlivened by no apostrophes or exclamations.

'Listen, my dear sir,' said he, in mysteriously confidential tones—'listen to an old soldier's advice. I have been to the mistress of the house (a very charming woman, with a genius for cookery!) to impress on her the necessity of making us some particularly strong and good coffee. You must drink this coffee in order to get rid of your little amiable exaltation of spirits before you think of going home—you *must*, my good and gracious friend! With all that money to take home tonight, it is a sacred duty to yourself to have your wits about you. You are known to be a winner to an enormous extent by several gentlemen present to-night, who, in a certain point of view, are very worthy and excellent fellows; but they are mortal men, my dear sir, and they have their amiable weaknesses! Need I say more? Ah, no, no! you understand me! Now, this is what you must do—send for a cabriolet when you feel quite well again—draw up all the windows when you get into it—and tell the driver to take you home only through the large and well-lighted thoroughfares. Do this; and you and your money will be safe. Do this; and to-morrow you will thank an old soldier for giving you a word of honest advice.'

Just as the ex-brave ended his oration in very lachrymose tones, the coffee came in, ready poured out in two cups. My attentive friend handed me one of the cups with a bow. I was parched with thirst, and drank it off at a draught. Almost instantly afterwards, I was seized with a fit of giddiness, and felt more completely intoxicated than ever. The room whirled round and round furiously; the old soldier seemed to be regularly bobbing up and down before me like the piston of a steam-engine. I was half deafened by a violent singing in my ears; a feeling of utter bewilderment, helplessness, idiocy, overcame me, I rose from my chair, holding on by the table to keep my balance; and stammered out, that I felt dreadfully unwell—so unwell that I did not know how I was to get home.

'My dear friend,' answered the old soldier, and even his voice seemed to be bobbing up and down as he spoke—'my dear friend, it would be madness to go home in *your* state; you would be sure to lose your money; you might be robbed and murdered with the greatest ease. *I* am going to sleep here: do *you* sleep here, too—they make up capital beds in this house—take one; sleep off the effects of the wine, and go home safely with your winnings to-morrow—to-morrow, in broad daylight.'

I had but two ideas left: one, that I must never let go hold of my handkerchief full of money; the other, that I must lie down somewhere immediately, and fall off into a comfortable sleep. So I agreed to the proposal about the bed, and took the offered arm of the old soldier, carrying my money with my disengaged hand. Preceded by the croupier, we passed along some passages and up a flight of stairs into the bedroom which I was to occupy. The ex-brave shook me warmly by the hand; proposed that we should breakfast together, and then, followed by the croupier, left me for the night.

I ran to the wash-hand stand; drank some of the water in my jug; poured the rest out, and plunged my face into it—then sat down in a chair and tried to compose myself. I soon felt better. The change for my lungs, from the fetid atmosphere of the gambling-room to the cool air of the apartment I now occupied; the almost equally refreshing change for my eyes, from the glaring gas-lights of the 'Salon' to the dim, quiet flicker of one bedroom candle; aided wonderfully the restorative effects of cold water. The giddiness left me, and I began to feel a little like a reasonable being again. My first thought was of the risk of sleeping all night in a gambling-house; my second, of the still greater risk of trying to get out after the house was closed, and of going home alone at night, through the streets of Paris with a large sum of money about me. I had slept in worse places than this on my travels, so I determined to lock, bolt, and barricade my door, and take my chance till the next morning.

Accordingly, I secured myself against all intrusion; looked under the bed, and into the cupboard; tried the fastening of the window; and then, satisfied that I had taken every proper precaution, pulled off my upper clothing, put my light, which was a dim one, on the hearth among a feathery litter of wood ashes, and got into bed, with the handkerchief full of money under my pillow.

I soon felt not only that I could not go to sleep, but that I could not even close my eyes. I was wide awake, and in a high fever. Every nerve in my body trembled—every one of my senses seemed to be preternaturally sharpened. I tossed and rolled, and tried every kind of position, and perseveringly sought out the cold corners of the bed, and all to no purpose. Now, I thrust my arms over the clothes; now, I poked them under the clothes; now, I violently shot my legs straight out down to the bottom of the bed; now, I convulsively coiled them up as near my chin as they would go; now, I shook out my crumpled pillow, changed it to the cool side, patted it flat, and lay down quietly on my back; now, I fiercely doubled it in two, set it up on end, thrust it against the board of the bed, and tried a sitting-posture. Every effort was in vain; I groaned with vexation, as I felt that I was in for a sleepless night.

What could I do? I had no book to read. And yet, unless I found out some method of diverting my mind, I felt certain that I was in the condition to imagine all sorts of horrors; to rack my brain with forebodings of every possible and impossible danger; in short, to pass the night in suffering all conceivable varieties of nervous terror.

I raised myself on my elbow, and looked about the room—which was brightened by a lovely moonlight pouring straight through the window—to see if it contained any pictures or ornaments that I could at all clearly distinguish. While my eyes wandered from wall to wall, a remembrance of Le Maistre's delightful little book, 'Voyage autour de ma Chambre,' occurred to me. I resolved to imitate the French author, and find occupation and amusement enough to relieve the tedium of my wakefulness, by making a mental inventory of every article of furniture I could see, and by following up to their sources the multitude of associations which even a chair, a table, or a wash-hand stand may be made to call forth.

In the nervous unsettled state of my mind at that moment, I found it much easier to make my inventory than to make my reflections, and thereupon soon gave up all hope of thinking in Le Maistre's fanciful track—or, indeed, of thinking at all. I looked about the room at the different articles of furniture, and did nothing more.

There was, first, the bed I was lying in; a four-post bed, of all things in the world to meet with in Paris!—yes, a thorough clumsy British four-poster, with the regular top lined with chintz— the regular fringed valance all round—the regular stifling unwholesome curtains, which I remembered having mechanically drawn back against the posts without particularly noticing the bed when I first got into the room. Then there was the marble-topped wash-hand stand, from which the water I had spilt, in my hurry to pour it out, was still dripping, slowly and more slowly, on to the brick-floor. Then two small chairs, with my coat, waistcoat, and trousers flung on them. Then a large elbow-chair covered with dirty-white dimity with my cravat and shirt-collar thrown over the back. Then a chest of drawers with two of the brass handles off, and a tawdry, broken china inkstand placed on it by way of ornament for the top. Then the dressing-table, adorned by a very small looking-glass, and a very large pin-cushion. Then the window—an unusually large window. Then a dark old picture, which the feeble candle dimly showed me. It was the picture of a fellow in a high Spanish hat, crowned with a plume of towering feathers. A swarthy sinister ruffian, looking upward, shading his eyes with his hand, and looking intently upward—it might be at some tall gallows at which he was going to be hanged. At any rate, he had the appearance of thoroughly deserving it.

This picture put a kind of constraint upon me to look upward too—at the top of the bed. It was a gloomy and not an interesting object, and I looked back at the picture. I counted the feathers in the man's hat—they stood out in relief—three white, two green. I observed the crown of his hat, which was of a conical shape, according to the fashion supposed to have been favored by Guido Fawkes. I wondered what he was looking up at. It couldn't be at the stars; such a desperado was neither astrologer nor astronomer. It must be at the high gallows, and he was going to be hanged presently. Would the executioner come into possession of his conical crowned hat and plume of feathers? I counted the feathers again—three white, two green.

While I still lingered over this very improving and intellectual employment, my thoughts insensibly began to wander. The moonlight shining into the room reminded me of a certain moonlight night in England—the night after a picnic party in a Welsh valley. Every incident of the drive homeward, through lovely scenery, which the moonlight made lovelier than ever, came back to my remembrance, though I had never given the picnic a thought for years; though, if I had *tried* to recollect it, I could certainly have recalled little or nothing of that scene long past. Of all the wonderful faculties that help to tell us we are immortal, which speaks the sublime truth more eloquently than memory? Here was I, in a strange house of the most suspicious character, in a situation of uncertainty, and even of peril, which might seem to make the cool exercise of my recollection almost out of the question; nevertheless, remembering, quite involuntarily, places, people, conversations, minute circumstances of every kind, which I had thought forgotten for ever, which I could not possibly have recalled at will even under the most favorable auspices. And what cause had produced in a moment the whole of this strange, complicated, mysterious effect? Nothing but some rays of moonlight shining in at my bedroom window.

I was still thinking of the picnic—of our merriment on the drive home—of the sentimental young lady who *would* quote Childe Harold because it was moonlight. I was absorbed by these past scenes and past amusements, when, in an instant, the thread on which my memories hung snapped asunder: my attention immediately came back to present things more vividly than ever, and I found myself, I neither knew why nor wherefore, looking hard at the picture again.

Looking for what?

Good God, the man had pulled his hat down on his brows!—No! the hat itself was gone! Where was the conical crown? Where the feathers—three white, two green?

Not there! In place of the hat and feathers, what dusky object was it that now hid his forehead, his eyes, his shading hand?

Was the bed moving?

I turned on my back and looked up. Was I mad? drunk? dreaming? giddy again? or was the top of the bed really moving down—sinking slowly, regularly, silently, horribly, right down throughout the whole of its length and breadth—right down upon Me, as I lay underneath?

My blood seemed to stand still. A deadly paralyzing coldness stole all over me, as I turned my head round on the pillow, and determined to test whether the bed-top was really moving or not, by keeping my eye on the man in the picture.

The next look in that direction was enough. The dull, black, frowsy outline of the valance above me was within an inch of being parallel with his waist. I still looked breathlessly. And steadily, and slowly—very slowly—I saw the figure, and the line of frame below the figure, vanish, as the valance moved down before it.

I am, constitutionally, anything but timid. I have been on more than one occasion in peril of my life, and have not lost my self-possession for an instant; but when the conviction first settled on my mind that the bed-top was really moving, was steadily and continuously sinking down upon me, I looked up shuddering, helpless, panic-stricken, beneath the hideous machinery for murder, which was advancing closer and closer to suffocate me where I lay.

I looked up, motionless, speechless, breathless. The candle, fully spent, went out; but the moonlight still brightened the room. Down and down, without pausing and without sounding, came the bed-top, and still my panic-terror seemed to bind me faster and faster to the mattress on which I lay—down and down it sank, till the dusty odor from the lining of the canopy came stealing into my nostrils.

At that final moment the instinct of self-preservation startled me out of my trance, and I moved at last. There was just room for me to roll myself sideways off the bed. As I dropped noiselessly to the floor, the edge of the murderous canopy touched me on the shoulder.

Without stopping to draw my breath, without wiping the cold sweat from my face, I rose instantly on my knees to watch the bed-top. I was literally spell-bound by it. If I had heard footsteps behind me, I could not have turned round; if a means of escape had been miraculously provided for me, I could not have moved to take advantage of it. The whole life in me was, at that moment, concentrated in my eyes.

It descended—the whole canopy, with the fringe round it, came down—down—close down; so close that there was not room now to squeeze my finger between the bed-top and the bed. I felt at the sides, and discovered that what had appeared to me from beneath to be the ordinary light canopy of a four-post bed, was in reality a thick, broad mattress, the substance of which was concealed by the valance and its fringe. I looked up and saw the four posts rising hideously bare. In the middle of the bed-top was a huge wooden screw that had evidently worked it down through a hole in the ceiling, just as ordinary presses are worked down on the substance selected for compression. The frightful apparatus moved without making the faintest noise. There had been no creaking as it came down; there was now not the faintest sound from the room above. Amid a dead and awful silence I beheld before me—in the nineteenth century, and in the civilized capital of France—such a machine for secret murder by suffocation as might have existed in the worst days of the Inquisition, in the lonely inns among the Hartz Mountains, in the mysterious tribunals of Westphalia! Still, as I looked on it, I could not move, I could hardly breathe, but I began to recover the power of thinking, and in a moment I discovered the murderous conspiracy framed against me in all its horror.

My cup of coffee had been drugged, and drugged too strongly. I had been saved from being smothered by having taken an overdose of some narcotic. How I had chafed and fretted at the fever-fit which had preserved my life by keeping me awake! How recklessly I had confided myself to the two wretches who had led me into this room, determined, for the sake of my winnings, to kill me in my sleep by the surest and most horrible contrivance for secretly accomplishing my destruction! How many men, winners like me, had slept, as I had proposed to sleep, in that bed, and had never been seen or heard of more! I shuddered at the bare idea of it.

But, erelong, all thought was again suspended by the sight of the murderous canopy moving once more. After it had remained on the bed—as nearly as I could guess—about ten minutes, it began to move up again. The villains who worked it from above evidently believed that their purpose was now accomplished. Slowly and silently, as it had descended, that horrible bed-top rose toward its former place. When it reached the upper extremities of the four posts, it reached the ceiling too. Neither hole nor screw could be seen; the bed became in appearance an ordinary bed again—the canopy an ordinary canopy, even to the most suspicious eyes.

Now, for the first time, I was able to move—to rise from my knees—to dress myself in my upper clothing—and to consider of how I should escape. If I betrayed, by the smallest noise, that the attempt to suffocate me had failed, I was certain to be murdered. Had I made any noise already? I listened intently, looking towards the door.

No! no footsteps in the passage outside—no sound of a tread, light or heavy, in the room above—absolute silence everywhere. Besides locking and bolting my door, I had moved an old wooden chest against it, which I had found under the bed. To remove this chest (my blood ran cold as I thought what its contents *might* be!) without making some disturbance was impossible; and, moreover, to think of escaping through the house, now barred up for the night, was sheer insanity. Only one chance was left me—the window. I stole to it on tiptoe.

My bedroom was on the first floor, above an *entresol,* and looked into the back street, which you have sketched in your view. I raised my hand to open the window, knowing that on that action hung, by the merest hair's-breadth, my chance of safety. They keep vigilant watch in a House of Murder. If any part of the frame cracked, if the hinge creaked, I was a lost man! It must have occupied me at least five minutes, reckoning by time—five *hours,* reckoning by suspense—to open that window. I succeeded in doing it silently—in doing it with all the dexterity of a housebreaker—and then looked down into the street. To leap the distance beneath me would be almost certain destruction! Next, I looked round at the sides of the house. Down the left side ran the thick water-pipe which you have drawn—it passed close by the outer edge of the window. The moment I saw the pipe, I knew I was saved. My breath came and went freely for the first time since I had seen the canopy of the bed moving down upon me!

To some men the means of escape which I had discovered might have seemed difficult and dangerous enough—to *me* the prospect of slipping down the pipe into the street did not suggest even a thought of peril. I had always been accustomed, by the practice of gymnastics, to keep up my schoolboy powers as a daring and expert climber; and knew that my head, hands, and feet would serve me faithfully in any hazards of ascent or descent. I had already got one leg over the window-sill, when I remembered the handkerchief filled with money under my pillow. I could well have afforded to leave it behind me, but I was revengefully determined that the miscreants of the gambling-house should miss their plunder as well as their victim. So I went back to the bed and tied the heavy handkerchief at my back by my cravat.

Just as I had made it tight and fixed it in a comfortable place, I thought I heard a sound of breathing outside the door. The chill feeling of horror ran through me again as I listened. No! dead silence still in the passage—I had only heard the night-air blowing softly into the room. The next moment I was on the window-sill— and the next I had a firm grip on the water-pipe with my hands and knees.

I slid down into the street easily and quietly, as I thought I should, and immediately set off at the top of my speed to a branch 'Prefecture' of Police, which I knew was situated in the immediate neighborhood. A 'Sub-prefect,' and several picked men among his subordinates, happened to be up, maturing, I believe, some scheme for discovering the perpetrator of a mysterious murder which all Paris was talking of just then. When I began my story, in a breathless hurry and in very bad French, I could see that the Sub-prefect suspected me of being a drunken Englishman who had robbed somebody; but he soon altered his opinion as I went on, and before I had anything like concluded, he shoved all the papers before him into a drawer, put on his hat, supplied me with another (for I was bare-headed), ordered a file of soldiers, desired his expert followers to get ready all sorts of tools for breaking open doors and ripping up brick-flooring, and took my arm, in the most friendly and familiar manner possible, to lead me with him out of the house. I will venture to say, that when the Sub-prefect was a little boy, and was taken for the first time to the Play, he was not half as much pleased as he was now at the job in prospect for him at the gambling-house!

Away we went through the streets, the Sub-prefect cross-examining and congratulating me in the same breath as we marched at the head of our formidable *posse comitatus*. Sentinels were placed at the back and front of the house the moment we got to it; a tremendous battery of knocks was directed against the door; a light appeared at a window; I was told to conceal myself behind the police—then came more knocks, and a cry of 'Open in the name of the law!' At that terrible summons bolts and locks gave way before an invisible hand, and the moment after the Sub-prefect was in the passage, confronting a waiter half-dressed and ghastly pale. This was the short dialogue which immediately took place:

'We want to see the Englishman who is sleeping in this house.'

'He went away hours ago.'

'He did no such thing. His friend went away; *he* remained. Show us to his bedroom!'

'I swear to you, Monsieur le Sous-prefet, he is not here! he—'

'I swear to you, Monsieur le Garçon, he is. He slept here—he didn't find your bed comfortable—he came to us to complain of it—here he is among my men—and here am I ready to look for a flea or two in his bedstead. Renaudin! (calling to one of the subordinates, and pointing to the waiter) collar that man, and tie his hands behind him. Now, then, gentlemen, let us walk up stairs!'

Every man and woman in the house was secured—the 'Old Soldier' the first. Then I identified the bed in which I had slept, and then we went into the room above.

No object that was at all extraordinary appeared in any part of it. The Sub-prefect looked round the place, commanded everybody to be silent, stamped twice on the floor, called for a candle, looked attentively at the spot he had stamped on, and ordered the flooring there to be carefully taken up. This was done in no time. Lights were produced, and we saw a deep raftered cavity between the floor of this room and the ceiling of the room beneath. Through this cavity there ran perpendicularly a sort of case of iron thickly greased; and inside the case appeared the screw, which communicated with the bed-top below. Extra lengths of screw, freshly oiled; levers covered with felt; all the complete upper works of a heavy press—constructed with infernal ingenuity so as to join the fixtures below, and when taken to pieces again to go into the smallest possible compass—were next discovered and pulled out on the floor. After some little difficulty the Sub-prefect succeeded in putting the machinery together, and, leaving his men to work it, descended with me to the bed-room. The smothering canopy was then lowered, but not so noiselessly as I had seen it lowered. When I mentioned this to the Sub-prefect, his answer, simple as it was, had a terrible significance. 'My men,' said he, 'are working down the bed-top for the first time—the men whose money you won were in better practice.'

We left the house in the sole possession of two police agents—every one of the inmates being removed to prison on the spot. The Sub-prefect, after taking down my *'procès-verbal'* in his office, returned with me to my hotel to get my passport. 'Do you think,' I asked, as I gave it to him, 'that any men have really been smothered in that bed, as they tried to smother *me*?'

'I have seen dozens of drowned men laid out at the Morgue,' answered the Sub-prefect, 'in whose pocket-books were found letters, stating that they had committed suicide in the Seine, because they had lost everything at the gaming-table. Do I know how many of those men entered the same gambling-house that *you* entered? won as *you* won? took that bed as *you* took it? slept in it? were smothered in it? and were privately thrown into the river, with a letter of explanation written by the murderers and placed in their pocket-books? No man can say how many or how few have suffered the fate from which you have escaped. The people of the gambling-house kept their bedstead machinery a secret from *us*—even from the police! The dead kept the rest of the secret for them. Good night, or rather good morning, Monsieur Faulkner! Be at my office again at nine o'clock—in the meantime, *au revoir!*'

The rest of my story is soon told. I was examined and re-examined; the gambling-house was strictly searched all through from top to bottom; the prisoners were separately interrogated; and two of the less guilty among them made a confession. *I* discovered that the Old Soldier was the master of the gambling-house—*justice* discovered that he had been drummed out of the army as a vagabond years ago; that he had been guilty of all sorts of villanies since; that he was in possession of stolen property, which the owners identified; and that he, the croupier, another accomplice, and the woman who had made my cup of coffee, were all in the secret of the bedstead. There appeared some reason to doubt whether the inferior persons attached to the house knew anything of the suffocating machinery; and they received the benefit of that doubt, by being treated simply as thieves and vagabonds. As for the Old Soldier and his two head-myrmidons, they went to the galleys; the woman who had drugged my coffee was imprisoned for I forget how many years; the regular attendants at the gambling-house were considered 'suspicious,' and placed under 'surveillance;' and I became, for one whole week (which is a long time), the head 'lion' in Parisian society. My adventure was dramatised by three illustrious playmakers, but never saw theatrical daylight; for the censorship forbade the introduction on the stage of a correct copy of the gambling-house bedstead.

One good result was produced by my adventure which any censorship must have approved: it cured me of ever again trying *Rouge et Noir* as an amusement. The sight of a green cloth, with packs of cards and heaps of money on it, will henceforth be for ever associated in my mind with the sight of a bed-canopy descending to suffocate me in the silence and darkness of the night.

THE THREE STRANGERS

THOMAS HARDY
(1840–1928)

Although not at all known as a writer of mystery fiction, Hardy's excellent suspense tale with its surprise ending has maintained its status as a minor classic ever since it was collected in his two-volume Wessex Tales *(1888). Buried in the Poet's Corner of Westminster Abbey for his great naturalistic novels, including* Tess of the D'Urbervilles, Far From the Madding Crowd, *and* The Return of the Native, *Hardy managed even in this short work to bring the force of nature into overwhelming prominence.*

MONG THE FEW FEATURES of agricultural England which retain an appearance but little modified by the lapse of centuries, may be reckoned the high, grassy, and furzy downs, coombs, or ewe-leases, as they are indifferently called, that fill a large area of certain counties in the south and southwest. If any mark of human occupation is met with hereon it usually takes the form of the solitary cottage of some shepherd.

Fifty years ago such a lonely cottage stood on such a down, and may possibly be standing there now. In spite of its loneliness, however, the spot, by actual measurement, was not more than five miles from a county town. Yet, what of that? Five miles of irregular upland, during the long inimical seasons, with their sleets, snows, rains, and mists, afford withdrawing space enough to isolate a Timon or a Nebuchadnezzar; much less, in fair weather, to please that less repellent tribe, the poets, philosophers, artists, and others who "conceive and meditate of pleasant things."

Some old earthen camp or barrow, some clump of trees, at least some starved fragment of ancient hedge, is usually taken advantage of in the erection of these forlorn dwellings. But, in the present case, such a kind of shelter had been disregarded. Higher Crowstairs, as the house was called, stood quite detached and undefended. The only reason for its precise situation seemed to be the crossing of two footpaths at right angles hard by, which may have crossed there and thus for a good five hundred years.

The house was thus exposed to the elements on all sides. But, though the wind up here blew unmistakably when it did blow, and the rain hit hard whenever it fell, the various weathers of the winter season were not quite so formidable on the coomb as they were imagined to be by dwellers on low ground. The raw rimes were not so pernicious as in the hollows, and the frosts were scarcely so severe. When the shepherd and his family who tenanted the house were pitied for their sufferings from the exposure, they said that upon the whole they were less inconvenienced by "wuzzes and flames" (hoarses and phlegms) than when they had lived by the stream of a snug neighbouring valley.

The night of March 28, 182–, was precisely one of the nights that were wont to call forth these expressions of commiseration. The level rainstorm smote walls, slopes, and hedges like the clothyard shafts of Senlac and Crecy. Such sheep and outdoor animals as had no shelter stood with their buttocks to the wind; while the tails of little birds trying to roost on some scraggy thorn were blown inside-out like umbrellas. The gable-end of the cottage was stained with wet, and the eaves-droppings flapped against the wall. Yet never was commiseration for the shepherd more misplaced. For that cheerful rustic was entertaining a large party in glorification of the christening of his second girl.

The guests had arrived before the rain began to fall, and they were all now assembled in the chief or living-room of the dwelling. A glance into the apartment at eight o'clock on this eventful evening would have resulted in the opinion that it was as cozy and comfortable a nook as could be wished for in boisterous weather. The calling of its inhabitant was proclaimed by a number of highly polished sheep-crooks without stems that were hung ornamentally over the fireplace, the curl of each shining crook varying from the antiquated type engraved in the patriarchal pictures of old family Bibles to the most approved fashion of the last local sheep-fair.

The room was lighted by half a dozen candles, having wicks only a trifle smaller than the grease which enveloped them, in candlesticks that were never used but at high-days, holy-days, and family feasts. The lights were scattered about the room, two of them standing on the chimney-piece. This position of candles was in itself significant. Candles on the chimney-piece always meant a party.

On the hearth, in front of a back-brand to give substance, blazed a fire of thorns, that crackled "like the laughter of the fool."

Nineteen persons were gathered here. Of these, five women, wearing gowns of various bright hues, sat in chairs along the wall; girls shy and not shy filled the window-bench; four men, including Charley Jake the hedge-carpenter, Elijah New the parish clerk, and John Pitcher, a neighbouring dairyman, the shepherd's father-in-law, lolled in the settle; a young man and maid, who were blushing over tentative *pourparlers* on a life-companionship, sat beneath the corner-cupboard; and an elderly engaged man of fifty or upward moved restlessly about from spots where his betrothed was not to the spot where she was.

Enjoyment was pretty general, and so much the more prevailed in being unhampered by conventional restrictions. Absolute confidence in each other's good opinion begat perfect ease, while the finishing stroke of manner, amounting to a truly princely serenity, was lent to the majority by the absence of any expression or trait denoting that they wished to get on in the world, enlarge their minds, or do any eclipsing thing whatever—which nowadays so generally nips the bloom and *bonhomie* of all except the two extremes of the social scale.

Shepherd Fennel had married well, his wife being a dairyman's daughter from the valley below, who brought fifty guineas in her pocket—and kept them there, till they should be required for ministering to the needs of a coming family. This frugal woman had been somewhat exercised as to the character that should be given to the gathering. A sit-still party had its advantages; but an undisturbed position of ease in chairs and settles was apt to lead on the men to such an unconscionable deal of toping that they would sometimes fairly drink the house dry. A dancing-party was the alternative; but this, while avoiding the foregoing objection on the score of good drink, had a counterbalancing disadvantage in the matter of good victuals, the ravenous appetites engendered by the exercise causing immense havoc in the buttery.

Shepherdess Fennel fell back upon the intermediate plan of mingling short dances with short periods of talk and singing, so as to hinder any ungovernable rage in either. But this scheme was entirely confined to her own gentle mind: the shepherd himself was in the mood to exhibit the most reckless phases of hospitality.

The fiddler was a boy of those parts, about twelve years of age, who had a wonderful dexterity in jigs and reels, though his fingers were so small and short as to necessitate a constant shifting for the high notes, from which he scrambled back to the first position with sounds not of unmixed purity of tone. At seven the shrill tweedle-dee of this youngster had begun, accompanied by a booming ground-bass from Elijah New, the parish clerk, who had thoughtfully brought with him his favourite musical instrument, the serpent. Dancing was instantaneous, Mrs. Fennel privately enjoining the players on no account to let the dance exceed the length of a quarter of an hour.

But Elijah and the boy, in the excitement of their position, quite forgot the injunction. Moreover, Oliver Giles, a man of seventeen, one of the dancers, who was enamoured of his partner, a fair girl of thirty-three rolling years, had recklessly handed a new crown-piece to the musicians, as a bribe to keep going as long as they had muscle and wind. Mrs. Fennel, seeing the steam begin to generate on the countenances of her guests, crossed over and touched the fiddler's elbow and put her hand on the serpent's mouth. But they took no notice, and fearing she might lose her character of genial hostess if she were to interfere too markedly, she retired and sat down helpless. And so the dance whizzed on with cumulative fury, the performers moving in their planet-like courses, direct and retrograde from apogee to perigee, till the hand of the well-kicked clock at the bottom of the room had travelled over the circumference of an hour.

While these cheerful events were in course of enactment within Fennel's pastoral dwelling, an incident having considerable bearing on the party had occurred in the gloomy night without. Mrs. Fennel's concern about the growing fierceness of the dance corresponded in point of time with the ascent of a human figure to the solitary hill of Higher Crowstairs from the direction of the distant town. This personage strode on through the rain without a pause, following the little-worn path which, further on in its course, skirted the shepherd's cottage.

It was nearly the time of full moon, and on this account, though the sky was lined with a uniform sheet of dripping cloud, ordinary objects out of doors were readily visible. The sad wan light revealed the lonely pedestrian to be a man of supple frame; his gait suggested that he had somewhat passed the period of perfect and instinctive agility, though not so far as to be otherwise than rapid of motion when occasion required. In point of fact he might have been about forty years of age. He appeared tall, but a recruiting sergeant, or other person accustomed to the judging of men's heights by the eye, would have discerned that this was chiefly owing to his gauntness, and that he was not more than five feet eight or nine.

Notwithstanding the regularity of his tread, there was caution in it, as in that of one who mentally feels his way; and despite the fact that it was not a black coat nor a dark garment of any sort that he wore, there was something about him which suggested that he naturally belonged to the black-coated tribes of men. His clothes were of fustian, and his boots hobnailed, yet in his progress he showed not the mud-accustomed bearing of hobnailed and fustianed peasantry.

By the time that he had arrived abreast of the shepherd's premises the rain came down, or rather came along, with yet more determined violence. The outskirts of the little homestead partially broke the force of wind and rain, and this induced him to stand still. The most salient of the shepherd's domestic erections was an empty sty at the forward corner of his hedgeless garden, for in these latitudes the principle of masking the homelier features of your establishment by a conventional frontage was unknown. The traveller's eye was attracted to this small building by the pallid shine of the wet slates that covered it. He turned aside, and, finding it empty, stood under the pent-roof for shelter.

While he stood, the boom of the serpent within, and the lesser strains of the fiddler, reached the spot as an accompaniment to the surging hiss of the flying rain on the sod, its louder beating on the cabbage-leaves of the garden, on the eight or ten bee-hives just discernible by the path, and its dripping from the eaves into a row of buckets and pans that had been placed under the walls of the cottage. For at Higher Crowstairs, as at all such elevated domiciles, the grand difficulty of housekeeping was an insufficiency of water; and a casual rainfall was utilised by turning out, as catchers, every utensil that the house contained. Some queer stories might be told of the contrivances for economy in suds and dish-waters that are absolutely necessitated in upland habitations during the droughts of summer. But at this season there were no such exigencies: a mere acceptance of what the skies bestowed was sufficient for an abundant store.

At last the notes of the serpent ceased and the house was silent. This cessation of activity aroused the solitary pedestrian from the reverie into which he had lapsed, and, emerging from the shed, with an apparently new intention, he walked up the path to the house-door. Arrived here, his first act was to kneel down on a large stone beside the row of vessels, and to drink a copious draught from one of them. Having quenched his thirst, he rose and lifted his hand to knock, but paused with his eye upon the panel. Since the dark surface of the wood revealed absolutely nothing, it was evident that he must be mentally looking through the door, as if he wished to measure thereby all the possibilities that a house of this sort might include, and how they might bear upon the question of his entry.

In his indecision he turned and surveyed the scene around. Not a soul was anywhere visible. The garden-path stretched downward from his feet, gleaming like the track of a snail; the roof of the little well, the well cover, the top rail of the garden-gate, were varnished with the same dull liquid glaze; while, far away in the vale, a faint whiteness of more than usual extent showed that the rivers were high in the meads. Beyond all this winked a few bleared lamplights through the beating drops, lights that denoted the situation of the country-town from which he had appeared to come. The absence of all notes of life in that direction seemed to clinch his intentions, and he knocked at the door.

Within, a desultory chat had taken the place of movement and musical sound. The hedge-carpenter was suggesting a song to the company, which nobody just then was inclined to undertake, so that the knock afforded a not unwelcome diversion.

"Walk in!" said the shepherd promptly.

The latch clicked upward, and out of the night our pedestrian appeared upon the door-mat. The shepherd arose, lifted two of the nearest candles, and turned to look at him.

Their light disclosed that the stranger was dark in complexion, and not unprepossessing as to feature. His hat, which for a moment he did not remove, hung low over his eyes, without concealing that they were large, open, and determined, moving with a flash rather than a glance round the room. He seemed pleased with the survey, and, baring his shaggy head, said, in a rich deep voice, "The rain is so heavy, friends, that I ask leave to come in and rest awhile."

"To be sure, stranger," said the shepherd. "And faith, you've been lucky in choosing your time, for we are having a bit of a fling for a glad cause—though to be sure a man could hardly wish that glad cause to happen more than once a year."

"Nor less," spoke up a woman. "For 'tis best to get your family over and done with, as soon as you can, so to be all the earlier out of the fag o't."

"And what may be this glad cause?" asked the stranger.

"A birth and christening," said the shepherd.

The stranger hoped his host might not be made unhappy either by too many or too few of such episodes, and being invited by a gesture to a pull at the mug, he readily acquiesced. His manner which, before entering, had been so dubious, was now altogether that of a carefree and candid man.

"Late to be traipsing athwart this coomb—hey?" said the engaged man of fifty.

"Late it is, master, as you say.—I'll take a seat in the chimney-corner, if you have nothing to urge against it, ma'am; for I am a little moist on the side that was next the rain."

Mrs. Shepherd Fennel assented, and made room for the self-invited comer, who, having got completely inside the chimney-corner, stretched out his legs and his arms with the expansiveness of a person quite at home.

"Yes, I am rather thin in the vamp," he said freely, seeing that the eyes of the shepherd's wife fell upon his boots, "and I am not well-fitted, either. I have had some rough times lately, and have been forced to pick up what I can get in the way of wearing, but I must find a suit better fit for working-days when I reach home."

"One of hereabouts?" she inquired.

"Not quite that—further up the country."

"I thought so. And so am I; and by your tongue you come from my neighbourhood."

"But you would hardly have heard of me," he said quickly. "My time would be long before yours, ma'am, you see."

This testimony to the youthfulness of his hostess had the effect of stopping her cross-examination.

"There is only one thing more wanted to make me happy," continued the new comer. "And that is a little baccy, which I am sorry to say I am out of."

"I'll fill your pipe," said the shepherd.

"I must ask you to lend me a pipe likewise."

"A smoker, and no pipe about ye?"

"I have dropped it somewhere on the road."

The shepherd filled and handed him a new clay pipe, saying as he did so, "Hand me your baccy-box—I'll fill that too, now I am about it."

The man went through the movement of searching his pockets.

"Lost that too?" said his entertainer, with some surprise.

"I am afraid so," said the man with some confusion. "Give it to me in a screw of paper."

Lighting his pipe at the candle with a suction that drew the whole flame into the bowl, he resettled himself in the corner, and bent his looks upon the faint steam from his damp legs, as if he wished to say no more.

Meanwhile the general body of guests had been taking little notice of this visitor by reason of an absorbing discussion in which they were engaged with the band about a tune for the next dance. The matter being settled, they were about to stand up, when an interruption came in the shape of another knock at the door.

At the sound the man in the chimney-corner took up the poker and began stirring the fire as if doing it thoroughly were the one aim of his existence; and a second time the shepherd said, "Walk in!"

In a moment another man stood upon the straw-woven doormat. He too was a stranger.

This individual was one of a type radically different from the first. There was more of the commonplace in his manner, and a certain jovial cosmopolitanism sat upon his features. He was several years older than the first arrival, his hair being slightly frosted, his eyebrows bristly, and his whiskers cut back from his cheeks. His face was rather full and flabby, and yet it was not altogether a face without power. A few grog-blossoms marked the neighbourhood of his nose.

He flung back his long drab greatcoat, revealing that beneath it he wore a suit of cider-grey shade throughout, large heavy seals, of some metal or other that would take a polish, dangling from his fob as his only personal ornament. Shaking the water-drops from his low-crowned glazed hat, he said, "I must ask for a few minutes' shelter, comrades, or I shall be wetted to my skin before I get to Casterbridge."

"Make yerself at home, master," said the shepherd, perhaps a trifle less heartily than on the first occasion. Not that Fennel had the least tinge of niggardliness in his composition; but the room was far from large, spare chairs were not numerous, and damp companions were not altogether comfortable at close quarters for the women and girls in their bright-coloured gowns.

However, the second comer, after taking off his greatcoat, and hanging his hat on a nail in one of the ceiling beams as if he had been specially invited to put it there, advanced and sat down at the table. This had been pushed so closely into the chimney-corner, to give all available room to the dancers, that its inner edge grazed the elbow of the man who had ensconced himself by the fire; and thus the two strangers were brought into close companionship.

They nodded to each other by way of breaking the ice of unacquaintance, and the first stranger handed his neighbour the large mug—a huge vessel of brown ware, having its upper edge worn away like a threshold by the rub of whole genealogies of thirsty lips that had gone the way of all flesh, and bearing the following inscription burnt upon its rotund side in yellow letters:

THERE IS NO FUN
UNTILL I CUM.

The other man, nothing loth, raised the mug to his lips, and drank on, and on, and on—till a curious blueness overspread the countenance of the shepherd's wife, who had regarded with no little surprise the first stranger's free offer to the second of what did not belong to him to dispense.

"I knew it!" said the toper to the shepherd with much satisfaction. "When I walked up your garden afore coming in, and saw the hives all of a row, I said to myself, 'Where there's bees there's honey, and where there's honey there's mead.' But mead of such a truly comfortable sort as this I really didn't expect to meet in my older days." He took yet another pull at the mug, till it assumed an ominous horizontality.

"Glad you enjoy it!" said the shepherd warmly.

"It is goodish mead," assented Mrs. Fennel with an absence of enthusiasm, which seemed to say that it was possible to buy praise for one's cellar at too heavy a price. "It is trouble enough to make—and really I hardly think we shall make any more. For honey sells well, and we can make shift with a drop o' small mead and metheglin for common use from the comb-washings."

"Oh, but you'll never have the heart!" reproachfully cried the stranger in cinder-grey, after taking up the mug a third time and setting it down empty. "I love mead, when 'tis old like this, as I love to go to church o' Sundays, or to relieve the needy any day of the week."

"Ha, ha, ha!" said the man in the chimney-corner, who, in spite of the taciturnity induced by the pipe of tobacco, could not or would not refrain from this slight testimony to his comrade's humour.

Now the old mead of those days, brewed of the purest first-year or maiden honey, four pounds to the gallon—with its due complement of whites of eggs, cinnamon, ginger, cloves, mace, rosemary, yeast, and processes of working, bottling, and cellaring—tasted remarkably strong; but it did not taste so strong as it actually was. Hence, presently, the stranger in cinder-grey at the table, moved by its creeping influence, unbuttoned his waistcoat, threw himself back in his chair, spread his legs, and made his presence felt in various ways.

"Well, well, as I say," he resumed, "I am going to Casterbridge, and to Casterbridge I must go. I should have been almost there by this time; but the rain drove me into ye; and I'm not sorry for it."

"You don't live in Casterbridge?" said the shepherd.

"Not as yet; though I shortly mean to move there."

"Going to set up in trade, perhaps?"

"No, no," said the shepherd's wife. "It is easy to see that the gentleman is rich, and don't want to work at anything."

The cinder-grey stranger paused, as if to consider whether he would accept that definition of himself. He presently rejected it by answering, "Rich is not quite the word for me, dame. I do work, and I must work. And even if I only get to Casterbridge by midnight I must begin work there at eight to-morrow morning. Yes, het or wet, blow or snow, famine or sword, my day's work to-morrow must be done."

"Poor man! Then, in spite o' seeming, you be worse off than we?" replied the shepherd's wife.

" 'Tis the nature of my trade, men and maidens. 'Tis the nature of my trade more than my poverty . . . But really and truly I must up and off, or I shan't get a lodging in the town." However, the speaker did not move, and directly added, "There's time for one more draught of friendship before I go; and I'd perform it at once if the mug were not dry."

"Here's a mug o' small," said Mrs. Fennel. "Small, we call it, though to be sure 'tis only the first wash o' the combs."

"No," said the stranger disdainfully. "I won't spoil your first kindness by partaking o' your second."

"Certainly not," broke in Fennel. "We don't increase and multiply every day, and I'll fill the mug again." He went away in the dark place under the stairs where the barrel stood. The shepherdess followed him.

"Why should you do this?" she said reproachfully, as soon as they were alone. "He's emptied it once, though it held enough for ten people; and now he's not contented wi' the small, but must needs call for more o' the strong! And a stranger unbeknown to any of us. For my part I don't like the look o' the man at all."

"But he's in the house, my honey; and 'tis a wet night, and a christening. Daze it, what's a cup of mead more or less? There'll be plenty more next bee-burning."

"Very well—this time, then," she answered, looking wistfully at the barrel. "But what is the man's calling, and where is he one of, that he should come in and join us like this!"

"I don't know. I'll ask him again."

The catastrophe of having the mug drained dry at one pull by the stranger in cinder-grey was effectually guarded against this time by Mrs. Fennel. She poured out his allowance in a small cup, keeping the large one at a discreet distance from him. When he had tossed off his portion the shepherd renewed his inquiry about the stranger's occupation.

The latter did not immediately reply, and the man in the chimney-corner, with a sudden demonstrativeness, said, "Anybody may know my trade—I'm a wheelwright."

"A very good trade for these parts," said the shepherd.

"And anybody may know mine—if they've the sense to find it out," said the stranger in cinder-grey.

"You may generally tell what a man is by his claws," observed the hedge-carpenter, looking at his hands. "My fingers be as full of thorns as an old pincushion is of pins."

The hands of the man in the chimney-corner instinctively sought the shade, and he gazed into the fire as he resumed his pipe. The man at the table took up the hedge-carpenter's remark, and added smartly, "True; but the oddity of my trade is that, instead of setting a mark upon me, it sets a mark upon my customers."

No observation being offered by anybody in elucidation of this enigma, the shepherd's wife once more called for a song. The same obstacles presented themselves as at the former time—one had no voice, another had forgotten the first verse. The stranger at the table, whose soul had now risen to a good working temperature, relieved the difficulty by exclaiming that, to start the company, he would sing himself. Thrusting one thumb into the arm-hole of his waistcoat, he waved the other hand in the air, and, with an extemporising gaze at the shining sheep-crooks above the mantel-piece, began:

> Oh my trade it is the rarest one,
> > Simple shepherds all—
> My trade is a sight to see;
> For my customers I tie, and take them up
> > on high,
> And waft 'em to a far countree.

The room was silent when he had finished the verse—with one exception, that of the man in the chimney-corner, who, at the singer's word, "Chorus!" joined him in a deep bass voice of musical relish—

> And waft 'em to a far countree.

Oliver Giles, John Pitcher the diaryman, the parish clerk, the engaged man of fifty, the row of young women against the wall, seemed lost in thought not of the gayest kind. The shepherd looked meditatively on the ground, the shepherdess gazed keenly at the singer, and with some suspicion; she was doubting whether this stranger was merely singing an old song from recollection, or was composing one there and then for the occasion. All were as perplexed at the obscure revelation as the guests at Belshazzar's Feast, except the man in the chimney-corner, who quietly said, "Second verse, stranger," and smoked on.

The singer thoroughly moistened himself from his lips inwards, and went on with the next stanza as requested:

> My tools are but common ones,
> Simple shepherds all,
> My tools are no sight to see:
> A little hempen string, and a post whereon
> to swing,
> Are implements enough for me.

Shepherd Fennel glanced round. There was no longer any doubt that the stranger was answering his question rhythmically. The guests one and all started back with suppressed exclamations. The young woman engaged to the man of fifty fainted half-way, and would have proceeded, but finding him wanting in alacrity for catching her she sat down trembling.

"Oh, he's the——!" whispered the people in the background, mentioning the name of an ominous public officer. "He's come to do it. 'Tis to be at Casterbridge gaol to-morrow—the man for sheep-stealing—the poor clock-maker we heard of, who used to live away at Anglebury and had no work to do—Timothy Sommers, whose family were a-starving, and so he went out of Anglebury by the high-road, and took a sheep in open daylight, defying the farmer and the farmer's wife and the farmer's man, and every man-jack among 'em. He" (and they nodded towards the stranger of the terrible trade) "is come from up the country to do it because there's not enough to do in his own county-town, and he's got the place here now our own county man's dead; he's going to live in the same cottage under the prison wall."

The stranger in cinder-grey took no notice of this whispered string of observations, but again wetted his lips. Seeing that his friend in the chimney-corner was the only one who reciprocated his joviality in any way, he held out his cup towards that appreciative comrade, who also held out his own. They clinked together, the eyes of the rest of the room hanging upon the singer's actions. He parted his lips for the third verse; but at that moment another knock was audible upon the door. This time the knock was faint and hesitating.

The company seemed scared; the shepherd looked with consternation towards the entrance, and it was with some effort that he resisted his alarmed wife's deprecatory glance, and uttered for the third time the welcome words, "Walk in!"

The door was gently opened, and another man stood upon the mat. He, like those who had preceded him, was a stranger. This time it was a short, small personage, of fair complexion, and dressed in a decent suit of dark clothes.

"Can you tell me the way to ——?" he began; when, gazing round the room to observe the nature of the company amongst whom he had fallen, his eyes lighted on the stranger in cinder-grey. It was just at the instant when the latter, who had thrown his mind into his song with such a will that he scarcely heeded the interruption, silenced all whispers and inquiries by bursting into his third verse:

> To-morrow is my working day,
> Simple shepherds all—
> To-morrow is a working day for me:
> For the farmer's sheep is slain, and the lad
> who did it ta'en,
> And on his soul may God ha' merc-y!

The stranger in the chimney-corner, waving cups with the singer so heartily that his mead splashed over on the hearth, repeated in his bass voice as before:

And on his soul may God ha' merc-y!

All this time the third stranger had been standing in the door-way. Finding now that he did not come forward or go on speaking, the guests particularly regarded him. They noticed to their surprise that he stood before them the picture of abject terror—his knees trembling, his hand shaking so violently that the door-latch by which he supported himself rattled audibly; his white lips were parted, and his eyes fixed on the merry officer of justice in the middle of the room. A moment more and he had turned, closed the door, and fled.

"What man can it be?" said the shepherd.

The rest, between the awfulness of their late discovery and the odd conduct of this third visitor, looked as if they knew not what to think, and said nothing. Instinctively they withdrew further and further from the grim gentleman in their midst, whom some of them seemed to take for the Prince of Darkness himself, till they formed a remote circle, an empty space of floor being left between them and him—

—circulus, cujus centrum diabolus.

The room was so silent—though there were more than twenty people in it—that nothing could be heard but the patter of the rain against the window-shutters, accompanied by the occasional hiss of a stray drop that fell down the chimney into the fire, and the steady puffing of the man in the corner, who had now resumed his pipe of long clay.

The stillness was unexpectedly broken. The distant sound of a gun reverberated through the air—apparently from the direction of the county town.

"Be jiggered!" cried the stranger who had sung the song, jumping up.

"What does that mean?" asked several.

"A prisoner escaped from the gaol—that's what it means."

All listened. The sound was repeated, and none of them spoke but the man in the chimney-corner, who said quietly, "I've often been told that in this county they fire a gun at such times; but I never heard it till now."

"I wonder if it is *my* man?" murmured the personage in cinder-grey.

"Surely it is!" said the shepherd involuntarily. "And surely we've seen him! That little man who looked in at the door by now, and quivered like a leaf when he seed ye and heard your song!"

"His teeth chattered, and the breath went out of his body," said the dairyman.

"And his heart seemed to sink within him like a stone," said Oliver Giles.

"And he bolted as if he'd been shot at," said the hedge-carpenter.

"True—his teeth chattered, and his heart seemed to sink; and he bolted as if he'd been shot at," slowly summed up the man in the chimney-corner.

"I didn't notice it," remarked the grim songster.

"We were all a-wondering what made him run off in such a fright," faltered one of the women against the wall, "and now 'tis explained."

The firing of the alarm-gun went on at intervals, low and sullenly, and their suspicions became a certainty. The sinister gentleman in cinder-grey roused himself. "Is there a constable here?" he asked in thick tones. "If so, let him step forward."

The engaged man of fifty stepped quavering out of the corner, his betrothed beginning to sob on the back of the chair.

"You are a sworn constable?"

"I be, sir."

"Then pursue the criminal at once, with assistance, and bring him back here. He can't have gone far."

"I will, sir, I will—when I've got my staff. I'll go home and get it, and come sharp here, and start in a body."

"Staff! Never mind your staff; the man'll be gone!"

"But I can't do nothing without my staff—can I, William, and John, and Charles Jake? No; for there's the king's royal crown a-painted on en in yaller and gold, and the lion and the unicorn, so as when I raise en up and hit my prisoner, 'tis made a lawful blow thereby. I wouldn't 'tempt to take up a man without my staff—no, not I. If I hadn't the law to gie me courage, why, instead o' my taking up him he might take up me!"

"Now, I'm a king's man myself, and can give you authority enough for this," said the formidable person in cinder-grey. "Now, then, all of ye, be ready. Have ye any lanterns?"

"Yes—have ye any lanterns?—I demand it," said the constable.

"And the rest of you able-bodied—"

"Able-bodied men—yes—the rest of ye," said the constable.

"Have you some good stout staves and pitchforks—"

"Staves and pitchforks—in the name o' the law. And take 'em in yer hands and go in quest, and do as we in authority tell yea."

Thus aroused, the men prepared to give chase. The evidence was, indeed, though circumstantial, so convincing, that but little argument was needed to show the shepherd's guests that after what they had seen it would look very much like connivance if they did not instantly pursue the unhappy third stranger, who could not as yet have gone more than a few hundred yards over such uneven country.

A shepherd is always well provided with lanterns; and, lighting these hastily, and with hurdle-staves in their hands, they poured out of the door, taking a direction along the crest of the hill, away from the town, the rain having fortunately a little abated.

Disturbed by the noise, or possibly by unpleasant dreams of her baptism, the child who had been christened began to cry heartbrokenly in the room overhead. These notes of grief came down through the chinks of the floor to the ears of the women below, who jumped up one by one, and seemed glad of the excuse to ascend and comfort the baby, for the incidents of the last half hour greatly oppressed them. Thus in the space of two or three minutes the room on the ground floor was deserted.

But it was not for long. Hardly had the sound of footsteps died away when a man returned round the corner of the house from the direction the pursuers had taken. Peeping in at the door, and seeing nobody there, he entered leisurely. It was the stranger of the chimney-corner, who had gone out with the rest. The motive of his return was shown by his helping himself to a cut piece of skimmer-cake that lay on a ledge beside where he had sat, and which he had apparently forgotten to take with him. He also poured out half a cup more mead from the quantity that remained, ravenously eating and drinking these as he stood. He had not finished when another figure came in just as quietly—the stranger in cinder-grey.

"Oh—you here?" said the latter smiling. "I thought you had gone to help in the capture." And this speaker also revealed the object of his return by looking solicitously round for the fascinating mug of old mead.

"And I thought you had gone," said the other, continuing his skimmer-cake with some effort.

"Well, on second thoughts, I felt there were enough without me," said the other, confidentially, "and such a night as it is, too. Besides, 'tis the business o' the Government to take care of its criminals—not mine."

"True; so it is. And I felt as you did, that there were enough without me."

"I don't want to break my limbs running over the humps and hollows of this wild country."

"Nor I neither, between you and me."

"These shepherd-people are used to it—simple-minded souls, you know, stirred up to anything in a moment. They'll have him ready for me before the morning, and no trouble to me at all."

"They'll have him, and we shall have saved ourselves all labour in the matter."

"True, true. Well, my way is to Casterbridge; and 'tis as much as my legs will do to take me that far. Going the same way?"

"No, I am sorry to say. I have to get home over there"—he nodded indefinitely to the right— "and I feel as you do, that it is quite enough for my legs to do before bedtime."

The other had by this time finished the mead in the mug, after which, shaking hands at the door, and wishing each other well, they went their several ways.

In the meantime the company of pursuers had reached the end of the hog's back elevation which dominated this part of the coomb. They had decided on no particular plan of action; and, finding that the man of the baleful trade was no longer in their company, they seemed quite unable to form any such plan now. They descended in all directions down the hill, and straightway several of the party fell into the snare set by Nature for all misguided midnight ramblers over the lower cretaceous formation. The "lynchets," or flint slopes, which belted the escarpment at intervals of a dozen yards, took the less cautious ones unawares, and losing their footing on the rubbly steep they slid sharply downwards, the lanterns rolling from their hands to the bottom, and there lying on their sides till the horn was scorched through.

When they had again gathered themselves together, the shepherd, as the man who knew the country best, took the lead, and guided them round these treacherous inclines. The lanterns, which seemed rather to dazzle their eyes and warn the fugitive than to assist them in the exploration, were extinguished, due silence was observed; and in this more rational order they plunged into the vale. It was a grassy, briary, moist channel, affording some shelter to any person who had sought it; but the party perambulated it in vain, and ascended on the other side.

Here they wandered apart, and after an interval closed together again to report progress. At the second time of closing in they found themselves near a lonely oak, the single tree on this part of the upland, probably sown there by a passing bird some hundred years before. And here, standing a little to one side of the trunk, as motionless as the trunk itself, appeared the man they were in quest of, his outline being well defined against the sky beyond. The band noiselessly drew up and faced him.

"Your money or your life!" said the constable sternly to the tall figure.

"No, no," whispered John Pitcher. "'Tisn't our side ought to say that. That's the doctrine of vagabonds like him, and we be on the side of the law."

"Well, well," replied the constable impatiently; "I must say something, mustn't I? And if you had all the weight o' this undertaking upon your mind, perhaps you'd say the wrong thing too.—Prisoner at the bar, surrender, in the name of the Fath—the Crown, I mane!"

The man under the tree seemed now to notice them for the first time, and, giving them no opportunity whatever for exhibiting their courage, he strolled slowly towards them. He was, indeed, the little man, the third stranger; but his trepidation had in a great measure gone.

"Well, travellers," he said, "did I hear ye speak to me?"

"You did: you've got to come and be our prisoner at once," said the constable. "We arrest ye on the charge of not biding in Casterbridge gaol in a decent proper manner to be hung to-morrow morning. Neighbours, do your duty, and seize the culpet!"

On hearing the charge, the man seemed enlightened, and, saying not another word, resigned himself with preternatural civility to the search-party, who, with their staves in their hands, surrounded him on all sides, and marched him back towards the shepherd's cottage.

It was eleven o'clock by the time they arrived. The light shining from the open door, a sound of men's voices within, proclaimed to them as they approached the house that some new events had arisen in their absence. On entering they discovered the shepherd's living-room to be invaded by two officers from Casterbridge gaol, and a well-known magistrate who lived at the nearest county seat, intelligence of the escape having become generally circulated.

"Gentlemen," said the constable, "I have brought back your man—not without risk and danger; but every one must do his duty. He is inside this circle of able-bodied persons, who have lent me useful aid considering their ignorance of Crown work. Men, bring forward your prisoner." And the third stranger was led to the light.

"Who is this?" said one of the officials.

"The man," said the constable.

"Certainly not," said the other turnkey; and the first corroborated his statement.

"But how can it be otherwise?" asked the constable. "Or why was he so terrified at sight o' the singing instrument of the law?" Here he related the strange behaviour of the third stranger on entering the house.

"Can't understand it," said the officer coolly. "All I know is that it is not the condemned man. He's quite a different character from this one; a gauntish fellow, with dark hair and eyes, rather good-looking, and with a musical bass voice that if you heard it once you'd never mistake as long as you lived."

"Why, souls—'twas the man in the chimney-corner!"

"Hey—what?" said the magistrate, coming forward after inquiring particulars from the shepherd in the background. "Haven't you got the man after all?"

"Well, sir," said the constable, "he's the man we were in search of, that's true; and yet he's not the man we were in search of. For the man we were in search of was not the man we wanted, sir, if you understand my everyday way; for 'twas the man in the chimney-corner."

"A pretty kettle of fish altogether!" said the magistrate. "You had better start for the other man at once."

The prisoner now spoke for the first time. The mention of the man in the chimney-corner seemed to have moved him as nothing else could do.

"Sir," he said, stepping forward to the magistrate, "take no more trouble about me. The time is come when I may as well speak. I have done nothing; my crime is that the condemned man is my brother. Early this afternoon I left home at Anglebury to tramp it all the way to Casterbridge gaol to bid him farewell. I was benighted, and called here to rest and ask the way. When I opened the door I saw before me the very man, my brother, that I thought to see in the condemned cell at Casterbridge. He was in this chimney-corner; and jammed close to him, so that he could not have got out if he had tried, was the executioner who'd come to take his life, singing a song about it and not knowing that it was his victim who was close by, joining in to save appearances. My brother looked a glance of agony at me, and I knew he meant, 'Don't reveal what you see; my life depends on it.' I was so terror-struck that I could hardly stand, and, not knowing what I did, I turned and hurried away."

The narrator's manner and tone had the stamp of truth, and his story made a great impression on all around. "And do you know where your brother is at the present time?" asked the magistrate.

"I do not. I have never seen him since I closed this door."

"I can testify to that, for we've been between ye ever since," said the constable.

"Where does he think to fly to?—what is his occupation?"

"He's a watch-and-clock maker, sir."

" 'A said 'a was a wheelwright—a wicked rogue," said the constable.

"The wheels o'clocks and watches he meant, no doubt," said Shepherd Fennel. "I thought his hands were palish for's trade."

"Well, it appears to me that nothing can be gained by retaining this poor man in custody," said the magistrate; "your business lies with the other, unquestionably."

And so the little man was released off-hand; but he looked nothing the less sad on that account, it being beyond the power of magistrate or constable to raze out the written troubles in his brain, for they concerned another whom he regarded with more solicitude than himself. When this was done, and the man had gone his way, the night was found to be so far advanced that it was deemed useless to renew the search before the next morning.

Next day, accordingly, the quest for the clever sheep-stealer became general and keen, to all appearance at least. But the intended punishment was cruelly disproportioned to the transgression, and the sympathy of a great many country folk in that district was strongly on the side of the fugitive. Moreover, his marvelous coolness and daring under the unprecedented circumstances of the shepherd's party won their admiration. So that it may be questioned if all those who ostensibly made themselves so busy in exploring woods and fields and lanes were quite so thorough when it came to the private examination of their own lofts and outhouses. Stories were afloat of a mysterious figure being occasionally seen in some old overgrown trackway or other, remote from turnpike roads; but when a search was instituted in any of these suspected quarters nobody was found. Thus the days and weeks passed without tidings.

In brief, the bass-voiced man of the chimney-corner was never recaptured. Some said that he went across the sea, others that he did not, but buried himself in the depths of a populous city. At any rate, the gentleman in cinder-grey never did his morning's work at Casterbridge, nor met anywhere at all, for business purposes, the comrade with whom he had passed an hour of relaxation in the lonely house on the coomb.

The grass has long been green on the graves of Shepherd Fennel and his frugal wife; the guests who made up the christening party have mainly followed their entertainers to the tomb; the baby in whose honour they all had met is a matron in the sere and yellow leaf. But the arrival of the three strangers at the shepherd's that night, and the details connected therewith, is a story as well known as ever in the country about Higher Crowstairs.

THE RED-HEADED LEAGUE

ARTHUR CONAN DOYLE
(1859–1930)

Although Sir Arthur always believed the Sherlock Holmes stories were trivial and that he would be remembered for his more serious historical novels, it is arguable that he created the most famous fictional character of all time, better known throughout the world than Hamlet, Alice, and Robinson Crusoe. It is difficult to realize now that he had had little success with his first two novels, A Study in Scarlet *and* The Sign of Four, *only finding his readership when his short stories appeared in* The Strand Magazine.

 HAD CALLED UPON MY FRIEND, Mr. Sherlock Holmes, one day in the autumn of last year, and found him in deep conversation with a very stout, florid-faced, elderly gentleman, with fiery red hair. With an apology for my intrusion, I was about to withdraw, when Holmes pulled me abruptly into the room, and closed the door behind me.

"You could not possibly have come at a better time, my dear Watson," he said cordially.

"I was afraid that you were engaged."

"So I am. Very much so."

"Then I can wait in the next room."

"Not at all. This gentleman, Mr. Wilson, has been my partner and helper in many of my most successful cases, and I have no doubt that he will be of the utmost use to me in yours also."

The stout gentleman half rose from his chair, and gave a bob of greeting, with a quick little questioning glance from his small, fat-encircled eyes.

"Try the settee," said Holmes, relapsing into his armchair, and putting his fingertips together, as was his custom when in judicial moods. "I know, my dear Watson, that you share my love of all that is bizarre and outside the conventions and humdrum routine of every-day life. You have shown your relish for it by the enthusiasm which has prompted you to chronicle, and, if you will excuse my saying so, somewhat to embellish so many of my own little adventures."

"Your cases have indeed been of the greatest interest to me," I observed.

"You will remember that I remarked the other day, just before we went into the very simple problem presented by Miss Mary Sutherland, that for strange effects and extraordinary combinations we must go to life itself, which is always far more daring than any effort of the imagination."

"A proposition which I took the liberty of doubting."

"You did, Doctor, but none the less you must come round to my view, for otherwise I shall keep on piling fact upon fact on you, until your reason breaks down under them and acknowledges me to be right. Now, Mr. Jabez

Wilson here has been good enough to call upon me this morning, and to begin a narrative which promises to be one of the most singular which I have listened to for some time. You have heard me remark that the strangest and most unique things are very often connected not with the larger but with the smaller crimes, and occasionally, indeed, where there is room for doubt whether any positive crime has been committed. As far as I have heard, it is impossible for me to say whether the present case is an instance of crime or not, but the course of events is certainly among the most singular that I have ever listened to. Perhaps, Mr. Wilson, you would have the great kindness to recommence your narrative. I ask you, not merely because my friend Dr. Watson has not heard the opening part, but also because the peculiar nature of the story makes me anxious to have every possible detail from your lips. As a rule, when I have heard some slight indication of the course of events I am able to guide myself by the thousands of other similar cases which occur to my memory. In the present instance I am forced to admit that the facts are, to the best of my belief, unique."

The portly client puffed out his chest with an appearance of some little pride, and pulled a dirty and wrinkled newspaper from the inside pocket of his greatcoat. As he glanced down the advertisement column, with his head thrust forward, and the paper flattened out upon his knee, I took a good look at the man, and endeavoured after the fashion of my companion to read the indications which might be presented by his dress or appearance.

I did not gain very much, however, by my inspection. Our visitor bore every mark of being an average commonplace British tradesman, obese, pompous, and slow. He wore rather baggy grey shepherd's check trousers, a not overclean black frockcoat, unbuttoned in the front, and a drab waistcoat with a heavy brassy Albert chain, and a square pierced bit of metal dangling down as an ornament. A frayed top hat and a faded brown overcoat with a wrinkled velvet collar lay upon a chair beside him. Altogether, look as I would, there was nothing remarkable about the man save his blazing red head, and the expression of extreme chagrin and discontent upon his features.

Sherlock Holmes' quick eye took in my occupation, and he shook his head with a smile as he noticed my questioning glances. "Beyond the obvious facts that he has at some time done manual labour, that he takes snuff, that he is a Freemason, that he has been in China, and that he has done a considerable amount of writing lately, I can deduce nothing else."

Mr. Jabez Wilson started up in his chair, with his forefinger upon the paper, but his eyes upon my companion.

"How, in the name of good fortune, did you know all that, Mr. Holmes?" he asked. "How did you know, for example, that I did manual labour. It's as true as gospel, for I began as a ship's carpenter."

"Your hands, my dear sir. Your right hand is quite a size larger than your left. You have worked with it, and the muscles are more developed."

"Well, the snuff, then, and the Freemasonry?"

"I won't insult your intelligence by telling you how I read that, especially as, rather against the strict rules of your order, you use an arc and compass breastpin."

"Ah, of course, I forgot that. But the writing?"

"What else can be indicated by that right cuff so very shiny for five inches, and the left one with the smooth patch near the elbow where you rest it upon the desk."

"Well, but China?"

"The fish which you have tattooed immediately above your right wrist could only have been done in China. I have made a small study of tattoo marks, and have even contributed to the literature of the subject. That trick of staining the fishes' scales of a delicate pink is quite peculiar to China. When, in addition, I see a Chinese coin hanging from your watch-chain, the matter becomes even more simple."

Mr. Jabez Wilson laughed heavily. "Well, I never!" said he. "I thought at first that you had done something clever, but I see that there was nothing in it after all."

"I begin to think, Watson," said Holmes, "that I make a mistake in explaining. 'Omne ignotum pro magnifico,' you know, and my poor little reputation, such as it is, will suffer shipwreck if I am so candid. Can you not find the advertisement, Mr. Wilson?"

"Yes, I have got it now," he answered, with his thick, red finger planted half-way down the column. "Here it is. This is what began it all. You just read it for yourself, sir."

I took the paper from him, and read as follows:

"TO THE RED-HEADED LEAGUE. On account of the bequest of the late Ezekiah Hopkins, of Lebanon, Penn., U.S.A., there is now another vacancy open which entitles a member of the League to a salary of four pounds a week for purely nominal services. All red-headed men who are sound in body and mind, and above the age of twenty-one years, are eligible. Apply in person on Monday, at eleven o'clock, to Duncan Ross, at the offices of the League, 7, Pope's-court, Fleet-street."

"What on earth does this mean?" I ejaculated, after I had twice read over the extraordinary announcement.

Holmes chuckled, and wriggled in his chair, as was his habit when in high spirits. "It is a little off the beaten track, isn't it?" said he. "And now, Mr. Wilson, off you go at scratch, and tell us all about yourself, your household, and the effect which this advertisement had upon your fortunes. You will first make a note, Doctor, of the paper and the date."

"It is *The Morning Chronicle,* of April 27, 1890. Just two months ago."

"Very good. Now, Mr. Wilson?"

"Well, it is just as I have been telling you, Mr. Sherlock Holmes," said Jabez Wilson, mopping his forehead, "I have a small pawnbroker's business at Coburg-square, near the City. It's not a very large affair, and of late years it has not done more than just give me a living. I used to be able to keep two assistants, but now I only keep one; and I would have a job to pay him, but that he is willing to come for half wages, so as to learn the business."

"What is the name of this obliging youth?" asked Sherlock Holmes.

"His name is Vincent Spaulding, and he's not such a youth either. It's hard to say his age. I should not wish a smarter assistant, Mr. Holmes; and I know very well that he could better himself, and earn twice what I am able to give him. But after all, if he is satisfied, why should I put ideas in his head?"

"Why, indeed? You seem most fortunate in having an *employé* who comes under the full market price. It is not a common experience among employers in this age. I don't know that your assistant is not as remarkable as your advertisement."

"Oh, he has his faults, too," said Mr. Wilson. "Never was such a fellow for photography. Snapping away with a camera when he ought to be improving his mind, and then diving down into the cellar like a rabbit into its hole to develop his pictures. That is his main fault; but, on the whole, he's a good worker. There's no vice in him."

"He is still with you, I presume?"

"Yes, sir. He and a girl of fourteen, who does a bit of simple cooking, and keeps the place clean—that's all I have in the house, for I am a widower, and never had any family. We live very quietly, sir, the three of us; and we keep a roof over our heads, and pay our debts, if we do nothing more.

"The first thing that put us out was that advertisement. Spaulding, he came down into the office just this day eight weeks with this very paper in his hand, and he says:

"'I wish to the Lord, Mr. Wilson, that I was a red-headed man.'

"'Why that?' I asks.

"'Why,' says he, 'here's another vacancy on the League of the Red-headed Men. It's worth quite a little fortune to any man who gets it, and I understand that there are more vacancies than there are men, so that the trustees are at their wits' end what to do with the money. If my hair would only change colour, here's a nice little crib all ready for me to step into.'

"'Why, what is it, then?' I asked. You see, Mr. Holmes, I am a very stay-at-home man, and, as my business came to me instead of my having to go to it, I was often weeks on end without putting my foot over the door-mat. In that way I didn't know much of what was going on outside, and I was always glad of a bit of news.

"'Have you ever heard of the League of the Red-headed Men?' he asked, with his eyes open.

"'Never.'

"'Why, I wonder at that, for you are eligible yourself for one of the vacancies.'

"'And what are they worth?' I asked.

"'Oh, merely a couple of hundred a year, but the work is slight, and it need not interfere very much with one's other occupations.'

"Well, you can easily think that that made me prick up my ears, for the business has not been over good for some years, and an extra couple of hundred would have been very handy.

"'Tell me all about it,' said I.

"'Well,' said he, showing me the advertisement, 'you can see for yourself that the League has a vacancy, and there is the address where you should apply for particulars. As far as I can make out, the League was founded by an American millionaire, Ezekiah Hopkins, who was very peculiar in his ways. He was himself red-headed, and he had a great sympathy for all red-headed men; so, when he died, it was found that he had left his enormous fortune in the hands of trustees, with instructions to apply the interest to the providing of easy berths to men whose hair is of that colour. From all I hear it is splendid pay, and very little to do.'

"'But,' said I, 'there would be millions of red-headed men who would apply.'

"'Not so many as you might think,' he answered. 'You see it is really confined to Londoners, and to grown men. This American had started from London when he was young, and he wanted to do the old town a good turn. Then, again, I have heard it is no use your applying if your hair is light red, or dark red, or anything but real, bright, blazing, fiery red. Now, if you cared to apply, Mr. Wilson, you would just walk in; but perhaps it would hardly be worth your while to put yourself out of the way for the sake of a few hundred pounds.'

"'Now, it is a fact, gentlemen, as you may see for yourselves, that my hair is of a very full and rich tint, so that it seemed to me that, if there was to be any competition in the matter, I stood as good a chance as any man that I had ever met. Vincent Spaulding seemed to know so much about it that I thought he might prove useful, so I just ordered him to put up the shutters for the day, and to come right away with me. He was very willing to have a holiday, so we shut the business up, and started off for the address that was given us in the advertisement.

"I never hope to see such a sight as that again, Mr. Holmes. From north, south, east, and west every man who had a shade of red in his hair had tramped into the City to answer the advertisement. Fleet-street was choked with red-headed folk, and Pope's-court looked like a coster's orange barrow. I should not have thought there were so many in the whole country as were brought together by that single advertisement. Every shade of colour they were—straw, lemon, orange, brick, Irish-setter, liver, clay; but, as Spaulding said, there were not many who had the real vivid flame-coloured tint. When I saw how many were waiting, I would have given it up in despair; but Spaulding would not hear of it. How he did it I could not imagine, but he pushed and pulled and butted until he got me through the crowd, and right up to the steps which led to the office. There was a double stream upon the stair, some going up in hope, and some coming back dejected; but we wedged in as well as we could, and soon found ourselves in the office."

"Your experience has been a most entertaining one," remarked Holmes, as his client paused and refreshed his memory with a huge pinch of snuff. "Pray continue your very interesting statement."

"There was nothing in the office but a couple of wooden chairs and a deal table, behind which sat a small man, with a head that was even redder than mine. He said a few words to each candidate as he came up, and then he always managed to find some fault in them which would disqualify them. Getting a vacancy did not seem to be such a very easy matter after all. However, when our turn came, the little man was much more favourable to me than to any of the others, and he closed the door as we entered, so that he might have a private word with us.

"'This is Mr. Jabez Wilson,' said my assistant, 'and he is willing to fill a vacancy in the League.'

"'And he is admirably suited for it,' the other answered. 'He has every requirement. I cannot recall when I have seen anything so fine.' He took a step backwards, cocked his head on one side, and gazed at my hair until I felt quite bashful. Then suddenly he plunged forward, wrung my hand, and congratulated me warmly on my success.

"'It would be injustice to hesitate,' said he. 'You will, however, I am sure, excuse me for taking an obvious precaution.' With that he seized my hair in both his hands, and tugged until I yelled with the pain. 'There is water in your eyes,' said he, as he released me. 'I perceive that all is as it should be. But we have to be careful, for we have twice been deceived by wigs and once by paint. I could tell you tales of cobbler's wax which would disgust you with human nature.' He stepped over to the window and shouted through it at the top of his voice that the vacancy was filled. A groan of disappointment came up from below, and the folk all trooped away in different directions, until there was not a red head to be seen except my own and that of the manager.

"'My name,' said he, 'is Mr. Duncan Ross, and I am myself one of the pensioners upon the fund left by our noble benefactor. Are you a married man, Mr. Wilson? Have you a family?'

"I answered that I had not.

"His face fell immediately.

"'Dear me!' he said, gravely, 'that is very serious indeed! I am sorry to hear you say that. The fund was, of course, for the propagation and spread of the red-heads as well as for their maintenance. It is exceedingly unfortunate that you should be a bachelor.'

"My face lengthened at this, Mr. Holmes, for I thought that I was not to have the vacancy after all; but, after thinking it over for a few minutes, he said that it would be all right.

"'In the case of another,' said he, 'the objection might be fatal, but we must stretch a point in favour of a man with such a head of hair as yours. When shall you be able to enter upon your new duties?'

"'Well, it is a little awkward, for I have a business already,' said I.

"'Oh, never mind about that, Mr. Wilson!' said Vincent Spaulding, 'I shall be able to look after that for you.'

"'What would be the hours?' I asked.

"'Ten to two.'

"Now a pawnbroker's business is mostly done of an evening, Mr. Holmes, especially Thursday and Friday evening, which is just before pay-day; so it would suit me very well to earn a little in the mornings. Besides, I knew that my assistant was a good man, and that he would see to anything that turned up.

"'That would suit me very well,' said I. 'And the pay?'

"'Is four pounds a week.'

"'And the work?'

"'Is purely nominal.'

"'What do you call purely nominal?'

"'Well, you have to be in the office, or at least in the building, the whole time. If you leave, you forfeit your whole position for ever. The will is very clear upon that point. You don't comply with the conditions if you budge from the office during that time.'

"'It's only four hours a day, and I should not think of leaving,' said I.

"'No excuse will avail,' said Mr. Duncan Ross, 'neither sickness, nor business, nor anything else. There you must stay, or you lose your billet.'

"'And the work?'

"'Is to copy out the "Encyclopædia Britannica." There is the first volume of it in that press. You must find your own ink, pens, and blotting-paper, but we provide this table and chair. Will you be ready to-morrow?'

"'Certainly,' I answered.

"'Then, good-bye, Mr. Jabez Wilson, and let me congratulate you once more on the important position which you have been fortunate enough to gain.' He bowed me out of the room, and I went home with my assistant, hardly knowing what to say or do, I was so pleased at my own good fortune.

"Well, I thought over the matter all day, and by evening I was in low spirits again; for I had quite persuaded myself that the whole affair must be some great hoax or fraud, though what its object might be I could not imagine. It seemed altogether past belief that anyone could make such a will, or that they would pay such a sum for doing anything so simple as copying out the 'Encyclopædia Britannica.' Vincent Spaulding did what he could to cheer me up, but by bedtime I had reasoned myself out of the whole thing. However, in the morning I determined to have a look at it anyhow, so I bought a penny bottle of ink, and with a quill pen, and seven sheets of foolscap paper, I started off for Pope's-court.

"Well, to my surprise and delight everything was right as possible. The table was set out ready for me, and Mr. Duncan Ross was there to see that I got fairly to work. He started me off upon the letter A, and then he left me; but he would drop in from time to time to see that all was right with me. At two o'clock he bade me good-day, complimented me upon the amount I had written, and locked the door of the office after me.

"This went on day after day, Mr. Holmes, and on Saturday the manager came in and planked down four golden sovereigns for my week's work. It was the same next

week, and the same the week after. Every morning I was there at ten, and every afternoon I left at two. By degrees Mr. Duncan Ross took to coming in only once of a morning, and then, after a time, he did not come in at all. Still, of course, I never dared to
leave the room for an instant, for I was not sure when he might come, and the billet
was such a good one, and suited me so well, that I would not risk the loss of it.

"Eight weeks passed away like this, and I had written about Abbots, and Archery,
and Armour, and Architecture, and Attica, and hoped with diligence that I might get on
to the Bs before very long. It cost me something in foolscap, and I had pretty nearly
filled a shelf with my writings. And then suddenly the whole business came to an end."

"To an end?"

"Yes, sir. And no later than this morning. I went to my work as usual at ten o'clock,
but the door was shut and locked, with a little square of cardboard hammered on to
the middle of the panel with a tack. Here it is, and you can read for yourself."

He held up a piece of white cardboard, about the size of a sheet of notepaper. It
read in this fashion:—

" THE RED-HEADED LEAGUE IS DISSOLVED. Oct. 9, 1890."

Sherlock Holmes and I surveyed this curt announcement and the rueful face
behind it, until the comical side of the affair so completely overtopped every other
consideration that we both burst out into a roar of laughter.

"I cannot see that there is anything very funny," cried our client, flushing up to
the roots of his flaming head. "If you can do nothing better than laugh at me, I can
go elsewhere."

"No, no," cried Holmes, shoving him back into the chair from which he had half
risen. "I really wouldn't miss your case for the world. It is most refreshingly unusual.
But there is, if you will excuse my saying so, something just a little funny about it.
Pray what steps did you take when you found the card upon the door?"

"I was staggered, sir. I did not know what to do. Then I called at the offices round,
but none of them seemed to know anything about it. Finally, I went to the landlord,
who is an accountant living on the ground floor, and I asked him if he could tell me
what had become of the Red-headed League. He said that he had never heard of any
such body. Then I asked him who Mr. Duncan Ross was. He answered that the name
was new to him."

" 'Well,' said I, 'the gentleman at No. 4.'

" 'What, the red-headed man?'

" 'Yes.'

" 'Oh,' said he, 'his name was William Morris. He was a solicitor, and was using
my room as a temporary convenience until his new premises were ready. He moved
out yesterday.'

" 'Where could I find him?'

" 'Oh, at his new offices. He did tell me the address. Yes, 17, King Edward-street,
near St. Paul's.'"

"I started off, Mr. Holmes, but when I got to that address it was a manufactory of
artificial kneecaps, and no one in it had ever heard of either Mr. William Morris, or
Mr. Duncan Ross."

"And what did you do then?" asked Holmes.

"I went home to Saxe-Coburg-square, and I took the advice of my assistant. But
he could not help me in any way. He could only say that if I waited I should hear by
post. But that was not quite good enough, Mr. Holmes. I did not wish to lose such a
place without a struggle, so, as I had heard that you were good enough to give
advice to poor folk who were in need of it, I came right away to you."

"And you did very wisely," said Holmes. "Your case is an exceedingly remarkable one, and I shall be happy to look into it. From what you have told me I think that it is possible that graver issues hang from it than might at first sight appear."

"Grave enough!" said Mr. Jabez Wilson. "Why, I have lost four pound a week."

"As far as you are personally concerned," remarked Holmes, "I do not see that you have any grievance against this extraordinary league. On the contrary, you are, as I understand, richer by some thirty pounds, to say nothing of the minute knowledge which you have gained on every subject which comes under the letter A. You have lost nothing by them."

"No, sir. But I want to find out about them, and who they are, and what their object was in playing this prank—if it was a prank—upon me. It was a pretty expensive joke for them, for it cost them two and thirty pounds."

"We shall endeavour to clear up these points for you. And, first, one or two questions, Mr. Wilson. The assistant of yours who first called your attention to the advertisement—how long had he been with you?"

"About a month then."

"How did he come?"

"In answer to an advertisement."

"Was he the only applicant?"

"No, I had a dozen."

"Why did you pick him?"

"Because he was handy, and would come cheap."

"At half wages, in fact."

"Yes."

"What is he like, this Vincent Spaulding?"

"Small, stout-built, very quick in his ways, no hair on his face, though he's not short of thirty. Has a white splash of acid upon his forehead."

Holmes sat up in his chair in considerable excitement. "I thought as much," said he. "Have you ever observed that his ears are pierced for earrings?"

"Yes, sir. He told me that a gipsy had done it for him when he was a lad."

"Hum!" said Holmes, sinking back in deep thought. "He is still with you?"

"Oh yes, sir; I have only just left him."

"And has your business been attended to in your absence?"

"Nothing to complain of, sir. There's never very much to do of a morning."

"That will do, Mr. Wilson. I shall be happy to give you an opinion upon the subject in the course of a day or two. To-day is Saturday, and I hope that by Monday we may come to a conclusion."

"Well, Watson," said Holmes, when our visitor had left us, "what do you make of it all?"

"I make nothing of it," I answered, frankly. "It is a most mysterious business."

"As a rule," said Holmes, "the more bizarre a thing is the less mysterious it proves to be. It is your commonplace, featureless crimes which are really puzzling, just as a commonplace face is the most difficult to identify. But I must be prompt over this matter."

"What are you going to do then?" I asked.

"To smoke," he answered. "It is quite a three pipe problem, and I beg that you won't speak to me for fifty minutes." He curled himself up in his chair, with his thin knees drawn up to his hawk-like nose, and there he sat with his eyes closed and his black clay pipe thrusting out like the bill of some strange bird. I had come to the conclusion that he had dropped asleep, and indeed was nodding myself, when he suddenly sprang out of his chair with the gesture of a man who has made up his mind, and put his pipe down upon the mantelpiece.

"Sarasate plays at the St. James's Hall this afternoon," he remarked. "What do you think, Watson? Could your patients spare you for a few hours?"

"I have no thing to do to-day. My practice is never very absorbing."

"Then, put on your hat, and come. I am going through the City first, and we can have some lunch on the way. I observe that there is a good deal of German music on the programme, which is rather more to my taste than Italian or French. It is introspective, and I want to introspect. Come along!"

We travelled by the Underground as far as Aldersgate; and a short walk took us to Saxe-Coburg-square, the scene of the singular story which we had listened to in the morning. It was a pokey, little, shabby-genteel place, where four lines of dingy two-storied brick houses looked out into a small railed-in enclosure, where a lawn of weedy grass, and a few clumps of faded laurel bushes made a hard fight against a smoke-laden and uncongenial atmosphere. Three gilt balls and a brown board with "JABEZ WILSON" in white letters, upon a corner house, announced the place where our red-headed client carried on his business. Sherlock Holmes stopped in front of it with his head on one side, and looked it all over, with his eyes shining brightly between puckered lids. Then he walked slowly up the street, and then down again to the corner, still looking keenly at the houses. Finally he returned to the pawnbroker's, and, having thumped vigorously upon the pavement with his stick two or three times, he went up to the door and knocked. It was instantly opened by a bright-looking, clean-shaven young fellow, who asked him to step in.

"Thank you," said Holmes, "I only wished to ask you how you would go from here to the Strand."

"Third right, fourth left," answered the assistant promptly, closing the door.

"Smart fellow, that," observed Holmes as we walked away. "He is, in my judgment, the fourth smartest man in London, and for daring I am not sure that he has not a claim to be third. I have known something of him before."

"Evidently," said I, "Mr. Wilson's assistant counts for a good deal in this mystery of the Red-headed League. I am sure that you inquired your way merely in order that you might see him."

"Not him."

"What then?"

"The knees of his trousers."

"And what did you see?"

"What I expected to see."

"Why did you beat the pavement?"

"My dear Doctor, this is a time for observation, not for talk. We are spies in an enemy's country. We know something of Saxe-Coburg-square. Let us now explore the parts which lie behind it."

The road in which we found ourselves as we turned round the corner from the retired Saxe-Coburg-square presented as great a contrast to it as the front of a picture does to the back. It was one of the main arteries which convey the traffic of the City to the north and west. The roadway was blocked with the immense stream of commerce flowing in a double tide inwards and outwards, while the footpaths were black with the hurrying swarm of pedestrians. It was difficult to realise as we looked at the line of fine shops and stately business premises that they really abutted on the other side upon the faded and stagnant square which we had just quitted.

"Let me see," said Holmes, standing at the corner, and glancing along the line, "I should like just to remember the order of the houses here. It is a hobby of mine to have an exact knowledge of London. There is Mortimer's, the tobacconist, the little newspaper shop, the Coburg branch of the City and Suburban Bank, the Vegetarian Restaurant, and McFarlane's carriage-building depot. That carries us right on to the other block. And now, Doctor, we've done our work, so it's time we had some play. A sandwich, and a cup of coffee, and then off to violin-land, where all is sweetness, and delicacy, and harmony, and there are no red-headed clients to vex us with their conundrums."

My friend was an enthusiastic musician, being himself not only a very capable performer, but a composer of no ordinary merit. All the afternoon he sat in the stalls wrapped in the most perfect happiness, gently waving his long thin fingers in time to the music, while his gently smiling face and his languid dreamy eyes were as unlike those of Holmes the sleuth-hound; Holmes the relentless, keen-witted, ready-handed criminal agent, as it was possible to conceive. In his singular character the dual nature alternately asserted itself, and his extreme exactness and astuteness represented, as I have often thought, the reaction against the poetic and contemplative mood which occasionally predominated in him. The swing of his nature took him from extreme languor to devouring energy; and, as I knew well, he was never so truly formidable as when, for days on end, he had been lounging in his armchair amid his improvisations and his black-letter editions. Then it was that the lust of the chase would suddenly come upon him, and that his brilliant reasoning power would rise to the level of intuition, until those who were unacquainted with his methods would look askance at him as on a man whose knowledge was not that of other mortals. When I saw him that afternoon so enwrapped in the music at St. James's Hall I felt that an evil time might be coming upon those whom he had set himself to hunt down.

"You want to go home, no doubt, Doctor," he remarked, as we emerged.

"Yes, it would be as well."

"And I have some business to do which will take some hours. This business at Coburg-square is serious."

"Why serious?"

"A considerable crime is in contemplation. I have every reason to believe that we shall be in time to stop it. But to-day being Saturday rather complicates matters. I shall want your help to-night."

"At what time?"

"Ten will be early enough."

"I shall be at Baker-street at ten."

"Very well. And, I say, Doctor! there may be some little danger, so kindly put your army revolver in your pocket." He waved his hand, turned on his heel, and disappeared in an instant among the crowd.

I trust that I am not more dense than my neighbours, but I was always oppressed with a sense of my own stupidity in my dealings with Sherlock Holmes. Here I had heard what he had heard, I had seen what he had seen, and yet from his words it was evident that he saw clearly not only what had happened, but what was about to happen, while to me the whole business was still confused and grotesque. As I drove home to my house in Kensington I thought over it all, from the extraordinary story of the red-headed copier of the "Encyclopædia" down to the visit to Saxe-Coburg-square, and the ominous words with which he had parted from me. What was this nocturnal expedition, and why should I go armed? Where were we going, and what were we to do? I had the hint from Holmes that this smooth-faced pawnbroker's assistant was a formidable man—a man who might play a deep game. I tried to puzzle it out, but gave it up in despair, and set the matter aside until night should bring an explanation.

It was a quarter past nine when I started from home and made my way across the Park, and so through Oxford-street to Baker-street. Two hansoms were standing at the door, and, as I entered the passage, I heard the sound of voices from above. On entering his room, I found Holmes in animated conversation with two men, one of whom I recognised as Peter Jones, the official police agent; while the other was a long, thin, sad-faced man, with a very shiny hat and oppressively respectable frock-coat.

"Ha! our party is complete," said Holmes, buttoning up his pea-jacket, and taking his heavy hunting crop from the rack. "Watson, I think you know Mr. Jones, of Scotland-yard? Let me introduce you to Mr. Merryweather, who is to be our companion in to-night's adventure."

"We're hunting in couples again, Doctor, you see," said Jones, in his consequential way. "Our friend here is a wonderful man for starting a chase. All he wants is an old dog to help him to do the running down."

"I hope a wild goose may not prove to be the end of our chase," observed Mr. Merryweather, gloomily.

"You may place considerable confidence in Mr. Holmes, sir," said the police agent, loftily. "He has his own little methods, which are, if he won't mind my saying so, just a little too theoretical and fantastic, but he has the makings of a detective in him. It is not too much to say that once or twice, as in that business of the Sholto murder and the Agra treasure, he has been more nearly correct than the official force."

"Oh, if you say so, Mr. Jones, it is all right!" said the stranger, with deference. "Still, I confess that I miss my rubber. It is the first Saturday night for seven-and-twenty years that I have not had my rubber."

"I think you will find," said Sherlock Holmes, "that you will play for a higher stake to-night than you have ever done yet, and that the play will be more exciting. For you, Mr. Merryweather, the stake will be some thirty thousand pounds; and for you, Jones, it will be the man upon whom you wish to lay your hands."

"John Clay, the murderer, thief, smasher and forger. He's a young man, Mr. Merryweather, but he is at the head of his profession, and I would rather have my bracelets on him than on any criminal in London. He's a remarkable man, is young John Clay. His grandfather was a Royal Duke, and he himself has been to Eton and Oxford. His brain is as cunning as his fingers, and though we meet signs of him at every turn, we never know where to find the man himself. He'll crack a crib in Scotland one week, and be raising money to build an orphanage in Cornwall the next. I've been on his track for years, and have never set eyes on him yet."

"I hope that I may have the pleasure of introducing you to-night. I've had one or two little turns also with Mr. John Clay, and I agree with you that he is at the head of his profession. It is past ten, however, and quite time that we started. If you two will take the first hansom, Watson and I will follow in the second."

Sherlock Holmes was not very communicative during the long drive, and lay back in the cab humming the tunes which he had heard in the afternoon. We rattled through an endless labyrinth of gas-lit streets until we emerged into Farringdon-street.

"We are close there now," my friend remarked. "This fellow Merryweather is a bank director and personally interested in the matter. I thought it as well to have Jones with us also. He is not a bad fellow, though an absolute imbecile in his profession. He has one positive virtue. He is as brave as a bulldog, and as tenacious as a lobster if he gets his claws upon anyone. Here we are, and they are waiting for us."

We had reached the same crowded thoroughfare in which we had found ourselves in the morning. Our cabs were dismissed, and, following the guidance of Mr. Merryweather, we passed down a narrow passage, and through a side door, which he opened for us. Within there was a small corridor, which ended in a very massive iron gate. This also was opened, and led down a flight of winding stone steps which terminated at another formidable gate. Mr. Merryweather stopped to light a lantern, and then conducted us down a dark, earth-smelling passage, and so, after opening a third door, into a huge vault or cellar, which was piled all round with crates and massive boxes.

"You are not very vulnerable from above," Holmes remarked, as he held up the lantern, and gazed about him.

"Nor from below," said Mr. Merryweather, striking his stick upon the flags which lined the floor. "Why, dear me, it sounds quite hollow!" he remarked, looking up in surprise.

"I must really ask you to be a little more quiet," said Holmes, severely. "You have already imperilled the whole success of our expedition. Might I beg that you would have the goodness to sit down upon one of those boxes, and not to interfere?"

The solemn Mr. Merryweather perched himself upon a crate, with a very injured expression upon his face, while Holmes fell upon his knees upon the floor and, with the lantern and a magnifying lens, began to examine minutely the cracks between the stones. A few seconds sufficed to satisfy him, for he sprang to his feet again, and put his glass in his pocket.

"We have at least an hour before us," he remarked, "for they can hardly take any steps until the good pawnbroker is safely in bed. Then they will not lose a minute, for the sooner they do their work the longer time they will have for their escape. We are at present, Doctor—as no doubt you have divined—in the cellar of the City branch of one of the principal London banks. Mr. Merryweather is the chairman of directors, and he will explain to you that there are reasons why the more daring criminals of London should take a considerable interest in this cellar at present."

"It is our French gold," whispered the director. "We have had several warnings that an attempt might be made upon it."

"Your French gold?"

"Yes. We had occasion some months ago to strengthen our resources, and borrowed, for that purpose, thirty thousand napoleons from the Bank of France. It has become known that we have never had occasion to unpack the money, and that it is still lying in our cellar. The crate upon which I sit contains two thousand napoleons packed between layers of lead foil. Our reserve bullion is much larger at present than is usually kept in a single branch office, and the directors have had misgivings upon the subject."

"Which were very well justified," observed Holmes. "And now it is time that we arranged our little plans. I expect that within an hour matters will come to a head. In the meantime, Mr. Merryweather, we must put the screen over that dark lantern."

"And sit in the dark?"

"I am afraid so. I had brought a pack of cards in my pocket, and I thought that, as we were a *partie carrée,* you might have your rubber after all. But I see that the enemy's preparations have gone so far that we cannot risk the presence of a light. And, first of all, we must choose our positions. These are daring men, and, though we shall take them at a disadvantage they may do us some harm, unless we are careful. I shall stand behind this crate, and do you conceal yourselves behind those. Then, when I flash a light upon them, close in swiftly. If they fire, Watson, have no compunction about shooting them down."

I placed my revolver, cocked, upon the top of the wooden case behind which I crouched. Holmes shot the slide across the front of his lantern, and left us in pitch darkness—such an absolute darkness as I have never before experienced. The smell of hot metal remained to assure us that the light was still there, ready to flash out at a moment's notice. To me, with my nerves worked up to a pitch of expectancy, there was something depressing and subduing in the sudden gloom, and in the cold, dank air of the vault.

"They have but one retreat," whispered Holmes. "That is back through the house into Saxe-Coburg-square. I hope that you have done what I asked you, Jones?"

"I have an inspector and two officers waiting at the front door."

"Then we have stopped all the holes. And now we must be silent and wait."

What a time it seemed! From comparing notes afterwards it was but an hour and a quarter, yet it appeared to me that the night must have almost gone, and the dawn be breaking above us. My limbs were weary and stiff, for I feared to change my position, yet my nerves were worked up to the highest pitch of tension, and my hearing was so acute that I could not hear the gentle breathing of my companions, but I could distinguish the deeper, heavier in-breath of the bulky Jones from the thin sighing note of the bank director. From my position I could look over the case in the direction of the floor. Suddenly my eyes caught the glint of a light.

At first it was but a lurid spark upon the stone pavement. Then it lengthened out until it became a yellow line, and then, without any warning or sound, a gash seemed to open and a hand appeared, a white, almost womanly hand, which felt about in the centre of the little area of light. For a minute or more the hand, with its writhing fingers, protruded out of the floor. Then it was withdrawn as suddenly as it appeared, and all was dark again save the single lurid spark, which marked a chink between the stones.

Its disappearance, however, was but momentary. With a rending, tearing sound, one of the broad, white stones turned over upon its side, and left a square, gaping hole, through which streamed the light of a lantern. Over the edge there peeped a clean-cut, boyish face, which looked keenly about it, and then, with a hand on either side of the aperture, drew itself shoulder high and waist high, until one knee rested upon the edge. In another instant he stood at the side of the hole, and was hauling after him a companion, lithe and small like himself, with a pale face and a shock of very red hair.

"It's all clear," he whispered. "Have you the chisel and the bags. Great Scott! Jump, Archie, jump, and I'll swing for it!"

Sherlock Holmes had sprung out and seized the intruder by the collar. The other dived down the hole, and I heard the sound of rending cloth as Jones clutched at his skirts. The light flashed upon the barrel of a revolver, but Holmes' hunting crop came down on the man's wrist, and the pistol clinked upon the stone floor.

"It's no use, John Clay," said Holmes blandly. "You have no chance at all."

"So I see," the other answered, with the utmost coolness. "I fancy that my pal is all right, though I see you have got his coat-tails."

"There are three men waiting for him at the door," said Holmes.

"Oh, indeed. You seem to have done the thing very completely. I must compliment you."

"And I you," Holmes answered. "Your red-headed idea was very new and effective."

"You'll see your pal again presently," said Jones. "He's quicker at climbing down holes than I am. Just hold out while I fix the derbies."

"I beg that you will not touch me with your filthy hands," remarked our prisoner, as the handcuffs clattered upon his wrists. "You may not be aware that I have royal blood in my veins. Have the goodness also when you address me always to say 'sir' and 'please.'"

"All right," said Jones, with a stare and a snigger. "Well, would you please, sir, march upstairs, where we can get a cab to carry your highness to the police-station."

"That is better," said John Clay, serenely. He made a sweeping bow to the three of us, and walked quietly off in the custody of the detective.

"Really, Mr. Holmes," said Mr. Merryweather, as we followed them from the cellar, "I do not know how the bank can thank you or repay you. There is no doubt that you have detected and defeated in the most complete manner one of the most determined attempts at bank robbery that have ever come into my experience."

"I have had one or two little scores of my own to settle with Mr. John Clay," said Holmes, "I have been at some small expense over this matter, which I shall expect the bank to refund, but beyond that I am amply repaid by having had an experience which is in many ways unique, and by hearing the very remarkable narrative of the Red-headed League."

"You see, Watson," he explained, in the early hours of the morning, as we sat over a glass of whisky and soda in Baker-street, "it was perfectly obvious from the first that the only possible object of this rather fantastic business of the advertisement of the League, and the copying of the 'Encyclopædia,' must be to get this not over-bright pawnbroker out of the way for a number of hours every day. It was a curious way of managing it, but really it would be difficult to suggest a better. The method was no doubt suggested to Clay's ingenious mind by the colour of his accomplice's hair. The four pounds a week was a lure which must draw him, and what was it to them, who were playing for thousands? They put in the advertisement, one rogue has the temporary office, the other rogue incites the man to apply for it, and together they manage to secure his absence every morning in the week. From the time that I heard of the assistant having come for half wages, it was obvious to me that he had some strong motive for securing the situation."

"But how could you guess what the motive was?"

"Had there been women in the house, I should have suspected a mere vulgar intrigue. That, however, was out of the question. The man's business was a small one, and there was nothing in his house which could account for such elaborate preparations, and such an expenditure as they were at. It must then be something out of the house. What could it be? I thought of the assistant's fondness for photography, and his trick of vanishing in the cellar. The cellar! There was the end of this tangled clue. Then I made inquiries as to this mysterious assistant, and found that I had to deal with one of the coolest and most daring criminals in London. He was doing something in the cellar—something which took many hours a day for months on end. What could it be, once more? I could think of nothing save that he was running a tunnel to some other building.

"So far I had got when we went to visit the scene of action. I surprised you by beating upon the pavement with my stick. I was ascertaining whether the cellar stretched out in front or behind. It was not in front. Then I rang the bell, and, as I hoped, the assistant answered it. We have had some skirmishes, but we had never set eyes upon each other before. I hardly looked at his face. His knees were what I wished to see. You must yourself have remarked how worn, wrinkled, and stained they were. They spoke of those hours of burrowing. The only remaining point was what they were burrowing for. I walked round the corner, saw that the City and Suburban Bank abutted on our friend's premises, and felt that I had solved my problem. When you drove home after the concert I called upon Scotland Yard, and upon the chairman of the bank directors, with the result that you have seen."

"And how could you tell that they would make their attempt to-night?" I asked.

"Well, when they closed their League offices that was a sign that they cared no longer about Mr. Jabez Wilson's presence, in other words, that they had completed their tunnel. But it was essential that they should use it soon as it might be discovered, or the bullion might be removed. Saturday would suit them better than any other day, as it would give them two days for their escape. For all these reasons I expected them to come to-night."

"You reasoned it out beautifully," I exclaimed in unfeigned admiration. "It is so long a chain, and yet every link rings true."

"It saved me from ennui," he answered, yawning. "Alas! I already feel it closing in upon me. My life is spent in one long effort to escape from the commonplaces of existence. These little problems help me to do so."

"And you are a benefactor of the race," said I.

He shrugged his shoulders. "Well, perhaps, after all, it is of some little use," he remarked. "'L'homme c'est rien—l'œuvre c'est tout,' as Gustave Flaubert wrote to Georges Sand."

THE CORPUS DELICTI

MELVILLE DAVISSON POST
(1869–1930)

Most anthologies feature a story about Uncle Abner, Post's most famous creation and a wonderfully moral character. But Randolph Mason is one of the great rogues of mystery fiction who brings the extraordinary viewpoint to a case that it doesn't matter in the least if a criminal is caught; he makes it his job to assure that he won't be punished. The character was so powerful that he influenced another author of legal mysteries, Erle Stanley Gardner, to use his name for his own creation, Perry Mason.

I

"THAT MAN MASON," SAID Samuel Walcott, "is the mysterious member of this club. He is more than that; he is the mysterious man of New York."

"I was much surprised to see him," answered his companion, Marshall St. Clair, of the great law firm of Seward, St. Clair, & De Muth. "I had lost track of him since he went to Paris as counsel for the American stockholders of the Canal Company. When did he come back to the States?"

"He turned up suddenly in his ancient haunts about four months ago," said Walcott, "as grand, gloomy, and peculiar as Napoleon ever was in his palmiest days. The younger members of the club call him 'Zanona Redivivus.' He wanders through the house usually late at night, apparently without noticing anything or anybody. His mind seems to be deeply and busily at work, leaving his bodily self to wander as it may happen. Naturally, strange stories are told of him; indeed, his individuality and his habit of doing some unexpected thing, and doing it in such a marvelously original manner that men who are experts at it look on in wonder, cannot fail to make him an object of interest.

"He has never been known to play at any game whatever, and yet one night he sat down to the chess table with old Admiral Du Brey. You know the Admiral is the great champion since he beat the French and English officers in the tournament last winter. Well, you also know that the conventional openings at chess are scientifically and accurately determined. To the utter disgust of Du Brey, Mason opened the game with an unheard of attack from the extremes of the board. The old Admiral stopped and, in a kindly patronizing way, pointed out the weak and absurd folly of his move and asked him to begin again with some one of the safe openings. Mason smiled and answered that if one had a head that he could trust he should use it; if not, then it was the part of wisdom to follow blindly the dead forms of some man who had a head. Du Brey was naturally angry and set himself to demolish Mason as quickly as possible. The game was rapid for a few moments. Mason lost piece after piece. His opening was broken and destroyed and its utter folly apparent to the lookers-on. The Admiral smiled and the game seemed all one-sided, when, suddenly, to his utter horror, Du Brey found that his king was in a trap. The foolish opening had been only a piece of shrewd strategy. The old Admiral fought and cursed and sacrificed his pieces, but it was of no use. He was gone. Mason checkmated him in two moves and arose wearily.

" 'Where in Heaven's name, man,' said the old Admiral, thunderstruck, 'did you learn that masterpiece?'

" 'Just here,' replied Mason. 'To play chess, one should know his opponent. How could the dead masters lay down rules by which you could be beaten, sir? They had never seen you'; and thereupon he turned and left the room. Of course, St. Clair, such a strange man would soon become an object of all kinds of mysterious rumors. Some are true and some are not. At any rate, I know that Mason is an unusual man with a gigantic intellect. Of late he seems to have taken a strange fancy to me. In face, I seem to be the only member of the club that he will talk with, and I confess that he startles and fascinates me. He is an original genius, St. Clair, of an unusual order."

"I recall vividly," said the younger man, "that before Mason went to Paris he was considered one of the greatest lawyers of this city and he was feared and hated by the bar at large. He came here, I believe, from Virginia and began with the high-grade criminal practice. He soon became famous for his powerful and ingenious defenses. He found holes in the law through which his clients escaped, holes that by the profession at large were not suspected to exist, and that frequently astonished the judges. His ability caught the attention of the great corporations. They tested him and found in him learning and unlimited resources. He pointed out methods by which they could evade obnoxious statutes, by which they could comply with the apparent letter of the law and yet violate its spirit, and advised them well in that most important of all things, just how far they could bend the law without breaking it. At the time he left for Paris he had a vast clientage and was in the midst of a brilliant career. The day he took passage from New York, the bar lost sight of him. No matter how great a man may be, the wave soon closes over him in a city like this. In a few years Mason was forgotten. Now only the older practitioners would recall him, and they would do so with hatred and bitterness. He was a tireless, savage, uncompromising fighter, always a recluse."

"Well," said Walcott, "he reminds me of a great world-weary cynic, transplanted from some ancient mysterious empire. When I come into the man's presence I feel instinctively the grip of his intellect. I tell you, St. Clair, Randolph Mason is the mysterious man of New York."

At this moment a messenger boy came into the room and handed Mr. Walcott a telegram. "St. Clair," said that gentleman, rising, "the directors of the Elevated are in session, and we must hurry." The two men put on their coats and left the house.

Samuel Walcott was not a club man after the manner of the Smart Set, and yet he was in fact a club man. He was a bachelor in the latter thirties, and resided in a great silent house on the avenue. On the street he was a man of substance, shrewd and progressive, backed by great wealth. He had various corporate interests in the larger syndicates, but the basis and foundation of his fortune was real estate. His houses on the avenue were the best possible property, and his elevator row in the importers' quarter was indeed a literal gold mine. It was known that, many years before, his grandfather had died and left him the property, which, at that time, was of no great value. Young Walcott had gone out onto the goldfields and had been lost of the forgotten. Ten years afterward he had turned up suddenly in New York and taken possession of his property, then vastly increased in value. His speculations were almost phenomenally successful, and, backed by the now enormous value of his real property, he was soon on a level with the merchant prince. His judgment was considered sound, and he had the full confidence of his business associates for safety and caution. Fortune heaped up riches around him with a lavish hand. He was unmarried and the halo of his wealth caught the keen eye of the matron with marriageable daughters. He was invited out, caught by the whirl of society, and tossed into its maelstrom. In a measure he reciprocated. He kept horses and a yacht. His dinners at Delmonico's and the club were above reproach. But with all he was a silent man with a shadow deep in his eyes, and seemed to court the society of his fellows, not because he loved them, but because he either hated or feared solitude. For years the strategy of the match-maker had gone gracefully afield, but Fate is relentless. If she shields the victim from the traps of men, it is not because she wishes him to escape, but because she is pleased to reserve him for her own trap. So it happened that, when Virginia St. Clair assisted Mrs. Miriam Steuvisant at her mid-winter reception, this same Samuel Walcott fell deeply and hopelessly and utterly in love, and it was so apparent to the beaten generals present, that Mrs. Miriam Steuvisant applauded herself, so to speak, with encore after encore. It was good to see this courteous, silent man literally at the feet of the young debutante. He was there of right. Even the mothers of marriageable daughters admitted that. The young girl was brown-haired, brown-eyed, and tall enough, said the experts, and of the blue blood royal, with all the grace, courtesy, and inbred genius of such princely heritage.

Perhaps it was objected by the censors of the Smart Set that Miss St. Clair's frankness and honesty were a trifle old-fashioned, and that she was a shadowy bit of a Puritan; and perhaps it was of these same qualities that Samuel Walcott received his hurt. At any rate the hurt was there and deep, and the new actor stepped up into the old time-worn, semi-tragic drama, and began his rôle with a tireless, utter sincerity that was deadly dangerous if he lost.

II

Perhaps a week after the conversation between St. Clair and Walcott, Randolph Mason stood in the private writing-room of the club with his hands behind his back.

He was a man apparently in the middle forties; tall and reasonably broad across the shoulders; muscular without being either stout or lean. His hair was thin and of a brown color, with erratic streaks of gray. His forehead was broad and high and of a faint reddish color. His eyes were restless inky black, and not over-large. The nose was big and muscular and bowed. The eyebrows were black and heavy, almost bushy. There were heavy furrows, running from the nose downward and outward to the corners of the mouth. The mouth was straight and the jaw was heavy, and square.

Looking at the face of Randolph Mason from above, the expression in repose was crafty and cynical; viewed from below upward, it was savage and vindictive, almost brutal; while from the front, if looked squarely in the face, the stranger was fascinated by the animation of the man and at once concluded that his expression was fearless and sneering. He was evidently of Southern extraction and a man of unusual power.

A fire smoldered on the hearth. It was a crisp evening in the early fall, and with that far-off touch of melancholy which ever heralds the coming winter, even in the midst of a city. The man's face looked tired and ugly. His long white hands were clasped tight together. His entire figure and face wore every mark of weakness and physical exhaustion; but his eyes contradicted. They were red and restless.

In the private dining-room the dinner party was in the best of spirits. Samuel Walcott was happy. Across the table from him was Miss Virginia St. Clair, radiant, a tinge of color in her cheeks. On either side, Mrs. Miriam Steuvisant and Marshall St. Clair were brilliant and light-hearted. Walcott looked at the young girl and the measure of his worship was full. He wondered for the thousandth time how she could possibly love him and by what earthly miracle she had come to accept him, and how it would be always to have her across the table from him, his own table in his own house.

They were about to rise from the table when one of the waiters entered the room and handed Walcott an envelope. He thrust it quickly into his pocket. In the confusion of rising the others did not notice him, but his face was ash-white and his hands trembled violently as he placed the wraps around the bewitching shoulders of Miss St. Clair.

"Marshall," he said, and despite the powerful effort his voice was hollow, "you will see the ladies safely cared for, I am called to attend a grave matter."

"All right, Walcott," answered the young man, with cheery good-nature, "you are too serious, old man, trot along."

"The poor dear," murmured Mrs. Steuvisant, after Walcott had helped them to the carriage and turned to go up to the steps of the club, "The poor dear is hard hit, and men are such funny creatures when they are hard hit."

Samuel Walcott, as his fate would, went direct to the private writing-room and opened the door. The lights were not turned on and in the dark he did not see Mason motionless by the mantel-shelf. He went quickly across the room to the writing-table, turned on one of the lights, and, taking the envelope from his pocket tore it open. Then he bent down by the light to read the contents. As his eyes ran over the paper, his jaw fell. The skin drew away from his cheek-bones and his face seemed literally to sink in. His knees gave way under him and he would have gone down in a heap had it not been for Mason's long arms that closed around him and held him up. The human economy is ever mysterious. The moment the new danger threatened, the latent power of the man as an animal, hidden away in the centers of intelligence, asserted itself. His hand clutched the paper and, with a half slide, he turned in Mason's arms. For a moment he stared up at the ugly man whose thin arms felt like wire ropes.

"You are under the dead-fall, aye," said Mason. "The cunning of my enemy is sublime."

"Your enemy?" gasped Walcott. "When did you come into it? How in God's name did you know it? How your enemy?"

Mason looked down at the wide bulging eyes of the man.

"Who should know better than I?" he said, "Haven't I broken through all the traps and plots that she could set?"

"She? She trap you?" The man's voice was full of horror.

"The old schemer," muttered Mason. "The cowardly old schemer, to strike in the back; but we can beat her. She did not count on my helping you—I, who know her so well."

Mason's face was red, and his eyes burned. In the midst of it all he dropped his hands and went over to the fire. Samuel Walcott arose, panting, and stood looking at Mason, with his hands behind him on the table. The naturally strong nature and the rigid school in which the man had been trained presently began to tell. His composure in part returned and he thought rapidly. What did this strange man know? Was he simply making shrewd guesses, or had he some mysterious knowledge of this matter? Walcott could not know that Mason meant only Fate, that he believed her to be his great enemy. Walcott had never before doubted his own ability to meet any emergency. This mighty jerk had carried him off his feet. He was unstrung and panic-stricken. At any rate this man had promised help. He would take it. He put the paper and envelope carefully into his pocket, smoothed out his rumpled coat, and going over to Mason touched him on the shoulder.

"Come," he said, "if you are to help me we must go."

The man turned and followed him without a word. In the hall Mason put on his hat and overcoat, and the two went out into the street. Walcott hailed a cab, and the two were driven to his house on the avenue. Walcott took out his latch-key, opened the door, and led the way into the library. He turned on the light and motioned Mason to seat himself at the table. Then he went into another room and presently returned with a bundle of papers and a decanter of brandy. He poured out a glass of the liquor and offered it to Mason. The man shook his head. Walcott poured the contents of the glass down his own throat. Then he set the decanter down and drew up a chair on the side of the table opposite Mason.

"Sir," said Walcott, in a voice deliberate, indeed, but as hollow as a sepulchre, "I am done for. God has finally gathered up the ends of the net, and it is knotted tight."

"Am I not here to help you?" said Mason, turning savagely. "I can beat Fate. Give me the details of her trap."

He bent forward and rested his arms on the table. His streaked gray hair was rumpled and on end, and his face was ugly. For a moment Walcott did not answer. He moved a little into the shadow; then he spread the bundle of old yellow papers out before him.

"To begin with," he said, "I am a living lie, a gilded crime-made sham, every bit of me. There is not an honest piece anywhere. It is all lie. I am a liar and a thief before men. The property which I possess is not mine, but stolen from a dead man. The very name which I bear is not my own, but is the bastard child of a crime. I am more than all that—I am a murderer; a murderer before the pure woman whom I love more than anything that God could make."

He paused for a moment and wiped the perspiration from his face.

"Sir," said Mason, "This is all drivel, infantile drivel. What you are is of no importance. How to get out is the problem, how to get out."

Samuel Walcott leaned forward, poured a glass of brandy and swallowed it.

"Well," he said, speaking slowly, "my right name is Richard Warren. In the spring of 1879 I came to New York and fell in with the real Samuel Walcott, a young man with a little money and some property which his grandfather had left him. We became friends, and concluded to go to the far west together. Accordingly we scraped together what money we could lay our hands on, and landed in the gold-mining regions of California. We were young and inexperienced, and our money went rapidly. One April morning we drifted into a little shack camp, away up in the Sierra Nevadas, called Hell's Elbow. Here we struggled and starved for perhaps a year. Finally, in utter desperation, Walcott married the daughter of a Mexican gambler, who ran an eating-house and a poker joint. With them we lived from hand to mouth in a wild God-forsaken way for several years. After a time the woman began to take a strange fancy to me. Walcott finally noticed it, and grew jealous.

"One night, in a drunken brawl, we quarreled, and I killed him. It was late at night, and, beside the woman, there were four of us in the poker room,—the Mexican gambler, a half-breed devil called Cherubim Pete, Walcott, and myself. When Walcott fell, the half-breed whipped out his weapon, and fired at me across the table; but the woman, Nina San Croix, struck his arm, and, instead of killing me, as he intended, the bullet mortally wounded her father, the Mexican gambler. I shot the half-breed through the forehead, and turned round, expecting the woman to attack me. On the contrary, she pointed to the window, and made me wait for her on the cross-trail below.

"It was fully three hours later before the woman joined me at the place indicated. She had a bag of gold dust, a few jewels that belonged to her father, and a package of papers. I asked her why she had stayed behind so long, and she replied that the men were not killed outright, and that she had brought a priest to them and waited until they had died. This was the truth, but not all the truth. Moved by superstition or foresight, the woman had induced the priest to take down the sworn statements of the two dying men, seal it, and give it to her. This paper she brought with her. All this I learned afterwards. At the time I knew nothing of this damning evidence.

"We struck out together for the Pacific coast. The country was lawless. The privations we endured were almost past belief. At times the woman exhibited cunning and ability that were almost genius, and through it all, often in the very fingers of death, her devotion to me never wavered. It was dog-like, and seemed to be her only object on earth. When we reached San Francisco, the woman put these papers into my hands." Walcott took up the yellow package, and pushed it across the table to Mason.

"She proposed that I assume Walcott's name, and that we come boldly to New York and claim the property. I examined the papers, found a copy of the will by which Walcott inherited the property, a bundle of correspondence, and sufficient documentary evidence to establish his identity beyond the shadow of a doubt. Desperate gambler as I now was, I quailed before the daring plan of Nina San Croix. I urged that I, Richard Warren, would be known, that the attempted fraud would be detected and would result in investigation, and perhaps unearth the whole horrible matter.

"The woman pointed out how much I resembled Walcott, what vast changes ten years of such life as we had led would naturally be expected to make in men, how utterly impossible it would be to trace back the fraud to Walcott's murder at Hell's Elbow, in the wild passes of the Sierra Nevadas. She bade me remember that we were both outcasts, both crime-branded, both enemies of man's law and God's; that we had nothing to lose; we were both sunk to the bottom. Then she laughed, and said that she had not found me a coward until now, but that if I had turned chicken-hearted, that was the end of it, of course. The result was, we sold the gold dust and jewels in San Francisco, took on such evidences of civilization as possible, and purchased passage to New York on the best steamer we could find.

"I was growing to depend on the bold gambler spirit of this woman, Nina San Croix; I felt the need of her strong, profligate nature. She was of a queer breed and a queerer school. Her mother was the daughter of a Spanish engineer, and had been stolen by the Mexican, her father. She herself had been raised and educated as best might be in one of the monasteries along the Rio Grande, and had there grown to womanhood before her father, fleeing into the mountains of California, carried her with him.

"When we landed in New York I offered to announce her as my wife, but she refused, saying that her presence would excite comment and perhaps attract the attention of Walcott's relatives. We therefore arranged that I should go alone into the city, claim the property, and announce myself as Samuel Walcott, and that she should remain under cover until such time as we would feel the ground safe under us.

"Every detail of the plan was fatally successful. I established my identity without difficulty and secured the property. It had increased vastly in value, and I, as Samuel Walcott, soon found myself a rich man. I went to Nina San Croix in hiding and gave her a large sum of money, with which she purchased a residence in a retired part of the city, far up in the northern suburb. Here she lived secluded and unknown while I remained in the city, living here as a wealthy bachelor.

"I did not attempt to abandon the woman, but went to her from time to time in disguise and under cover of the greatest secrecy. For a time everything ran smooth, the woman was still devoted to me above everything else, and thought always of my welfare first and seemed content to wait so long as I thought best. My business expanded. I was sought after and consulted and drawn into the higher life of New York, and more and more felt that the woman was an albatross on my neck. I put her off with one excuse after another. Finally she began to suspect me and demanded that I should recognize her as my wife. I attempted to point out the difficulties. She met them all by saying that we should both go to Spain, there I could marry her and we could return to America and drop into my place in society without causing more than a passing comment.

"I concluded to meet the matter squarely once for all. I said that I would convert half of the property into money and give it to her, but that I would not marry her. She did not fly into a storming rage as I had expected, but went quietly out of the room and presently returned with two papers, which she read. One was the certificate of her marriage to Walcott duly authenticated; the other was the dying statement of her father, the Mexican gambler, and of Samuel Walcott, charging me with murder. It was in proper form and certified by the Jesuit priest.

" 'Now,' she said, sweetly, when she had finished, 'which do you prefer, to recognize your wife, or to turn all the property over to Samuel Walcott's widow and hang for his murder?'

"I was dumbfounded and horrified. I saw the trap that I was in and I consented to do anything she should say if she would only destroy the papers. This she refused to do. I pleaded with her and implored her to destroy them. Finally she gave them to me with a great show of returning confidence, and I tore them into bits and threw them into the fire.

"That was three months ago. We arranged to go to Spain and do as she said. She was to sail this morning and I was to follow. Of course I never intended to go. I congratulated myself on the fact that all trace of evidence against me was destroyed and that her grip was now broken. My plan was to induce her to sail, believing that I would follow. When she was gone I would marry Miss St. Clair, and if Nina San Croix should return I would defy her and lock her up as a lunatic. But I was reckoning like an infernal ass, to imagine for a moment that I could thus hoodwink such a woman as Nina San Croix.

"To-night I received this." Walcott took the envelope from his pocket and gave it to Mason. "You saw the effect of it; read it and you will understand why I felt the death hand when I saw her writing on the envelope."

Mason took the paper from the envelope. It was written in Spanish, and ran:

"Greeting to RICHARD WARREN

"The great Señor does his little Nina injustice to think she would go away to

Spain and leave him to the beautiful American. She is not so thoughtless. Before she goes, she shall be, Oh so very rich! And the dear Señor shall be, Oh so very safe! The Archbishop and the kind Church hate murderers.

"NINA SAN CROIX

"Of course, fool, the papers you destroyed were copies.

"N. SAN C"

To this was pinned a line in a delicate aristocratic hand, saying that the Archbishop would willingly listen to Madam San Croix's statement if she would come to him on Friday morning at eleven.

"You see," said Walcott, desperately, "there is no possible way out. I know the woman—when she decides to do a thing that is the end of it. She has decided to do this."

Mason turned around from the table, stretched out his long legs, and thrust his hands deep into his pockets. Walcott sat with his head down, watching Mason hopelessly, almost indifferently, his face blank and sunken. The ticking of the bronze clock on the mantel-shelf was loud, painfully loud. Suddenly Mason drew his knees in and bent over, put both his bony hands on the table, and looked at Walcott.

"Sir," he said, "this matter is in such shape that there is only one thing to do. This growth must be cut at the roots, and cut out quickly. This is the first fact to be determined, and a fool would know it. The second fact is that you must do it yourself. Hired killers are like the grave and the daughters of the horse-leech,—they cry always, 'Give, Give.' They are only palliatives, not cures. By using them you swap perils. You simply take a stay of execution at best. The common criminal would know this. These are the facts of your problem. The master plotters of crime would see here but two difficulties to meet:

"A practical method for accomplishing the body of the crime.

"A cover for the criminal agent.

"They would see no farther, and attempt to guard no farther. After they had provided a plan for the killing, and a means by which the killer could cover his trail and escape from the theater of the homicide, they would believe all the requirements of the problems met, and would stop. The greatest, the very giants among them, have stopped here and have been in great error.

"In every crime, especially in the great ones, there exists a third element, preeminently vital. This third element the master plotters have either overlooked or else have not had the genius to construct. They plan with rare cunning to baffle the victim. They plan with vast wisdom, almost genius, to baffle the trailer. But they fail utterly to provide any plan for baffling the punisher. Ergo, their plots are fatally defective and often result in ruin. Hence the vital necessity for providing the third element—the *escape ipso jure.*"

Mason arose, walked around the table, and put his hand firmly on Samuel Walcott's shoulder. "This must be done to-morrow night," he continued; "you must arrange your business matters to-morrow and announce that you are going on a yacht cruise, by order of your physician, and may not return for some weeks. You must prepare your yacht for a voyage, instruct your men to touch at a certain point on Staten Island, and wait until six o'clock day after to-morrow morning. If you do not come aboard by that time, they are to go to one of the South American ports and remain until further orders. By this means your absence for an indefinite period will be explained. You will go to Nina San Croix in the disguise which you have always used, and from her to the yacht, and by this means step out of your real status and back into it without leaving traces. I will come here to-morrow evening and furnish you with everything that you shall need and give you full and exact instructions in every particular. These details you must execute with the greatest care, as they will be vitally essential to the success of my plan."

Through it all Walcott had been silent and motionless. Now he arose, and in his face there must have been some premonition of protest, for Mason stepped back and put out his hand. "Sir," he said, with brutal emphasis, "not a word. Remember that you are only the hand, and the hand does not think." Then he turned around abruptly and went out of the house.

III

The place which Samuel Walcott had selected for the residence of Nina San Croix was far up in the northern suburb of New York. The place was very old. The lawn was large and ill-kept; the house, a square old-fashioned brick, was set far back from the street, and partly hidden by trees. Around it all was a rusty iron fence. The place had the air of genteel ruin, such as one finds in the Virginias.

On a Thursday of November, about three o'clock in the afternoon, a little man, driving a dray, stopped in the alley at the rear of the house. As he opened the back gate an old negro woman came down the steps from the kitchen and demanded to know what he wanted. The drayman asked if the lady of the house was in. The old negro answered that she was asleep at this hour and could not be seen.

"That is good," said the little man, "now there won't be any row. I brought up some cases of wine which she ordered from our house last week and which the Boss told me to deliver at once, but I forgot it until to-day. Just let me put it in the cellar now, Auntie, and don't say a word to the lady about it and she won't ever know that it was not brought up on time."

The drayman stopped, fished a silver dollar out of his pocket, and gave it to the old negro. "There now, Auntie," he said, "my job depends upon the lady not knowing about this wine; keep it mum."

"Dat's all right, honey," said the old servant, beaming like a May morning. "De cellar door is open, carry it all in and put it in de back part and nobody aint never going to know how long it has been in 'dar."

The old negro went back into the kitchen and the little man began to unload the dray. He carried in five wine cases and stowed them away in the back part of the cellar as the old woman had directed. Then, after having satisfied himself that no one was watching, he took from the dray two heavy paper sacks, presumably filled with flour, and a little bundle wrapped in an old newspaper; these he carefully hid behind the wine cases in the cellar. After a while he closed the door, climbed on his dray, and drove off down the alley.

About eight o'clock in the evening of the same day, a Mexican sailor dodged in the front gate and slipped down to the side of the house. He stopped by the window and tapped on it with his finger. In a moment a woman opened the door. She was tall, lithe, and splendidly proportioned, with a dark Spanish face and straight hair. The man stepped inside. The woman bolted the door and turned round.

"Ah," she said, smiling, "it is you, Señor? How good of you."

The man started. "Whom else did you expect?" he said quickly.

"Oh!" laughed the woman, "perhaps the Archbishop."

"Nina!" said the man, in a broken voice that expressed love, humility, and reproach. His face was white under the black sunburn.

For a moment the woman wavered. A shadow flitted over her eyes, then she stepped back. "No," she said, "not yet."

The man walked across to the fire, sank down in a chair, and covered his face with his hands. The woman stepped up noiselessly behind him and leaned over the chair. The man was either in great agony or else he was a superb actor, for the muscles of his neck twitched violently and his shoulders trembled.

"Oh," he muttered, as though echoing his thoughts, "I can't do it, I can't!"

The woman caught the words and leaped up as though some one had struck her in the face. She threw back her head. Her nostrils dilated and her eyes flashed.

"You can't do it!" she cried. "Then you do love her! You shall do it! Do you hear me? You shall do it! You killed him! You got rid of him! but you shall not get rid of me. I have the evidence, all of it. The Archbishop will have it to-morrow. They shall hang you! Do you hear me? They shall hang you!"

The woman's voice rose, it was loud and shrill. The man turned slowly round without looking up, and stretched out his arms toward the woman. She stopped and looked down at him. The fire glittered for a moment and then died out of her eyes, her bosom heaved and her lips began to tremble. With a cry she flung herself into his arms, caught him around the neck, and pressed his face up close against her cheek.

"Oh! Dick, Dick," she sobbed, "I do love you so! I can't live without you! Not another hour, Dick! I do want you so much, so much, Dick!"

The man shifted his right arm quickly, slipped a great Mexican knife out of his sleeve, and passed his fingers slowly up the woman's side until he felt the heart beat under his hand, then he raised the knife, gripped the handle tight, and drove the keen blade into the woman's bosom. The hot blood gushed out over his arm, and down on his leg. The body, warm and limp, slipped down in his arms. The man got up, pulled out the knife, and thrust it into a sheath at his belt, unbuttoned the dress, and slipped it off of the body. As he did this a bundle of papers dropped upon the floor; these he glanced at hastily and put into his pocket. Then he took the dead woman up in his arms, went out into the hall, and started to go up the stairway. The body was relaxed and heavy, and for that reason difficult to carry. He doubled it up into an awful heap, with the knees against the chin, and walked slowly and heavily up the stairs and out into the bath-room. There he laid the corpse down on the tiled floor. Then he opened the window, closed the shutters, and lighted the gas. The bath-room was small and contained an ordinary steel tub, porcelain-lined, standing near the window and raised about six inches above the floor. The sailor went over to the tub, pried up the metal rim of the outlet with his knife, removed it, and fitted into its place a porcelain disk which he took from his pocket; to this disk was attached a long platinum wire, the end of which he fastened on the outside of the tub. After he had done this he went back to the body, stripped off its clothing, put it down in the tub and began to dismember it with the great Mexican knife. The blade was strong and sharp as a razor. The man worked rapidly and with the greatest care.

When he had finally cut the body into as small pieces as possible, he replaced the knife in its sheath, washed his hands, and went out of the bath-room and down stairs to the lower hall. The sailor seemed perfectly familiar with the house. By a side door he passed into the cellar. There he lighted the gas, opened one of the wine cases, and, taking up all the bottles that he could conveniently carry, returned to the bath-room. There he poured the contents into the tub on the dismembered body, and then returned to the cellar with the empty bottles, which he replaced in the wine cases. This he continued to do until all the cases but one were emptied and the bath tub was more than half full of liquid. This liquid was sulphuric acid.

When the sailor returned to the cellar with the last empty wine bottles, he opened the fifth case, which really contained wine, took some of it out, and poured a little into each of the empty bottles in order to remove any possible odor of the sulphuric acid. Then he turned out the gas and brought up to the bath-room with him the two paper flour sacks and the little heavy bundle. These sacks were filled with nitrate of soda. He set them down by the door, opened the little bundle, and took out two long rubber tubes, each attached to a heavy gas burner, not unlike the ordinary burners of a small gas-stove. He fastened the tubes to two of the gas jets, put the burners under the tub, turned the gas on full, and lighted it. Then he threw into the tub the woman's clothing and the papers which he had found on her body, after which he took up the two heavy sacks of nitrate of soda and dropped them carefully into the sulphuric acid. When he had done this he went quickly out of the bath-room and closed the door.

The deadly acids at once attacked the body and began to destroy it; as the heat increased, the acids boiled and the destructive process was rapid and awful. From time to time the sailor opened the door of the bath-room cautiously, and, holding a wet towel over his mouth and nose, looked in at his horrible work. At the end of a few hours there was only a swimming mass in the tub. When the man looked at four o'clock, it was all a thick murky liquid. He turned off the gas quickly and stepped back out of the room. For perhaps half an hour he waited in the hall; finally, when the acids had cooled so that they no longer gave off fumes, he opened the door and went in, took hold of the platinum wire and, pulling the porcelain disk from the stop-cock, allowed the awful contents of the tub to run out. Then he turned on the hot water, rinsed the tub clean, and replaced the metal outlet. Removing the rubber tubes, he cut them into pieces, broke the porcelain disk and, rolling up the platinum wire, washed it all down the sewer pipe.

The fumes had escaped through the open window; this he now closed and set himself to putting the bath-room in order, and effectually removing every trace of his night's work. The sailor moved around with the very greatest degree of care. Finally, when he had arranged everything to his complete satisfaction, he picked up the two burners, turned out the gas, and left the bath-room, closing the door after him. From the bath-room he went directly to the attic, concealed the two rusty burners under a heap of rubbish, and then walked carefully and noiselessly down the stairs and through the lower hall. As he opened the door and stepped into the room where he had killed the woman, two police-officers sprang out and seized him. The man screamed like a wild beast taken in a trap and sank down.

"Oh! oh!" he cried, "it was no use! it was no use to do it!" Then he recovered himself in a manner and was silent. The officers handcuffed him, summoned the patrol, and took him at once to the stationhouse. There he said he was a Mexican sailor and that his name was Victor Ancona; but he would say nothing further. The following morning he sent for Randolph Mason and the two were long together.

IV

The obscure defendant charged with murder has little reason to complain of the law's delays. The morning following the arrest of Victor Ancona, the newspapers published long sensational articles, denounced him as a fiend, and convicted him. The grand jury, as it happened, was in session. The preliminaries were soon arranged and the case was railroaded into trial. The indictment contained a great many counts, and charged the prisoner with the murder of Nina San Croix by striking, stabbing, choking, poisoning, and so forth.

The trial had continued for three days and had appeared so overwhelmingly one-sided that the spectators who were crowded in the court-room had grown to be violent and bitter partisans, to such an extent that the police watched them closely. The attorneys for the People were dramatic and denunciatory, and forced their case with arrogant confidence. Mason, as counsel for the prisoner, was indifferent and listless. Throughout the entire trial he had sat almost motionless at the table, his gaunt form bent over, his long legs drawn up under his chair, and his weary, heavy-muscled face, with its restless eyes, fixed and staring out over the heads of the jury, was like a tragic mask. The bar, and even the judge, believed that the prisoner's counsel had abandoned his case.

The evidence was all in and the People rested. It had been shown that Nina San Croix had resided for many years in the house in which the prisoner was arrested; that she had lived by herself, with no other companion than an old negro servant; that her past was unknown, and that she received no visitors, save the Mexican sailor, who came to her house at long intervals. Nothing whatever was shown tending to explain who the prisoner was or whence he had come. It was shown that on Tuesday preceding the killing the Archbishop had received a communication from Nina San Croix, in which she said she desired to make a statement of the greatest import, and asking for an audience. To this the Archbishop replied that he would willingly grant her a hearing if she would come to him at eleven o'clock on Friday morning. Two policemen testified that about eight o'clock on the night of Thursday they had noticed the prisoner slip into the gate of Nina San Croix's residence and go down to the side of the house where he was admitted; that his appearance and seeming haste had attracted their attention; that they had concluded that it was some clandestine armour, and out of curiosity had both slipped down to the house and endeavored to find a position from which they could see into the room, but were unable to do so, and were about to go back to the street when they heard a woman's voice cry out in great anger: "I know that you love her and that you want to get rid of me, but you should not do it! You murdered him but you shall not murder me! I have all the evidence to convict you of murdering him! The Archbishop will have it to-morrow! They shall hang you! Do you hear me? They shall hang you for his murder!" that thereupon one of the policemen proposed that they should break into the house and see what was wrong, but the other had urged that it was only the usual lovers' quarrel and if they should interfere they would find nothing upon which a charge could be based and would only be laughed at by the chief; that they had waited and listened for a time, but hearing nothing further had gone back to the street and contented themselves with keeping a strict watch on the house.

The People proved further, that on Thursday evening Nina San Croix had given the old negro domestic a sum of money and dismissed her, with the instruction that she was not to return until sent for. The old woman testified that she had gone directly to the house of her son, and later had discovered that she had forgotten some articles of clothing which she needed; that thereupon she had returned to the house and had gone up the back way to her room—this was about eight o'clock; that while there she had heard Nina San Croix's voice in great passion and remembered that she had used the words stated by the policemen; that these sudden, violent cries had frightened her greatly and she had bolted the door and been afraid to leave the room; shortly thereafter, she had heard heavy footsteps ascending the stairs, slowly and with great difficulty, as though some one were carrying a heavy burden; that therefore her fear had increased and that she had put out the light and hidden under the bed. She remembered hearing the footsteps moving about up-stairs for many hours, how long she could not tell. Finally, about half-past four in the morning, she crept out, opened the door, slipped down stairs, and ran out into the street. There she had found the policemen and requested them to search the house.

The two officers had gone to the house with the woman. She had opened the door and they had had just time to step back into the shadow when the prisoner entered. When arrested, Victor Ancona had screamed with terror, and cried out, "It was no use! it was no use to do it!"

The Chief of Police had come to the house and instituted a careful search. In the room below, from which the cries had come, he found a dress which was identified as belonging to Nina San Croix and which she was wearing when last seen by the domestic, about six o'clock that evening. This dress was covered with blood, and had a slit about two inches long in the left side of the bosom, into which the Mexican knife, found on the prisoner, fitted perfectly. These articles were introduced in evidence, and it was shown that the slit would be exactly over the heart of the wearer, and that such a wound would certainly result in death. There was much blood on one of the chairs and on the floor. There was also blood on the prisoner's coat and the leg of his trousers, and the heavy Mexican knife was also bloody. The blood was shown by the experts to be human blood.

The body of the woman was not found, and the most rigid and tireless search failed to develop the slightest trace of the corpse, or the manner of its disposal. The body of the woman had disappeared as completely as though it had vanished into the air.

When counsel announced that he had closed for the People, the judge turned and looked gravely down at Mason. "Sir," he said, "the evidence for the defense may now be introduced."

Randolph Mason arose slowly and faced the judge.

"If your Honor please," he said, speaking slowly and distinctly, "the defendant has no evidence to offer." He paused while a murmur of astonishment ran over the court-room. "But, if your Honor please," he continued, "I move that the jury be directed to find the prisoner not guilty."

The crowd stirred. The counsel for the People smiled. The judge looked sharply at the speaker over his glasses. "On what ground?" he said curtly.

"On the ground," replied Mason, "that the *corpus delicti* has not been proven."

"Ah!" said the judge, for once losing his judicial gravity.

Mason sat down abruptly. The senior counsel for the prosecution was on his feet in a moment.

"What!" he said, "the gentleman bases his motion on a failure to establish the *corpus delicti*? Does he jest, or has he forgotten the evidence? The term '*corpus delicti*' is technical, and means the body of the crime, or the substantial fact that a crime has been committed. Does any one doubt it in this case? It is true that no one actually saw the prisoner kill the decedent, and that he has so successfully hidden the body that it has not been found, but the powerful chain of circumstances, clear and close-linked, proving motive, the criminal agency, and the criminal act, is overwhelming.

"The victim in this case is on the eve of making a statement that would prove fatal to the prisoner. The night before the statement is to be made he goes to her

65

residence. They quarrel. Her voice is heard, raised high in the greatest passion, denouncing him, and charging that he is a murderer, that she has the evidence and will reveal it, that he shall be hanged, and that he shall not be rid of her. Here is the motive for the crime, clear as light. Are not the bloody knife, the bloody dress, the bloody clothes of the prisoner, unimpeachable witnesses to the criminal act? The criminal agency of the prisoner has not the shadow of a possibility to obscure it. His motive is gigantic. The blood on him, and his despair when arrested, cry 'Murder! murder!' with a thousand tongues.

"Men may lie, but circumstances cannot. The thousand hopes and fears and passions of men may delude, or bias the witness. Yet it is beyond the human mind to conceive that a clear, complete chain of concatenated circumstances can be in error. Hence it is that the greatest jurists have declared that such evidence, being rarely liable to delusion or fraud, is safest and most powerful. The machinery of human justice cannot guard against the remote and improbable doubt. The inference is persistent in the affairs of men. It is the only means by which the human mind reaches the truth. If you forbid the jury to exercise it, you bid them work after first striking off their hands. Rule out the irresistible inference, and the end of justice is come in this land; and you may as well leave the spider to weave his web through the abandoned court-room."

The attorney stopped, looked down at Mason with a pompous sneer, and retired to his place at the table. The judge sat thoughtful and motionless. The jurymen leaned forward in their seats.

"If your Honor please," said Mason, rising, "this is a matter of law, plain, clear, and so well settled in the State of New York the even counsel for the People should know it. The question before your Honor is simple. If the *corpus delicti,* the body of the crime, has been proven, as required by the laws of the commonwealth, then this case should go to the jury. If not, then it is the duty of this Court to direct the jury to find the prisoner not guilty. There is here no room for judicial discretion. Your Honor has but to recall and apply the rigid rule announced by our courts prescribing distinctly how the *corpus delicti* in murder must be proven.

"The prisoner here stands charged with the highest crime. The law demands, first, that the crime, as a fact, be established. The fact that the victim is indeed dead must first be made certain before any one can be convicted for her killing, because, so long as there remains the remotest doubt as to the death, there can be no certainty as to the criminal agent, although the circumstantial evidence indicating the guilt of the accused may be positive, complete, and utterly irresistible. In murder, the *corpus delicti,* or body of the crime, is composed of two elements:

"Death, as a result.

"The criminal agency of another as the means.

"It is the fixed and immutable law of this State, laid down in the leading case of Ruloff *v.* The People, and binding upon this Court, that both components of the *corpus delicti* shall not be established by circumstantial evidence. There must be direct proof of one or the other of these two component elements of the *corpus delicti.* If one is proven by direct evidence, the other may be presumed; but both shall not be presumed from circumstances, no matter how powerful, how cogent, or how completely overwhelming the circumstances may be. In other words, no man can be convicted of murder in the State of New York, unless the body of the victim be found and identified, or there be direct proof that the prisoner did some act adequate to produce death, and did it in such a manner as to account for the disappearance of the body."

The face of the judge cleared and grew hard. The members of the bar were attentive and alert; they were beginning to see the legal escape open up. The audience were puzzled; they did not yet understand. Mason turned to the counsel for the People. His ugly face was bitter with contempt.

"For three days," he said, "I have been tortured by this useless and expensive farce. If counsel for the People had been other than play-actors, they would have known in the beginning that Victor Ancona could not be convicted for murder, unless he were confronted in this court-room with a living witness, who had looked into the dead face of Nina San Croix; or, if not that, a living witness who had seen him drive the dagger into her bosom.

"I care not if the circumstantial evidence in this case were so strong and irresistible as to be overpowering; if the judge on the bench, if the jury, if every man within sound of my voice, were convinced of the guilt of the prisoner to the degree of certainty that is absolute; if the circumstantial evidence left in the mind no shadow of the remotest improbable doubt; yet, in the absence of the eye-witness, this prisoner cannot be punished, and this Court must compel the jury to acquit him."

The audience now understood, and they were dumbfounded. Surely this was not the law. They had been taught that the law was common sense, and this,—this was anything else.

Mason saw it all, and grinned. "In its tenderness," he sneered, "the law shields the innocent. The good law of New York reaches out its hand and lifts the prisoner out of the clutches of the fierce jury that would hang him."

Mason sat down. The room was silent. The jurymen looked at each other in amazement. The counsel for the People arose. His face was white with anger, and incredulous.

"Your Honor," he said, "this doctrine is monstrous. Can it be said that, in order to evade punishment, the murderer has only to hide or destroy the body of the victim, or sink it into the sea? Then, if he is not seen to kill, the law is powerless and the murderer can snap his finger in the face of retributive justice. If this is the law, then the law for the highest crime is a dead letter. The great commonwealth winks at murder and invites every man to kill his enemy, provided he kill him in secret and hide him. I repeat, your Honor,"—the man's voice was now loud and angry and rang through the court-room—"that this doctrine is monstrous!"

"So said Best, and Story, and many another," muttered Mason, "and the law remained."

"The Court," said the judge, abruptly, "desires no further argument."

The counsel for the People resumed his seat. His face lighted up with triumph. The Court was going to sustain him.

The judge turned and looked down at the jury. He was grave, and spoke with deliberate emphasis.

"Gentlemen of the jury," he said, "the rule of Lord Hale obtains in this State and is binding upon me. It is the law as stated by counsel for the prisoner: that to warrant conviction of murder there must be direct proof either of the death, as of the finding and identification of the corpse, or of criminal violence adequate to produce death, and exerted in such a manner as to account for the disappearance of the body; and it is only when there is direct proof of the one that the other can be established by circumstantial evidence. This is the law, and cannot now be departed from. I do not presume to explain its wisdom. Chief-Justice Johnson has observed, in the leading case, that it may have its probable foundation in the idea that where direct proof is absent as to both the fact of the death and of criminal violence capable of producing death, no evidence can rise to the degree of moral certainty that the individual is dead by criminal intervention, or even lead by direct inference to this result; and that, where the fact of death is not certainly ascertained, all inculpatory circumstantial evidence wants the key necessary for its satisfactory interpretation, and cannot be depended on to furnish more than probable results. It may be, also, that such a rule has some reference to the dangerous possibility that a general preconception of guilt, or a general excitement of popular feeling, may creep in to supply the place of evidence, if upon other than direct proof of death or a cause of death, a jury are permitted to pronounce a prisoner guilty.

"In this case the body has not been found and there is no direct proof of criminal agency on the part of the prisoner, although the chain of circumstantial evidence is complete and irresistible in the highest degree. Nevertheless, it is all circumstantial evidence, and under the laws of New York the prisoner cannot be punished. I have no right of discretion. The law does not permit a conviction in this case, although every one of us may be morally certain of the prisoner's guilt. I am, therefore, gentlemen of the jury, compelled to direct you to find the prisoner not guilty."

"Judge," interrupted the foreman, jumping up in the box, "we cannot find that verdict under our oath; we know that this man is guilty."

"Sir," said the judge, "this is a matter of law in which the wishes of the jury cannot be considered. The clerk will write a verdict of not guilty, which you, as foreman, will sign."

The spectators broke out into a threatening murmur that began to grow and gather volume. The judge rapped on his desk and ordered the bailiffs promptly to suppress any demonstration on the part of the audience. Then he directed the foreman to sign the verdict prepared by the clerk. When this was done he turned to Victor Ancona; his face was hard and there was a cold glitter in his eyes.

"Prisoner at the bar," he said, "you have been put to trial before this tribunal on a charge of cold-blooded and atrocious murder. The evidence produced against you was of such powerful and overwhelming character that it seems to have left no doubt in the minds of the jury, nor indeed in the mind of any person present in this court-room.

"Had the question of your guilt been submitted to these twelve arbiters, a conviction would certainly have resulted and the death penalty would have been imposed. But the law, rigid, passionless, even-eyed, has thrust in between you and the wrath of your fellows and saved you from it. I do not cry out against the impotency of the law; it is perhaps as wise as imperfect humanity could make it. I deplore, rather, the genius of evil men who, by cunning design, are enabled to slip through the fingers of this law. I have no word of censure or admonition for you, Victor Ancona. The law of New York compels me to acquit you. I am only its mouthpiece, with my individual wishes throttled. I speak only those things which the law directs I shall speak.

"You are now at liberty to leave this court-room, not guiltless of the crime of murder, perhaps, but at least rid of its punishment. The eyes of men may see Cain's mark on your brow, but the eyes of the Law are blind to it."

When the audience fully realized what the judge had said they were amazed and silent. They knew as well as men could know, that Victor Ancona was guilty of murder, and yet he was now going out of the court-room free. Could it happen that the law protected only against the blundering rogue? They had heard always of the boasted completeness of the law which magistrates from time immemorial had labored to perfect, and now when the skillful villain sought to evade it, they saw how weak a thing it was.

V

The wedding march of Lohengrin floated out from the Episcopal Church of St. Mark, clear and sweet, and perhaps heavy with its paradox of warning. The theater of this coming contract before high leaven was a wilderness of roses worth the taxes of a county. The high caste of Manhattan, by the grace of the check-book, were present, clothed in Parisian purple and fine linen, cunningly and marvelously wrought.

Over in her private pew, ablaze with jewels, and decked with fabrics from the deft hand of many a weaver, sat Mrs. Miriam Steuvisant as imperious and self-complacent as a queen. To her it was all a kind of triumphal procession, proclaiming her ability as a general. With her were a choice few of the *genus homo,* which obtains at the five-o'clock teas, instituted, say the sages, for the purpose of sprinkling the holy water of Lethe.

"Czarina," whispered Reggie Du Puyster, leaning forward, "I salute you. The ceremony *sub jugum* is superb."

"Walcott is an excellent fellow," answered Mrs. Steuvisant; "not a vice, you know, Reggie."

"Aye, Empress," put in the others, "a purist taken in the net. The clean-skirted one has come to the altar. Vive la vertu!"

Samuel Walcott, still sunburned from his cruise, stood before the chancel with the only daughter of the blue-blooded St. Clairs. His face was clear and honest and his voice firm. This was life and not romance. The lid of the sepulchre had closed and he had slipped from under it. And now, and ever after, the hand red with murder was clean as any.

The minister raised his voice, proclaiming the holy union before God, and this twain, half pure, half foul, now by divine ordinance one flesh, bowed down before it. No blood cried from the ground. The sunlight of high noon streamed down through the window panes like a benediction.

Back in the pew of Mrs. Miriam Steuvisant, Reggie Du Puyster turned down his thumb. "Habet!" he said.

GENTLEMEN AND PLAYERS

E. W. HORNUNG
(1866–1921)

Soon after marrying Constance, the sister of Arthur Conan Doyle, Hornung began to write stories about A. J. Raffles, the greatest thief in literature. The dashing cricket player and man-about-town became briefly almost as popular as Doyle's much more moral creation, Sherlock Holmes. It is a commonly held theory that Hornung invented Raffles mainly to tweak his somewhat stodgy brother-in-law, to whom he dedicated his first book, The Amateur Cracksman *(1898).*

LD RAFFLES MAY OR MAY NOT have been an exceptional criminal, but as a cricketer I dare swear he was unique. Himself a dangerous bat, a brilliant field, and perhaps the very finest slow bowler of his decade, he took incredibly little interest in the game at large. He never went up to Lord's without his cricket-bag, or showed the slightest interest in the result of a match in which he was not himself engaged. Nor was this mere hateful egotism on his part. He professed to have lost all enthusiasm for the game, and to keep it up only from the very lowest motives.

'Cricket,' said Raffles, 'like everything else, is good enough sport until you discover a better. As a source of excitement it isn't in it with other things you wot of, Bunny, and the involuntary comparison becomes a bore. What's the satisfaction of taking a man's wicket when you want his spoons? Still, if you can bowl a bit your low cunning won't get rusty, and always looking for the weak spot's just the kind of mental exercise one wants.

Yes, perhaps there's some affinity between the two things after all. But I'd chuck up cricket to-morrow, Bunny, if it wasn't for the glorious protection it affords a person of my proclivities.'

'How so?' said I. 'It brings you before the public, I should have thought, far more than is either safe or wise.'

'My dear Bunny, that's exactly where you make a mistake. To follow crime with reasonable impunity you simply must have a parallel ostensible career—the more public the better. The principle is obvious. Mr. Peace, of pious memory, disarmed suspicion by acquiring a local reputation for playing the fiddle and taming animals, and it's my profound conviction that Jack the Ripper was a really eminent public man, whose speeches were very likely reported alongside his atrocities. Fill the bill in some prominent part, and you'll never be suspected of doubling it with another of equal prominence. That's why I want you to cultivate journalism, my boy, and sign all you can. And it's the one and only reason why I don't burn my bats for firewood.'

Nevertheless, when he did play there was no keener performer on the field, nor one more anxious to do well for his side. I remember how he went to the nets, before the first match of the season, with his pocket full of sovereigns, which he put on the stumps instead of bails. It was a sight to see the professionals bowling like demons for the hard cash, for whenever a stump was hit a pound was tossed to the bowler and another balanced in its stead, while one man took £3 with a ball that spread-eagled the wicket. Raffles's practice cost him either eight or nine sovereigns; but he had absolutely first-class bowling all the time, and he made fifty-seven runs next day.

It became my pleasure to accompany him to all his matches, to watch every ball he bowled, or played, or fielded, and to sit chatting with him in the pavilion when he was doing none of these three things. You might have seen us there, side by side, during the greater part of the Gentlemen's first innings against the Players (who had lost the toss) on the second Monday in July. We were to be seen, but not heard, for Raffles had failed to score, and was uncommonly cross for a player who cared so little for the game. Merely taciturn with me, he was positively rude to more than one member who wanted to know how it had happened, or who ventured to commiserate him on his luck; there he sat, with a straw hat tilted over his nose and a cigarette stuck between lips that curled disagreeably at every advance. I was, therefore, much surprised when a young fellow of the exquisite type came and squeezed himself in between us, and met with a perfectly civil reception despite the liberty. I did not know the boy by sight, nor did Raffles introduce us; but their conversation proclaimed at once a slightness of acquaintanceship and a licence on the lad's part which combined to puzzle me. Mystification reached its height when Raffles was informed that the other's father was anxious to meet him, and he instantly consented to gratify that whim.

'He's in the Ladies' Enclosure. Will you come round now?'

'With pleasure,' says Raffles.—'Keep a place for me, Bunny.'

And they were gone.

'Young Crowley,' said some voice further back. 'Last year's Harrow Eleven.'

'I remember him. Worst man in the team.'

'Keen cricketer, however. Stopped till he was twenty to get his colours. Governor made him. Keen breed. Oh, pretty, sir! Very pretty!'

The game was boring me. I only came to see old Raffles perform. Soon I was looking wistfully for his return, and at length I saw him beckoning me from the palings to the right.

'Want to introduce you to old Amersteth,' he whispered, when I joined him. 'They've a cricket week next month, when this boy Crowley comes of age, and we've both got to go down and play.'

'Both!' I echoed. 'But I'm no cricketer!'

'Shut up,' says Raffles. 'Leave that to me. I've been lying for all I'm worth,' he added sepulchrally, as we reached the bottom of the steps. 'I trust to you not to give the show away.'

There was the gleam in his eye that I knew well enough elsewhere, but was unprepared for in those healthy, sane surroundings; and it was with very definite misgivings and surmises that I followed the Zingari blazer through the vast flower-bed of hats and bonnets that bloomed beneath the ladies' awning.

Lord Amersteth was a fine-looking man with a short moustache and a double chin. He received me with much dry courtesy, through which, however, it was not difficult to read a less flattering tale. I was accepted as the inevitable appendage of the invaluable Raffles, with whom I felt deeply incensed as I made my bow.

'I have been bold enough,' said Lord Amersteth, 'to ask one of the Gentlemen of England to come down and play some rustic cricket for us next month. He is kind enough to say that he would have liked nothing better, but for this little fishing expedition of yours, Mr _____, Mr _____,' and Lord Amersteth succeeded in remembering my name.

It was, of course, the first I had ever heard of that fishing expedition, but I made haste to say that it could easily, and should certainly, be put off. Raffles gleamed approval through his eyelashes. Lord Amersteth bowed and shrugged.

'You're very good, I'm sure,' said he. 'But I understand you're a cricketer yourself?'

'He was one at school,' said Raffles, with infamous readiness.

'Not a real cricketer,' I was stammering meanwhile.

'In the eleven?' said Lord Amersteth.

'I'm afraid not,' said I.

'But only just out of it,' declared Raffles, to my horror.

'Well, well, we can't all play for the Gentlemen,' said Lord Amersteth slyly. 'My son Crowley only just scraped into the eleven at Harrow, and he's going to play. I may even come in myself at a pinch; so you won't be the only duffer, if you are one, and I shall be very glad if you will come down and help us too. You shall flog a stream before breakfast and after dinner, if you like.'

'I should be very proud,' I was beginning, as the mere prelude to resolute excuses; but the eye of Raffles opened wide upon me; and I hesitated weakly, to be duly lost.

'Then that's settled,' said Lord Amersteth, with the slightest suspicion of grimness. 'It's to be a little week, you know, when my son comes of age. We play the Free Foresters, the Dorsetshire Gentlemen, and probably some local lot as well. But Mr Raffles will tell you all about it, and Crowley shall write.—Another wicket! By Jove, they're all out! Then I rely on you both.' And, with a little nod, Lord Amersteth rose and sidled to the gangway.

Raffles rose also, but I caught the sleeve of his blazer.

'What are you thinking of?' I whispered savagely. 'I was nowhere near the eleven. I'm no sort of cricketer. I shall have to get out of this!'

'Not you,' he whispered back. 'You needn't play, but come you must. If you wait for me after half-past six I'll tell you why.'

But I could guess the reason; and I am ashamed to say that it revolted me much less than did the notion of making a public fool of myself on a cricket-field. My gorge rose at this as it no longer rose at crime, and it was in no tranquil humour that I strolled about the ground while Raffles disappeared in the pavilion. Nor was my annoyance lessened by a little meeting I witnessed between young Crowley and his father, who shrugged as he stopped and stooped to convey some information which made the young man look a little blank. It may have been pure self-consciousness on my part, but I could have sworn that the trouble was their inability to secure the great Raffles without his insignificant friend.

Then the bell rang, and I climbed to the top of the pavilion to watch Raffles bowl. No subtleties are lost up there; and if ever a bowler was full of them, it was A. J. Raffles on this day, as, indeed, all the cricket world remembers. One had not to be a cricketer oneself to appreciate his perfect command of pitch and break, his beautifully easy action, which never varied with the varying pace, his great ball on the leg-stump— his dropping head-ball—in a word, the infinite ingenuity of that versatile attack. It was no mere exhibition of athletic prowess, it was an intellectual treat, and one with a special significance in my eyes. I saw the 'affinity between the two things,' saw it in that afternoon's tireless warfare against the flower of professional cricket. It was not that Raffles took many wickets for few runs; he was too fine a bowler to mind being hit; and time was short, and the wicket good. What I admired, and what I remember, was the combination of resource and cunning, of patience and precision, of head-work and handiwork, which made every over an artistic whole. It was all so characteristic of that other Raffles whom I alone knew!

'I felt like bowling this afternoon,' he told me later—in the hansom. 'With a pitch to help me, I'd have done something big; as it is, three for forty-one, out of the four that tell, isn't so bad for a slow bowler on a plumb wicket against those fellows. But I felt venomous! Nothing riles me more than being asked about for my cricket as though I were a pro. myself.'

'Then why on earth go?'

'To punish them, and—because we shall be jolly hard up, Bunny, before the season's over!'

'Ah!' said I. 'I thought it was that.'

'Of course it was! It seems they're going to have the very devil of a week of it—balls—dinner-parties—swagger house-party—general junketings—and obviously a houseful of diamonds as well. Diamonds galore! As a general rule nothing would induce me to abuse my position as a guest. I've never done it, Bunny. But in this case we're engaged like the waiters and the band, and by heaven we'll take our toll! Let's have a quiet dinner somewhere and talk it over.'

'It seems rather a vulgar sort of theft,' I could not help saying; and to this, my single protest, Raffles instantly assented.

'It is a vulgar sort,' said he; 'but I can't help that. We're getting vulgarly hard up again, and there's end on't. Besides, these people deserve it, and can afford it. And don't you run away with the idea that all will be plain sailing; nothing will be easier than getting some stuff, and nothing harder than avoiding all suspicion, as, of course, we must. We may come away with no more than a good working plan of the premises. Who knows? In any case there's weeks of thinking in it for you and me.'

But with those weeks I will not weary you further than by remarking that the 'thinking' was done entirely by Raffles, who did not always trouble to communicate his thoughts to me. His reticence, however, was no longer an irritant. I began to accept it as a necessary convention of these little enterprises. And, after our last adventure of the kind, more especially after its *dénouement,* my trust in Raffles was much too solid to be shaken by a want of trust in me, which I still believe to have been more the instinct of the criminal than the judgment of the man.

It was on Monday, August 10, that we were due at Milchester Abbey, Dorset; and the beginning of the month found us cruising about that very county, with fly-rods actually in our hands. The idea was that we should acquire at once a local reputation as decent fishermen, and some knowledge of the country-side, with a view to further and more deliberate operations in the event of an unprofitable week. There was another idea which Raffles kept to himself until he had got me down there. Then one day he produced a cricket-ball in a meadow we were crossing, and threw me catches for an hour together. More hours he spent in bowling to me on the nearest green; and, if I was never a cricketer, at least I came nearer to being one by the end of that week than ever before or since.

Incident began early on the Monday. We had sallied forth from a desolate little junction within quite a few miles of Milchester, had been caught in a shower, had run for shelter to a wayside inn. A florid, over-dressed man was drinking in the parlour, and I could have sworn it was at the sight of him that Raffles recoiled on the threshold, and afterwards insisted on returning to the station through the rain. He assured me, however, that the odour of stale ale had almost knocked him down. And I had to make what I could of his speculative, downcast eyes and knitted brows.

Milchester Abbey is a grey, quadrangular pile, deep-set in rich woody country, and twinkling with triple rows of quaint windows, every one of which seemed alight as we drove up just in time to dress for dinner. The carriage had whirled us under I know not how many triumphal arches in process of construction, and past the tents and flag-poles of a juicy-looking cricket-field, on which Raffles undertook to bowl up to his reputation. But the chief signs of festival were within, where we found an enormous house-party assembled, including more persons of pomp, majesty, and dominion than I had ever encountered in one room before. I confess I felt overpowered. Our errand and my own pretences combined to rob me of an address upon which I had sometimes plumed myself; and I have a grim recollection of my nervous relief when dinner was at last announced. I little knew what an ordeal it was to prove.

I had taken in a much less formidable young lady than might have fallen to my lot. Indeed I began by blessing my good fortune in this respect. Miss Melhuish was merely the rector's daughter, and she had only been asked to make an even number. She informed me of both facts before the soup reached us, and her subsequent conversation was characterised by the same engaging candour. It exposed what was little short of a mania for imparting information. I had simply to listen, to nod, and to be thankful. When I confessed to knowing very few of those present, even by sight, my entertaining companion proceeded to tell me who everybody was, beginning on my left and working conscientiously round to her right. This lasted quite a long time, and really interested me; but a great deal that followed did not; and, obviously to recapture my unworthy attention, Miss Melhuish suddenly asked me, in a sensational whisper, whether I could keep a secret.

I said I thought I might, whereupon another question followed, in still lower and more thrilling accents:

'Are you afraid of burglars?'

Burglars! I was roused at last. The word stabbed me. I repeated it in a horrified query.

'So I've found something to interest you at last!' said Miss Melhuish, in naïve triumph. 'Yes—burglars! But don't speak so loud. It's supposed to be kept a great secret. I really oughtn't to tell you at all!'

'But what is there to tell?' I whispered with satisfactory impatience.

'You promise not to speak of it?'

'Of course!'

'Well, then, there are burglars in the neighbourhood.'

'Have they committed any robberies?'

'Not yet.'

'Then how do you know?'

'They've been seen. In the district. Two well-known London thieves!'

Two! I looked at Raffles. I had done so often during the evening, envying him his high spirits, his iron nerve, his buoyant wit, his perfect ease and self-possession. But now I pitied him; through all my own terror and consternation, I pitied him as he sat eating and drinking, and laughing, and talking, without a cloud of fear or of embarrassment on his handsome, talking, dare-devil face. I caught up my champagne and emptied the glass.

'Who has seen them?' I then asked calmly.

'A detective. They were traced down from town a few days ago. They are believed to have designs on the Abbey!'

'But why aren't they run in?'

'Exactly what I asked papa on the way here this evening. He says there is no warrant out against the men at present, and all that can be done is to watch their movements.'

'Oh! so they are being watched?'

'Yes, by a detective who is down here on purpose. And I heard Lord Amersteth tell papa that they had been seen this afternoon at Warbeck Junction.'

The very place where Raffles and I had been caught in the rain! Our stampede from the inn was now explained; on the other hand, I was no longer to be taken by surprise by anything that my companion might have to tell me; and I succeeded in looking her in the face with a smile.

'This is really quite exciting, Miss Melhuish,' said I. 'May I ask how you come to know so much about it?'

'It's papa,' was the confidential reply. 'Lord Amersteth consulted him, and he consulted me. But for goodness' sake don't let it get about! I can't think what tempted me to tell you!'

'You may trust me, Miss Melhuish. But—aren't you frightened?'

Miss Melhuish giggled.

'Not a bit! They won't come to the rectory. There's nothing for them there. But look round the table: look at the diamonds: look at old Lady Melrose's necklace alone!'

The Dowager-Marchioness of Melrose was one of the few persons whom it had been unnecessary to point out to me. She sat on Lord Amersteth's right, flourishing her ear-trumpet, and drinking champagne with her usual notorious freedom, as dissipated and kindly a dame as the world has ever seen. It was a necklace of diamonds and sapphires that rose and fell about her ample neck.

'They say it's worth five thousand pounds at least,' continued my companion. 'Lady Margaret told me so this morning (that's Lady Margaret next to your Mr Raffles, you know); and the old dear will wear them every night. Think what a haul they would be! No; we don't feel in danger at the rectory.'

When the ladies rose, Miss Melhuish bound me to fresh vows of secrecy; and left me, I should think, with some remorse for her indiscretion, but more satisfaction at the importance which it had undoubtedly given her in my eyes. The opinion may smack of vanity, though, in reality, the very springs of conversation reside in that same human, universal itch to thrill the auditor. The peculiarity of Miss Melhuish was that she must be thrilling at all costs. And thrilling she had surely been.

I spare you my feelings of the next two hours. I tried hard to get a word with Raffles, but again and again I failed. In the dining-room he and Crowley lit their cigarettes with the same match, and had their heads together all the time. In the drawing-room I had the mortification of hearing him talk interminable nonsense into the trumpet-ear of Lady Melrose, whom he knew in town. Lastly, in the billiard-room, they had a great and lengthy pool, while I sat aloof and chafed more than ever in the company of a very serious Scotchman, who had arrived since dinner, and who would talk of nothing but the recent improvements in instantaneous photography. He had not come to play in the matches (he told me), but to obtain for Lord Amersteth such a series of cricket photographs as had never been taken before; whether as an amateur or a professional photographer I was unable to determine. I remember, however, seeking distraction in little bursts of resolute attention to the conversation of this bore. And so at last the long ordeal ended; glasses were emptied, men said good-night, and I followed Raffles to his room.

'It's all up!' I gasped, as he turned up the gas and I shut the door. 'We're being watched. We've been followed down from town. There's a detective here on the spot!'

'How do you know?' asked Raffles, turning upon me quite sharply, but without the least dismay. And I told him how I knew.

'Of course,' I added, 'it was the fellow we saw in the inn this afternoon.'

'The detective?' said Raffles. 'Do you mean to say you don't know a detective when you see one, Bunny?'

'If that wasn't the fellow, which is?'

Raffles shook his head.

'To think that you've been talking to him for the last hour in the billiard-room, and couldn't spot what he was!'

'The Scotch photographer—'

I paused aghast.

'Scotch he is,' said Raffles, 'and photographer he may be. He is also Inspector Mackenzie of Scotland Yard—the very man I sent the message to that night last April. And you couldn't spot who he was in a whole hour! Oh, Bunny, Bunny, you were never built for crime!'

'But,' said I, 'if that was Mackenzie, who was the fellow you bolted from at Warbeck?'

'The man he's watching.'

'But he's watching us!'

Raffles looked at me with a pitying eye, and shook his head again before handing me his open cigarette-case.

'I don't know whether smoking's forbidden in one's bed-room, but you'd better take one of these and stand tight, Bunny, because I'm going to say something offensive.'

I helped myself with a laugh.

'Say what you like, my dear fellow, if it really isn't you and I that Mackenzie's after.'

'Well, then, it isn't and it couldn't be, and nobody but a born Bunny would suppose for a moment that it was! Do you seriously think he would sit there and knowingly watch his man playing pool under his nose? Well, he might; he's a cool hand, Mackenzie; but I'm not cool enough to win a pool under such conditions. At least, I don't think I am; it would be interesting to see. The situation wasn't free from strain as it was, though I knew he wasn't thinking of us. Crowley told me all about it after dinner, you see, and then I'd seen one of the men for myself this afternoon. You thought it was a detective who made me turn tail at that inn. I really don't know why I didn't tell you at the time, but it was just the opposite. That loud, red-faced brute is one of the cleverest thieves in London, and I once had a drink with him and our mutual fence. I was an East-ender from tongue to toe at the moment, but you will understand that I don't run unnecessary risks of recognition by a brute like that.'

'He's not alone, I hear.'

'By no means; there's at least one other man with him; and it's suggested that there may be an accomplice here in the house.'

'Did Lord Crowley tell you so?'

'Crowley and the champagne between them. In confidence, of course, just as your girl told you; but even in confidence he never let on about Mackenzie. He told me there was a detective in the background, but that was all. Putting him up as a guest is evidently their big secret, to be kept from the other guests because it might offend them, but more particularly from the servants whom he's here to watch. That's my reading of the situation, Bunny, and you will agree with me that it's infinitely more interesting than we could have imagined it would prove.'

'But infinitely more difficult for us,' said I, with a sigh of pusillanimous relief. 'Our hands are tied for this week, at all events.'

'Not necessarily, my dear Bunny, though I admit that the chances are against us. Yet I'm not so sure of that either. There are all sorts of possibilities in these three-cornered combinations. Set A to watch B, and he won't have an eye left for C. That's the obvious theory, but then Mackenzie's a very big A. I should be sorry to have any boodle about me with that man in the house. Yet it would be great to nip in between A and B and score off them both at once! It would be worth a risk, Bunny, to do that; it would be worth risking something merely to take on old hands like B and his men at their own old game! Eh, Bunny? That would be something like a match. Gentlemen and Players at single wicket, by Jove!'

His eyes were brighter than I had known them for many a day. They shone with the perverted enthusiasm which was roused in him only by the contemplation of some new audacity. He kicked off his shoes and began pacing his room with noiseless rapidity; not since the night of the Old Bohemian dinner to Reuben Rosenthall had Raffles exhibited such excitement in my presence; and I was not sorry at the moment to be reminded of the fiasco to which that banquet had been the prelude.

'My dear A. J.,' said I in his very own tone, 'you're far too fond of the uphill game; you will eventually fall a victim to the sporting spirit and nothing else. Take a lesson from our last escape, and fly lower as you value our skins. Study the house as much as you like, but do—not—go and shove your head into Mackenzie's mouth!'

My wealth of metaphor brought him to a standstill, with his cigarette between his fingers and a grin beneath his shining eyes.

'You're quite right, Bunny, I won't. I really won't. Yet—you saw old Lady Melrose's necklace? I've been wanting it for years! But I'm not going to play the fool, honour bright, I'm not; yet—by Jove!—to get the windward of the professors and Mackenzie too! It would be a great game, Bunny, it would be a great game!'

'Well, you mustn't play it this week.'

'No, no, I won't. But I wonder how the professors think of going to work? That's what one wants to know. I wonder if they've really got an accomplice in the house? How I wish I knew their game! But it's all right, Bunny; don't you be jealous; it shall be as you wish.'

And with that assurance I went off to my own room and so to bed with an incredibly light heart. I had still enough of the honest man in me to welcome the postponement of our actual felonies, to dread their performance, to deplore their necessity: which is merely another way of stating the too patent fact that I was an incomparably weaker man than Raffles, while every whit as wicked. I had, however, one rather strong point. I possessed the gift of dismissing unpleasant considerations, not intimately connected with the passing moment, entirely from my mind. Through the exercise of this faculty I had lately been living my frivolous life in town with as much ignoble enjoyment as I had derived from it the year before; and similarly, here at Milchester, in the long-dreaded cricket week, I had after all a quite excellent time.

It is true that there were other factors in this pleasing disappointment. In the first place, *mirabile dictu*, there were one or two even greater duffers than I on the Abbey cricket field. Indeed, quite early in the week, when it was of most value to me, I gained considerable kudos for a lucky catch; a ball, of which I had merely heard the hum, stuck fast in my hand, which Lord Amersteth himself grasped in public congratulation. This happy accident was not to be undone even by me, and, as nothing succeeds like success, and the constant encouragement of the one great cricketer on the field was in itself an immense stimulus, I actually made a run or two in my very next innings. Miss Melhuish said pretty things to me that night at the great ball in honour of Viscount Crowley's majority; she also told me that was the night on which the robbers would assuredly make their raid, and was full of arch tremors when we sat out in the garden, though the entire premises were illuminated all night long. Meanwhile the quiet Scotchman took countless photographs by day, which he developed by night in a dark room admirably situated in the servants' part of the house; and it is my firm belief that only two of his fellow guests knew Mr Clephane of Dundee for Inspector Mackenzie of Scotland Yard.

The week was to end with a trumpery match on the Saturday, which two or three of us intended abandoning early in order to return to town that night. The match, however, was never played. In the small hours of the Saturday morning a tragedy took place at Milchester Abbey.

Let me tell of the thing as I saw and heard it. My room opened upon the central gallery, and was not even on the same floor as that on which Raffles—and I think all the other men—were quartered. I had been put, in fact, into the dressing-room of one of the grand suites, and my two near neighbours were old Lady Melrose and my host and hostess. Now, by the Friday evening the actual festivities were at an end, and, for the first time that week, I must have been sound asleep since midnight, when all at once I found myself sitting up breathless. A heavy thud had come against my door, and now I heard hard breathing and the dull stamp of muffled feet.

'I've got ye,' muttered a voice. 'It's no use struggling.'

It was the Scotch detective, and a new fear turned me cold. There was no reply, but the hard breathing grew harder still, and the muffled feet beat the floor to a quicker measure. In sudden panic I sprang out of bed and flung open my door. A light burnt low on the landing, and by it I could see Mackenzie swaying and staggering in a silent tussle with some powerful adversary.

'Hold this man!' he cried, as I appeared. 'Hold the rascal!'

But I stood like a fool until the pair of them backed into me, when, with a deep breath, I flung myself on the fellow, whose face I had seen at last. He was one of the footmen who waited at table; and no sooner had I pinned him than the detective loosed his hold.

'Hang on to him,' he cried. 'There's more of 'em below.'

And he went leaping down the stairs, as other doors opened and Lord Amersteth and his son appeared simultaneously in their pyjamas. At that my man ceased struggling; but I was still holding him when Crowley turned up the gas.

'What the devil's all this?' asked Lord Amersteth, blinking. 'Who was that ran downstairs?'

'MacClephane!' said I hastily.

'Aha!' said he, turning to the footman. 'So you're the scoundrel, are you?—Well done! Well done! Where was he caught?'

I had no idea.

'Here's Lady Melrose's door open,' said Crowley.—'Lady Melrose! Lady Melrose!'

'You forget she's deaf,' said Lord Amersteth. 'Ah! that'll be her maid.'

An inner door had opened; next instant there was a little shriek, and a white figure gesticulated on the threshold.

'Où donc est l'écrin de Madame la Marquise? La fenêtre est ouverte. Il a disparu!'

'Window open and jewel-case gone, by Jove!' exclaimed Lord Amersteth. 'Mais comment est Madame la Marquise? Est-elle bien?'

'Out, milor. Elle dort.'

'Sleeps through it all,' said my lord. 'She's the only one, then!'

'What made Mackenzie—Clephane—bolt?' young Crowley asked me.

'Said there were more of them below.'

'Why the devil couldn't you tell us so before?' he cried, and went leaping downstairs in his turn.

He was followed by nearly all the cricketers, who now burst upon the scene in a body, only to desert it for the chase. Raffles was one of them, and I would gladly have been another, had not the footman chosen this moment to hurl me from him, and to make a dash in the direction from which they had come. Lord Amersteth had him in an instant; but the fellow fought desperately, and it took the two of us to drag him downstairs, amid a terrified chorus from half-open doors. Eventually we handed him over to two other footmen who appeared with their night-shirts tucked into their trousers, and my host was good enough to compliment me as he led the way outside.

'I thought I heard a shot,' he added. 'Didn't you?'

'I thought I heard three.'

And out we dashed into the darkness.

I remember how the gravel pricked my feet, how the wet grass numbed them as we made for the sound of voices on an outlying lawn. So dark was the night that we were in the cricketers' midst before we saw the shimmer of their pyjamas, and then Lord Amersteth almost trod on Mackenzie as he lay prostrate in the dew.

'Who's this?' he cried. 'What on earth's happened?'

'It's Clephane,' said a man who knelt over him. 'He's got a bullet in him somewhere.'

'Is he alive?'

'Barely.'

'Good God! Where's Crowley?'

'Here I am,' called a breathless voice. 'It's not good, you fellows. There's nothing to show which way they've gone. Here's Raffles; he's chucked it, too.' And they ran up panting.

'Well, we've got one of them, at all events,' muttered Lord Amersteth. 'The next thing is to get this poor fellow indoors. Take his shoulders, somebody. Now his middle. Join hands under him. All together now; that's the way. Poor fellow! Poor fellow! His name isn't Clephane at all. He's a Scotland Yard detective, down here for these very villains!'

Raffles was the first to express surprise; but he had also been the first to raise the wounded man. Nor had any of them a stronger or more tender hand in the slow procession to the house. In a little we had the senseless man stretched on a sofa in the library. And there, with ice on his wound and brandy in his throat, his eyes opened and his lips moved.

Lord Amersteth bent down to catch the words.

'Yes, yes,' said he; 'we've got one of them safe and sound. The brute you collared upstairs.' Lord Amersteth bent lower. 'By Jove! Lowered the jewel-case out of the window, did he? And they've got clean away with it. Well, well! I only hope we'll be able to pull this good fellow through. He's off again.'

An hour passed: the sun was rising.

It found a dozen young fellows on the settees in the billiard-room, drinking whisky and soda-water in their overcoats and pyjamas, and still talking excitedly in one breath. A time-table was being passed from hand to hand: the doctor was still in the library. At last the door opened, and Lord Amersteth put in his head.

'It isn't hopeless,' said he, 'but it's bad enough. There'll be no cricket today.'

Another hour, and most of us were on our way to catch the early train; between us we filled a compartment almost to suffocation. And still we talked all together of the night's event; and still I was a little hero in my way, for having kept my hold of the one ruffian who had been taken; and my gratification was subtle and intense. Raffles watched me under lowered lids. Not a word had we had together; not a word did we have until we had left the others at Paddington, and were skimming through the streets in a hansom with noiseless tyres and a tinkling bell.

'Well, Bunny,' said Raffles, 'so the professors have it, eh?'

'Yes,' said I. 'And I'm jolly glad!'

'That poor Mackenzie has a ball in his chest?'

'That you and I have been on the decent side for once.'

He shrugged his shoulders.

'You're hopeless, Bunny, quite hopeless! I take it you wouldn't have refused your share if the boodle had fallen to us? Yet you positively enjoy coming off second best—for the second time running! I confess, however, that the professors' methods were full of interest to me. I, for one, have probably gained as much in experience as I have lost in other things. That lowering the jewel-case out of the window was a very simple and effective expedient; two of them had been waiting below for it for hours.'

'How do you know?' I asked.

'I saw them from my own window, which was just above the dear old lady's. I was fretting for that necklace in particular, when I went up to turn in for our last night—and I happened to look out of the window. In point of fact, I wanted to see whether the one below was open, and whether there was the slightest chance of working the oracle with my sheet for a rope. Of course I took the precaution of turning my light off first, and it was a lucky thing I did, I saw the pros. right down below, and they never saw me. I saw a little tiny luminous disc just for an instant, and then again for an instant a few minutes later. Of course I knew what it was, for I have my own watch-dial daubed with luminous paint; it makes a lantern of sorts when you can get no better. But these fellows were not using theirs as a lantern. They were under the old lady's window. They were watching the time. The whole thing was arranged with their accomplice inside. Set a thief to catch a thief: in a minute I had guessed what the whole thing proved to be.'

'And you did nothing!' I exclaimed.

'On the contrary, I went downstairs and straight into Lady Melrose's room—'

'You did?'

'Without a moment's hesitation. To save her jewels. And I was prepared to yell as much into her ear-trumpet for all the house to hear. But the dear lady is too deaf and too fond of her dinner to wake easily.'

'Well?'

'She didn't stir.'

'And yet you allowed the professors, as you call them, to take her jewels, case and all!'

'All but this,' said Raffles, thrusting his fist into my lap. 'I would have shown it you before, but really, old fellow, your face all day has been worth a fortune to the firm!'

And he opened his fist, to shut it next instant on the bunch of diamonds and of sapphires that I had last seen encircling the neck of Lady Melrose.

A JOURNEY

EDITH WHARTON
(1862–1937)

Having been powerfully influenced by Henry James in her literary vision, Edith Wharton did not write mystery fiction in the ordinary sense. Her very civilized novels of manners, such as Ethan Frome *and* The Age of Innocence, *made her reputation. Still, in the following story, it is abundantly clear that she was able to create an atmosphere of terrific suspense. Curiously, this most American of authors lived most of her life in France.*

S SHE LAY IN HER BERTH, staring at the shadows overhead, the rush of the wheels was in her brain, driving her deeper and deeper into circles of wakeful lucidity. The sleeping-car had sunk into its night-silence. Through the wet window-pane she watched the sudden lights, the long stretches of hurrying blackness. Now and then she turned her head and looked through the opening in the hangings at her husband's curtains across the aisle. . . .

She wondered restlessly if he wanted anything and if she could hear him if he called. His voice had grown very weak within the last months and it irritated him when she did not hear. This irritability, this increasing childish petulance seemed to give expression to their imperceptible estrangement. Like two faces looking at one another through a sheet of glass they were close together, almost touching, but they could not hear or feel each other: the conductivity between them was broken. She, at least, had this sense of separation, and she fancied sometimes that she saw it reflected in the look with which he supplemented his failing words. Doubtless the fault was hers. She was too impenetrably healthy to be touched by the irrelevancies of disease. Her self-reproachful tenderness was tinged with the sense of his irrationality: she had a vague feeling that there was a purpose in his helpless tyrannies. The suddenness of the change had found her so unprepared. A year ago their pulses had beat to one robust measure; both had the same prodigal confidence in an exhaustless future. Now their energies no longer kept step: hers still bounded ahead of life, pre-empting unclaimed regions of hope and activity, while his lagged behind, vainly struggling to overtake her.

When they married, she had such arrears of living to make up: her days had been as bare as the whitewashed school-room where she forced innutritious facts upon reluctant children. His coming had broken in on the slumber of circumstance, widening the present till it became the encloser of remotest chances. But imperceptibly the horizon narrowed. Life had a grudge against her: she was never to be allowed to spread her wings.

At first the doctors had said that six weeks of mild air would set him right; but when he came back this assurance was explained as having of course included a winter in a dry climate. They gave up their pretty house, storing the wedding presents and new furniture, and went to Colorado. She had hated it there from the first. Nobody knew her or cared about her; there was no one to wonder at the good match she had made, or to envy her the new dresses and the visiting-cards which were still a surprise to her. And he kept growing worse. She felt herself beset with difficulties too evasive to be fought by so direct a temperament. She still loved him, of course; but he was gradually, undefinably ceasing to be himself. The man she had married had been strong, active, gently masterful: the male whose pleasure it is to clear a way through the material obstructions of life; but now it was she who was the protector, he who must be shielded from importunities and given his drops or his beef-juice though the skies were falling. The routine of the sick-room bewildered her; this punctual administering of medicine seemed as idle as some uncomprehended religious mummery.

There were moments, indeed, when warm gushes of pity swept away her instinctive resentment of his condition, when she still found his old self in his eyes as they groped for each other through the dense medium of his weakness. But these moments had grown rare. Sometimes he frightened her: his sunken expressionless face seemed that of a stranger; his voice was weak and hoarse; his thin-lipped smile a mere muscular contraction. Her hand avoided his damp soft skin, which had lost the familiar roughness of health: she caught herself furtively watching him as she might have watched a strange animal. It frightened her to feel that this was the man she loved; there were hours when to tell him what she suffered seemed the one escape from her fears. But in general she judged herself more leniently, reflecting that she had perhaps been too long alone with him, and that she would feel differently when they were at home again, surrounded by her robust and buoyant family. How she had rejoiced when the doctors at last gave their consent to his going home! She knew, of course, what the decision meant: they both knew. It meant that he was to die; but they dressed the truth in hopeful euphuisms, and at times, in the joy of preparation, she really forgot the purpose of their journey, and slipped into an eager allusion to next year's plans.

At last the day of leaving came. She had a dreadful fear that they would never get away; that somehow at the last moment he would fail her; that the doctors held one of their accustomed treacheries in reserve; but nothing happened. They drove to the station, he was installed in a seat with a rug over his knees and a cushion at his back, and she hung out of the window waving unregretful farewells to the acquaintances she had really never liked till then.

The first twenty-four hours had passed off well. He revived a little and it amused him to look out of the window and to observe the humors of the car. The second day he began to grow weary and to chafe under the dispassionate stare of the freckled child with the lump of chewing-gum. She had to explain to the child's mother that her husband was too ill to be disturbed: a statement received by that lady with a resentment visibly supported by the maternal sentiment of the whole car. . . .

That night he slept badly and the next morning his temperature frightened her: she was sure he was growing worse. The day passed slowly, punctuated by the small irritations of travel. Watching his tired face, she traced in its contractions every rattle and jolt of the train, till her own body vibrated with sympathetic fatigue. She felt the others observing him too, and hovered restlessly between him and the line of interrogative eyes. The freckled child hung about him like a fly: offers of candy and picture-books failed to dislodge her: she twisted one leg around the other and watched him imperturbably. The porter, as he passed, lingered with vague proffers of help, probably inspired by philanthropic passengers swelling with the sense that "something ought to be done"; and one nervous man in a skull-cap was audibly concerned as to the possible effect on his wife's health.

The hours dragged on in a dreary inoccupation. Toward dusk she sat down beside him and he laid his hand on hers. The touch startled her. He seemed to be calling her from far off. She looked at him helplessly and his smile went through her like a physical pang.

"Are you very tired?" she asked.

"No, not very."

"We'll be there soon now."

"Yes, very soon."

"This time tomorrow—"

He nodded and they sat silent. When she had put him to bed and crawled into her own berth she tried to cheer herself with the thought that in less than twenty-four hours they would be in New York. Her people would all be at the station to meet her—she pictured their round unanxious faces pressing through the crowd. She only hoped that they would not tell him too loudly that he was looking splendidly and would be all right in no time: the subtler sympathies developed by long contact with suffering were making her aware of a certain coarseness of texture in the family sensibilities.

Suddenly she thought she heard him call. She parted the curtains and listened. No, it was only a man snoring at the other end of the car. His snores had a greasy sound, as though they passed through tallow. She lay down and tried to sleep. . . . Had she not heard him move? She started up trembling. . . . The silence frightened her more than any sound. He might not be able to make her hear—he might be calling her now. . . . What made her think of such things? It was merely the familiar tendency of an over-tired mind to fasten itself on the most intolerable chance within the range of its forebodings. . . . Putting her head out, she listened; but she could not distinguish his breathing from that of the other pairs of lungs about her. She longed to get up and look at him, but she knew the impulse was a mere vent for her restlessness, and the fear of disturbing him restrained her. . . . The regular movement of his curtain reassured her, she knew not why; she remembered that he had wished her a cheerful goodnight; and the sheer inability to endure her fears a moment longer made her put them from her with an effort of her whole sound tired body. She turned on her side and slept.

She sat up stiffly, staring out at the dawn. The train was rushing through a region of bare hillocks huddled against a lifeless sky. It looked like the first day of creation. The air of the car was close, and she pushed up her window to let in the keen wind. Then she looked at her watch: it was seven o'clock, and soon the people about her would be stirring. She slipped into her clothes, smoothed her disheveled hair and crept to the dressing-room. When she had washed her face and adjusted her dress she felt more hopeful. It was always a struggle for her not to be cheerful in the morning. Her cheeks burned deliciously under the coarse towel, and the wet hair about her temples broke into strong upward tendrils. Every inch of her was full of life and elasticity. And in ten hours they would be at home!

She stepped to her husband's berth: it was time for him to take his early glass of milk. The window-shade was down, and in the dusk of the curtained enclosure she could just see that he lay sideways, with his face away from her. She leaned over him and drew up the shade. As she did so she touched one of his hands. It felt cold. . . .

She bent closer, laying her hand on his arm and calling him by name. He did not move. She spoke again more loudly; she grasped his shoulder and gently shook it. He lay motionless. She caught hold of his hand again: it slipped from her limply, like a dead thing. A dead thing? . . . Her breath caught. She must see his face. She leaned forward, and hurriedly, shrinkingly, with a sickening reluctance of the flesh, laid her hands on his shoulders and turned him over. His head fell back; his face looked small and smooth; he gazed at her with steady eyes.

She remained motionless for a long time, holding him thus; and they looked at each other. Suddenly she shrank back: the longing to scream, to call out, to fly from him, had almost overpowered her. But a strong hand arrested her. Good God! If it were known that he was dead they would be put off the train at the next station—

In a terrifying flash of remembrance there arose before her a scene she had once witnessed in traveling, when a husband and wife, whose child had died in the train, had been thrust out at some chance station. She saw them standing on the platform with the child's body between them; she had never forgotten the dazed look with which they followed the receding train. And this was what would happen to her. Within the next hour she might find herself on the platform of some strange station, alone with her husband's body. . . . Anything but that! It was too horrible—She quivered like a creature at bay.

As she cowered there, she felt the train moving more slowly. It was coming then—they were approaching a station! She saw again the husband and wife standing on the lonely platform; and with a violent gesture she drew down the shade to hide her husband's face.

Feeling dizzy, she sank down on the edge of the berth, keeping away from his outstretched body, and pulling the curtains close, so that he and she were shut into a kind of sepulchral twilight. She tried to think. At all costs she must conceal the fact that he was dead. But how? Her mind refused to act: she could not plan, combine. She could think of no way but to sit there, clutching the curtains, all day long. . . .

She heard the porter making up her bed; people were beginning to move about the car; the dressing-room door was being opened and shut. She tried to rouse herself. At length with a supreme effort she rose to her feet, stepping into the aisle of the car and drawing the curtains tight behind her. She noticed that they still parted slightly with the motion of the car, and finding a pin in her dress she fastened them together. Now she was safe. She looked around and saw the porter. She fancied he was watching her.

"Ain't he awake yet?" he inquired.

"No," she faltered.

"I got his milk all ready when he wants it. You know you told me to have it for him by seven."

She nodded silently and crept into her seat.

At half-past eight the train reached Buffalo. By this time the other passengers were dressed and the berths had been folded back for the day. The porter, moving to and fro under his burden of sheets and pillows, glanced at her as he passed. At length he said: "Ain't he going to get up? You know we're ordered to make up the berths as early as we can."

She turned cold with fear. They were just entering the station.

"Oh, not yet," she stammered. "Not till he's had his milk. Won't you get it, please?"

"All right. Soon as we start again."

When the train moved on he reappeared with the milk. She took it from him and sat vaguely looking at it: her brain moved slowly from one idea to another, as though they were stepping-stones set far apart across a whirling flood. At length she became aware that the porter still hovered expectantly.

"Will I give it to him?" he suggested.

"Oh, no," she cried, rising. "He—he's asleep yet, I think—"

She waited till the porter had passed on; then she unpinned the curtains and slipped behind them. In the semi-obscurity her husband's face stared up at her like a marble mask with agate eyes. The eyes were dreadful. She put out her hand and drew down the lids. Then she remembered the glass of milk in her other hand: what was she to do with it? She thought of raising the window and throwing it out; but to do so she would have to lean across his body and bring her face close to his. She decided to drink the milk.

She returned to the seat with the empty glass and after a while the porter came back to get it.

"When'll I fold up his bed?" he asked.

"Oh, not now—not yet; he's ill—he's very ill. Can't you let him stay as he is? The doctor wants him to lie down as much as possible."

He scratched his head. "Well, if he's really sick—"

He took the empty glass and walked away, explaining to the passengers that the party behind the curtains was too sick to get up just yet.

She found herself the center of sympathetic eyes. A motherly woman with an intimate smile sat down beside her.

"I'm really sorry to hear your husband's sick. I've had a remarkable amount of sickness in my family and maybe I could assist you. Can I take a look at him?"

"Oh, no—no, please! He mustn't be disturbed."

The lady accepted the rebuff indulgently.

"Well, it's just as you say, of course, but you don't look to me as if you'd had much experience in sickness and I'd have been glad to assist you. What do you generally do when your husband's taken this way?"

"I—I let him sleep."

"Too much sleep ain't any too healthful either. Don't you give him any medicine?"

"Y-yes."

"Don't you wake him to take it?"

"Yes."

"When does he take the next dose?"

"Not for—two hours—"

The lady looked disappointed. "Well, if I was you I'd try giving it oftener. That's what I do with my folks."

After that many faces seemed to press upon her. The passengers were on their way to the dining-car, and she was conscious that as they passed down the aisle they glanced curiously at the closed curtains. One lantern-jawed man with prominent eyes stood still and tried to shoot his projecting glance through the division between the folds. The freckled child, returning from breakfast, waylaid the passers with a buttery clutch, saying in a loud whisper, "He's sick"; and once the conductor came by, asking for tickets. She shrank into her corner and looked out of the window at the flying trees and houses, meaningless hieroglyphs on an endlessly unrolled papyrus.

Now and then the train stopped, and the newcomers on entering the car stared in turn at the closed curtains. More and more people seemed to pass—their faces began to blend fantastically with the images surging in her brain. . . .

Later in the day a fat man detached himself from the mist of faces. He had a creased stomach and soft pale lips. As he pressed himself into the seat facing her she noticed that he was dressed in black broadcloth, with a soiled white tie.

"Husband's pretty bad this morning, is he?"

"Yes."

"Dear, dear! Now that's terribly distressing, ain't it?" An apostolic smile revealed his gold-filled teeth. "Of course you know there's no sech thing as sickness. Ain't that a lovely thought? Death itself is but a deloosion of our grosser senses. On'y lay yourself open to the influx of the sperrit, submit yourself passively to the action of the divine force, and disease and dissolution will cease to exist for you. If you could indooce your husband to read this little pamphlet—"

The faces about her again grew indistinct. She had a vague recollection of hearing the motherly lady and the parent of the freckled child ardently disputing the relative advantages of trying several medicines at once, or of taking each in turn; the motherly lady maintaining that the competitive system saved time; the other objecting that you couldn't tell which remedy had effected the cure; their voices went on and on, like bell-buoys droning through a fog. . . . The porter came up now and then with questions that she did not understand, but that somehow she must have answered since he went away again without repeating them; every two hours the motherly lady reminded her that her husband ought to have his drops; people left the car and others replaced them. . . .

Her head was spinning and she tried to steady herself by clutching at her thoughts as they swept by, but they slipped away from her like bushes on the side of a sheer precipice down which she seemed to be falling. Suddenly her mind grew clear again and she found herself vividly picturing what would happen when the train reached New York. She shuddered as it occurred to her that he would be quite cold and that someone might perceive he had been dead since morning.

She thought hurriedly: "If they see I am not surprised they will suspect something. They will ask questions; and if I tell them the truth they won't believe me— no one would believe me! It will be terrible"—and she kept repeating to herself: "I must pretend I don't know. I must pretend I don't know. When they open the curtains I must go up to him quite naturally—and then I must scream." . . . She had an idea that the scream would be very hard to do.

Gradually new thoughts crowded upon her, vivid and urgent: she tried to separate and restrain them, but they beset her clamorously, like her school-children at the end of a hot day, when she was too tired to silence them. Her head grew confused, and she felt a sick fear of forgetting her part, of betraying herself by some unguarded word or look.

"I must pretend I don't know," she went on murmuring. The words had lost their significance, but she repeated them mechanically, as though they had been a magic formula, until she heard herself saying: "I can't remember, I can't remember!"

Her voice sounded very loud, and she looked about her in terror; but no one seemed to notice that she had spoken.

As she glanced down the car her eye caught the curtains of her husband's berth, and she began to examine the monotonous arabesques woven through their heavy folds. The pattern was intricate and difficult to trace; she gazed fixedly at the curtains, and as she did so the thick stuff grew transparent and through it she saw her husband's face—his dead face. She struggled to avert her look, but her eyes refused to move and her head seemed to be held in a vice. At last, with an effort that left her weak and shaking, she turned away; but it was of no use; close in front of her, small and smooth, was her husband's face. It seemed to be suspended in the air between her and the false braids of the woman who sat in front of her. With an uncontrollable gesture she stretched out her hand to push the face away, and suddenly she felt the touch of his smooth skin. She repressed a cry and half started from her seat. The woman with the false braids looked around, and feeling that she must justify her movement in some way she rose and lifted her traveling-bag from the opposite seat. She unlocked the bag and looked into it; but the first object her hand met was a small flask of her husband's, thrust there at the last moment, in the haste of departure. She locked the bag and closed her eyes . . . his face was there again, hanging between her eye-balls and lids like a waxen mask against a red curtain. . . .

She roused herself with a shiver. Had she fainted or slept? Hours seemed to have elapsed; but it was still broad day, and the people about her were sitting in the same attitudes as before.

A sudden sense of hunger made her aware that she had eaten nothing since morning. The thought of food filled her with disgust, but she dreaded a return of faintness, and remembering that she had some biscuits in her bag she took one out and ate it. The dry crumbs choked her, and she hastily swallowed a little brandy from her husband's flask. The burning sensation in her throat acted as a counter-irritant, momentarily relieving the dull ache of her nerves. Then she felt a gently stealing warmth, as though a soft air fanned her, and the swarming fears relaxed their clutch, receding through the stillness that enclosed her, a stillness soothing as the spacious quietude of a summer day. She slept.

Through her sleep she felt the impetuous rush of the train. It seemed to be life itself that was sweeping her on with headlong inexorable force—sweeping her into darkness and terror, and the awe of unknown day. Now all at once everything was still—not a sound, not a pulsation. . . . She was dead in her turn, and lay beside him with smooth upstaring face. How quiet it was!— and yet she heard feet coming, the feet of men who were to carry them away. . . . She could feel too—she felt a sudden prolonged vibration, a series of hard shocks, and then another plunge into darkness: the darkness of death this time—a black whirlwind on which they were both spinning like leaves, in wild uncoiling spirals, with millions and millions of the dead. . . .

She sprang up in terror. Her sleep must have lasted a long time, for the winter day had paled and the lights had been lit. The car was in confusion, and as she regained her self-possession she saw that the passengers were gathering up their wraps and bags. The woman with the false braids had brought from the dressing-room a sickly ivy-plant in a bottle, and the Christian Scientist was reversing his cuffs. The porter passed down the aisle with his impartial brush. An impersonal figure with a gold-banded cap asked for her husband's ticket. A voice shouted "Baig-gage express!" and she heard the clicking of metal as the passengers handed over their checks.

Presently her window was blocked by an expanse of sooty wall, and the train passed into the Harlem tunnel. The journey was over; in a few minutes she would see her family pushing their joyous way through the throng at the station. Her heart dilated. The worst terror was past. . . .

"We'd better get him up now, hadn't we?" asked the porter, touching her arm.

He had her husband's hat in his hand and was meditatively revolving it under his brush.

She looked at the hat and tried to speak; but suddenly the car grew dark. She flung up her arms, struggling to catch at something, and fell face downward, striking her head against the dead man's berth.

THE LEOPARD MAN'S STORY

JACK LONDON
(1876–1916)

At one time described as the world's most popular, best-selling, and best-paid author, London was also a self-proclaimed Socialist who was broke when he died almost certainly of an overdose of morphine and sleeping pills, having spent his fortune on alcohol and a huge castle that was destroyed by fire before he could complete it. His forays into mystery fiction were restricted to a few short stories and The Assassination Bureau, *a spy novel he abandoned, later to be completed by Robert L. Fish.*

E HAD A DREAMY, FARAWAY look in his eyes, and his sad, insistent voice, gentle-spoken as a maid's, seemed the placid embodiment of some deep-seated melancholy. He was the Leopard Man, but he did not look it. His business in life, whereby he lived, was to appear in a cage of performing leopards before vast audiences, and to thrill those audiences by certain exhibitions of nerve for which his employers rewarded him on a scale commensurate with the thrills he produced.

As I say, he did not look it. He was narrow-hipped, narrow-shouldered, and anemic, while he seemed not so much oppressed by gloom as by a sweet and gentle sadness, the weight of which was as sweetly and gently borne. For an hour I had been trying to get a story out of him, but he appeared to lack imagination. To him there was no romance in his gorgeous career, no deeds of daring, no thrills—nothing but a gray sameness and infinite boredom.

Lions? Oh, yes! He had fought with them. It was nothing. All you had to do was to stay sober. Anybody could whip a lion to a standstill with an ordinary stick. He had fought one for half an hour once. Just hit him on the nose every time he rushed, and when he got artful and rushed with his head down, why, the thing to do was to stick out your leg. When he grabbed at the leg you drew it back and hit him on the nose again. That was all.

With the faraway look in his eyes and his soft flow of words he showed me his scars. There were many of them, and one recent one where a tigress had reached for his shoulder and gone down to the bone. I could see the neatly mended rents in the coat he had on. His right arm, from the elbow down, looked as though it had gone through a threshing machine, such was the ravage wrought by claws and fangs. But it was nothing, he said, only the old wounds bothered him somewhat when rainy weather came on.

Suddenly his face brightened with a recollection, for he was really as anxious to give me a story as I was to get it.

"I suppose you've heard of the lion tamer who was hated by another man?" he asked.

He paused and looked pensively at a sick lion in the cage opposite.

"Got the toothache," he explained. "Well, the lion tamer's big play to the audience was putting his head in a lion's mouth. The man who hated him attended every performance in the hope sometime of seeing that lion crunch down. He followed the circus about all over the country. The years went by and he grew old, and the lion tamer grew old, and the lion grew old. And at last one day, sitting in a front seat, he saw what he had waited for. The lion crunched down, and there wasn't any need to call a doctor."

The Leopard Man glanced casually over his fingernails in a manner which would have been critical had it not been so sad.

"Now, that's what I call patience," he continued, "and it's my style. But it was not the style of a fellow I knew. He was a little, thin, sawed-off, sword-swallowing and juggling Frenchman. De Ville, he called himself, and he had a nice wife. She did trapeze work and used to dive from under the roof into a net, turning over once on the way as nice as you please.

"De Ville had a quick temper, as quick as his hand, and his hand was as quick as the paw of a tiger. One day, because the ringmaster called him a frog eater, or something like that and maybe a little worse, he shoved him against the soft pine background he used in his knife-throwing act, so quick the ringmaster didn't have time to think, and there, before the audience, de Ville kept the air on fire with his knives, sinking them into the wood all round the ringmaster so close that they passed through his clothes and most of them bit into his skin.

"The clowns had to pull the knives out to get him loose, for he was pinned fast. So the word went around to watch out for de Ville, and no one dared be more than barely civil to his wife. And she was a sly bit of baggage, too, only all hands were afraid of de Ville.

"But there was one man, Wallace, who was afraid of nothing. He was the lion tamer, and he had the selfsame trick of putting his head into the lion's mouth. He'd put it into the mouths of any of them, though he preferred Augustus, a big, good-natured beast who could always be depended upon.

"As I was saying, Wallace—'King' Wallace we called him—was afraid of nothing alive or dead. He was a king and no mistake. I've seen him drunk, and on a wager go into the cage of a lion that had turned nasty, and without a stick beat him to a finish. Just did it with his fist on the nose.

"Madame de Ville—"

At an uproar behind us the Leopard Man turned quietly around. It was a divided cage, and a monkey, poking through the bars and around the partition, had had its paw seized by a big gray wolf that was trying to pull off the paw by main strength. The arm seemed stretching out longer and longer like a thick elastic, and the unfortunate monkey's mates were raising a terrible din. No keeper was at hand, so the Leopard Man stepped over a couple of paces, dealt the wolf a sharp blow on the nose with the light cane he carried, and returned with a sadly apologetic smile to take up his unfinished sentence as though there had been no interruption.

"—looked at King Wallace and King Wallace looked at her, while de Ville looked back. We warned Wallace, but it was no use. He laughed at us, as he laughed at de Ville one day when he shoved de Ville's head into a bucket of paste because he wanted to fight.

"De Ville was in a pretty mess—I helped to scrape him off; but he was cool as a cucumber and made no threats at all. But I saw a glitter in his eyes which I had seen often in the eyes of wild beasts, and I went out of my way to give Wallace a final warning. He laughed, but he did not look so much in Madame de Ville's direction after that.

"Several months passed by. Nothing had happened and I was beginning to think it all a scare over nothing. We were West by that time, showing in 'Frisco. It was during the afternoon performance, and the big tent was filled with women and children, when I went looking for Red Denny, the head canvasman, who had walked off with my pocketknife.

"Passing by one of the dressing tents I glanced in through a hole in the canvas to see if I could locate him. He wasn't there, but directly in front of me was King Wallace, in tights, waiting for his turn to go on with his cage of performing lions. He was watching with much amusement a quarrel between a couple of trapeze artists. All the rest of the people in the dressing tent were watching the same thing, with the exception of de Ville, whom I noticed staring at Wallace with undisguised hatred. Wallace and the rest were all too busy following the quarrel to notice this or what followed.

"But I saw it through the hole in the canvas. De Ville drew his handkerchief from his pocket, made as though to mop the sweat from his face with it—it was a hot day—and at the same time walked past Wallace's back. He never stopped, but with a flirt of the handkerchief kept right on to the doorway, where he turned his head, while passing out, and shot a swift look back. The look troubled me at the time, for not only did I see hatred in it, but I saw triumph as well.

"'De Ville will bear watching,' I said to myself, and I really breathed easier when I saw him go out the entrance to the circus grounds and board an electric car for downtown. A few minutes later I was in the big tent, where I had overhauled Red Denny. King Wallace was doing his turn and holding the audience spellbound. He was in a particularly vicious mood, and he kept the lions stirred up till they were all snarling—that is, all of them except old Augustus, and he was just too fat and lazy and old to get stirred up over anything.

"Finally Wallace cracked the old lion's knees with his whip and got him into position. Old Augustus, blinking good-naturedly, opened his mouth and in popped Wallace's head. Then the jaws came together, *crunch*, just like that."

The Leopard Man smiled in a sweetly wistful fashion, and the faraway look came into his eyes.

"And that was the end of King Wallace," he went on in his sad, low voice. "After the excitement cooled down I watched my chance and bent over and smelled Wallace's head. Then I sneezed."

"It . . . it was . . .?" I queried with halting eagerness.

"Snuff—that de Ville dropped on his hair in the dressing tent. Old Augustus never meant to do it. He only sneezed."

A RETRIEVED REFORMATION

CRIMINAL: JIMMY VALENTINE

O. HENRY
(1862–1910)

William Sydney Porter was in jail for embezzlement when he was befriended by a prison guard, Orrin Henry, thus inspiring the famous pseudonym. The following story became one of the most famous mystery plays in the American theater under the title Alias Jimmy Valentine, *which opened on Broadway in 1910 and was revived in 1921 with Otto Kruger as the star. Four motion pictures between 1920 and 1942 also recount the affairs of the beleaguered safecracker.*

A GUARD CAME TO THE PRISON shoe shop, where Jimmy Valentine was assiduously stitching uppers, and escorted him to the front office. There the warden handed Jimmy his pardon, which had been signed that morning by the governor.

Jimmy took it in a tired kind of way. He had served nearly ten months of a four-year sentence. He had expected to stay only about three months, at the longest. When a man with as many friends on the outside as Jimmy Valentine had is received in the "stir" it is hardly worth while to cut his hair.

"Now, Valentine," said the warden, "you'll go out in the morning. Brace up, and make a man of yourself. You're not a bad fellow at heart. Stop cracking safes, and live straight."

"Me?" said Jimmy, in surprise. "Why, I never cracked a safe in my life."

"Oh, no," laughed the warden. "Of course not. Let's see, now. How was it

you happened to get sent up on that Springfield job? Was it because you wouldn't prove an alibi for fear of compromising somebody in extremely high-toned society? Or was it simply a case of a mean old jury that had it in for you? It's always one or the other with you innocent victims."

"Me?" said Jimmy, still blankly virtuous. "Why, Warden, I never was in Springfield in my life!"

"Take him back, Cronin," smiled the warden, "and fix him up with outgoing clothes. Unlock him at seven in the morning, and let him come to the bullpen. Better think over my advice, Valentine."

At a quarter past seven on the next morning Jimmy stood in the warden's outer office. He had on a suit of the villainously fitting, ready-made clothes and a pair of the stiff, squeaky shoes that the state furnishes to its discharged compulsory guests.

The clerk handed him a railroad

ticket and the five-dollar bill with which the law expected him to rehabilitate himself into good citizenship and prosperity. The warden gave him a cigar, and shook hands. Valentine, 9762, was chronicled on the books "Pardoned by Governor," and Mr. James Valentine walked out into the sunshine.

Disregarding the song of the birds, the waving green trees, and the smell of the flowers, Jimmy headed straight for a restaurant. There he tasted the first sweet joys of liberty in the shape of a broiled chicken and a bottle of wine—followed by a cigar a grade better than the one the warden had given him.

From there he proceeded leisurely to the depot. He tossed a quarter into the hat of a blind man sitting by the door, and boarded his train. Three hours set him down in a little town near the state line. He went to the café of one Mike Dolan and shook hands with Mike, who was alone behind the bar.

"Sorry we couldn't make it sooner, Jimmy, me boy," said Mike. "But we had that protest from Springfield to buck against, and the governor nearly balked. Feeling all right?"

"Fine," said Jimmy. "Got my key?"

He got his key and went upstairs, unlocking the door of a room at the rear. Everything was just as he had left it. There on the floor was still Ben Price's collar button that had been torn from that eminent detective's shirt when they had overpowered Jimmy to arrest him.

Pulling out from the wall a folding bed, Jimmy slid back a panel in the wall, and dragged out a dust-covered suitcase. He opened this and gazed fondly at the finest set of burglar's tools in the East. It was a complete set, made of specially tempered steel, the latest designs in drills, punches, braces and bits, jimmies, clamps, and augers, with two or three novelties invented by Jimmy himself, in which he took pride.

In half an hour Jimmy went downstairs and through the café. He was now dressed in tasteful and well-fitting clothes, and carried his dusted and cleaned suitcase in his hand.

"Got anything on?" asked Mike Dolan, genially.

"Me?" said Jimmy, in a puzzled tone. "I don't understand. I'm representing the New York Amalgamated Short Snap Biscuit Cracker and Frazzled Wheat Company."

This statement delighted Mike to such an extent that Jimmy had to take a seltzer-and-milk on the spot. He never touched "hard" drinks.

A week after the release of Valentine, 9762, there was a neat job of safe burglary done in Richmond, Indiana, with no clue to the author. A scant $800 was all that was secured.

Two weeks after that a patented, improved, burglar-proof safe in Logansport was opened like a cheese to the tune of $1500.

That began to interest the rogue-catchers. Then an old-fashioned bank-safe in Jefferson City became active and threw out of its crater an eruption of banknotes amounting to $5000.

The losses were now high enough to bring the matter up into Ben Price's class of work. By comparing notes, a remarkable similarity in the methods of the burglaries was noticed. Ben Price investigated the scenes of the robberies, and was heard to remark: "That's Dandy Jim Valentine's autograph. He's resumed business. Look at that combination knob—jerked out as easy as pulling up a radish in wet weather. He's got the only clamps that can do it. And look how clean those tumblers were punched out! Jimmy never has to drill but one hole. Yes, I guess I want Mr. Valentine. He'll do his bit next time without any short-time or clemency foolishness."

Ben Price knew Jimmy's habits. He had learned them while working up the

Springfield case. Long jumps, quick getaways, no confederates, and a taste for good society—these ways had helped Mr. Valentine to become noted as a successful dodger of retribution. It was given out that Ben Price had taken up the trail of the elusive cracksman, and other people with burglar-proof safes felt more at ease.

One afternoon Jimmy Valentine and his suitcase climbed out of the mailback in Elmore, a little town five miles off the railroad down in the black-jack country of Arkansas. Jimmy, looking like an athletic young senior just home from college, went down the broad sidewalk toward the hotel.

A young lady crossed the street, passed him at the corner, and entered a door over which was the sign "The Elmore Bank." Jimmy Valentine looked into her eyes, forgot what he was, and became another man. She lowered her eyes and colored slightly. Young men of Jimmy's style and looks were scarce in Elmore.

Jimmy collared a boy loafing on the steps of the bank as if he were one of the stockholders and began to ask him questions about the town, feeding him dimes at intervals. By and by the young lady came out, looking royally unconscious of the young man with the suitcase, and went her way.

"Isn't that young lady Miss Polly Simpson?" asked Jimmy, with specious guile.

"Naw," said the boy. "She's Annabel Adams. Her pa owns this bank. What'd you come to Elmore for? Is that a gold watch-chain? I'm going to get a bulldog. Got any more dimes?"

Jimmy went to the Planters' Hotel, registered as Ralph D. Spencer, and engaged a room. He leaned on the desk and declared his platform to the clerk. He said he had come to Elmore to look for a location to go into business. How was the shoe business, now, in the town? He had thought of the shoe business. Was there an opening?

The clerk was impressed by the clothes and manner of Jimmy. He, himself, was something of a pattern of fashion to the thinly gilded youth of Elmore, but he now perceived his shortcomings. While trying to figure out Jimmy's manner of tying his four-in-hand he cordially gave information.

Yes, there ought to be a good opening in the shoe line. There wasn't an exclusive shoe store in the place. The dry goods and general stores handled them. Business in all lines was fairly good. Hoped Mr. Spencer would decide to locate in Elmore. He would find it a pleasant town to live in, and the people very sociable.

Mr. Spencer thought he would stop over in the town a few days and look over the situation. No, the clerk needn't call the boy. He would carry up his suitcase himself; it was rather heavy.

Mr. Ralph Spencer, the phoenix that arose from Jimmy Valentine's ashes—ashes left by the flame of a sudden and alterative attack of love—remained in Elmore, and prospered. He opened a shoe store and secured a good run of trade.

Socially he was also a success, and made many friends. And he accomplished the wish of his heart. He met Miss Annabel Adams and became more and more captivated by her charms.

At the end of a year the situation of Mr. Ralph Spencer was this: he had won the respect of the community, his shoe store was flourishing, and he and Annabel were engaged to be married in two weeks. Mr. Adams, the typical, plodding, country banker, approved of Spencer. Annabel's pride in him almost equalled her affection. He was as much at home in the family of Mr. Adams and that of Annabel's married sister as if he were already a member.

One day Jimmy sat down in his room and wrote this letter, which he mailed to the address of one of his old friends in St. Louis:

Dear Old Pal:

I want you to be at Sullivan's place, in Little Rock, next Wednesday night, at nine o'clock. I want you to wind up some little matters for me. And, also, I want to make you a present of my kit of tools. I know you'll be glad to get them—you couldn't duplicate the lot for a thousand dollars. Say, Billy, I've quit the old business—a year ago. I've got a nice store. I'm making an honest living, and I'm going to marry the finest girl on earth two weeks from now. It's the only life, Billy—the straight one. I wouldn't touch a dollar of another man's money now for a million. After I get married I'm going to sell out and go West, where there won't be so much danger of having old scores brought up against me. I tell you, Billy, she's an angel. She believes in me; and I wouldn't do another crooked thing for the whole world. Be sure to be at Sully's, for I must see you.

Your old friend,
Jimmy

On the Monday night after Jimmy wrote this letter, Ben Price jogged unobtrusively into Elmore in a livery buggy. He lounged about town in his quiet way until he found out what he wanted to know. From the drug store across the street from Spencer's shoe store he got a good look at Ralph D. Spencer.

Going to marry the banker's daughter, are you, Jimmy? said Ben to himself, softly. Well, I don't know!

The next morning Jimmy took breakfast at the Adamses. He was going to Little Rock that day to order his wedding suit and buy something nice for Annabel. That would be the first time he had left town since he came to Elmore. It had been more than a year now since those last professional "jobs," and he thought he could safely venture out.

After breakfast quite a family party went downtown together—Mr. Adams, Annabel, Jimmy, and Annabel's married sister with her two little girls, aged five and nine. They came by the hotel where Jimmy still boarded, and he ran up to his room and brought down his suitcase. Then they went on to the bank. There stood Jimmy's horse and buggy and Dolph Gibson, who was going to drive him over to the railroad station.

All went inside the high, carved-oak railings into the banking room—Jimmy included, for Mr. Adams' future son-in-law was welcome anywhere. The clerks were pleased to be greeted by the good-looking, agreeable young man who was going to marry Miss Annabel.

Jimmy set his suitcase down. Annabel, whose heart was bubbling with happiness and lively youth, put on Jimmy's hat and picked up the suitcase. "Wouldn't I make a nice drummer?" said Annabel. "My, Ralph, how heavy it is. Feels like it was full of gold bricks."

"Lot of nickel-plated shoehorns in there," said Jimmy coolly, "that I'm going to return. Thought I'd save express charges by taking them up. I'm getting economical."

The Elmore Bank had just put in a new safe and vault. Mr. Adams was very proud of it, and insisted on an inspection by everyone. The vault was a small one, but it had a new patented door. It fastened with three solid steel bolts thrown simultaneously with a single handle, and had a time lock.

Mr. Adams beamingly explained its workings to Mr. Spencer, who showed a courteous but not too intelligent interest. The two children, May and Agatha, were delighted by the shining metal and funny clock and knobs.

While they were thus engaged, Ben Price sauntered in and leaned on his elbow, looking casually inside between the railings. He told the teller he didn't want anything; he was just waiting for a man he knew.

Suddenly there were screams from the women, and a commotion. Unperceived by the elders, May, the nine-year-old girl, in a spirit of play, had shut Agatha in the vault. She had then shot the bolts and turned the knob of the combination as she had seen Mr. Adams do.

The old banker sprang to the handle and tugged at it.

"The door can't be opened," he groaned. "The clock hasn't been wound nor the combination set."

Agatha's mother screamed again, hysterically.

"Hush!" said Mr. Adams, raising his trembling hand. "All be quiet for a moment. Agatha!" he called as loudly as he could. "Listen to me." During the following silence they could just hear the faint sound of the child wildly shrieking in the dark vault in a panic of terror.

"My precious darling!" wailed the mother. "She will die of fright! Open the door! Oh, break it open! Can't you men do something?"

"There isn't a man nearer than Little Rock who can open that door," said Mr. Adams, in a shaky voice. "My God! Spencer, what shall we do? That child—she can't stand it long in there. There isn't enough air, and, besides, she'll go into convulsions from fright."

Agatha's mother, frantic now, beat the door of the vault with her hands. Somebody wildly suggested dynamite. Annabel turned to Jimmy, her large eyes full of anguish, but not yet despairing. To a woman nothing seems quite impossible to the powers of the man she worships.

"Can't you do something, Ralph—*try*, won't you?"

He looked at her with a queer, soft smile in his keen eyes.

"Annabel," he said, "give me that rose you are wearing, will you?"

Hardly believing that she heard him aright, she unpinned the bud from the bosom of her dress and placed it in his hand. Jimmy stuffed it into his vest pocket, threw off his coat, and pulled up his shirt sleeves. With that act Ralph D. Spencer passed away and Jimmy Valentine took his place.

"Get away from the door, all of you," he commanded.

He set his suitcase on the table and opened it out flat. From that time on he seemed to be unconscious of the presence of anyone else. He laid out the shining, queer implements swiftly and orderly, whistling softly to himself as he always did when at work. In a deep silence and immovable, the others watched him as if under a spell.

In a minute Jimmy's pet drill was biting smoothly into the steel door. In ten minutes—breaking his own burglarious record—he threw back the bolts and opened the door.

Agatha, almost collapsed, but safe, was gathered into her mother's arms.

Jimmy Valentine put on his coat, and walked outside the railings toward the front door. As he went he thought he heard a faraway voice that he once knew call "Ralph!" But he never hesitated.

At the door a big man stood somewhat in his way.

"Hello, Ben!" said Jimmy, still with his strange smile. "Got around at last, have you? Well, let's go. I don't know that it makes much difference, now."

Then Ben Price acted strangely.

"Guess you're mistaken, Mr. Spencer," he said. "Don't believe I recognize you. Your buggy's waiting for you, ain't it?"

And Ben Price turned and strolled down the street.

THE PROBLEM OF CELL 13

JACQUES FUTRELLE
(1875–1912)

A mystery might be how a Georgia-born child could have such a foreign-sounding name, but Jacques Futrelle was entirely American, moving from the South to work for the Boston American newspaper, which ran the following story as a contest. Eventually, 42 more stories were written about the eccentric Thinking Machine. Futrelle died heroically when the Titanic went down, reportedly saving his wife and many others, refusing to enter a lifeboat that would have saved him.

RACTICALLY ALL THOSE LETters remaining in the alphabet after Augustus S.F.X. Van Dusen was named were afterward acquired by that gentleman in the course of a brilliant scientific career, and, being honorably acquired, were tacked on to the other end. His name, therefore, taken with all that belonged to it, was a wonderfully imposing structure. He was a Ph.D., an LL.D., an F.R.S., an M.D., and an M.D.S. He was also some other things—just what he himself couldn't say—through recognition of his ability by various foreign educational and scientific institutions.

In appearance he was no less striking than in nomenclature. He was slender with the droop of the student in his thin shoulders and the pallor of a close, sedentary life on his clean-shaven face. His eyes wore a perpetual, forbidding squint—the squint of a man who studies little things—and when they could be seen at all through his thick spectacles, were mere slits of watery blue. But above his eyes was his most striking feature. This was a tall, broad brow, almost abnormal in height and width, crowned by a heavy shock of bushy, yellow hair. All these things conspired to give him a peculiar, almost grotesque, personality.

Professor Van Dusen was remotely German. For generations his ancestors had been noted in the sciences; he was the logical result, the mastermind. First and above all he was a logician. At least thirty-five years of the half century or so of his existence had been devoted exclusively to proving that two and two always equal four, except in unusual cases, where they equal three or five, as the case may be. He stood broadly on the general proposition that all things that start must go somewhere, and was able to bring the concentrated mental force of his forefathers to bear on a given problem. Incidentally it may be remarked that Professor Van Dusen wore a No. 8 hat.

The world at large had heard vaguely of Professor Van Dusen as The Thinking Machine. It was a newspaper catchphrase applied to him at the time of a remarkable exhibition at chess; he had demonstrated then that a stranger to the game might, by the force of inevitable logic, defeat a champion who had devoted a lifetime to its study. The Thinking Machine! Perhaps that more nearly described him than all his honorary initials, for he spent week after week, month after month, in the seclusion of his small laboratory from which had gone forth thoughts that staggered scientific associates and deeply stirred the world at large.

It was only occasionally that The Thinking Machine had visitors, and these were usually men who, themselves high in the sciences, dropped in to argue a point and perhaps convince themselves. Two of these men, Dr. Charles Ransome and Alfred Fielding, called one evening to discuss some theory which is not of consequence here.

"Such a thing is impossible," declared Dr. Ransome emphatically, in the course of the conversation.

"Nothing is impossible," declared The Thinking Machine with equal emphasis. He always spoke petulantly. "The mind is master of all things. When science fully recognizes that fact a great advance will have been made."

"How about the airship?" asked Dr. Ransome.

"That's not impossible at all," asserted The Thinking Machine. "It will be invented sometime. I'd do it myself, but I'm busy."

Dr. Ransome laughed tolerantly.

"I've heard you say such things before," he said. "But they mean nothing. Mind may be master of matter, but it hasn't yet found a way to apply itself. There are some things that can't be *thought* out of existence, or rather which would not yield to any amount of thinking."

"What, for instance?" demanded The Thinking Machine.

Dr. Ransome was thoughtful for a moment as he smoked.

"Well, say prison walls," he replied. "No man can *think* himself out of a cell. If he could, there would be no prisoners."

"A man can so apply his brain and ingenuity that he can leave a cell, which is the same thing," snapped The Thinking Machine.

Dr. Ransome was slightly amused.

"Let's suppose a case," he said, after a moment. "Take a cell where prisoners under sentence of death are confined—men who are desperate and, maddened by fear, would take any chance to escape—suppose you were locked in such a cell. Could you escape?"

"Certainly," declared The Thinking Machine.

"Of course," said Mr. Fielding, who entered the conversation for the first time, "you might wreck the cell with an explosive—but inside, a prisoner, you couldn't have that."

"There would be nothing of that kind," said The Thinking Machine. "You might treat me precisely as you treated prisoners under sentence of death, and I would leave the cell."

"Not unless you entered it with tools prepared to get out," said Dr. Ransome.

The Thinking Machine was visibly annoyed and his blue eyes snapped.

"Lock me in any cell in any prison anywhere at any time, wearing only what is necessary, and I'll escape in a week," he declared, sharply.

Dr. Ransome sat up straight in the chair, interested. Mr. Fielding lighted a new cigar.

"You mean you could actually *think* yourself out?" asked Dr. Ransome.

"I would get out," was the response.

"Are you serious?"

"Certainly I am serious."

Dr. Ransome and Mr. Fielding were silent for a long time.

"Would you be willing to try it?" asked Mr. Fielding, finally.

"Certainly," said Professor Van Dusen, and there was a trace of irony in his voice. "I have done more asinine things than that to convince other men of less important truths."

The tone was offensive and there was an undercurrent strongly resembling anger on both sides. Of course it was an absurd thing, but Professor Van Dusen reiterated his willingness to undertake the escape and it was decided upon.

"To begin now," added Dr. Ransome.

"I'd prefer that it begin tomorrow," said The Thinking Machine, "because—"

"No, now," said Mr. Fielding, flatly. "You are arrested, figuratively, of course, without any warning locked in a cell with no chance to communicate with friends, and left there with identically the same care and attention that would be given to a man under sentence of death. Are you willing?"

"All right, now, then," said The Thinking Machine, and he arose.

"Say, the death cell in Chisholm Prison."

"The death cell in Chisholm Prison."

"And what will you wear?"

"As little as possible," said The Thinking Machine. "Shoes, stockings, trousers, and a shirt."

"You will permit yourself to be searched, of course?"

"I am to be treated precisely as all prisoners are treated," said The Thinking Machine. "No more attention and no less."

There were some preliminaries to be arranged in the matter of obtaining permission for the test, but all three were influential men and everything was done satisfactorily by telephone, albeit the prison commissioners, to whom the experiment was explained on purely scientific grounds, were sadly bewildered. Professor Van Dusen would be the most distinguished prisoner they had ever entertained.

When The Thinking Machine had donned those things which he was to wear during his incarceration he called the little old woman who was his housekeeper, cook, and maidservant all in one.

"Martha," he said, "it is now twenty-seven minutes past nine o'clock. I am going away. One week from tonight, at half past nine, these gentlemen and one, possibly two, others will take supper with me here. Remember Dr. Ransome is very fond of artichokes."

The three men were driven to Chisholm Prison, where the warden was awaiting them, having been informed of the matter by telephone. He understood merely that the eminent Professor Van Dusen was to be his prisoner, if he could keep him, for one week; that he had committed no crime, but that he was to be treated as all other prisoners were treated.

"Search him," instructed Dr. Ransome.

The Thinking Machine was searched. Nothing was found on him; the pockets of the trousers were empty; the white, stiff-bosomed shirt had no pocket. The shoes and stockings were removed, examined, then replaced. As he watched all these preliminaries, and noted the pitiful, childlike physical weakness of the man—the colorless face, and the thin, white hands—Dr. Ransome almost regretted his part in the affair.

"Are you sure you want to do this?" he asked.

"Would you be convinced if I did not?" inquired The Thinking Machine in turn.

"No."

"All right, I'll do it."

What sympathy Dr. Ransome had was dissipated by the tone. It nettled him, and he resolved to see the experiment to the end; it would be a stinging reproof to egotism.

"It will be impossible for him to communicate with anyone outside?" he asked.

"Absolutely impossible," replied the warden. "He will not be permitted writing materials of any sort."

"And your jailers, would they deliver a message from him?"

"Not one word, directly or indirectly," said the warden. "You may rest assured of that. They will report anything he might say or turn over to me, anything he might give them."

"That seems entirely satisfactory," said Mr. Fielding, who was frankly interested in the problem.

"Of course, in the event he fails," said Dr. Ransome, "and asks for his liberty, you understand you are to set him free?"

"I understand," replied the warden.

The Thinking Machine stood listening, but had nothing to say until this was all ended, then:

"I should like to make three small requests. You may grant them or not, as you wish."

"No special favors, now," warned Mr. Fielding.

"I am asking none," was the stiff response. "I should like to have some tooth powder—buy it yourself to see that it is tooth powder—and I should like to have one five-dollar and two ten-dollar bills."

Dr. Ransome, Mr. Fielding, and the warden exchanged astonished glances. They were not surprised at the request for tooth powder, but were at the request for money.

"Is there any man with whom our friend would come in contact that he could bribe with twenty-five dollars?"

"Not for twenty-five hundred dollars," was the positive reply.

"Well, let him have them," said Mr. Fielding. "I think they are harmless enough."

"And what is the third request?" asked Dr. Ransome.

"I should like to have my shoes polished."

Again the astonished glances were exchanged. This last request was the height of absurdity, so they agreed to it. These things all being attended to, The Thinking Machine was led back into the prison from which he had undertaken to escape.

"Here is Cell Thirteen," said the warden, stopping three doors down the steel corridor. "This is where we keep condemned murderers. No one can leave it without my permission; and no one in it can communicate with the outside. I'll stake my reputation on that. It's only three doors back of my office and I can readily hear any unusual noise."

"Will this cell do, gentlemen?" asked The Thinking Machine. There was a touch of irony in his voice.

"Admirably," was the reply.

The heavy steel door was thrown open, there was a great scurrying and scampering of tiny feet, and The Thinking Machine passed into the gloom of the cell. Then the door was closed and double-locked by the warden.

"What is that noise in there?" asked Dr. Ransome, through the bars.

"Rats—dozens of them," replied The Thinking Machine, tersely.

The three men, with final good nights, were turning away when The Thinking Machine called:

"What time is it exactly, Warden?"

"Eleven-seventeen," replied the warden.

"Thanks. I will join you gentlemen in your office at half past eight o'clock one week from tonight," said The Thinking Machine.

"And if you do not?"

"There is no 'if' about it."

Chisholm Prison was a great, spreading structure of granite, four stories in all, which stood in the center of acres of open space. It was surrounded by a wall of solid masonry eighteen feet high, and so smoothly finished inside and out as to offer no foothold to a climber, no matter how expert. Atop this fence, as a further precaution, was a five-foot fence of steel rods, each terminating in a keen point. This fence in itself marked an absolute deadline between freedom and imprisonment, for, even if a man escaped from his cell, it would seem impossible for him to pass the wall.

The yard, which on all sides of the prison building was twenty-five feet wide, that being the distance from the building to the wall, was by day an exercise ground for those prisoners to whom was granted the boon of occasional semi-liberty. But that was not for those in Cell 13. At all times of the day there were armed guards in the yard, four of them, one patrolling each side of the prison building.

By night the yard was almost as brilliantly lighted as by day. On each of the four sides was a great arc light which rose above the prison wall and gave to the guards a clear sight. The lights, too, brightly illuminated the spiked top of the wall. The wires which fed the arc lights ran up the side of the prison building on insulators and from the top story led out to the poles supporting the arc lights.

All these things were seen and comprehended by The Thinking Machine, who was only enabled to see out his closely barred cell window by standing on his bed. This was on the morning following his incarceration. He gathered, too, that the river lay over there beyond the wall somewhere, because he heard faintly the pulsation of a motor boat and high up in the air saw a river bird. From that same direction came the shouts of boys at play and the occasional crack of a batted ball. He knew then that between the prison wall and the river was an open space, a playground.

Chisholm Prison was regarded as absolutely safe. No man had ever escaped from it. The Thinking Machine, from his perch on the bed, seeing what he saw, could readily understand why. The walls of the cell, though built he judged twenty years before, were perfectly solid, and the window bars of new iron had not a shadow of rust on them. The window itself, even with the bars out, would be a difficult mode of egress because it was small.

Yet, seeing these things, The Thinking Machine was not discouraged. Instead, he thoughtfully squinted at the great arc light—there was bright sunlight now—and traced with his eyes the wire which led from it to the building. That electric wire, he reasoned, must come down the side of the building not a great distance from his cell. That might be worth knowing.

Cell 13 was on the same floor with the offices of the prison—that is, not in the basement, nor yet upstairs. There were only four steps up to the office floor, therefore the level of the floor must be only three or four feet above ground. He couldn't see the ground directly beneath his window, but he could see it further out toward the wall. It would be an easy drop from the window. Well and good.

Then The Thinking Machine fell to remembering how he had come to the cell. First, there was the outside guard's booth, a part of the wall. There were two heavily barred gates there, both of steel. At this gate was one man always on guard. He admitted persons to the prison after much clanking of keys and locks, and let them out when ordered to do so. The warden's office was in the prison building, and in order to reach that official from the prison yard one had to pass a gate of solid steel with only a peephole in it. Then coming from that inner office to Cell 13, where he was now, one must pass a heavy wooden door and two steel doors into the corridors of the prison; and always there was the double-locked door of Cell 13 to reckon with.

There were then, The Thinking Machine recalled, seven doors to be overcome before one could pass from Cell 13 into the outer world, a free man. But against this was the fact that he was rarely interrupted. A jailer appeared at his cell door at six in the morning with a breakfast of prison fare; he would come again at noon, and again at six in the afternoon. At nine o'clock at night would come the inspection hour. That would be all.

"It's admirably arranged, this prison system," was the mental tribute paid by The Thinking Machine. "I'll have to study it a little when I get out. I had no idea there was such great care exercised in the prisons."

There was nothing, positively nothing, in his cell, except his iron bed, so firmly put together that no man could tear it to pieces save with sledges or a file. He had neither of these. There was not even a chair, or a small table, or a bit of tin or crockery. Nothing! The jailer stood by when he ate, then took away the wooden spoon and bowl which he had used.

One by one these things sank into the brain of The Thinking Machine. When the last possibility had been considered he began an examination of his cell. From the roof, down the walls on all sides, he examined the stones and the cement between them. He stamped over the floor carefully time after time, but it was cement, perfectly solid. After the examination he sat on the edge of the iron bed and was lost in thought for a long time. For Professor Augustus S.F.X. Van Dusen, The Thinking Machine, had something to think about.

He was disturbed by a rat, which ran across his foot, then scampered away into a dark corner of the cell, frightened by its own daring. After a while The Thinking Machine, squinting steadily into the darkness of the corner where the rat had gone, was able to make out in the gloom many little beady eyes staring at him. He counted six pair, and there were perhaps others; he didn't see very well.

Then The Thinking Machine, from his seat on the bed, noticed for the first time the bottom of his cell door. There was an opening there of two inches between the steel bar and the floor. Still looking steadily at this opening, The Thinking Machine backed suddenly into the corner where he had seen the beady eyes. There was a great scampering of tiny feet, several squeaks of frightened rodents, and then silence.

None of the rats had gone out the door, yet there were none in the cell. Therefore there must be another way out of the cell, however small. The Thinking Machine, on hands and knees, started a search for this spot, feeling in the darkness with his long, slender fingers.

At last his search was rewarded. He came upon a small opening in the floor, level with the cement. It was perfectly round and somewhat larger than a silver dollar. This was the way the rats had gone. He put his fingers deep into the opening; it seemed to be a disused drainage pipe and was dry and dusty.

Having satisfied himself on this point, he sat on the bed again for an hour, then made another inspection of his surroundings through the small cell window. One of the outside guards stood directly opposite, beside the wall, and happened to be looking at the window of Cell 13 when the head of The Thinking Machine appeared. But the scientist didn't notice the guard.

Noon came and the jailer appeared with the prison dinner of repulsively plain food. At home The Thinking Machine merely ate to live; here he took what was offered without comment. Occasionally he spoke to the jailer who stood outside the door watching him.

"Any improvements made here in the last few years?" he asked.

"Nothing particularly," replied the jailer. "New wall was built four years ago."

"Anything done to the prison proper?"

"Painted the woodwork outside, and I believe about seven years ago a new system of plumbing was put in."

"Ah!" said the prisoner. "How far is the river over there?"

"About three hundred feet. The boys have a baseball ground between the wall and the river."

The Thinking Machine had nothing further to say just then, but when the jailer was ready to go he asked for some water.

"I get very thirsty here," he explained. "Would it be possible for you to leave a little water in a bowl for me?"

"I'll ask the warden," replied the jailer, and he went away.

Half an hour later he returned with water in a small earthen bowl.

"The warden says you may keep this bowl," he informed the prisoner. "But you must show it to me when I ask for it. If it is broken, it will be the last."

"Thank you," said The Thinking Machine. "I shan't break it."

The jailer went on about his duties. For just the fraction of a second it seemed that The Thinking Machine wanted to ask a question, but he didn't.

Two hours later this same jailer, in passing the door of Cell No. 13, heard a noise inside and stopped. The Thinking Machine was down on his hands and knees in a corner of the cell, and from that same corner came several frightened squeaks. The jailer looked on interestedly.

"Ah, I've got you," he heard the prisoner say.

"Got what?" he asked, sharply.

"One of these rats," was the reply. "See?" And between the scientist's long fingers the jailer saw a small gray rat struggling. The prisoner brought it over to the light and looked at it closely.

"It's a water rat," he said.

"Ain't you got anything better to do than to catch rats?" ask the jailer.

"It's disgraceful that they should be here at all," was the irritated reply. "Take this one away and kill it. There are dozens more where it came from."

The jailer took the wriggling, squirmy rodent and flung it down on the floor violently. It gave one squeak and lay still. Later he reported the incident to the warden, who only smiled.

Still later that afternoon the outside armed guard on the Cell 13 side of the prison looked up again at the window and saw the prisoner looking out. He saw a hand raised to the barred window and then something white fluttered to the ground, directly under the window of Cell 13. It was a little roll of linen, evidently of white shirting material, and tied around it was a five-dollar bill. The guard looked up at the window again, but the face had disappeared.

With a grim smile he took the little linen roll and the five-dollar bill to the warden's office. There together they deciphered something which was written on it with a queer sort of ink, frequently blurred. On the outside was this:

"Finder of this please deliver to Dr. Charles Ransome."

"Ah," said the warden, with a chuckle. "Plan of escape number one has gone wrong." Then, as an afterthought: "But why did he address it to Dr. Ransome?"

"And where did he get the pen and ink to write with?" asked the guard.

The warden looked at the guard and the guard looked at the warden. There was no apparent solution of that mystery. The warden studied the writing carefully, then shook his head.

"Well, let's see what he was going to say to Dr. Ransome," he said at length, still puzzled, and he unrolled the inner piece of linen.

"Well, if that—what—what do you think of that?" he asked, dazed.

The guard took the bit of linen and read this:

"Epa cseot d'net niiy awe htto n'si sih. T."

The warden spent an hour wondering what sort of a cipher it was, and half an hour wondering why his prisoner should attempt to communicate with Dr. Ransome, who was the cause of his being there. After this the warden devoted some thought to the question of where the prisoner got writing materials, and what sort of writing materials he had. With the idea of illuminating this point, he examined the linen again. It was torn apart of a white shirt and had ragged edges.

Now it was possible to account for the linen, but what the prisoner had used to write with was another matter. The warden knew it would have been impossible for him to have either pen or pencil, and, besides, neither pen nor pencil had been used in this writing. What, then? The warden decided to investigate personally. The Thinking Machine was his prisoner; he had orders to hold his prisoners; if this one sought to escape by sending cipher messages to persons outside, he would stop it, as he would have stopped it in the case of any other prisoner.

The warden went back to Cell 13 and found The Thinking Machine on his hands and knees on the floor, engaged in nothing more alarming than catching rats. The prisoner heard the warden's step and turned to him quickly.

"It's disgraceful," he snapped, "these rats. There are scores of them."

"Other men have been able to stand them," said the warden. "Here is another shirt for you—let me have the one you have on."

"Why?" demanded The Thinking Machine, quickly. His tone was hardly natural, his manner suggested actual perturbation.

"You have attempted to communicate with Dr. Ransome," said the warden severely. "As my prisoner, it is my duty to put a stop to it."

The Thinking Machine was silent for a moment.

"All right," he said, finally. "Do your duty."

The warden smiled grimly. The prisoner arose from the floor and removed the white shirt the warden had brought. The warden took the white shirt eagerly, and then and there compared the pieces of linen on which was written the cipher with certain torn places in the shirt. The Thinking Machine looked on curiously.

"The guard brought *you* those, then?" he asked.

"He certainly did," replied the warden triumphantly. "And that ends your first attempt to escape."

The Thinking Machine watched the warden as he, by comparison, established to his own satisfaction that only two pieces of linen had been torn from the white shirt.

"What did you write this with?" demanded the warden.

"I should think it a part of your duty to find out," said The Thinking Machine, irritably.

The warden started to say some harsh things, then restrained himself and made a minute search of the cell and of the prisoner instead. He found absolutely nothing; not even a match or toothpick which might have been used for a pen. The same mystery surrounded the fluid with which the cipher had been written. Although the warden left Cell 13 visibly annoyed, he took the torn shirt in triumph.

"Well, writing notes on a shirt won't get him out, that's certain," he told himself with some complacency. He put the linen scraps into his desk to await developments. "If that man escapes from that cell I'll—hang it—I'll resign."

On the third day of his incarceration The Thinking Machine openly attempted to bribe his way out. The jailer had brought his dinner and was leaning against the barred door, waiting, when The Thinking Machine began the conversation.

"The drainage pipes of the prison lead to the river, don't they?" he asked.

"Yes," said the jailer.

"I suppose they are very small."

"Too small to crawl through, if that's what you're thinking about," was the grinning response.

There was silence until The Thinking Machine finished his meal. Then:

"You know I'm not a criminal, don't you?"

"Yes."

"And that I've a perfect right to be freed if I demand it?"

"Yes."

"Well, I came here believing that I could make my escape," said the prisoner, and his squint eyes studied the face of the jailer. "Would you consider a financial reward for aiding me to escape?"

The jailer, who happened to be an honest man, looked at the slender, weak figure of the prisoner, at the large head with its mass of yellow hair, and was almost sorry.

"I guess prisons like these were not built for the likes of you to get out of," he said, at last.

"But would you consider a proposition to help me get out?" the prisoner insisted, almost beseechingly.

"No," said the jailer, shortly.

"Five hundred dollars," urged The Thinking Machine. "I am not a criminal."

"No," said the jailer.

"A thousand?"

"No," again said the jailer, and he started away hurriedly to escape further temptation. Then he turned back. "If you should give me ten thousand dollars I couldn't get you out. You'd have to pass through seven doors, and I only have the keys to two."

Then he told the warden all about it.

"Plan number two fails," said the warden, smiling grimly. "First a cipher, then bribery."

When the jailer was on his way to Cell 13 at six o'clock, again bearing food to The Thinking Machine, he paused, startled by the unmistakable scrape, scrape of steel against steel. It stopped at the sound of his steps, then craftily the jailer, who was beyond the prisoner's range of vision, resumed his tramping, the sound apparently that of a man going away from Cell 13. As a matter of fact he was in the same spot.

After a moment there came again the steady scrape, scrape, and the jailer crept cautiously on tiptoes to the door and peered between the bars. The Thinking Machine was standing on the iron bed working at the bars of the little window. He was using a file, judging from the backward and forward swing of his arms.

Cautiously the jailer crept back to the office, summoned the warden in person, and they returned to Cell 13 on tiptoes. The steady scrape was still audible. The warden listened to satisfy himself and then suddenly appeared at the door.

"Well?" he demanded, and there was a smile on his face.

The Thinking Machine glanced back from his perch on the bed and leaped to the floor, making frantic efforts to hide something. The warden went in, with hand extended.

"Give it up," he said.

"No," said the prisoner, sharply.

"Come, give it up," urged the warden. "I don't want to have to search you again."

"No," repeated the prisoner.

"What was it—a file?" asked the warden.

The Thinking Machine was silent and stood squinting at the warden with something very nearly approaching disappointment on his face—nearly, but not quite. The warden was almost sympathetic.

"Plan number three fails, eh?" he asked, good-naturedly. "Too bad, isn't it?"

The prisoner didn't say.

"Search him," instructed the warden.

The jailer searched the prisoner carefully. At last, artfully concealed in the waistband of the trousers, he found a piece of steel about two inches long, with one side curved like a half moon.

"Ah," said the warden, as he received it from the jailer, "from your shoe heel," and he smiled pleasantly.

The jailer continued his search and on the other side of the trousers waistband found another piece of steel identical with the first. The edge showed where they had been worn against the bars of the window.

"You couldn't saw a way through those bars with these," said the warden.

"I could have," said The Thinking Machine firmly.

"In six months, perhaps," said the warden, good-naturedly.

The warden shook his head slowly as he gazed into the slightly flushed face of his prisoner.

"Ready to give it up?" he asked.

"I haven't started yet," was the prompt reply.

Then came another extensive search of the cell. Carefully the two men went over it, finally turning out the bed and searching that. Nothing. The warden in person climbed upon the bed and examined the bars of the window where the prisoner had been sawing. When he looked he was amused.

"Just made it a little bright by hard rubbing," he said to the prisoner, who stood looking on with a somewhat crestfallen air. The warden grasped the iron bars in his strong hands and tried to shake them. They were immovable, set firmly in the solid granite. He examined each in turn and found them all satisfactory. Finally he climbed down from the bed.

"Give it up, Professor," he advised.

The Thinking Machine shook his head and the warden and jailer passed on again. As they disappeared down the corridor The Thinking Machine sat on the edge of the bed with his head in his hands.

"He's crazy to try to get out of that cell," commented the jailer.

"Of course he can't get out," said the warden. "But he's clever. I would like to know what he wrote that cipher with."

It was four o'clock next morning when an awful, heart-racking shriek of terror resounded through the great prison. It came from a cell, somewhere about the center, and its tone told a tale of horror, agony, terrible fear. The warden heard and with three of his men rushed into the long corridor leading to Cell 13.

As they ran there came again that awful cry. It died away in a sort of wail. The white faces of prisoners appeared at cell doors upstairs and down, staring out wonderingly, frightened.

"It's that fool in Cell Thirteen," grumbled the warden.

He stopped and stared in as one of the jailers flashed a lantern. "That fool in Cell Thirteen" lay comfortably on his cot, flat on his back with his mouth open, snoring. Even as they looked there came again the piercing cry, from somewhere above. The warden's face blanched a little as he started up the stairs. There on the top floor he found a man in Cell 43, directly above Cell 13, but two floors higher, cowering in a corner of his cell.

"What's the matter?" demanded the warden.

"Thank God you've come," exclaimed the prisoner, and he cast himself against the bars of his cell.

"What is it?" demanded the warden again.

He threw open the door and went in. The prisoner dropped on his knees and clasped the warden about the body. His face was white with terror, his eyes were widely distended, and he was shuddering. His hands, icy cold, clutched at the warden's.

"Take me out of this cell, please take me out," he pleaded.

"What's the matter with you, anyhow?" insisted the warden, impatiently.

"I heard something—something," said the prisoner, and his eyes roved nervously around the cell.

"What did you hear?"

"I—I can't tell you," stammered the prisoner. Then, in a sudden burst of terror: "Take me out of this cell—put me anywhere—but take me out of here."

The warden and the three jailers exchanged glances.

"Who is this fellow? What's he accused of?" asked the warden.

"Joseph Ballard," said one of the jailers. "He's accused of throwing acid in a woman's face. She died from it."

"But they can't prove it," gasped the prisoner. "They can't prove it. Please put me in some other cell."

He was still clinging to the warden, and that official threw his arms off roughly. Then for a time he stood looking at the cowering wretch, who seemed possessed of all the wild, unreasoning terror of a child.

"Look here, Ballard," said the warden, finally, "if you heard anything, I want to know what it was. Now tell me."

"I can't, I can't," was the reply. He was sobbing.

"Where did it come from?"

"I don't know. Everywhere—nowhere. I just heard it."

"What was it—a voice?"

"Please don't make me answer," pleaded the prisoner.

"You must answer," said the warden, sharply.

"It was a voice—but—but it wasn't human," was the sobbing reply.

"Voice, but not human?" repeated the warden, puzzled.

"It wounded muffled and—and far away—and ghostly," explained the man.

"Did it come from inside or outside the prison?"

"It didn't seem to come from anywhere—it was just here, here, everywhere. I heard it. I heard it."

For an hour the warden tried to get the story, but Ballard had become suddenly obstinate and would say nothing—only pleaded to be placed in another cell, or to have one of the jailers remain near him until daylight. These requests were gruffly refused.

"And see here," said the warden, in conclusion, "if there's any more of this scream-ing I'll put you in the padded cell."

Then the warden went his way, a sadly puzzled man. Ballard sat at his cell door until daylight, his face, drawn and white with terror, pressed against the bars, and looked out into the prison with wide, staring eyes.

That day, the fourth since the incarceration of The Thinking Machine, was en-livened considerably by the volunteer prisoner, who spent most of his time at the lit-tle window of his cell. He began proceedings by throwing another piece of linen down to the guard, who picked it up dutifully and took it to the warden. On it was written:

"Only three days more."

The warden was in no way surprised at what he read; he understood that The Thinking Machine meant only three days more of his imprisonment, and he regarded the note as a boast. But how was the thing written? Where had The Think-ing Machine found his new piece of linen? Where? How? He carefully examined the linen. It was white, of fine texture, shirting material. He took the shirt which he had taken and carefully fitted the two original pieces of the linen to the torn places. This third piece was entirely superfluous; it didn't fit anywhere, and yet it was unmis-takably the same goods.

"And where—where does he get anything to write with?" demanded the warden of the world at large.

Still later on the fourth day The Thinking Machine, through the window of his cell, spoke to the armed guard outside.

"What day of the month is it?" he asked.

"The fifteenth," was the answer.

The Thinking Machine made a mental astronomical calculation and satisfied him-self that the moon would not rise until after nine o'clock that night. Then he asked another question:

"Who attends to those arc lights?"

"Man from the company."

"You have no electricians in the building?"

"No."

"I should think you could save money if you had your own man."

"None of my business," replied the guard.

The guard noticed The Thinking Machine at the cell window frequently during that day, but always the face seemed listless and there was a certain wistfulness in the squint eyes behind the glasses. After a while he accepted the presence of the leonine head as a matter of course. He had seen other prisoners do the same thing; it was the longing for the outside world.

That afternoon, just before the day guard was relieved, the head appeared at the window again, and The Thinking Machine's hand held something out between the bars. It fluttered to the ground and the guard picked it up. It was a five-dollar bill.

"That's for you," called the prisoner.

As usual, the guard took it to the warden. That gentleman looked at it suspi-ciously; he looked at everything that came from Cell 13 with suspicion.

"He said it was for me," explained the guard.

"It's a sort of a tip, I suppose," said the warden. "I see no particular reason why you shouldn't accept—"

Suddenly he stopped. He had remembered that The Thinking Machine had gone into Cell 13 with one five-dollar bill and two ten-dollar bills; twenty-five dollars in all. Now a five-dollar bill had been tied around the first pieces of linen that came from the cell. The warden still had it, and to convince himself he took it out and looked at it. It was five dollars; yet here was another five dollars, and The Thinking Machine had only had ten-dollar bills.

"Perhaps somebody changed one of the bills for him," he thought at last, with a sigh of relief.

But then and there he made up his mind. He would search Cell 13 as a cell was never before searched in this world. When a man could write at will, and change money, and do other wholly inexplicable things, there was something radically wrong with his prison. He planned to enter the cell at night—three o'clock would be an excellent time. The Thinking Machine must do all the weird things he did some-time. Night seemed the most reasonable.

Thus it happened that the warden stealthily descended upon Cell 13 that night at three o'clock. He paused at the door and listened. There was no sound save the steady, regular breathing of the prisoner. The keys unfastened the double locks with scarcely a clank, and the warden entered, locking the door behind him. Suddenly he flashed his dark lantern in the face of the recumbent figure.

If the warden had planned to startle The Thinking Machine he was mistaken, for that individual merely opened his eyes quietly, reached for his glasses, and inquired, in a most matter-of-fact tone:

"Who is it?"

It would be useless to describe the search that the warden made. It was minute. Not one inch of the cell or the bed was overlooked. He found the round hole in the floor, and with a flash of inspiration thrust his thick fingers into it. After a moment of fumbling there he drew up something and looked at it in the light of his lantern.

"Ugh!" he exclaimed.

The thing he had taken out was a rat—a dead rat. His inspiration fled as a mist before the sun. But he continued the search. The Thinking Machine, without a word, arose and kicked the rat out of the cell into the corridor.

The warden climbed on the bed and tried the steel bars in the tiny window. They were perfectly rigid; every bar of the door was the same.

Then the warden searched the prisoner's clothing, beginning at the shoes. Nothing hidden in them! Then the trousers waistband. Still nothing! Then the pockets of the trousers. From one side he drew out some paper money and examined it.

"Five one-dollar bills," he gasped.

"That's right," said the prisoner.

"But the—you had two tens and a five—what the—how do you do it?"

"That's my business," said The Thinking Machine.

"Did any of my men change this money for you—on your word of honor?"

The Thinking Machine paused just a fraction of a second.

"No," he said.

"Well, do you make it?" asked the warden, He was prepared to believe anything.

"That's my business," again said the prisoner.

The warden glared at the eminent scientist fiercely. He felt—he knew—that this man was making a fool of him, yet he didn't know how. If he were a real prisoner he would get the truth—but, then, perhaps, those inexplicable things which had happened would not have been brought before him so sharply. Neither of the men spoke for a long time, then suddenly the warden turned fiercely and left the cell, slamming the door behind him. He didn't dare to speak, then.

He glanced at the clock. It was ten minutes to four. He had hardly settled himself in bed when again came that heart-breaking shriek through the prison. With a few muttered words, which, while not elegant, were highly expressive, he relighted his lantern and rushed through the prison again to the cell on the upper floor.

Again Ballard was crushing himself against the steel door, shrieking, shrieking at the top of his voice. He stopped only when the warden flashed his lamp in the cell.

"Take me out, take me out," he screamed. "I did it, I did it, I killed her. Take it away."

"Take what away?" asked the warden.

"I threw the acid in her face—I did it—I confess. Take me out of here."

Ballard's condition was pitiable; it was only an act of mercy to let him out into the corridor. There he crouched in a corner, like an animal at bay, and clasped his hands to his ears. It took half an hour to calm him sufficiently for him to speak. Then he told incoherently what had happened. On the night before at four o'clock he had heard a voice—a sepulchral voice, muffled and wailing in tone.

"What did it say?" asked the warden, curiously.

"Acid—acid—acid!" gasped the prisoner. "It accused me. Acid! I threw the acid, and the woman died. Oh!" It was a long, shuddering wail of terror.

"Acid?" echoed the warden, puzzled. The case was beyond him.

"Acid. That's all I heard—that one word, repeated several times. There were other things, too, but I didn't hear them."

"That was last night, eh?" asked the warden. "What happened tonight—what frightened you just now?"

"It was the same thing," gasped the prisoner. "Acid—acid—acid!" He covered his face with his hands and sat shivering. "It was acid I used on her, but I didn't mean to kill her. I just heard the words. It was something accusing me—accusing me." He mumbled, and was silent.

"Did you hear anything else?"

"Yes—but I couldn't understand—only a little bit—just a word or two."

"Well, what was it?"

"I heard 'acid' three times, then I heard a long, moaning sound, then—then—I heard 'number eight hat.' I heard that twice."

"Number eight hat," repeated the warden. "What the devil—number eight hat? Accusing voices of conscience have never talked about number eight hats, so far as I ever heard."

"He's insane," said one of the jailers, with an air of finality.

"I believe you," said the warden. "He must be. He probably heard something and got frightened. He's trembling now. Number eight hat! What the—"

When the fifth day of The Thinking Machine's imprisonment rolled around the warden was wearing a hunted look. He was anxious for the end of the thing. He could not help but feel that his distinguished prisoner had been amusing himself. And if this were so, The Thinking Machine had lost none of his sense of humor. For on this fifth day he flung down another linen note to the outside guard, bearing the words "Only two days more." Also he flung down half a dollar.

Now the warden knew—he *knew*—that the man in Cell 13 didn't have any half dollars—he *couldn't* have any half dollars, no more than he could have pen and ink and linen, and yet he did have them. It was a condition, not a theory; that is one reason why the warden was wearing a hunted look.

That ghastly, uncanny thing, too, about "acid" and "number eight hat" clung to him tenaciously. They didn't mean anything, of course, merely the ravings of an insane murderer who had been driven by fear to confess his crime, still there were so many things that "didn't mean anything" happening in the prison now since The Thinking Machine was there.

On the sixth day the warden received a postal stating that Dr. Ransome and Mr. Fielding would be at Chisholm Prison on the following evening, Thursday, and in the event Professor Van Dusen had not yet escaped—and they presumed he had not because they had not heard from him—they would meet him there.

"In the event he had not yet escaped!" The warden smiled grimly. Escaped!

The Thinking Machine enlivened this day for the warden with three notes. They were on the usual linen and bore generally on the appointment at half past eight o'clock Thursday night, which appointment the scientist had made at the time of his imprisonment.

On the afternoon of the seventh day the warden passed Cell 13 and glanced in. The Thinking Machine was lying on the iron bed, apparently sleeping lightly. The cell appeared precisely as it always did from a casual glance. The warden would swear that no man was going to leave it between that hour—it was then four o'clock—and half past eight o'clock that evening.

On his way back past the cell the warden heard the steady breathing again, and coming closer to the door looked in. He wouldn't have done so if The Thinking Machine had been looking, but now—well, it was different.

A ray of light came through the high window and fell on the face of the sleeping man. It occurred to the warden for the first time that his prisoner appeared haggard and weary. Just then The Thinking Machine stirred slightly and the warden hurried on up the corridor guiltily. That evening after six o'clock he saw the jailer.

"Everything all right in Cell Thirteen?" he asked.

"Yes, sir," replied the jailer. "He didn't eat much, though."

It was with a feeling of having done his duty that the warden received Dr. Ransome and Mr. Fielding shortly after seven o'clock. He intended to show them the linen notes and lay before them the full story of his woes, which was a long one. But before this came to pass the guard from the river side of the prison yard entered the office.

"The arc light in my side of the yard won't light," he informed the warden.

"Confound it, that man's a hoodoo," thundered the official. "Everything has happened since he's been here."

The guard went back to his post in the darkness, and the warden phoned to the electric light company.

"This is Chisholm Prison," he said through the phone.

"Send three or four men down here quick, to fix an arc light."

The reply was evidently satisfactory, for the warden hung up the receiver and passed out into the yard. While Dr. Ransome and Mr. Fielding sat waiting the guard at the outer gate came in with a special-delivery letter. Dr. Ransome happened to notice the address, and, when the guard went out, looked at the letter more closely.

"By George!" he exclaimed.

"What is it?" asked Mr. Fielding.

Silently the doctor offered the letter. Mr. Fielding examined it closely.

"Coincidence," he said. "It must be."

It was nearly eight o'clock when the warden returned to his office. The electricians had arrived in a wagon, and were now at work. The warden pressed the buzz-button communicating with the man at the outer gate in the wall.

"How many electricians came in?" he asked, over the short phone. "Four? Three workmen in jumpers and overalls and the manager? Frock coat and silk hat? All right. Be certain that only four go out. That's all."

He turned to Dr. Ransome and Mr. Fielding.

"We have to be careful here—particularly," and there was broad sarcasm in his tone, "since we have scientists locked up."

The warden picked up the special-delivery letter carelessly, and then began to open it.

"When I read this I want to tell you gentlemen something about how—Great Caesar!" he ended, suddenly, as he glanced at the letter. He sat with mouth open, motionless, from astonishment.

"What is it?" asked Mr. Fielding.

"A special-delivery letter from Cell Thirteen," gasped the warden. "An invitation to supper."

"What?" and the two others arose, unanimously.

The warden sat dazed, staring at the letter for a moment, then called sharply to a guard outside in the corridor.

"Run down to Cell Thirteen and see if that man's in there."

The guard went as directed, while Dr. Ransome and Mr. Fielding examined the letter.

"It's Van Dusen's handwriting; there's no question of that," said Dr. Ransome. "I've seen too much of it."

Just then the buzz on the telephone from the outer gate sounded, and the warden, in a semitrance, picked up the receiver.

"Hello! Two reporters, eh? Let 'em come in." He turned suddenly to the doctor and Mr. Fielding. "Why, the man *can't* be out. He must be in his cell."

Just at that moment the guard returned.

"He's still in his cell, sir," he reported. "I saw him. He's lying down."

"There, I told you so," said the warden, and he breathed freely again. "But how did he mail that letter?"

There was a rap on the steel door which led from the jail yard into the warden's office.

"It's the reporters," said the warden. "Let them in," he instructed the guard; then to the two other gentlemen: "Don't say anything about this before them, because I'd never hear the last of it."

The door opened, and the two men from the front gate entered.

"Good evening, gentlemen," said one. That was Hutchinson Hatch; the warden knew him well.

"Well?" demanded the other, irritably. "I'm here."

That was The Thinking Machine.

He squinted belligerently at the warden, who sat with mouth agape. For the moment that official had nothing to say. Dr. Ransome and Mr. Fielding were amazed, but they didn't know what the warden knew. They were only amazed; he was paralyzed. Hutchinson Hatch, the reporter, took in the scene with greedy eyes.

"How—how—how did you do it?" gasped the warden, finally.

"Come back to the cell," said The Thinking Machine, in the irritated voice which his scientific associates knew so well.

The warden, still in a condition bordering on trance, led the way.

"Flash your light in there," directed The Thinking Machine.

The warden did so. There was nothing unusual in the appearance of the cell, and there—there on the bed lay the figure of The Thinking Machine. Certainly! There was the yellow hair! Again the warden looked at the man beside him and wondered at the strangeness of his own dreams.

With trembling hands he unlocked the cell door and The Thinking Machine passed inside.

"See here," he said.

He kicked at the steel bars in the bottom of the cell door and three of them were pushed out of place. A fourth broke off and rolled away in the corridor.

"And here, too," directed the erstwhile prisoner as he stood on the bed to reach the small window. He swept his hand across the opening and every bar came out.

"What's this in bed?" demanded the warden, who was slowly recovering.

"A wig," was the reply. "Turn down the cover."

The warden did so. Beneath it lay a large coil of strong rope, thirty feet or more, a dagger, three files, ten feet of electric wire, a thin, powerful pair of steel pliers, a small tack hammer with its handle, and—and a derringer pistol.

"How did you do it?" demanded the warden.

"You gentlemen have an engagement to supper with me at half past nine o'clock," said The Thinking Machine.

"Come on, or we shall be late."

"But how did you do it?" insisted the warden.

"Don't ever think you can hold any man who can use his brain," said The Thinking Machine. "Come on; we shall be late."

It was an impatient supper party in the rooms of Professor Van Dusen and a somewhat silent one. The guests were Dr. Ransome, Alfred Fielding, the warden, and Hutchinson Hatch, reporter. The meal was served to the minute, in accordance with Professor Van Dusen's instructions of one week before; Dr. Ransome found the artichokes delicious. At last the supper was finished and The Thinking Machine turned full on Dr. Ransome and squinted at him fiercely.

"Do you believe it now?" he demanded.

"I do," replied Dr. Ransome.

"Do you admit that it was a fair test?"

"I do."

With the others, particularly the warden, he was waiting anxiously for the explanation.

"Suppose you tell us how—" began Mr. Fielding.

"Yes, tell us how," said the warden.

The Thinking Machine readjusted his glasses, took a couple of preparatory squints at his audience, and began the story. He told it from the beginning logically; and no man ever talked to more interested listeners.

"My agreement was," he began, "to go into a cell, carrying nothing except what was necessary to wear, and to leave that cell within a week. I had never seen Chisholm Prison. When I went into the cell I asked for tooth powder, two ten- and one five-dollar bills, and also to have my shoes blacked. Even if these requests had been refused it would not have mattered seriously. But you agreed to them.

"I knew there would be nothing in the cell which you thought I might use to advantage. So when the warden locked the door on me I was apparently helpless, unless I could turn three seemingly innocent things to use. They were things which would have been permitted any prisoner under sentence of death, were they not, warden?"

"Tooth powder and polished shoes, yes, but not money," replied the warden.

"Anything is dangerous in the hands of a man who knows how to use it," went on The Thinking Machine. "I did nothing that first night but sleep and chase rats." He glared at the warden. "When the matter was broached I knew I could do nothing that night, so suggested next day. You gentlemen thought I wanted time to arrange an escape with outside assistance, but this was not true. I knew I could communicate with whom I pleased, when I pleased."

The warden stared at him a moment, then went on smoking solemnly.

"I was aroused next morning at six o'clock by the jailer with my breakfast," continued the scientist. "He told me dinner was at twelve and supper at six. Between these times, I gathered, I would be pretty much to myself. So immediately after breakfast I examined my outside surroundings from my cell window. One look told me it would be useless to try to scale the wall, even should I decide to leave my cell by the window, for my purpose was to leave not only the cell, but the prison. Of course, I could have gone over the wall, but it would have taken me longer to lay my plans that way. Therefore, for the moment, I dismissed all idea of that.

"From this first observation I knew the river was on that side of the prison, and that there was also a playground there. Subsequently these surmises were verified by a keeper. I knew then one important thing—that anyone might approach the prison wall from that side if necessary without attracting any particular attention. That was well to remember. I remembered it.

"But the outside thing which most attracted my attention was the feed wire to the arc light which ran within a few feet—probably three or four—of my cell window. I knew that would be valuable in the event I found it necessary to cut off that arc light."

"Oh, you shut it off tonight, then?" asked the warden.

"Having learned all I could from that window," resumed The Thinking Machine, without heeding the interruption, "I considered the idea of escaping through the prison proper. I recalled just how I had come into the cell, which I knew would be the only way. Seven doors lay between me and the outside. So, also for the time being, I gave up the idea of escaping that way. And I couldn't go through the solid granite walls of the cell."

The Thinking Machine paused for a moment and Dr. Ransome lighted a new cigar. For several minutes there was silence, then the scientific jailbreaker went on:

"While I was thinking about these things a rat ran across my foot. It suggested a new line of thought. There were at least half a dozen rats in the cell—I could see their beady eyes. Yet I had noticed none come under the cell door. I frightened them purposely and watched the cell door to see if they went out that way. They did not, but they were gone. Obviously they went another way. Another way meant another opening.

"I searched for this opening and found it. It was an old drain pipe, long unused and partly choked with dirt and dust. But this was the way the rats had come. They came from somewhere. Where? Drain pipes usually lead outside prison grounds. This one probably led to the river, or near it. The rats must therefore come from that direction. If they came a part of the way, I reasoned that they came all the way, because it was extremely unlikely that a solid iron or lead pipe would have any hole in it except at the exit.

"When the jailer came with my luncheon he told me two important things, although he didn't know it. One was that a new system of plumbing had been put in the prison seven years before; another that the river was only three hundred feet away. Then I knew positively that the pipe was a part of an old system; I knew, too, that it slanted generally toward the river. But did the pipe end in the water or on land?

"This was the next question to be decided. I decided it by catching several of the rats in the cell. My jailer was surprised to see me engaged in this work. I examined at least a dozen of them. They were perfectly dry; they had come through the pipe, and, most important of all, they were *not house rats, but field rats.* The other end of the pipe was on land, then, outside the prison walls. So far, so good.

"Then, I knew that if I worked freely from this point I must attract the warden's attention in another direction. You see, by telling the warden that I had come there to escape you made the test more severe, because I had to trick him by false scents."

The warden looked up with a sad expression in his eyes.

"The first thing was to make him think I was trying to communicate with you, Dr. Ransome. So I wrote a note on a piece of linen I tore from my shirt, addressed it to Dr. Ransome, tied a five-dollar bill around it, and threw it out the window. I knew the guard would take it to the warden, but I rather hoped the warden would send it as addressed. Have you that first linen note, Warden?"

The warden produced the cipher.

"What the deuce does it mean, anyhow? he asked.

"Read it backward, beginning with the *T* signature and disregard the division into words," instructed The Thinking Machine.

The warden did so.

"*T-h-i-s,* this," he spelled, studied it a moment, then read it off, grinning;
"This is not the way I intend to escape."

"Well, now what do you think o' that?" he demanded, still grinning.

"I knew that would attract your attention, just as it did," said The Thinking Machine, "and if you really found out what it was it would be a sort of gentle rebuke."

"What did you write it with?" asked Dr. Ransome, after he had examined the linen and passed it to Mr. Fielding.

"This," said the erstwhile prisoner, and he extended his foot. On it was the shoe he had worn in prison, though the polish was gone—scraped off clean. "The shoe blacking, moistened with water, was my ink; the metal tip of the shoelace made a fairly good pen."

The warden looked up and suddenly burst into a laugh, half of relief, half of amusement.

"You're a wonder," he said, admiringly. "Go on."

"That precipitated a search of my cell by the warden, as I had intended," continued The Thinking Machine. "I was anxious to get the warden into the habit of searching my cell, so that finally, constantly finding nothing, he would get disgusted and quit. This at last happened, practically."

The warden blushed.

"He then took my white shirt away and gave me a prison shirt. He was satisfied that those two pieces of the shirt were all that was missing. But while he was searching my cell I had another piece of that same shirt, about nine inches square, rolled into a small ball in my mouth."

"Nine inches of that shirt?' demanded the warden. "Where did it come from?"

"The bosoms of all stiff white shirts are of triple thickness," was the explanation. "I tore out the inside thickness, leaving the bosom only two thicknesses. I knew you wouldn't see it. So much for that."

There was a little pause, and the warden looked from one to another of the men with a sheepish grin.

"Having disposed of the warden for the time being by giving him something else to think about, I took my first serious step toward freedom," said Professor Van

Dusen. "I knew, within reason, that the pipe led somewhere to the playground outside; I knew a great many boys played there; I knew that rats came into my cell from out there. Could I communicate with some one outside with these things at hand?

"First was necessary, I saw, a long and fairly reliable thread, so—but here," he pulled up his trousers legs and showed that the tops of both stockings, of fine, strong lisle, were gone. "I unraveled those—after I got them started it wasn't difficult—and I had easily a quarter of a mile of thread that I could depend on.

"Then on half of my remaining linen I wrote, laboriously enough I assure you, a letter explaining my situation to this gentleman here," and he indicated Hutchinson Hatch. "I knew he would assist me—for the value of the newspaper story. I tied firmly to this linen letter a ten-dollar bill—there is no surer way of attracting the eye of anyone—and wrote on the linen: 'Finder of this deliver to Hutchinson Hatch, *Daily American,* who will give another ten dollars for the information.

"The next thing was to get this note outside on that playground where a boy might find it. There were two ways, but I chose the best. I took one of the rats—I became adept in catching them—tied the linen and money firmly to one leg, fastened my lisle thread to another, and turned him loose in the drain pipe. I reasoned that the natural fright of the rodent would make him run until he was outside the pipe and then out on earth he would probably stop to gnaw off the linen and money.

"From the moment the rat disappeared into that dusty pipe I became anxious. I was taking some many chances. The rat might gnaw the string, of which I held one end; other rats might gnaw it; the rat might run out of the pipe and leave the linen and money where they would never be found; a thousand other things might have happened. So began some nervous hours, but the fact that the rat ran on until only a few feet of the string remained in my cell made me think he was outside the pipe. I had carefully instructed Mr. Hatch what to do in case the note reached him. The question was: would it reach him?

"This done, I could only wait and make other plans in case this one failed. I openly attempted to bribe my jailer, and learned from him that he held the keys to only two of seven doors between me and freedom. Then I did something else to make the warden nervous. I took the steel supports out of the heels of my shoes and made a pretense of sawing the bars of my cell window. The warden raised a pretty row about that. He developed, too, the habit of shaking the bars of my cell window to see if they were solid. They were—then."

Again the warden grinned. He had ceased being astonished.

"With this one plan I had done all I could and could only wait to see what happened," the scientist went on. "I couldn't know whether my note had been delivered or even found, or whether the mouse had gnawed it up. And I didn't dare to draw back through the pipe that one slender thread which connected me with the outside.

"When I went to bed that night I didn't sleep, for fear there would come the slight signal twitch at the thread which was to tell me that Mr. Hatch had received the note. At half past three o'clock, I judge, I felt this twitch, and no prisoner actually under sentence of death ever welcomed a thing more heartily."

The Thinking Machine stopped and turned to the reporter.

"You'd better explain just what you did," he said.

"The linen note was brought to me by a small boy who had been playing baseball," said Mr. Hatch. "I immediately saw a big story in it, so I gave the boy another ten dollars, and got several spools of silk, some twine, and a roll of light, pliable wire. The professor's note suggested that I have the finder of the note show me just where it was picked up, and told me to make my search from there, beginning at two o'clock in the morning. If I found the other end of the thread I was to twitch it gently three times, then a fourth.

"I began the search with a small-bulb electric light. It was an hour and twenty minutes before I found the end of the drain pipe, half-hidden in weeds. Then I found the end of the lisle thread, twitched it as directed and immediately I got an answering twitch.

"Then I fastened the silk to this and Professor Van Dusen began to pull it into his cell. I nearly had heart disease for fear the string would break. To the end of the silk I fastened the twine, and when that had been pulled in I tied on the wire. Then that was drawn into the pipe and we had a substantial line, which rats couldn't gnaw, from the mouth of the drain into the cell."

The Thinking Machine raised his hand and Hatch stopped.

"All this was done in absolute silence," said the scientist. "But when the wire reached my hand I could have shouted. Then we tried another experiment, which Mr. Hatch was prepared for. I tested the pipe as a speaking tube. Neither of us could hear very clearly, but I dared not speak loud for fear of attracting attention in the prison. At last I made him understand what I wanted immediately. He seemed to have great difficulty in understanding when I asked for nitric acid, and I repeated the word 'acid' several times.

"Then I heard a shriek from a cell above me. I knew instantly that someone had overheard, and when I heard you coming, Mr. Warden, I feigned sleep. If you had entered my cell at that moment that whole plan of escape would have ended there. But you passed on. That was the nearest I ever came to being caught.

"Having established this improvised trolley it is easy to see how I got things in the cell and made them disappear at will. I merely dropped them back into the pipe. You, Mr. Warden, could not have reached the connecting wire with your fingers; they are too large. My fingers, you see, are longer and more slender. In addition I guarded the top of that pipe with a rat—you remember how."

"I remember," said the warden, with a grimace.

"I thought that if anyone were tempted to investigate that hole the rat would dampen his ardor. Mr. Hatch could not send me anything useful through the pipe until next night, although he did send me change for ten dollars as a test, so I proceeded with other parts of my plan. Then I evolved the method of escape which I finally employed.

"In order to carry this out successfully it was necessary for the guard in the yard to get accustomed to seeing me at the cell window. I arranged this by dropping linen notes to him, boastful in tone, to make the warden believe, if possible, one of his assistants was communicating with the outside for me. I would stand at my window for hours gazing out, so the guard could see, and occasionally I spoke to him. In that way I learned that the prison had no electricians of its own, but was dependent upon the lighting company if anything should go wrong.

"That cleared the way to freedom perfectly. Early in the evening of the last day of my imprisonment, when it was dark, I planned to cut the feed wire which was only a few feet from my window, reaching it with an acid-tipped wire I had. That would make that side of the prison perfectly dark while the electricians were searching for the break. That would also bring Mr. Hatch into the prison yard.

"There was only one more thing to do before I actually began the work of setting myself free. This was to arrange final details with Mr. Hatch through our speaking tube. I did this within half an hour after the warden left my cell on the fourth night of my imprisonment. Mr. Hatch again had serious difficulty in understanding me, and I repeated the word 'acid' to him several times, and later on the words 'number eight hat'—that's my size—and these were the things which made a prisoner upstairs confess to murder, so one of the jailers told me next day. This prisoner heard our voices, confused of course, through the pipe, which also went to his cell. The cell directly over me was not occupied, hence no one else heard.

"Of course the actual work of cutting the steel bars out of the window and door was comparatively easy with nitric acid, which I got through the pipe in tin bottles, but it took time. Hour after hour on the fifth and sixth and seventh days the guard below was looking at me as I worked on the bars of the window with the acid on a piece of wire. I used the tooth powder to prevent the acid spreading. I looked away abstractedly as I worked and each minute the acid cut deeper into the metal. I noticed that the jailers always tried the door by shaking the upper part, never the lower bars; therefore I cut the lower bars, leaving them hanging in place by thin strips of metal. But that was a bit of daredeviltry. I could not have gone that way so easily."

The Thinking Machine sat silent for several minutes.

"I think that makes everything clear," he went on. "Whatever points I have not explained were merely to confuse the warden and jailers. These things in my bed I brought in to please Mr. Hatch, who wanted to improve the story. Of course, the wig was necessary in my plan. The special-delivery letter I wrote and directed in my cell with Mr. Hatch's fountain pen, then sent it out to him and he mailed it. That's all, I think."

"But your actually leaving the prison grounds and then coming in through the outer gate to my office?" asked the warden.

"Perfectly simple," said the scientist. "I cut the electric light wire with acid, as I said, when the current was off. Therefore when the current was turned on the arc didn't light. I knew it would take some time to find out what was the matter and make repairs. When the guard went to report to you the yard was dark, I crept out the window—it was a tight fit, too—replaced the bars by standing on a narrow ledge, and remained in a shadow until the force of electricians arrived. Mr. Hatch was one of them.

"When I saw him I spoke and he handed me a cap, a jumper, and overalls, which I put on within ten feet of you, Mr. Warden, while you were in the yard. Later Mr. Hatch called me, presumably as a workman, and together we went out the gate to get something out of the wagon. The gate guard let us pass out readily as two workmen who have just passed in. We changed our clothing and reappeared, asking to see you. We saw you. That's all."

There was silence for several minutes. Dr. Ransome was first to speak.

"Wonderful!" he exclaimed. "Perfectly amazing."

"How did Mr. Hatch happen to come with the electricians?" asked Mr. Fielding.

"His father is manager of the company," replied The Thinking Machine.

"But what if there had been no Mr. Hatch outside to help?"

"Every prisoner has one friend outside who would help him escape if he could."

"Suppose—just suppose—there had been no old plumbing system there?" asked the warden, curiously.

"There were two other ways out," said The Thinking Machine, enigmatically.

Ten minutes later the telephone bell rang. It was a request for the warden.

"Light all right, eh?" the warden asked, through the phone. "Good. Wire cut beside Cell Thirteen? Yes, I know. One electrician too many? What's that? Two came out?"

The warden turned to the others with a puzzled expression.

"He only let in four electricians; he has let out two and says there are three left."

"I was the odd one," said The Thinking Machine.

"Oh," said the warden. "I see." Then through the phone: "Let the fifth man go. He's all right."

THE ABSENT-MINDED COTERIE

ROBERT BARR
(1850–1912)

The British journalist and short story writer Barr is best known today for his creation of Eugène Valmont, probably the first important humorous sleuth in the history of detective fiction. His overwhelming ego, ready wit, and elegant attire conspire to make him resemble Agatha Christie's famous Belgian sleuth, Hercule Poirot. Valmont appeared in only one volume of tales, The Triumph of Eugène Valmont *(1906). Poirot, incidentally, made his debut in 1920.*

 WELL REMEMBER THE NOVEMber day when I first heard of the Summertrees case, because there hung over London a fog so thick that two or three times I lost my way, and no cab was to be had at any price. The few cabmen then in the streets were leading their animals slowly along, making for their stables. It was one of those depressing London days which filled me with ennui and a yearning for my own clear city of Paris, where, if we are ever visited by a slight mist, it is at least clean, white vapor, and not this horrible London mixture saturated with suffocating carbon. The fog was too thick for any passer to read the contents bills of the newspapers plastered on the pavement, and as there were probably no races that day the newsboys were shouting what they considered the next most important event—the election of an American President. I bought a paper and thrust it into my pocket. It was late when I reached my flat, and, after dining there, which was an unusual thing for me to do, I put on my slippers, took an easy-chair before the fire, and began to read my evening journal. I was distressed to learn that the eloquent Mr. Bryan had been defeated. I knew little about the silver question, but the man's oratorical powers had appealed to me, and my sympathy was aroused because he owned many silver mines, and yet the price of the metal was so low that apparently he could not make a living through the operation of them. But, of course, the cry that he was a plutocrat, and a reputed millionaire over and over again, was bound to defeat him in a democracy where the average voter is exceedingly poor and not comfortably well-to-do, as is the case with our peasants in France. I always took great interest in the affairs of the huge republic to the West, having been at some pains to inform myself accurately regarding its politics; and although, as my readers know, I seldom quote anything complimentary that is said of me, nevertheless, an American client of mine once admitted that he never knew the true inwardness—I think that was the phrase he used—of American politics until he heard me discourse upon them. But then, he added, he had been a very busy man all his life.

I had allowed my paper to slip to the floor, for in very truth the fog was penetrating even into my flat, and it was becoming difficult to read, notwithstanding the electric light. My man came in, and announced that Mr. Spenser Hale wished to see me, and, indeed, any night, but especially when there is rain or fog outside, I am more pleased to talk with a friend than to read a newspaper.

"*Mon Dieu,* my dear Monsieur Hale, it is a brave man you are to venture out in such a fog as is abroad tonight."

"Ah, Monsieur Valmont," said Hale with pride, "you cannot raise a fog like this in Paris!"

"No. There you are supreme," I admitted, rising and saluting my visitor, then offering him a chair.

"I see you are reading the latest news," he said, indicating my newspaper. "I am very glad that man Bryan is defeated. Now we shall have better times."

I waved my hand as I took my chair again. I will discuss many things with Spenser Hale, but not American politics; he does not understand them. It is a common defect of the English to suffer complete ignorance regarding the internal affairs of other countries.

"It is surely an important thing that brought you out on such a night as this. The fog must be very thick in Scotland Yard."

This delicate shaft of fancy completely missed him, and he answered stolidly:

"It's thick all over London, and, indeed, throughout most of England."

"Yes, it is," I agreed, but he did not see that either.

Still, a moment later, he made a remark which, if it had come from some people I know, might have indicated a glimmer of comprehension.

"You are a very, very clever man, Monsieur Valmont, so all I need say is that the question which brought me here is the same as that on which the American election was fought. Now, to a countryman, I should be compelled to give further explanation, but to you, monsieur, that will not be necessary."

There are times when I dislike the crafty smile and partial closing of the eyes which always distinguishes Spenser Hale when he places on the table a problem which he expects will baffle me. If I said he never did baffle me, I would be wrong, of course, for sometimes the utter simplicity of the puzzles which trouble him leads me into an intricate involution entirely unnecessary in the circumstances.

I pressed my finger tips together, and gazed for a few moments at the ceiling. Hale had lit his black pipe, and my silent servant placed at his elbow the whisky and soda, then tiptoed out of the room. As the door closed my eyes came from the ceiling to the level of Hale's expansive countenance.

"Have they eluded you?" I asked quietly.

"Who?"

"The coiners."

Hale's pipe dropped from his jaw, but he managed to catch it before it reached the floor. Then he took a gulp from the tumbler.

"That was just a lucky shot," he said.

"*Parfaitement,*" I replied carelessly.

"Now, own up, Valmont, wasn't it?"

I shrugged my shoulders. A man cannot contradict a guest in his own house.

"Oh, stow that!" cried Hale impolitely. He is a trifle prone to strong and even slangy expressions when puzzled. "Tell me how you guessed it."

"It is very simple, *mon ami*. The question on which the American election was fought is the price of silver, which is so low that it has ruined Mr. Bryan, and threatens to ruin all the farmers of the West who possess silver mines on their farms. Silver troubled America, *ergo* silver troubles Scotland Yard.

"Very well; the natural inference is that some one has stolen bars of silver. But such a theft happened three months ago, when the metal was being uploaded from a German steamer at Southampton, and my dear friend Spenser Hale ran down the thieves very cleverly as they were trying to dissolve the marks off the bars with acid. Now crimes do not run in series, like the numbers in roulette at Monte Carlo. The thieves are men of brains. They say to themselves, 'What chance is there successfully to steal bars of silver while Mr. Hale is at Scotland Yard?' Eh, my good friend?"

"Really, Valmont," said Hale, taking another sip, "sometimes you almost persuade me that you have reasoning powers."

"Thanks, comrade. Then it is not a *theft* of silver we have now to deal with. But the American election was fought on the *price* of silver. If silver had been high in cost, there would have been no silver question. So the crime that is bothering you arises through the low price of silver, and this suggests that it must be a case of illicit coinage, for there the low price of the metal comes in. You have, perhaps, found a more subtle illegitimate act going forward than heretofore. Some one is making your shillings and your half crowns from real silver, instead of from baser metal, and yet there is a large profit which has not hitherto been possible through the high price of silver. With the old conditions you were familiar, but this new element sets at naught all your previous formulas. That is how I reasoned the matter out."

"Well, Valmont, you have hit it, I'll say that for you; you have hit it. There is a gang of expert coiners who are putting out real silver money, and making a clear shilling on the half crown. We can find no trace of the coiners, but we know the man who is shoving the stuff."

"That ought to be sufficient," I suggested.

"Yes, it should, but it hasn't proved so up to date. Now I came tonight to see if you would do one of your French tricks for us, right on the quiet."

"What French trick, Monsieur Spenser Hale?" I inquired with some asperity, forgetting for the moment that the man invariably became impolite when he grew excited.

"No offense intended," said the blundering officer, who really is a good-natured fellow, but always puts his foot in it, and then apologizes. "I want some one to go through a man's house without a search warrant, spot the evidence, let me know, and then we'll rush the place before he has time to hide his tracks."

"Who is this man, and where does he live?"

"His name is Ralph Summertrees, and he lives in a very natty little *bijou* residence, as the advertisements call it, situated in no less a fashionable street than Park Lane."

"I see. What has aroused your suspicions against him?"

"Well, you know, that's an expensive district to live in; it takes a bit of money to do the trick. This Summertrees has no ostensible business, yet every Friday he goes to the United Capital Bank in Piccadilly, and deposits a bag of swag, usually all silver coin."

"Yes; and this money?"

"This money, so far as we can learn, contains a good many of these new pieces which never saw the British Mint."

"It's not all the new coinage, then?"

"Oh, no, he's a bit too artful for that! You see, a man can go round London, his pockets filled with new-coined five-shilling pieces, buy this, that, and the other, and come home with his change in legitimate coins of the realm—half crowns, florins, shillings, six-pences, and all that."

"I see. Then why don't you nab him one day when his pockets are stuffed with illegitimate five-shilling pieces?"

"That could be done, of course, and I've thought of it, but, you see, we want to land the whole gang. Once we arrested him, without knowing where the money came from, the real coiners would take flight."

"How do you know he is not the real coiner himself?"

Now poor Hale is as easy to read as a book. He hesitated before answering this question, and looked confused as a culprit caught in some dishonest act.

"You need not be afraid to tell me," I said soothingly, after a pause. "You have had one of your men in Mr. Summertrees' house, and so learned that he is not the coiner. But your man has not succeeded in getting you evidence to incriminate other people."

"You've about hit it again, Monsieur Valmont. One of my men has been Summertrees' butler for two weeks, but, as you say, he has found no evidence."

"Is he still butler?"

"Yes."

"Now tell me how far you have got. You know that Summertrees deposits a bag of coin every Friday in the Piccadilly Bank, and I suppose the bank has allowed you to examine one or two of the bags."

"Yes, sir, they have, but, you see, banks are very difficult to treat with. They don't like detectives bothering round, and while they do not stand out against the law, still they never answer any more questions than they're asked, and Mr. Summertrees has been a good customer at the United Capital for many years."

"Haven't you found out where the money comes from?"

"Yes, we have; it is brought there night after night by a man who looks like a respectable city clerk, and he puts it into a large safe, of which he holds the key, this safe being on the ground floor, in the dining room."

"Haven't you followed the clerk?"

"Yes. He sleeps in the Park Lane house every night and goes up in the morning to an old curiosity shop in Tottenham Court Road, where he stays all day, returning with his bag of money in the evening."

"Why don't you arrest and question him?"

"Well, Monsieur Valmont, there is just the same objection to his arrest as to that of Summertrees himself. We could easily arrest both, but we have not the slightest evidence against either of them, and then, although we put the go-betweens in clink, the worst criminals of the lot would escape."

"Nothing suspicious about the old curiosity shop?"

"No. It appears to be perfectly regular."

"This game has been going on under your noses for how long?"

"For about six weeks."

"Is Summertrees a married man?"

"No."

"Are there any women servants in the house?"

"No, except that three charwomen come in every morning to do up the rooms."

"Of what is his household comprised?"

"There is the butler, then the valet, and last the French cook."

"Ah," cried I, "the French cook! This case interests me. So Summertrees has succeeded in completely disconcerting your man. Has he prevented him going from top to bottom of the house?"

"Oh, no! He has rather assisted him than otherwise. On one occasion he went to the safe, took out the money, had Podgers—that's my chap's name—help him to count it, and then actually sent Podgers to the bank with the bag of coin."

"And Podgers has been all over the place?"

"Yes."

"Saw no signs of a coining establishment?"

"No. It is absolutely impossible that any coining can be done there. Besides, as I tell you, that respectable clerk brings him the money."

"I suppose you want me to take Podgers's position?"

"Well, Monsieur Valmont, to tell you the truth, I would rather you didn't. Podgers has done everything a man can do, but I thought if you got into the house, Podgers assisting, you might go through it night after night at your leisure."

"I see. That's just a little dangerous in England. I think I should prefer to assure myself the legitimate standing of being amiable Podgers's successor. You say that Summertrees has no business?"

"Well, sir, not what you might call a business. He is by way of being an author, but I don't count that any business."

"Oh, an author, is he? When does he do his writing?"

"He locks himself up most of the day in his study."

"Does he come out for lunch?"

"No; he lights a little spirit lamp inside, Podgers tells me, and makes himself a cup of coffee, which he takes with a sandwich or two."

"That's rather frugal fare for Park Lane."

"Yes, Monsieur Valmont, it is, but he makes it up in the evening, when he has a long dinner, with all them foreign kickshaws you people like, done by his French cook."

"Sensible man! Well, Hale, I see I shall look forward with pleasure to making the acquaintance of Mr. Summertrees. Is there any restriction on the going and coming of your man Podgers?"

"None in the least. He can get away either night or day."

"Very good, friend Hale; bring him here tomorrow, as soon as our author locks himself up in his study, or rather, I should say, as soon as the respectable clerk leaves for Tottenham Court Road, which I should guess, as you put it, is about half an hour after his master turns the key of the room in which he writes."

"You are quite right in that guess, Valmont. How did you hit it?"

"Merely a surmise, Hale. There is a good deal of oddity about that Park Lane house, so it doesn't surprise me in the least that the master gets to work earlier in the morning than the man. I have also a suspicion that Ralph Summertrees knows perfectly well what the estimable Podgers is there for."

"What makes you think that?"

"I can give no reason except that my opinion of the acuteness of Summertrees has been gradually rising all the while you were speaking, and at the same time my estimate of Podgers's craft has been as steadily declining. However, bring the man here tomorrow, that I may ask him a few questions."

Next day, about eleven o'clock, the ponderous Podgers, hat in hand, followed his chief into my room. His broad, impassive, immobile, smooth face gave him rather more the air of a genuine butler than I had expected, and this appearance, of course, was enhanced by his livery. His replies to my questions were those of a well-trained servant who will not say too much unless it is made worth his while. All in all, Podgers exceeded my expectations, and really my friend Hale had some justification for regarding him, as he evidently did, a triumph in his line.

"Sit down, Mr. Hale, and you, Podgers."

The man disregarded my invitation, standing like a statue until his chief made a motion; then he dropped into a chair. The English are great on discipline.

"Now, Mr. Hale, I must first congratulate you on the make-up of Podgers. It is excellent. You depend less on artificial assistance than we do in France, and in that I think you are right."

"Oh, we know a bit over here, Monsieur Valmont!" said Hale, with pardonable pride.

"Now then, Podgers, I want to ask you about this clerk. What time does he arrive in the evening?"

"At prompt six, sir."

"Does he ring, or let himself in with a latchkey?"

"With a latchkey, sir."

"How does he carry the money?"

"In a little locked leather satchel, sir, flung over his shoulder."

"Does he go direct to the dining room?"

"Yes, sir."

"Have you seen him unlock the safe, and put in the money?"

"Yes, sir."

"Does the safe unlock with a word or a key?"

"With the key, sir. It's one of the old-fashioned kind."

"Then the clerk unlocks his leather money bag?"

"Yes, sir."

"That's three keys used within as many minutes. Are they separate or in a bunch?"

"In a bunch, sir."

"Did you ever see your master with this bunch of keys?"

"No, sir."

"You saw him open the safe once, I am told?"

"Yes, sir."

"Did he use a separate key, or one of a bunch?"

Podgers slowly scratched his head, then said:

"I don't just remember, sir."

"Ah, Podgers, you are neglecting the big things in that house! Sure you can't remember?"

"No, sir."

"Once the money is in the safe locked up, what does the clerk do?"

"Goes to his room, sir."

"Where is this room?"

"On the third floor, sir."

"Where do you sleep?"

"On the fourth floor with the rest of the servants, sir."

"Where does the master sleep?"

"On the second floor, adjoining his study."

"The house consists of four stories and a basement, does it?"

"Yes, sir."

"I have somehow arrived at the suspicion that it is a very narrow house. Is that true?"

"Yes, sir."

"Does the clerk ever dine with your master?"

"No, sir. The clerk don't eat in the house at all, sir."

"Does he go away before breakfast?"

"No, sir."

"No one takes breakfast to his room?"

"No, sir."

"What time does he leave the house?"

"At ten o'clock, sir."

"When is breakfast served?"

"At nine o'clock, sir."

"At what hour does your master retire to his study?"

"At half past nine, sir."

"Locks the door on the inside?"

"Yes, sir."

"Never rings for anything during the day?"

"Not that I know of, sir."

"What sort of man is he?"

Here Podgers was on familiar ground, and he rattled off a description minute in every particular.

"What I meant was, Podgers, is he silent, or talkative, or does he get angry? Does he seem furtive, suspicious, anxious, terrorized, calm, excitable, or what?"

"Well, sir, he is by way of being very quiet, never has much to say for hisself; never saw him angry or excited."

"Now, Podgers, you've been at Park Lane for a fortnight or more. You are a sharp, alert, observant man. What happens there that strikes you as unusual?"

"Well, I can't exactly say, sir," replied Podgers, looking rather helplessly from his chief to myself, and back again.

"Your professional duties have often compelled you to enact the part of butler before, otherwise you wouldn't do it so well. Isn't that the case?"

Podgers did not reply, but glanced at his chief. This was evidently a question pertaining to the service, which a subordinate was not allowed to answer. However, Hale said at once:

"Certainly. Podgers has been in dozens of places."

"Well, Podgers, just call to mind some of the other households where you have been employed, and tell me any particulars in which Mr. Summertrees's establishment differs from them."

Podgers pondered a long time.

"Well, sir, he do stick to writing pretty close."

"Ah, that's his profession, you see, Podgers. Hard at it from half past nine till toward seven, I imagine?"

"Yes, sir."

"Anything else, Podgers? No matter how trivial."

"Well, sir, he's fond of reading, too; leastways, he's fond of newspapers."

"When does he read?"

"I never seen him read 'em, sir; indeed, so far as I can tell, I never knew the papers to be opened, but he takes them all in, sir."

"What, all the morning papers?"

"Yes, sir, and all the evening papers, too."

"Where are the morning papers placed?"

"On the table in his study, sir."

"And the evening papers?"

"Well, sir, when the evening papers come, the study is locked. They are put on a side table in the dining room, and he takes them upstairs with him to his study."

"This has happened every day since you've been there?"

"Yes, sir."

"You reported that very striking fact to your chief, of course?"

"No, sir, I don't think I did," said Podgers, confused.

"You should have done so. Mr. Hale would have known how to make the most of a point so vital."

"Oh, come now, Valmont," interrupted Hale, "you're chaffing us! Plenty of people take in all the papers!"

"I think not. Even clubs and hotels subscribe to the leading journals only. You said *all,* I think, Podgers?"

"Well, *nearly* all, sir."

"But which is it? There's a vast difference."

"He takes a good many, sir."

"How many?"

"I don't just know, sir."

"That's easily found out, Valmont," cried Hale, with some impatience, "if you think it really important."

"I think it so important that I'm going back with Podgers myself. You can take me into the house, I suppose, when you return?"

"Oh, yes, sir!"

"Coming back to these newspapers for a moment, Podgers. What is done with them?"

"They are sold to the ragman, sir, once a week."

"Who takes them from the study?"

"I do, sir."

"Do they appear to have been read very carefully?"

"Well, no, sir; leastways, some of them seem never to have been opened, or else folded up very carefully again."

"Did you notice that extracts have been clipped from any of them?"

"No, sir."

"Does Mr. Summertrees keep a scrapbook?"

"Not that I know of, sir."

"Oh, the case is perfectly plain!" said I, leaning back in my chair, and regarding the puzzled Hale with that cherubic expression of self-satisfaction which I know is so annoying to him.

"*What's* perfectly plain?" he demanded, more gruffly perhaps than etiquette would have sanctioned.

"Summertrees is no coiner, nor is he linked with any band of coiners."

"What is he, then?"

"Ah, that opens another avenue of inquiry! For all I know to the contrary, he may be the most honest of men. On the surface it would appear that he is a reasonably industrious tradesman in Tottenham Court Road, who is anxious that there should be no visible connection between a plebeian employment and so aristocratic a residence as that in Park Lane."

At this point Spenser Hale gave expression to one of those rare flashes of reason which are always an astonishment to his friends.

"That is nonsense, Monsieur Valmont," he said; "the man who is ashamed of the connection between his business and his house is one who is trying to get into society, or else the women of his family are trying it, as is usually the case. Now Summertrees has no family. He himself goes nowhere, gives no entertainments, and accepts no invitations. He belongs to no club; therefore, to say that he is ashamed of his connection with the Tottenham Court Road shop is absurd. He is concealing the connection for some other reason that will bear looking into."

"My dear Hale, the Goddess of Wisdom herself could not have made a more sensible series of remarks. Now, *mon ami*, do you want my assistance, or have you enough to go on with?"

"Enough to go on with? We have nothing more than we had when I called on you last night."

"Last night, my dear Hale, you supposed this man was in league with coiners. Today you know he is not."

"I know you *say* he is not."

I shrugged my shoulders, and raised my eyebrows, smiling at him.

"It is the same thing, Monsieur Hale."

"Well, of all the conceited—" and the good Hale could get no farther.

"If you wish my assistance, it is yours."

"Very good. Not to put too fine a point upon it, I do."

"In that case, my dear Podgers, you will return to the residence of our friend Summertrees, and get together for me in a bundle all of yesterday's morning and evening papers that were delivered to the house. Can you do that, or are they mixed up in a heap in the coal cellar?"

"I can do it, sir. I have instructions to place each day's papers in a pile by itself in case they should be wanted again. There is always one week's supply in the cellar, and we sell the papers of the week before to the ragman."

"Excellent. Well, take the risk of abstracting one day's journals, and have them ready for me. I will call upon you at half past three o'clock exactly, and then I want you to take me upstairs to the clerk's bedroom in the third story, which I suppose is not locked during the daytime?"

"No, sir, it is not."

With this the patient Podgers took his departure. Spenser Hale rose when his assistant left.

"Anything further I can do?" he asked.

"Yes; give me the address of the shop in Tottenham Court Road. Do you happen to have about you one of those new five-shilling pieces which you believe to be illegally coined?"

He opened his pocket book, took out the bit of white metal, and handed it to me.

"I'm going to pass this off before evening," I said, putting it in my pocket, "and I hope none of your men will arrest me."

"That's all right," laughed Hales as he took his leave.

At half past three Podgers was waiting for me, and opened the front door as I came up the steps, thus saving me the necessity of ringing. The house seemed strangely quiet. The French cook was evidently down in the basement, and we had probably all the upper part to ourselves, unless Summertrees was in his study, which I doubted. Podgers led me directly upstairs to the clerk's room on the third floor, walking on tiptoe, with an elephantine air of silence and secrecy combined, which struck me as unnecessary.

"I will make an examination of this room," I said. "Kindly wait for me down by the door of the study."

The bedroom proved to be of respectable size when one considers the smallness of the house. The bed was all nicely made up, and there were two chairs in the room, but the usual washstand and swing mirror were not visible. However, seeing a curtain at the farther end of the room, I drew it aside, and found, as I expected, a fixed lavatory in an alcove of perhaps four feet deep by five in width. As the room was about fifteen feet wide, this left two thirds of the space unaccounted for. A moment later I opened a door which exhibited a closet filled with clothes hanging on hooks. This left a space of five feet between the clothes closet and the lavatory. I thought at first that the entrance to the secret stairway must have issued from the lavatory, but examining the boards closely, although they sounded hollow to the knuckles, they were quite evidently plain match boarding, and not a concealed door. The entrance to the stairway, therefore, must issue from the clothes closet. The right-hand wall proved similar to the match boarding of the lavatory, so far as the casual eye or touch was concerned, but I saw at once it was a door. The latch turned out to be somewhat ingeniously operated by one of the hooks which held a pair of old trousers. I found that the hook, if pressed upward, allowed the door to swing outward, over the stairhead. Descending to the second floor, a similar latch let me into a similar clothes closet in the room beneath. The two rooms were identical in size, one directly above the other, the only difference being that the lower-room door gave into the study, instead of into the hall, as was the case with the upper chamber.

The study was extremely neat, either not much used, or the abode of a very methodical man. There was nothing on the table except a pile of that morning's papers. I walked to the farther end, turned the key in the lock, and came upon the astonished Podgers.

"Well, I'm blowed!" exclaimed he.

"Quite so," I rejoined; "you've been tiptoeing past an empty room for the last two weeks. Now, if you'll come with me, Podgers, I'll show you how the trick is done."

When he entered the study I locked the door once more, and led the assumed butler, still tiptoeing through force of habit, up the stair into the top bedroom, and so out again, leaving everything exactly as we found it. We went down the main stair to the front hall, and there Podgers had my parcel of papers all neatly wrapped up. This bundle I carried to my flat, gave one of my assistants some instructions, and left him at work on the papers.

I took a cab to the foot of Tottenham Court Road, and walked up the street till I came to J. Simpson's old curiosity shop. After gazing at the well-filled windows for some time, I stepped inside, having selected a little iron crucifix displayed behind the pane; the work of some ancient craftsman.

I knew at once from Podgers's description that I was waited upon by the veritable respectable clerk who brought the bag of money each night to Park Lane, and who, I was certain, was no other than Ralph Summertrees himself.

There was nothing in his manner differing from that of any other quiet salesman. The price of the crucifix proved to be seven-and-six, and I threw down a sovereign to pay for it.

"Do you mind the change being all in silver, sir?" he asked, and I answered without any eagerness, although the question aroused a suspicion that had begun to be allayed:

"Not in the least."

He gave me half a crown, three two-shilling pieces, and four separate shillings, all coins being well-worn silver of the realm, the undoubted inartistic product of the reputable British Mint. This seemed to dispose of the theory that he was palming off illegitimate money. He asked me if I were interested in any particular branch of antiquity, and I replied that my curiosity was merely general, and exceedingly amateurish, whereupon he invited me to look around. This I proceeded to do, while he resumed the addressing and stamping of some wrapped-up pamphlets which I surmised to be copies of his catalogue.

He made no attempt either to watch me or to press his wares upon me. I selected at random a little inkstand, and asked its price. It was two shillings, he said, whereupon I produced my fraudulent five-shilling piece. He took it, gave me the change without comment, and the last doubt about his connection with coiners flickered from my mind.

At this moment a young man came in who, I saw at once, was not a customer. He walked briskly to the farther end of the shop, and disappeared behind a partition which had one pane of glass in it that gave an outlook toward the front door.

"Excuse me a moment," said the shopkeeper, and he followed the young man into the private office.

As I examined the curious heterogeneous collection of things for sale, I heard the clink of coins being poured out on the lid of a desk or an uncovered table, and the murmur of voices floated out to me. I was now near the entrance of the shop, and by a sleight-of-hand trick, keeping the corner of my eye on the glass pane of the private office, I removed the key of the front door without a sound, and took an impression of it in wax, returning the key to its place unobserved. At this moment another young man came in, and walked straight past me into the private office. I heard him say:

"Oh, I beg pardon, Mr. Simpson! How are you, Rogers?"

"Hello, Macpherson," saluted Rogers, who then came out, bidding good night to Mr. Simpson, and departed, whistling, down the street, but not before he had repeated his phrase to another young man entering, to whom he gave the name of Tyrrel.

I noted these three names in my mind. Two others came in together, but I was compelled to content myself with memorizing their features, for I did not learn their names. These men were evidently collectors, for I heard the rattle of money in every case; yet here was a small shop, doing apparently very little business, for I had been within it for more than half an hour, and yet remained the only customer. If credit were given, one collector would certainly have been sufficient, yet five had come in, and had poured their contributions into the pile Summertrees was to take home with him that night.

I determined to secure one of the pamphlets which the man had been addressing. They were piled on a shelf behind the counter, but I had no difficulty in reaching across and taking the one on top, which I slipped into my pocket. When the fifth young man went down the street Summertrees himself emerged, and this time he carried in his hand the well-filled locked leather satchel, with the straps dangling. It was now approaching half past five, and I saw he was eager to close up and get away.

"Anything else you fancy, sir?" he asked me.

"No, or, rather, yes and no. You have a very interesting collection here, but it's getting so dark I can hardly see."

"I close at half past five, sir."

"Ah! in that case," I said, consulting my watch, "I shall be pleased to call some other time."

"Thank you, sir," replied Summertrees quietly, and with that I took my leave.

From the corner of an alley on the other side of the street I saw him put up the shutters with his own hands, then he emerged with overcoat on, and the money satchel slung across his shoulder. He locked the door, tested it with his knuckles, and walked down the street, carrying under one arm the pamphlets he had been addressing. I followed him at some distance, saw him drop the pamphlets into the box at the first post office he passed, and walk rapidly toward his house in Park Lane.

When I returned to my flat and called in my assistant, he said:

"After putting to one side the regular advertisements of pills, soap, and what not, here is the only one common to all the newspapers, morning and evening alike. The advertisements are not identical, sir, but they have two points of similarity, or perhaps I should say three. They all profess to furnish a cure for absent-mindedness; they all ask that the applicant's chief hobby shall be stated, and they all bear the same address: Dr. Willoughby, in Tottenham Court Road."

"Thank you," said I, as he placed the scissored advertisements before me.

I read several of the announcements. They were all small, and perhaps that is why I had never noticed one of them in the newspapers, for certainly they were odd enough. Some asked for lists of absent-minded men, with the hobbies of each, and for these lists, prizes of from one shilling to six were offered. In other clippings Dr. Willoughby professed to be able to cure absent-mindedness. There were no fees and no treatment, but a pamphlet would be sent, which, if it did not benefit the receiver, could do no harm. The Doctor was unable to meet the patients personally, nor could he enter into correspondence with them. The address was the same as that of the old curiosity shop in Tottenham Court Road. At this juncture I pulled the pamphlet from my pocket, and saw it was entitled, "Christian Science and Absent-Mindedness," by Dr. Stamford Willoughby, and at the end of the article was the statement contained in the advertisements, that Dr. Willoughby would neither see patients nor hold any correspondence with them.

I drew a sheet of paper toward me, wrote to Dr. Willoughby, alleging that I was a very absent-minded man, and would be glad of his pamphlet, adding that my special hobby was the collecting of first editions. I then signed myself, "Alport Webster, Imperial Flats, London, W."

I may here explain that it is often necessary for me to see people under some other name than the well-known appellation of Eugène Valmont. There are two doors to my flat, and on one of these is painted, "Eugène Valmont"; on the other there is a receptacle, into which can be slipped a sliding panel bearing any *nom de guerre* I choose. The same device is arranged on the ground floor, where the names of all occupants of the building appear on the right-hand wall.

I sealed, addressed, and stamped my letter, then told my man to put out the name of Alport Webster, and if I did not happen to be in when any one called upon that mythical person, he was to make an appointment for me.

It was nearly six o'clock next afternoon when the card of Angus Macpherson was brought in to Mr. Alport Webster. I recognized the young man at once as the second who had entered the little shop, carrying his tribute to Mr. Simpson the day before. He held three volumes under his arm, and spoke in such a pleasant, insinuating sort of way, that I knew at once he was an adept in his profession of canvasser.

"Will you be seated, Mr. Macpherson? In what way can I serve you?"

He placed the three volumes, backs upward, on my table.

"Are you interested at all in first editions, Mr. Webster?"

"It is the one thing I am interested in," I replied; "but unfortunately they often run into a lot of money."

"That is true," said Macpherson sympathetically, "and I have here three books, one of which is an exemplification of what you say. This one costs a hundred pounds. The last copy that was sold by auction in London brought a hundred and twenty-three pounds. This next one is forty pounds, and the third ten pounds. At these prices I am certain you could not duplicate three such treasures in any bookshop in Britain."

I examined them critically, and saw at once that what he said was true. He was still standing on the opposite side of the table.

"Please take a chair, Mr. Macpherson. Do you mean to say you go round London with a hundred and fifty pounds' worth of goods under your arm in this careless way?"

The young man laughed.

"I run very little risk, Mr. Webster. I don't suppose anyone I meet imagines for a moment there is more under my arm than perhaps a trio of volumes I have picked up in the fourpenny box to take home with me."

I lingered over the volume for which he asked a hundred pounds, then said, looking across at him:

"How came you to be possessed of this book, for instance?"

He turned upon me a fine, open countenance, and answered without hesitation in the frankest possible manner:

"I am not in actual possession of it, Mr. Webster. I am by way of being a connoisseur in rare and valuable books myself, although, of course, I have little money with which to indulge in the collection of them. I am acquainted, however, with the lovers of desirable books in different quarters of London. These three volumes, for instance, are from the library of a private gentleman in the West End. I have sold many books to him, and he knows I am trustworthy. He wishes to dispose of them at something under their real value, and has kindly allowed me to conduct the negotiations. I make it my business to find out those who are interested in rare books, and by such trading I add considerably to my income."

"How, for instance, did you learn that I was a bibliophile?"

Mr. Macpherson laughed genially.

"Well, Mr. Webster, I must confess that I chanced it. I do that very often. I take a flat like this, and send in my card to the name on the door. If I am invited in, I ask the occupant the question I asked you just now: 'Are you interested in rare editions?' If he says no, I simply beg pardon and retire. If he says yes, then I show my wares."

"I see," said I, nodding. What a glib liar he was, with that innocent face of his, and yet my next question brought forth the truth.

"As this is the first time you have called upon me, Mr. Macpherson, you have no objection to my making some further inquiry, I suppose. Would you mind telling me the name of the owner of these books in the West End?"

"His name is Mr. Ralph Summertrees, of Park Lane."

"Of Park Lane? Ah, indeed!"

"I shall be glad to leave the books with you, Mr. Webster, and if you care to make an appointment with Mr. Summertrees, I am sure he will not object to say a word in my favor."

"Oh, I do not in the least doubt it, and should not think of troubling the gentleman."

"I was going to tell you," went on the young man, "that I have a friend, a capitalist, who, in a way, is my supporter; for, as I said, I have little money of my own. I find it is often inconvenient for people to pay down any considerable sum. When, however, I strike a bargain, my capitalist buys the books, and I make an arrangement with my customer to pay a certain amount each week, and so even a large purchase is not felt, as I make the installments small enough to suit my client."

"You are employed during the day, I take it?"

"Yes, I am a clerk in the City."

Again we were in the blissful realms of fiction!

"Suppose I take this book at ten pounds, what installments should I have to pay each week?"

"Oh, what you like, sir. Would five shillings be too much?"

"I think not."

"Very well, sir; if you pay me five shillings now, I will leave the book with you, and shall have pleasure in calling this day week for the next installment."

I put my hand into my pocket, and drew out two half crowns, which I passed over to him.

"Do I need to sign any form or undertaking to pay the rest?"

The young man laughed cordially.

"Oh, no, sir, there is no formality necessary. You see, sir, this is largely a labor of love with me, although I don't deny I have my eye on the future. I am getting together what I hope will be a very valuable connection with gentlemen like yourself who are fond of books, and I trust some day that I may be able to resign my place with the insurance company and set up a choice little business of my own, where my knowledge of values in literature will prove useful."

And then, after making a note in a little book he took from his pocket, he bade me a most graceful good-by and departed, leaving me cogitating over what it all meant.

Next morning two articles were handed to me. The first came by post and was a pamphlet on "Christian Science and Absent-Mindedness," exactly similar to the one I had taken away from the old curiosity shop; the second was a small key made from my wax impression that would fit the front door of the same shop—a key fashioned by an excellent anarchist friend of mine in an obscure street near Holborn.

That night at ten o'clock I was inside the old curiosity shop, with a small storage battery in my pocket, and a little electric glowlamp at my buttonhole, a most useful instrument for either burglar or detective.

I had expected to find the books of the establishment in a safe, which, if it was similar to the one in Park Lane, I was prepared to open with the false keys in my possession, or to take an impression of the keyhole and trust to my anarchist friend for the rest. But to my amazement I discovered all the papers pertaining to the concern in a desk which was not even locked. The books, three in number, were the ordinary daybook, journal, and ledger referring to the shop; bookkeeping of the older fashion; but in a portfolio lay half a dozen foolscap sheets, headed, "Mr. Rogers's List," "Mr. Macpherson's," "Mr. Tyrrel's," the names I had already learned, and three others. These lists contained in the first column, names; in the second column, addresses; in the third, sums of money; and then in the small, square places following were amounts ranging from two-and-sixpence to a pound. At the bottom of Mr. Macpherson's list was the name Alport Webster, Imperial Flats, £10; then in the small, square place, five shillings. These six sheets, each headed by a canvasser's name, were evidently the record of current collections, and the innocence of the whole thing was so apparent that, if it were not for my fixed rule never to believe that I am at the bottom of any case until I have come on something suspicious, I would have gone out empty-handed as I came in.

The six sheets were loose in a thin portfolio, but standing on a shelf above the desk were a number of fat volumes, one of which I took down, and saw that it contained similar lists running back several years. I noticed on Mr. Macpherson's current list the name of Lord Semptam, an eccentric old nobleman I knew slightly. Then turning to the list immediately before the current one the name was still there; I traced it back through list after list until I found the first entry, which was no less than three years previous, and there Lord Semptam was down for a piece of furniture costing fifty pounds, and on that account he had paid a pound a week for more than three years, totaling a hundred and seventy pounds at the least, and instantly the glorious simplicity of the scheme dawned upon me, and I became so interested in the swindle that I lit the gas, fearing my little lamp would be exhausted before my investigation ended, for it promised to be a long one.

In several instances the intended victim proved shrewder than old Simpson had counted upon, and the word "Settled" had been written on the line carrying the name when the exact number of installments was paid. But as these shrewd persons dropped out, others took their places, and Simpson's dependence on their absent-mindedness seemed to be justified in nine cases out of ten. His collectors were collecting long after the debt had been paid. In Lord Semptam's case, the payment had evidently become chronic, and the old man was giving away his pound a week to the suave Macpherson two years after his debt had been liquidated.

From the big volume I detached the loose leaf, dated 1893, which recorded Lord Semptam's purchase of a carved table for fifty pounds, and on which he had been paying a pound a week from that time to the date of which I am writing, which was November, 1896. This single document, taken from the file of three years previous, was not likely to be missed, as would have been the case if I had selected a current sheet. I nevertheless made a copy of the names and addresses of Macpherson's present clients; then, carefully placing everything exactly as I had found it, I extinguished the gas, and went out of the shop, locking the door behind me. With the 1893 sheet in my pocket I resolved to prepare a pleasant little surprise for my suave friend Macpherson when he called to get his next installment of five shillings.

Late as was the hour when I reached Trafalgar Square, I could not deprive myself of the felicity of calling on Mr. Spenser Hale, who I knew was then on duty. He never appeared at his best during office hours, because officialism stiffened his stalwart frame. Mentally he was impressed with the importance of his position, and added to this he was not then allowed to smoke his big black pipe and terrible tobacco. He received me with the curtness I had been taught to expect when I inflicted myself upon him at his office. He greeted me abruptly with:

"I say, Valmont, how long do you expect to be on this job?"

"What job?" I asked mildly.

"Oh, you know what I mean: the Summertrees affair?"

"Oh, *that!*" I exclaimed, with surprise. "The Summertrees case is already completed, of course. If I had known you were in a hurry, I should have finished up everything yesterday, but as you and Podgers, and I don't know how many more, have been at it sixteen or seventeen days, if not longer, I thought I might venture to take as many hours, as I am working entirely alone. You said nothing about haste, you know."

"Oh, come now, Valmont, that's a bit thick. Do you mean to say you have already got evidence against the man?"

"Evidence absolute and complete."

"Then who are the coiners?"

"My most estimable friend, how often have I told you not to jump at conclusions? I informed you when you first spoke to me about the matter that Summertrees was neither a coiner nor a confederate of coiners. I secured evidence sufficient to convict him of quite another offense, which is probably unique in the annals of crime. I have penetrated the mystery of the shop, and discovered the reason for all those suspicious actions which quite properly set you on his trail. Now I wish you to come to my flat next Wednesday night at a quarter to six, prepared to make an arrest."

"I must know whom I am to arrest, and on what counts."

"Quite so, *mon ami* Hale; I did not say you were to make an arrest, but merely warned you to be prepared. If you have time now to listen to the disclosures, I am quite at your service. I promise you there are some original features in the case. If, however, the present moment is inopportune, drop in on me at your convenience, previously telephoning so that you may know whether I am there or not, and thus your valuable time will not be expended purposelessly."

With this I presented to him my most courteous bow, and although his mystified expression hinted a suspicion that he thought I was chaffing him, as he would call it, official dignity dissolved somewhat, and he intimated his desire to hear all about it then and there. I had succeeded in arousing my friend Hale's curiosity. He listened to the evidence with perplexed brow, and at last ejaculated he would be blessed.

"This young man," I said, in conclusion, "will call upon me at six on Wednesday afternoon, to receive his second five shillings. I propose that you, in your uniform, shall be seated there with me to receive him, and I am anxious to study Mr. Macpherson's countenance when he realizes he has walked in to confront a policeman. If you will then allow me to cross-examine him for a few moments, not after the manner of Scotland Yard, with a warning lest he incriminate himself, but in the free and easy fashion we adopt in Paris, I shall afterwards turn the case over to you to be dealt with at your discretion."

"You have a wonderful flow of language, Monsieur Valmont," was the officer's tribute to me. "I shall be on hand at a quarter to six on Wednesday."

"Meanwhile," said I, "kindly say nothing of this to any one. We must arrange a complete surprise for Macpherson. That is essential. Please make no move in the matter at all until Wednesday night."

Spenser Hale, much impressed, nodded acquiescence, and I took a polite leave of him.

The question of lighting is an important one in a room such as mine, and electricity offers a good deal of scope to the ingenious. Of this fact I have taken full advantage. I can manipulate the lighting of my room so that any particular spot is bathed in brilliancy, while the rest of the space remains in comparative gloom, and I arranged the lamps so that the full force of their rays impinged against the door that Wednesday evening, while I sat on one side of the table in semidarkness and Hale sat on the other, with a light beating down on him from above which gave him the odd, sculptured look of a living statue of Justice, stern and triumphant. Any one entering the room would first be dazzled by the light, and next would see the gigantic form of Hale in the full uniform of his order.

When Angus Macpherson was shown into this room, he was quite visibly taken aback, and paused abruptly on the threshold, his gaze riveted on the huge policeman. I think his first purpose was to turn and run, but the door closed behind him, and he doubtless heard, as we all did, the sound of the bolt being thrust in its place, thus locking him in.

"I—I beg your pardon," he stammered, "I expected to meet Mr. Webster."

As he said this, I pressed the button under my table, and was instantly enshrouded with light. A sickly smile overspread the countenance of Macpherson as he caught sight of me, and he made a very creditable attempt to carry off the situation with nonchalance.

"Oh, there you are, Mr. Webster; I did not notice you at first."

It was a tense moment. I spoke slowly and impressively.

"Sir, perhaps you are not unacquainted with the name of Eugène Valmont."

He replied brazenly:

"I am sorry to say, sir, I never heard of the gentleman before."

At this came a most inopportune "Haw-haw" from that blockhead Spenser Hale, completely spoiling the dramatic situation I had elaborated with such thought and care. It is little wonder the English possess no drama, for they show scant appreciation of the sensational moments in life; they are not quickly alive to the lights and shadows of events.

"Haw-haw," brayed Spenser Hale, and at once reduced the emotional atmosphere to a fog of commonplace. However, what is a man to do? He must handle the tools with which it pleases Providence to provide him. I ignored Hale's untimely laughter.

"Sit down, sir," I said to Macpherson, and he obeyed.

"You have called on Lord Semptam this week," I continued sternly.

"Yes, sir."

"And collected a pound from him?"

"Yes, sir."

"In October, 1893, you sold Lord Semptam a carved antique table for fifty pounds?"

"Quite right, sir."

"When you were here last week you gave me Ralph Summertrees as the name of a gentleman living in Park Lane. You knew at the time that this man was your employer?"

Macpherson was now looking fixedly at me, and on this occasion made no reply. I went on calmly:

"You also knew that Summertrees, of Park Lane, was identical with Simpson, of Tottenham Court Road?"

"Well, sir," said Macpherson, "I don't exactly see what you're driving at, but it's quite usual for a man to carry on a business under an assumed name. There is nothing illegal about that."

"We will come to the illegality in a moment, Mr. Macpherson. You and Rogers and Tyrrel and three others are confederates of this man Simpson."

"We are in his employ; yes, sir, but no more confederates than clerks usually are."

"I think, Mr. Macpherson, I have said enough to show you that the game is what you call up. You are now in the presence of Mr. Spenser Hale, from Scotland Yard, who is waiting to hear your confession."

Here the stupid Hale broke in with his:

"And remember, sir, that anything you say will be—"

"Excuse me, Mr. Hale," I interrupted hastily, "I shall turn over the case to you in a very few moments, but I ask you to remember our compact, and to leave it for the present entirely in my hands. Now, Mr. Macpherson, I want your confession, and I want it at once."

"Confession? Confederates?" protested Macpherson, with admirably simulated surprise. "I must say you use extraordinary terms, Mr.—Mr.—What did you say the name was?"

"Haw-haw," roared Hale. "His name is Monsieur Valmont."

"I implore you, Mr. Hale, to leave this man to me for a very few moments. Now, Macpherson, what have you to say in your defense?"

"Where nothing criminal has been alleged, Monsieur Valmont, I see no necessity for defense. If you wish me to admit that somehow you have acquired a number of details regarding our business, I am perfectly willing to do so, and to subscribe to their accuracy. If you will be good enough to let me know of what you complain, I shall endeavor to make the point clear to you, if I can. There has evidently been some misapprehension, but for the life of me, without further explanation, I am as much in a fog as I was on my way coming here, for it is getting a little thick outside."

Macpherson certainly was conducting himself with great discretion, and presented, quite unconsciously, a much more diplomatic figure than my friend Spenser Hale, sitting stiffly opposite me. His tone was one of mild expostulation, mitigated by the intimation that all misunderstanding speedily would be cleared away. To outward view he offered a perfect picture of innocence, neither protesting too much nor too little. I had, however, another surprise in store for him, a trump card, as it were, and I played it down on the table.

"There!" I cried with vim, "have you ever seen that sheet before?"

He glanced at it without offering to take it in his hand.

"Oh, yes," he said, "that has been abstracted from our file. It is what I call my visiting list."

"Come, come, sir," I cried sternly, "you refuse to confess, but I warn you we know all about it. You never heard of Dr. Willoughby, I suppose."

"Yes, he is the author of the silly pamphlet on Christian Science."

"You are in the right, Mr. Macpherson; on Christian Science and Absent-Mindedness."

"Possibly. I haven't read it for a long while."

"Have you ever met this learned doctor, Mr. Macpherson?"

"Oh, yes. Dr. Willoughby is the pen name of Mr. Summertrees. He believes in Christian Science and that sort of thing, and writes about it."

"Ah, really. We are getting your confession bit by bit, Mr. Macpherson. I think it would be better to be quite frank with us."

"I was just going to make the same suggestion to you, Monsieur Valmont. If you will tell me in a few words exactly what is your charge against either Mr. Summertrees or myself, I will know then what to say."

"We charge you, sir, with obtaining money under false pretenses, which is a crime that has landed more than one distinguished financier in prison."

Spenser Hale shook his fat forefinger at me, and said:

"Tut, tut, Valmont; we mustn't threaten, we mustn't threaten, you know"; but I went on without heeding him.

"Take for instance, Lord Semptam. You sold him a table for fifty pounds, on the installment plan. He was to pay a pound a week, and in less than a year the debt was liquidated. But he is an absent-minded man, as all your clients are. That is why you came to me. I had answered the bogus Willoughby's advertisement. And so you kept on collecting and collecting for something more than three years. Now do you understand the charge?"

Mr. Macpherson's head, during this accusation, was held slightly inclined to one side. At first his face was clouded by the most clever imitation of anxious concentration of mind I had ever seen, and this was gradually cleared away by the dawn of awakening perception. When I had finished, an ingratiating smile hovered about his lips.

"Really, you know," he said, "that is rather a capital scheme. The absent-minded league, as one might call them. Most ingenious. Summertrees, if he had any sense of humor, which he hasn't, would be rather taken by the idea that his innocent fad for Christian Science had led him to be suspected of obtaining money under false pretenses. But, really, there are no pretensions about the matter at all. As I understand it, I simply call and receive the money through the forgetfulness of the persons on my list, but where I think you would have both Summertrees and myself, it there was anything in your audacious theory, would be an indictment for conspiracy. Still, I quite see how the mistake arises. You have jumped to the conclusion that we sold nothing to Lord Semptam except that carved table three years ago. I have pleasure in pointing out to you that his lordship is a frequent customer of ours, and has had many things from us at one time or another. Sometimes he is in our debt; sometimes we are in his. We keep a sort of running contract with him by which he pays us a pound a week. He and several other customers deal on the same plan, and in return, for an income that we can count upon, they get the first offer of anything in which they are supposed to be interested. As I have told you, we call these sheets in the office our visiting lists, but to make the visiting lists complete you need what we term our encyclopedia. We call it that because it is in so many volumes; a volume for each year, running back I don't know how long. You will notice little figures here from time to time above the amount stated on this visiting list. These figures refer to the page of the encyclopedia for the current year, and on that page is noted the new sale and the amount of it, as it might be set down, say, in a ledger."

"That is a very entertaining explanation, Mr. Macpherson. I suppose this encyclopedia, as you call it, is in the shop at Tottenham Court Road?"

"Oh, no, sir. Each volume of the encyclopedia is self-locking. These books contain the real secret of our business, and they are kept in the safe at Mr. Summertrees's house in Park Lane. Take Lord Semptam's account, for instance. You will find, in faint figures under a certain date, 102. If you turn to page 102 of the encyclopedia for that year, you will then see a list of what Lord Semptam has bought, and the prices he was charged for them. It is really a very simple matter. If you will allow me to use your telephone for a moment, I will ask Mr. Summertrees, who has not yet begun dinner, to bring with him here the volume for 1893, and within a quarter of an hour you will be perfectly satisfied that everything is quite legitimate."

I must confess that the young man's naturalness and confidence staggered me, the more so as I saw by the sarcastic smile on Hale's lips that he did not believe a single word spoken. A portable telephone stood on the table, and as Macpherson finished his explanation, he reached over and drew it toward him. Then Spenser Hale interfered.

"Excuse *me*," he said, "I'll do the telephoning. What is the call number of Mr. Summertrees?"

"One forty Hyde Park."

Hale at once called up Central, and presently was answered from Park Lane. We heard him say:

"Is this the residence of Mr. Summertrees? Oh, is that you, Podgers? Is Mr. Summertrees in? Very well. This is Hale. I am in Valmont's flat—Imperial Flats—you know. Yes, where you went with me the other day. Very well, go to Mr. Summertrees, and say to him that Mr. Macpherson wants the encyclopedia for 1893. Do you get that? Yes, encyclopedia. Oh, don't understand what it is. Mr. Macpherson. No, don't mention my name at all. Just say Mr. Macpherson wants the encyclopedia for the year 1893, and that you are to bring it. Yes, you may tell him that Mr. Macpherson is at Imperial Flats, but don't mention my name at all. Exactly. As soon as he gives you the book, get a cab, and come here as quickly as possible with it. If Summertrees doesn't want to let the book go, then tell him to come with you. If he won't do that, place him under arrest, and bring both him and the book here. All right. Be as quick as you can; we're waiting."

Macpherson made no protest against Hale's use of the telephone; he merely sat back in his chair with a resigned expression on his face which, if painted on canvas, might have been entitled, "The Falsely Accused." When Hale rang off, Macpherson said:

"Of course you know your business best, but if your man arrests Summertrees, he will make you a laughingstock of London. There is such a thing as unjustifiable arrest, as well as getting money under false pretenses, and Mr. Summertrees is not the man to forgive an insult. And then, if you will allow me to say so, the more I think over your absent-minded theory the more absolutely grotesque it seems, and if the case ever gets into the newspapers, I am sure, Mr. Hale, you'll experience an uncomfortable half hour with your chiefs at Scotland Yard."

"I'll take the risk of that, thank you," said Hale stubbornly.

"Am I to consider myself under arrest?" inquired the young man.

"No, sir."

"Then, if you will pardon me, I shall withdraw. Mr. Summertrees will show you everything you wish to see in his books, and can explain his business much more capably than I, because he knows more about it; therefore, gentlemen, I bid you good night."

"No, you don't. Not just yet awhile," exclaimed Hale, rising to his feet simultaneously with the young man.

"Then I *am* under arrest," protested Macpherson.

"You're not going to leave this room until Podgers brings that book."

"Oh, very well," and he sat down again.

And now, as talking is dry work, I set out something to drink, a box of cigars, and a box of cigarettes. Hale mixed his favorite brew, but Macpherson, shunning the wine of his country, contented himself with a glass of plain mineral water, and lit a cigarette. Then he awoke my high regard by saying pleasantly, as if nothing had happened:

"While we are waiting, Monsieur Valmont, may I remind you that you owe me five shillings?"

I laughed, took the coin from my pocket, and paid him, whereupon he thanked me.

"Are you connected with Scotland Yard, Monsieur Valmont?" asked Macpherson, with the air of a man trying to make conversation to bridge over a tedious interval; but before I could reply Hale blurted out:

"Not likely!"

"You have an official standing as a detective, then, Monsieur Valmont?"

"None whatever," I replied quickly, thus getting in my oar ahead of Hale.

"That is a loss to our country," pursued this admirable young man, with evident sincerity.

I began to see I could make a good deal of so clever a fellow if he came under my tuition.

"The blunders of our police," he went on, "are something deplorable. If they would but take lessons in strategy, say, from France, their unpleasant duties would be so much more acceptably performed, with much less discomfort to their victims."

"France," snorted Hale in derision, "why, they call a man guilty there until he's proven innocent."

"Yes, Mr. Hale, and the same seems to be the case in Imperial Flats. You have quite made up your mind that Mr. Summertrees is guilty, and will not be content until he proves his innocence. I venture to predict that you will hear from him before long in a manner that may astonish you."

Hale grunted and looked at his watch. The minutes passed very slowly as we sat there smoking and at last even I began to get uneasy. Macpherson, seeing our anxiety, said that when he came in the fog was almost as thick as it had been the week before, and that there might be some difficulty in getting a cab. Just as he was speaking the door was unlocked from the outside, and Podgers entered, bearing a thick volume in his hand. This he gave to his superior, who turned over its pages in amazement, and then looked at the back, crying:

"*Encyclopedia of Sport, 1893!* What sort of a joke is this, Mr. Macpherson?"

There was a pained look on Mr. Macpherson's face as he reached forward and took the book. He said with a sigh:

"If you had allowed me to telephone, Mr. Hale, I should have made it perfectly plain to Summertrees what was wanted. I might have known this mistake was liable to occur. There is an increasing demand for out-of-date books of sport, and no doubt Mr. Summertrees thought this was what I meant. There is nothing for it but to send your man back to Park Lane and tell Mr. Summertrees that what we want is the locked volume of accounts for 1893, which we call the encyclopedia. Allow me to write an order that will bring it. Oh, I'll show you what I have written before your man takes it," he said, as Hale stood ready to look over his shoulder.

On my note paper he dashed off a request such as he had outlined, and handed it to Hale, who read it and gave it to Podgers.

"Take that to Summertrees, and get back as quickly as possible. Have you a cab at the door?"

"Yes, sir."

"Is it foggy outside?"

"Not so much, sir, as it was an hour ago. No difficulty about the traffic now, sir."

"Very well, get back as soon as you can."

Podgers saluted, and left with the book under his arm. Again the door was locked, and again we sat smoking in silence until the stillness was broken by the tinkle of the telephone. Hale put the receiver to his ear.

"Yes, this is the Imperial Flats. Yes. Valmont. Oh, yes; Macpherson is here. What? Out of what? Can't hear you. Out of print. What, the encyclopedia's out of print? Who is that speaking? Dr. Willoughby; thanks."

Macpherson rose as if he would go to the telephone, but instead (and he acted so quietly that I did not notice what he was doing until the thing was done) he picked up the sheet which he called his visiting list, and walking quite without haste, held it in the glowing coals of the fireplace until it disappeared in a flash of flame up the chimney. I sprang to my feet indignant, but too late to make even a motion toward saving the sheet. Macpherson regarded us both with that self-depreciatory smile which had several times lighted up his face.

"How dared you burn that sheet?" I demanded.

"Because, Monsieur Valmont, it did not belong to you; because you do not belong to Scotland Yard; because you stole it; because you had no right to it; and because you have no official standing in this country. If it had been in Mr. Hale's possession I should not have dared, as you put it, to destroy the sheet, but as this sheet was abstracted from my master's premises by you, an entirely unauthorized person, whom he would have been justified in shooting dead if he had found you housebreaking, and you had resisted him on his discovery, I took the liberty of destroying the document. I have always held that these sheets should not have been kept, for, as has been the case, if they fell under the scrutiny of so intelligent a person as Eugène Valmont, improper inferences might have been drawn. Mr. Summertrees, however, persisted in keeping them, but made this concession, that if I ever telegraphed him or telephoned him the word 'Encyclopedia,' he would at once burn these records, and he, on his part, was to telegraph or telephone to me 'The encyclopedia is out of print,' whereupon I would know that he had succeeded.

"Now, gentlemen, open this door, which will save me the trouble of forcing it. Either put me formally under arrest, or cease to restrict my liberty. I am very much obliged to Mr. Hale for telephoning, and I have made no protest to so gallant a host as Monsieur Valmont is, because of the locked door. However, the farce is now terminated. The proceedings I have sat through were entirely illegal, and if you will pardon me, Mr. Hale, they have been a little too French to down here in old England, or to make a report in the newspapers that would be quite satisfactory to your chiefs. I demand either my formal arrest, or the unlocking of that door."

In silence, I pressed a button, and my man threw open the door. Macpherson walked to the threshold, paused, and looked back at Spenser Hale, who sat there silent as a sphinx.

"Good evening, Mr. Hale."

There being no reply, he turned to me with the same ingratiating smile:

"Good evening, Monsieur Eugène Valmont," he said, "I shall give myself the pleasure of calling next Wednesday at six for my five shillings."

THE INVISIBLE MAN*

G. K. CHESTERTON
(1874–1936)

For all his intellectual activity, G. K. Chesterton is read today mainly as a writer of detective stories, especially those involving Father Brown, the gentle Roman Catholic priest who views wrongdoers not as criminals to be brought to justice and punished but as souls needing salvation. Based on Father John O'Connor, a real-life clergyman whom Chesterton knew, he has been portrayed in the movies by Walter Connolly (in 1934) and Alec Guinness (in 1954).

IN THE COOL BLUE TWILIGHT of two steep streets in Camden Town, the shop at the corner, a confectioner's, glowed like the butt of a firework, for the light was of many colours and some complexity, broken up by many mirrors and dancing on many gilt and gaily-coloured cakes and sweetmeats. Against this one fiery glass were glued the noses of many gutter-snipes, for the chocolates were all wrapped in those red and gold and green metallic colours which are almost better than chocolate itself; and the huge white wedding-cake in the window was somehow at once remote and satisfying, just as if the whole North Pole were good to eat. Such rainbow provocations could naturally collect the youth of the neighbourhood up to the ages of ten or twelve. But this corner was also attractive to youth at a later stage; and a young man, not less than twenty-four, was staring into the same shop window. To him, also, the shop was of fiery charm, but this attraction was not wholly to be explained by chocolates; which, however, he was far from despising.

He was a tall, burly, red-haired young man, with a resolute face but a listless manner. He carried under his arm a flat, grey portfolio of black-and-white sketches, which he had sold with more or less success to publishers ever since his uncle (who was an admiral) had disinherited him for Socialism, because of a lecture which he had delivered against that economic theory. His name was John Turnbull Angus.[1]

---

* How could a murderer enter the victim's apartment in daylight and remove his body without being seen? This is perhaps the best known, most anthologized of all Father Brown stories. It first appeared, with pictures by Sidney Lucas, in *Cassell's Magazine* (February 1911).

[1] This young red-haired Scotsman may be a relative of James Turnbull, the Scottish atheist in Chesterton's fantasy *The Ball and the Cross*.

Entering at last, he walked through the confectioner's shop into the back room, which was a sort of pastry-cook restaurant, merely raising his hat to the young lady who was serving there. She was a dark, elegant, alert girl in black, with a high colour and very quick, dark eyes; and after the ordinary interval she followed him into the inner room to take his order.

His order was evidently a usual one. 'I want, please,' he said with precision, 'one halfpenny bun and a small cup of black coffee.' An instant before the girl could turn away he added, 'Also, I want you to marry me.'

The young lady of the shop stiffened suddenly, and said, 'Those are jokes I don't allow.'[2]

The red-haired young man lifted grey eyes of an unexpected gravity.

'Really and truly,' he said, 'it's as serious—as serious as the halfpenny bun. It is expensive, like the bun; one pays for it. It is indigestible, like the bun. It hurts.'

The dark young lady had never taken her dark eyes off him, but seemed to be studying him with almost tragic exactitude. At the end of her scrutiny she had something like the shadow of a smile, and she sat down in a chair.

'Don't you think,' observed Angus, absently, 'that it's rather cruel to eat these halfpenny buns? They might grow up into penny buns. I shall give up these brutal sports when we are married.'

The dark young lady rose from her chair and walked to the window, evidently in a state of strong but unsympathetic cogitation. When at last she swung round again with an air of resolution she was bewildered to observe that the young man was carefully laying out on the table various objects from the shop window. They included a pyramid of highly coloured sweets, several plates of sandwiches, and the two decanters containing that mysterious port and sherry which are peculiar to pastry-cooks. In the middle of this neat arrangement he had carefully let down the enormous load of white sugared cake which had been the huge ornament of the window.

'What on earth are you doing?' she asked.

'Duty, my dear Laura,' he began.

'Oh, for Lord's sake, stop a minute,' she cried, 'and don't talk to me in that way. I mean, what is all that?'

'A ceremonial meal, Miss Hope.'

'And what is *that*?' she asked impatiently, pointing to the mountain of sugar.

'The wedding-cake, Mrs. Angus,' he said.

The girl marched to that article, removed it with some clatter, and put it back in the shop window; she then returned, and, putting her elegant elbows on the table, regarded the young man not unfavourably but with considerable exasperation.

'You don't give me any time to think,' she said.

'I'm not such a fool,' he answered; 'that's my Christian humility.'

She was still looking at him; but she had grown considerably graver behind the smile. 'Mr Angus,' she said steadily, 'before there is a minute more of this nonsense I must tell you something about myself as shortly as I can.'

'Delighted,' replied Angus gravely. 'You might tell me something about myself, too, while you are about it.'

'Oh, do hold your tongue and listen,' she said. 'It's nothing that I'm ashamed of,

---

2   In the magazine text Chesterton adds that the woman made her remark 'with a snap of her black eyes.'

and it isn't even anything that I'm specially sorry about. But what would you say if there were something that is no business of mine and yet is my nightmare?'

'In that case,' said the man seriously, 'I should suggest that you bring back the cake.'

'Well, you must listen to the story first,' said Laura, persistently. 'To begin with, I must tell you that my father owned the inn called the "Red Fish" at Ludbury,[3] and I used to serve people in the bar.'

'I have often wondered,' he said, 'why there was a kind of a Christian air about this one confectioner's shop.'

'Ludbury is a sleepy, grassy little hole in the Eastern Counties, and the only kind of people who ever came to the "Red Fish" were occasional commercial travellers, and for the rest, the most awful people you can see, only you've never seen them. I mean little, loungy men, who had just enough to live on and had nothing to do but lean about in bar-rooms and bet on horses, in bad clothes that were just too good for them. Even these wretched young rotters were not very common at our house; but there were two of them that were a lot too common—common in every sort of way. They both lived on money of their own, and were wearisomely idle and over-dressed. But yet I was a bit sorry for them, because I half believe they slunk into our little empty bar because each of them had a slight deformity; the sort of thing that some yokels laugh at. It wasn't exactly a deformity either; it was more an oddity. One of them was a surprisingly small man, something like a dwarf, or at least like a jockey. He was not at all jockeyish to look at, though; he had a round black head and a well-trimmed black beard, bright eyes like a bird's; he jingled money in his pockets; he jangled a great gold watch chain; and he never turned up except dressed just too much like a gentleman to be one. He was no fool though, though a futile idler; he was curiously clever at all kinds of things that couldn't be the slightest use; a sort of impromptu conjuring; making fifteen matches set fire to each other like a regular firework; or cutting a banana or some such thing into a dancing doll. His name was Isidore Smythe; and I can see him still, with his little dark face, just coming up to the counter, making a jumping kangaroo out of five cigars.

'The other fellow was more silent and more ordinary; but somehow he alarmed me much more than poor little Smythe. He was very tall and slight, and light-haired; his nose had a high bridge, and he might almost have been handsome in a spectral sort of way; but he had one of the most appalling squints I have ever seen or heard of. When he looked straight at you, you didn't know where you were yourself, let alone what he was looking at. I fancy this sort of disfigurement embittered the poor chap a little; for while Smythe was ready to show off his monkey tricks anywhere, James Welkin (that was the squinting man's name) never did anything except soak in our bar parlour, and go for great walks by himself in the flat, grey country all round. All the same, I think Smythe, too, was a little sensitive about being so small, though he carried it off more smartly. And so it was that I was really puzzled, as well as startled, and very sorry, when they both offered to marry me in the same week.

'Well, I did what I've since thought was perhaps a silly thing. But, after all, these

---

[3]   Chesterton invented the name of Ludbury, but in the story's magazine form it is Sudbury, an actual town on the River Stour in Suffolk. The famous English painter John Gainsborough was born in Sudbury and for a time lived there. Chesterton may have disguised the name because he described some unpleasant characters who frequented one of the town's inns. I assume that the inn's name, The Red Fish, was also invented by G.K.

freaks were my friends in a way; and I had a horror of their thinking I refused them for the real reason, which was that they were so impossibly ugly. So I made up some gas of another sort, about never meaning to marry anyone who hadn't carved his way in the world. I said it was a point of principle with me not to live on money that was just inherited like theirs. Two days after I had talked in this well-meaning sort of way, the whole trouble began. The first thing I heard was that both of them had gone off to seek their fortunes, as if they were in some silly fairy tale.

'Well, I've never seen either of them from that day to this. But I've had two letters from the little man called Smythe, and really they were rather exciting.'

'Ever heard of the other man?' asked Angus.

'No, he never wrote,' said the girl, after an instant's hesitation. 'Smythe's first letter was simply to say that he had started out walking with Welkin to London; but Welkin was such a good walker that the little man dropped out of it, and took a rest by the roadside. He happened to be picked up by some travelling show, and, partly because he was nearly a dwarf, and partly because he was really a clever little wretch, he got on quite well in the show business, and was soon sent up to the Aquarium, to do some tricks that I forget. That was his first letter. His second was much more of a startler, and I only got it last week.'

The man called Angus emptied his coffee-cup and regarded her with mild and patient eyes. Her own mouth took a slight twist of laughter as she resumed, 'I suppose you've seen on the hoardings[4] all about this "Smythe's Silent Service"? Or you must be the only person that hasn't. Oh, I don't know much about it, it's some clockwork invention[5] for doing all the housework by machinery. You know the sort of thing: "Press a button—A Butler who Never Drinks." "Turn a Handle—Ten Housemaids who Never Flirt." You must have seen the advertisements. Well, whatever these machines are, they are making pots of money; and they are making it all for that little imp whom I knew down in Ludbury. I can't help feeling pleased the poor little chap has fallen on his feet; but the plain fact is, I'm in terror of his turning up any minute and telling me he's carved his way in the world—as he certainly has.'

'And the other man?' repeated Angus with a sort of obstinate quietude.

Laura Hope got to her feet suddenly. 'My friend,' she said, 'I think you are a witch. Yes, you are quite right. I have not seen a line of the other man's writing; and I have no more notion than the dead of what or where he is. But it is of him that I

---

4 'Hoardings' is a British term for a board fence on which bills and advertisements are posted.
5 In Chesterton's time no one anticipated electronic, computer-controlled machines; the best G.K. could imagine was an elaborate clockwork robot similar to L. Frank Baum's Tik-Tok of Oz except it was headless. Had anyone suggested that before the century was over robots would be constructing cars, Chesterton would have been incredulous. Today the 'butler who never drinks' and the 'housemaid who never flirts' are no more impossible than the automated factory workers who never tire or go on strike.

The headless robots of G.K.'s story are, of course, symbols of how some members of the upper classes look upon their servants, seeing them as little more than useful machines, faceless robots with no individuality. This heartless tendency not to comprehend the complexity of simple, ordinary people returns as a theme in one of the best of the later Father Brown stories, 'The Blast of the Book' (*The Scandal of Father Brown*). The tale is about an erudite professor who is easily hoodwinked by his clerk Berridge. The professor liked to call him Babbage (after Charles Babbage, inventor of a pioneering mechanical computer) because he considered Berridge no more than an inhuman 'calculating machine'.

am frightened. It is he who is all about my path. It is he who has half driven me mad. Indeed, I think he had driven me mad; for I have felt him where he could not have been, and I have heard his voice when he could not have spoken.'

'Well, my dear,' said the young man, cheerfully, 'if he were Satan himself, he is done for now you have told somebody. One goes mad all alone, old girl. But when was it you fancied you felt and heard our squinting friend?'

'I hear James Welkin laugh as plainly as I hear you speak,' said the girl, steadily. 'There was nobody there, for I stood just outside the shop at the corner, and could see down both streets at once. I had forgotten how he laughed, though his laugh was as odd as his squint. I had not thought of him for nearly a year. But it's a solemn truth that a few seconds later the first letter came from his rival.'

'Did you ever make the spectre speak or squeak, or anything?' asked Angus, with some interest.

Laura suddenly shuddered, and then said, with an unshaken voice, 'Yes. Just when I had finished reading the second letter from Isidore Smythe announcing his success, just then, I heard Welkin say, "He shan't have you, though." It was quite plain, as if he were in the room. It is awful; I think I must be mad.'

'If you really were mad,' said the young man, 'you would think you must be sane. But certainly there seems to me to be something a little rum about this unseen gentleman. Two heads are better than one—I spare you allusions to any other organs— and really, if you would allow me, as a sturdy, practical man, to bring back the wedding-cake out of the window—'

Even as he spoke, there was a sort of steely shriek in the street outside, and a small motor, driven at devilish speed, shot up to the door of the shop and stuck there. In the same flash of time a small man in a shiny top hat stood stamping in the outer room.

Angus, who had hitherto maintained hilarious ease from motives of mental hygiene, revealed the strain of his soul by striding abruptly out of the inner room and confronting the newcomer. A glance at him was quite sufficient to confirm the savage guesswork of a man in love. This very dapper but dwarfish figure, with the spike of black beard carried insolently forward, the clever unrestful eyes, the neat but very nervous fingers, could be none other than the man just described to him: Isidore Smythe, who made dolls out of banana skins and match-boxes; Isidore Smythe, who made millions out of undrinking butlers and unflirting housemaids of metal. For a moment the two men, instinctively understanding each other's air of possession, looked at each other with that curious cold generosity which is the soul of rivalry.[6]

Mr Smythe, however, made no allusion to the ultimate ground of their antagonism, but said simply and explosively, 'Has Miss Hope seen that thing on the window?'

'On the window?' repeated the staring Angus.

'There's no time to explain other things,' said the small millionaire shortly. 'There's some tomfoolery going on here that has to be investigated.'

He pointed his polished walking-stick at the window, recently depleted by the bridal preparations of Mr Angus; and that gentleman was astonished to see along the front of the glass a long strip of paper pasted, which had certainly not been on the window when he had looked through it some time before. Following the energetic Smythe outside into the street, he found that some yard and a half of stamp

---

[6] In *Cassell's Magazine* Chesterton added to this sentence: 'and goes down to the roots of the soul.'

paper[7] had been carefully gummed along the glass outside, and on this was written in straggly characters, 'If you marry Smythe, he will die.'

'Laura,' said Angus, putting his big red head into the shop, 'you're not mad.'

'It's the writing of that fellow Welkin,' said Smythe gruffly. 'I haven't seen him for years, but he's always bothering me. Five times in the last fortnight he's had threatening letters left at my flat, and I can't even find out who leaves them, let alone if it is Welkin himself. The porter of the flats swears that no suspicious characters have been seen, and here he has pasted up a sort of dado[8] on a public shop window, while the people in the shop—'

'Quite so,' said Angus modestly, 'while the people in the shop were having tea. Well, sir, I can assure you I appreciate your common sense in dealing so directly with the matter. We can talk about other things afterwards. The fellow cannot be very far off yet, for I swear there was no paper there when I went last to the window, ten or fifteen minutes ago. On the other hand, he's too far off to be chased, as we don't even know the direction. If you'll take my advice, Mr Smythe, you'll put this at once in the hands of some energetic inquiry man, private rather than public. I know an extremely clever fellow, who has set up in business five minutes from here in your car. His name's Flambeau, and though his youth was a bit stormy, he's a strictly honest man now, and his brains are worth money.[9] He lives in Lucknow Mansions, Hampstead.'

'That is odd,' said the little man, arching his black eyebrows. 'I live, myself, in Himalaya Mansions, round the corner. Perhaps you might care to come with me; I can go to my rooms and sort out these queer Welkin documents, while you run round and get your friend the detective.'

'You are very good,' said Angus politely. 'Well, the sooner we act the better.'

Both men, with a queer kind of impromptu fairness, took the same sort of formal farewell of the lady, and both jumped into the brisk little car. As Smythe took the handles and they turned the great corner of the street, Angus was amused to see a gigantesque poster of 'Smythe's Silent Service,' with a picture of a huge headless iron doll, carrying a saucepan with legend, 'A Cook Who is Never Cross.'

'I use them in my own flat,' said the little black-bearded man, laughing, 'partly for advertisement, and partly for real convenience. Honestly, and all above board, those big clockwork dolls of mine do bring you coals or claret or a time-table quicker than any live servants I've ever known, if you know which knob to press. But I'll never deny, between ourselves, that such servants have their disadvantages, too.'

'Indeed?' said Angus; 'is there something they can't do?'

---

[7] Stamp paper is the blank marginal paper on sheets of postage stamps, often used at the time as paper sticking tape.

[8] Dado: 'Any lining, painting, or papering of the lower part of an interior wall, of a different material or colour from that of the upper part' (*OED*).

[9] Flambeau's business is that of private detective, and his office (we learn in later stories) is in Westminster across from the Abbey. His specialty is catching jewel thieves. On one occasion ('The Insoluble Problem,' the last story in the last Father Brown book) 'he had torn the tiara of the Duchess of Dulwich out of the very hand of the bandit as he bolted through the garden.' Indeed, his exploits as a crime investigator soon rival in flamboyance some of his youthful crimes. 'He laid so ingenious a trap for the criminal who planned to carry off the celebrated Sapphire Necklace,' to continue the above quote, 'that the artist in question actually carried off the copy which he had himself planned to leave as a substitute.'

'Yes,' replied Smythe coolly; 'they can't tell me who left those threatening letters at my flat.'

The man's motor was small and swift like himself; in fact, like his domestic service, it was of his own invention. If he was an advertising quack, he was one who believed in his own wares. The sense of something tiny and flying was accentuated as they swept up long white curves of road in the dead but open daylight of evening. Soon the white curves came sharper and dizzier; they were upon ascending spirals, as they say in the modern religions. For, indeed, they were cresting a corner of London which is almost as precipitous as Edinburgh, if not quite so picturesque. Terrace rose above terrace, and the special tower of flats they sought rose above them all to almost Egyptian height, gilt by the level sunset. The change, as they turned the corner and entered the crescent known as Himalaya Mansions, was as abrupt as the opening of a window; for they found that pile of flats sitting above London as above a green sea of slate. Opposite to the mansions, on the other side of the gravel crescent, was a bushy enclosure more like a steep hedge or dyke than a garden, and some way below that ran a strip of artificial water, a sort of canal, like the moat of that embowered fortress. As the car swept round the crescent it passed, at one corner, the stray stall of a man selling chestnuts; and right away at the other end of the curve, Angus could see a dim blue policeman walking slowly. These were the only human shapes in that high suburban solitude; but he had an irrational sense that they expressed the speechless poetry of London. He felt as if they were figures in a story.

The little car shot up to the right house like a bullet, and shot out its owner like a bomb shell. He was immediately inquiring of a tall commissionaire in shining braid, and a short porter in shirt sleeves, whether anybody or anything had been seeking his apartments. He was assured that nobody and nothing had passed these officials since his last inquiries; whereupon he and the slightly bewildered Angus were shot up in the lift like a rocket, till they reached the top floor.

'Just come in for a minute,' said the breathless Smythe. 'I want to show you those Welkin letters. Then you might run round the corner and fetch your friend.' He pressed a button concealed in the wall, and the door opened of itself.

It opened on a long, commodious ante-room, of which the only arresting features, ordinarily speaking, were the rows of tall half-human mechanical figures that stood up on both sides like tailors' dummies. Like tailors' dummies they were headless; and like tailors' dummies they had a handsome unnecessary humpiness in the shoulders, and a pigeon-breasted protuberance of chest; but barring this, they were not much more like a human figure than any automatic machine at a station that is about the human height. They had two great hooks like arms, for carrying trays; and they were painted pea-green, or vermilion, or black for convenience of distinction; in every other way they were only automatic machines and nobody would have looked twice at them. On this occasion, at least, nobody did. For between the two rows of these domestic dummies lay something more interesting than most of the mechanics of the world. It was a white, tattered scrap of paper scrawled with red ink; and the agile inventor had snatched it up almost as soon as the door flew open. He handed it to Angus without a word. The red ink on it actually was not dry, and the message ran, 'If you have been to see her today, I shall kill you.'

There was a short silence, and then Isidore Smythe said quietly, 'Would you like a little whisky? I rather feel as if I should.'

'Thank you; I should like a little Flambeau,'[10] said Angus, gloomily. 'This business seems to me to be getting rather grave. I'm going around at once to fetch him.'

'Right you are,' said the other, with admirable cheerfulness. 'Bring him round here as quick as you can.'

But as Angus closed the front door behind him he saw Smythe push back a button, and one of the clockwork images glided from its place and slid along a groove in the floor carrying a tray with syphon and decanter. There did seem something a trifle weird about leaving the little man alone among those dead servants, who were coming to life as the door closed.

Six steps from Smythe's landing the man in shirt sleeves was doing something with a pail. Angus stopped to extract a promise, fortified with a prospective bribe, that he would remain in that place until the return with the detective, and would keep count of any kind of stranger coming up those stairs. Dashing down to the front hall he then laid similar charges of vigilance on the commissionaire at the front door, from whom he learned the simplifying circumstance that there was no back door. Not content with this, he captured the floating policeman and induced him to stand opposite the entrance and watch it; and finally paused an instant for a pennyworth of chestnuts, and an inquiry as to the probable length of the merchant's stay in the neighbourhood.

The chestnut seller, turning up the collar of his coat, told him he should probably be moving shortly, as he thought it was going to snow. Indeed, the evening was growing grey and bitter, but Angus, with all his eloquence, proceeded to nail the chestnut man to his post.

'Keep yourself warm on your own chestnuts,' he said earnestly. 'Eat up your whole stock; I'll make it worth your while. I'll give you a sovereign if you'll wait here till I come back, and then tell me whether any man, woman, or child has gone into that house where the commissionaire is standing.'

He then walked away smartly, with a last look at the besieged tower.

'I've made a ring round that room, anyhow,' he said. 'They can't all four of them be Mr Welkin's accomplices.'

Lucknow Mansions were, so to speak, on a lower platform of that hill of houses, of which Himalaya Mansions might be called the peak. Mr Flambeau's semi-official flat was on the ground floor, and presented in every way a marked contrast to the American machinery and cold hotel-like luxury of the flat of the Silent Service. Flambeau, who was a friend of Angus, received him in a rococo artistic den behind his office, of which the ornaments were sabres, harquebuses,[11] Eastern curiosities, flasks of Italian wine, savage cooking-pots, a plumy Persian cat, and a small dusty-looking Roman Catholic priest, who looked particularly out of place.

'This is my friend Father Brown,' said Flambeau. 'I've often wanted you to meet him. Splendid weather, this; a little cold for Southerners like me.'

'Yes, I think it will keep clear,' said Angus, sitting down on a violet-striped Eastern ottoman.

'No,' said the priest quietly, 'it has begun to snow.'

And, indeed, as he spoke, the first few flakes, foreseen by the man of chestnuts, began to drift across the darkening windowpane.

---

[10] I take it that Angus means he wants some light shed on the situation.

[11] 'Harquebuses' comes from the German 'hook-gun', a sixteenth-century military gun. Too heavy to be held, it was supported on a tripod or some similar device. A hook on the barrel allowed it to be attached to its support.

'Well,' said Angus heavily. 'I'm afraid I've come on business, and rather jumpy business at that. The fact is, Flambeau, within a stone's throw of your house is a fellow who badly wants your help; he's perpetually being haunted and threatened by an invisible enemy—a scoundrel whom nobody has even seen.' As Angus proceeded to tell the whole tale of Smythe and Welkin, beginning with Laura's story, and going on with his own, the supernatural laugh at the corner of two empty streets, the strange distinct words spoken in an empty room, Flambeau grew more and more vividly concerned, and the little priest seemed to be left out of it, like a piece of furniture. When it came to the scribbled stamp paper pasted on the window, Flambeau rose, seeming to fill the room with his huge shoulders.

'If you don't mind,' he said, 'I think you had better tell me the rest of the nearest road to this man's house. It strikes me, somehow, that there is no time to be lost.'

'Delighted,' said Angus, rising also, 'though he's safe enough for the present, for I've set four men to watch the only hole to his burrow.'

They turned out into the street, the small priest trundling after them with the docility of a small dog. He merely said, in a cheerful way, like one making conversation, 'How quick the snow gets thick on the ground.'

As they threaded the steep side streets already powdered with silver, Angus finished his story; and by the time they reached the crescent with the towering flat, he had leisure to turn his attention to the four sentinels. The chestnut seller, both before and after receiving a sovereign, swore stubbornly that he had watched the door and seen no visitor enter. The policeman was even more emphatic. He said he had had experience of crooks of all kinds, in top hats and in rags; he wasn't so green as to expect suspicious characters to look suspicious; he looked out for anybody, and, so help him, there had been nobody. And when all three men gathered round the gilded commissionaire, who still stood smiling astride of the porch, the verdict was more final still.

'I've got a right to ask any man, duke or dustman, what he wants in these flats,' said the genial and gold-laced giant, 'and I'll swear there's been nobody to ask since this gentleman went away.'

The unimportant Father Brown, who stood back, looking modestly at the pavement, here ventured to say meekly, 'Has nobody been up and down stairs, then, since the snow began to fall? It began while we were all round at Flambeau's.'

'Nobody's been in here, sir, you can take it from me,' said the official, with beaming authority.

'Then I wonder what that is?' said the priest, and stared at the ground blankly like a fish.

The others all looked down also; and Flambeau used a fierce exclamation and a French gesture. For it was unquestionably true that down the middle of the entrance guarded by the man in gold lace, actually between the arrogant, stretched legs of that colossus, ran a stringy pattern of grey footprints stamped upon the white snow.

'God!' cried Angus involuntarily, 'the Invisible Man!'[12]

Without another word he turned and dashed up the stairs, with Flambeau following;

---

[12] When Chesterton entitled this story he may have had in mind the popular short novel (1897) of the same title by his friend and antagonist H. G. Wells. Ralph Ellison's 1925 novel, *Invisible Man,* has a theme essentially the same as G.K.'s story. Ellison's black protagonist is a man who loses his identity, becoming as invisible to blacks as he is to whites.

(continued on next page)

but Father Brown still stood looking about him in the snowclad street as if he had lost interest in his query.

Flambeau was plainly in a mood to break down the door with his big shoulder; but the Scotsman, with more reason, if less intuition, fumbled about on the frame of the door till he found the invisible button; and the door swung slowly open.

It showed substantially the same serried interior;[13] the hall had grown darker, though it was still struck here and there with the last crimson shafts of sunset, and one or two of the headless machines had been moved from their places for this or that purpose, and stood here and there about the twilit place. The green and red of their coats were all darkened in the dusk; and their likeness to human shapes slightly increased by their very shapelessness. But in the middle of them all, exactly where the paper with the red ink had lain, there lay something that looked very like red ink spilt out of its bottle. But it was not red ink.

With a French combination of reason and violence Flambeau simply said 'Murder!' and, plunging into the flat, had explored every corner and cupboard of it in five minutes. But if he expected to find a corpse he found none. Isidore Smythe simply was not in the place, either dead or alive. After the most tearing search the two men met each other in the outer hall, with streaming faces and staring eyes. 'My friend,' said Flambeau, talking French in his excitement, 'not only is your murderer invisible, but he makes invisible also the murdered man.'

Angus looked round at the dim room full of dummies, and in some Celtic corner of his Scotch soul a shudder started. One of the life-size dolls stood immediately overshadowing the blood stain, summoned, perhaps, by the slain man an instant before he fell. One of the high-shouldered hooks that served the thing for arms, was a little lifted, and Angus had suddenly the horrid fancy that poor Smythe's own iron child had struck him down. Matter had rebelled, and these machines had killed their master.[14] But even so, what had they done with him?

'Eaten him?' said the nightmare at his ear; and he sickened for an instant at the idea of rent, human remains absorbed and crushed into all that acephalous clockwork.

He recovered his mental health by an emphatic effort, and said to Flambeau, 'Well, there it is. The poor fellow has evaporated like a cloud and left a red streak on the floor. The tale does not belong to this world.'

'There is only one thing to be done,' said Flambeau, 'whether it belongs to this world or the other, I must go down and talk to my friend.'

---

12 (continued) Chesterton's story is often likened to Poe's 'The Purloined Letter', in which an important document is concealed by putting it in a spot too obvious to be noticed by the police.

I must add an anecdote about the renowned physicist Eugene Wigner that involves a brown sack like the postman's—though one of paper, not cloth. When Enrico Fermi obtained the first nuclear chain reaction in a laboratory under the University of Chicago's football stadium, Wigner suddenly produced a bottle of wine to celebrate. Because no one had seen him carry in a bottle, the wine seemed to appear by magic. Some of those present thought he had concealed the bottle for hours under his jacket. I once had the pleasure of asking Wigner how he had performed this miracle. He laughed, reminded me of Poe's story, and said he had brought the bottle in an ordinary brown paper sack which he simply placed unobtrusively aside until he needed it.

13 'Serried' is commonly used to describe ranks of soldiers who stand shoulder to shoulder.

14 Chesterton probably had in mind the famous story by Ambrose Bierce, 'Moxon's Master', in which an angry clockwork chess machine kills its inventor after losing a game.

They descended, passing the man with the pail, who again asseverated that he had let no intruder pass, down to the commissionaire and the hovering chestnut man, who rigidly reasserted their own watchfulness. But when Angus looked round for his fourth confirmation he could not see it, and called out with some nervousness, 'Where is the policeman?'

'I beg your pardon,' said Father Brown; 'that is my fault. I just sent him down the road to investigate something—that I just thought worth investigating.'

'Well, we want him back pretty soon,' said Angus abruptly, 'for the wretched man upstairs has not only been murdered, but wiped out.'

'How?' asked the priest.

'Father,' said Flambeau, after a pause, 'upon my soul I believe it is more in your department than mine. No friend or foe has entered the house, but Smythe is gone, as if stolen by the fairies. If that is not supernatural, I—'

As he spoke they were all checked by an unusual sight; the big blue policeman came round the corner of the crescent, running. He came straight up to Brown.

'You're right, sir,' he panted, 'they've just found poor Mr Smythe's body in the canal down below.'

Angus put his hand wildly to his head. 'Did he run down and drown himself?' he asked.

'He never came down, I'll swear,' said the constable, 'and he wasn't drowned either, for he died of a great stab over the heart.'

'And yet you saw no one enter?' said Flambeau in a grave voice.

'Let us walk down the road a little,' said the priest.

As they reached the other end of the crescent he observed abruptly, 'Stupid of me! I forgot to ask the policeman something. I wonder if they found a light brown sack.'

'Why a light brown sack?' asked Angus, astonished.

'Because if it was any other coloured sack, the case must begin over again,' said Father Brown; 'but if it was a light brown sack, why, the case is finished.'

'I am pleased to hear it,' said Angus with hearty irony. 'It hasn't begun, so far as I am concerned.'

'You must tell us all about it,' said Flambeau with a strange heavy simplicity, like a child.

Unconsciously they were walking with quickening steps down the long sweep of road on the other side of the high crescent, Father Brown leading briskly, though in silence. At last he said with an almost touching vagueness, 'Well, I'm afraid you'll think it so prosy. We always begin at the abstract end of things, and you can't begin this story anywhere else.

'Have you ever noticed this—that people never answer what you say? They answer what you mean—or what they think you mean. Suppose one lady says to another in a country house, "Is anybody staying with you?" the lady doesn't answer "Yes; the butler, the three footmen, the parlourmaid, and so on," though the parlourmaid may be in the room, or the butler behind her chair. She says "There is *nobody* staying with us," meaning nobody of the sort you mean. But suppose a doctor inquiring into an epidemic asks, "Who is staying in the house?" then the lady will remember the butler, parlourmaid, and the rest. All language is used like that; you never get a question answered literally, even when you get it answered truly. When those four quite honest men said that no man had gone into the Mansions, they did not really mean that *no man* had gone into them. They meant no man whom they could suspect of being your man. A man did go into the house, and did come out of it, but they never noticed him.'

'An invisible man?' inquired Angus, raising his red eyebrows.

'A mentally invisible man,' said Father Brown.

A minute or two after he resumed in the same unassuming voice, like a man thinking his way. 'Of course you can't think of such a man, until you do think of him. That's where his cleverness comes in. But I came to think of him through two or three little things in the tale Mr Angus told us. First, there was the fact that this Welkin went for long walks. And then there was the vast lot of stamp paper on the window. And then, most of all, there were the two things the young lady said—things that couldn't be true. Don't get annoyed,' he added hastily, noting a sudden movement of the Scotsman's head; 'she thought they were true all right, but they couldn't be true. A person can't be quite alone in a street when she starts reading a letter just received. There must be somebody pretty near her; he must be mentally invisible.'

'Why must there be somebody near her?' asked Angus.

'Because,' said Father Brown, 'barring carrier-pigeons, somebody must have brought her the letter.'

'Do you really mean to say,' asked Flambeau, with energy, 'that Welkin carried his rival's letters to his lady?'

'Yes,' said the priest. 'Welkin carried his rival's letters to his lady. You see, he had to.'

'Oh, I can't stand much more of this,' exploded Flambeau. 'Who is this fellow? What does he look like? What is the usual get-up of a mentally invisible man?'

'He is dressed rather handsomely in red, blue and gold,' replied the priest promptly with precision, 'and in this striking, and even showy, costume he entered Himalaya Mansions under eight human eyes; he killed Smythe in cold blood, and came down into the street again carrying the dead body in his arms—'

'Reverend sir,' cried Angus, standing still, 'are you raving mad, or am I?'

'You are not mad,' said Brown, 'only a little unobservant. You have not noticed such a man as this, for example.'

He took three quick strides forward, and put his hand on the shoulder of an ordinary passing postman who had bustled by them unnoticed under the shade of the trees.

'Nobody ever notices postmen somehow,' he said thoughtfully; 'yet they have passions like other men, and even carry large bags where a small corpse can be stowed quite easily.'

The postman, instead of turning naturally, had ducked and tumbled against the garden fence. He was a lean fair-bearded man of very ordinary appearance, but as he turned an alarmed face over his shoulder, all three men were fixed with an almost fiendish squint.

⨏⨏

Flambeau went back to his sabres, purple rugs and Persian cat, having many things to attend to. John Turnbull Angus went back to the lady at the shop, with whom that imprudent young man contrives to be extremely comfortable. But Father Brown walked those snow-covered hills under the stars for many hours with a murderer, and what they said to each other will never be known.

Afterword

Perhaps a tiny midget could be stowed in a postman's bag, but a small man? This has often been cited as an example of unbelievable aspects of Father Brown plots.

'Surely no postman ever at any time carried a bag large enough to conceal even a small man's body,' writes Gertrude M. White in *The Chesterton Review* (May 1984).

In a later issue of the same magazine (May 1985) Bernard Bell disagreed. 'In those far-off days, the postman delivered both letters and parcels in a large mail bag, and he became the model for drawings of Santa Claus and his bag of goodies. Even I dimly remember that, when I was young, I used a surplus mail bag as a sleeping bag on weekend hikes.'

Not knowing anything about the size of bags carried by postmen in Edwardian London, I must leave this question open. In any case, the tale is clearly a semi-fantasy with an eternal moral. Servants and tradespeople with whom we come in frequent contact should never be invisible.

THE INFALLIBLE GODAHL

FREDERICK IRVING ANDERSON
(1877–1947)

One of the most popular writers for the Saturday Evening Post *when it was the top fiction magazine in the country, Anderson is remembered today, if at all, for his brilliant tales about Sophie Lang, the beautiful young jewel thief whose exploits were recounted in one book and three motion pictures, and the Infallible Godahl, who was such an effective criminal that he had never even been suspected of a crime, much less arrested for one.*

LIVER ARMISTON NEVER WAS much of a sportsman with a rod or gun—though he could do fancy work with a pistol in a shooting gallery. He had, however, one game from which he derived the utmost satisfaction. Whenever he went traveling, which was often, he invariably caught his trains by the tip of the tail, so to speak, and hung on till he could climb aboard. In other words he believed in close connections. He had a theory that more valuable dollars-and-cents time and good animal heat are wasted warming seats in stations waiting for trains than by missing them. The sum of joy to his methodical mind was to halt the slamming gates at the last fraction of the last second with majestic upraised hand, and to stroll aboard his parlor car with studied deliberation, while the train crew were gnashing their teeth in rage and swearing to get even with the gateman for letting him through.

Yet Mr Armiston never missed a train. A good many of them tried to miss him, but none ever succeeded. He reckoned time and distance so nicely that it really seemed as if his trains had nothing else half so important as waiting until Mr Oliver Armiston got aboard.

On this particular June day he was due in New Haven at two. If he failed to get there at two o'clock he could very easily arrive at three. But an hour is sixty minutes, and a minute is sixty seconds; and, further, Mr Armiston having passed his word that he would be there at two o'clock, surely would be.

On this particular day, by the time Armiston finally got to the Grand Central the train looked like an odds-on favourite. In the first place he was still in his bed at an hour when another and less experienced traveler would have been watching the clock in the station waiting room. In the second place, after kissing his wife in that absent-minded manner characteristic of true love, he became tangled in a Broadway traffic crush at the first corner. Scarcely was he extricated from this when he ran into a Socialist mass meeting at Union Square. It was due only to the wits of his chauffeur that the taxi-cab was extricated with very little damage to the surrounding human scenery. But our man of method did not fret. Instead he buried himself in his book, a treatise on Cause and Effect, which at that moment was lulling him with soothing sentiment:

'There is no such thing as accident. The so-called accidents of everyday life are due to the preordained action of correlated causes, which is inevitable and over which man has no control.'

This was comforting, but not much to the point, when Oliver Armiston looked up and discovered he had reached 23rd Street and had come to a halt. A sixty-foot truck, with an underslung burden consisting of a sixty-ton steel girder, had at this point suddenly developed weakness in its off hindwheel and settled down on the pavement across the right of way like a tired elephant. This, of course, was not an accident. It was due to a weakness in the construction of that wheel—a weakness that had from the beginning been destined to block street cars and taxicabs at this particular spot at this particular hour.

Mr Armiston dismounted and walked a block. Here he hailed a second taxicab and soon was spinning north again at a fair speed, albeit the extensive building operations in Fourth Avenue had made the street well-nigh impassable.

The roughness of the pavement merely shook up his digestive apparatus and gave it zest for the fine luncheon he was promising himself the minute he stepped aboard his train. His new chauffeur got lost three times in the maze of traffic about the Grand Central Station. This, however, was only human, seeing that the railroad company changed the map of 42nd Street every twenty-four hours during the course of the building of its new terminal.

Mr Armiston at length stepped from his taxicab, gave his grip to a porter and paid the driver from a huge roll of bills. This same roll was no sooner transferred back to his pocket than a nimble-fingered pickpocket removed it. This again was not an accident. That pickpocket had been waiting there for the last hour for that roll of bills. It was preordained, inevitable. And Oliver Armiston had just thirty seconds to catch his train by the tail and climb aboard. He smiled contentedly to himself.

It was not until he called for his ticket that he discovered his loss. For a full precious second he gazed at the hand that came away empty from his money pocket, and then:

'I find I left my purse at home,' he said with a grand air he knew how to assume on occasions. 'My name is Mr Oliver Armiston.'

Now Oliver Armiston was a name to conjure with.

'I don't doubt it,' said the ticket agent dryly. 'Mr Andrew Carnegie was here yesterday begging car fare to 125th Street, and Mr John D. Rockefeller quite frequently drops in and leaves his dollar watch in hock. Next!'

And the ticket agent glared at the man blocking the impatient line and told him to move on.

Armiston flushed crimson. He glanced at the clock. For once in his life he was about to experience that awful feeling of missing his train. For once in his life he was about to be robbed of that delicious sensation of hypnotising the gatekeeper and walking majestically down that train platform that extends northwards under the train-shed a considerable part of the distance toward Yonkers. Twenty seconds. Armiston turned round, still holding his ground, and glared concentrated malice at the man next in line. That man was in a hurry. In his hand he held a bundle of bills. For a second, the thief-instinct that is latent in us all suggested itself to Armiston. There within reach of his hand was the money, the precious paltry dollar bills that stood between him and his train. It scared him to discover that he, an upright and honoured citizen, was almost in the act of grabbing them like a common pickpocket.

Then a truly remarkable thing happened. The man thrust his handful of bills at Armiston.

'The only way I can raise this blockade is to bribe you,' he said, returning Armiston's glare. 'Here—take what you want—and give the rest of us a chance.'

With the alacrity of a blind beggar miraculously cured by the sight of much money, Armiston grabbed the handful, extracted what he needed for his ticket, and thrust the rest back into the waiting hand of his unknown benefactor. He caught the gate by a hair. So did his unknown friend. Together they walked down the platform, each matching the other's leisurely pace with his own. They might have been two potentates, so deliberately did they catch this train. Armiston would have liked to thank this person, but the other presented so forbidding an exterior that it was hard to find a point of attack. By force of habit Armiston boarded the parlour car, quite forgetting he did not have money for a seat. So did the other. The unknown thrust a bill at the porter. 'Get me two chairs,' he said. 'One is for this gentleman.'

Once inside and settled, Armiston renewed his efforts to thank this strange person. That person took a card from his pocket and handed it to Armiston.

'Don't run away with the foolish idea,' he said tartly, 'that I have done you a service willingly. You were making me miss my train, and I took this means of bribing you to get you out of my way. That is all, sir. At your leisure you may send me your check for the trifle.'

'A most extraordinary person!' said Armiston to himself. 'Let me give you my card,' he said to the other. 'As to the service rendered, you are welcome to your own ideas on that. For my part I am very grateful.'

The unknown took the proffered card and thrust it in his waistcoat pocket without glancing at it. He swung his chair round and opened a magazine, displaying a pair of broad unneighbourly shoulders. This was rather disconcerting to Armiston, who was accustomed to have his card act as an Open Sesame!

'Damn his impudence!' he said to himself. 'He takes me for a mendicant. I'll make copy of him!'

This was the popular author's way of getting even with those who offended his tender sensibilities.

Two things worried Armiston: One was his luncheon—or rather the absence of it; and the other was his neighbor. This neighbour, now that Armiston had a chance to study him, was a young man, well set up. He had a fine bronzed face that was not half so surly as his manner. He was now buried up to his ears in a magazine, oblivious of everything about him, even the dining-car porter, who strode down the aisle and announced the first call to lunch in the dining car.

'I wonder what the fellow is reading,' said Armiston to himself. He peeped over the man's shoulder and was interested at once, for the stranger was reading a copy of a magazine called by the vulgar 'The Whited Sepulchre'. It was the pride of this magazine that no man on earth could read it without the aid of a dictionary. Yet this person seemed to be enthralled. And what was more to the point, and vastly pleasing to Armiston, the man was at that moment engrossed in one of Armiston's own effusions. It was one of his crime stories that had won him praise and lucre. It concerned the Infallible Godahl.

These stories were pure reason incarnate in the person of a scientific thief. The plot was invariably so logical that is seemed more like the output of some machine than of a human mind. Of course the plots were impossible, because the fiction thief had to be an incredible genius to carry out the details. But nevertheless they were highly entertaining, fascinating and dramatic at one and the same time.

And this individual read the story through without winking an eyelash—as though the mental effort cost him nothing—and then, to Armiston's delight, turned back to the beginning and read it again. The author threw out his chest and shot his cuffs. It was not often that such unconscious tribute fell to his lot. He took the card of his unknown benefactor. It read:

Mr J. Borden Benson

THE TOWERS   NEW YORK CITY

'Humph!' snorted Armiston. 'An aristocrat—and a snob too!'

At this moment the aristocrat turned his chair and handed the magazine to his companion. All his bad humor was gone.

'Are you familiar,' he asked, 'with this man Armiston's work? I mean these scientific thief stories that are running now.'

'Ye-yes. Oh, yes,' sputtered Armiston, hastily putting the other's card away. 'I—in fact, you know—I take them every morning before breakfast.'

In a way this was the truth, for Armiston always began his day's writing before breakfasting.

Mr Benson smiled—a very fine smile at once boyish and sophisticated.

'Rather a heavy diet early in the morning, I should say,' he replied. 'Have you read this last one then?'

'Oh, yes,' said the delighted author.

'What do you think of it?' asked Benson.

The author puckered his lips.

'It is on a par with the others,' he said.

'Yes,' said Benson thoughtfully. 'I should say the same thing. And when we have said that there is nothing left to say. They are a truly remarkable product. Quite unique, you know. And yet,' he said, frowning at Armiston, 'I believe that this man Armiston is to be ranked as the most dangerous man in the world today.'

'Oh, I say—' began Armiston. But he checked himself, chuckling. He was very glad Mr Benson had not looked at his card.

'I mean it,' said the other decidedly. 'And you think so yourself, I fully believe. No thinking man could do otherwise.'

'In just what way? I must confess I have never thought of his work as anything but pure invention.'

It was truly delicious. Armiston would certainly make copy of this person.

'I will grant,' said Benson, 'that there is not a thief in the world today clever enough—brainy enough—to take advantage of the suggestions put forth in these stories. But some day there will arise a man to whom they will be as simple as an ordinary blueprint, and he will profit accordingly. This magazine, by printing these stories, is merely furnishing him with his tools, showing him how to work. And the worst of it is—'

'Just a minute,' said the author. 'Agreeing for the moment that these stories will be the tools of Armiston's hero in real life some day, how about the popular magazines? They print ten such stories to one of these by Armiston.'

'Ah, my friend,' said Benson, 'you forget one thing: the popular magazines deal with real life—the possible, the usual. And in that very thing they protect the public against sharpers, by exposing the methods of those same sharpers. But with Armiston—no. Much as I enjoy him as an intellectual treat, I am afraid—'

He didn't finish his sentence. Instead he fell to shaking his head, as though in amazement at the devilish ingenuity of the author under discussion.

'I am certainly delighted,' thought that author, 'that my disagreeable benefactor did not have the good grace to look at my card. This really is most entertaining.' And then aloud, and treading on thin ice. 'I should be very glad to tell Oliver what you say and see what he has to say about it.'

Benson's face broke into a wreath of wrinkles:

'Do you know him? Well, I declare! That is a privilege. I heartily wish you would tell him.'

'Would you like to meet him? I am under obligation to you. I can arrange a little dinner for a few of us.'

'No,' said Benson, shaking his head: 'I would rather go on reading him without knowing him. Authors are so disappointing in real life. He may be some puny, anaemic little half-portion, with dirty fingernails and all the rest that goes with genius. No offence to your friend! Besides, I am afraid I might quarrel with him.'

'Last call for lunch in the dinin' cy-yah-aa,' sang the porter. Armiston was looking at his fingernails as the porter passed. They were manicured once a day.

'Come lunch with me,' said Benson heartily. 'I should be pleased to have you as my guest. I apologize for being rude to you at the ticket window, but I did want to catch this train mighty bad.'

Armiston laughed. 'Well, you have paid my car fare,' he said, 'and I won't deny I am hungry enough to eat a hundred-and-ten-pound rail. I will let you buy me a meal, being penniless.'

Benson arose, and as he drew out his handkerchief the card Armiston had given him fluttered into that worthy's lap. Armiston closed his hand over it, chuckling again. Fate had given him the chance of preserving his incognito with this person as long as he wished. It would be a rare treat to get him ranting again about the author Armiston.

But Armiston's host did not rant against his favourite author. In fact he was so enthusiastic over that man's genius that the same qualities which he decried as a danger to society in his opinion only added lustre to the work. Benson asked his guest innumerable questions as to the personal qualities of his ideal, and Armiston shamelessly constructed a truly remarkable person. The other listened entranced.

'No, I don't want to know him,' he said. 'In the first place I haven't the time, and in the second I'd be sure to start a row. And then there is another thing: if he is half the man I take him to be from what you say, he wouldn't stand for people fawning on him and telling him what a wonder he is. That's about what I should be doing, I am afraid.'

'Oh,' said Armiston, 'he isn't so bad as that. He is a—well, a sensible chap, with clean fingernails and all that. You know, and he gets a haircut once every three weeks, the same as the rest of us.'

'I am glad to hear you say so, Mr—er . . .'

Benson fell to chuckling.

'By gad,' he said, 'here we have been talking with each other for an hour, and I haven't so much as taken a squint at your card to see who you are!'

He searched for the card Armiston had given him.

'Call it Brown,' said Armiston, lying gorgeously and with a feeling of utmost righteousness. 'Martin Brown, single, read-and-write, colour, white, laced shoes and derby hat, as the police say.'

'All right, Mr Brown; glad to know you. We will have some cigars. You have no idea how much you interest me, Mr Brown. How much does Armiston get for his stories?'

'Every word he writes brings him the price of a good cigar. I should say he makes forty thousand a year.'

'Humph! That is better than Godahl, his star creation, could bag as a thief, I imagine, let alone the danger of getting snipped with a pistol ball on a venture.'

Armiston puffed up his chest and shot his cuffs again.

'How does he get his plots?'

Armiston knitted his ponderous brows. 'There's the rub,' he said. 'You can talk about so-and-so much a word until you are deaf, dumb and blind. But, after all, it isn't the number of words or how they are strung together that makes a story. It is the idea. And ideas are scarce.'

'I have an idea that I have always wanted to have Armiston get hold of, just to see what he could do with it. If you will pardon me, to my way of thinking the really important thing isn't the ideas, but how to work out the details.'

'What's your idea?' asked Armiston hastily. He was not averse to appropriating anything he encountered in real life and dressing it up to suit his taste. 'I'll pass it on to Armiston, if you say so.'

'Will you? That's capital. To begin with,' Mr Benson said as he twirled his brandy glass with long, lean, silky fingers—a hand Armiston thought he would not like to have handle him in a rage—'to begin with, Godahl, this thief, is not an ordinary thief, he is a high-brow. He has made some big hauls. He must be a very rich man now—eh? You see that he is quite real to me. By this time, I should say, Godahl has acquired such a fortune that thieving for mere money is no longer an object. What does he do? Sit down and live on his income? Not much. He is a person of refined tastes with an eye for the aesthetic. He desires art objects, rare porcelains, a gem of rare cut or colour set by Benvenuto Cellini, a Leonardo da Vinci—did Godahl steal the Mona Lisa, by the way? He is the most likely person I can think of—or perhaps a Gutenberg Bible. Treasures, things of exquisite beauty to look at, to enjoy in secret, not to show to other people. That is the natural development of this man Godahl, eh?'

'Splendid!' exclaimed Armiston, his enthusiasm getting the better of him.

'Have you ever heard of Mrs Billy Wentworth?' asked Benson.

'Indeed, I know her well,' said Armiston, his guard down.

'Then you must surely have seen her white ruby?'

'White ruby! I never heard of such a thing. A white ruby?'

'Exactly. That's just the point. Neither have I. But if Godahl heard of a white ruby the chances are he would possess it—especially if it were the only one of its kind in the world.'

'Gad! I do believe he would, from what I know of him.'

'And especially,' went on Benson, 'under the circumstances. You know the Wentworths have been round a good deal. They haven't been over-scrupulous in getting things they wanted. Now Mrs Wentworth—but before I go on with this weird tale I want you to understand me. It is pure fiction—an idea for Armiston and his wonderful Godahl. I am merely suggesting the Wentworths as fictitious characters.'

'I understand,' said Armiston.

'Mrs Wentworth might very well possess this white ruby. Let us say she stole it from some potentate's household in the Straits Settlements. She gained admittance by means of the official position of her husband. They can't accuse her of theft. All they can do is to steal the gem back from her. It is a sacred stone of course. They always are in fiction stories. And the usual tribe of jugglers, rug-peddlers, and so on—all disguised, you understand—have followed her to America, seeking a chance, not on her life, not to commit violence of any kind, but to steal that stone.

'She can't wear it,' went on Benson. 'All she can do is hide it away in some safe place. What is a safe place? Not a bank. Godahl could crack a bank with his little finger. So might those East Indian fellows, labouring under the call of religion. Not in a safe. That would be folly.'

'How then?' put in Armiston eagerly.

'Ah, there you are! That's for Godahl to find out. He knows, let us say, that these foreigners in one way or another have turned Mrs Wentworth's apartments upside down. They haven't found anything. He knows that she keeps that white ruby in that house. Where is it? Ask Godahl! Do you see the point? Has Godahl ever cracked a nut like that? No. Here he must be the cleverest detective in the world and the cleverest thief at the same time. Before he can begin thieving he must make his blue-prints.'

'When I read Armiston,' continued Benson, 'that is the kind of problem that springs up in my mind. I am always trying to think of some knot this wonderful thief would have to employ his best powers to unravel. I think of some weird situation like this one. I say to myself: "Good! I will write that. I will be as famous as Armiston. I will create another Godahl." But,' he said with a wave of his hands, 'what is the result? I tie the knot, but I can't untie it. The trouble is, I am not a Godahl. And this man Armiston, as I read him, is Godahl. He must be, or else Godahl could not be made to do the wonderful things he does. Hello! New Haven already? Mighty sorry to have you go, old chap. Great pleasure. When you get to town let me know. Maybe I will consent to meet Armiston.'

Armiston's first care on returning to New York was to remember the providential loan by which he had been able to keep clean his record of never missing a train. He counted out the sum in bills, wrote a polite note, signed it 'Martin Brown,' and dispatched it by messenger to J. Borden Benson, The Towers. The Towers, the address Mr Benson's card bore, is an ultra-fashionable apartment hotel in Lower Fifth Avenue. It maintains all the pomp and solemnity of an English ducal castle. Armiston remembered having on a remote occasion taken dinner there with a friend and the recollection always gave him a chill. It was like dining among ghosts of kings, so grand and funereal was the air that pervaded everything.

Armiston, who could not forbear curiosity as to his queer benefactor, took occasion to look him up in the Blue Book and the Club Directory, and found that J. Borden Benson was quite some personage, several lines being devoted to him. This was extremely pleasing. Armiston had been thinking of that white-ruby yarn. It appealed to his sense of the dramatic. He would work it up in his best style, and on publication have a fine laugh on Benson by sending him an autographed copy and thus waking that gentleman up to the fact that it really had been the great Armiston in person he had befriended and entertained. What a joke it would be on Benson, thought the author; not without an intermixture of personal vanity, for even a genius such as he was not blind to flattery properly applied, and Benson unknowingly had laid it on thick.

'And, by gad,' thought the author, 'I will use the Wentworths as the main characters, as the victims of Godahl! They are just the people to fit into such a romance. Benson put money in my pocket, though he didn't suspect it. Lucky he didn't know what shifts we popular authors are put to for plots.'

Suiting the action to the word, Armiston and his wife accepted the next invitation they received from the Wentworths.

Mrs Wentworth, be it understood, was a lion hunter. She was forever trying to gather about her such celebrities as Armiston the author, Brackens the painter, Johanssen the explorer, and others. Armiston had always withstood her wiles. He always had some excuse to keep him away from her gorgeous table, where she exhibited her lions to her simpering friends.

There were many undesirables sitting at the table, idle-rich youths, girls of the fast hunting set, and so on, and they all gravely shook the great author by the hand and told him what a wonderful man he was. As for Mrs Wentworth, she was too highly elated at her success in roping him for sane speech, and she fluttered about him like a hysterical bridesmaid. But, Armiston noted with relief, one of his pals was there—Johanssen. Over cigars and cognac he managed to buttonhole the explorer.

'Johanssen,' he said, 'you have been everywhere.'

'You are mistaken there,' said Johanssen. 'I have never before tonight been north of 59th Street in New York.'

'Yes, but you have been in Java and Ceylon and the Settlements. Tell me, have you ever heard of such a thing as a white ruby?'

The explorer narrowed his eyes to a slit and looked queerly at his questioner. 'That's a queer question,' he said in a low voice, 'to ask in this house.'

Armiston felt his pulse quicken. 'Why?' he asked, assuming an air of surprised innocence.

'If you don't know,' said the explorer shortly, 'I certainly will not enlighten you.'

'All right; as you please. But you haven't answered my question yet. Have you ever heard of a white ruby?'

'I don't mind telling you that I have heard of such a thing—that is, I have heard there is a ruby in existence that is called the white ruby. It isn't really white, you know; it has a purplish tinge. But the old heathen who rightly owns it likes to call it white, just as he likes to call his blue and gray elephants white.'

'Who owns it?' asked Armiston, trying his best to make his voice sound natural. To find in this manner that there was some parallel for the mystical white ruby of which Benson had told him appealed strongly to his superdeveloped dramatic sense. He was now as keen on the scent as a hound.

Johanssen took to drumming on the tablecloth. He smiled to himself and his eyes glowed. Then he turned and looked sharply at his questioner.

'I suppose,' he said, 'that all things are grist to a man of your trade. If you are thinking of building a story round a white ruby I can think of nothing more fascinating. But, Armiston,' he said, suddenly altering his tone and almost whispering, 'if you are on the track of *the* white ruby let me advise you now to call off your dogs and keep your throat whole. I think I am a brave man. I have shot tigers at ten paces—held my fire purposely to see how charmed a life I really did bear. I have been charged by mad rhinos and by wounded buffaloes, have walked across a clearing where the air was being punctured with bullets as thick as holes in a mosquito screen. But,' he said, laying his hand on Armiston's arm, 'I have never had the nerve to hunt the white ruby.'

'Capital!' exclaimed the author.

'Capital, yes, for a man who earns his bread and gets his excitement by sitting at a typewriter and dreaming about these things. But take my word for it, it isn't capital for a man who gets his excitement by doing this thing. Hands off, my friend!'

'It really does exist then?'

Johanssen puckered his lips. 'So they say,' he said.

'What's it worth?'

'Worth? What do you mean by worth? Dollars and cents? What is your child worth to you. A million, a billion—how much? Tell me. No, you can't. Well, that's just what the miserable stone is worth to the man who rightfully owns it. Now let's quit talking nonsense. There's Billy Wentworth shooing the men into the drawing-room. I suppose we shall be entertained this evening by some of the hundred-dollar-a-minute songbirds, as usual. It's amazing what these people will spend for mere vulgar display when there are hundreds of families starving within a mile of this spot!'

Two famous singers sang that night. Armiston did not have much opportunity to look over the house. He was now fully determined to lay the scene of his story in this very house. At leave-taking the sugar-sweet Mrs Billy Wentworth drew Armiston aside and said:

'It's rather hard on you to ask you to sit through an evening with these people. I will make amends by asking you to come to me some night when we can be by ourselves. Are you interested in rare curios? Yes, we all are. I have some really wonderful things I want you to see. Let us make it next Tuesday, with a little informal dinner, just for ourselves.'

Armiston then and there made the lion hunter radiantly happy by accepting her invitation to sit at her board as a family friend instead of as a lion.

As he put his wife into their automobile he turned and looked at the house. It stood opposite Central Park. It was a copy of some French château in gray sandstone, with a barbican, and overhanging towers, and all the rest of it. The windows of the street floor peeped out through deep embrasures and were heavily guarded with iron latticework.

'Godahl will have the very devil of a time breaking in there,' he chuckled to himself. Late that night his wife awakened him to find out why he was tossing about so.

'That white ruby has got on my nerves,' he said cryptically, and she, thinking he was dreaming, persuaded him to try to sleep again.

Great authors must really live in the flesh, at times at least, the lives of their great characters. Otherwise these great characters would not be so real as they are. Here was Armiston, who had created a superman in the person of Godahl the thief. For ten years he had written nothing else. He had laid the life of Godahl out in squares, thought for him, dreamed about him, set him to new tasks, gone through all sorts of queer adventures with him. And this same Godahl had amply repaid him. He had raised the author from the ranks of struggling amateurs to a position among the most highly paid fiction writers in the United States. He had brought him ease and luxury. Armiston did not need the money any more. The serial rights telling of the exploits of this Godahl had paid him handsomely. The book of Godahl's adventures had paid him even better, and had furnished him yearly with a never-failing income, like government bonds, but at a much higher rate of interest. Even though the crimes this Godahl had committed were all on paper, nevertheless Godahl was a living being to his creator. More—he was Armiston, and Armiston was Godahl.

It was not surprising, then, that when Tuesday came Armiston awaited the hour with feverish impatience. Here, as his strange friend had so thoughtlessly and casually told him, was an opportunity for the great Godahl to outdo even himself. Here was an opportunity for Godahl to be the greatest detective in the world, in the first place, before he could carry out one of his sensational thefts.

So it was Godahl, not Armiston, who helped his wife out of their automobile that evening and mounted the splendid steps of the Wentworth mansion. He cast his eyes aloft; took in every inch of the facade.

'No,' he said, 'Godahl cannot break in from the street. I must have a look at the back of the house.'

He cast his eyes on the ironwork that guarded the deep windows giving on the street.

It was not iron after all, but chilled steel sunk into armoured concrete. The outposts of this house were as safely guarded as the vault of the United States Mint.

'It's got to be from the inside,' he said, making mental note of this fact.

The butler was stone-deaf. This was rather singular. Why should a family of the standing of the Wentworths employ a man as head of their city establishment who was stone-deaf? Armiston looked at the man with curiosity. He was still in middle age. Surely, then, he was not retained because of years of service. No, there was something more than charity behind this. He addressed a casual word to the man as he handed him his hat and cane. His back was turned and the man did not reply. Armiston turned and repeated the sentence in the same tone. The man watched his lips in the bright light of the hall.

'A lip-reader, and a dandy,' thought Armiston, for the butler seemed to catch every word he said.

'Fact Number 2!' said the creator of Godahl the thief.

He felt no compunction at thus noting the most intimate details of the Wentworth establishment. An accident had put him on the track of a rare good story, and it was all copy. Besides, he told himself, when he came to write the story he would disguise it in such a way that no-one reading it would know it was about the Wentworths. If their establishment happened to possess the requisite setting for a great story, surely there was no reason why he should not take advantage of that fact.

The great thief—he made no bones of the fact to himself that he had come here to help Godahl—accepted the flattering greeting of his hostess with the grand air that so well fitted him. Armiston was tall and thin, with slender fingers and a touch of grey in his wavy hair, for all his youthful years, and he knew how to wear clothes. Mrs Wentworth was proud of him as a social ornament, even aside from his glittering fame as an author. And Mrs Armiston was well born, so there was no jar in their being received in the best house of the town.

The dinner was truly delightful. Here Armiston saw, or thought he saw, one of the reasons for the deaf butler. The hostess had him so trained that she was able to catch her servant's eye and instruct him in this or that trifle by merely moving her lips. It was almost uncanny, thought the author, this silent conversation the deaf man and his mistress were able to carry on unnoticed by the others.

'By gad, it's wonderful! Godahl, my friend, underscore that note of yours referring to the deaf butler. Don't miss it. It will take a trick.'

Armiston gave his undivided attention to his hostess as soon as he found Wentworth entertaining Mrs Armiston and thus properly dividing the party. He persuaded her to talk by a cleverly pointed question here and there; and as she talked, he studied her.

'We are going to rob you of your precious white ruby, my friend,' he thought humorously to himself; 'and while we are laying our wires there is nothing about you too small to be worthy of our attention.'

Did she really possess the white ruby? Did this man Benson know anything about the white ruby? And what was the meaning of the strange actions of his friend Johanssen when approached on the subject in this house? His hostess came to have a wonderful fascination for him. He pictured this beautiful creature so avid in her lust for rare gems that she actually did penetrate the establishment of some heathen potentate in the Straits simply for the purpose of stealing the mystic stone. 'Have you ever, by any chance, been in the Straits?' he asked indifferently.

'Wait,' Mrs Wentworth said with a laugh as she touched his hand lightly; 'I have some curios from the Straits, and I will venture to say you have never seen their like.'

Half an hour later they were all seated over coffee and cigarettes in Mrs Wentworth's boudoir. It was indeed a strange place. There was scarcely a single corner of the world that had not contributed something to its furnishing. Carvings of teak and ivory; hangings of sweet-scented vegetable fibres; lamps of jade; queer little gods, all sitting like Buddha with their legs drawn up under them, carved out of jade or sardonyx; scarfs of baroque pearls; Darjeeling turquoises—Armiston had never before seen such a collection. And each item had its story. He began to look on this frail little woman with different eyes. She had been and seen and done, and the tale of her life, what she had actually lived, outshone even that of the glittering rascal Godahl, who was standing beside him now and directing his ceaseless questions. 'Have you any rubies?' he asked.

Mrs Wentworth bent before a safe in the wall. With swift fingers she whirled the combination. The keen eyes of Armiston followed the bright knob like a cat.

'Fact Number 3!' said the Godahl in him as he mentally made note of the numbers. 'Five—eight—seven—four—six. That's the combination.'

Mrs Wentworth showed him six pigeon-blood rubies.

'This one is pale,' he said carelessly, holding a particularly large stone up to the light. 'Is it true that occasionally they are found white?'

His hostess looked at him before answering. He was intent on a deep-red stone he held in the palm of his hand. It seemed a thousand miles deep.

'What a fantastic idea!' she said. She glanced at her husband, who had reached out and taken her hand in a naturally affectionate manner.

'Fact Number 4!' mentally noted Armiston. 'Are you not in mortal fear of robbery with all this wealth?'

Mrs Wentworth laughed lightly.

'That is why we live in a fortress,' she said.

'Have you never, then, been visited by thieves?' asked the author boldly.

'Never!' she said.

'A lie,' thought Armiston. 'Fact Number 5! We are getting on swimmingly.'

'I do not believe that even your Godahl the Infallible could get in here,' Mrs Wentworth said. 'Not even the servants enter this room. That door is not locked with a key; yet it locks. I am not much of a housekeeper,' she said lazily, 'but such housekeeping as is done in this room is all done by these poor little hands of mine.'

'No! Most amazing! May I look at the door?'

'Yes, Mr Godahl,' said the woman, who had lived more lives than Godahl himself.

Armiston examined the door, this strange device that locked without a key, apparently indeed without a lock, and came away disappointed.

'Well, Mr Godahl?' his hostess said tauntingly. He shook his head in perplexity.

'Most ingenious,' he said; and then suddenly: 'Yet I will venture that if I turned Godahl loose on this problem he would solve it.'

'What fun!' she cried, clapping her hands.

'You challenge him?' asked Armiston.

'What nonsense is this!' cried Wentworth, coming forward.

'No nonsense at all,' said Mrs Wentworth. 'Mr Armiston has just said that his Godahl could rob me. Let him try. If he can—if mortal man can gain the secrets of ingress and egress of this room—I want to know it. I don't believe mortal man can enter this room.'

Armiston noted a strange glitter in her eyes.

'Gad! She was born to the part! What a woman!' he thought. And then aloud:

'I will set him to work. I will lay the scene of his exploit in—say—Hungary, where this room might very well exist in some feudal castle. How many people have entered this room since it was made the storehouse of all this wealth?'

'Not six besides yourself,' replied Mrs Wentworth.

'Then no one can recognize it if I describe it in a story—in fact, I will change the material details. We will say that it is not jewels Godahl is seeking. We will say that it is a—'

Mrs Wentworth's hand touched his own. The tips of her fingers were cold. 'A white ruby,' she said.

'Gad! What a thoroughbred!' he exclaimed to himself—or to Godahl. And then aloud: 'Capital! I will send you a copy of the story autographed.'

The next day he called at The Towers and sent up his card to Mr Benson's apartments. Surely a man of Benson's standing could be trusted with such a secret. In fact it was evidently not a secret to Benson, who in all probability was one of the six Mrs Wentworth said had entered that room. Armiston wanted to talk the matter over with Benson. He had given up his idea of having fun with him by sending him a marked copy of the magazine containing his tale. His story had taken complete possession of him, as always had been the case when he was at work dispatching Godahl on his adventures.

'If that ruby really exists,' Armiston said, 'I don't know whether I shall write the story or steal the ruby for myself. Benson is right. Godahl should not steal any more for mere money. He is after rare, unique things now. And I am Godahl. I feel the same way myself.'

A valet appeared, attired in a gorgeous livery. Armiston wondered why any self-respecting American would consent to don such raiment, even though it was the livery of the great Benson family.

'Mr Armiston, sir,' said the valet, looking at the author's card he held in his hand. 'Mr Benson sailed for Europe yesterday morning. He is spending the summer in Norway. I am to follow on the next steamer. Is there any message I can take to him, sir? I have heard him speak of you, sir.'

Armiston took the card and wrote on it in pencil:

I called to apologise. I am Martin Brown. The chance was too good to miss. You will pardon me, won't you?

For the next two weeks Armiston gave himself over to his dissipation, which was accompanying Godahl on this adventure. It was a formidable task. The secret room he placed in a Hungarian castle, as he had promised. A beautiful countess was his heroine. She had seen the world, mostly in man's attire, and her escapades had furnished vivacious reading for two continents. No one could possibly connect her with Mrs Billy Wentworth. So far it was easy. But how was Godahl to get into this wonderful room where the countess had hidden this wonderful rare white ruby? The room was lined with chilled steel. Even the door—this he had noted when he was examining that peculiar portal—was lined with layers of steel. It could withstand any known tool.

However, Armiston was Armiston, and Godahl was Godahl. He got into that room. He got the white ruby!

The manuscript went to the printers, and the publishers said that Armiston had never done anything like it since he started Godahl on his astonishing career.

He banked the cheque for his tale, and as he did so he said: 'Gad I would a hundred times rather possess that white ruby. Confound the thing! I feel as if I had not heard the last of it.'

Armiston and his wife went to Maine for the summer without leaving their address. Along in the early fall he received by registered mail, forwarded by his trusted servant at the town house, a package containing the envelope he had addressed to J. Borden Benson, The Towers. Furthermore it contained the dollar bill he had dispatched to that individual, together with his note which he had signed 'Martin Brown.' And across the note, in the most insulting manner, was written in coarse, greasy blue-pencil lines:

Damnable impertinence. I'll cane you the first time I see you.

And no more. That was enough of course—quite sufficient.

In the same mail came a note from Armiston's publishers, saying that his story 'The White Ruby' was scheduled for publication in the October number, out September 25th. This cheered him up. He was anxious to see it in print. Late in September they started back to town.

'Aha!' he said as he sat reading his paper in the parlor car. He had caught this train by the veriest tip of its tail and upset the running schedule in the act. 'Aha! I see my genial friend, J. Borden Benson, is in town, contrary to custom at this time of year. Life must be a great bore to that snob.'

A few days after arriving in town he received a package of advance copies of the magazine containing his story, and he read the tale of 'The White Ruby' as if he had never seen it before. On the cover of one copy, which he was to dispatch to his grumpy benefactor, J. Borden Benson, he wrote:

Charmed to be caned. Call any time. See contents.
Oliver Armiston.

On another he wrote:

Dear Mrs Wentworth,
See how simple it is to pierce your fancied security!

He dispatched these two magazines with a feeling of glee. No sooner had he done so, however, than he learned that the Wentworths had not yet returned from Newport. The magazine would be forwarded to them no doubt. The Wentworths' absence made the tale all the better, in fact, for in his story Armiston had insisted on Godahl's breaking into the castle and solving the mystery of the keyless door during the season when the château was closed and strung with a perfect network of burglar alarms connecting with the *Gendarmerie* in the nearby village.

That was the twenty-fifth day of September. The magazine was put on sale that morning.

On the twenty-sixth day of September Armiston bought a late edition of an afternoon paper from a leather-lunged boy who was hawking 'Extra'! in the street. Across the first page the headlines met his eye:

ROBBERY AND MURDER IN THE
WENTWORTH MANSION!

Private watchmen, summoned by burglar alarm at ten o'clock this morning, find servant with skull crushed on floor of mysterious steel-doored
room. Murdered man's pockets filled with rare jewels. Police believe he
was murdered by a confederate who escaped.

THE WENTWORTH BUTLER, STONE-DEAF, HAD JUST RETURNED
FROM NEWPORT TO OPEN HOUSE AT TIME OF MURDER.

It was ten o'clock that night when an automobile drew up at Armiston's door, and a
tall man with a square jaw, square shoes and a square moustache alighted. This was
Deputy Police Commissioner Byrnes, a professional detective whom the new admin-
istration had drafted into the city's service from the government secret service.

Byrnes was admitted and as he advanced to the middle of the drawing-room,
without so much as a nod to the ghostlike Armiston who stood shivering before
him, he drew a package of papers from his pocket.

'I presume you have seen all the evening papers,' he said, spitting his words
through his half-closed teeth with so much show of personal malice that Armiston—
never a brave man in spite of his Godahl—cowered before him.

Armiston shook his head dumbly at first, but at length he managed to say: 'Not
all; no.'

The Deputy Commissioner with much deliberation drew out the latest extra and
handed it to Armiston without a word.

It was the *Evening News*. The first page was divided down its entire length by a
black line. On one side, and occupying four columns, was a word-for-word reprint
of Armiston's story, 'The White Ruby.'

On the other, the facts in deadly parallel, was a graphic account of the robbery
and murder at the home of Billy Wentworth. The parallel was glaring in the intensity of its dumb accusation. On the one side was the theoretical Godahl, working his
masterly way of crime, step by step; and on the other was the plagiarism of Armiston's story, following the intricacies of the master mind with copy-book accuracy.

The editor, who must have been a genius in his way, did not accuse. He simply
placed the fiction and the fact side by side and let the reader judge for himself. It
was masterly. If, as the law says, the mind that conceives, the intelligence that
directs, a crime is more guilty than the very hand that acts, then Armiston here was
both thief and murderer. Thief, because the white ruby had actually been stolen.
Mrs Billy Wentworth, rushed to the city by special train, attended by doctors and
nurses, now confirmed the story of the theft of the ruby. Murderer, because in the
story Godahl had for once in his career stooped to murder as the means, and had
triumphed over the dead body of his confederate, scorning, in his joy at possessing
the white ruby, the paltry diamonds, pearls, and red rubies with which his confederate had crammed his pockets.

Armiston seized the police official by his lapels.

'The butler!' he screamed. 'The butler! Yes, the butler. Quick, or he will have
flown!'

Byrnes gently disengaged the hands that had grasped him.

'Too late,' he said. 'He has already flown. Sit down and quiet your nerves. We need your help. You are the only man in the world who can help us now.'

When Armiston was himself again he told the whole tale, beginning with his strange meeting with J. Borden Benson on the train, and ending with his accepting Mrs Wentworth's challenge to have Godahl break into the room and steal the white ruby. Byrnes nodded over the last part. He had already heard that from Mrs Wentworth, and there was the autographed copy of the magazine to show for it.

'You say that J. Borden Benson told you of this white ruby in the first place.'

Armiston again told, in great detail, the circumstances, all the humor now turned into grim tragedy.

'That is strange,' said the ex-secret-service chief. 'Did you leave your purse at home or was your pocket picked?'

'I thought at first that I had absent-mindedly left it at home. Then I remembered having paid the chauffeur out of the roll of bills, so my pocket must have been picked.'

'What kind of a looking man was this Benson?'

'You must know him,' said Armiston.

'Yes, I know him; but I want to know what he looked like to you. I want to find out how he happened to be so handy when you were in need of money.'

Armiston described the man minutely.

The Deputy sprang to his feet. 'Come with me,' he said; and they hurried into the automobile and soon drew up in front of The Towers.

Five minutes later they were ushered into the magnificent apartment of J. Borden Benson. That worthy was in his bath preparing to retire for the night.

'I don't catch the name,' Armiston and the Deputy heard him cry through the bathroom door to his valet.

'Mr Oliver Armiston, sir.'

'Ah, he has come for his caning, I expect. I'll be there directly.'

He did not wait to complete his toilet, so eager was he to see the author. He strode out in a brilliant bathrobe and in one hand he carried an alpenstock. His eyes glowed in anger. But the sight of Byrnes surprised as well as halted him.

'Do you mean to say this is J. Borden Benson?' cried Armiston to Byrnes, rising to his feet and pointing at the man.

'The same,' said the Deputy; 'I swear to it. I know him well! I take it he is not the gentleman who paid your car fare to New Haven.'

'Not by a hundred pounds!' exclaimed Armiston as he surveyed the huge bulk of the elephantine clubman.

The forced realisation that the stranger he had hitherto regarded as a benefactor was not J. Borden Benson at all, but someone who had merely assumed that worthy's name while he was playing the conceited author as an easy dupe, did more to quiet Armiston's nerves than all the sedatives his doctor had given him. It was a badly dashed popular author who sat down with the Deputy Commissioner in his library an hour later. He would gladly have consigned Godahl to the bottom of the sea; but it was too late. Godahl had taken the trick.

'How do you figure it?' Armiston asked, turning to the Deputy.

'The beginning is simple enough. It is the end that bothers me,' said the official. 'Your bogus J. Borden Benson is, of course, the brains of the whole combination. Your infernal Godahl has told us exactly how this crime was committed. Now your infernal Godahl must bring the guilty parties to justice.'

It was plain to be seen that the police official hated Godahl worse than poison, and feared him too.

'Why not look in the Rogues' Gallery for this man who befriended me on the train?'
The chief laughed.

'For the love of Heaven, Armiston, do you, who pretend to know all about scientific thievery, think for a moment that the man who took your measure so easily is of the class of crooks who get their pictures in the Rogues' Gallery? Talk sense!'

'I can't believe you when you say he picked my pocket.'

'I don't care whether you believe me or not; he did, or one of his pals did. It all amounts to the same thing, don't you see? First, he wanted to get acquainted with you. Now the best way to get into your good graces was to put you unsuspectingly under obligation to him. So he robs you of your money. From what I have seen of you in the last few hours it must have been like taking candy from a child. Then he gets next to you in line. He pretends that you are merely some troublesome toad in his path. He gives you money for your ticket, to get you out of his way so he won't miss his train. His train! Of course his train is your train. He puts you in a position where you have to make advances to him. And then, grinning to himself all the time at your conceit and gullibility, he plays you through your pride, your Godahl. Think of the creator of the great Godahl falling for a trick like that!'

Byrnes's last words were the acme of biting sarcasm.

'You admit yourself that he is too clever for you to put your hands on.'

'And then,' went on Byrnes, not heeding the interruption, 'he invites you to lunch and tells you what he wants you to do for him. And you follow his lead like a sheep at the tail of the bellwether! Great Scott, Armiston! I would give a year's salary for one hour's conversation with that man.'

Armiston was beginning to see the part this queer character had played; but he was in a semi-hysterical state, and, like a woman in such a position, he wanted a calm mind to tell him the whole thing in words of one syllable, to verify his own dread.

'What do you mean?' he asked. 'I don't quite follow. You say he tells me what he wants me to do.'

Byrnes shrugged his shoulders in disgust; then, as if resigned to the task before him, he began his explanation.

'Here, man. I will draw a diagram for you. This gentleman friend of yours—we will call him John Smith for convenience—wants to get possession of this white ruby. He knows that it is in the keeping of Mrs Billy Wentworth. He knows you know Mrs Wentworth and have access to her house. He knows that she stole this bauble and is frightened to death all the time. Now John Smith is a pretty clever chap. He handled the great Armiston like hot putty. He had exhausted his resources. He is baffled and needs help. What does he do? He reads the stories about the great Godahl. Confidentially, Mr Armiston, I will tell you that I think your great Godahl is mush. But that is neither here nor there. If you can sell him as a gold brick, all right. But Mr John Smith is struck by the wonderful ingenuity of this Godahl. He says, 'Ha! I will get Godahl to tell me how to get this gem!'

'So he gets hold of yourself, sir, and persuades you that you are playing a joke on him to rant and rave about the great Godahl. Then—and here the villain enters—he says: "Here is a thing the great Godahl cannot do. I dare him to do it." He tells you about the gem, whose very existence is quite fantastic enough to excite the imagination of the wonderful Armiston. And by clever suggestion he persuades you to play the plot at the home of Mrs Wentworth. And all the time you are chuckling to yourself, thinking what a rare joke you are going to have on J. Borden Benson when you send him an autographed copy and show him that he was talking to the distinguished genius all the time and didn't know it. That's the whole story, sir. Now wake up!'

Byrnes sat back in his chair and regarded Armiston with the smile a pedagogue bestows on a refractory boy whom he has just flogged soundly.

'I will explain further,' he continued. 'You haven't visited the house yet. You can't. Mrs Wentworth, for all she is in bed with four dozen hot-water bottles, would tear you limb from limb if you went there. And don't you think for a minute she isn't able to. That woman is a vixen.'

Armiston nodded gloomily. The very thought of her now sent him into a cold sweat.

'Mr Godahl, the obliging,' continued the Deputy, 'notes one thing to begin with: the house cannot be entered from the outside. So it must be an inside job. How can this be accomplished? Well, there is the deaf butler. Why is he deaf? Godahl ponders. Ha! He has it! The Wentworths are so dependent on servants that they must have them round at all times. This butler is the one who is constantly about them. They are worried to death by their possession of this white ruby. Their house has been raided from the inside a dozen times. Nothing is taken, mind you. They suspect their servants. This thing haunts them, but the woman will not give up this foolish bauble. So she has as her major domo a man who cannot understand a word in any language unless he is looking at the speaker and is in a bright light. He can only understand the lips. Handy, isn't it? In a dull light or with their backs turned they can talk about anything they want to. This is a jewel of a butler.'

'But,' added Byrnes, 'one day a man calls. He is a lawyer. He tells the butler he is heir to a fortune—fifty thousand dollars. He must go to Ireland to claim it. Your friend on the train—he is the man of course—sends your butler to Ireland. So this precious butler is lost. They must have another. Only a deaf one will do. And they find just the man they want—quite accidentally, you understand. Of course it is Godahl, with forged letters saying he has been in service in great houses. Presto! The great Godahl himself is now the butler. It is simple enough to play deaf. You say this is fiction. Let me tell you this: six weeks ago the Wentworths actually changed butlers. That hasn't come out in the papers yet.'

Armiston, who had listened to the Deputy's review of his story listlessly, now sat up with a start. He suddenly exclaimed gleefully:

'But my story didn't come out till two days ago!'

'Ah, yes; but you forget that it has been in the hands of your publishers for three months. A man who was clever enough to dupe the great Armiston wouldn't shirk the task of getting hold of a proof of that story.'

Armiston sank deeper into his chair.

'Once Godahl got inside the house the rest was simple. He corrupted one of the servants. He opened the steel-lined door with the flame of an oxyacetylene blast. As you say in your story that flame cuts steel like wax; he didn't have to bother about the lock. He simply cut the door down. Then he put his confederate in a good humour by telling him to fill his pockets with the diamonds and other junk in the safe, which he obligingly opens. One thing bothers me, Armiston. How did you find out about that infernal contraption that killed the confederate?'

Armiston buried his face in his hands. Byrnes rudely shook him.

'Come,' he said; 'you murdered that man, though you are innocent. Tell me how.'

'Is this the third degree?' said Armiston.

'It looks like it,' said the Deputy grimly as he gnawed at his stubby moustache. Armiston drew a long breath, like one who realises how hopeless is his situation. He began to speak in a low tone. All the while the Deputy glared at Godahl's inventor with his accusing eye.

'When I was sitting in the treasure room with the Wentworths and my wife, playing auction bridge, I dismissed the puzzle of the door as easily solved by means of the brazing flame. The problem was not to get into the house, or into this room, but to find the ruby. It was not in the safe.'

'No, of course not. I suppose your friend on the train was kind enough to tell you that. He had probably looked there himself.'

'Gad! He did tell me that, come to think of it. Well, I studied that room. I was sure the white ruby, if it really existed, was within ten feet of me. I examined the floor, the ceiling, the walls. No result. But,' he said, shivering as if in a draught of cold air, 'there was a chest in that room made of Lombardy oak.' The harassed author buried his face in his hands. 'Oh, this is terrible!' he moaned.

'Go on,' said the Deputy in his colourless voice.

'I can't. I tell it all in the story, Heaven help me!'

'I know you tell it all in the story,' came the rasping voice of Byrnes; 'but I want you to tell me it to me. I want to hear it from your own lips—as Armiston; you understand, whose devilry has just killed a man; not as your damnable Godahl.'

'The chest was not solid oak,' went on Armiston. 'It was solid steel covered with oak to disguise it.'

'How did you know that?'

'I had seen it before.'

'Where?'

'In Italy fifteen years ago, in a decayed castle, back through the Soldini Pass from Lugano. It was the possession of an old nobleman, a friend of a friend of mine.'

'Humph!' grunted the Deputy. And then: 'Well, how did you know it was the same one?'

'By the inscription carved on the front. It was—but I have told all this in print already. Why need I go over it all again?'

'I want to hear it again from your own lips. Maybe there are some points you did not tell in print. Go on!'

'The inscription was "*Sanctus Dominus*".'

The Deputy smiled grimly.

'Very fitting, I should say. Praise the Lord with the most diabolical engine of destruction I have ever seen.'

'And then,' said Armiston, 'there was the owner's name—"Arno Petronii." Queer name that.'

'Yes,' said the Deputy dryly. 'How did you hit on this as the receptacle for the white ruby?'

'If it were the same one I saw in Lugano—and I felt sure it was—it was certain death to attempt to open it—that is, for one who did not know how. Such machines were common enough in the Middle Ages. There was an obvious way to open it. It was meant to be obvious. To open it that way was inevitable death. It released tremendous springs that crushed anything within a radius of five feet. You saw that?'

'I did,' said the Deputy, and he shuddered as he spoke. Then, bringing his fierce face within an inch of the cowering Armiston, he said:

'You knew the secret spring by which that safe could be opened as simply as a shoebox, eh?'

Armiston nodded his head.

'But Godahl did not,' he said. 'Having recognized this terrible chest,' went on the author, 'I guessed it must be the hiding place of the jewel—for two reasons: in the first place Mrs Wentworth had avoided showing it to us. She passed it by as a mere bit of curious furniture. Second, it was too big to go through the door or any one of the windows. They must have gone to the trouble of taking down the wall to get that thing in there. Something of a task, too, considering it weighs about two tons.'

'You didn't bring out that point in your story.'

'Didn't I? I fully intended to.'

'Maybe,' said the Deputy, watching his man sharply, 'it so impressed your friend who paid your car fare to New Haven that he clipped it out of the manuscript when he borrowed it.'

'There is no humour in this affair, sir, if you will pardon me,' said Armiston.

'That is quite true. Go ahead.'

'The rest you know. Godahl, in my story—the thief in real life—had to sacrifice to a life to open that chest. So he corrupted a small kitchen servant, filling his pockets with these other jewels, and told him to touch the spring.'

'You murdered that man in cold blood,' said the Deputy, rising and pacing the floor. 'The poor deluded devil, from the looks of what's left of him, never let out a whimper, never knew what hit him. Here, take some more of this brandy. Your nerves are in a bad way.'

'What I can't make out is this,' said Armiston after a time. 'There was a million dollars' worth of stuff in that room that could have been put into a quart measure. Why did not this thief, who was willing to go to all the trouble to get the white ruby, take some of the jewels? Nothing is missing besides the white ruby, as I understand it. Is there?'

'No,' said the Deputy. 'Not a thing. Here comes a messenger boy.'

'For Mr Armiston? Yes,' he said to the entering maid. The boy handed him a package for which the Deputy signed.

'This is for you,' he said, turning to Armiston as he closed the door. 'Open it.'

When the package was opened the first object to greet their eyes was a roll of bills.

'This grows interesting,' said Byrnes. He counted the money. 'Thirty-nine dollars. Your friend evidently is returning the money he stole from you at the station. What does he have to say for himself? I see there is a note.'

He reached over and took the paper out of Armiston's hands. It was ordinary bond stationery, with no identifying marks of any consequence. The note was written in bronze ink, in a careful copperplate hand, very small and precise. It read:

> *Most Excellency Sir:*
> *Herewith, most honoured dollars I am dispatching complete. Regretful extremely of sad blood being not to be prevented. Accept trifle from true friend.*

That was all.

'There's a jeweller's box,' said Byrnes. 'Open it.'

Inside the box was a lozenge-shaped diamond about the size of a little fingernail. It hung from a tiny bar of silver, highly polished and devoid of ornament. On the back under the clasp-pin were several microscopic characters.

There were several obvious clues to be followed—the messenger boy, the lawyers who induced the deaf butler to go to Ireland on what later proved to be a wild-goose chase, the employment agency through which the new butler had been secured, and so on. But all of these avenues proved too respectable to yield results. Deputy Byrnes had early arrived at his own conclusions, by virtue of the knowledge he had gained as government agent, yet to appease the popular indignation he kept up a desultory search for the criminal.

It was natural that Armiston should think of his friend Johanssen at this juncture. Johanssen possessed that wonderful Oriental capacity of aloofness which we Westerners are so ready to term indifference or lack of curiosity.

'No, I thank you,' said Johanssen. 'I'd rather not mix in.'

The pleadings of the author were in vain. His words fell on deaf ears.

'If you will not lift a hand because of your friendship for me,' said Armiston bitterly, 'then think of the law. Surely there is something due to justice, when both robbery and bloody murder have been committed!'

'Justice!' cried Johanssen in scorn. 'Justice, you say! My friend, if you steal for me, and I reclaim by force that which is mine, is that injustice? If you cannot see the idea behind that surely, then, I cannot explain it to you.'

'Answer one question,' said Armiston. 'Have you any idea who the man was I met on the train?'

'For your own peace of mind—yes. As a clue leading to what you so glibly term justice—pshaw! Tonight's sundown would be easier for you to catch than his man if I know him. Mind you, Armiston, I do not know. But I believe. Here is what I believe:

'In a dozen courts of kings and petty princelings that I know of in the East there are Westerners retained as advisers—fiscal agents they usually call them. Usually they are American or English, or occasionally German.

'Now I ask you a question. Say that you were in the hire of a heathen prince, and a grievous wrong were done that prince, say, by a thoughtless woman who had not the least conception of the beauty of an idea she has outraged. Merely for the possession of a bauble, valueless to her except to appease vanity, she ruthlessly rode down a superstition that was as holy to this prince as your own belief in Christ is to you. What would you do?'

Without waiting for Armiston to answer, Johanssen went on:

'I know a man—You say this man you met on the train had wonderful hands, did he not? Yes, I thought so. Armiston I know a man who would not sit idly by and smile to himself over the ridiculous fuss occasioned by the loss of an imperfect stone—off-colour, badly cut, and everything else. Neither would he laugh at the superstition behind it. He would say to himself: 'This superstition is older by several thousand years than I or my people.' And this man, whom I know, is brave enough to right that wrong himself if his underlings failed.'

'I follow,' said Armiston dully.

'But,' said Johanssen, leaning forward and tapping the author on the knee—'but the task proves too big for him. What did he do? He asked the cleverest man in the world to help him. And Godahl helped him. That,' said Johanssen, interrupting Armiston with a raised finger, 'is the story of the white ruby. The Story of the White Ruby, you see, is something infinitely finer than mere vulgar robbery and murder, as the author of Godahl the Infallible conceived it.'

Johanssen said a great deal more. In the end he took the lozenge-shaped diamond pendant and put the glass on the silver bar, that his friend might see the inscription on the back. He told him what the inscription signified—'Brother of a King,' and, furthermore, how few men alive possessed the capacity for brotherhood.

'I think,' said Armiston as he was about to take his leave, 'that I will travel in the Straits this winter.'

'If you do,' said Johanssen, 'I earnestly advise you to leave your Godahl and his decoration at home.'

THE ADVENTURE OF
THE UNIQUE "HAMLET"

Being an Unrecorded Adventure of Mr. Sherlock Holmes

VINCENT STARRETT
(1886–1974)

One of the greatest bibliophiles in this century, Starrett wrote his "Books Alive" column for the Chicago Tribune *for many years. His numerous essays and books often centered on detective fiction in general and Sherlock Holmes specifically. This story appeared originally in a small volume believed to have been printed in an edition of 110 copies, one of the great rarities in the world of collectable Sherlock Holmes material and valued in the thousands of dollars.*

1

OLMES," SAID I ONE MORNING, as I stood in our bay window, looking idly into the street, "surely here comes a madman. Someone has incautiously left the door open and the poor fellow has slipped out. What a pity!"

It was a glorious morning in the spring, with a fresh breeze and inviting sunlight, but as it was early few persons were as yet astir. Birds twittered under the neighboring eaves, and from the far end of the thoroughfare came faintly the droning cry of an umbrella repairman; a lean cat slunk across the cobbles and disappeared into a courtway; but for the most part the street was deserted, save for the eccentric individual who had called forth my exclamation.

Sherlock Holmes rose lazily from the chair in which he had been lounging and came to my side, standing with long legs spread and hands in the pockets of his dressing gown. He smiled as he saw the singular personage coming along; and a personage the man seemed to be, despite his curious actions, for he was tall and portly, with elderly whiskers of the variety called mutton-chop, and eminently respectable. He was loping curiously, like a tired hound, lifting his knees high as he ran, and a heavy double watch chain bounced against and rebounded from the plump line of his figured waistcoat. With one hand he clutched despairingly at his tall silk hat, while with the other he made strange

---

* A pastiche, uncanonical and un-Conanical, and fairly satirical. It may also be read as a good-humored satire on book collectors.

gestures in the air, in a state of emotion bordering on distraction. We could almost see the spasmodic workings of his countenance.

"What in the world can ail him?" I cried. "See how he glances at the houses as he passes."

"He is looking at the numbers," responded Sherlock Holmes with dancing eyes, "and I fancy it is ours that will give him the greatest happiness. His profession, of course, is obvious."

"A banker, I should imagine, or at least a person of affluence," I ventured, wondering what curious detail had betrayed the man's vocation to my remarkable companion in a single glance.

"Affluent, yes," said Holmes with a mischievous twinkle, "but not exactly a banker, Watson. Notice the sagging pockets, despite the excellence of his clothing, and the rather exaggerated madness of his eye. He is a collector, or I am very much mistaken."

"My dear fellow!" I exclaimed. "At his age and in his station! And why should he be seeking us? When we settled that last bill—"

"Of books," said my friend severely. "He is a book collector. His line is Caxtons, Elzevirs, and Gutenberg Bibles, not the sordid reminders of unpaid grocery accounts. See, he is turning in, as I expected, and in a moment he will stand upon our hearthrug and tell the harrowing tale of a unique volume and its extraordinary disappearance."

His eyes gleamed and he rubbed his hands together in satisfaction. I could not hope that his conjecture was correct, for he had had little recently to occupy his mind, and I lived in constant fear that he would seek that stimulation his active brain required in the long-tabooed cocaine bottle.

As Holmes finished speaking, the doorbell echoed through the house; then hurried feet were sounding on the stairs, while the wailing voice of Mrs. Hudson, raised in protest, could only have been occasioned by frustration of her coveted privilege of bearing up our caller's card. Then the door burst violently inward and the object of our analysis staggered to the center of the room and pitched headforemost upon our center rug. There he lay, a magnificent ruin, with his head on the fringed border and his feet in the coal scuttle; and sealed within his motionless lips was the amazing story he had come to tell—for that it was amazing we could not doubt in the light of our client's extraordinary behavior.

Sherlock Holmes ran quickly for the brandy, while I knelt beside the stricken man and loosened his wilted neckband. He was not dead, and when we had forced the flask beneath his teeth he sat up in groggy fashion, passing a dazed hand across his eyes. Then he scrambled to his feet with an embarrassed apology for his weakness, and fell into the chair which Holmes invitingly held toward him.

"That is right, Mr. Harrington Edwards," said my companion soothingly. "Be quite calm, my dear sir, and when you have recovered your composure you will find us ready to listen."

"You know me then?" cried our visitor. There was pride in his voice and he lifted his eyebrows in surprise.

"I had never heard of you until this moment; but if you wish to conceal your identity it would be well," said Sherlock Holmes, "for you to leave your bookplates at home." As Holmes spoke he returned a little package of folded paper slips, which he had picked from the floor. "They fell from your hat when you had the misfortune to collapse," he added whimsically.

"Yes, yes," cried the collector, a deep blush spreading across his features. "I remember now; my hat was a little large and I folded a number of them and placed them beneath the sweatband. I had forgotten."

"Rather shabby usage for a handsome etched plate," smiled my companion; "but that is your affair. And now, sir, if you are quite at ease, let us hear what it is that has brought you, a collector of books, from Poke Stogis Manor—the name is on the plate—to the office of Sherlock Holmes, consulting expert in crime. Surely nothing but the theft of Mahomet's own copy of the Koran can have affected you so strongly."

Mr. Harrington Edwards smiled feebly at the jest, then sighed. "Alas," he murmured, "if that were all! But I shall begin at the beginning.

"You must know, then, that I am the greatest Shakespearean commentator in the world. My collection of *ana* is unrivaled and much of the world's collection (and consequently its knowledge of the veritable Shakespeare) has emanated from my pen. One book I did not possess: it was unique, in the correct sense of that abused word, the greatest Shakespeare rarity in the world. Few knew that it existed, for its existence was kept a profound secret among a chosen few. Had it become known that this book was in England—anywhere, indeed—its owner would have been hounded to his grave by wealthy Americans.

"It was in the possession of my friend—I tell you this in strictest confidence—of my friend, Sir Nathaniel Brooke-Bannerman, whose place at Walton-on-Walton is next to my own. A scant two hundred yards separate our dwellings; so intimate has been our friendship that a few years ago the fence between our estates was removed, and each of us roamed or loitered at will in the other's preserves.

"For some years, now, I have been at work upon my greatest book—my magnum opus. It was to be my last book also embodying the results of a lifetime of study and research. Sir, I know Elizabethan London better than any man alive; better than any man who ever lived, I think—." He burst suddenly into tears.

"There, there," said Sherlock Holmes gently. "Do not be distressed. Pray continue with your interesting narrative. What was this book—which, I take it, in some manner has disappeared? You borrowed it from your friend?"

"That is what I am coming to," said Mr. Harrington Edwards, drying his tears, "but as for help, Mr. Holmes, I fear that is beyond even you. As you surmise, I needed this book. Knowing its value, which could not be fixed, for the book is priceless, and knowing Sir Nathaniel's idolatry of it, I hesitated before asking for the loan of it. But I had to have it, for without it my work could not have been completed, and at length I made my request. I suggested that I visit him and go through the volume under his eyes, he sitting at my side throughout my entire examination, and servants stationed at every door and window, with fowling pieces in their hands.

"You can imagine my astonishment when Sir Nathaniel laughed at my precautions. 'My dear Edwards,' he said, 'that would be all very well were you Arthur Rambidge or Sir Homer Nantes (mentioning the two great men of the British Museum), or were you Mr. Henry Hutterson, the American railway magnate; but you are my friend Harrington Edwards, and you shall take the book home with you for as long as you like.' I protested vigorously, I can assure you; but he would have it so, and as I was touched by this mark of his esteem, at length I permitted him to have his way. My God! If I had remained adamant! If I had only—."

He broke off and for a moment stared blindly into space. His eyes were directed at the Persian slipper on the wall, in the toe of which Holmes kept his tobacco, but we could see that his thoughts were far away.

"Come, Mr. Edwards," said Holmes firmly. "You are agitating yourself unduly. And you are unreasonably prolonging our curiosity. You have not yet told us what this book is."

Mr. Harrington Edwards gripped the arm of the chair in which he sat. Then he spoke, and his voice was low and thrilling.

"The book was a *Hamlet* quarto, dated 1602, presented by Shakespeare to his friend Drayton, with an inscription four lines in length, written and signed by the Master, himself!"

"My dear sir!" I exclaimed. Holmes blew a long, slow whistle of astonishment.

"It is true," cried the collector. "That is the book I borrowed, and that is the book I lost! The long-sought quarto of 1602, actually inscribed in Shakespeare's own hand! His greatest drama, in an edition dated a year earlier than any that is known; a perfect copy, and with four lines in his own handwriting! Unique! Extraordinary! Amazing! Astounding! Colossal! Incredible! Un—."

He seemed wound up to continue indefinitely; but Holmes, who had sat quite still at first, shocked by the importance of the loss, interrupted the flow of adjectives.

"I appreciate your emotion, Mr. Edwards," he said, "and the book is indeed all that you say it is. Indeed, it is so important that we must at once attack the problem of rediscovering it. The book, I take it, is readily identifiable?"

"Mr. Holmes," said our client, earnestly, "it would be impossible to hide it. It is so important a volume that, upon coming into its possession, Sir Nathaniel Brooke-Bannerman called a consultation of the great binders of the Empire, at which were present Mr. Riviere, Messrs. Sangorski and Sutcliffe, Mr. Zaehnsdorf, and certain others. They and myself, with two others, alone know of the book's existence. When I tell you that it is bound in brown levant morocco, with leather joints and brown levant doublures and flyleaves, the whole elaborately gold-tooled, inlaid with seven hundred and fifty separate pieces of various colored leathers, and enriched by the insertion of eighty-seven precious stones, I need not add that it is a design that never will be duplicated, and I mention only a few of its glories. The binding was personally done by Messrs. Riviere, Sangorski, Sutcliffe, and Zaehnsdorf, working alternately, and is a work of such enchantment that any man might gladly die a thousand deaths for the privilege of owning it for twenty minutes."

"Dear me," quoth Sherlock Holmes, "it must indeed be a handsome volume, and from your description, together with a realization of its importance by reason of its association, I gather that it is something beyond what might be termed a valuable book."

"Priceless!" cried Mr. Harrington Edwards. "The combined wealth of India, Mexico, and Wall Street would be all too little for its purchase."

"You are anxious to recover this book?" asked Sherlock Holmes, looking at him keenly.

"My God!" shrieked the collector, rolling up his eyes and clawing at the air with his hands. "Do you suppose—?"

"Tut, tut!" Holmes interrupted. "I was only teasing you. It is a book that might move even you, Mr. Harrington Edwards, to theft—but we may put aside that notion. Your emotion is too sincere, and besides you know too well the difficulties of hiding such a volume as you describe. Indeed, only a very daring man would purloin it and keep it long in his possession. Pray tell us how you came to lose it."

Mr. Harrington Edwards seized the brandy flask, which stood at his elbow, and drained it at a gulp. With the renewed strength thus obtained, he continued his story:

"As I have said, Sir Nathaniel forced me to accept the loan of the book, much against my wishes. On the evening that I called for it, he told me that two of his servants, heavily armed, would accompany me across the grounds to my home. 'There is no danger,' he said, 'but you will feel better'; and I heartily agreed with him. How shall I tell you what happened? Mr. Holmes, it was those very servants who assailed me and robbed me of my priceless borrowing!"

Sherlock Holmes rubbed his lean hands with satisfaction. "Splendid!" he murmured. "This is a case after my own heart. Watson, these are deep waters in which we are adventuring. But you are rather lengthy about this, Mr. Edwards. Perhaps it will help matters if I ask you a few questions. By what road did you go to your home?"

"By the main road, a good highway which lies in front of our estates. I preferred it to the shadows of the wood."

"And there were some two hundred yards between your doors. At what point did the assault occur?"

"Almost midway between the two entrance drives, I should say."

"There was no light?"

"That of the moon only."

"Did you know these servants who accompanied you?"

"One I knew slightly; the other I had not seen before."

"Describe them to me, please."

"The man who is known to me is called Miles. He is clean-shaven, short and powerful, although somewhat elderly. He was known, I believe, as Sir Nathaniel's most trusted servant; he had been with Sir Nathaniel for years. I cannot describe him minutely for, of course, I never paid much attention to him. The other was tall and thickset, and wore a heavy beard. He was a silent fellow; I do not believe that he spoke a word during the journey."

"Miles was more communicative?"

"Oh yes—even garrulous, perhaps. He talked about the weather and the moon, and I forget what else."

"Never about books?"

"There was no mention of books between any of us."

"Just how did the attack occur?"

"It was very sudden. We had reached, as I say, about the halfway point, when the big man seized me by the throat—to prevent outcry, I suppose—and on the instant, Miles snatched the volume from my grasp and was off. In a moment his companion followed him. I had been half throttled and could not immediately cry out; but when I could articulate, I made the countryside ring with my cries. I ran after them, but failed even to catch another sight of them. They had disappeared completely."

"Did you all leave the house together?"

"Miles and I left together; the second man joined us at the porter's lodge. He had been attending to some of his duties."

"And Sir Nathaniel—where was he?"

"He said good-night on the threshold."

"What has he had to say about all this?"

"I have not told him."

"You have not told him?" echoed Sherlock Holmes, in astonishment.

"I have not dared," confessed our client miserably. "It will kill him. That book was the breath of his life."

"When did all this occur?" I put in, with a glance at Holmes.

"Excellent, Watson," said my friend, answering my glance. "I was just about to ask the same question."

"Just last night," was Mr. Harrington Edwards' reply. "I was crazy most of the night, and didn't sleep a wink. I came to you the first thing this morning. Indeed, I tried to raise you on the telephone, last night, but could not establish a connection."

"Yes," said Holmes, reminiscently, "we were attending Mme Trentini's first night. We dined later at Albani's."

"Oh, Mr. Holmes, do you think you can help me?" cried the abject collector.

"I trust so," answered my friend, cheerfully. "Indeed, I am certain I can. Such a book, as you remark, is not easily hidden. What say you, Watson, to a run down to Walton-on-Walton?"

"There is a train in half an hour," said Mr. Harrington Edwards, looking at his watch. "Will you return with me?"

"No, no," laughed Holmes, "that would never do. We must not be seen together just yet, Mr. Edwards. Go back yourself on the first train, by all means, unless you have further business in London. My friend and I will go together. There is another train this morning?"

"An hour later."

"Excellent. Until we meet, then!"

2

We took the train from Paddington Station an hour later, as we had promised, and began our journey to Walton-on-Walton, a pleasant, aristocratic little village and the scene of the curious accident to our friend of Poke Stogis manor. Sherlock Holmes, lying back in his seat, blew earnest smoke rings at the ceiling of our compartment, which fortunately was empty, while I devoted myself to the morning paper. After a bit I tired of this occupation and turned to Holmes to find him looking out of the window, wreathed in smiles, and quoting Horace softly under his breath.

"You have a theory?" I asked, in surprise.

"It is a capital mistake to theorize in advance of the evidence," he replied. "Still, I have given some thought to the interesting problem of our friend, Mr. Harrington Edwards, and there are several indications which can point to only one conclusion."

"And whom do you believe to be the thief?"

"My dear fellow," said Sherlock Holmes, "you forget we already know the thief. Edwards has testified quite clearly that it was Miles who snatched the volume."

"True," I admitted, abashed. "I had forgotten. All we must do then, is to find Miles."

"And a motive," added my friend, chuckling. "What would you say, Watson, was the motive in this case?"

"Jealousy," I replied.

"You surprise me!"

"Miles had been bribed by a rival collector, who in some manner had learned about this remarkable volume. You remember Edwards told us this second man joined them at the lodge. That would give an excellent opportunity for the substitution of a man other than the servant intended by Sir Nathaniel. Is not that good reasoning?"

"You surpass yourself, my dear Watson," murmured Holmes. "It is excellently reasoned, and as you justly observe, the opportunity for a substitution was perfect."

"Do you not agree with me?"

"Hardly, Watson. A rival collector, in order to accomplishment this remarkable coup, first would have to have known of the volume, as you suggest, but also he must have known upon what night Mr. Harrington Edwards would go to Sir Nathaniel's to get it, which would point to collaboration on the part of our client.

As a matter of fact, however, Mr. Edwards' decision to accept the loan was, I believe, sudden and without previous determination."

"I do not recall his saying so."

"He did not say so, but it is a simple deduction. A book collector is mad enough to begin with, Watson; but tempt him with such bait as this Shakespeare quarto and he is bereft of all sanity. Mr. Edwards would not have been able to wait. It was just the night before that Sir Nathaniel promised him the book, and it was just last night that he flew to accept the offer—flying, incidentally, to disaster also. The miracle is that he was able to wait an entire day."

"Wonderful!" I cried.

"Elementary," said Holmes. "If you are interested, you will do well to read Harley Graham on *Transcendental Emotion*; while I have myself been guilty of a small brochure in which I catalogue some twelve hundred professions and the emotional effect upon their members of unusual tidings, good and bad."

We were the only passengers to alight at Walton-on-Walton, but rapid inquiry developed that Mr. Harrington Edwards had returned on the previous train. Holmes, who had disguised himself before leaving the coach, did all the talking. He wore his cap peak backward, carried a pencil behind his ear, and had turned up the bottoms of his trousers; while from one pocket dangled the end of a linen tape measure. He was a municipal surveyor to the life, and I could not but think that, meeting him suddenly in the highway I should not myself have known him. At his suggestion, I dented the crown of my hat and turned my jacket inside out. Then he gave me an end of the tape measure, while he, carrying the other, went on ahead. In this fashion, stopping from time to time to kneel in the dust and ostensibly to measure sections of the roadway, we proceeded toward Poke Stogis Manor. The occasional villagers whom we encountered on their way to the station paid us no more attention than if we had been rabbits.

Shortly we came in sight of our friend's dwelling, a picturesque and rambling abode, sitting far back in its own grounds and bordered by a square of sentinel oaks. A gravel pathway led from the roadway to the house entrance and, as we passed, the sunlight struck fire from an antique brass knocker on the door. The whole picture, with its background of gleaming countryside, was one of rural calm and comfort; we could with difficulty believe it the scene of the curious problem we had come to investigate.

"We shall not enter yet," said Sherlock Holmes, passing the gate leading into our client's acreage; "but we shall endeavor to be back in time for luncheon."

From this point the road progressed downward in a gentle decline and the vegetation grew more thickly on either side of the road. Sherlock Holmes kept his eyes stolidly on the path before us, and when we had covered about a hundred yards he stopped. "Here," he said, pointing, "the assault occurred."

I looked closely at the earth, but could see no sign of struggle.

"You recall it was midway between the two houses that it happened," he continued. "No, there are few signs; there was no violent tussle. Fortunately, however, we had our proverbial fall of rain last evening and the earth has retained impressions nicely." He indicated the faint imprint of a foot, then another, and still another. Kneeling down, I was able to see that, indeed, many feet had passed along the road.

Holmes flung himself at full length in the dirt and wriggled swiftly about, his nose to the earth, muttering rapidly in French. Then he whipped out a glass, the better to examine something that had caught his eye; but in a moment he shook his head in disappointment and continued with his exploration. I was irresistibly reminded of a noble hound, at fault, sniffing in circles in an effort to re-establish a lost scent. In a moment, however, he had it, for with a little cry of pleasure he rose to his feet, zigzagged curiously across the road and paused before a bridge, a lean finger pointing accusingly at a break in the thicket.

"No wonder they disappeared," he smiled as I came up. "Edwards thought they continued up the road, but here is where they broke through." Then stepping back a little distance, he ran forward lightly and cleared the hedge at a bound.

"Follow me carefully," he warned, "for we must not allow our own footprints to confuse us." I fell more heavily than my companion, but in a moment he had me up and helped me to steady myself. "See," he cried, examining the earth; and deep in the mud and grass I saw the prints of two pairs of feet.

"The small man broke through," said Sherlock Holmes, exultantly, "but the larger rascal leaped over the hedge. See how deeply his prints are marked; he landed heavily here in the soft ooze. It is significant, Watson, that they came this way. Does it suggest nothing to you?"

"That they were men who knew Edwards' grounds as well as the Brooke-Bannerman estate," I answered; and thrilled with pleasure at my friend's nod of approbation.

He flung himself upon the ground without further conversation, and for some moments we both crawled painfully across the grass. Then a shocking thought occurred to me.

"Holmes," I whispered in dismay, "do you see where these footprints tend? They are directed toward the home of our client, Mr. Harrington Edwards!"

He nodded his head slowly, and his lips were tight and thin. The double line of impressions ended abruptly at the back door of Poke Stogis Manor!

Sherlock Holmes rose to his feet and looked at his watch.

"We are just in time for luncheon," he announced, and brushed off his garments. Then, deliberately, he knocked upon the door. In a few moments we were in the presence of our client.

"We have been roaming about in the neighborhood," apologized the detective, "and took the liberty of coming to your rear door."

"You have a clue?" asked Mr. Harrington Edwards eagerly.

A queer smile of triumph sat upon Holmes's lips.

"Indeed," he said quietly, "I believe I have solved your little problem, Mr. Harrington Edwards."

"My dear Holmes!" I cried, and "My dear sir!" cried our client.

"I have yet to establish a motive," confessed my friend; "but as to the main facts there can be no question."

Mr. Harrington Edwards fell into a chair; he was white and shaking.

"The book," he croaked. "Tell me."

"Patience, my good sir," counseled Holmes kindly. "We have had nothing to eat since sunup, and we are famished. All in good time. Let us first have luncheon and then all shall be made clear. Meanwhile, I should like to telephone to Sir Nathaniel Brooke-Bannerman, for I wish him also to hear what I have to say."

Our client's pleas were in vain. Holmes would have his little joke and his luncheon. In the end, Mr. Harrington Edwards staggered away to the kitchen to order a repast, and Sherlock Holmes talked rapidly and unintelligibly into the telephone and came back with a smile on his face. But I asked no questions; in good time this extraordinary man would tell his story in his own way. I had heard all that he had heard, and had seen all that he had seen; yet I was completely at sea. Still, our host's ghastly smile hung heavily in my mind, and come what would I felt sorry for him. In a little time we were seated at table. Our client, haggard and nervous, ate slowly and with apparent discomfort; his eyes were never long absent from Holmes's inscrutable face. I was little better off, but Sherlock Holmes ate with gusto, relating meanwhile a number of his earlier adventures—which I may some day give to the world, if I am able to read my illegible notes made on the occasion.

When the dreary meal had been concluded we went into the library, where Sherlock Holmes took possession of the easiest chair with an air of proprietorship that would have been amusing in other circumstances. He screwed together his long pipe and lighted it with almost malicious lack of haste, while Mr. Harrington Edwards perspired against the mantel in an agony of apprehension.

"Why must you keep us waiting, Mr. Holmes?" he whispered. "Tell us, at once, please, who— who—." His voice trailed off into a moan.

"The criminal," said Sherlock Holmes smoothly, "is—."

"Sir Nathaniel Brooke-Bannerman!" said a maid, suddenly putting her head in at the door; and on the heels of her announcement stalked the handsome baronet, whose priceless volume had caused all this commotion and unhappiness.

Sir Nathaniel was white, and he appeared ill. He burst at once into talk.

"I have been much upset by your call," he said, looking meanwhile at our client. "You say you have something to tell me about the quarto. Don't say—that—anything— has happened—to it!" He clutched nervously at the wall to steady himself, and I felt deep pity for the unhappy man.

Mr. Harrington Edwards looked at Sherlock Holmes. "Oh, Mr. Holmes," he cried pathetically, "why did you send for him?"

"Because," said my friend, "I wish him to hear the truth about the Shakespeare quarto. Sir Nathaniel, I believe you have not been told as yet that Mr. Edwards was robbed, last night, of your precious volume—robbed by the trusted servants whom you sent with him to protect it."

"What!" screamed the titled collector. He staggered and fumbled madly at his heart, then collapsed into a chair. "My God!" he muttered, and then again: "My God!"

"I should have thought you would have been suspicious of evil when your servants did not return," pursued the detective.

"I have not seen them," whispered Sir Nathaniel. "I do not mingle with my servants. I did not know they had failed to return. Tell me—tell me all!"

"Mr. Edwards," said Sherlock Holmes, turning to our client, "will you repeat your story, please?"

Mr. Harrington Edwards, thus adjured, told the unhappy tale again, ending with a heartbroken cry of "Oh, Nathaniel, can you ever forgive me?"

"I do not know that it was entirely your fault," observed Holmes cheerfully. "Sir Nathaniel's own servants are the guilty ones, and surely he sent them with you."

"But you said you had solved the case, Mr. Holmes," cried our client, in a frenzy of despair.

"Yes," agreed Holmes, "it is solved. You have had the clue in your own hands ever since the occurrence, but you did not know how to use it. It all turns upon the curious actions of the taller servant, prior to the assault."

"The actions of—?" stammered Mr. Harrington Edwards. "Why, he did nothing— said nothing!"

"That is the curious circumstance," said Sherlock Holmes. Sir Nathaniel got to his feet with difficulty.

"Mr. Holmes," he said, "this has upset me more than I can tell you. Spare no pains to recover the book and to bring to justice the scoundrels who stole it. But I must go away and think—think—."

"Stay," said my friend. "I have already caught one of them."

"What? Where?" cried the two collectors together.

"Here," said Sherlock Holmes, and stepping forward he laid a hand on the baronet's shoulder. "You, Sir Nathaniel, were the taller servant, you were one of the thieves who throttled Mr. Harrington Edwards and took from him your own book. And now, sir, will you tell us why you did it?"

Sir Nathaniel Brooke-Bannerman staggered and would have fallen had I not rushed forward and supported him. I placed him in a chair. As we looked at him we saw confession in his eyes; guilt was written in his haggard face.

"Come, come," said Holmes impatiently. "Or will it make it easier for you to tell the story as it occurred? Let it be so, then. You parted with Mr. Harrington Edwards on your doorsill, Sir Nathaniel, bidding your best friend good-night with a smile on your lips and evil in your heart. And as soon as you had crossed the door, you slipped into an enveloping raincoat, turned up your collar, and hastened by a shorter road to the porter's lodge, where you joined Mr. Edwards and Miles as one of your own servants. You spoke no word at any time, because you feared to speak. You were afraid Mr. Edwards would recognize your voice, while your beard, hastily assumed, protected your face and in the darkness your figure passed unnoticed.

"Having strangled and robbed your best friend, then, of your own book, you and your scoundrelly assistant fled across Mr. Edwards' fields to his own back door, thinking that, if investigation followed, I would be called in, and would trace those footprints and fix the crime upon Mr. Harrington Edwards—as part of a criminal plan, prearranged with your rascally servants, who would be supposed to be in the pay of Mr. Edwards and the ringleaders in a counterfeit assault upon his person. Your mistake, sir, was in ending your trail abruptly at Mr. Edwards' back door. Had you left another trail, then, leading back to your own domicile, I should unhesitatingly have arrested Mr. Harrington Edwards for the theft.

"Surely you must know that in criminal cases handled by me, it is never the obvious solution that is the correct one. The mere fact that the finger of suspicion is made to point at a certain individual is sufficient to absolve that individual from guilt. Had you read the little works of my friend and colleague, Dr. Watson, you would not have made such a mistake. Yet you claim to be a bookman!"

A low moan from the unhappy baronet was his only answer.

"To continue, however; there at Mr. Edwards' own back door you ended your trail, entering his house—his own house—and spending the night under his roof, while his cries and ravings over his loss filled the night and brought joy to your unspeakable soul. And in the morning, when he had gone forth to consult me, you quietly left—you and Miles—and returned to your own place by the beaten highway."

"Mercy!" cried the defeated wretch, cowering in his chair. "If it is made public, I am ruined. I was driven to it. I could not let Mr. Edwards examine the book, for that way exposure would follow; yet I could not refuse him—my best friend—when he asked its loan."

"Your words tell me all that I did not know," said Sherlock Holmes sternly. "The motive now is only too plain. The work, sir, was a forgery, and knowing that your erudite friend would discover it, you chose to blacken his name to save your own. Was the book insured?"

"Insured for £100,000, he told me," interrupted Mr. Harrington Edwards excitedly.

"So that he planned at once to dispose of this dangerous and dubious item, and to reap a golden reward," commented Holmes. "Come, sir, tell us about it. How much of it was forgery? Merely the inscription?"

"I will tell you," said the baronet suddenly, "and throw myself upon the mercy of my friend, Mr. Edwards. The whole book, in effect, was a forgery. It was originally made up of two imperfect copies of the 1604 quarto. Out of the pair I made one perfect volume, and a skillful workman, now dead, changed the date for me so cleverly that only an expert of the first water could have detected it. Such an expert, however, is Mr. Harrington Edwards—the one man in the world who could have unmasked me."

"Thank you, Nathaniel," said Mr. Harrington Edwards gratefully.

"The inscription, of course, also was forged," continued the baronet. "You may as well know everything."

"And the book?" asked Holmes. "Where did you destroy it?"

A grim smile settled on Sir Nathaniel's features. "It is even now burning in Mr. Edwards' own furnace," he said.

"Then it cannot yet be consumed," cried Holmes, and dashed into the cellar, to emerge some moments later, in high spirits, carrying a charred leaf of paper in his hand.

"It is a pity," he cried, "a pity! In spite of its questionable authenticity, it was a noble specimen. It is only half consumed; but let it burn away. I have preserved one leaf as a souvenir of the occasion." He folded it carefully and placed it in his wallet. "Mr. Harrington Edwards, I fancy the decision in this matter is for you to announce. Sir Nathaniel, of course, must make no effort to collect the insurance."

"Let us forget it, then," said Mr. Harrington Edwards, with a sigh. "Let it be a sealed chapter in the history of bibliomania." He looked at Sir Nathaniel Brooke-Bannerman for a long moment, then held out his hand. "I forgive you, Nathaniel," he said simply.

Their hands met; tears stood in the baronet's eyes. Powerfully moved, Holmes and I turned from the affecting scene and crept to the door unnoticed. In a moment the free air was blowing on our temples, and we were coughing the dust of the library from our lungs.

3

"They are a strange people, these book collectors," mused Sherlock Holmes as we rattled back to town.

"My only regret is that I shall be unable to publish my notes on this interesting case," I responded.

"Wait a bit, my dear Doctor," counseled Holmes, "and it will be possible. In time both of them will come to look upon it as a hugely diverting episode, and will tell it upon themselves. Then your notes shall be brought forth and the history of another of Mr. Sherlock Holmes's little problems shall be given to the world."

"It will always be a reflection upon Sir Nathaniel," I demurred.

"He will glory in it," prophesied Sherlock Holmes. "He will go down in bookish circles with Chatterton, and Ireland, and Payne Collier. Mark my words, he is not blind even now to the chance this gives him for a sinister immortality. He will be the first to tell it."

"But why did you preserve the leaf from *Hamlet?*" I inquired. "Why not a jewel from the binding?"

Sherlock Holmes laughed heartily. Then he slowly unfolded the leaf in question, and directed a humorous finger to a spot upon the page.

"A fancy," he responded, "to preserve so accurate a characterization of either of our friends. The line is a real jewel. See, the good Polonius says: 'That he is mad, 'tis true; 'tis true 'tis pittie; and pittie 'tis 'tis true.' There is as much sense in Master Will as in Hafiz or Confucius, and a greater felicity of expression . . . Here is London, and now, my dear Watson, if we hasten we shall be just in time for Zabriski's matinee!"

THE GIOCONDA SMILE

ALDOUS HUXLEY
(1894–1963)

The author of highly praised novels of societal decadence such as Crome Yellow *and* Antic Hay *and then of the futuristic "Utopian" novel* Brave New World, *Huxley's only crime story is this famous tale of slowly engulfing terror. It was collected in* Mortal Coils *(1922) and was later adapted for the stage as a three-act play called* The Gioconda Smile *in Great Britain and* Mortal Coils *in the United States. It opened in 1947 but enjoyed little success.*

ISS SPENCE WILL BE DOWN directly, sir."

"Thank you," said Mr. Hutton, without turning round. Janet Spence's parlormaid was so ugly—ugly on purpose, it always seemed to him, malignantly, criminally ugly—that he could not bear to look at her more than was necessary. The door closed. Left to himself, Mr. Hutton got up and began to wander round the room, looking with meditative eyes at the familiar objects it contained.

Photographs of Greek statuary, photographs of the Roman Forum, colored prints of Italian masterpieces, all very safe and well known. Poor, dear Janet, what a prig—what an intellectual snob! Her real taste was illustrated in that water-color by the pavement artist, the one she had paid half a crown for (and thirty-five shillings for the frame). How often he had heard her tell the story, how often expatiate on the beauties of that skillful imitation of an oleograph! "A real Artist in the streets," and you could hear the capital A in Artist as she spoke the words. She made you feel

that part of his glory had entered into Janet Spence when she tendered him that half crown for the copy of the oleograph. She was implying a compliment to her own taste and penetration. A genuine Old Master for half a crown. Poor, dear Janet!

Mr. Hutton came to a pause in front of a small oblong mirror. Stooping a little to get a full view of his face, he passed a white, well-manicured finger over his mustache. It was as curly, as freshly auburn as it had been twenty years ago. His hair still retained its color, and there was no sign of baldness yet—only a certain elevation of the brow. "Shakespearean," thought Mr. Hutton, with a smile, as he surveyed the smooth and polished expanse of his forehead.

Others abide our question, thou art free. . . . Footsteps in the sea . . . Majesty . . . Shakespeare, thou shouldst be living at this hour. No, that was Milton, wasn't it? Milton, the Lady of Christ's. There was no lady about him. He was what the women would call a manly man. That was why they liked him—for the curly auburn mustache and the discreet redolence of tobacco. Mr. Hutton smiled again; he enjoyed making fun of himself. Lady of Christ's? No, no. He was the Christ of Ladies. Very pretty, very pretty. The Christ of Ladies. Mr. Hutton wished there were somebody he could tell the joke to. Poor, dear Janet wouldn't appreciate it, alas!

He straightened himself up, patted his hair, and resumed his peregrination. Damn the Roman Forum; he hated those dreary photographs.

Suddenly he became aware that Janet Spence was in the room, standing near the door. Mr. Hutton started, as though he had been taken in some felonious act. To make these silent and spectral appearances was one of Janet Spence's peculiar talents. Perhaps she had been there all the time, had seen him looking at himself in the mirror. Impossible! But, still, it was disquieting.

"Oh, you gave me such a surprise," said Mr. Hutton, recovering his smile and advancing with outstretched hand to meet her.

Miss Spence was smiling too: her Gioconda smile, he had once called it in a moment of half-ironical flattery. Miss Spence had taken the compliment seriously, and had always tried to live up to the Leonardo standard. She smiled on his silence while Mr. Hutton shook hands; that was part of the Gioconda business.

"I hope you're well," said Mr. Hutton. "You look it."

What a queer face she had! That small mouth pursed forward by the Gioconda expression into a little snout with a round hole in the middle as though for whistling—it was like a penholder seen from the front. Above the mouth a well-shaped nose, finely aquiline. Eyes large, lustrous, and dark, with the largeness, luster, and darkness that seems to invite sties and an occasional bloodshot suffusion. They were fine eyes, unchangingly grave. The penholder might do its Gioconda trick, but the eyes never altered in their earnestness. Above them, a pair of boldly arched, heavily penciled black eyebrows lent a surprising air of power, as of a Roman matron, to the upper portion of the face. Her hair was dark and equally Roman; Agrippina from the brows upward.

"I thought I'd just look in on my way home," Mr. Hutton went on. "Ah, it's good to be back here"—he indicated with a wave of his hand the flowers in the vases, the sunshine and greenery beyond the windows—"it's good to be back in the country after a stuffy day of business in town."

Miss Spence, who had sat down, pointed to a chair at her side.

"No, really, I can't sit down," Mr. Hutton protested. "I must get back to see how poor Emily is. She was rather seedy this morning." He sat down, nevertheless. "It's these wretched liver chills. She's always getting them. Women—" He broke off and coughed, so as to hide the fact that he had uttered. He was about to say that women with weak digestions ought not to marry; but the remark was too cruel, and he didn't really believe it. Janet Spence, moreover, was a believer in eternal flames and spiritual attachments. "She hopes to be well enough," he added, "to see you at luncheon tomorrow. Can you come? Do!" He smiled persuasively. "It's my invitation too, you know."

She dropped her eyes, and Mr. Hutton almost thought that he detected a certain reddening of the cheek. It was a tribute; he stroked his mustache.

"I should like to come if you think Emily's really well enough to have a visitor."

"Of course. You'll do her good. You'll do us both good. In married life three is often better company than two."

"Oh, you're cynical."

Mr. Hutton always had a desire to say "Bow-wow-wow" whenever that last word was spoken. It irritated him more than any other word in the language. But instead of barking he made haste to protest.

"No, no. I'm only speaking a melancholy truth. Reality doesn't always come up to the ideal, you know. But that doesn't make me believe any less in the ideal. Indeed, I believe in it passionately—the ideal of a matrimony between two people in perfect accord. I think it's realizable. I'm sure it is."

He paused significantly and looked at her with an arch expression. A virgin of thirty-six, but still unwithered; she had her charms. And there was something really rather enigmatic about her. Miss Spence made no reply but continued to smile. There were times when Mr. Hutton got rather bored with the Gioconda. He stood up.

"I must really be going now. Farewell, mysterious Gioconda." The smile grew intenser, focused itself, as it were, in a narrower snout. Mr. Hutton made a cinque-cento gesture, and kissed her extended hand. It was the first time he had done such a thing; the action seemed not to be resented. "I look forward to tomorrow."

"Do you?"

For answer Mr. Hutton once more kissed her hand, then turned to go. Miss Spence accompanied him to the porch.

"Where's your car?" she asked.

"I left it at the gate of the drive."

"I'll come and see you off."

"No, no." Mr. Hutton was playful, but determined. "You must do no such thing. I simply forbid you."

"But I should like to come," Miss Spence protested, throwing a rapid Gioconda at him.

Mr. Hutton held up his hand. "No," he repeated, and then, with a gesture that was almost the blowing of a kiss, he started to run down the drive, lightly on his toes, with long, bounding strides like a boy's. He was proud of that run; it was quite marvelously youthful. Still, he was glad the drive was no longer. At the last bend, before passing out of sight of the house, he halted and turned round. Miss Spence was still standing on the steps, smiling her smile. He waved his hand, and this time quite definitely and overtly wafted a kiss in her direction. Then, breaking once more into his magnificent canter, he rounded the last dark promontory of trees. Once out of sight of the house he let his high paces decline to a trot, and finally to a walk. He took out his handkerchief and began wiping his neck inside his collar. What fools, what fools! Had there ever been such an ass as poor, dear Janet Spence? Never, unless it was himself. Decidedly he was the more malignant fool, since he, at least, was aware of his folly and still persisted in it. Why did he persist? Ah, the problem that was himself, the problem that was other people.

He had reached the gate. A large, prosperous-looking motor was standing at the side of the road.

"Home, M'Nab." The chauffeur touched his cap. "And stop at the crossroads on the way, as usual," Mr. Hutton added, as he opened the door of the car. "Well?" he said, speaking into the obscurity that lurked within.

"Oh, Teddy Bear, what an age you've been!" It was a fresh and childish voice that spoke the words. There was the faintest hint of Cockney impurity about the vowel sounds.

Mr. Hutton bent his large form and darted into the car with the agility of an animal regaining its burrow.

"Have I?" he said, as he shut the door. The machine began to move. "You must have missed me a lot if you found the time so long." He sat back in the low seat; a cherishing warmth enveloped him.

"Teddy Bear . . ." and with a sigh of contentment a charming little head declined on to Mr. Hutton's shoulder. Ravished, he looked down sideways at the round, babyish face.

"Do you know, Doris, you look like the pictures of Louise de Kerouaille." He passed his fingers through a mass of curly hair.

"Who's Louise de Kera-whatever-it-is?" Doris spoke from remote distances.

"She was, alas! *Fuit*. We shall all be 'was' one of these days. Meanwhile . . ."

Mr. Hutton covered the babyish face with kisses. The car rushed smoothly along. M'Nab's back, through the front window was stonily impassive, the back of a statue.

"Your hands," Doris whispered. "Oh, you mustn't touch me. They give me electric shocks."

Mr. Hutton adored her for the virgin imbecility of the words. How late in one's existence one makes the discovery of one's body!

"The electricity isn't in me, it's in you." He kissed her again, whispering her name several times: Doris, Doris, Doris. The scientific appellation of the sea mouse, he was thinking as he kissed the throat she offered him, white and extended like the throat of a victim awaiting the sacrificial knife. The sea mouse was a sausage with iridescent fur: very peculiar. Or was Doris the sea cucumber, which turns itself inside out in moments of alarm? He would really have to go to Naples again, just to see the aquarium. These sea creatures were fabulous, unbelievably fantastic.

"Oh, Teddy Bear!" (More zoology; but he was only a land animal. His poor little jokes!) "Teddy Bear, I'm so happy."

"So am I," said Mr. Hutton. Was it true?

"But I wish I knew if it were right. Tell me, Teddy Bear, is it right or wrong?"

"Ah, my dear, that's just what I've been wondering for the last thirty years."

"Be serious, Teddy Bear. I want to know if this is right; if it's right that I should be here with you and that we should love one another, and that it should give me electric shocks when you touch me."

"Right? Well, it's certainly good that you should have electric shocks rather than sexual repressions. Read Freud; repressions are the devil."

"Oh, you don't help me. Why aren't you ever serious? If only you knew how miserable I am sometimes, thinking it's not right. Perhaps, you know, there is a hell, and all that. I don't know what to do. Sometimes I think I ought to stop loving you."

"But could you?" asked Mr. Hutton, confident in the powers of his seduction and his mustache.

"No, Teddy Bear, you know I couldn't. But I could run away, I could hide from you, I could lock myself up and force myself not to come to you."

"Silly little thing!" He tightened his embrace.

"Oh, dear, I hope it isn't wrong. And there are times when I don't care if it is."

Mr. Hutton was touched. He had a certain protective affection for this little creature. He laid his cheek against her hair and so, interlaced, they sat in silence, while the car, swaying and pitching a little as it hastened along, seemed to draw in the white road and the dusty hedges towards it devouringly.

"Good-by, good-by."

The car moved on, gathered speed, vanished round a curve, and Doris was left standing by the signpost at the crossroads, still dizzy and weak with the languor born of those kisses and the electrical touch of those gentle hands. She had to take a deep breath, to draw herself up deliberately, before she was strong enough to start her homeward walk. She had half a mile in which to invent the necessary lies.

Alone, Mr. Hutton suddenly found himself the prey of an appalling boredom.

Mrs. Hutton was lying on the sofa in her boudoir, playing Patience. In spite of the warmth of the July evening a wood fire was burning on the hearth. A black Pomeranian, extenuated by the heat and the fatigues of digestion, slept before the blaze.

"Phew! Isn't it rather hot in here?" Mr. Hutton asked as he entered the room.

"You know I have to keep warm, dear." The voice seemed breaking on the verge of tears. "I get so shivery."

"I hope you're better this evening."

"Not much, I'm afraid."

The conversation stagnated. Mr. Hutton stood leaning his back against the mantelpiece. He looked down at the Pomeranian lying at his feet, and with the toe of his right boot he rolled the little dog over and rubbed its white-flecked chest and belly. The creature lay in an inert ecstasy. Mrs. Hutton continued to play Patience. Arrived at an impasse, she altered the position of one card, took back another, and went on playing. Her Patiences always came out.

"Dr. Libbard thinks I ought to go to Llandrindod Wells this summer."

"Well—go, my dear—go, most certainly."

Mr. Hutton was thinking of the events of the afternoon: how they had driven, Doris and he, up to the hanging wood, had left the car to wait for them under the shade of the trees, and walked together out into the windless sunshine of the chalk down.

"I'm to drink the waters for my liver, and he thinks I ought to have massage and electric treatment, too."

Hat in hand, Doris had stalked four blue butterflies that were dancing together round a scabious flower with a motion that was like the flickering of blue fire. The blue fire burst and scattered into whirling sparks; she had given chase, laughing and shouting like a child.

"I'm sure it will do you good, my dear."

"I was wondering if you'd come with me, dear."

"But you know I'm going to Scotland at the end of the month."

Mrs. Hutton looked up at him entreatingly. "It's the journey," she said. "The thought of it is such a nightmare. I don't know if I can manage it. And you know I can't sleep in hotels. And then there's the luggage and all the worries. I can't go alone."

"But you won't be alone. You'll have your maid with you." He spoke impatiently. The sick woman was usurping the place of the healthy one. He was being dragged back from the memory of the sunlit down and the quick, laughing girl, back to this unhealthy, overheated room and its complaining occupant.

"I don't think I shall be able to go."

"But you must, my dear, if the doctor tells you to. And, besides, a change will do you good."

"I don't think so."

"But Libbard thinks so, and he knows what he's talking about."

"No, I can't face it. I'm too weak. I can't go alone." Mrs. Hutton pulled a handkerchief out of her black silk bag, and put it to her eyes.

"Nonsense, my dear, you must make the effort."

"I had rather be left in peace to die here." She was crying in earnest now.

"O Lord! Now do be reasonable. Listen now, please." Mrs. Hutton only sobbed more violently. "Oh, what is one to do?" He shrugged his shoulders and walked out of the room.

Mr. Hutton was aware that he had not behaved with proper patience; but he could not help it. Very early in his manhood he had discovered that not only did he not feel sympathy for the poor, the weak, the diseased, and deformed; he actually hated them. Once, as an undergraduate, he spent three days at a mission in the East End. He had returned, filled with a profound and ineradicable disgust. Instead of pitying, he loathed the unfortunate. It was not, he knew, a very comely emotion; and he had been ashamed of it at first. In the end he had decided that it was temperamental, inevitable, and had felt no further qualms. Emily had been healthy and beautiful when he married her. He had loved her then. But now—was it his fault that she was like this?

Mr. Hutton dined alone. Food and drink left him more benevolent than he had been before dinner. To make amends for his show of exasperation he went up to his wife's room and offered to read to her. She was touched, gratefully accepted the offer, and Mr. Hutton, who was particularly proud of his accent, suggested a little light reading in French.

"French? I am so fond of French." Mrs. Hutton spoke of the language of Racine as though it were a dish of green peas.

Mr. Hutton ran down to the library and returned with a yellow volume. He began reading. The effort of pronouncing perfectly absorbed his whole attention. But how good his accent was! The fact of its goodness seemed to improve the quality of the novel he was reading.

At the end of fifteen pages an unmistakable sound aroused him. He looked up; Mrs. Hutton had gone to sleep. He sat still for a little while, looking with a dispassionate curiosity at the sleeping face. Once it had been beautiful; once, long ago, the sight of it, the recollection of it, had moved him with an emotion profounder, perhaps, than any he had felt before or since. Now it was lined and cadaverous. The skin was stretched tightly over the cheekbones, across the bridge of the sharp, birdlike nose. The closed eyes were set in profound bone-rimmed sockets. The lamplight striking on the face from the side emphasized with light and shade its cavities and projections. It was the face of a dead Christ by Morales.

> Le squelette était invisible
> Au temps heureux de l'art païen.

He shivered a little, and tiptoed out of the room.

On the following day Mrs. Hutton came down to luncheon. She had had some unpleasant palpitations during the night, but she was feeling better now. Besides, she wanted to do honor to her guest. Miss Spence listened to her complaints about Llandrindod Wells, and was loud in sympathy, lavish with advice. Whatever she said was always said with intensity. She leaned forward, aimed, so to speak, like a gun, and fired her words. Bang! the charge in her soul was ignited, the words whizzed forth at the narrow barrel of her mouth. She was a machine gun riddling her hostess with sympathy. Mr. Hutton had undergone similar bombardments, mostly of a literary or philosophic character—bombardments of Maeterlinck, of Mrs. Besant, of Bergson, of William James. Today the missiles were medical. She talked about insomnia, she expatiated on the virtues of harmless drugs and beneficent specialists. Under the bombardment Mrs. Hutton opened out, like a flower in the sun.

Mr. Hutton looked on in silence. The spectacle of Janet Spence evoked in him an unfailing curiosity. He was not romantic enough to imagine that every face masked an interior physiognomy of beauty or strangeness, that every woman's small talk was like a vapor hanging over mysterious gulfs. His wife, for example, and Doris;

they were nothing more than what they seemed to be. But with Janet Spence it was somehow different. Here one could be sure that there was some kind of queer face behind the Gioconda smile and the Roman eyebrows. The only question was: What exactly was there? Mr. Hutton could never quite make out.

"But perhaps you won't have to go to Llandrindod after all," Miss Spence was saying. "If you get well quickly Dr. Libbard will let you off."

"I only hope so. Indeed, I do really feel rather better today."

Mr. Hutton felt ashamed. How much was it his own lack of sympathy that prevented her from feeling well every day? But he comforted himself by reflecting that it was only a case of feeling, not of being better. Sympathy does not mend a diseased liver or a weak heart.

"My dear, I wouldn't eat those red currants if I were you," he said, suddenly solicitous. "You know that Libbard has banned everything with skins and pips."

"But I am so fond of them," Mrs. Hutton protested, "and I feel so well today."

"Don't be a tyrant," said Miss Spence, looking first at him and then at his wife. "Let the poor invalid have what she fancies; it will do her good." She laid her hand on Mrs. Hutton's arm and patted it affectionately two or three times.

"Thank you, my dear." Mrs. Hutton helped herself to the stewed currants.

"Well, don't blame me if they make you ill again."

"Do I ever blame you, dear?"

"You have nothing to blame me for," Mr. Hutton answered playfully. "I am the perfect husband."

They sat in the garden after luncheon. From the island of shade under the old cypress tree they looked out across a flat expanse of lawn, in which the parterres of flowers shone with a metallic brilliance.

Mr. Hutton took a deep breath of the warm and fragrant air. "It's good to be alive," he said.

"Just to be alive," his wife echoed, stretching one pale, knot-jointed hand into the sunlight.

A maid brought the coffee; the silver pots and the little blue cups were set on a folding table near the group of chairs.

"Oh, my medicine!" exclaimed Mrs. Hutton. "Run in and fetch it, Clara, will you? The white bottle on the sideboard."

"I'll go," said Mr. Hutton. "I've got to go and fetch a cigar in any case."

He ran in towards the house. On the threshold he turned round for an instant. The maid was walking back across the lawn. His wife was sitting up in her deck chair, engaged in opening her white parasol. Miss Spence was bending over the table, pouring out the coffee. He passed into the cool obscurity of the house.

"Do you like sugar in your coffee?" Miss Spence inquired.

"Yes, please. Give me rather a lot. I'll drink it after my medicine to take the taste away."

Mrs. Hutton leaned back in her chair, lowering the sunshade over her eyes, so as to shut out from her vision the burning sky.

Behind her, Miss Spence was making a delicate clinking among the coffee cups.

"I've given you three large spoonfuls. That ought to take the taste away. And here comes the medicine."

Mr. Hutton had reappeared, carrying a wineglass, half full of a pale liquid.

"It smells delicious," he said, as he handed it to his wife.

"That's only the flavoring." She drank it off at a gulp, shuddered, and made a grimace. "Ugh, it's so nasty. Give me my coffee."

Miss Spence gave her the cup; she sipped at it. "You've made it like syrup. But it's very nice, after that atrocious medicine."

At half-past three Mrs. Hutton complained that she did not feel as well as she had done, and went indoors to lie down. Her husband would have said something about the red currants, but checked himself; the triumph of an "I told you so" was too cheaply won. Instead, he was sympathetic, and gave her his arm to the house.

"A rest will do you good," he said. "By the way, I shan't be back till after dinner."

"But why? Where are you going?"

"I promised to go to Johnson's this evening. We have to discuss the war memorial you know."

"Oh, I wish you weren't going." Mrs. Hutton was almost in tears. "Can't you stay? I don't like being alone in the house."

"But, my dear, I promised—weeks ago." It was a bother having to lie like this. "And now I must get back and look after Miss Spence."

He kissed her on the forehead and went out again into the garden. Miss Spence received him aimed and intense.

"Your wife is dreadfully ill," she fired off at him.

"I thought she cheered up so much when you came."

"That was purely nervous, purely nervous. I was watching her closely. With a heart in that condition and her digestion wrecked—yes, wrecked—anything might happen."

"Libbard doesn't take so gloomy a view of poor Emily's health." Mr. Hutton held open the gate that led from the garden into the drive; Miss Spence's car was standing by the front door.

"Libbard is only a country doctor. You ought to see a specialist."

He could not refrain from laughing. "You have a macabre passion for specialists."

Miss Spence held up her hand in protest. "I am serious. I think poor Emily is in a very bad state. Anything might happen—at any moment."

He handed her into the car and shut the door. The chauffeur started the engine and climbed into his place, ready to drive off.

"Shall I tell him to start?" He had no desire to continue the conversation.

Miss Spence leaned forward and shot a Gioconda in his direction. "Remember, I expect you to come and see me again soon."

Mechanically he grinned, made a polite noise, and, as the car moved forward, waved his hand. He was happy to be alone.

A few minutes afterwards Mr. Hutton himself drove away. Doris was waiting at the crossroads. They dined together twenty miles from home, at a roadside hotel. It was one of those bad, expensive meals which are only cooked in country hotels frequented by motorists. It revolted Mr. Hutton, but Doris enjoyed it. She always enjoyed things. Mr. Hutton ordered a not very good brand of champagne. He was wishing he had spent the evening in his library.

When they started homewards Doris was a little tipsy and extremely affectionate. It was very dark inside the car, but looking forward, past the motionless form of M'Nab, they could see a bright and narrow universe of forms and colors scooped out of the night by the electric head lamps.

It was after eleven when Mr. Hutton reached home. Dr. Libbard met him in the hall. He was a small man with delicate hands and well-formed features that were almost feminine. His brown eyes were large and melancholy. He used to waste a great deal of time sitting at the bedside of his patients, looking sadness through those eyes and talking in a sad, low voice about nothing in particular. His person exhaled a pleasing odor, decidedly antiseptic but at the same time suave and discreetly delicious.

"Libbard?" said Mr. Hutton in surprise. "You here? Is my wife ill?"

"We tried to fetch you earlier," the soft, melancholy voice replied. "It was thought you were at Mr. Johnson's, but they had no news of you there."

"No, I was detained. I had a breakdown," Mr. Hutton answered irritably. It was tiresome to be caught out in a lie.

"Your wife wanted to see you urgently."

"Well, I can go now." Mr. Hutton moved toward the stairs.

Dr. Libbard laid a hand on his arm. "I'm afraid it's too late."

"Too late?" He began fumbling with his watch; it wouldn't come out of the pocket.

"Mrs. Hutton passed away half an hour ago."

The voice remained even in its softness, the melancholy of the eyes did not deepen. Dr. Libbard spoke of death as he would speak of a local cricket match. All things were equally vain and equally deplorable.

Mr. Hutton found himself thinking of Janet Spence's words. At any moment—at any moment. She had been extraordinarily right.

"What happened?" he asked. "What was the cause?"

Dr. Libbard explained. It was heart failure brought on by a violent attack of nausea, caused in its turn by the eating of something of an irritant nature. Red currants? Mr. Hutton suggested. Very likely. It had been too much for the heart. There was chronic valvular disease: something had collapsed under the strain. It was all over; she could not have suffered much.

"It's a pity they should have chosen the day of the Eton and Harrow match for the funeral," old General Grego was saying as he stood, his top hat in his hand, under the shadow of the lych gate, wiping his face with his handkerchief.

Mr. Hutton overheard the remark and with difficulty restrained a desire to inflict grievous bodily pain on the General. He would have liked to hit the old brute in the middle of his big red face. Monstrous great mulberry, spotted with meal! Was there no respect for the dead? Did nobody care? In theory he didn't much care; let the dead bury the dead. But here, at the graveside, he had found himself actually sobbing. Poor Emily, they had been pretty happy once. Now she was lying at the bottom of a seven-foot hole. And here was Grego complaining that he couldn't go to the Eton and Harrow match.

Mr. Hutton looked round at the groups of black figures that were drifting slowly out of the churchyard towards the fleet of cabs and motors assembled in the road outside. Against the brilliant background of the July grass and flowers and foliage, they had a horribly alien and unnatural appearance. It pleased him to think that all these people would soon be dead, too.

That evening Mr. Hutton sat up late in his library reading the life of Milton. There was no particular reason why he should have chosen Milton; it was the book that first came to hand, that was all. It was after midnight when he had finished. He got up from his armchair, unbolted the French windows, and stepped out on to the little paved terrace. The night was quiet and clear. Mr. Hutton looked at the stars and at the holes between them, dropped his eyes to the dim lawns and hueless flowers of the garden, and let them wander over the farther landscape, black and gray under the moon.

He began to think with a kind of confused violence. There were the stars, there was Milton. A man can be somehow the peer of stars and night. Greatness, nobility. But is there seriously a difference between the noble and the ignoble? Milton, the stars, death, and himself—himself. The soul, the body; the higher and the lower nature. Perhaps there was something in it, after all. Milton had a god on his side and righteousness. What had he? Nothing, nothing whatever. There were only Doris's little breasts. What was the point of it all? Milton, the stars, death, and Emily in her grave, Doris and himself—always himself . . .

Oh, he was a futile and disgusting being. Everything convinced him of it. It was a solemn moment. He spoke aloud: "I will, I will." The sound of his own voice in the darkness was appalling; it seemed to him that he had sworn that infernal oath which binds even the gods: "I will, I will." There had been New Year's days and solemn anniversaries in the past, when he had felt the same contritions and recorded similar resolutions. They had all thinned away, these resolutions, like smoke, into nothingness. But this was a greater moment and he had pronounced a more fearful oath. In the future it was to be different. Yes, he would live by reason, he would be industrious, he would curb his appetites, he would devote his life to some good purpose. It was resolved and it would be so.

In practice he saw himself spending his mornings in agricultural pursuits, riding round with the bailiff, seeing that his land was farmed in the best modern way— silos and artificial manures and continuous cropping and all that. The remainder of the day should be devoted to serious study. There was that book he had been intending to write for so long—*The Effect of Diseases on Civilization*.

Mr. Hutton went to bed humble and contrite, but with a sense that grace had entered into him. He slept for seven and a half hours, and woke to find the sun brilliantly shining. The emotions of the evening had been transformed by a good night's rest into his customary cheerfulness. It was not until a good many seconds after his return to conscious life that he remembered his resolution, his Stygian oath. Milton and death seemed somehow different in the sunlight. As for the stars, they were not here. But the resolutions were good; even in the daytime he could see that. He had his horse saddled after breakfast, and rode round the farm with the bailiff. After luncheon he read Thucydides on the plague at Athens. In the evening he made a few notes on malaria in Southern Italy. While he was undressing he remembered that there was a good anecdote in Skelton's jest-book about the Sweating Sickness. He would have made a note of it if only he could have found a pencil.

On the sixth morning of his new life Mr. Hutton found among his correspondence an envelope addressed in that peculiarly vulgar handwriting which he knew to be Doris's. He opened it, and began to read. She didn't know what to say; words were so inadequate. His wife dying like that, and so suddenly—it was too terrible. Mr. Hutton sighed, but his interest revived somewhat as he read on:

> "Death is so frightening, I never think of it when I can help it. But when something like this happens, or when I am feeling ill or depressed, then I can't help remembering it is there so close, and I think about all the wicked things I have done and about you and me, and I wonder what will happen. And I am so frightened. I am so lonely, Teddy Bear, and so unhappy, and I don't know what to do. I can't get rid of the idea of dying, I am so wretched and helpless without you. I didn't mean to write to you; I meant to wait till you were out of mourning and could come and see me again, but I was so lonely and miserable, Teddy Bear, I had to write. I couldn't help it. Forgive me, I want you so

much; I have nobody in the world but you. You are so good and gentle and understanding; there is nobody like you. I shall never forget how good and kind you have been to me, and you are so clever and know so much, I can't understand how you ever came to pay any attention to me, I am so dull and stupid, much less like me and love me, because you do love me a little, don't you, Teddy Bear?"

Mr. Hutton was touched with shame and remorse. To be thanked like this, worshiped for having seduced the girl—it was too much. It had just been a piece of imbecile wantonness. Imbecile, idiotic: there was no other way to describe it. For, when all was said, he had derived very little pleasure from it. Taking all things together, he had probably been more bored than amused. Once upon a time he had believed himself to be a hedonist. But to be a hedonist implies a certain process of reasoning, a deliberate choice of known pleasures, a rejection of known pains. This had been done without reason, against it. For he knew beforehand—so well, so well—that there was no interest or pleasure to be derived from these wretched affairs. And yet each time the vague itch came upon him he succumbed, involving himself once more in the old stupidity. There had been Maggie, his wife's maid, and Edith, the girl on the farm, and Mrs. Pringle, and the waitress in London, and others—there seemed to be dozens of them. It had all been so stale and boring. He knew it would be; he always knew. And yet, and yet . . . Experience doesn't teach.

Poor little Doris! He would write to her kindly, comfortingly, but he wouldn't see her again. A servant came to tell him that his horse was saddled and waiting. He mounted and rode off. That morning the old bailiff was more irritating than usual.

Five days later Doris and Mr. Hutton were sitting together on the pier at Southend; Doris, in white muslin with pink garnishings, radiated happiness; Mr. Hutton, legs outstretched and chair tilted, had pushed the panama back from his forehead, and was trying to feel like a tripper. That night, when Doris was asleep, breathing and warm by his side, he recaptured, in this moment of darkness and physical fatigue, the rather cosmic emotion which had possessed him that evening, not a fortnight ago, when he had made his great resolution. And so his solemn oath had already gone the way of so many other resolutions. Unreason had triumphed; at the first itch of desire he had given way. He was hopeless, hopeless.

For a long time he lay with closed eyes, ruminating his humiliation. The girl stirred in her sleep. Mr. Hutton turned over and looked in her direction. Enough faint light crept in between the half-drawn curtains to show her bare arm and shoulder, her neck, and the dark tangle of hair on the pillow. She was beautiful, desirable. Why did he lie there moaning over his sins? What did it matter? If he were hopeless, then so be it; he would make the best of his hopelessness. A glorious sense of irresponsibility suddenly filled him. He was free, magnificently free. In a kind of exaltation he drew the girl towards him. She woke, bewildered, almost frightened under his rough kisses.

The storm of his desire subsided into a kind of serene merriment. The whole atmosphere seemed to be quivering with enormous silent laughter.

"Could anyone love you as much as I do, Teddy Bear?" The question came faintly from distant worlds of love.

"I think I know somebody who does," Mr. Hutton replied. The submarine laughter was swelling, rising, ready to break the surface of silence and resound.

"Who? Tell me. What do you mean?" The voice had come very close; charged with suspicion, anguish, indignation, it belonged to this immediate world.

"A—ah!"

"Who?"

"You'll never guess." Mr. Hutton kept up the joke until it began to grow tedious, and then pronounced the name "Janet Spence."

Doris was incredulous. "Miss Spence of the Manor? That old woman?" It was too ridiculous. Mr. Hutton laughed too.

"But it's quite true," he said. "She adores me." Oh, the vast joke. He would go and see her as soon as he returned—see and conquer. "I believe she wants to marry me," he added.

"But you wouldn't . . . you don't intend . . ."

The air was fairly crepitating with humor. Mr. Hutton laughed aloud. "I intend to marry you," he said. It seemed to him the best joke he had ever made in his life.

When Mr. Hutton left Southend he was once more a married man. It was agreed that, for the time being, the fact should be kept secret. In the autumn they would go abroad together, and the world should be informed. Meanwhile he was to go back to his own house and Doris to hers.

The day after his return he walked over in the afternoon to see Miss Spence. She received him with the old Gioconda.

"I was expecting you to come."

"I couldn't keep away," Mr. Hutton gallantly replied.

They sat in the summerhouse. It was a pleasant place—a little old stucco temple bowered among dense bushes of evergreen. Miss Spence had left her mark on it by hanging up over the seat a blue-and-white Della Robbia plaque.

"I am thinking of going to Italy this autumn," said Mr. Hutton. He felt like a ginger-beer bottle, ready to pop with bubbling humorous excitement.

"Italy . . ." Miss Spence closed her eyes ecstatically. "I feel drawn there too."

"Why not let yourself be drawn?"

"I don't know. One somehow hasn't the energy and initiative to set out alone."

"Alone . . ." Ah, sound of guitars and throaty singing! "Yes, traveling alone isn't much fun."

Miss Spence lay back in her chair without speaking. Her eyes were still closed. Mr. Hutton stroked his mustache. The silence prolonged itself for what seemed a very long time.

Pressed to stay to dinner, Mr. Hutton did not refuse. The fun had hardly started. The table was laid in the loggia. Through its arches they looked out on to the sloping garden, to the valley below and the farther hills. Light ebbed away; the heat and silence were oppressive. A huge cloud was mounting up the sky, and there were distant breathings of thunder. The thunder drew nearer, a wind began to blow, and the first drops of rain fell. The table was cleared. Miss Spence and Mr. Hutton sat on in the growing darkness.

Miss Spence broke a long silence by saying meditatively:

"I think everyone has a right to a certain amount of happiness, don't you?"

"Most certainly." But what was she leading up to? Nobody makes generalizations about life unless they mean to talk about themselves. Happiness: he looked back on his own life, and saw a cheerful, placid existence disturbed by no great griefs or discomforts or alarms. He had always had money and freedom; he had been able to do very much as he wanted. Yes, he supposed he had been happy—happier than most men. And now he was not merely happy; he had discovered in irresponsibility the secret of gaiety. He was about to say something about his happiness when Miss Spence went on speaking.

"People like you and me have a right to be happy some time in our lives."

"Me?" said Mr. Hutton surprised.

"Poor Henry! Fate hasn't treated either of us very well."

"Oh, well, it might have treated me worse."

"You're being cheerful. That's brave of you. But don't think I can't see behind the mask."

Miss Spence spoke louder and louder as the rain came down more and more heavily. Periodically the thunder cut across her utterances. She talked on, shouting against the noise.

"I have understood you so well and for so long."

A flash revealed her, aimed and intent, leaning towards him. Her eyes were two profound and menacing gun barrels. The darkness re-engulfed her.

"You were a lonely soul seeking a companion soul. I could sympathize with you in your solitude. Your marriage . . ."

The thunder cut short the sentence. Miss Spence's voice became audible once more with the words:

". . . could offer no companionship to a man of your stamp. You needed a soul mate."

A soul mate—he! A soul mate. It was incredibly fantastic. "Georgette Leblanc, the ex-soul mate of Maurice Maeterlinck." He had seen that in the paper a few days ago. So it was thus that Janet Spence had painted him in her imagination—a soul-mater. And for Doris he was a picture of goodness and the cleverest man in the world. And actually, really, he was what? Who knows?

"My heart went out to you. I could understand; I was lonely, too." Miss Spence laid her hand on his knee. "You were so patient." Another flash. She was still aimed, dangerously. "You never complained. But I could guess—I could guess."

"How wonderful of you!" So he was an âme incomprise. "Only a woman's intuition . . ."

The thunder crashed and rumbled, died away, and only the sound of the rain was left. The thunder was his laughter, magnified, externalized. Flash and crash, there it was again, right on top of them.

"Don't you feel that you have within you something that is akin to this storm?" He could imagine her leaning forward as she uttered the words. "Passion makes one the equal of the elements."

What was his gambit now? Why, obviously, he should have said "Yes," and ventured on some unequivocal gesture. But Mr. Hutton suddenly took fright. The ginger beer in him had gone flat. The woman was serious—terribly serious. He was appalled.

Passion? "No," he desperately answered. "I am without passion."

But his remark was either unheard or unheeded, for Miss Spence went on with a growing exaltation, speaking so rapidly, however, and in such a burningly intimate whisper that Mr. Hutton found it very difficult to distinguish what she was saying. She was telling him, as far as he could make out, the story of her life. The lightning was less frequent now, and there were long intervals of darkness. But at each flash he saw her still aiming towards him, still yearning forward with a terrifying intensity. Darkness, the rain, and then flash! her face was there, close at hand. A pale mask, greenish white; the large eyes, the narrow barrel of the mouth, the heavy eyebrows. Agrippina, or wasn't it rather—yes, wasn't it rather George Robey?

He began devising absurd plans for escaping. He might suddenly jump up, pretending he had seen a burglar—Stop thief! stop thief!—and dash off into the night in pursuit. Or should he say that he felt faint, a heart attack? or that he had seen a ghost—Emily's ghost—in the garden? Absorbed in his childish plotting, he had ceased to pay attention to Miss Spence's words. The spasmodic clutching of her hand recalled his thoughts.

"I honored you for that, Henry," she was saying.

Honored him for what?

"Marriage is a sacred tie, and your respect for it, even when the marriage was, as it was in your case, an unhappy one, made me respect you and admire you and— shall I dare say the word?"

Oh, the burglar, the ghost in the garden! But it was too late.

". . . yes, love you, Henry, all the more. But we're free now, Henry."

Free? There was a movement in the dark, and she was kneeling on the floor by his chair.

"Oh, Henry, Henry, I have been unhappy too."

Her arms embraced him, and by the shaking of her body he could feel that she was sobbing. She might have been a suppliant crying for mercy.

"You mustn't, Janet," he protested. Those tears were terrible, terrible. "Not now, not now! You must be calm; you must go to bed." He patted her shoulder, then got up, disengaging himself from her embrace. He left her still crouching on the floor beside the chair on which he had been sitting.

Groping his way into the hall, and without waiting to look for his hat, he went out of the house, taking infinite pains to close the door noiselessly behind him. The clouds had blown over, and the moon was shining from a clear sky. There were puddles all along the road, and a noise of running water rose from the gutters and ditches. Mr. Hutton splashed along, not caring if he got wet.

How heart-rendingly she had sobbed! With the emotions of pity and remorse that the recollection evoked in him there was a certain resentment: why couldn't she have played the game that he was playing—the heartless, amusing game? Yes, but he had known all the time that she wouldn't, she couldn't play that game; he had known and persisted.

What had she said about passion and the elements? Something absurdly stale, but true, true. There she was, a cloud black bosomed and charged with thunder, and he, like some absurd little Benjamin Franklin, had sent up a kite into the heart of the menace. Now he was complaining that his toy had drawn the lightning.

She was probably still kneeling by that chair in the loggia, crying.

But why hadn't he been able to keep up the game? Why had his irresponsibility deserted him, leaving him suddenly sober in a cold world? There were no answers to any of his questions. One idea burned steady and luminous in his mind—the idea of flight. He must get away at once.

"What are you thinking about, Teddy Bear?"

"Nothing."

There was a silence. Mr. Hutton remained motionless, his elbows on the parapet of the terrace, his chin in his hands, looking down over Florence. He had taken a villa on one of the hilltops to the south of the city. From a little raised terrace at the end of the garden one looked down a long fertile valley on to the town and beyond it to the bleak mass of Monte Morello and, eastward of it, to the peopled hill of Fiesole, dotted with white houses. Everything was clear and luminous in the September sunshine.

"Are you worried about anything?"

"No, thank you."

"Tell me, Teddy Bear."

"But, my dear, there's nothing to tell." Mr. Hutton turned round, smiled, and patted the girl's hand. "I think you'd better go in and have your siesta. It's too hot for you here."

"Very well, Teddy Bear. Are you coming too?"

"When I've finished my cigar."

"All right. But do hurry up and finish it, Teddy Bear." Slowly, reluctantly, she descended the steps of the terrace and walked towards the house.

Mr. Hutton continued his contemplation of Florence. He had need to be alone. It was good sometimes to escape from Doris and the restless solicitude of her passion. He had never known the pains of loving hopelessly, but he was experiencing now the pains of being loved. These last weeks had been a period of growing discomfort. Doris was always with him, like an obsession, like a guilty conscience. Yes, it was good to be alone.

He pulled an envelope out of his pocket and opened it; not without reluctance. He hated letters; they always contained something unpleasant—nowadays, since his second marriage. This was from his sister. He began skimming through the insulting home truths of which it was composed. The words "indecent haste," "social suicide," "scarcely cold in her grave," "person of the lower classes," all occurred. They were inevitable now in any communication from a well-meaning and right-thinking relative. Impatient, he was about to tear the stupid letter to pieces when his eye fell on a sentence at the bottom of the third page. His heart beat with uncomfortable violence as he read it. It was too monstrous! Janet Spence was going about telling everyone that he had poisoned his wife in order to marry Doris. What damnable malice! Ordinarily a man of the suavest temper, Mr. Hutton found himself trembling with rage. He took the childish satisfaction of calling names—he cursed the woman.

Then suddenly he saw the ridiculous side of the situation. The notion that he should have murdered anyone in order to marry Doris! If they only knew how miserably bored he was. Poor, dear Janet! She had tried to be malicious; she had only succeeded in being stupid.

A sound of footsteps aroused him; he looked round. In the garden below the little terrace the servant girl of the house was picking fruit. A Neapolitan, strayed somehow as far north as Florence, she was a specimen of the classical type—a little debased. Her profile might have been taken from a Sicilian coin of a bad period. Her features, carved floridly in the grand tradition, expressed an almost perfect stupidity. Her mouth was the most beautiful thing about her; the calligraphic hand of nature had richly curved it into an expression of mulish bad temper. . . . Under her hideous black clothes, Mr. Hutton divined a powerful body, firm and massive. He had looked at her before with a vague interest and curiosity. Today the curiosity defined and focused itself into a desire. An idyll of Theocritus. Here was the woman; he, alas, was not precisely like a goatherd on the volcanic hills. He called to her.

"Armida!"

The smile with which she answered him was so provocative, attested so easy a virtue, that Mr. Hutton took fright. He was on the brink once more—on the brink. He must draw back, oh! quickly, quickly, before it was too late. The girl continued to look up at him.

"Ha chiamato?" she asked at last.

Stupidity or reason? Oh, there was no choice now. It was imbecility every time.

"Scendo," he called back to her. Twelve steps led from the garden to the terrace. Mr. Hutton counted them. Down, down, down, down . . . He saw a vision of himself descending from one circle of the inferno to the next—from a darkness full of wind and hail to an abyss of stinking mud.

For a good many days the Hutton case had a place on the front page of every news-paper. There had been no more popular murder trial since George Smith had tem-porarily eclipsed the European War by drowning in a warm bath his seventh bride. The public imagination was stirred by this tale of murder brought to light months after the date of the crime. Here, it was felt, was one of those incidents in human life, so notable because they are so rare, which do definitely justify the ways of God to man. A wicked man had been moved by an illicit passion to kill his wife. For months he had lived in sin and fancied security—only to be dashed at last more horribly into the pit he had prepared for himself. Murder will out, and here was a case of it. The readers of the newspapers were in a position to follow every move-ment of the hand of God. There had been vague, but persistent, rumors in the neigh-borhood; the police had taken action at last. Then came the exhumation order, the post-mortem examination, the inquest, the evidence of the experts, the verdict of the coroner's jury, the trial, the condemnation. For once Providence had done its duty, obviously, grossly, didactically, as in a melodrama. The newspapers were right in making of the case the staple intellectual food of a whole season.

Mr. Hutton's first emotion when he was summoned from Italy to give evidence at the inquest was one of indignation. It was a monstrous, a scandalous thing that the police should take such idle, malicious gossip seriously. When the inquest was over he would bring an action for malicious prosecution against the Chief Constable; he would sue the Spence woman for slander.

The inquest was opened; the astonishing evidence unrolled itself. The experts had examined the body, and had found traces of arsenic; they were of opinion that the late Mrs. Hutton had died of arsenic poisoning.

Arsenic poisoning . . . Emily had died of arsenic poisoning? After that, Mr. Hutton learned with surprise that there was enough arsenicated insecticide in his green-houses to poison an army.

It was now, quite suddenly, that he saw it: there was a case against him. Fascinated, he watched it growing, growing, like some monstrous tropical plant. It was envelop-ing him, surrounding him; he was lost in a tangled forest.

When was the poison administered? The experts agreed that it must have been swallowed eight or nine hours before death. About lunchtime? Yes, about lunchtime. Clara, the parlormaid, was called. Mrs. Hutton, she remembered, had asked her to go and fetch her medicine. Mr. Hutton had volunteered to go instead; he had gone alone. Miss Spence—ah, the memory of the storm, the white, aimed face! the horror of it all!—Miss Spence confirmed Clara's statement, and added that Mr. Hutton had come back with the medicine already poured out in a wineglass, not in the bottle.

Mr. Hutton's indignation evaporated. He was dismayed, frightened. It was all too fantastic to be taken seriously, and yet this nightmare was a fact—it was actually happening.

M'Nab had seen them kissing, often. He had taken them for a drive on the day of Mrs. Hutton's death. He could see them reflected in the windscreen, sometimes out of the tail of his eye.

The inquest was adjourned. That evening Doris went to bed with a headache. When he went to her room after dinner, Mr. Hutton found her crying.

"What's the matter?" He sat down on the edge of her bed and began to stroke her hair. For a long time she did not answer, and he went on stroking her hair mechanically, almost unconsciously; sometimes, even, he bent down and kissed her bare shoulder. He had his own affairs, however, to think about. What had happened? How was it that the stupid gossip had actually come true? Emily had died of arsenic poisoning. It was absurd, impossible. The order of things had been broken, and he was at the mercy of an irresponsibility. What had happened, what was going to happen? He was interrupted in the midst of his thoughts.

"It's my fault—it's my fault!" Doris suddenly sobbed out. "I shouldn't have loved you; I oughtn't to have let you love me. Why was I ever born?"

Mr. Hutton didn't say anything, but looked down in silence at the abject figure of misery lying on the bed.

"If they do anything to you I shall kill myself."

She sat up, held him for a moment at arm's length, and looked at him with a kind of violence, as though she were never to see him again.

"I love you, I love you, I love you." She drew him, inert and passive, towards her, clasped him, pressed herself against him. "I didn't know you loved me as much as that, Teddy Bear. But why did you do it—why did you do it?"

Mr. Hutton undid her clasping arms and got up. His face became very red. "You seem to take it for granted that I murdered my wife," he said. "It's really too grotesque. What do you all take me for? A cinema hero?" He had begun to lose his temper. All the exasperation, all the fear and bewilderment of the day, was transformed into a violent anger against her. "It's all such damned stupidity. Haven't you any conception of a civilized man's mentality? Do I look the sort of man who'd go about slaughtering people? I suppose you imagined I was so insanely in love with you that I could commit any folly. When will you women understand that one isn't insanely in love? All one asks for is a quiet life, which you won't allow one to have. I don't know what the devil ever induced me to marry you. It was all a damned stupid, practical joke. And now you go about saying I'm a murderer. I won't stand it."

Mr. Hutton stamped towards the door. He had said horrible things, he knew—odious things that he ought speedily to unsay. But he wouldn't. He closed the door behind him.

"Teddy Bear!" He turned the handle; the latch clicked into place. "Teddy Bear!" The voice that came to him through the closed door was agonized. Should he go back? He ought to go back. He touched the handle, then withdrew his fingers and quickly walked away. When he was halfway down the stairs he halted. She might try to do something silly—throw herself out of the window or God knows what! He listened attentively; there was no sound. But he pictured her very clearly, tiptoeing across the room, lifting the sash as high as it would go, leaning out into the cold night air. It was raining a little. Under the window lay the paved terrace. How far below? Twenty-five or thirty feet? Once, when he was walking along Picadilly, a dog had jumped out of a third-story window of the Ritz. He had seen it fall; he had heard it strike the pavement. Should he go back? He was damned if he would; he hated her.

He sat for a long time in the library. What had happened? What was happening? He turned the question over and over in his mind and could find no answer. Suppose the nightmare dreamed itself out to its horrible conclusion. Death was waiting for him. His eyes filled with tears; he wanted so passionately to live. "Just to be alive." Poor Emily had wished it too, he remembered: "Just to be alive." There were still so many places in this astonishing world unvisited, so many queer delightful people still unknown, so many lovely women never so much as seen. The huge white oxen would still be dragging their wains along the Tuscan roads, the cypresses would still go up, straight as pillars, to the blue heaven; but he would not be there to see them. And the sweet southern wines—Tear of Christ and Blood of Judas—others would drink them, not he. Others would walk down the obscure and narrow lanes between the bookshelves in the London Library, sniffing the dusty perfume of good literature, peering at strange titles, discovering unknown names, exploring the fringes of vast domains of knowledge. He would be lying in a hole in the ground. And why, why? Confusedly he felt that some extraordinary kind of justice was being done. In the past he had been wanton and imbecile and irresponsible. Now Fate was playing as wantonly, as irresponsibly, with him. It was tit for tat, and God existed after all.

He felt that he would like to pray. Forty years ago he used to kneel by his bed every evening. The nightly formula of his childhood came to him almost unsought from some long unopened chamber of the memory. "God bless Father and Mother, Tom and Cissie and the Baby, Mademoiselle and Nurse, and everyone that I love, and make me a good boy. Amen." They were all dead now—all except Cissie.

His mind seemed to soften and dissolve; a great calm descended upon his spirit. He went upstairs to ask Doris's forgiveness. He found her lying on the couch at the foot of the bed. On the floor beside her stood a blue bottle of liniment, marked "Not to be taken"; she seemed to have drunk about half of it.

"You didn't love me," was all she said when she opened her eyes to find him bending over her.

Dr. Libbard arrived in time to prevent any very serious consequences. "You mustn't do this again," he said while Mr. Hutton was out of the room.

"What's to prevent me?" she asked defiantly.

Dr. Libbard looked at her with his large, sad eyes. "There's nothing to prevent you," he said. "Only yourself and your baby. Isn't it rather bad luck on your baby, not allowing it to come into the world because you want to go out of it?"

Doris was silent for a time. "All right," she whispered. "I won't."

Mr. Hutton sat by her bedside for the rest of the night. He felt himself now to be indeed a murderer. For a time he persuaded himself that he loved this pitiable child. Dozing in his chair, he woke up, stiff and cold, to find himself drained dry, as it were, of every emotion. He had become nothing but a tired and suffering carcass. At six o'clock he undressed and went to bed for a couple of hours' sleep. In the course of the same afternoon the coroner's jury brought in a verdict of "Willful Murder," and Mr. Hutton was committed for trial.

Miss Spence was not at all well. She had found her public appearances in the witness box very trying, and when it was all over she had something that was very nearly a breakdown. She slept badly, and suffered from nervous indigestion. Dr. Libbard used to call every other day. She talked to him a great deal—mostly about the Hutton case. . . . Her moral indignation was always on the boil. Wasn't it appalling to think that one had had a murderer in one's house. Wasn't it extraordinary that one could have been for so long mistaken about the man's character? (But she had had an inkling from the first.) And then the girl he had gone off with—so low class, so little better than a prostitute. The news that the second Mrs. Hutton was expecting a baby—the posthumous child of a condemned and executed criminal—revolted her; the thing was shocking—an obscenity. Dr. Libbard answered her gently and vaguely, and prescribed bromide.

One morning he interrupted her in the midst of her customary tirade. "By the way," he said in his soft, melancholy voice, "I suppose it was really you who poisoned Mrs. Hutton."

Miss Spence stared at him for two or three seconds with enormous eyes, and then quietly said, "Yes." After that she started to cry.

"In the coffee, I suppose."

She seemed to nod assent. Dr. Libbard took out his fountain pen, and in his neat, meticulous calligraphy wrote out a prescription for a sleeping draught.

HAIRCUT

RING LARDNER
(1885–1933)

It was one of the banes of Ring Lardner's life that he was never able to distance himself from the fact that he'd begun his professional writing career as a sports reporter. His humorous observations made him enormously popular in his time but there was always a dark underside to the funny stuff and he has been described as the sincerest pessimist America has produced. His outright hatred for boors and dopes is evident in virtually all his stories, including the one that follows.

GOT *ANOTHER* BARBER THAT comes over from Carterville and helps me out Saturdays, but the rest of the time I can get along all right alone. You can see for yourself that this ain't no New York City and besides that, the most of the boys works all day and don't have no leisure to drop in here and get themselves prettied up.

You're a newcomer, ain't you? I thought I hadn't seen you round before. I hope you like it good enough to stay. As I say, we ain't no New York City or Chicago, but we have pretty good times. Not as good, though, since Jim Kendall got killed. When he was alive, him and Hod Meyers used to keep this town in an uproar. I bet they was more laughin' done here than any town its size in America.

Jim was comical, and Hod was pretty near a match for him. Since Jim's gone, Hod tries to hold his end up just the same as ever, but it's tough goin' when you ain't got nobody to kind of work with.

They used to be plenty fun in here Saturdays. This place is jam-packed Saturdays, from four o'clock on. Jim and Hod would show up right after their supper, round six o'clock. Jim would set himself down in that big chair, nearest the blue spittoon. Whoever had been settin' in that chair, why they'd get up when Jim come in and give it to him.

You'd of thought it was a reserved seat like they have sometimes in a theayter. Hod would generally always stand or walk up and down, or some Saturdays, of course, he'd be settin' in his chair part of the time, gettin' a haircut.

Well, Jim would set there a w'ile without openin' his mouth only to spit, and then finally he'd say to me, "Whitey"—my right name, that is, my right first name, is Dick, but everybody round here calls me Whitey—Jim would say, "Whitey, your nose looks like a rosebud tonight. You must of been drinkin' some of your aw de cologne."

So I'd say, "No, Jim, but you look like you'd been drinkin' somethin' of that kind or somethin' worse."

Jim would have to laugh at that, but then he'd speak up and say, "No, I ain't had nothin' to drink, but that ain't sayin' I wouldn't like somethin'. I wouldn't even mind if it was wood alcohol."

Then Hod Meyers would say, "Neither would your wife." That would set everybody to laughin' because Jim and his wife wasn't on very good terms. She'd of divorced him only they wasn't no chance to get alimony and she didn't have no way to take care of herself and the kids. She couldn't never understand Jim. He *was* kind of rough, but a good fella at heart.

Him and Hod had all kinds of sport with Milt Sheppard. I don't suppose you've seen Milt. Well, he's got an Adam's apple that looks more like a mushmelon. So I'd shavin' Milt and when I'd start to shave down here on his neck, Hod would holler, "Hey, Whitey, wait a minute! Before you cut into it, let's make up a pool and see who can guess closest to the number of seeds."

And Jim would say, "If Milt hadn't of been so hoggish, he'd of ordered a half a cantaloupe instead of a whole one and it might not of stuck in his throat."

All the boys would roar at this and Milt himself would force a smile, though the joke was on him. Jim certainly was a card!

There's his shavin' mug, settin' on the shelf, right next to Charley Vail's. "Charles M. Vail." That's the druggist. He comes in regular for his shave, three times a week. And Jim's is the cup next to Charley's. "James H. Kendall." Jim won't need no shavin' mug no more, but I'll leave it there just the same for old time's sake. Jim certainly was a character!

Years ago, Jim used to travel for a canned goods concern over in Carterville. They sold canned goods. Jim had the whole northern half of the state and was on the road five days out of every week. He'd drop in here Saturdays and tell his experiences for that week. It was rich.

I guess he paid more attention to playin' jokes than makin' sales. Finally the concern let him out and he come right home here and told everybody he'd been fired instead of sayin' he'd resigned like most fellas would of.

It was a Saturday and the shop was full and Jim got up out of that chair and says, "Gentlemen, I got an important announcement to make. I been fired from my job."

Well, they asked him if he was in earnest and he said he was and nobody could think of nothin' to say till Jim finally broke the ice himself. He says, "I been sellin' canned goods and now I'm canned goods myself."

You see, the concern he'd been workin' for was a factory that made canned goods. Over in Carterville. And now Jim said he was canned himself. He was certainly a card!

Jim had a great trick that he used to play w'ile he was travelin'. For instance, he'd be ridin' on a train and they'd come to some little town like, well, like, we'll say, like Benton. Jim would look out the train window and read the signs on the stores.

For instance, they'd be a sign, "Henry Smith, Dry Goods." Well, Jim would write down the name and the name of the town and when he got to wherever he was goin' he'd mail back a postal card to Henry Smith at Benton and not sign no name to it, but he'd write on the card, well, somethin' like "Ask your wife about that book agent that spent the afternoon last week," or "Ask your Missus who kept her from gettin' lonesome the last time you was in Carterville." And he'd sign the card, "A Friend."

Of course, he never knew what really come of none of those jokes, but he could picture what *probably* happened and that was enough. Jim didn't work very steady after he lost his position with the Carterville people. What he did earn, doin' odd jobs round town, why he spent pretty near all of it on gin and his family might of starved if the stores hadn't of carried them along. Jim's wife tried her hand at dress-makin', but they ain't nobody goin' to get rich makin' dresses in this town.

As I say, she'd of divorced Jim, only she seen that she couldn't support herself and the kids and she was always hopin' that some day Jim would cut out his habits and give her more than two or three dollars a week.

They was a time when she would go to whoever he was workin' for and ask them to give her his wages, but after she done this once or twice, he beat her to it by bor-rowin' most of his pay in advance. He told it all round town, how he had outfoxed his Missus. He certainly was a caution!

But he wasn't satisfied with just outwittin' her. He was sore the way she had acted, tryin' to grab off his pay. And he made up his mind he'd get even. Well, he waited till Evans's Circus was advertised to come to town. Then he told his wife and two kiddies that he was goin' to take them to the circus. The day of the circus, he told them he would get the tickets and meet them outside the entrance to the tent.

Well, he didn't have no intentions of bein' there or buyin' tickets or nothin'. He got full of gin and laid round Wright's poolroom all day. His wife and kids waited and waited and of course he didn't show up. His wife didn't have a dime with her, or nowhere else, I guess. So she finally had to tell the kids it was all off and they cried like they wasn't never goin' to stop.

Well, it seems, w'ile they was cryin', Doc Stair came along and he asked what was the matter, but Mrs. Kendall was stubborn and wouldn't tell him, but the kids told him and he insisted on takin' them and their mother in to the show. Jim found this out afterwards and it was one reason why he had it in for Doc Stair.

Doc Stair come here about a year and a half ago. He's a mighty handsome young fella and his clothes always look like he has them made to order. He goes to Detroit two or three times a year and w'ile he's there he must have a tailor take his mea-sure and then make him a suit to order. They cost pretty near twice as much, but they fit a whole lot better than if you just bought them in a store.

For a w'ile everybody was wonderin' why a young doctor like Doc Stair should come to a town like this where we already got old Doc Gamble and Doc Foote that's both been here for years and all the practice in town was always divided between the two of them.

Then they was a story got round that Doc Stair's gal had throwed him over, a gal up in the Northern Peninsula somewheres, and the reason he come here was to hide himself away and forget it. He said himself that he thought they wasn't nothin' like general practice in a place like ours to fit a man to be a good all round doctor. And that's why he'd came.

Anyways, it wasn't long before he was makin' enough to live on, though they tell me that he never dunned nobody for what they owed him, and the folks here cer-tainly has got the owin' habit, even in my business. If I had all that was comin' to me for just shaves alone, I could go to Carterville and put up at the Mercer for a week and see a different picture every night. For instance, they's old George Purdy—but I guess I shouldn't ought to be gossipin'.

Well, last year, our coroner died, died of the flu. Ken Beatty, that was his name. He was the coroner. So they had to choose another man to be coroner in his place and they picked Doc Stair. He laughed at first and said he didn't want it, but they made him take it. It ain't no job that anybody would fight for and what a man makes out of it in a year would just about buy seeds for their garden. Doc's the kind, though, that can't say no to nothin' if you keep at him long enough.

But I was goin' to tell you about a poor boy we got here in town—Paul Dickson.

He fell out of a tree when he was about ten years old. Lit on his head and it done somethin' to him and he ain't never been right. No harm in him, but just silly. Jim Kendall used to call him cuckoo; that's a name Jim had for anybody that was off their head, only he called people's head their bean. That was another of his gags, callin' head bean and callin' crazy people cuckoo. Only poor Paul ain't crazy, but just silly.

You can imagine that Jim used to have all kinds of fun with Paul. He'd send him to the White Front Garage for a left-handed monkey wrench. Of course they ain't no such a thing as a left-handed monkey wrench.

And once we had a kind of a fair here and they was a baseball game between the fats and the leans and before the game started Jim called Paul over and sent him way down to Schrader's hardware store to get a key for the pitcher's box.

They wasn't nothin' in the way of gags that Jim couldn't think up, when he put his mind to it.

Poor Paul was always kind of suspicious of people, maybe on account of how Jim had kept foolin' him. Paul wouldn't have much to do with anybody only his own mother and Doc Stair and a girl here in town named Julie Gregg. That is, she ain't a girl no more, but pretty near thirty or over.

When Doc first came to town, Paul seemed to feel like here was a real friend and he hung around Doc's office most of the w'ile; the only time he wasn't there was when he'd go home to eat or sleep or when he seen Julie Gregg doin' her shoppin'.

When he looked out Doc's window and seen her, he'd run downstairs and join her and tag along with her to the different stores. The poor boy was crazy about Julie and she always treated him mighty nice and made him feel like he was welcome, though of course it wasn't nothin' but pity on her side.

Doc done all he could to improve Paul's mind and he told me once that he really thought the boy was gettin' better, that they was times when he was as bright and sensible as anybody else.

But I was goin' to tell you about Julie Gregg. Old Man Gregg was in the lumber business, but got to drinkin' and lost the most of his money and when he died, he didn't leave nothin' but the house and just enough insurance for the girl to skimp along on.

Her mother was a kind of a half invalid and didn't hardly ever leave the house. Julie wanted to sell the place and move somewheres else after the old man died, but the mother said she was born here and would die here. It was tough on Julie, as the young people round this town—well, she's too good for them.

She's been away to school and Chicago and New York and different places and they ain't no subject she can't talk on, where you take the rest of the young folks here and you mention anything to them outside of Gloria Swanson or Tommy Meighan and they think you're delirious. Did you see Gloria in *Wages of Virtue*? You missed somethin'!

Well, Doc Stair hadn't been here more than a week when he come in one day to get shaved and I recognized who he was as he had been pointed out to me, so I told him about my old lady. She's been ailin' for a couple years and either Doc Gamble or Doc Foote, neither one, seemed to be helpin' her. So he said he would come out and see her, but if she was able to get out herself, it would be better to bring her to his office where he could make a complete examination.

So I took her to his office and w'ile I was waiting' for her in the reception room, in come Julie Gregg. When somebody comes in Doc Stair's office, they's a bell that rings in his inside office so he can tell they's somebody to see him.

So he left my old lady inside and come out to the front office and that's the first time him and Julie met and I guess it was what they call love at first sight. But it wasn't fifty-fifty. This young fella was the slickest lookin' fella she'd ever seen in this town and she went wild over him. To him she was just a young lady that wanted to see the doctor.

She'd came on about the same business I had. Her mother had been doctorin' for years with Doc Gamble and Doc Foote and with no results. So she'd heard they was a new doc in town and decided to give him a try. He promised to call and see her mother that same day.

I said a minute ago that it was love at first sight on her part. I'm not only judgin' by how she acted afterwards but how she looked at him that first day in his office. I ain't no mind reader, but it was wrote all over her face that she was gone.

Now Jim Kendall, besides bein' a jokesmith and a pretty good drinker, well, Jim was quite a lady-killer. I guess he run pretty wild durin' the time he was on the road for them Carterville people, and besides that, he'd had a couple little affairs of the heart right here in town. As I say, his wife could of divorced him, only she couldn't.

But Jim was like the majority of men, and women, too, I guess. He wanted what he couldn't get. He wanted Julie Gregg and worked his head off tryin' to land her. Only he'd of said bean instead of head.

Well, Jim's habits and his jokes didn't appeal to Julie and of course he was a married man, so he didn't have no more chance than, well, than a rabbit. That's an expression of Jim's himself. When somebody didn't have no chance to get elected or somethin', Jim would always say they didn't have no more chance than a rabbit.

He didn't make no bones about how he felt. Right in here, more than once, in front of the whole crowd, he said he was stuck on Julie and anybody that could get her for him was welcome to his house and his wife and kids included. But she wouldn't have nothin' to do with him; wouldn't even speak to him on the street. He finally seen he wasn't gettin' nowheres with his usual line so he decided to try the rough stuff. He went right up to her house one evenin' and when she opened the door he forced his way in and grabbed her. But she broke loose and before he could stop her, she run in the next room and locked the door and phoned to Joe Barnes. Joe's the marshal. Jim could hear who she was phonin' to and he beat it before Joe got there.

Joe was an old friend of Julie's pa. Joe went to Jim the next day and told him what would happen if he ever done it again.

I don't know how the news of this little affair leaked out. Chances is that Joe Barnes told his wife and she told somebody else's wife and they told their husband. Anyways, it did leak out and Hod Meyers had the nerve to kid Jim about it, right here in this shop. Jim didn't deny nothin' and kind of laughed it off and said for us all to wait; that lots of people had tried to make a monkey out of him, but he always got even.

Meanw'ile everybody in town was wise to Julie's bein' wild mad over the Doc. I don't suppose she had any idea how her face changed when him and her was together; of course she couldn't of, or she'd kept away from him. And she didn't know that we was all noticin' how many times she made excuses to go up to his office or pass it on the other side of the street and look up in his window to see if he was there. I felt sorry for her and so did most other people.

Hod Meyers kept rubbin' it into Jim about how the Doc had cut him out. Jim didn't pay no attention to the kiddin' and you could see he was plannin' one of his jokes.

One trick Jim had was the knack of changin' his voice. He could make you think he was a girl talkin' and he could mimic any man's voice. To show you how good he was along this line, I'll tell you the joke he played on me once.

You know, in most towns of any size, when a man is dead and needs a shave, why the barber that shaves him soaks him five dollars for the job; that is, he don't soak *him,* but whoever ordered the shave. I just charge three dollars because personally I don't mind much shavin' a dead person. They lay a whole lot stiller than live customers. The only thing is that you don't feel like talkin' to them and you get kind of lonesome.

Well, about the coldest day we ever had here, two years ago last winter, the phone rung at the house w'ile I was home to dinner and I answered the phone and it was a woman's voice and she said she was Mrs. John Scott and her husband was dead and would I come out and shave him.

Old John had always been a good customer of mine. But they live seven miles out in the country, on the Streeter road. Still I didn't see how I could say no.

So I said I would be there, but would have to come in a jitney and it might cost three or four dollars besides the price of the shave. So she, or the voice, it said that was all right, so I got Frank Abbott to drive me out to the place and when I got there, who should open the door but old John himself! He wasn't no more dead than, well, than a rabbit.

It didn't take no private detective to figure out who had played me this little joke. Nobody could of thought it up but Jim Kendall. He certainly was a card!

I tell you this incident just to show you how he could disguise his voice and make you believe it was somebody else talkin'. I'd of swore it was Mrs. Scott had called me. Anyways, some woman.

Well, Jim waited till he had Doc Stair's voice down pat; then he went after revenge.

He called Julie up on a night when he knew Doc was over in Carterville. She never questioned but what it was Doc's voice. Jim said he must see her that night; he couldn't wait no longer to tell her somethin'. She was all excited and told him to come to the house. But he said he was expectin' an important long distance call and wouldn't she please forget her manners for once and come to his office. He said they couldn't nothin' hurt her and nobody would see her and he just *must* talk to her a little w'ile. Well, poor Julie fell for it.

Doc always keeps a night light in his office, so it looked to Julie like they was somebody there.

Meanw'ile Jim Kendall had went to Wright's poolroom, where they was a whole gang amusin' themselves. The most of them had drank plenty of gin, and they was a rough bunch even when sober. They was always strong for Jim's jokes and when he told them to come with him and see some fun they give up their card games and pool games and followed along.

Doc's office is on the second floor. Right outside his door they's a flight of stairs leadin' to the floor above. Jim and his gang hid in the dark behind these stairs.

Well, Julie come up to Doc's door and rung the bell and they was nothin' doin'. She rung it again and she rung it seven or eight times. Then she tried the door and found it locked. Then Jim made some kind of a noise and she heard it and waited a minute, and then she says, "Is that you, Ralph?' Ralph is Doc's first name.

They was no answer and it must of came to her all of a sudden that she'd been bunked. She pretty near fell downstairs and the whole gang after her. They chased her all the way home, hollerin', "Is that you, Ralph?" and "Oh, Ralphie, dear, is that you?" Jim says he couldn't holler it himself, as he was laughin' too hard.

Poor Julie! She didn't show up here on Main Street for a long, long time afterward.

And of course Jim and his gang told everybody in town, everybody but Doc Stair. They was scared to tell him, and he might of never knowed only for Paul Dickson. The poor cuckoo, as Jim called him, he was here in the shop one night when Jim was still gloatin' yet over what he'd done to Julie. And Paul took in as much of it as he could understand and he run to Doc with the story.

It's a cinch Doc went up in the air and swore he'd make Jim suffer. But it was a kind of a delicate thing, because if it got out that he had beat Jim up, Julie was bound to hear of it and then she'd know that Doc knew and of course knowin' that he knew would make it worse for her than ever. He was goin' to do somethin', but it took a lot of figurin'.

Well, it was a couple of days later when Jim was here in the shop again, and so was the cuckoo. Jim was goin' duck-shootin' the next day and had come in lookin' for Hod Meyers to go with him. I happened to know that Hod had went over to Carterville and wouldn't be home till the end of the week. So Jim said he hated to go alone and he guessed he would call it off. Then poor Paul spoke up and said if Jim would take him he would go along. Jim thought a w'ile and then he said, well, he guessed a half-wit was better than nothin'.

I suppose he was plottin' to get Paul out in the boat and play some joke on him, like pushin' him in the water. Anyways, he said Paul could go. He asked him had he ever shot a duck and Paul said no, he'd never even had a gun in his hands. So Jim said he could set in the boat and watch him and if he behaved himself, he might lend him his gun for a couple of shots. They made a date to meet in the mornin' and that's the last I seen of Jim alive.

Next mornin', I hadn't been open more than ten minutes when Doc Stair come in. He looked kind of nervous. He asked me had I seen Paul Dickson. I said no, but I knew where he was, out duck-shootin' with Jim Kendall. So Doc says that's what he had heard, and he couldn't understand it because Paul had told him he wouldn't never have no more to do with Jim as long as he lived.

He said Paul had told him about the joke Jim had played on Julie. He said Paul had asked him what he thought of the joke and the Doc had told him that anybody that would do a thing like that ought not to be let live.

I said it had been a kind of a raw thing, but Jim just couldn't resist no kind of a joke, no matter how raw. I said I thought he was all right at heart, but just bubblin' over with mischief. Doc turned and walked out.

At noon he got a phone call from old John Scott. The lake where Jim and Paul had went shootin' is on John's place. Paul had came runnin' up to the house a few minutes before and said they'd been an accident. Jim had shot a few ducks and then give the gun to Paul and told him to try his luck. Paul hadn't never handled a gun and he was nervous. He was shakin' so hard that he couldn't control the gun. He let fire and Jim sunk back in the boat, dead.

Doc Stair, bein' the coroner, jumped in Frank Abbott's flivver and rushed out to Scott's farm. Paul and old John was down on the shore of the lake. Paul had rowed the boat to shore, but they'd left the body in it, waitin' for Doc to come.

Doc examined the body and said they might as well fetch it back to town. They was no use leavin' it there or callin' a jury, as it was a plain case of accidental shootin'.

Personally I wouldn't never leave a person shoot a gun in the same boat I was in unless I was sure they knew somethin' about guns. Jim was a sucker to leave a new beginner have his gun, let alone a half-wit. It probably served Jim right, what he got. But still we miss him round here. He certainly was a card!

Comb it wet or dry?

THE KILLERS

ERNEST HEMINGWAY
(1894–1961)

Arguably the greatest writer of the twentieth century and certainly the most influential, Hemingway's many tales and novels involved violence and death but seldom mystery and crime. One exception is To Have and Have Not (1937) and this story, possibly his most famous. As influential as his style of writing was on most American male writers, Andre Gide notes that the major influence on his own style was Dashiell Hammett, the first important hard-boiled writer.

HE DOOR OF HENRY'S LUNCH-room opened and two men came in. They sat down at the counter.

"What's yours?" George asked them.

"I don't know," one of the men said. "What do you want to eat, Al?"

"I don't know," said Al. "I don't know what I want to eat."

Outside it was getting dark. The street light came on outside the window. The two men at the counter read the menu. From the other end of the counter Nick Adams watched them. He had been talking to George when they came in.

"I'll have a roast pork tenderloin with apple sauce and mashed potatoes," the first man said.

"It isn't ready yet."

"What the hell do you put it on the card for?"

"That's the dinner," George explained. "You can get that at six o'clock."

George looked at the clock on the wall behind the counter.

"It's five o'clock."

"The clock says twenty minutes past five," the second man said.

"It's twenty minutes fast."

"Oh, to hell with the clock," the first man said. "What have you got to eat?"

"I can give you any kind of sandwiches," George said. "You can have ham and eggs, bacon and eggs, liver and bacon, or a steak."

"Give me chicken croquettes with green peas and cream sauce and mashed potatoes."

"That's the dinner."

"Everything we want's the dinner, eh? That's the way you work it."

"I can give you ham and eggs, bacon and eggs, liver—"

"I'll take ham and eggs," the man called Al said. He wore a derby hat and a black overcoat buttoned across the chest. His face was small and white and he had tight lips. He wore a silk muffler and gloves.

"Give me bacon and eggs," said the other man. He was about the same size as Al. Their faces were different, but they were dressed like twins. Both wore overcoats too tight for them. They sat leaning forward, their elbows on the counter.

"Got anything to drink?" Al asked.

"Silver beer, bevo, ginger-ale," George said.

"I mean you got anything to *drink*?"

"Just those I said."

"This is a hot town," said the other. "What do they call it?"

"Summit."

"Ever hear of it?" Al asked his friend.

"No," said the friend.

"What do you do here nights?" Al asked.

"They eat the dinner," his friend said. "They all come here and eat the big dinner."

"That's right," George said.

"So you think that's right?" Al asked George.

"Sure."

"You're a pretty bright boy, aren't you?"

"Sure," said George.

"Well, you're not," said the other little man. "Is he, Al?"

"He's dumb," said Al. He turned to Nick. "What's your name?"

"Adams."

"Another bright boy," Al said. "Ain't he a bright boy, Max?"

"The town's full of bright boys," Max said.

George put the two platters, one of ham and eggs, the other of bacon and eggs, on the counter. He set down two side dishes of fried potatoes and closed the wicket into the kitchen.

"Which is yours?" he asked Al.

"Don't you remember?"

"Ham and eggs."

"Just a bright boy," Max said. He leaned forward and took the ham and eggs. Both men ate with their gloves on. George watched them eat.

"What are *you* looking at?" Max looked at George.

"Nothing."

"The hell you were. You were looking at me."

"Maybe the boy meant it for a joke, Max," Al said.

George laughed.

"*You* don't have to laugh," Max said to him. "*You* don't have to laugh at all, see?"

"All right," said George.

"So he thinks it's all right." Max turned to Al. "He thinks it's all right. That's a good one."

"Oh, he's a thinker," Al said. They went on eating.

"What's the bright boy's name down the counter?" Al asked Max.

"Hey, bright boy," Max said to Nick. "You go around on the other side of the counter with your boy friend."

"What's the idea?" Nick asked.

"There isn't any idea."

"You better go around, bright boy," Al said. Nick went around behind the counter.

"What's the idea?" George asked.

"None of your damn business," Al said. "Who's out in the kitchen?"

"The nigger."

"What do you mean the nigger?"

"The nigger that cooks."

"Tell him to come in."

"What's the idea?"

"Tell him to come in."

"Where do you think you are?"

"We know damn well where we are," the man called Max said. "Do we look silly?"

"You talk silly," Al said to him. "What the hell do you argue with this kid for? Listen," he said to George, "tell the nigger to come out here."

"What are you going to do to him?"

"Nothing. Use your head, bright boy. What would we do to a nigger?"

George opened the slit that opened back into the kitchen. "Sam," he called. "Come in here a minute."

The door to the kitchen opened and the nigger came in. "What was it?" he asked. The two men at the counter took a look at him.

"All right, nigger. You stand right there," Al said.

Sam, the nigger, standing in his apron, looked at the two men sitting at the counter. "Yes, sir," he said. Al got down from his stool.

"I'm going back to the kitchen with the nigger and bright boy," he said. "Go on back to the kitchen, nigger. You go with him, bright boy." The little man walked after Nick and Sam, the cook, back into the kitchen. The door shut after them. The man called Max sat at the counter opposite George. He didn't look at George but looked in the mirror that ran along back of the counter. Henry's had been made over from a saloon into a lunch counter.

"Well, bright boy," Max said, looking into the mirror, "why don't you say something?"

"What's it all about?"

"Hey, Al," Max called, "bright boy wants to know what it's all about."

"Why don't you tell him?" Al's voice came from the kitchen.

"What do you think it's all about?"

"I don't know."

"What do you think?"

Max looked into the mirror all the time he was talking.

"I wouldn't say."

"Hey, Al, bright boy says he wouldn't say what he thinks it's all about."

"I can hear you, all right," Al said from the kitchen. He had propped open the slit that dishes passed through into the kitchen with a catsup bottle. "Listen, bright boy," he said from the kitchen to George. "Stand a little further along the bar. You move a little to the left, Max." He was like a photographer arranging for a group picture.

"Talk to me, bright boy," Max said. "What do you think's going to happen?"

George did not say anything.

"I'll tell you," Max said. "We're going to kill a Swede. Do you know a big Swede named Ole Andreson?"

"Yes."

"He comes here to eat every night, don't he?"

"Sometimes he comes here."

"He comes here at six o'clock, don't he?"

"If he comes."

"We know all that, bright boy," Max said. "Talk about something else. Ever go to the movies?"

"Once in a while."

"You ought to go to the movies more. The movies are fine for a bright boy like you."

"What are you going to kill Ole Andreson for? What did he ever do to you?"

"He never had a chance to do anything to us. He never even seen us."

"And he's only going to see us once," Al said from the kitchen.

"What are you going to kill him for, then?" George asked.

"We're killing him for a friend. Just to oblige a friend, bright boy."

"Shut up," said Al from the kitchen. "You talk too goddam much."

"Well, I got to keep bright boy amused. Don't I, bright boy?"

"You talk too damn much," Al said. "The nigger and my bright boy are amused by themselves. I got them tied up like a couple of girl friends in the convent."

"I suppose you were in a convent."

"You never know."

"You were in a kosher convent. That's where you were."

George looked up at the clock.

"If anybody comes in you tell them the cook is off, and if they keep after it, you tell them you'll go back and cook yourself. Do you get that, bright boy?"

"All right," George said. "What are you going to do with us afterward?"

"That'll depend," Max said. "That's one of those things you never know at the time."

George looked up at the clock. It was a quarter past six. The door from the street opened. A street-car motorman came in.

"Hello, George," he said. "Can I get supper?"

"Sam's gone out," George said. "He'll be back in about half an hour."

"I'd better go up the street," the motorman said. George looked at the clock. It was twenty minutes past six.

"That was nice, bright boy," Max said. "You're a regular little gentleman."

"He knew I'd blow his head off," Al said from the kitchen.

"No," said Max. "It ain't that. Bright boy is nice. He's a nice boy. I like him."

At six-fifty-five George said: "He's not coming."

Two other people had been in the lunchroom. Once George had gone out to the kitchen and made a ham-and-egg sandwich "to go" that a man wanted to take with him. Inside the kitchen he saw Al, his derby hat tipped back, sitting on a stool beside the wicket with the muzzle of a sawed-off shotgun resting on the ledge. Nick and the cook were back to back in the corner, a towel tied in each of their mouths. George had cooked the sandwich, wrapped it up in oiled paper, put it in a bag, brought it in, and the man had paid for it and gone out.

"Bright boy can do everything," Max said. "He can cook and everything. You'd make some girl a nice wife, bright boy."

"Yes?" George said. "Your friend, Ole Andreson, isn't going to come."

"We'll give him ten minutes," Max said.

Max watched the mirror and the clock. The hands of the clock marked seven o'clock, and then five minutes past seven.

"Come on, Al," said Max. "We better go. He's not coming."

"Better give him five minutes," Al said from the kitchen.

In the five minutes a man came in, and George explained that the cook was sick.

"Why the hell don't you get another cook?" the man asked. "Aren't you running a lunch counter?" He went out.

"Come on, Al," Max said.

"What about the two bright boys and the nigger?"

"They're all right."

"You think so?"

"Sure. We're through with it."

"I don't like it," said Al. "It's sloppy. You talk too much."

"Oh, what the hell," said Max. "We got to keep amused, haven't we?"

"You talk too much all the same," Al said. He came out from the kitchen. The cut-off barrels of the shotgun made a slight bulge under the waist of his too-tight-fitting overcoat. He straightened his coat with his gloved hands.

"So long, bright boy," he said to George. "You got a lot of luck."

"That's the truth," Max said. "You ought to play the races, bright boy."

The two of them went out the door. George watched them, through the window, pass under the arc light and across the street. In their tight overcoats and derby hats they looked like a vaudeville team. George went back through the swinging door into the kitchen and untied Nick and the cook.

"I don't want any more of that," said Sam, the cook. "I don't want any more of that."

Nick stood up. He had never had a towel in his mouth before. "Say," he said. "What the hell?" He was trying to swagger it off.

"They were going to kill Ole Andreson," George said. "They were going to shoot him when he came in to eat."

"Ole Andreson?"

"Sure."

The cook felt the corners of his mouth with his thumbs.

"They all gone?" he asked.

"Yeah," said George. "They're gone now."

"I don't like it," said the cook. "I don't like any of it at all."

"Listen," George said to Nick. "You better go see Ole Andreson."

"All right."

"You better not have anything to do with it at all," Sam, the cook, said. "You better stay way out of it."

"Don't go if you don't want to," George said.

"Mixing up in this ain't going to get you anywhere," the cook said. "You stay out of it."

"I'll go see him," Nick said to George. "Where does he live?" The cook turned away.

"Little boys always know what they want to do," he said.

"He lives up at Hirsch's rooming house," George said to Nick.

"I'll go up there."

Outside the arc light shone through the bare branches of a tree. Nick walked up the street beside the car tracks and turned at the next arc light down a side street. Three houses up the street was Hirsch's rooming house. Nick walked up the two steps and pushed the bell. A woman came to the door.

"Is Ole Andreson here?"

"Do you want to see him?"

"Yes, if he's in."

Nick followed the woman up a flight of stairs and back to the end of a corridor. She knocked on the door.

"Who is it?"

"It's somebody to see you, Mr. Andreson," the woman said.

"It's Nick Adams."

"Come in."

Nick opened the door and went into the room. Ole Andreson was lying on the bed with all his clothes on. He had been a heavyweight prizefighter and he was too long for the bed. He lay with his head on two pillows. He did not look at Nick.

"What was it?" he asked.

"I was up at Henry's," Nick said, "and two fellows came in and tied me up and the cook, and they said they were going to kill you."

It sounded silly when he said it. Ole Andreson said nothing.

"They put us out in the kitchen." Nick went on. "They were going to shoot you when you came in to supper."

Ole Andreson looked at the wall and did not say anything.

"George thought I better come and tell you about it."

"There isn't anything I can do about it," Ole Andreson said.

"I'll tell you what they were like."

"I don't want to know what they were like," Ole Andreson said. He looked at the wall. "Thanks for coming to tell me about it."

"That's all right."

Nick looked at the big man lying on the bed.

"Don't you want me to go and see the police?"

"No," Ole Andreson said. "That wouldn't do any good."

"Isn't there something I could do?"

"No. There ain't anything to do."

"Maybe it was just a bluff."

"No. It ain't just a bluff."

Ole Andreson rolled over toward the wall.

"The only thing is," he said, talking toward the wall, "I just can't make up my mind to go out. I been in here all day."

"Couldn't you get out of town?"

"No," Ole Andreson said. "I'm through with all that running around."

He looked at the wall.

"There ain't anything to do now."

"Couldn't you fix it up some way?"

"No, I got in wrong." He talked in the same flat voice. "There ain't anything to do. After a while I'll make up my mind to go out."

"I better go back and see George," Nick said.

"So long," said Ole Andreson. He did not look toward Nick. "Thanks for coming around."

Nick went out. As he shut the door he saw Ole Andreson with all his clothes on, lying on the bed looking at the wall.

"He's been in his room all day," the landlady said downstairs. "I guess he don't feel well. I said to him: 'Mr. Andreson, you ought to go out and take a walk on a nice fall day like this,' but he didn't feel like it."

"He doesn't want to go out."

"I'm sorry he don't feel well," the woman said. "He's an awfully nice man. He was in the ring, you know."

"I know it."

"You never know it except from the way his face is," the woman said. They stood talking just inside the street door. "He's just as gentle."

"Well, good night, Mrs. Hirsch," Nick said.

"I'm not Mrs. Hirsch," the woman said. "She owns the place. I just look after it for her. I'm Mrs. Bell."

"Well, good night, Mrs. Bell," Nick said.

"Good night," the woman said.

Nick walked up the dark street to the corner under the arc light, and then along the car tracks to Henry's eating house. George was inside, back of the counter. "Did you see Ole?"

"Yes," said Nick. "He's in his room and he won't go out."

The cook opened the door from the kitchen when he heard Nick's voice. "I don't even listen to it," he said and shut the door.

"Did you tell him about it?" George asked.

"Sure. I told him but he knows what it's all about."

"What's he going to do?"

"Nothing."

"They'll kill him."

"I guess they will."

"He must have got mixed up in something in Chicago."

"I guess so," said Nick.

"It's a hell of a thing."

"It's an awful thing," Nick said.

They did not say anything. George reached down for a towel and wiped the counter.

"I wonder what he did?" Nick said.

"Double-crossed somebody. That's what they kill them for."

"I'm going to get out of this town," Nick said.

"Yes," said George. "That's a good thing to do."

"I can't stand to think about him waiting in the room and knowing he's going to get it. It's too damned awful."

"Well," said George, "you better not think about it."

THE HANDS OF
MR. OTTERMOLE

THOMAS BURKE
(1886–1945)

Twelve of the most distinguished literary critics in the world of mystery fiction were polled some years ago to determine the best detective stories of all time. The number one story is the one that follows. Oddly, it is untypical of Burke's work, which was mainly devoted to stories set in London's Limehouse district. He was rare among his contemporaries in portraying Orientals as sympathetic characters, not sinister stereotypes. The most famous of these stories was "Broken Blossoms," filmed with Richard Barthelmess and Lillian Gish.

T SIX O'CLOCK OF A JANUARY evening Mr. Whybrow was walking home through the cobweb alleys of London's East End. He had left the golden clamour of the great High Street to which the tram had brought him from the river and his daily work, and was now in the chessboard of byways that is called Mallon End. None of the rush and gleam of the High Street trickled into these byways. A few paces south— a flood tide of life, foaming and beating. Here—only slow-shuffling figures and muffled pulses. He was in the sink of London, the last refuge of European vagrants.

As though in tune with the street's spirit, he too walked slowly, with head down. It seemed that he was pondering some pressing trouble, but he was not. He had no trouble. He was walking slowly because he had been on his feet all day, and he was bent in abstraction because he was wondering whether the Missis would have herrings for his tea, or haddock; and he was trying to decide which would be the more tasty on a night like this. A wretched night it was, of damp and mist, and the mist wandered into his throat and his eyes, and the damp had settled on pavement and roadway, and where the sparse lamplight fell it sent up a greasy sparkle that chilled one to look at. By contrast it made his speculations more agreeable, and made him ready for that tea—whether herring or haddock. His eye turned from the glum bricks that made his horizon, and went forward half a mile. He saw a gas-lit kitchen, a flamy fire, and a spread tea table. There was toast in the hearth and a singing kettle on the side and a piquant effusion of herrings, or maybe of haddock, or perhaps sausages. The vision gave his aching feet a throb of energy. He shook imperceptible damp from his shoulders, and hastened towards its reality.

But Mr. Whybrow wasn't going to get any tea that evening—or any other evening. Mr. Whybrow was going to die. Somewhere within a hundred yards of him another man was walking: a man much like Mr. Whybrow and much like any other man, but without the only quality that enables mankind to live peaceably together and not as madmen in a jungle. A man with a dead heart eating into itself and bringing forth the foul organisms that arise from death and corruption. And that thing in man's shape, on a whim or a settled idea—one cannot know—had said within himself that Mr. Whybrow should never taste another herring. Not that Mr. Whybrow had injured him. Not that he had any dislike of Mr. Whybrow. Indeed, he knew nothing of him save as a familiar figure about the streets. But, moved by a force that had taken possession of his empty cells, he had picked Mr. Whybrow with that blind choice that makes us pick one restaurant table that has nothing to mark it from four or five other tables, or one apple from a dish of half a dozen equal apples; or that drives nature to send a cyclone upon one corner of this planet, and destroy five hundred lives in that corner, and leave another five hundred in the same corner unharmed. So this man had picked on Mr. Whybrow, as he might have picked on you or me, had we been within his daily observation; and even now he was creeping through the blue-toned streets, nursing his large white hands, moving ever closer to Mr. Whybrow's tea table, and so closer to Mr. Whybrow himself.

He wasn't, this man, a bad man. Indeed, he had many of the social and amiable qualities, and passed as a respectable man, as most successful criminals do. But the thought had come into his mouldering mind that he would like to murder somebody, and, as he held no fear of God or man, he was going to do it, and would then go home to *his* tea. I don't say that flippantly, but as a statement of fact. Strange as it may seem to the humane, murderers must and do sit down to meals after a murder. There is no reason why they shouldn't, and many reasons why they should. For one thing, they need to keep their physical and mental vitality at full beat for the business of covering their crime. For another, the strain of their effort makes them hungry, and satisfaction at the accomplishment of a desired thing brings a feeling of relaxation towards human pleasures. It is accepted among nonmurderers that the murderer is always overcome by fear for his safety and horror at his act; but this type is rare. His own safety is, of course, his immediate concern, but vanity is a marked quality of most murderers, and that, together with the thrill of conquest, makes him confident that he can secure it, and when he has restored his strength with food he goes about securing it as a young hostess goes about the arranging of her first big dinner—a little anxious, but no more. Criminologists and detectives tell us that *every* murderer, however intelligent or cunning, always makes one slip in his tactics—one little slip that brings the affair home to him. But that is only half-true. It is true only of the murderers who are caught. Scores of murderers are not caught: therefore scores of murderers do not make any mistake at all. This man didn't.

As for horror or remorse, prison chaplains, doctors, and lawyers have told us that of murderers they have interviewed under condemnation and the shadow of death, only one here and there has expressed any contrition for this act, or shown any sign of mental misery. Most of them display only exasperation at having been caught when so many have gone undiscovered, or indignation at being condemned for a perfectly reasonable act. However normal and humane they may have been before the murder, they are utterly without conscience after it. For what is conscience? Simply a polite nickname for superstition, which is a polite nickname for fear. Those who associate remorse with murder are, no doubt, basing their ideas on the world legend of the remorse of Cain, or are projecting their own frail minds into the mind of the murderer, and getting false reactions. Peaceable folk cannot hope to make contact with this mind, for they are not merely different in mental type from the murderer: they are different in their personal chemistry and construction. Some men can and do kill, not one man, but two or three, and go calmly about their daily affairs. Other men could not, under the most agonising provocation, bring themselves even to wound. It is men of this sort who imagine the murderer in torments of remorse and fear of the law, whereas he is actually sitting down to his tea.

The man with the large white hands was as ready for his tea as Mr. Whybrow was, but he had something to do before he went to it. When he had done that something, and made no mistake about it, he would be even more ready for it, and would go to it as comfortably as he went to it the day before, when his hands were stainless.

Walk on, then, Mr. Whybrow, walk on; and as you walk, look you last upon the familiar features of your nightly journey. Follow your jack-o'-lantern tea table. Look well upon its warmth and colour and kindness; feed your eyes with it, and tease your nose with its gently domestic odours; for you will never sit down to it. Within ten minutes' pacing of you a pursuing phantom has spoken in his heart, and you are doomed. There you go—you and phantom—two nebulous dabs of mortality, moving through green air along pavements of powder-blue, the one to kill, the other to be killed. Walk on. Don't annoy your burning feet by hurrying, for the more slowly you walk, the longer you will breathe the green air of this January dusk, and see the dreamy lamplight and the little shops, and hear the agreeable commerce of the London crowd and the haunting pathos of the street organ. These things are dear to you, Mr. Whybrow. You don't know it now, but in fifteen minutes you will have two seconds in which to realise how inexpressibly dear they are.

Walk on, then, across this crazy chessboard. You are in Lagos Street now, among the tents of the wanderers of Eastern Europe. A minute or so, and you are in Loyal Lane, among the lodging houses that shelter the useless and the beaten of London's camp followers. The lane holds the smell of them, and its soft darkness seems heavy with the wail of the futile. But you are not sensitive to impalpable things, and you plod through it, unseeing, as you do every evening, and come to Blean Street, and plod through that. From basement to sky rise the tenements of an alien colony. Their windows slot the ebony of their walls with lemon. Behind those windows strange life is moving, dressed with forms that are not of London or of England, yet, in essence, the same agreeable life that you have been living, and tonight will live no more. From high above you comes a voice crooning *The Song of Katta*. Through a window you see a family keeping a religious rite. Through another you see a woman pouring out tea for her husband. You see a man mending a pair of boots; a mother bathing her baby. You have seen all these things before, and never noticed them. You do not notice them now, but if you knew that you were never going to see them again, you would notice them. You never *will* see them again, not because your life has run its natural course, but because a man whom you have often passed in the street has at his own solitary pleasure decided to usurp the awful authority of nature, and destroy you. So perhaps it's as well that you don't notice them, for your part in them is ended. No more for you these pretty moments of our earthly travail: only one moment of terror, and then a plunging darkness.

Closer to you this shadow of massacre moves, and now he is twenty yards behind you. You can hear his footfall, but you do not turn your head. You are familiar with footfalls. You are in London, in the easy security of your daily territory, and footfalls behind you, your instinct tells you, are no more than a message of human company.

But you can't hear something in those footfalls—something that goes with a wid-dershins beat? Something that says: *Look out, look out. Beware, beware.* Can't you hear the very syllables of *mur-der-er, mur-der-er*? No; there is nothing in footfalls. They are neutral. The foot of villainy falls with the same quiet note as the foot of hon-esty. But those footfalls, Mr. Whybrow, are bearing on to you a pair of hands, and there is something in hands. Behind you that pair of hands is even now stretching its muscles in preparation for your end. Every minute of your days you have been see-ing human hands. Have you ever realised the sheer horror of hands—those appendages that are a symbol for our moments of trust and affection and salutation? Have you thought of the sickening potentialities that lie within the scope of that five-tentacled member? No, you never have; for all the human hands that you have seen have been stretched to you in kindness or fellowship. Yet, though the eyes can hate, and the lips can sting, it is only that dangling member that can gather the accu-mulated essence of evil, and electrify it into currents of destruction. Satan may enter into man by many doors, but in the hands alone can he find the servants of his will.

Another minute, Mr. Whybrow, and you will know all about the horror of human hands.

You are nearly home now. You have turned into your street—Caspar Street—and you are in the centre of the chessboard. You can see the front window of your little four-roomed house. The street is dark, and its three lamps give only a smut of light that is more confusing than darkness. It is dark—empty, too. Nobody about; no lights in the front parlours of the houses, for the families are at tea in their kitchens; and only a random glow in a few upper rooms occupied by lodgers. Nobody about but you and your following companion, and you don't notice him. You see him so often that he is never seen. Even if you turned your head and saw him, you would only say good evening to him, and walk on. A suggestion that he was a possible mur-derer would not even make you laugh. It would be too silly.

And now you are at your gate. And now you have found your door key. And now you are in, and hanging up your hat and coat. The Missis has just called a greeting from the kitchen, whose smell is an echo of that greeting (herrings!) and you have answered it, when the door shakes under a sharp knock.

Go away, Mr. Whybrow. Go away from that door. Don't touch it. Get right away from it. Get out of the house. Run with the Missis to the back garden, and over the fence. Or call the neighbours. But don't touch that door. Don't, Mr. Whybrow, don't open . . .

Mr. Whybrow opened the door.

That was the beginning of what became known as London's Strangling Horrors. Horrors they were called because they were something more than murders: they were motiveless, and there was an air of black magic about them. Each murder was committed at a time when the street where the bodies were found was empty of any perceptible or possible murderer. There would be an empty alley. There would be a policeman at its end. He would turn his back on the empty alley for less than a minute. Then he would look round and run into the night with news of another strangling. And in any direction he looked nobody to be seen and no report to be had of anybody being seen. Or he would be on duty in a long-quiet street, and sud-denly be called to a house of dead people whom a few seconds earlier he had seen alive. And again, whichever way he looked nobody to be seen; and although police whistles put an immediate cordon around the area, and searched all houses, no possible murderer to be found.

The first news of the murder of Mr. and Mrs. Whybrow was brought by the station sergeant. He had been walking through Caspar Street on his way to the station for duty, when he noticed the open door of No. 98. Glancing in, he saw by the gaslight of the passage a motionless body on the floor. After a second look he blew his whistle, and when the constables answered him he took one to join him in a search of the house, and sent others to watch all neighbouring streets, and make inquiries at adjoining houses. But neither in the house nor in the streets was anything found to indicate the murderer. Neighbours on either side, and opposite, were questioned, but they had seen nobody about, and had heard nothing. One had heard Mr. Whybrow come home—the scrape of his latchkey in the door was so regular an evening sound, he said, that you could set your watch by it for half past six—but he had heard nothing more than the sound of the opening door until the sergeant's whistle. Nobody had been seen to enter the house or leave it, by front or back, and the necks of the dead people carried no fingerprints or other traces. A nephew was called in to go over the house, but he could find nothing missing; and anyway his uncle possessed nothing worth stealing. The little money in the house was untouched, and there were no signs of any disturbance of the property, or even of struggle. No signs of anything but brutal and wanton murder.

Mr. Whybrow was known to neighbours and workmates as a quiet, likeable, home-loving man; such a man as could not have any enemies. But, then, murdered men seldom have. A relentless enemy who hates a man to the point of wanting to hurt him seldom wants to murder him, since to do that puts him beyond suffering. So the police were left with an impossible situation: no clue to the murderer and no motive for the murders; only the fact that they had been done.

The first news of the affair sent a tremor through London generally, and an electric thrill through all Mallon End. Here was a murder of two inoffensive people, not for gain and not for revenge; and the murderer, to whom, apparently, killing was a casual impulse, was at large. He had left no traces, and, provided he had no companions, there seemed no reason why he should not remain at large. Any clear-headed man who stands alone, and has no fear of God or man, can, if he chooses, hold a city, even a nation, in subjection; but your everyday criminal is seldom clear-headed, and dislikes being lonely. He needs, if not the support of confederates, at least somebody to talk to; his vanity needs the satisfaction of perceiving at first hand the effect of his work. For this he will frequent bars and coffee shops and other public places. Then, sooner or later, in a glow of comradeship, he will utter the one word too much; and the nark, who is everywhere, has an easy job.

But though the doss houses and saloons and other places were combed and set with watches, and it was made known by whispers that good money and protection were assured to those with information, nothing attaching to the Whybrow case could be found. The murderer clearly had no friends and kept no company. Known men of this type were called up and questioned, but each was able to give a good account of himself; and in a few days the police were at a dead end. Against the constant public gibe that the thing had been done almost under their noses, they became restive, and for four days each man of the force was working his daily beat under a strain. On the fifth day they became still more restive.

It was the season of annual teas and entertainments for the children of the Sunday schools, and on an evening of fog, when London was a world of groping phantoms, a small girl, in the bravery of best Sunday frock and shoes, shining face and new-washed hair, set out from Logan Passage for St. Michael's Parish Hall. She never got there. She was not actually dead until half past six, but she was as good as dead from the moment she left her mother's door. Somebody like a man, pacing the street from which the passage led, saw her come out; and from that moment she was dead. Through the fog somebody's large white hands reached after her, and in fifteen minutes they were about her.

At half past six a whistle screamed trouble, and those answering it found the body of little Nellie Vrinoff in a warehouse entry in Minnow Street. The sergeant was first among them, and he posted his men to useful points, ordering them here and there in the tart tones of repressed rage, and berating the officer whose beat the street was. "I saw you, Magson, at the end of the lane. What were you up to there? You were there ten minutes before you turned." Magson began an explanation about keeping an eye on a suspicious-looking character at that end, but the sergeant cut him short: "Suspicious characters be damned. You don't want to look for suspicious characters. You want to look for *murderers*. Messing about . . . and then this happens right where you ought to be. Now think what they'll say."

With the speed of ill news came the crowd, pale and perturbed; and on the story that the unknown monster had appeared again, and this time to a child, their faces streaked the fog with spots of hate and horror. But then came the ambulance and more police, and swiftly they broke up the crowd; and as it broke the sergeant's thought was thickened into words, and from all sides came low murmurs of "Right under their noses." Later inquiries showed that four people of the district, above suspicion, had passed that entry at intervals of seconds before the murder, and seen nothing and heard nothing. None of them had passed the child alive or seen her dead. None of them had seen anybody in the street except themselves. Again the police were left with no motive and with no clue.

And now the district, as you will remember, was given over, not to panic, for the London public never yields to that, but to apprehension and dismay. If these things were happening in their familiar streets, then anything might happen. Wherever people met—in the streets, the markets and the shops—they debated the one topic. Women took to bolting their windows and doors at the first fall of dusk. They kept their children closely under their eye. They did their shopping before dark, and watched anxiously, while pretending they weren't watching, for the return of their husbands from work. Under the Cockney's semihumorous resignation to disaster, they hid an hourly foreboding. By the whim of one man with a pair of hands the structure and tenor of their daily life were shaken, as they always can be shaken by any man contemptuous of humanity and fearless of its laws. They began to realise that the pillars that supported the peaceable society in which they lived were mere straws that anybody could snap; that laws were powerful only so long as they were obeyed; that the police were potent only so long as they were feared. By the power of his hands this one man had made a whole community do something new: he had made it think, and left it gasping at the obvious.

And then, while it was yet gasping under his first two strokes, he made his third. Conscious of the horror that his hands had created, and hungry as an actor who has once tasted the thrill of the multitude, he made fresh advertisement of his presence; and on Wednesday morning, three days after the murder of the child, the papers carried to the breakfast tables of England the story of a still more shocking outrage.

At 9:32 on Tuesday night a constable was on duty in Jarnigan Road, and at that time spoke to a fellow officer named Petersen at the top of Clemming Street. He had seen this officer walk down that street. He could swear that the street was empty at that time, except for a lame bootblack whom he knew by sight, and who passed him and entered a tenement on the side opposite that on which his fellow officer was walking. He had the habit, as all constables had just then, of looking constantly behind him and around him, whichever way he was walking, and he was certain that the street was empty. He passed his sergeant at 9:33, saluted him, and answered his inquiry for anything seen. He reported that he had seen nothing, and passed on. His beat ended at a short distance from Clemming Street, and, having paced it, he turned and came again at 9:34 to the top of the street. He had scarcely reached it before he heard the hoarse voice of the sergeant: "Gregory! You there? Quick. Here's another. My God, it's Petersen! Garrotted. Quick, call 'em up!"

That was the third of the Strangling Horrors, of which there would be a fourth and a fifth; and the five horrors were to pass into the unknown and unknowable. That is, unknown as far as authority and the public were concerned. The identity of the murderer *was* known, but to two men only. One was the murderer himself; the other was a young journalist.

This young man, who was covering the affairs for his paper, the *Daily Torch,* was no smarter than the other zealous newspapermen who were hanging about these byways in the hope of a sudden story. But he was patient, and he hung a little closer to the case than the other fellows, and by continually staring at it he at last raised the figure of the murderer like a genie from the stones on which he had stood to do his murders.

After the first few days the men had given up any attempt at exclusive stories, for there was none to be had. They met regularly at the police station, and what little information there was they shared. The officials were agreeable to them, but no more. The sergeant discussed with them the details of each murder; suggested possible explanations of the man's methods; recalled from the past those cases that had some similarity; and on the matter of motive reminded them of the motiveless Neil Cream and the wanton John Williams, and hinted that work was being done which would soon bring the business to an end; but about that work he would not say a word. The inspector, too, was gracefully garrulous on the thesis of Murder, but whenever one of the party edged the talk towards what was being done in this immediate matter, he glided past it. Whatever the officials knew, they were not giving it to newspapermen. The business had fallen heavily upon them, and only by a capture made by their own efforts could they rehabilitate themselves in official and public esteem. Scotland Yard, of course, was at work, and had all the station's material; but the station's hope was that they themselves would have the honour of settling the affair; and however useful the cooperation of the press might be in other cases, they did not want to risk a defeat by a premature disclosure of their theories and plans.

So the sergeant talked at large, and propounded one interesting theory after another, all of which the newspaper men had thought of themselves.

The young man soon gave up these morning lectures on the Philosophy of Crime, and took to wandering about the streets and making bright stories out of the effect of the murders on the normal life of the people. A melancholy job made more melancholy by the district. The littered roadways, the crestfallen houses, the bleared windows—all held the acid misery that evokes no sympathy: the misery of the frustrated poet. The misery was the creation of the aliens, who were living in this makeshift fashion because they had no settled homes, and would neither take the trouble to make a home where they *could* settle nor get on with their wandering.

There was little to be picked up. All he saw and heard were indignant faces, and wild conjectures of the murderer's identity and of the secret of his trick of appearing and disappearing unseen. Since a policeman himself had fallen a victim, denunciations of the force had ceased, and the unknown was now invested with a cloak of legend. Men eyed other men, as though thinking: "It might be *him*. It might be *him*." They were no longer looking for a man who had the air of a Madame Tussaud murderer; they were looking for a man, or perhaps some harridan woman, who had done these particular murders. Their thoughts ran mainly on the foreign set. Such ruffianism could scarcely belong to England, nor could the bewildering cleverness of the thing. So they turned to Romanian gipsies and Turkish carpet sellers. There, clearly, would be found the warm spot. These Eastern fellows—they knew all sorts of tricks, and they had no real religion—nothing to hold them within bounds. Sailors returning from those parts had told tales of conjurors who made themselves invisible; and there were tales of Egyptian and Arab potions that were used for abysmally queer purposes. Perhaps it *was* possible to them; you never knew. They were so slick and cunning, and they had such gliding movements; no Englishman could melt away as they could. Almost certainly the murderer would be found to be one of that sort—with some dark trick of his own—and just because they were sure that he *was* a magician, they felt that it was useless to look for him. He was a power, able to hold them in subjection and to hold himself untouchable. Superstition, which so easily cracks the frail shell of reason, had got into them. He could do anything he chose: he would never be discovered. These two points they settled, and they went about the streets in a mood of resentful fatalism.

They talked of their ideas to the journalist in half tones, looking right and left, as though *he* might overhear them and visit them. And though all the district was thinking of him and ready to pounce upon him, yet so strongly had he worked upon them that if any man in the street—say, a small man of commonplace features and form—had cried, "*I* am the monster!" would their stifled fury have broken into flood and have borne him down and engulfed him? Or would they not suddenly have seen something unearthly in that everyday face and figure, something unearthly in his everyday boots, something unearthly about his hat, something that marked him as one whom none of their weapons could alarm or pierce? And would they not momentarily have fallen back from this devil, as the devil fell back from the Cross made by the sword of Faust, and so have given him time to escape? I do not know; but so fixed was their belief in his invincibility that it is at least likely that they would have made this hesitation, had such an occasion arisen. But it never did. Today this commonplace fellow, his murder lust glutted, is still seen and observed among them as he was seen and observed all the time; but because nobody then dreamt, or now dreams, that he was what he was, they observed him then, and observe him now, as people observe a lamppost.

Almost was their belief in his invincibility justified; for, five days after the murder of the policeman Petersen, when the experience and inspiration of the whole detective force of London were turned towards his identification and capture, he made his fourth and fifth strokes.

At nine o'clock that evening, the young newspaperman, who hung about every night until his paper was away, was strolling along Richards Lane. Richards Lane is a narrow street, partly a stall market, and partly residential. The young man was in the residential section, which carries on one side small working-class cottages, and on the other the wall of a railway goods yard. The great wall hung a blanket of shadow over the lane, and the shadow and the cadaverous outline of the now deserted market stalls gave it the appearance of a living lane that had been turned to frost in the moment between breath and death. The very lamps, that elsewhere were nimbuses of gold, had here the rigidity of gems. The journalist, feeling this message of frozen eternity, was telling himself that he was tired of the whole thing, when in one stroke the frost was broken. In the moment between one pace and another silence and darkness were racked by a high scream and through the scream a voice: "Help! help! *He's here!*"

Before he could think what movement to make, the lane came to life. As though its invisible populace had been waiting on that cry, the door of every cottage was flung open, and from them and from the alleys poured shadowy figures bent in question mark form. For a second or so they stood as rigid as lamps; then a police whistle gave them direction, and the flock of shadows sloped up the street. The journalist followed them, and others followed him. From the main street and from surrounding streets they came, some risen from unfinished suppers, some disturbed in their ease of slippers and shirt sleeves, some stumbling on infirm limbs, and some upright, and armed with pokers or the tools of their trade. Here and there above the wavering cloud of heads moved the bold helmets of policemen. In one dim mass they surged upon a cottage whose doorway was marked by the sergeant and two constables; and voices of those behind urged them on with "Get in! Find him! Run round the back! Over the wall!" and those in front cried: "Keep back! Keep back!"

And now the fury of a mob held in thrall by unknown peril broke loose. He was here—on the spot. Surely this time he *could not* escape. All minds were bent upon the cottage; all energies thrust towards its doors and windows and roof; all thought was turned upon one unknown man and his extermination. So that no one man saw any other man. No man saw the narrow, packed lane and the mass of struggling shadows, and all forgot to look among themselves for the monster who never lingered upon his victims. All forgot, indeed, that they, by their mass crusade of vengeance, were affording him the perfect hiding place. They saw only the house, and they heard only the rendering of woodwork and the smash of glass at back and front, and the police giving orders or crying with the chase; and they pressed on.

But they found no murderer. All they found was news of murder and a glimpse of the ambulance, and for their fury there was no other object than the police themselves, who fought against this hampering of their work.

The journalist managed to struggle through to the cottage door, and to get the story from the constable stationed there. The cottage was the home of a pensioned sailor and his wife and daughter. They had been at supper, and at first it appeared that some obnoxious gas had smitten all three in midaction. The daughter lay dead on the hearthrug, with a piece of bread and butter in her hand. The father had fallen sideways from his chair, leaving on his plate a filled spoon of rice pudding. The mother lay half under the table, her lap filled with the pieces of a broken cup and splashes of cocoa. But in three seconds the idea of gas was dismissed. One glance at their necks showed that this was the Strangler again; and the police stood and looked at the room and momentarily shared the fatalism of the public. They were helpless.

This was his fourth visit, making seven murders in all. He was to do, as you know, one more—and to do it that night; and then he was to pass into history as the unknown London horror, and return to the decent life that he had always led, remembering little of what he had done, and worried not at all by the memory. Why did he stop? Impossible to say. Why did he begin? Impossible again. It just happened like that; and if he thinks at all of those days and nights, I surmise that he thinks of them as we think of foolish or dirty little sins that we committed in childhood. We say that they were not really sins, because we were not then consciously ourselves: we had not come to realisation; and we look back at that foolish little creature that we once were, and forgive him because he didn't know. So, I think, with this man.

There are plenty like him. Eugene Aram, after the murder of Daniel Clarke, lived a quiet, contented life for fourteen years, unhaunted by his crime and unshaken in his self-esteem. Dr. Crippen murdered his wife, and then lived pleasantly with his mistress in the house under whose floor he had buried the wife. Constance Kent, found not guilty of the murder of her young brother, led a peaceful life for five years before she confessed. George Joseph Smith and William Palmer lived amiably among their fellows untroubled by fear or by remorse for their poisonings and drownings. Charles Peace, at the time he made his one unfortunate essay, had settled down into a respectable citizen with an interest in antiques. It happened that, after a lapse of time, these men were discovered, but more murderers than we guess are living decent lives today, and will die in decency undiscovered and unsuspected. As this man will.

But he had a narrow escape, and it was perhaps this narrow escape that brought him to a stop. The escape was due to an error of judgement on the part of the journalist.

As soon as he had the full story of the affair, which took some time, he spent fifteen minutes on the telephone, sending the story through, and at the end of the fifteen minutes, when the stimulus of the business had left him, he felt physically tired and mentally dishevelled. He was not yet free to go home; the paper would not go away for another hour; so he turned into a bar for a drink and some sandwiches.

It was then, when he had dismissed the whole business from his mind, and was looking about the bar and admiring the landlord's taste in watch chains and his air of domination, and was thinking that the landlord of a well-conducted tavern had a more comfortable life than a newspaperman, that his mind received from nowhere a spark of light. He was not thinking about the Strangling Horrors; his mind was on his sandwich. As a public-house sandwich, it was a curiosity. The bread had been thinly cut, it was buttered, and the ham was not two months stale; it was ham as it should be. His mind turned to the inventor of this refreshment, the earl of Sandwich, and then to George IV, and then to the Georges, and to the legend of that George who was worried to know how the apple got into the apple dumpling. He wondered whether George would have been equally puzzled to know how the ham got into the ham sandwich, and how long it would have been before it occurred to him that the ham could not have got there unless somebody had put it there. He got up to order another sandwich, and in that moment a little active corner of his mind settled the affair. If there was ham in his sandwich, somebody must have put it there. If seven people had been murdered, somebody must have been there to murder them. There was no aeroplane or automobile that would go into a man's pocket; therefore that somebody must have escaped either by running away or standing still; and again therefore—

He was visualising the front-page story that his paper would carry if his theory were correct, and if—a matter of conjecture—his editor had the necessary nerve to make a bold stroke, when a cry of "Time, gentlemen, please! All out!" reminded him of the hour. He got up and went out into a world of mist, broken by the ragged discs of roadside puddles and the streaming lightning of motor buses. He was certain that he had *the* story, but, even if it were proved, he was doubtful whether the policy of his paper would permit him to print it. It had one great fault. It was truth, but it was impossible truth. It rocked the foundations of everything that newspaper readers believed and that newspaper editors helped them to believe. They might believe that Turkish carpet sellers had the gift of making themselves invisible. They would not believe this.

As it happened, they were not asked to, for the story was never written. As his paper had by now gone away, and as he was nourished by his refreshment and stimulated by his theory, he thought he might put in an extra half hour by testing that theory. So he began to look about for the man he had in mind—a man with white hair, and large white hands; otherwise an everyday figure whom nobody would look twice at. He wanted to spring his idea on this man without warning, and he was going to place himself within reach of a man armoured in legends of dreadfulness and grue. This might appear to be an act of supreme courage—that one man, with no hope of immediate outside support, should place himself at the mercy of one who was holding a whole parish in terror. But it wasn't. He didn't think about the risk. He didn't think about his duty to his employers or loyalty to his paper. He was moved simply by an instinct to follow a story to its end.

He walked slowly from the tavern and crossed into Fingal Street, making for Deever Market, where he had hope of finding his man. But his journey was shortened. At the corner of Lotus Street he saw him—or a man who looked like him. This street was poorly lit, and he could see a little of the man: but he *could* see white hands. For some twenty paces he stalked him; then drew level with him; and at a point where the arch of a railway crossed the street, he saw that this was his man. He approached him with the current conversational phrase of the district: "Well, seen anything of the murderer?" The man stopped to look sharply at him; then, satisfied that the journalist was not the murderer, said:

"Eh? No, nor's anybody else, curse it. Doubt if they ever will."

"I don't know. I've been thinking about them, and I've got an idea."

"So?"

"Yes. Came to me all of a sudden. Quarter of an hour ago. And I'd felt that we'd all been blind. It's been staring us in the face."

The man turned again to look at him, and the look and the movement held suspicion of this man who seemed to know so much. "Oh? Has it? Well, if you're so sure, why not give us the benefit of it?"

"I'm going to." They walked level, and were nearly at the end of the little street where it meets Deever Market, when the journalist turned casually to the man. He put a finger on his arm. "Yes, it seems to me quite simple now. But there's still one point I don't understand. One little thing I'd like to clear up. I mean the motive. Now, as man to man, tell me, Sergeant Ottermole, just *why* did you kill all those inoffensive people?"

The sergeant stopped, and the journalist stopped. There was just enough light from the sky, which held the reflected light of the continent of London, to give him a sight of the sergeant's face, and the sergeant's face was turned to him with a wide smile of such urbanity and charm that the journalist's eyes were frozen as they met it. The smile stayed for some seconds. Then said the sergeant: "Well, to tell you the truth, Mr. Newspaperman, I don't know. I really don't know. In fact, I've been worried about it myself. But I've got an idea—just like you. Everybody knows that we can't control the workings of our minds. Don't they? Ideas come into our minds without asking. But everybody's supposed to be able to control his body. Why? Eh? We get our minds from Lord-knows-where—from people who were dead hundreds of years before we were born. Mayn't we get our bodies in the same way? Our faces—our legs—our heads—they aren't completely ours. We don't make 'em. They come to us. And couldn't ideas come into our bodies like ideas come into our minds? Eh? Can't ideas live in nerve and muscle as well as in brain? Couldn't it be that parts of our bodies aren't really us, and couldn't ideas come into—into"—he shot his arms out, showing the great white-gloved hands and hairy wrists; shot them out so swiftly to the journalist's throat that his eyes never saw them—"into *my hands!*"

THE LITTLE HOUSE
AT CROIX-ROUSSE

GEORGES SIMENON
(1903–1989)

(TRANSLATED BY ANTHONY BOUCHER)

Best known for the long series of novels involving Inspector Jules Maigret, Simenon tired of the famous policeman he had created at the age of twenty-six and abandoned him for many years while he wrote deep, complex psychological crime novels. He eventually returned to Maigret as a rest from his more strenuous work. In his early years, he was able to write a book in three or four days, but later settled into the more leisurely pace of every two weeks.

HAD NEVER SEEN JOSEPH Leborgne at work before. I received something of a shock when I entered his room that day.

His blond hair, usually plastered down, was in complete disorder. The individual hairs, stiffened by brilliantine, stuck out all over his head. His face was pale and worn. Nervous twitches distorted his features.

He threw a grudging glare at me which almost drove me from the room. But since I could see that he was hunched over a diagram, my curiosity was stronger than my sensitivity. I advanced into the room and took off my hat and coat.

"A fine time you've picked!" he grumbled.

This was hardly encouraging. I stammered, "A tricky case?"

"That's putting it mildly. Look at that paper."

"It's the plan of a house? A small house?"

"The subtlety of your mind! A child of four could guess that. You know the Croix-Rousse district in Lyons?"

"I've passed through there."

"Good! This little house lies in one of the most deserted sections of the district—not a district, I might add, which is distinguished by its liveliness."

"What do these black crosses mean, in the garden and on the street?"

"Policemen."

"Good Lord! And the crosses mark where they've been killed?"

"Who said anything about dead policemen? The crosses indicate policemen who were on duty at these several spots on the night of the eighth-to-ninth. The cross that's heavier than the others is Corporal Manchard."

I dared not utter a word or move a muscle. It felt wisest not to interrupt

Leborgne, who was favoring the plan with the same furious glares which he had bestowed upon me.

"Well? Aren't you going to ask me *why* policemen were stationed there—six of them, no less—on the night of the eighth-to-ninth? Or maybe you're going to pretend that you've figured it out?"

I said nothing.

"They were there because the Lyons police had received, the day before, the following letter:

"Dr. Luigi Ceccioni will be murdered, at his home,
on the night of the eighth-to-ninth instant."

"And the doctor had been warned?" I asked at last.

"No! Since Ceccioni was an Italian exile and it seemed more than likely that the affair had political aspects, the police preferred to take their precautions without warning the party involved."

"And he was murdered anyway?"

"Patience! Dr. Ceccioni, fifty years of age, lived alone in this wretched little hovel. He kept house for himself and ate his evening meal every day in an Italian restaurant nearby. On the eighth he left home at seven o'clock, as usual, for the restaurant. And Corporal Manchard, one of the best police officers in France and a pupil, to boot, of the great Lyons criminologist Dr. Eugène Locard, searched the house from basement to attic. He proved to himself that no one was hidden there and that it was impossible to get in by any other means than the ordinary doors and windows visible from the outside. No subterranean passages nor any such hocus-pocus. Nothing out of a mystery novel . . . You understand?"

I was careful to say nothing, but Leborgne's vindictive tone seemed to accuse me of willfully interpolating hocus-pocus.

"No one in the house! Nothing to watch but two doors and three windows! A lesser man than Corporal Manchard would have been content to set up the watch with only himself and one policeman. But Manchard requisitioned five, one for each entrance, with himself to watch the watchers. At nine p.m. the shadow of the doctor appeared in the street. He re-entered his house, *absolutely alone.* His room was upstairs; a light went on in there promptly. And then the police vigil began. Not one of them dozed! Not one of them deserted his post! Not one of them lost sight of the precise point which he had been delegated to watch!

"Every fifteen minutes Manchard made the round of the group. Around three a.m. the petroleum lamp upstairs went out slowly, as though it had run out of fuel. The corporal hesitated. At last he decided to use his lock-picking gadget and go in. Upstairs, in the bedroom, seated—or rather half lying—on the edge of the bed was Dr. Luigi Ceccioni. His hands were clutched to his chest and he was dead. He was completely dressed, even to the cape which still hung over his shoulders. His hat had fallen to the floor. His underclothing and suit were saturated with blood and his hands were soaked in it. One bullet from a six-millimeter Browning had penetrated less than a centimeter above his heart."

I gazed at Joseph Leborgne with awe. I saw his lip tremble.

"No one had entered the house! No one had left!" he groaned. "I'll swear to that as though I'd stood guard myself: I know my Corporal Manchard. And don't go thinking that they found the revolver in the house. *There wasn't any revolver!* Not in sight and not hidden. Not in the fireplace, or even in the roof gutter. Not in the garden—

not anywhere at all! In other words, a bullet was fired in a place where there was no one save the victim himself and where there was no firearm!

"As for the windows, they were closed and undamaged; a bullet fired from outside would have shattered the panes. Besides, a revolver doesn't carry far enough to have been fired from outside the range covered by the cordon of policemen. Look at the plan! Eat it up with your eyes! And you may restore some hope of life to poor Corporal Manchard, who has given up sleeping and looks upon himself virtually as a murderer."

I timidly ventured, "What do you know about Ceccioni?"

"That he used to be rich. That he's hardly practiced medicine at all, but rather devoted himself to politics—which made it healthier for him to leave Italy."

"Married? Bachelor?"

"Widower. One child, a son, at present studying in Argentina."

"What did he live on in Lyons?"

"A little of everything and nothing. Indefinite subsidies from his political colleagues. Occasional consultations, but those chiefly *gratis* among the poor of the Italian colony."

"Was anything stolen from the house?"

"Not a trace of any larcenous entry or of anything stolen."

I don't know why, but at this moment I wanted to laugh. It suddenly seemed to me that some master of mystification had amused himself by presenting Joseph Leborgne with a totally impossible problem, simply to give him a needed lesson in modesty.

He noticed the broadening of my lips. Seizing the plan, he crossed the room to plunge himself angrily into his armchair.

"Let me know when you've solved it!" he snapped.

"I can certainly solve nothing before you," I said tactfully.

"Thanks," he observed.

I began to fill my pipe. I lit it, disregarding my companion's rage which was reaching the point of paroxysm.

"All I ask of you is that you sit quietly," he pronounced. "And don't breathe so loudly," he added.

Ten minutes passed as unpleasantly as possible. Despite myself, I called up the image of the plan, with the six black crosses marking the policemen.

And the impossibility of this story, which had at first so amused me, began to seem curiously disquieting.

After all, this was not a matter of psychology or of detective *flair,* but of pure geometry.

"This Manchard," I asked suddenly. "Has he ever served as a subject for hypnotism?"

Joseph Leborgne did not even deign to answer that one.

"Did Ceccioni have any political enemies in Lyons?"

Leborgne shrugged.

"And it's been proved that the son is in Argentina?"

This time he merely took the pipe out of my mouth and tossed it on the mantelpiece.

"You have the names of all the policemen?"

He handed me a sheet of paper:

> *Jérôme Pallois, 28, married*
> *Jean-Joseph Stockman, 31, single*
> *Armand Dubois, 26, married*
> *Hubert Trajanu, 43, divorced*
> *Germain Garros, 32, married*

I reread these lines three times. The names were in the order in which the men had been stationed around the building, starting from the left.

I was ready to accept the craziest notions. Desperately I exclaimed at last, "It *is* impossible!"

And I looked at Joseph Leborgne. A moment before his face had been pale, his eyes encircled, his lips bitter. Now, to my astonishment, I saw him smilingly head for a pot of jam.

As he passed a mirror he noticed himself and seemed scandalized by the incongruous contortions of his hair. He combed it meticulously. He adjusted the knot of his cravat.

Once again Joseph Leborgne was his habitual self. As he looked for a spoon with which to consume his horrible jam of leaves-of-God-knows-what, he favored me with a sarcastic smile.

"How simple it would always be to reach the truth if preconceived ideas did not falsify our judgment!" he sighed. "You have just said, 'It *is* impossible!' So therefore . . ."

I waited for him to contradict me. I'm used to that.

"So, therefore," he went on, "it *is* impossible. Just so. And all that we needed to do from the very beginning was simply to admit that fact. There was no revolver in the house, no murderer hidden there. Very well: then there was no shot fired there."

"But then . . . ?"

"Then, very simply, Luigi Ceccioni arrived *with the bullet already in his chest.* I've every reason to believe that he fired the bullet himself. He was a doctor; he knew just where to aim—'less than a centimeter above the heart,' you'll recall—so that the wound would not be *instantly* fatal, but would allow him to move about for a short time."

Joseph Leborgne closed his eyes.

"Imagine this poor hopeless man. He has only one son. The boy is studying abroad, but the father no longer has any money to send him. Ceccioni insures his life with the boy as beneficiary. His next step is to die—but somehow to die with no suspicion of suicide, or the insurance company will refuse to pay.

"By means of an anonymous letter he summons the police themselves as witnesses. They see him enter his house where there is no weapon and they find him dead several hours later.

"It was enough, once he was seated on his bed, to massage his chest, forcing the bullet to penetrate more deeply, at last to touch the heart . . ."

I let out an involuntary cry of pain. But Leborgne did not stir. He was no longer concerned with me.

It was not until a week later that he showed me a telegram from Corporal Manchard:

AUTOPSY REVEALS ECCHYMOSIS AROUND WOUNDS AND
TRACES FINGER PRESSURE STOP DOCTOR AND SELF PUZZLED
POSSIBLE CAUSE STOP REQUEST YOUR ADVICE IMMEDIATELY

"You answered?"

He looked at me reproachfully. "It requires both great courage and great imagination to massage oneself to death. Why should the poor man have done that in vain? The insurance company has a capital of four hundred million . . ."

THE CASE OF THE MISSING PATRIARCHS

SHERLOCK HOLMES IS DEAD . . .

LOGAN CLENDENING, M.D.
(1884–1945)

This minor work is probably not one of the greatest mystery stories ever written. It is a bit short to have allowed great character development or a rich tapestry of philosophical insights, or even a fully textured atmosphere. Still, it is so lovely in its simplicity that I have always smiled when I recall it or reread it. It was privately printed as a Christmas gift in an edition of only 30 copies and is one of the most sought-after books in the world of Sherlock Holmes collecting.

HERLOCK HOLMES IS DEAD. AT the age of 80 he passed away quietly in his sleep. And at once ascended to Heaven.

The arrival of few recent immigrants to the celestial streets has caused so much excitement. Only Napoleon's appearance in Hell is said to have equaled the great detective's reception. In spite of the heavy fog which rolled in from the Jordan, Holmes was immediately bowled in a hansom to audience with the Divine Presence. After the customary exchange of amenities, Jehovah said:

"Mr. Holmes, we too have our problems. Adam and Eve are missing. Have been, 's a matter of fact, for nearly two eons. They used to be quite an attraction to visitors and we would like to commission you to discover them."

Holmes looked thoughtful for a moment.

"We fear that their appearance when last seen would furnish no clue," continued Jehovah. "A man is bound to change in two eons."

Holmes held up his long thin hand. "Could you make a general announcement that a contest between an immovable body and an irresistible force will be staged in that large field at the end of the street—Lord's, I presume it is?"

The announcement was made and soon the streets were filled with a slowly moving crowd. Holmes stood idly in the divine portico watching them.

Suddenly he darted into the crowd and seized a patriarch and his whimpering old mate; he brought them to the Divine Presence.

"Adam," said Deity, "you have been giving us a great deal of anxiety. But, Mr. Holmes, tell me how you found them."

"Elementary, my dear God," said Sherlock Holmes, "they have no navels."

CLERICAL ERROR

JAMES GOULD COZZENS
(1903–1978)

Known mainly for such widely popular novels of love and lust as By Love Possessed *(which was successfully and appropriately filmed), Cozzens nevertheless wrote a crime novel,* The Just and the Unjust *(1942), that was regarded as important enough to be included on the Haycraft-Queen Definitive Library of Detective-Crime Mystery Fiction, the best list of the cornerstones of mysteries ever compiled by two of the best scholars in that world.*

HERE WERE THREE STEPS down from the street door. Then the store extended, narrow and low between the book-packed walls, sixty or seventy feet to a little cubbyhole of an office where a large sallow man worked under a shaded desk-lamp. He had heard the street door open, and he looked that way a moment, peering intently through his spectacles. Seeing only a thin, stiffly erect gentleman with a small cropped white mustache, standing hesitant before the table with the sign *Any Book 50 Cents,* he returned to the folded copy of a religious weekly on the desk in front of him. He looked at the obituary column again, pulled a pad toward him, and made a note. When he had finished, he saw, on looking up again, that the gentleman with the white mustache had come all the way down the store.

"Yes, sir?" he said, pushing the papers aside. "What can I do for you?"

The gentleman with the white mustache stared at him keenly. "I am addressing the proprietor, Mr. Joreth?" he said.

"Yes, sir. You are."

"Quite so. My name is Ingalls—Colonel Ingalls."

"I'm glad to know you, Colonel. What can I—"

"I see that the name does not mean anything to you."

Mr. Joreth took off his spectacles, looked searchingly. "Why, no, sir. I am afraid not. Ingalls. No. I don't know anyone by that name."

Colonel Ingalls thrust his stick under his arm and drew an envelope from his inner pocket. He took a sheet of paper from it, unfolded the sheet, scowled at it a moment, and tossed it onto the desk. "Perhaps," he said, "this will refresh your memory."

Mr. Joreth pulled his nose a moment, looked harder at Colonel Ingalls, replaced his spectacles. "Oh," he said, "a bill. Yes. You must excuse me. I do much of my business by mail with people I've never met personally. 'The Reverend Doctor Godfrey Ingalls, Saint John's Rectory.' Ah, yes, yes—"

"The late Doctor Ingalls was my brother. This bill is obviously an error.

He would never have ordered, received, or wished to read any of these works. Naturally, no such volumes were found among his effects."

"Hm," said Mr. Joreth. "Yes, I see." He read down the itemized list, coughed, as though in embarrassment. "I see. Now, let me check my records for a moment." He dragged down a vast battered folio from the shelf before him. "G, H, I—" he muttered. "*Ingalls.* Ah, now—"

"There is no necessity for that," said Colonel Ingalls. "It is, of course, a mistake. A strange one, it seems to me. I advise you strongly to be more careful. If you choose to debase yourself by surreptitiously selling works of the sort, that is your business. But—"

Mr. Joreth nodded several times, leaned back. "Well, Colonel," he said, "you're entitled to your opinion. I don't sit in judgment on the tastes of my customers. Now, in this case, there seems unquestionably to have been an order for the books noted from the source indicated. On the fifteenth of last May I filled the order. Presumably they arrived. What became of them, then, is no affair of mine; but in view of your imputation I might point out that such literature is likely to be kept in a private place and read privately. For eight successive months I sent a statement. I have never received payment. Of course, I was unaware that the customer was, didn't you say, deceased. Hence my reference to legal action on this last. I'm very sorry to have—"

"You unmitigated scoundrel!" roared Colonel Ingalls. "Do you really mean definitely to maintain that Doctor Ingalls purchased such books? Let me tell you—"

Mr. Joreth said, "My dear sir, one moment, if you please! Are you in a position to be so positive? I imply nothing about the purchaser. I mean to maintain nothing, except that I furnished goods, for which I am entitled to payment. I am a poor man. When people do not pay me, what can I do but—"

"Why, you infamous—"

Mr. Joreth held up his hand. "Please, please!" he protested. "I think you are taking a most unjust and unjustified attitude, Colonel. This account has run a long while. I've taken no action. I am well aware of the unpleasantness which would be caused for many customers if a bill for books of this sort was made public. The circumstances aren't by any means unique, my dear sir; a list of my confidential customers would no doubt surprise you."

Colonel Ingalls said carefully, "Be good enough to show me my brother's original order."

"Ah," said Mr. Joreth. He pursed his lips. "That's unfair of you, Colonel. You are quite able to see that I wouldn't have it. It would be the utmost imprudence for me to keep on file anything which could cause so much trouble. I have the carbon of an invoice, which is legally sufficient, under the circumstances, I think. You see my position."

"Clearly," said Colonel Ingalls. "It is the position of a dirty knave and a blackguard, and I shall give myself the satisfaction of thrashing you."

He whipped the stick from under his arm. Mr. Joreth slid agilely from his seat, caught the telephone off the desk, kicking a chair into the Colonel's path.

"Operator," he said, "I want a policeman." Then he jerked open a drawer, plucked a revolver from it. "Now, my good sir," he said, his back against the wall, "we shall soon see. I have put up with a great deal of abuse from you, but there are limits. To a degree I understand your provocation, though it doesn't excuse your conduct. If you choose to take yourself out of here at once and send me a check for the amount due me, we will say no more."

Colonel Ingalls held the stick tight in his hand. "I think I will wait for the officer," he said with surprising composure. "I was too hasty. In view of your list of so-called customers, which you think would surprise me, there are doubtless other people to be considered—"

The stick in his hand leaped, sudden and slashing, catching Mr. Joreth over the wrist. The revolver flew free, clattered along the floor, and Colonel Ingalls kicked it behind him. "It isn't the sort of thing the relatives of a clergyman would like to have made public, is it? When you read of the death of one, what is to keep you from sending a bill? Very often they must pay and shut up. A most ingenious scheme, sir."

Mr. Joreth clasped his wrist, wincing. "I am at a loss to understand this nonsense," he said. "How dare you—"

"Indeed?" said Colonel Ingalls. "Ordinarily, I might be at loss myself, sir; but in this case I think you put your foot in it, sir! I happen to be certain that my late brother ordered no books from you, that he did not keep them in private or read them in private. It was doubtless not mentioned in the obituary, but for fifteen years previous to his death Doctor Ingalls had the misfortune to be totally blind . . . There, sir, is the policeman you sent for."

THE TWO BOTTLES OF RELISH

LORD DUNSANY
(1878–1957)

Noted primarily as an author of fantasy and supernatural fiction, the eighteenth Baron Dunsany's first play was produced by William Butler Yeats at Dublin's Abbey Theatre in 1909. Titled The Glittering Gate, *it is the story of two dead burglars who, realizing that they are unlikely to get into heaven in the usual way, simply jimmy the pearly gates. The present story, his most famous, although not without whimsey, is a trifle darker.*

MITHERS IS MY NAME. I'M what you might call a small man and in a small way of business. I travel for Num-numo, a relish for meats and savouries—the world-famous relish, I ought to say. It's really quite good, no deleterious acids in it, and does not affect the heart; so it is quite easy to push. I wouldn't have gotten the job if it weren't. But I hope some day to get something that's harder to push, as of course the harder they are to push, the better the pay. At present I can just make my way, with nothing at all over; but then I live in a very expensive flat. It happened like this, and that brings me to my story. And it isn't the story you'd expect from a small man like me, yet there's nobody else to tell it. Those that know anything of it besides me are all for hushing it up. Well, I was looking for a room to live in in London when first I got my job. It had to be in London, to be central; and I went to a block of buildings, very gloomy they looked, and saw the man that ran them and asked him for what I wanted. Flats they called them; just a bedroom and a sort

of a cupboard. Well, he was showing a man round at the time who was a gent, in fact more than that, so he didn't take much notice of me—the man that ran all those flats didn't, I mean. So I just ran behind for a bit, seeing all sorts of rooms and waiting till I could be shown my class of thing. We came to a very nice flat, a sitting room, bedroom and bathroom, and a sort of little place that they called a hall. And that's how I came to know Linley. He was the bloke that was being shown round.

"Bit expensive," he said.

And the man that ran the flats turned away to the window and picked his teeth. It's funny how much you can show by a simple thing like that. What he meant to say was that he'd hundreds of flats like that, and thousands of people looking for them, and he didn't care who had them or whether they all went on looking. There was no mistaking him, somehow. And yet he never said a word, only looked away out of the window and picked his teeth. And I ventured to speak to Mr. Linley then; and I said, "How about it, sir, if I paid half, and shared it? I wouldn't be in the way, and I'm out all day, and whatever you said would go, and really I wouldn't be no more in your way than a cat."

You may be surprised at my doing it; and you'll be much more surprised at him accepting it—at least, you would if you knew me, just a small man in a small way of business. And yet I could see at once that he was taking to me more than he was taking to the man at the window.

"But there's only one bedroom," he said.

"I could make up my bed easy in that little room there," I said.

"The hall," said the man, looking round from the window, without taking his toothpick out.

"And I'd have the bed out of the way and hid in the cupboard by any hour you like," I said.

He looked thoughtful, and the other man looked out over London; and in the end, do you know, he accepted.

"Friend of yours?" said the flat man.

"Yes," answered Mr. Linley.

It was really very nice of him.

I'll tell you why I did it. Able to afford it? Of course not. But I heard him tell the flat man that he had just come down from Oxford and wanted to live for a few months in London. It turned out he wanted just to be comfortable and do nothing for a bit while he looked things over and chose a job, or probably just as long as he could afford it. Well, I said to myself, what's the Oxford manner worth in business, especially a business like mine? Why, simply everything you've got. If I picked up only a quarter of it from this Mr. Linley I'd be able to double my sales, and that would soon mean I'd be given something a lot harder to push, with perhaps treble the pay. Worth it every time. And you can make a quarter of an education go twice as far again, if you're careful with it. I mean you don't have to quote the whole of the *Inferno* to show that you've read Milton; half a line may do it.

Well, about the story I have to tell. And you mightn't think that a little man like me could make you shudder. Well, I soon forgot about the Oxford manner when we settled down in our flat. I forgot it in the sheer wonder of the man himself. He had a mind like an acrobat's body, like a bird's body. It didn't want education. You didn't notice whether he was educated or not. Ideas were always leaping up in him, things you'd never have thought of. And not only that, but if any ideas were about, he'd sort of catch them. Time and again I've found him knowing just what I was going to say. Not thought reading, but what they call intuition. I used to try to learn a bit about chess, just to take my thoughts off Num-numo in the evening, when I'd done with it. But problems I never could do. Yet he'd come along and glance at my problem and say, "You probably move that piece first," and I'd say, "But where?" and he'd say, "Oh, one of those three squares." And I'd say, "But it will be taken on all of them." And the piece a queen all the time, mind you. And he'd say, "Yes, it's doing no good there: you're probably meant to lose it."

And, do you know, he'd be right.

You see, he'd been following out what the other man had been thinking. That's what he'd been doing.

Well, one day there was that ghastly murder at Unge. I don't know if you remember it. But Steeger had gone down to live with a girl in a bungalow on the North Downs, and that was the first we had heard of him.

The girl had two hundred pounds, and he got every penny of it, and she utterly disappeared. And Scotland Yard couldn't find her.

Well, I'd happened to read that Steeger had bought two bottles of Num-numo; for the Otherthorpe police had found out everything about him, except what he did with the girl; and that of course attracted my attention, or I should have never thought again about the case or said a word of it to Linley. Num-numo was always on my mind, as I always spent every day pushing it, and that kept me from forgetting the other thing. And so one day I said to Linley, "I wonder with all that knack you have for seeing through a chess problem, and thinking of one thing and another, that you don't have a go at that Otherthorpe mystery. It's a problem as much as chess," I said.

"There's not the mystery in ten murders that there is in one game of chess," he answered.

"It's beaten Scotland Yard," I said.

"Has it?" he asked.

"Knocked them endwise," I said.

"It shouldn't have done that," he said. And almost immediately after he said, "What are the facts?"

We were both sitting at supper, and I told him the facts, as I had them straight from the papers. She was a pretty blonde, she was small, she was called Nancy Elth, she had two hundred pounds, they lived at the bungalow for five days. After that he stayed there for another fortnight, but nobody ever saw her alive again. Steeger said she had gone to South America, but later said he had never said South America, but South Africa. None of her money remained in the bank where she had kept it, and Steeger was shown to have come by at least a hundred fifty pounds just at that time. Then Steeger turned out to be vegetarian, getting all his food from the greengrocer, and that made the constable in the village of Unge suspicious of him, for a vegetarian was something new to the constable. He watched Steeger after that, and it's well he did, for there was nothing that Scotland Yard asked him that he couldn't tell them about him, except of course one thing. And he told the police at Otherthorpe five or six miles away, and they came and took a hand at it too. They were able to say for one thing that he never went outside the bungalow and its tidy garden ever since she disappeared. You see, the more they watched him the more suspicious they got, as you naturally do if you're watching a man; so that very soon they were watching every move he made, but if it hadn't been for his being a vegetarian they'd never have started to suspect him, and there wouldn't have been enough evidence even for Linley. Not that they found out anything much against him, except that hundred fifty pounds dropping in from nowhere, and it was Scotland Yard that found that, not the police of Otherthorpe. No, what the constable of Unge found out was about the larch trees, and that beat Scotland Yard utterly, and beat Linley up to the very last, and of course it beat me. There were ten larch trees in the bit of a garden, and he'd made some sort of arrangement with the landlord, Steeger had, before he took the bungalow, by which he could do what he liked with the larch trees. And then from about the time that little Nancy Elth must have died he cut every one of them down. Three times a day he went at it for nearly a week, and when they were all down he cut them all up into logs no more than two feet long and laid them all in neat heaps. You never saw such work. And what for? To give an excuse for the axe was one theory. But the excuse was bigger than the axe; it took him a fortnight, hard work every day. And he could have killed a little thing like Nancy Elth without an axe, and cut her up too. Another theory was that he wanted firewood, to make away with the body. But he never used it. He left it all standing there in those neat stacks. It fairly beat everybody.

Well, those are the facts I told Linley. Oh yes, and he bought a big butcher's knife. Funny thing, they all do. And yet it isn't so funny after all; if you've got to cut a woman up, you've got to cut her up; and you can't do that without a knife. Then, there were some negative facts. He hadn't burned her. Only had a fire in the small stove now and then; and only used it for cooking. They got on to that pretty smartly, the Unge constable did, and the men that were lending him a hand from Otherthorpe. There were some little woody places lying round, shaws they call them in that part of the country, the country people do, and they could climb a tree handy and unobserved and get a sniff at the smoke in almost any direction it might be blowing. They did that now and then, and there was no smell of flesh burning, just ordinary cooking. Pretty smart of the Otherthorpe police that was, though of course it didn't help to hang Steeger. Then later on the Scotland Yard men went down and got another fact—negative, but narrowing things down all the while. And that was that the chalk under the bungalow and under the little garden had none of it been disturbed. And he'd never been outside it since Nancy disappeared. Oh yes, and he had a big file besides the knife. But there was no sign of any ground bones found on the file, or any blood on the knife. He's washed them of course. I told all that to Linley.

Now I ought to warn you before I go any further. I am a small man myself and you probably don't expect anything horrible from me. But I ought to warn you this man was a murderer, or at any rate somebody was; the woman had been made away with, a nice pretty little girl too, and the man that had done that wasn't necessarily going to stop at things you might think he'd stop at. With the mind to do a thing like that, and with the long thin shadow of the rope to drive him further, you can't say what he'll stop at. Murder tales seem nice things sometimes for a lady to sit and read all by herself by the fire. But murder isn't a nice thing, and when a murderer's desperate and trying to hide his tracks he isn't even as nice as he was before. I'll ask you to bear that in mind. Well, I've warned you.

So I says to Linley, "And what do you make of it?"

"Drains?" said Linley.

"No," I says, "you're wrong there. Scotland Yard has been into that. And the Otherthorpe people before them. They've had a look in the drains, such as they are, a little thing running into a cesspool beyond the garden; and nothing has gone down it—nothing that oughtn't to have, I mean."

He made one or two suggestions, but Scotland Yard had been before him in every case. That's really the crab of my story, if you'll excuse the expression. You want a man who sets out to be a detective to take his magnifying glass and go down to the spot; to go to the spot before everything; and then to measure the footmarks and pick up the clues and find the knife that the police have overlooked. But Linley never even went near the place, and he hadn't got a magnifying glass, not as I ever saw, and Scotland Yard were before him every time.

In fact they had more clues than anybody could make head or tail of. Every kind of clue to show that he'd murdered the poor little girl; every kind of clue to show that he hadn't disposed of the body; and yet the body wasn't there. It wasn't in South America either, and not much more likely in South Africa. And all the time, mind you, that enormous bunch of chopped larchwood, a clue that was staring everyone in the face and leading nowhere. No, we didn't seem to want any more clues, and Linley never went near the place. The trouble was to deal with the clues we'd got. I was completely mystified; so was Scotland Yard; and Linley seemed to be getting no forwarder; and all the while the mystery was hanging on me. I mean if it were not for the trifle I'd chanced to remember, and if it were not for one chance word I said to Linley, that mystery would have gone the way of all the other mysteries that men have made nothing of, a darkness, a little patch of night in history.

Well, the fact was Linley didn't take much interest in it at first, but I was so absolutely sure that he could do it that I kept him to the idea. "You can do chess problems," I said.

"That's ten times harder," he said, sticking to his point.

"Then why don't you do this?" I said.

"Then go and take a look at the board for me," said Linley.

That was his way of talking. We'd been a fortnight together, and I knew it by now. He meant to go down to the bungalow at Unge. I know you'll say why didn't he go himself; but the plain truth of it is that if he'd been tearing about the countryside he'd never have been thinking, whereas sitting there in his chair by the fire in our flat there was no limit to the ground he could cover, if you follow my meaning. So down I went by train next day, and got out at Unge station. And there were the North Downs rising up before me, somehow like music.

"It's up there, isn't it?" I said to the porter.

"That's right," he said. "Up there by the lane; and mind to turn to your right when you get to the old yew tree, a very big tree, you can't mistake it, and then . . ." and he told me the way so that I couldn't go wrong. I found them all like that, very nice and helpful. You see, it was Unge's day at last. Everyone had heard of Unge now; you could have got a letter there any time just then without putting the county or post down; and this was what Unge had to show. I dare say if you tried to find Unge now . . . well, anyway, they were making hay while the sun shone.

Well, there the hill was, going up into sunlight, going up like a song. You don't want to hear about the spring, and all the May rioting, and the colour that came down over everything later on in the day, and all those birds; but I thought, "What a nice place to bring a girl to." And then when I thought that he'd killed her there, well, I'm only a small man, as I said, but when I thought of her on that hill with all the birds singing, I said to myself, "Wouldn't it be odd if it turned out to be me after all that got that man killed, if he did murder her." So I soon found my way up to the bungalow and began prying about, looking over the hedge into the garden. And I didn't find much, and I found nothing at all that the police hadn't found already, but there were those heaps of larch logs staring me in the face and looking very queer.

I did a lot of thinking, leaning against the hedge, breathing the smell of the may, and looking over the top of it at the larch logs, and the neat little bungalow the other side of the garden. Lots of theories I thought of, till I came to the best thought of all; and that was that if I left the thinking to Linley, with his Oxford and Cambridge education, and only brought him the facts, as he had told me, I should be doing more good in my way than if I tried to do any big thinking. I forgot to tell you that I had gone to Scotland Yard in the morning. Well, there wasn't really much to tell. What they asked me was what I wanted. And, not having an answer exactly ready, I didn't find out very much from them. But it was quite different at Unge; everyone was obliging; it was their day there, as I said. The constable let me go indoors, so long as I didn't touch anything, and he gave me a look at the garden from the inside. And I saw the stumps of the ten larch trees, and I noticed one thing that Linley said was very observant of me, not that it turned out to be any use, but anyway I was doing my best: I noticed that the stumps had been all chopped anyhow. And from that I thought that the man that did it didn't know much about chopping. The constable said that was a deduction. So then I said that the axe was blunt when he used it; and that certainly made the constable think, though he didn't actually say I was right this time. Did I tell you that Steeger never went outdoors, except to the little garden to chop wood, ever since Nancy disappeared? I think I did. Well, it was perfectly true. They'd watched him night and day, one or another of them, and the Unge constable told me that himself. That limited things a good deal. The only thing I didn't like about it was that I felt Linley ought to have found all that out instead of ordinary policemen, and I felt that he could have too. There'd have been romance in a story like that. And they'd never have done it if the news hadn't gone round that the man was a vegetarian and only dealt at the greengrocer's. Likely as not even that was only started out of pique by the butcher. It's queer what little things may trip a man up. Best to keep straight is my motto. But perhaps I'm straying a bit away from my story. I should like to do that forever—forget that it ever was; but I can't.

Well, I picked up all sorts of information; clues I suppose I should call it in a story like this, though they none of them seemed to lead anywhere. For instance, I found out everything he ever bought at the village, I could even tell you the kind of salt he bought, quite plain with no phosphates in it, that they sometimes put in to make it tidy. And then he got ice from the fishmonger's, and plenty of vegetables, as I said, from the greengrocer, Mergin & Sons. And I had a bit of a talk over it all with the constable. Slugger he said his name was. I wondered why he hadn't come in and searched the place as soon as the girl was missing. "Well, you can't do that," he said. "And besides, we didn't suspect at once, not about the girl, that is. We only suspected there was something wrong about him on account of him being a vegetarian. He stayed a good fortnight after the last that was seen of her. And then we slipped in like a knife. But, you see, no one had been inquiring about her; there was no warrant out."

"And what did you find," I asked Slugger, "when you went in?"

"Just a big file," he said, "and the knife and the axe that he must have got to chop her up with."

"But he got the axe to chop trees with," I said.

"Well, yes," he said, but rather grudgingly.

"And what did he chop them for?" I asked.

"Well, of course, my superiors has theories about that," he said, "that they mightn't tell to everybody."

You see, it was those logs that were beating them.

"But did he cut her up at all?" I asked.

"Well, he said that she was going to South America," he answered. Which was really very fair-minded of him.

I don't remember now much else that he told me. Steeger left the plates and dishes all washed up and very neat, he said.

Well, I brought all this back to Linley, going up by the train that started just about sunset. I'd like to tell you about the late spring evening, so calm over that grim bungalow, closing in with a glory all round it as though it were blessing it; but you'll want to hear of the murder. Well, I told Linley everything, though much of it didn't seem to me to be worth the telling. The trouble was that the moment I began to leave anything out, he'd know it, and make me drag it in. "You can't tell what may be vital," he'd say. "A tin tack swept away by a housemaid might hang a man."

All very well, but be consistent, even if you are educated at Eton and Harrow, and whenever I mentioned Num-numo, which after all was the beginning of the whole story, because he wouldn't have heard of it if it hadn't been for me, and my noticing that Steeger had bought two bottles of it, why then he said that things like that were trivial and we should keep to the main issues. I naturally talked a bit about Num-numo, because only that day I pushed close on fifty bottles of it in Unge. A murder certainly stimulates people's minds, and Steeger's two bottles gave me an opportunity that only a fool could have failed to make something of. But of course all that was nothing at all to Linley.

You can't see a man's thoughts, and you can't look into his mind, so that all the most exciting things in the world can never be told of. But what I think happened all that evening with Linley, while I talked to him before supper, and all through supper, and sitting smoking afterwards in front of our fire, was that his thoughts were stuck at a barrier there was no getting over. And the barrier wasn't the difficulty of finding ways and means by which Steeger might have made away with the body, but the impossibility of finding why he chopped those masses of wood every day for a fortnight, and paid, as I'd just found out, twenty-five pounds to his landlord to be allowed to do it. That's what was beating Linley. As for the ways by which Steeger might have hidden the body, it seemed to me that every way was blocked by the police. If you said he buried it, they said the chalk was undisturbed; if you said he carried it away, they said he never left the place; if you said he burned it, they said no smell of burning was ever noticed when the smoke blew low, and when it didn't they climbed trees after it. I'd taken to Linley wonderfully, and I didn't have to be educated to see there was something big in a mind like his, and I thought that he could have done it. When I saw the police getting in before him like that, and no way that I could see of getting past them, I felt real sorry.

Did anyone come to the house, he asked me once or twice. Did anyone take anything from it? But we couldn't account for it that way. Then perhaps I made some suggestion that was no good, or perhaps I started talking of Num-numo again, and he interrupted me rather sharply.

"But what would you do, Smithers?" he said. "What would you do yourself?"

"If I'd murdered poor Nancy Elth?" I asked.

"Yes," he said.

"I can't ever imagine doing such a thing," I told him.

He sighed at that, as though it were something against me.

"I suppose I should never be a detective," I said. And he just shook his head.

Then he looked broodingly into the fire for what seemed an hour. And then he shook his head again. We both went to bed after that.

I shall remember the next day all my life. I was till evening, as usual, pushing Num-numo. And we sat down to supper about nine. You couldn't get things cooked at those flats, so of course we had it cold. And Linley began with a salad. I can see it now, every bit of it. Well, I was still a bit full of what I'd done in Unge, pushing Num-numo. Only a fool, I know, would have been unable to push it there; but still, I *had* pushed it; and about fifty bottles, forty-eight to be exact, are something in a small village, whatever the circumstances. So I was talking about it a bit; and then all of a sudden I realized that Num-numo was nothing to Linley, and I pulled myself up with a jerk. It was really very kind of him; do you know what he did? He must have known at once why I stopped talking, and he just stretched out a hand and said, "Would you give me a little of your Num-numo for my salad?"

I was so touched I nearly gave it to him. But of course you don't take Num-numo with salad. Only for meats and savouries. That's on the bottle.

So I just said to him, "Only for meats and savouries." Though I don't know what savouries are. Never had any.

I never saw a man's face go like that before.

He seemed still for a whole minute. And nothing speaking about him but that expression. Like a man that's seen something that no one has ever looked at before, something he thought couldn't be.

And then he said in a voice that was all quite changed, more low and gentle and quiet it seemed, "No good for vegetables, eh?"

"Not a bit," I said.

And at that he gave a kind of sob in his throat. I hadn't thought he could feel things like that. Of course I didn't know what it was all about; but, whatever it was, I thought all that sort of thing would have been knocked out of him at Eton and Harrow, an educated man like that. There were no tears in his eyes, but he was feeling something horribly.

And then he began to speak with big spaces between his words, saying, "A man might make a mistake perhaps, and use Num-numo with vegetables."

"Not twice," I said. What else could I say?

And he repeated that after me as though I had told of the end of the world, and adding an awful emphasis to my words, till they seemed all clammy with some frightful significance, and shaking his head as he said it.

Then he was quite silent.

"What is it?" I asked.

"Smithers," said he.

And I said, "Well?"

"Look here, Smithers," he said, "you must phone down to the grocer at Unge and find out from him this."

"Yes?" I said.

"Whether Steeger bought those two bottles, as I expect he did, on the same day, and not a few days apart. He couldn't have done that."

I waited to see if any more was coming, and then I ran out and did what I was told. It took me some time, being after nine o'clock, and only then with the help of the police. About six days apart they said; and so I came back and told Linley. He looked up at me so hopefully when I came in, but I saw that it was the wrong answer by his eyes.

You can't take things to heart like that without being ill, and when he didn't speak I said, "What you want is a good brandy, and go to bed early."

And he said, "No. I must see someone from Scotland Yard. Phone round to them. Say here at once."

But I said, "I can't get an inspector from Scotland Yard to call on us at this hour."

His eyes were all lit up. He was all there all right.

"Then tell them," he said, "they'll never find Nancy Elth. Tell one of them to come here, and I'll tell him why." And he added, I think only for me, "They must watch Steeger, till one day they get him over something else."

And, do you know, he came. Inspector Ulton; he came himself.

While we were waiting I tried to talk to Linley. Partly curiosity, I admit. But I didn't want to leave him to those thoughts of his, brooding away by the fire. I tried to ask him what it was all about. But he wouldn't tell me. "Murder is horrible," is all he would say. "And as a man covers his tracks up it only gets worse."

He wouldn't tell me. "There are tales," he said, "that one never wants to hear."

That's true enough. I wish I'd never heard this one. I never did actually. But I guessed it from Linley's last words to Inspector Ulton, the only ones that I overheard. And perhaps this is the point at which to stop reading my story, so that you don't guess it too; even if you think you want murder stories. For don't you rather want a murder story with a bit of a romantic twist, and not a story about real foul murder? Well, just as you like.

In came Inspector Ulton, and Linley shook hands in silence, and pointed the way to his bedroom; and they went in there and talked in low voices, and I never heard a word.

A fairly hearty-looking man was the inspector when they went into that room.

They walked through our sitting room in silence when they came out, and together they went into the hall, and there I heard the only words they said to each other. It was the inspector that first broke that silence.

"But why," he said, "did he cut down the trees?"

"Solely," said Linley, "in order to get an appetite."

THE CHASER

JOHN COLLIER
(1901–1980)

John Collier's short stories are as impossible to define as the works of Patricia Highsmith and Stanley Ellin, mixing crime and mystery and suspense and fantasy and whatever else seems needed to produce perfect little gems. The story you are about to read was collected in Fancies and Goodnights, *selected by Ellery Queen for his critical compilation,* Queen's Quorum, *as one of the 106 greatest mystery short story collections of all time.*

LAN AUSTEN, AS NERVOUS AS a kitten, went up certain dark and creaky stairs in the neighbourhood of Pell Street, and peered about for a long time on the dim landing before he found the name he wanted written obscurely on one of the doors.

He pushed open this door, as he had been told to do, and found himself in a tiny room, which contained no furniture but a plain kitchen table, a rocking chair, and an ordinary chair. On one of the dirty buff-colored walls were a couple of shelves, containing in all perhaps a dozen bottles and jars.

An old man sat in the rocking chair, reading a newspaper. Alan, without a word, handed him the card he had been given. "Sit down, Mr. Austen," said the old man very politely. "I am glad to make your acquaintance."

"Is it true," asked Alan, "that you have a certain mixture that has—er—quite extraordinary effects?"

"My dear sir," replied the old man, "my stock in trade is not very large—I don't deal in laxatives and teething mixtures—but such as it is, it is varied. I think nothing I sell has effects which could be precisely described as ordinary."

"Well, the fact is—" began Alan.

"Here, for example," interrupted the old man, reaching for a bottle from the shelf. "Here is a liquid as colourless as water, almost tasteless, quite imperceptible in coffee, milk, wine, or any other beverage. It is also quite imperceptible to any known method of autopsy."

"Do you mean it is a poison?" cried Alan, very much horrified.

"Call it cleaning fluid if you like," said the old man indifferently "Lives need cleaning. Call it a spot-remover. 'Out, damned spot!' Eh? 'Out, brief candle!'"

"I want nothing of that sort," said Alan.

"Probably it is just as well," said the old man. "Do you know the price of this? For one teaspoonful, which is sufficient, I ask five thousand dollars. Never less. Not a penny less."

"I hope all your mixtures are not as expensive," said Alan apprehensively.

"Oh, dear, no," said the old man. "It would be no good charging that sort of price for a love potion, for example.

Young people who need a love potion very seldom have five thousand dollars. Otherwise they would not need a love potion."

"I'm glad to hear you say so," said Alan.

"I look at it like this," said the old man. "Please a customer with one article, and he will come back when he needs another. Even if it *is* more costly. He will save up for it, if necessary."

"So," said Alan, "you really do sell love potions?"

"If I did not sell love potions," said the old man, reaching for another bottle, "I should not have mentioned the other matter to you. It is only when one is in a position to oblige that one can afford to be so confidential."

"And these potions," said Alan. "They are not just—just—er—"

"Oh, no," said the old man. "Their effects are permanent, and extend far beyond the mere casual impulse. But they include it. Oh, yes, they include it. Bountifully. Insistently. Everlastingly."

"Dear me!" said Alan, attempting a look of scientific detachment. "How very interesting!"

"But consider the spiritual side," said the old man.

"I do, indeed," said Alan.

"For indifference," said the old man, "they substitute devotion. For scorn, adoration. Give one tiny measure of this to the young lady—its flavour is imperceptible in orange juice, soup, or cocktails—and however gay and giddy she is, she will change altogether. She'll want nothing but solitude, and you."

"I can hardly believe it," said Alan. "She is so fond of parties."

"She will not like them any more," said the old man. "She'll be afraid of the pretty girls you may meet."

"She'll actually be jealous?" cried Alan in a rapture. "Of me?"

"Yes, she will want to be everything to you."

"She is, already. Only she doesn't care about it."

"She will, when she has taken this. She will care intensely. You'll be her sole interest in life."

"Wonderful!" cried Alan.

"She'll want to know all you do," said the old man. "All that has happened to you during the day. Every word of it. She'll want to know what you are thinking about, why you smile suddenly, why you are looking sad."

"That is love!" cried Alan.

"Yes," said the old man. "How carefully she'll look after you! She'll never allow you to be tired, to sit in a draught, to neglect your food. If you are an hour late, she'll be terrified. She'll think you are killed, or that some siren has caught you."

"I can hardly imagine Diana like that!" cried Alan, overwhelmed with joy.

"You will not have to use your imagination," said the old man. "And, by the way, since there are always sirens, if by any chance you *should,* later on, slip a little, you need not worry. She will forgive you, in the end. She'll be terribly hurt, of course, but she'll forgive you—in the end."

"That will not happen," said Alan fervently.

"Of course not," said the old man. "But, if it does, you need not worry. She'll never divorce you. Oh, no! And, of course, she herself will never give you the least, the very least, grounds for—not divorce, of course—but even uneasiness."

"And how much," said Alan, "how much is this wonderful mixture?"

"It is not so dear," said the old man, "as the spot remover, as I think we agreed to call it. No. That is five thousand dollars; never a penny less. One has to be older than you are, to indulge in that sort of thing. One has to save up for it."

"But the love potion?" said Alan.

"Oh, that," said the old man, opening the drawer in the kitchen table, and taking out a tiny, rather dirty-looking phial. "That is just a dollar."

"I can't tell you how grateful I am," said Alan, watching him fill it.

"I like to oblige," said the old man. "Then customers come back, later in life, when they are rather better off, and want more expensive things. Here you are. You will find it very effective."

"Thank you again," said Alan. "Goodbye."

"*Au revoir,*" said the old man.

THE PERFECT CRIME

BEN RAY REDMAN
(1896–1961)

When Ellery Queen assembled the first great anthology of detective fiction, 101 Years' Entertainment, *in 1941, he filled its many pages with the greatest of the great, from Poe and Doyle to the masters of the twentieth century. He chose to end the book with this story, calling it "the detective story to end detective stories." He was right, of course, as it features a great detective faced with a great crime, a unique motive, a brilliant criminal—everything we could want and more.*

HE WORLD'S GREATEST DETECtive complacently sipped a port some years older than himself and intently gazed across the table at his most intimate acquaintance; for many years the detective had not permitted himself the luxury of friends. Gregory Hare looked back at him, waiting, listening.

"There is no doubt about it," Trevor reiterated, putting down his glass, "the perfect crime is a possibility; it requires only the perfect criminal."

"Naturally," assented Hare with a shrug, "but the perfect criminal . . ."

"You mean he is a mythical fellow, not apt to be met with in the flesh?"

"Exactly," said Hare, nodding his big head.

Trevor sighed, sipped again, and adjusted the eyeglasses on his thin, sharp nose. "No, I admit I haven't encountered him as yet, but I am always hopeful."

"Hoping to be done in the eye, eh?"

"No, hoping to see the perfect methods of detection tested to the limits of their possibilities. You know, a gifted detector of crime is something more than an inspired policeman with a little bloodhound blood in his veins, something more than a precise scientist; he's an art critic as well, and no art critic likes to be condemned to a steady diet of second-rate stuff."

"Quite."

"Second-rate stuff is bad enough, but it's not the worst. Think of the third, fourth, fifth, and heaven-knows-what-rate crimes that come along every day! And even the masterpieces, the 'classics,' are pretty poor daubs when you look at them closely: a bad tone here and a wrong line there; something false, something botched."

"Most murderers are rather foolish," interjected Hare.

"Foolish! Of course they are. You should know, man, you've defended enough of them. The trouble is that murder almost never evokes the best efforts of the best minds. As a rule it is the work of an inferior mind, cunningly striving towards a perfection that is beyond its reach, or of a superior mind so blinded by passion that its faculties are temporarily impaired. Of course, there are your homicidal maniacs, and they are often clever, but they lack imagination and variety; sooner or later their inability to do anything but repeat themselves brings them up with a sharp jerk."

"Repetition is dullness," murmured Hare, "and dullness, as somebody has remarked, is the one unforgivable sin."

"Right," agreed Trevor. "It is, and plenty of murderers have suffered for it. But they have suffered from vanity almost as often. Practically every murderer, unless he has been accidentally impelled to crime, is an egregious egotist. You know that as well as I do. His sense of power is tremendous, and as a rule he can't keep his mouth shut."

Dr. Harrison Trevor's glasses shone brightly, and he plucked continually at the black cord depending from them as he jerked out his sentences with rapidity and precision. He was on his own ground, and he knew what he was talking about. For twenty years criminals had been his specialty and his legitimate prey. He had hunted them through all lands, and he hunted them successfully. Upstairs, in a chiffonier drawer in his bedroom, there was a large red-leather box holding visible symbols of that success: small decorations of gold and silver and bright ribbons bore mute witness to the gratitude that various European governments had felt, on notable occasions, towards the greatest man hunter of his generation. If Trevor was a dogmatist on murder he was entitled to be one.

Hare, on the other hand, was a good and respectful listener, but, being a criminal lawyer of long experience, he was a man with ideas of his own; and he always expressed them when there was no legal advantage to be gained by withholding them. He expressed one now, when he drawled softly, "All murderers are great egotists, are they? How about great detectives?"

Trevor blinked, then smiled coldly, clutching at his black cord. "Most detectives are asses, I grant you, complete asses and vain as peacocks; very few of them are great. I know only three. One of them is now in Vienna, the second is in Paris, and the third is . . ."

Hare raised his hand in interruption and said, "The third, or rather the first, is in this room."

The greatest detective in the world nodded briskly. "Of course. There's no point in false modesty, is there?"

"None at all. And it might be a little difficult to maintain such an attitude so soon after the Harrington case. The poor chap was put out of his misery week before last, wasn't he?"

Trevor snorted. "Yes, if you want to call him a poor chap; he was a deliberate murderer. But let's get back to that perfect crime of ours."

"Of yours, you mean," Hare corrected him politely. "I haven't subscribed to the possibility of it as yet. And how would you know about a perfect crime if it ever were committed? The criminal would never be discovered."

"If he had any artistic pride, he would leave a full account of it to be published after his death. Besides, you are forgetting the perfect methods of detection."

Hare whistled softly. "There's a pretty theoretical problem for you. What would happen when the perfect detector set out to catch the perfect criminal? Rather like the immovable object and the irresistible force business, and just about as sensible. The fly in the ointment, of course, is that there is no such thing as perfection."

Dr. Trevor sat up rigidly and glared at the speaker. "There is perfection in the detection of crime."

"Well, perhaps there is." Hare laughed amiably, "You should know, Trevor. But I think what you really mean is that there is a perfect method for detecting imperfect crimes."

The doctor's rigidity had vanished, and now he was smiling with as much geniality as he ever displayed. "Perhaps that is what I do mean, perhaps it is. But there is a little experiment that I should like to try, just the same."

"And that is?"

"And that is, or rather would be, the experiment of exercising all my intelligence in the commission of a crime, then, forgetting every detail of it utterly, using my skill and knowledge to solve the riddle of my own creation. Should I catch myself, or should I escape myself? That's the question."

"It would be a nice sporting event," agreed Hare, "but I'm afraid it's one that can't be pulled off. The little trifle of forgetting is the difficulty. But it would be interesting to see the outcome."

"Yes, it would," said the other, speaking rather more dreamily than was his habit, "but we can never see quite as far as we should like to. My Japanese man, Tanaka, has a saying that he resorts to whenever he is asked a difficult question. He simply smiles and answers, 'Fuji san ni nobottara sazo tōku made miemashō.' It means, I believe, that if one were to ascend Mount Fuji one could see far. The trouble is that, as in the case of so many problems, we can't climb the mountain."

"Wise Tanaka. But tell me, Trevor, what is your conception of a perfect crime?"

"I'm afraid it isn't precisely formulated; but I have a rough outline in my mind, and I'll give it to you as well as I can. First, though, let's go up to the library; we shall be more comfortable there, and it will give Tanaka a chance to clear the table. Bring your cigar, and come along."

Together the two men climbed the narrow staircase, the host leading. Dr. Trevor's house was a compact, brick building in the East Fifties, not far from Madison Avenue. Its picturesqueness was rather uncharacteristic of its owner, but its neatness was entirely like him. It was not a large house according to the standards of wealthy New York, but it was a perfectly appointed one, and considerably more spacious than it looked from the street, for the doctor had built on an addition that completely covered the plot which had once been the back yard; and this new section, as well as housing the kitchen and servants' quarters below, held a laboratory and workroom two stories high. An industrial or research chemist might have coveted the equipment of that room; and the filing cases that completely lined the encircling gallery would have furnished any newspaper with a complete reference department. A door opened from the library into the laboratory, and the library itself came close to being the ideal chamber of every student. Dr. Harrison Trevor's house was, in short, an ideal bachelor's establishment, and he had never been tempted to transform it into anything else. More than one male visitor had found reason to remark, "Old Trevor does well for himself."

The same idea flitted across Hare's mind as he puffed at his host's excellent cigar and tasted the liqueur that Tanaka had placed on the table beside his chair. He, too, enjoyed the pleasures of bachelorhood, but he had never learned the knack of enjoying them quite so thoroughly. He would make a few improvements in the routine of his life; he could afford them.

"The perfect crime must, of course, be a murder." Trevor's voice broke the silence that had followed their entrance into the library.

Hare shifted his bulk a little and inquired, "Yes? Why?"

"Because it is, according to our accepted standards, the most reprehensible of all crimes and, therefore, according to my interests, the best. Human life is what we prize most and do our best to protect; to take human life with an art that eludes all detection is unquestionably the ideal criminal action. In it there is a degree of beauty possible in no other crime."

"Humph!" grunted Hare, "you make it sound pleasant."

"I am speaking at once as an amateur and as a professor of crime. You have heard surgeons talk of 'beautiful cases.' Well, that is my attitude precisely; and in my cases invariably, as in most of theirs, the patient dies."

"I see."

Trevor blinked, tugged at his eyeglass cord, and then continued. "The crime must be murder, and it must be murder of a particular kind, the purest kind. Now that is the 'purest' kind? Let us see. The *crime passionel* can be ruled out at once, for it is almost impossible that it should be perfect. Passion does not make for art; hot blood begets innumerable blunders. What about the murder for gain? Murderers of this kind make murder a means, not an end in itself; they kill not for the sake of eliminating the victim but in order to profit by the victim's death. No, we can't look to murder for profit as the type that might produce our perfect crime."

The sharp-nosed doctor paused and held his cigar for a moment between his thin lips. Hare studied his face curiously; the man's complete lack of emotion in discussing such matters was not wholly pleasant, he reflected.

Trevor put down his cigar. "Now, how about political and religious murders? They can be counted out almost immediately, for the simple reason that the murderer in such cases is always convinced that he is either serving the public or serving God and, therefore, seldom makes any attempt to conceal his guilt. But there is another class to be considered—those who kill for the sheer joy of killing, those who are dominated by the blood lust. Offhand you would think that their killing would be of the purest type. But as I have said before, the maniac invariably repeats himself, and his repetition leads to his discovery. And even more important is the consideration that the artist must possess the faculty of choice, and that the born killer has no choice. His actions are not willed by himself, they are compelled; whereas the perfect crime must be a work of art, not of necessity."

"You seem to have written off all the possibilities pretty well," remarked Hare.

The doctor shook his head quickly. "Not all. There is one type of murder left, and it is the kind we are looking for: the murder of elimination, the murder in which the sole and pure object is to remove the victim from the world, to get rid of a person whose continued existence is not desirable to the murderer."

"But that brings you back to your *crime passionel,* doesn't it? Practically all murders of jealousy, for example, are murders of elimination, aren't they?"

"In a sense, yes, but not in the purest sense. And, as I have said before, passion can never produce the perfect crime. It must be studied, carefully meditated, and performed in absolutely cold blood. Otherwise it is sure to be imperfect."

"You do go at this in a rather fish-blooded way," remarked the good listener as the doctor paused for a moment.

"Of course I do, and that is the only way the perfect crime could be committed. Now I can imagine a pure murder of elimination that would be ideal so far as motives and circumstances were concerned. Suppose you had spent fifteen years establishing a certain reading of a dubious passage in one of Pindar's odes."

"Ha, ha!" interrupted Hare jocosely. "Suppose I had."

"And suppose," continued Dr. Harrison Trevor, not noticing the interruption, "that another scholar had managed to build up an argument which completely invalidated your interpretation. Suppose, further, that he communicated his proofs to you, and that he had as yet mentioned them to no one else. There you would have a perfect motive and a perfect set of circumstances; only the method of the murder would remain to be worked out."

Gregory Hare sat bolt upright. "Good God, man! What do you mean, 'the method of the murder'?"

The doctor blinked. "Why, don't you understand? You would have excellent reasons for eliminating your rival and thereby saving your own interpretation of the text from confutation; and no one, once your victim was dead and the proofs destroyed, could suspect that you had any such motive. You could work with perfect freedom, you could concentrate on two essentials: the method of the murder and, of course, the disposition of the body."

"The disposition of the body?" Hare seemed to echo the speaker's last words involuntarily.

"To be sure; that is a very important item, most important in fact. But I flatter myself," and here the doctor chuckled softly, "that I have done some very valuable research work along that line."

"You have, eh?" murmured Hare. "And what have you found out?"

"I'll tell you later," Trevor assured him, "and I don't think I would tell any other man alive, because it's really too simple and too dangerous. But at the moment I want to impress on you that the disposition of the body is perhaps the most important step of all in the commission of the perfect crime. The absence of a *corpus delicti* is curiously troublesome to the police. Harrington should really have managed to get rid of West's body, although it probably wouldn't have kept him from sitting in the electric chair two weeks ago. He was too careless."

Hare again sat up sharply and exclaimed, "Was he? Speaking of that, it was the Harrington case that I chiefly wanted to talk to you about tonight."

"Oh, was it? Well, we can get around to that in a minute. And, by the way, that came pretty close to being a murder of elimination, if you like; but the money element figured in it, big money, and gold is apt to have a fairly strong smell when it is mixed up with crime. Harrington's motive was easily traced, but his position made it impossible to touch him until we had our case absolutely water-tight."

"Water-tight, eh? That's what I want to hear about. You see I was abroad until last week, and didn't even know Harrington had been arrested until just before I sailed. The North African newspapers aren't so informative. I was particularly interested, you see, because I knew both men fairly well, and West's wife even better."

"Oh, yes, his wife, gorgeous woman. They were separated, and she's been in Europe for the last two and a half years."

"Yes, I know she has—most of the time."

"All the time. She hasn't been in the United States during that period."

"Hasn't she? Well, I last saw her at Monte Carlo, but that's not important at the moment. I want to hear how you tracked down Harrington."

Dr. Harrison Trevor smiled complacently, adjusted his eyeglasses, and then launched forth in his characteristic manner. "It was really simplicity itself. The only flaw was that Harrington finally confessed. That rather annoyed me, for we didn't need a confession; the circumstantial evidence was complete."

"Circumstantial?"

"Of course. You know as well as I do that most convictions for murder are based on circumstantial evidence. One doesn't send out invitations for a killing."

"No, of course not. Sorry."

"Well, as you probably know, Ernest West, Wall Street operator and multimillionaire (as the papers had it), was found shot through the heart one night a little more than a year ago. He had a shack down on Long Island, near Smithtown, that he used as a base for duck shooting and fishing. The only servant he kept there was an old housekeeper, a local inhabitant; he liked to lead the simple life when he could. Never even used to take a chauffeur down with him. The evening he was killed the housekeeper was absent, spending the night with a sick daughter of hers in Jamaica. She testified that West had sent her off, saying that he could pick up a light supper and breakfast for himself. She turned up the next morning, and nearly died of the shock. West was shot in what was a kind of gun room where he kept all his gear and a few books—cosy sort of place and the best room in the house. There was no sign of a struggle. He was sitting slumped in a big armchair. The bullet that killed him was a .25 caliber. Furst, of the Homicide Bureau, called me up as soon as the regulars failed to locate any scent, and I went down there immediately. West was an important man, you know." The doctor tugged self-consciously at his black cord. "I went down there at once, and I discovered various things. First of all, the house was isolated, and there was no one in the neighborhood who could give any useful evidence whatsoever. The body had been discovered by a messenger boy with a telegram at about seven-thirty; medical examination indicated that the murder had been committed about an hour before. Inside the house I found only one item that I thought useful. After going over the dust and so forth which I swept up from the gun-room floor, I had several tiny thread ends that had pretty obviously come from a tweed suit; and those threads could not be matched in West's wardrobe. But they might have been months old, so I didn't concentrate on them at first. Outside the house there was more to go on. The ground was damp, and two sets of footprints were visible: a man's and a woman's . . ."

"A woman's?" Hare was all attention now.

"Yes, the housekeeper's, of course."

"Oh, yes, the housekeeper's."

"Certainly, But it was difficult to identify them, for the reason that the man, apparently through nervousness, had walked up and down the lane leading to the road several times before finally leaving the scene of his crime; and he had trampled over almost every one of the woman's footprints, scarcely leaving one intact."

"That was odd, wasn't it?

"Very, at first glance, but really simple enough when you think it over. The murderer had hurried out of the house after firing the fatal shot; then he hesitated. He was flurried and couldn't make up his mind as to his next step, even though he had an automobile waiting for him at the end of the lane. So he walked up and down for a few minutes, to calm his nerves and collect his ideas. It was a narrow lane, and the obliteration of the other tracks was at once accidental and inevitable."

"He had a car waiting?"

"Yes, a heavy touring car. Its tire marks were plain, as were those of the public hack that West had ordered for his housekeeper that afternoon. And there was one interesting feature about the marks. There was a big, hard blister on one of the shoes, and it left a perfectly defined indentation in the mud every time it came around."

"I see. And both sets of footprints ended at the same spot?"

"Naturally. The hack stopped for the woman just where the murderer later parked his car."

"Hum." Hare had now lighted a new cigar, and he puffed at it reflectively before asking, "And you are quite sure the woman did not get into the car with the man?"

Trevor stared at the speaker blankly and exclaimed, "You must be wool gathering, Hare. The woman was the housekeeper, and she went off in a public hack at least two hours before the crime was committed. In any event, Harrington confirmed the correctness of all my deductions when he finally confessed." Dr. Harrison Trevor was obviously nettled.

"Oh, yes, of course he did; I'd forgotten. Sorry, Let's hear how you nabbed him."

For a moment the detective looked at his companion doubtfully, as though he feared the other might be baiting him; for Hare's questions had not been of the sort that his alert mind usually asked. He seemed to have something up his sleeve. But Trevor thrust his suspicions aside and returned to the pleasant task of describing his triumph.

"With the bullet, the footprints, the tire marks, and the threads, I had considerable to go on. All I had to do was to relate them unmistakably to one man, and I had my murderer. But the trail soon let into quarters where we had to move cautiously. With my material evidence in front of me, I set out to fasten upon some individual who might have had a motive for killing West. So far as anyone could say, he had no enemies; but on the other hand he had few friends. He believed in the maxim that he travels fastest who travels alone. However, he had nipped some men pretty badly in the Street; and it was upon his financial operations that I soon concentrated my attention. There, with the facilities for investigation at my command, I discovered some very interesting facts. During the three weeks prior to West's death the common stock of Elliott Light and Power had risen fifty-seven points; four days after he had been shot it had dropped back no less than sixty-three points. Investigation showed that on the day West was murdered Harrington was short one hundred and thirty-odd thousand shares of that particular stock. He had been selling it short all the way up, and West had been buying all that was offered. Harrington's resources, great as they were, weren't equal to his rival's. He knew that unless he could break Elliott Common wide open he was a ruined man, and he took the one sure way to do it that he could think of. He eliminated West. It was murder for millions."

Trevor paused impressively; Hare did not say a word.

"That's about all there is to the story; the rest of it was routine sleuthing. One of my men found four tires, three in perfect condition, which had been taken from Harrington's touring car and replaced on the day following the murder. They had been put in a loft of the garage on Harrington's country place. Three perfect tires, mind you; and on the fourth there was a large, hard blister. Harrington's shoes fitted the footprints in West's lane, and the thread ends matched the threads in one of Harrington's suits. And, to top it all off, after the man was arrested, we found a .25, pearl-handled revolver in his wall safe. One shot had been fired, and the weapon hadn't been cleaned since. Harrington's chauffeur testified that his master had taken out the big touring car alone on the afternoon of the murder; the man remembered the date because it had been his wife's birthday. It was all very simple, and even such elements of interest as it possessed were lessened by Harrington's confession. The press made much too much of a stir about my part in the affair." The doctor smiled deprecatingly. "It was really no mystery at all, and if the men involved had not been so rich and so prominent the case would have been virtually ignored. But we nailed him just in time; he was sailing for Europe the following week."

"What kind of a revolver did you say it was?" Hare asked the question so abruptly that Trevor started before answering.

"Why, it was a .25, pearl-handled and nickel-finished. Rather a dainty weapon altogether; Harrington was a bit apologetic about owning such a toy."

"I should think he might have been. Was the handle slightly chipped on the right side?"

Trevor leaned forward suddenly. "Yes, it was. How the devil did you know?"

"Why it got chipped when Alice dropped it on a rock at Davos. The four of us were target shooting back of the hotel."

"Alice!" exclaimed Trevor. "What Alice? And what do you mean by the four of you?"

Hare answered quietly, "Alice West, my dear fellow. You see, it was her gun. And the four of us were West, Alice, Harrington, and myself; we were all staying at the same hotel in Switzerland four years ago."

"Her gun?" The doctor was speaking excitedly now. "You mean she gave it to him?"

"I doubt it, much as she loved him," drawled Hare. "He probably took it away from her, too late."

"You're talking in riddles," snapped the detective. "What do you mean?"

"Simply that that little weapon helped to execute the wrong man," said Hare wearily.

"The wrong man!"

"Well, that's one way of putting it; but in this case I am very much afraid that the right 'man' was a woman."

Trevor's apparent excitement had vanished abruptly, and now he was as calm as a sphinx. "Tell me exactly what you mean," he demanded.

Hare put aside the butt of his cigar. "It all began back in Davos, four years ago. Harrington fell in love with Alice West, and she fell in love with him. West played dog in the manger: he wouldn't let his wife divorce him and he wouldn't divorce her. They separated, of course, but that didn't help Alice and Harrington towards getting married. I was on the inside of the affair from the first, you see; accidentally to begin with, and afterwards because they all made me their confidant in various degrees. West behaved like a swine, because he really didn't love the woman any more. He simply had made up his mind that no other man was going to have her, legally at least. And he stuck to it—until she killed him."

"She killed him?" The great detective spoke softly.

"I'm as sure of it as though I had seen her do it. To begin with, it was her revolver that fired the shot, as you have proved to me. I've seen it a hundred times when we were firing at bottles and what not for fun. There was no reason for Harrington to borrow it; he had a nice little armory of his own, hadn't he?"

"Yes, we did find a couple of heavy service revolvers and an automatic."

"Exactly. He never would have used a toy like that in a thousand years; and besides he would never have committed a murder. He was too level-headed. Alice, on the other hand, is an extremely hysterical type; I've seen her go completely off her head with anger. Beautiful, Lord, yes! But dangerous, and in the last analysis a coward. She's proved that. I never did envy Harrington."

"But she was in Europe, man, when the murder was committed."

"She was not, Trevor. She was in Montreal that very month, to my certain knowledge, and Montreal isn't so far from Long Island. Harry Sands ran into her at the Ritz there; they were reminiscing about it at Monte Carlo the last time I saw her. She was in Europe before and after the murder, but she wasn't there when it happened. Anyway, that's not the whole story."

"Well, what is it?" Trevor's mouth was grim.

Hare's fingers were playing with a silver match box, and he hesitated a minute before answering. Then he spoke quickly and to the point.

"The rest of it is this. As I told you, Alice is hysterical, and during the past few years drink and dope haven't helped her any. Well, one night at Monte, just before I left, she went off the deep end. We had been talking about her husband's death, and I had been speculating as to who could have done it. Harrington hadn't been arrested then. And I'd been asking her, too, if she and Harrington weren't going to get married soon. She dodged that question, obviously embarrassed. Then suddenly she burst out into a wild tirade against the dead man, called him every name under heaven, and finally dived into her evening bag and fished out a letter. It was addressed to her, and the post mark was more than a year old; it was almost broken at the creases from having been read over and over again. She shoved it at me, and insisted that I read it. It was from West, and it was a cruel letter if I've ever read one. It was the letter of a cat to a mouse, of a jailer to his prisoner: West had her where he wanted her, and he intended to keep her there. He didn't miss a trick when it came to rubbing it in. It was so bad that I didn't want to finish it, but she made me. When I gave it back to her her eyes were blazing; and she grabbed my hand and cried, 'What would you do to a man like that?' I hemmed and hawed for a minute, and she answered herself by exclaiming, 'Kill him! Kill him! Wouldn't you?' As calmly as I could I pointed out to her that someone had already done just that; and she burst into a fit of the wickedest laughter I've ever heard. Then she calmed down, powdered her nose, and said quietly, 'It's funny that you can shoot the heads off all the innocent bottles you like and no one says a word, but if you kill a human snake they hang you for it. And I don't want to hang, thank you very much.'"

Hare paused as though he were very tired, and then he added, "That's about all there was to it; it wasn't very nice. I left for Africa the next day, and I scarcely ever saw the papers there. But I hadn't any doubts as to who had bumped off Ernest West."

While the minute hand on the mantel clock jumped three times there was silence in the book-lined room. Then Trevor spoke, and his voice was strained. "So you think I made a mistake?"

Hare looked him straight in the eye. "What do you think?"

The detective took refuge in another question. "Have you any theory as to what really happened?"

"It's hard to say exactly, but I'm sure she did it. Her reference to the bottles showed that she knew what weapon had been used; she must have done in a thousand bottles with it at various times. My guess is that she and Harrington went down to see West together, to see if they couldn't make him change his mind after all, and that they failed. Then she pulled out that little toy of hers. She always carried it around in her bag. I use to tell her it was a bad habit. She shot West before he could move; she was a better shot than Harrington, he could never have found the man's heart. Then they left the house and drove off in Harrington's car; but first of all he went back and thoughtfully trampled out every one of her footprints, and, just to make sure he wasn't missing any, he walked over the housekeeper's as well. There were three sets of tracks there, Trevor, not two; I'll bet on that. Then Harrington took the gun away from her—if he hadn't taken it before—and drove her to wherever she wanted to go. She left him; she left him to stand the gaff if he was suspected, and it was like him to do what he did. He loved her if any man ever loved a woman; and she loved him in her own way, but it wasn't the best way in the world. She loved her own white neck considerably more." Hare smiled a wry smile. "She had forgotten that New York State doesn't go in for hanging. Altogether it is not a pretty tale. But Harrington, poor devil, wanted to save the woman even if she wasn't worth it. You see, to him she was."

"It's impossible!" Trevor snapped out the words as if despite himself.

"What is?"

"That I made a mistake."

"We all make mistakes, my dear fellow."

"I don't." The tight mouth was tighter than ever.

"Well, it's a shame, but what's done is done." Hare shrugged his shoulders.

Trevor looked at him with cold eyes. "Obviously you do not understand. My reputation does not permit of mistakes. I simply can't make them. That's all."

Hare mustered a genial smile; he was genuinely sorry that Trevor was so distressed and he sought to reassure him. "But your reputation isn't going to suffer. The facts won't come out. Alice West will be dead of dope inside of two years, if I'm any judge, and no one else knows."

"You do."

"Yes, I do; but we can forget about that."

Trevor nodded nervously. "Yes, we must. Do you understand, Hare, we *must.*"

Hare studied him quizzically. "Don't worry, old chap, your reputation's safe with me; I'll keep my mouth shut."

Trevor nodded again, more nervously and more emphatically. "Yes, yes, I know you will, of course. I know you will."

"And how about a drink?" Hare swung himself out of his chair.

"On the table there. Help yourself. I'm going into the laboratory for a minute."

The doctor disappeared through the low door, and Hare busied himself with the decanters and the bottles in a preoccupied manner. He was sorry that Trevor was so upset; but what colossal egotism! Perhaps he should have held his tongue; nothing had been gained. He would never mention the subject again. It was a stiff drink of brandy that Hare finally poured himself, and he held it up to the light studying it, with his back to the laboratory door. But he never drank it; for he dropped the glass as he felt the lean fingers at his throat and the chloroform pad smothering his mouth and nostrils. He managed to say only the two words, "My God . . ."

About fifteen minutes later, Dr. Harrison Trevor peered cautiously over the banister of his own stairway. There was no one below, and he descended swiftly. In the kitchen Tanaka heard the front door slam, and almost immediately afterwards his master's voice calling him from the first-floor landing. Tanaka responded briskly.

"Mr. Hare has just left," said the doctor, "and he forgot his cigarette case. Run after him; he may still be in sight."

Tanaka sped upon his errand. Yes, there on the corner was a tall man, obviously Hare *san*; but he was getting into a taxi. Tanaka ran, but before he was half way down the block Hare *san* had driven off. Tanaka returned to report failure.

"Too bad," said his master, who met him on the landing. "But it doesn't really matter. Telephone Mr. Hare's apartment and tell his man that Mr. Hare left his case here, and that he is not to worry about it. You can take it to him in the morning."

Tanaka went downstairs to obey orders; and his master was left to wonder at the coincidence of the man who looked like Hare getting into the taxi. The accidental evidence might prove useful, but it was quite unnecessary, quite unnecessary; he had no need of accidental aid. At the door of his library the detective paused and surveyed the scene with a critical eye: everything was in place, comfortably, conventionally, indisputably in place. There were no fragments of the broken tumbler on the floor; only a dark, wet spot on the carpet that was drying rapidly. Brandy and soda would leave no stain. Dr. Harrison Trevor smiled a chilly smile and then walked resolutely toward the laboratory where his task awaited him. Once the door had been locked behind him, his first act was to switch on the electric ventilator fan which carried off all obnoxious odors through a concealed flue. After that he worked on into the morning hours.

The disappearance of Mr. Gregory Hare, eminent criminal lawyer, within a week after his return from abroad, furnished the front pages of the newspapers with rather more than a nine days' wonder. It was Dr. Trevor who was the first to insist upon foul play; and it was Dr. Trevor who worked fervently upon the case, with all the assistance that the police could give him. Naturally he was deeply concerned, for Hare had been an intimate acquaintance, and he had been among the last to see the man alive; but the body was never found, and there was no evidence to go on with. Tanaka repeated what he knew, reiterating the story of the taxi; and a patrolman on fixed post confirmed the Japanese's testimony. The tall gentleman had come from the direction of Dr. Trevor's house, and had driven off just as the servant had come running after him. All of which helped not at all. A certain "Limping" Louie, whom Hare, years before when he was District Attorney, had sent up for a long term, was dragged in by the police net; but he had a perfect alibi. The mystery remained a mystery.

Dr. Trevor and Inspector Furst were discussing the case one afternoon, long after it had been abandoned. Furst still toyed with the idea that it might not have been murder, but the doctor was positive.

"I'm absolutely sure of it, Furst, absolutely sure. Hare was killed."

"Well," said the Inspector, "if you are so sure, I'm inclined to agree. You've never made a mistake."

YOURS TRULY, JACK THE RIPPER

ROBERT BLOCH
(1917–1994)

Had he never written another word, Robert Bloch's place in the history of crime and suspense fiction would be secure because of his superb novel Psycho *(1959), which was brilliantly filmed by Alfred Hitchcock the following year. The story which follows was widely praised when it was adapted for television by Barré Lyndon for* Thriller, *to which Bloch contributed many other stories, as he also did for* Alfred Hitchcock Presents.

 LOOKED AT THE STAGE Englishman. He looked at me.

"Sir Guy Hollis?" I asked.

"Indeed. Have I the pleasure of addressing John Carmody, the psychiatrist?"

I nodded. My eyes swept over the figure of my distinguished visitor. Tall, lean, sandy-haired—with the traditional tufted mustache. And the tweeds. I suspected a monocle concealed in a vest pocket, and wondered if he'd left his umbrella in the outer office.

But more than that, I wondered what the devil had impelled Sir Guy Hollis of the British Embassy to seek out a total stranger here in Chicago.

Sir Guy didn't help matters any as he sat down. He cleared his throat, glanced around nervously, tapped his pipe against the side of the desk. Then he opened his mouth.

"What do you think of London?" he said.

"Why—"

"I'd like to discuss London with you, Mr. Carmody."

I meet all kinds. So I merely smiled, sat back, and gave him his head.

"Have you ever noticed anything strange about that city?" he asked.

"Well, the fog is famous."

"Yes, the fog. That's important. It usually provides the perfect setting."

"Setting for what?"

Sir Guy Hollis gave me an enigmatic grin.

"Murder," he murmured.

"Murder?"

"Yes. Hasn't it struck you that London, of all cities, has a peculiar affinity for those who contemplate homicide?"

They don't talk that way, except in books. Still, it was an interesting thought. London as an ideal spot for a murder!

"As you mentioned," said Sir Guy, "there is a natural reason for this. The fog is an ideal background. And then too the British have a peculiar attitude in such matters. You might call it their sporting instinct. They regard murder as a sort of a game."

I sat up straight. Here was a theory.

"Yes, I needn't bore you with homicide statistics. The record is there. Aesthetically, temperamentally, the Englishman is interested in crimes of violence.

"A man commits murder. Then the excitement begins. The game starts. Will the criminal outwit the police? You can read between the lines in their newspaper stories. Everybody is waiting to see who will score.

"British law regards a prisoner as guilty until proven innocent. That's *their* advantage. But first they must catch their prisoner. And London bobbies are not allowed to carry firearms. That's a point for the fugitive. You see? All part of the rules of the game."

I wondered what Sir Guy was driving at. Either a point or a strait-jacket. But I kept my mouth shut and let him continue.

"The logical result of this British attitude toward murder is—Sherlock Holmes," he said.

"Have you ever noticed how popular the theme of murder is in British fiction and drama?"

I smiled. I was back on familiar ground.

"*Angel Street*," I suggested.

"*Ladies in Retirement*," he continued. "*Night Must Fall.*"

"*Payment Deferred*," I added. "*Laburnum Grove. King Lady. Love from a Stranger. Portrait of a Man with Red Hair. Black Limelight.*"

He nodded. "Think of the motion pictures of Alfred Hitchcock and Emlyn Williams. The actors—Wilfred Lawson and Leslie Banks."

"Charles Laughton," I continued for him. "Edmund Gwenn. Basil Rathbone. Raymond Massey. Sir Cedric Hardwicke."

"You're quite an expert on this sort of thing yourself," he told me.

"Not at all," I smiled. "I'm a psychiatrist."

Then I leaned forward. I didn't change my tone of voice. "All I want to know," I said sweetly, "is why the hell you come up to my office and discuss murder melodramas with me."

It stung him. He sat back and blinked a little.

"That isn't my intention," he murmured. "No. Not at all. I was just advancing a theory—"

"Stalling," I said. "Stalling. Come on, Sir Guy—spit it out."

Talking like a gangster is all a part of the applied psychiatric technique. At least, it worked for me.

It worked this time.

Sir Guy stopped bleating. His eyes narrowed. When he leaned forward again he meant business.

"Mr. Carmody," he said, "have you ever heard of—Jack the Ripper?"

"The murderer?" I asked.

"Exactly. The greatest monster of them all. Worse than Springheel Jack or Crippen. Jack the Ripper. Red Jack."

"I've heard of him," I said.

"Do you know his history?"

I got tough again. "Listen, Sir Guy," I muttered. "I don't think we'll get any place swapping old wives' tales about famous crimes of history."

Another bulls-eye. He took a deep breath.

"This is no old wives' tale. It's a matter of life or death."

He was so wrapped up in his obsession he even talked that way. Well—I was willing to listen. We psychiatrists get paid for listening.

"Go ahead," I told him. "Let's have the story."

Sir Guy lit a cigarette and began to talk.

"London, 1888," he began. "Late summer and early fall. That was the time. Out of nowhere came the shadowy figure of Jack the Ripper—a stalking shadow with a knife, prowling through London's East End. Haunting the squalid dives of Whitechapel, Spitalfields. Where he came from no one knew. But he brought death. Death in a knife.

"Six times that knife descended to slash the throats and bodies of London's women. Drabs and alley sluts. August 7th was the date of the first butchery. They found her body lying there with 39 stab wounds. A ghastly murder. On August 31st, another victim. The press became interested. The slum inhabitants were more deeply interested still.

"Who was this unknown killer who prowled in their midst and struck at will in the deserted alley-ways of night-town? And what was more important—when would he strike again?

"September 8th was the date. Scotland Yard assigned special deputies. Rumors ran rampant. The atrocious nature of the slayings was the subject for shocking speculation.

"The killer used a knife—expertly. He cut throats and removed—certain portions— of the bodies after death. He chose victims and settings with a fiendish deliberation. No one saw him or heard him. But watchmen making their gray rounds in the dawn would stumble across the hacked and horrid thing that was the Ripper's handiwork.

"Who was he? What was he? A mad surgeon? A butcher? An insane scientist? A pathological degenerate escaped from an asylum? A deranged nobleman? A member of the London police?

"Then the poem appeared in the newspapers. The anonymous poem, designed to put a stop to speculations—but which only aroused public interest to a further frenzy. A mocking little stanza:

> *I'm not a butcher, I'm not a kid*
> *Nor yet a foreign skipper,*
> *But I'm your own true loving friend,*
> *Yours truly—Jack the Ripper.*

"And on September 30th, two more throats were slashed open."

I interrupted Sir Guy for a moment.

"Very interesting," I commented. I'm afraid a faint hint of sarcasm crept into my voice.

He winced, but didn't falter in his narrative.

"There was silence, then, in London for a time. Silence, and a nameless fear. When would Red Jack strike again? They waited through October. Every figment of fog concealed his phantom presence. Concealed it well—for nothing was learned of the Ripper's identity, or his purpose. The drabs of London shivered in the raw wind of early November. Shivered, and were thankful for the coming of each morning's sun.

"November 9th. They found her in her room. She lay there very quietly, limbs neatly arranged. And beside her, with equal neatness, were laid her head and heart. The Ripper had outdone himself in execution.

"Then, panic. But needless panic. For though press, police, and populace alike awaited in sick dread, Jack the Ripper did not strike again.

"Months passed. A year. The immediate interest died, but not the memory. They said Jack had skipped to America. That he had committed suicide. They said—and they wrote. They've written ever since. Theories, hypotheses, arguments, treatises. But to this day no one knows who Jack the Ripper was. Or why he killed. Or why he stopped killing."

Sir Guy was silent. Obviously he expected some comment from me.

"You tell the story well," I remarked. "Though with a slight emotional bias."

"I've got all the documents," said Sir Guy Hollis. "I've made a collection of existing data and studied it."

I stood up. "Well," I yawned, in mock fatigue, "I've enjoyed your little bedtime story a great deal, Sir Guy. It was kind of you to abandon your duties at the British Embassy to drop in on a poor psychiatrist and regale him with your anecdotes."

Goading him always did the trick.

"I suppose you want to know why I'm interested?" he snapped.

"Yes. That's exactly what I'd like to know. Why are you interested?"

"Because," said Sir Guy Hollis, "I am on the trail of Jack the Ripper now. I think he's here—in Chicago!"

I sat down again. This time I did the blinking act.

"Say that again," I stuttered.

"Jack the Ripper is alive, in Chicago, and I'm out to find him."

"Wait a minute," I said. "Wait—a—minute!"

He wasn't smiling. It wasn't a joke.

"See here," I said. "What was the date of these murders?"

"August to November, 1888."

"1888? But if Jack the Ripper was an able-bodied man in 1888, he'd surely be dead today! Why look, man—if he were merely *born* in that year, he'd be 55 years old today!"

"Would he?" smiled Sir Guy Hollis. "Or should I say, 'Would she?' Because Jack the Ripper may have been a woman. Or any number of things."

"Sir Guy," I said. "You came to the right person when you looked me up. You definitely need the services of a psychiatrist."

"Perhaps. Tell me, Mr. Carmody, do you think I'm crazy?"

I looked at him and shrugged. But I had to give him a truthful answer.

"Frankly—no."

"Then you might listen to the reasons I believe Jack the Ripper is alive today."

"I might."

"I've studied these cases for thirty years. Been over the actual ground. Talked to officials. Talked to friends and acquaintances of the poor drabs who were killed. Visited with men and women in the neighborhood. Collected an entire library of material touching on Jack the Ripper. Studied all the wild theories or crazy notions.

"I learned a little. Not much, but a little. I won't bore you with my conclusions. But there was another branch of inquiry that yielded more fruitful returns. I have studied unsolved crimes. Murders.

"I could show you clippings from the papers of half the world's great cities. San Francisco. Shanghai. Calcutta. Omsk. Paris. Berlin. Pretoria. Cairo. Milan. Adelaide.

"The trail is there, the pattern. Unsolved crimes. Slashed throats of women. With the peculiar disfigurations and removals. Yes, I've followed a trail of blood. From New York westward across the continent. Then to the Pacific. From there to Africa. During the World War of 1914–18 it was Europe. After that, South America. And since 1930, the United States again. Eighty-seven such murders—and to the trained criminologist, all bear the stigma of the Ripper's handiwork.

"Recently there were the so-called Cleveland torso slayings. Remember? A shocking series. And finally, two recent deaths in Chicago. Within the past six months. One out on South Dearborn. The other somewhere up on Halsted. Same type of crime, same technique. I tell you, there are unmistakable indications in all these affairs—indications of the work of Jack the Ripper!"

I smiled.

"A very tight theory," I said. "I'll not question your evidence at all, or the deductions you draw. You're the criminologist, and I'll take your word for it. Just one thing remains to be explained. A minor point, perhaps, but worth mentioning."

"And what is that?" asked Sir Guy.

"Just how could a man of, let us say, 85 years commit these crimes? For if Jack the Ripper was around 30 in 1888 and lived, he'd be 85 today."

Sir Guy was silent. I had him there. But—

"Suppose he didn't get any older?" whispered Sir Guy.

"What's that?"

"Suppose Jack the Ripper didn't grow old? Suppose he is still a young man today?"

"All right," I said. "I'll suppose for a moment. Then I'll stop supposing and call for my nurse to restrain you."

"I'm serious," said Sir Guy.

"They all are," I told him. "That's the pity of it all, isn't it? They *know* they hear voices and see demons. But we lock them up just the same."

It was cruel, but it got results. He rose and faced me.

"It's a crazy theory, I grant you," he said. "All the theories about the Ripper are crazy. The idea that he was a doctor. Or a maniac. Or a woman. The reasons advanced for such beliefs are flimsy enough. There's nothing to go by. So why should my notion be any worse?"

"Because people grow older," I reasoned with him. "Doctors, maniacs, and women alike."

"What about—*sorcerers*?"

"Sorcerers?"

"Necromancers. Wizards. Practicers of Black Magic?"

"What's the point?"

"I studied," said Sir Guy. "I studied everything. After awhile I began to study the dates of the murders. The pattern those dates formed. The rhythm. The solar, lunar, stellar rhythm. The sidereal aspect. The astrological significance."

He *was* crazy. But I still listened.

"Suppose Jack the Ripper didn't murder for murder's sake alone? Suppose he wanted to make—a sacrifice?"

"What kind of a sacrifice?"

Sir Guy shrugged. "It is said that if you offer blood to the dark gods that they grant boons. Yes, if a blood offering is made at the proper time—when the moon and the stars are right—and with the proper ceremonies—they grant boons. Boons of youth. Eternal youth."

"But that's nonsense!"

"No. That's—Jack the Ripper."

I stood up. "A most interesting theory," I told him. "But Sir Guy—there's one thing I'm interested in. Why do you come here and tell it to me? I'm not an authority on witchcraft. I'm not a police official or criminologist. I'm a practicing psychiatrist. What's the connection?"

Sir Guy smiled.

"You are interested, then?"

"Well, yes. There must be some point."

"There is. But I wished to be assured of your interest first. Now I can tell you my plan."

"And just what is that plan?"

Sir Guy gave me a long look. Then he spoke.

"John Carmody," he said, "you and I are going to capture Jack the Ripper."

2

That's the way it happened. I've given the gist of that first interview in all its intricate and somewhat boring detail, because I think it's important. It helps to throw some light on Sir Guy's character and attitude. And in view of what happened after that—

But I'm coming to those matters.

Sir Guy's thought was simple. It wasn't even a thought. Just a hunch.

"You know the people here," he told me. "I've inquired. That's why I came to you as the ideal man for my purpose. You number amongst your acquaintances many writers, painters, poets. The so-called intelligentsia. The Bohemians. The lunatic fringe from the near north side.

"For certain reasons—never mind what they are—my clues lead me to infer that Jack the Ripper is a member of that element. He chooses to pose as an eccentric. I've a feeling that with you to take me around and introduce me to your set, I might hit upon the right person."

"It's all right with me," I said. "But just how are you going to look for him? As you say, he might be anybody, anywhere. And you have no idea what he looks like. He might be young or old. Jack the Ripper—a Jack of all trades? Rich man, poor man, beggar man, thief, doctor, lawyer—how will you know?"

"We shall see." Sir Guy sighed heavily. "But I must find him. At once."

"Why the hurry?"

Sir Guy sighed again. "Because in two days he will kill again."

"Are you sure?"

"Sure as the stars. I've plotted his chart, you see. All 87 of the murders correspond to certain astrological rhythm patterns. If, as I suspect, he makes a blood sacrifice to renew his youth, he must murder within two days. Notice the pattern of his first crimes in London. August 7th. Then August 31. September 8th. September 30th. November 9th. Intervals of 24 days, 9 days, 22 days—he killed two this time—and then 40 days. Of course there were crimes in between. There had to be. But they weren't discovered and pinned on him.

"At any rate, I've worked out a pattern for him, based on all my data. And I say that within the next two days he kills. So I must seek him out, somehow, before then."

"And I'm still asking you what you want me to do."

"Take me out," said Sir Guy. "Introduce me to your friends. Take me to parties."

"But where do I begin? As far as I know, my artistic friends, despite their eccentricities, are all normal people."

"So is the Ripper. Perfectly normal. Except on certain nights." Again that faraway look in Sir Guy's eyes. "Then he becomes an ageless pathological monster, crouching to kill, on evenings when the stars blaze down in the blazing patterns of death."

"All right," I said. "All right. I'll take you to parties, Sir Guy. I want to go myself, anyway. I need the drinks they'll serve there, after listening to your kind of talk."

We made our plans. And that evening I took him over to Lester Baston's studio.

As we ascended to the penthouse roof in the elevator I took the opportunity to warn Sir Guy.

"Baston's a real screwball," I cautioned him. "So are his guests. Be prepared for anything and everything."

"I am." Sir Guy Hollis was perfectly serious. He put his hand in his trousers pocket and pulled out a gun.

"What the—" I began.

"If I see him I'll be ready," Sir Guy said. He didn't smile, either.

"But you can't go running around at a party with a loaded revolver in your pocket, man!"

"Don't worry, I won't behave foolishly."

I wondered. Sir Guy Hollis was not, to my way of thinking, a normal man.

We stepped out of the elevator, went toward Baston's apartment door.

"By the way," I murmured, "just how do you wish to be introduced? Shall I tell them who you are and what you are looking for?"

"I don't care. Perhaps it would be best to be frank."

"But don't you think that the Ripper—if by some miracle he or she is present— will immediately get the wind up and take cover?"

"I think the shock of the announcement that I am hunting the Ripper would provoke some kind of a betraying gesture on his part," said Sir Guy.

"You'd make a pretty good psychiatrist yourself," I conceded. "It's a fine theory. But I warn you, you're going to be in for a lot of ribbing. This is a wild bunch."

Sir Guy smiled.

"I'm ready," he announced. "I have a little plan of my own. Don't be shocked by anything I do," he warned me.

I nodded and knocked on the door.

Baston opened it and poured out into the hall. His eyes were as red as the maraschino cherries in his Manhattan. He teetered back and forth regarding us very gravely. He squinted at my square-cut homburg hat and Sir Guy's mustache.

"Aha," he intoned. "The Walrus and the Carpenter."

I introduced Sir Guy.

"Welcome," said Baston, gesturing us inside with over-elaborate courtesy. He stumbled after us into the garish parlor.

I stared at the crowd that moved restlessly through the fog of cigarette smoke.

It was the shank of the evening for this mob. Every hand held a drink. Every face held a slightly hectic flush. Over in one corner the piano was going full blast, but the imperious strains of the *March* from *The Love for Three Oranges* couldn't drown out the profanity from the crap-game in the other corner.

Prokofieff had no chance against African polo, and one set of ivories rattled louder than the other.

Sir Guy got a monocle-full right away. He saw LaVerne Gonnister, the poetess, hit Hymie Kralik in the eye. He saw Hymie sit down on the floor and cry until Dick Pool accidentally stepped on his stomach as he walked through to the dining room for a drink.

He heard Nadia Vilinoff the commercial artist tell Johnny Odcutt that she thought his tattooing was in dreadful taste, and he saw Barclay Melton crawl under the dining room table with Johnny Odcutt's wife.

His zoological observations might have continued indefinitely if Lester Baston hadn't stepped to the center of the room and called for silence by dropping a vase on the floor.

"We have distinguished visitors in our midst," bawled Lester, waving his empty glass in our direction. "None other than the Walrus and the Carpenter. The Walrus is Sir Guy Hollis, a something-or-other from the British Embassy. The Carpenter, as you all know, is our own John Carmody, the prominent dispenser of libido-liniment."

He turned and grabbed Sir Guy by the arm, dragging him to the middle of the carpet. For a moment I thought Hollis might object, but a quick wink reassured me. He was prepared for this.

"It is our custom, Sir Guy," said Baston, loudly, "to subject our new friends to a little cross-examination. Just a little formality at these very formal gatherings, you understand. Are you prepared to answer questions?"

Sir Guy nodded and grinned.

"Very well," Baston muttered. "Friends—I give you this bundle from Britain. Your witness."

Then the ribbing started. I meant to listen, but at that moment Lydia Dare saw me and dragged me off into the vestibule for one of those Darling-I-waited-for-your-call-all-day routines.

By the time I got rid of her and went back, the impromptu quiz session was in full swing. From the attitude of the crowd, I gathered that Sir Guy was doing all right for himself.

Then Baston himself interjected a question that upset the apple-cart.

"And what, may I ask, brings you to our midst tonight? What is your mission, oh Walrus?"

"I'm looking for Jack the Ripper."

Nobody laughed.

Perhaps it struck them all the way it did me. I glanced at my neighbors and began to *wonder*.

LaVerne Gonnister. Hymie Kralik. Harmless. Dick Pool. Nadia Vilinoff. Johnny Odcutt and his wife. Barclay Melton. Lydia Dare. All harmless.

But what a forced smile on Dick Pool's face! And that sly, self-conscious smirk that Barclay Melton wore!

Oh, it was absurd, I grant you. But for the first time I saw these people in a new light. I wondered about their lives—their secret lives beyond the scenes of parties.

How many of them were playing a part, concealing something?

Who here would worship Hecate and grant that horrid goddess the dark boon of blood?

Even Lester Baston might be masquerading.

The mood was upon us all, for a moment. I saw questions flicker in the circle of eyes around the room.

Sir Guy stood there, and I could swear he was fully conscious of the situation he'd created, and enjoyed it.

I wondered idly just what was *really* wrong with him. Why he had this odd fixation concerning Jack the Ripper. Maybe he was hiding secrets, too. . . .

Baston, as usual, broke the mood. He burlesqued it.

"The Walrus isn't kidding, friends," he said. He slapped Sir Guy on the back and put his arm around him as he orated. "Our English cousin is really on the trail of the fabulous Jack the Ripper. You all remember Jack the Ripper, I presume? Quite a cutup in the old days, as I recall. Really had some ripping good times when he went out on a tear.

"The Walrus has some idea that the Ripper is still alive, probably prowling around Chicago with a Boy Scout knife. In fact"—Baston paused impressively and shot it out in a rasping stage-whisper—"in fact, he has reason to believe that Jack the Ripper might even be right here in our midst tonight."

There was the expected reaction of giggles and grins. Baston eyed Lydia Dare reprovingly. "You girls needn't laugh," he smirked. "Jack the Ripper might be a woman, too, you know. Sort of a Jill the Ripper."

"You mean you actually suspect one of us?" shrieked LaVerne Gonnister, simpering up to Sir Guy. "But that Jack the Ripper person disappeared ages ago, didn't he? In 1888?"

"Aha!" interrupted Baston. "How do you know so much about it, young lady? Sounds suspicious! Watch her, Sir Guy—she may not be as young as she appears. These lady poets have dark pasts."

The tension was gone, the mood was shattered, and the whole thing was beginning to degenerate into a trivial party joke. The man who had played the *March* was eyeing the piano with a *Scherzo* gleam in his eye that augured ill for Prokofieff. Lydia Dare was glancing at the kitchen, waiting to make a break for another drink.

Then Baston caught it.

"Guess what?" he yelled. "The Walrus has a gun."

His embracing arm had slipped and encountered the hard outline of the gun in Sir Guy's pocket. He snatched it out before Hollis had the opportunity to protest.

I stared hard at Sir Guy, wondering if this thing had carried far enough. But he flicked a wink my way and I remembered he had told me not to be alarmed.

So I waited as Baston broached a drunken inspiration.

"Let's play fair with our friend the Walrus," he cried. "He came all the way from England to our party on this mission. If none of you is willing to confess, I suggest we give him a chance to find out—the hard way."

"What's up?" asked Johnny Odcutt.

"I'll turn out the lights for one minute. Sir Guy can stand here with his gun. If anyone in this room is the Ripper he can either run for it or take the opportunity to— well, eradicate his pursuer. Fair enough?"

It was even sillier that it sounds, but it caught the popular fancy. Sir Guy's protests were unheard in the ensuing babble. And before I could stride over and put in my two cents' worth, Lester Baston had reached the light switch.

"Don't anybody move," he announced, with fake solemnity. "For one minute we will remain in darkness—perhaps at the mercy of a killer. At the end of that time, I'll turn up the lights again and look for bodies. Choose your partners, ladies and gentlemen."

The lights went out.

Somebody giggles.

I heard footsteps in the darkness. Mutterings.

A hand brushed my face.

The watch on my wrist ticked violently. But even louder, rising above it, I heard another thumping. The beating of my heart.

Absurd. Standing in the dark with a group of tipsy fools. And yet there was real terror lurking here, rustling through the velvet blackness.

Jack the Ripper prowled in darkness like this. And Jack the Ripper had a knife. Jack the Ripper had a madman's brain and a madman's purpose.

But Jack the Ripper was dead, dead and dust these many years—by every human law.

Only there are no human laws when you feel yourself in the darkness, when the darkness hides and protects and the outer mask slips off your face and you feel something welling up within you, a brooding shapeless purpose that is brother to the blackness.

Sir Guy Hollis shrieked.

There was a grisly thud.

Baston had the lights on.

Everybody screamed.

Sir Guy Hollis lay sprawled on the floor in the center of the room. The gun still clutched in his hand.

I glanced at the faces, marveling at the variety of expressions human beings can assume when confronting horror.

All the faces were present in the circle. Nobody had fled. And yet Sir Guy Hollis lay there . . .

LaVerne Gonnister was wailing and hiding her face.

"All right."

Sir Guy rolled over and jumped to his feet. He was smiling.

"Just an experiment, eh? If Jack the Ripper *were* among those present, and thought I had been murdered, he would have betrayed himself in some way when the lights went on and he saw me lying there.

"I am convinced of your individual and collective innocence. Just a gentle spoof, my friends."

Hollis stared at the goggling Baston and the rest of them crowding in behind him.

"Shall we leave, John?" he called to me. "It's getting late, I think."

Turning, he headed for the closet. I followed him. Nobody said a word.

It was a pretty dull party after that.

3

I met Sir Guy the following evening as we agreed, on the corner of 29th and South Halsted.

After what happened the night before, I was prepared for almost anything. But Sir Guy seemed matter-of-fact enough as he stood huddled against a grimy doorway and waited for me to appear.

"Boo!" I said, jumping out suddenly. He smiled. Only the betraying gesture of his left hand indicated that he'd instinctively reached for his gun when I startled him.

"All ready for our wild goose chase?" I asked.

"Yes." He nodded. "I'm glad that you agreed to meet me without asking questions," he told me. "It shows you trust my judgment." He took my arm and edged me along the street slowly.

"It's foggy tonight, John," said Sir Guy Hollis. "Like London."

I nodded.

"Cold, too, for November."

I nodded again and half-shivered my agreement.

"Curious," mused Sir Guy. "London fog and November. The place and the time of the Ripper murders."

I grinned through the darkness. "Let me remind, you, Sir Guy, that this isn't London, but Chicago. And it isn't November, 1888. It's over fifty years later."

Sir Guy returned my grin, but without mirth. "I'm not so sure, at that," he murmured. "Look about you. These tangled alleys and twisted streets. They're like the East End. Mitre Square. And surely they are as ancient as fifty years, at least."

"You're in the colored neighborhood off South Clark Street," I said, shortly. "And why you dragged me down here I still don't know."

"It's a hunch," Sir Guy admitted. "Just a hunch on my part, John. I want to wander around down here. There's the same geographical conformation in these streets as in those courts where the Ripper roamed and slew. That's where we'll find him, John. Not in the bright lights of the Bohemian neighborhood, but down here in the darkness. The darkness where he waits and crouches."

"Is that why you brought a gun?" I asked. I was unable to keep a trace of sarcastic nervousness from my voice. All of this talk, this incessant obsession with Jack the Ripper, got on my nerves more than I cared to admit.

"We may need the gun," said Sir Guy, gravely. "After all, tonight is the appointed night."

I sighed. We wandered on through the foggy, deserted streets. Here and there a dim light burned above a gin-mill door-way. Otherwise, all was darkness and shadow. Deep, gaping alley-ways loomed as we proceeded down a slanting side-street.

We crawled through that fog, alone and silent, like two tiny maggots floundering within a shroud.

When that thought hit me, I winced. The atmosphere was beginning to get *me*, too. If I didn't watch my step I'd go as loony as Sir Guy.

"Can't you see there's not a soul around these streets?" I said, tugging at his coat impatiently.

"He's bound to come," said Sir Guy. "He'll be drawn here. This is what I've been looking for. A *genius loci*. An evil spot that attracts evil. Always, when he slays, it's in the slums.

"You see, that must be one of his weaknesses. He has a fascination for squalor. Besides, the women he needs for sacrifice are more easily found in the dives and stew-pots of a great city."

I smiled. "Well, let's go into one of the dives or stew-pots," I suggested. "I'm cold. Need a drink. This damned fog gets into your bones. You Britishers can stand it, but I like warmth and dry heat."

We emerged from our side-street and stood upon the threshold of an alley.

Through the white clouds of mist ahead, I discerned a dim blue light, a naked bulb dangling from a beer sign above an alley tavern.

"Let's take a chance," I said. "I'm beginning to shiver."

"Lead the way," said Sir Guy. I led him down the alley passage. We halted before the door of the dive.

"What are you waiting for?" he asked.

"Just looking in," I told him. "This is a rough neighborhood, Sir Guy. Never know what you're liable to run into. And I'd prefer we didn't get into the wrong company. Some of these Negro places resent white customers."

"Good idea, John."

I finished my inspection through the doorway. "Looks deserted," I murmured. "Let's try it."

We entered a dingy bar. A feeble light flickered above the counter and railing, but failed to penetrate the further gloom of the back booths.

A gigantic Negro lolled across the bar—a black giant with prognathous jaw and ape-like torso. He scarcely stirred as we came in, but his eyes flickered open quite suddenly and I knew he noted our presence and was judging us.

"Evening," I said.

He took his time before replying. Still sizing us up. Then, he grinned.

"Evening, gents. What's your pleasure?"

"Gin," I said. "Two gins. It's a cold night."

"That's right, gents."

He poured, I paid, and took the glasses over to one of the booths. We wasted no time in emptying them. The fiery liquor warmed.

I went over to the bar and got the bottle. Sir Guy and I poured ourselves another drink. The big Negro went back into his doze, with one wary eye half-open against any sudden activity.

The clock over the bar ticked on. The wind was rising outside, tearing the shroud of fog to ragged shreds. Sir Guy and I sat in the warm booth and drank our gin.

He began to talk, and the shadows crept up about us to listen.

He rambled a great deal. He went over everything he'd said in the office when I met him, just as though I hadn't heard it before. The poor devils with obsessions are like that.

I listened very patiently. I poured Sir Guy another drink. And another.

But the liquor only made him more talkative. How he did run on! About ritual killings and prolonging life unnaturally—the whole fantastic tale came out again. And of course, he maintained his unyielding conviction that the Ripper was abroad tonight.

I suppose I was guilty of goading him.

"Very well," I said, unable to keep the impatience from my voice. "Let us say that your theory is correct—even though we must overlook every natural law and swallow a lot of superstition to give it any credence.

"But let us say, for the sake of argument, that you are right. Jack the Ripper was a man who discovered how to prolong his own life through making human sacrifices. He did travel around the world as you believe. He is in Chicago now and he is planning to kill. In other words, let us suppose that everything you claim is gospel truth. So what?"

"What do you mean, 'so what'?" said Sir Guy.

"I mean—so what?" I answered. "If all this is true, it still doesn't prove that by sitting down in a dingy gin-mill on the South Side, Jack the Ripper is going to walk in here and let you kill him, or turn him over to the police. And come to think of it, I don't even know now just what you intend to *do* with him if you ever did find him."

Sir Guy gulped his gin. "I'd capture the bloody swine," he said. "Capture him and turn him over to the government, together with all the papers and documentary evidence I've collected against him over a period of many years. I've spent a fortune investigating this affair, I tell you, a fortune! His capture will mean the solution of hundreds of unsolved crimes, of that I am convinced.

"I tell you, a mad beast is loose on this world! An ageless, eternal beast, sacrificing to Hecate and the dark gods!"

In vino veritas. Or was all this babbling the result of too much gin? It didn't matter. Sir Guy Hollis had another. I sat there and wondered what to do with him. The man was rapidly working up to a climax of hysterical drunkenness.

"One other point," I said, more for the sake of conversation than in any hopes of obtaining information. "You still don't explain how it is that you hope to just blunder into the Ripper."

"He'll be around," said Sir Guy. "I'm psychic. I know."

Sir Guy wasn't psychic. He was maudlin.

The whole business was beginning to infuriate me. We'd been sitting here an hour, and during all this time I'd been forced to play nursemaid and audience to a babbling idiot. After all, he wasn't a regular patient of mine.

"That's enough," I said, putting out my hand as Sir Guy reached for the half-emptied bottle again. "You've had plenty. Now I've got a suggestion to make. Let's call a cab and get out of here. It's getting late and it doesn't look as though your elusive friend is going to put in his appearance. Tomorrow, if I were you, I'd plan to turn all those papers and documents over to the F.B.I. If you're so convinced of the truth of your wild theory, they are competent enough to make a very thorough investigation, and find your man."

"No." Sir Guy was drunkenly obstinate. "No cab."

"But let's get out of here anyway," I said, glancing at my watch. "It's past midnight."

He sighed, shrugged, and rose steadily. As he started for the door, he tugged the gun free from his pocket.

"Here, give me that!" I whispered. "You can't walk around the street brandishing that thing."

I took the gun and slipped it inside my coat. Then I got hold of his right arm and steered him out of the door. The Negro didn't look up as we departed.

We stood shivering in the alleyway. The fog had increased. I couldn't see either end of the alley from where we stood. It was cold. Damp. Dark. Fog or no fog, a little wind was whispering secrets to the shadows at our backs.

The fresh air hit Sir Guy just as I expected it would. Fog and gin-fumes don't mingle very well. He lurched as I guided him slowly through the mist.

Sir Guy, despite his incapacity, still stared apprehensively at the alley, as though he expected to see a figure approaching.

Disgust got the better of me.

"Childish foolishness," I snorted. "Jack the Ripper, indeed! I call this carrying a hobby too far."

"Hobby?" He faced me. Through the fog I could see his distorted face. "You call this a hobby?"

"Well, what is it?" I grumbled. "Just why else are you so interested in tracking down this mythical killer?"

My arm held him. But his stare held me.

"In London," he whispered. "In 1888 . . . one of those nameless drabs the Ripper slew . . . was my mother."

"What?"

"Later I was recognized by my father, and legitimatized. We swore to give our lives to find the Ripper. My father was the first to search. He died in Hollywood in 1926—on the trail of the Ripper. They said he was stabbed by an unknown assailant in a brawl. But I know who that assailant was.

"So I've taken up his work, do you see, John? I've carried on. And I will carry on until I do find him and kill him with my own hands.

"He took my mother's life and the lives of hundreds to keep his own hellish being alive. Like a vampire, he battens on blood. Like a ghoul, he is nourished by death. Like a fiend, he stalks the world to kill. He is cunning, devilishly cunning. But I'll never rest until I find him, never!"

I believed him them. He wouldn't give up. He wasn't just a drunken babbler any more. He was as fanatical, as determined, as relentless as the Ripper himself.

Tomorrow he'd be sober. He'd continue the search. Perhaps he'd turn those papers over to the F.B.I. Sooner or later, with such persistence—and with his motive—he'd be successful. I'd always known he had a motive.

"Let's go," I said, steering him down the alley.

"Wait a minute," said Sir Guy. "Give me back my gun." He lurched a little. "I'd feel better with the gun on me."

He pressed me into the dark shadows of a little recess.

I tried to shrug him off, but he was insistent.

"Let me carry the gun, now, John," he mumbled.

"All right," I said.

I reached into my coat, brought my hand out.

"But that's not a gun," he protested. "That's a knife."

"I know."

I bore down on him swiftly.

"John!" he screamed.

"Never mind the 'John'," I whispered, raising the knife. "Just call me . . . Jack."

THE BLIND SPOT

BARRY PEROWNE
(1908–1985)

Barry Perowne was able to secure the rights to continue the Raffles series. He began by making him more of a two-fisted adventurer in the mold of.The Saint, but in later years returned to the intellectual capers for which E. W. Hornung was known and produced many stories that were the equal of the originals. The following tale is not about the amateur cracksman but stands in the front rank of the most ingenious stories of all time.

 NNIXTER LOVED THE LITTLE man like a brother. He put an arm around the little man's shoulders, partly from affection and partly to prevent himself from falling. He had been drinking earnestly since seven o'clock the previous evening. It was now nudging midnight, and things were a bit hazy. The lobby was full of the thump of hot music; down two steps, there were a lot of tables, a lot of people, a lot of noise. Annixter had no idea what this place was called, or how he had got here, or when. He had been in so many places since seven o'clock the previous evening.

'In a nutshell,' confided Annixter, leaning heavily on the little man, 'a woman fetched you a kick in the face, or fate fetches you a kick in the face. Same thing, really—a woman and fate. So what? So you think it's the finish, an' you go out and get plastered. You get good an' plastered,' said Annixter, 'an' you brood.

'You sit there an' you drink an' you brood—an' in the end you find you've brooded up just about the best idea you ever had in your life! 'At's the way it goes,' said Annixter, 'an' 'at's my philosophy—the harder you kick a playwright, the better he works.'

He gestured with such vehemence that he would have collapsed if the little man hadn't steadied him. The little man was poker-backed, his grip was firm. His mouth was firm, too—a straight line, almost colourless. He wore hexagonal rimless spectacles, a black hard-felt hat, a neat pepper-and-salt suit. He looked pale and prim beside the flushed, rumpled Annixter.

From her counter, the hat-check girl watched them indifferently.

'Don't you think,' the little man said to Annixter, 'you ought to go home now? I've been honoured you should tell me the scenario of your play, but—'

'I had to tell someone,' said Annixter, 'or blow my top! Oh, boy, what a play, what a play! What a murder, eh? That climax—'

The full, dazzling perfection of it struck him again. He stood frowning, considering, swaying a little—then nodded abruptly, groped for the little man's hand, warmly pumphandled it.

'Sorry I can't stick around,' said Annixter, 'I got work to do.'

He crammed his hat on shapelessly, headed on a slightly elliptical course across the lobby, thrust the double doors open with both hands, lurched out into the night.

It was, to his inflamed imagination, full of lights, winking and tilting across the dark. *Sealed Room* by James Annixter. No. *Room Reserved* by James—No, no. *Blue Room. Room Blue* by James Annixter—

He stepped, oblivious, off the curb, and a taxi, swinging in toward the place he had just left, skidded with suddenly locked, squealing wheels on the wet road.

Something hit Annixter violently in the chest, and all the lights he had been seeing exploded in his face.

Then there weren't any lights.

Mr. James Annixter, the playwright, was knocked down by a taxi late last night when leaving the Casa Havana. After hospital treatment for shock and superficial injuries, he returned to his home.

The lobby of the Casa Havana was full of the thump of music; down two steps there were a lot of tables, a lot of people, a lot of noise. The hat-check girl looked wonderingly at Annixter—at the plaster on his forehead, the black sling which supported his left arm.

'My,' said the hat-check girl, 'I certainly didn't expect to see *you* again so soon!'

'You remember me, then?' said Annixter, smiling.

'I ought to,' said the hat-check girl. 'You cost me a night's sleep! I heard those brakes squeal after you went out the door that night—and there was a sort of thud!' She shuddered. 'I kept hearing it all night long. I can still hear it now—a week after! Horrible!'

'You're sensitive,' said Annixter.

'I got too much imagination,' the hat-check girl admitted. 'F'instance, I just *knew* it was you even before I run to the door and see you lying there. That man you was with was standing just outside. "My heavens," I say to him, "it's your friend!"'

'What did he say?' Annixter asked.

'He says, "He's not my friend. He's just someone I met." Funny, eh?'

Annixter moistened his lips.

'How d'you mean,' he said carefully, 'funny? I *was* just someone he'd met.'

'Yes, but—man you been drinking with,' said the hat-check girl, 'killed before your eyes. Because he must have seen it; he went out right after you. You'd think he'd 'a' been interested, at least. But when the taxi driver starts shouting for witnesses, it wasn't his fault, I looks around for that man—an' he's gone!'

Annixter exchanged a glance with Ransome, his producer, who was with him. It was a slightly puzzled, slightly anxious glance. But he smiled, then, at the hat-check girl.

'Not quite "killed before his eyes",' said Annixter. 'Just shaken up a bit, that's all.'

There was no need to explain to her how curious, how eccentric, had been the effect of that 'shaking up' upon his mind.

'If you could 'a' seen yourself lying there with the taxi's lights shining on you—'

'Ah, there's that imagination of yours!' said Annixter.

He hesitated for just an instant, then asked the question he had come to ask—the question which had assumed so profound an importance for him.

He asked, 'That man I was with—who was he?'

The hat-check girl looked from one to the other. She shook her head.

'I never saw him before,' she said, 'and I haven't seen him since.'

Annixter felt as though she had struck him in the face. He had hoped, hoped desperately, for a different answer; he had counted on it.

Ransome put a hand on his arm, restrainingly.

'Anyway,' said Ransome, 'as we're here, let's have a drink.'

They went down the two steps into the room where the band thumped. A waiter led them to a table, and Ransome gave him an order.

'There was no point in pressing that girl,' Ransome said to Annixter. 'She doesn't know the man, and that's that. My advice to you, James, is: Don't worry. Get your mind on something else. Give yourself a chance. After all, it's barely a week since—'

'A week!' Annixter said. 'Hell, look what I've done in that week! The whole of the first two acts, and the third act right up to that crucial point—the climax of the whole thing: the solution: the scene that the play stands or falls on! It would have been done, Bill—the whole play, the best thing I ever did in my life—it would have been finished two days ago if it hadn't been for this—' he knuckled his forehead—'this extraordinary blind spot, this damnable little trick of memory!'

'You had a very rough shaking up—'

'That?' Annixter said contemptuously. He glanced down at the sling on his arm. 'I never even felt it; it didn't bother me. I woke up in the ambulance with my play as vivid in my mind as the moment the taxi hit me—more so, maybe, because I was stone cold sober then, and knew what I had. A winner—a thing that just couldn't miss!'

'If you'd rested,' Ransome said, 'as the doc told you, instead of sitting up in bed there scribbling night and day—'

'I had to get it on paper. Rest?' said Annixter, and laughed harshly. 'You don't get rest when you've got a thing like that. That's what you live for—if you're a playwright. That *is* living! I've lived eight whole lifetimes, in those eight characters, during the past five days. I've lived so utterly in them, Bill, that it wasn't till I actually came to write that last scene that I realized what I'd lost! Only my whole play, that's all! How was Cynthia stabbed in that windowless room into which she had locked and bolted herself? How did the killer get to her? *How was it done?*

'Hell,' Annixter said, 'scores of writers, better men than I am, have tried to put that sealed room murder over—and never quite done it convincingly: never quite got away with it: been overelaborate, phoney! I had it—heaven help me, *I* had it! Simple, perfect, glaringly obvious when you've once seen it! And it's my whole play—the curtain rises on that sealed room and falls on it! That was my revelation— *how it was done!* That was what I got, by the way of playwright's compensation, because a woman I thought I loved kicked me in the face—I brooded up the answer to the sealed room! And a taxi knocked it out of my head!'

He drew a long breath.

'I've spent two days and two nights, Bill, trying to get that idea back—*how it was done!* It won't come. I'm a competent playwright; I know my job; I could finish my play, but it'd be like all those others—not quite right, phoney! It wouldn't be *my play*! But there's a little man walking around this city somewhere—a little man with hexagonal glasses—who's got my idea in his head! He's got it because I told it to him. I'm going to find that little man, and get back what belongs to me! I've got to! Don't you see that, Bill? I've *got* to!'

If the gentleman who, at the Casa Havana on the night of January 27th so patiently listened to a playwright's outlining of an idea for a drama will communicate with the Box No. below, he will hear of something to his advantage.

A little man who had said, 'He's not my friend. He's just someone I met—'

A little man who'd seen an accident but hadn't waited to give evidence—

The hat-check girl had been right. There *was* something a little queer about that. A little queer?

During the next few days, when the advertisements he'd inserted failed to bring any reply, it began to seem to Annixter very queer indeed.

His arm was out of its sling now, but he couldn't work. Time and again, he sat down before his almost completed manuscript, read it through with close, grim attention, thinking, 'It's *bound* to come back this time!'—only to find himself up against that blind spot again, that blank wall, that maddening hiatus in his memory.

He left his work and prowled the streets; he haunted bars and saloons; he rode for miles on 'buses and subways, especially at the rush hours. He saw a million faces, but the face of the little man with hexagonal glasses he did not see.

The thought of him obsessed Annixter. It was infuriating, it was unjust, it was torture to think that a little, ordinary, chance-met citizen was walking blandly around somewhere with the last link of his, the celebrated James Annixter's, play—the best thing he'd ever done—locked away in his head. And with no idea of what he had: without the imagination, probably, to appreciate what he had! And certainly with no idea of what it meant to Annixter!

Or *had* he some idea? Was he, perhaps, not quite so ordinary as he'd seemed? Had he seen those advertisements, drawn from them tortuous inferences of his own? Was he holding back with some scheme for shaking Annixter down for a packet?

The more Annixter thought about it, the more he felt that the hat-check girl had been right, that there was something very queer indeed about the way the little man had behaved after the accident.

Annixter's imagination played around the man he was seeking, tried to probe into his mind, conceived reasons for his fading away after the accident, for his failure to reply to the advertisements.

Annixter's was an active and dramatic imagination. The little man who had seemed so ordinary began to take on a sinister shape in Annixter's mind—

But the moment he actually saw the little man again, he realized how absurd it was. It was so absurd that it was laughable. The little man was so respectable; his shoulders were so straight; his pepper-and-salt suit was so neat; his black hard-felt hat was set so squarely on his head—

The doors of the subway train were just closing when Annixter saw him, standing on the platform with a briefcase in one hand, a folded evening paper under his other arm. Light from the train shone on his prim, pale face; his hexagonal spectacles flashed. He turned toward the exit as Annixter lunged for the closing doors of the train, squeezed between them on to the platform.

Craning his head to see above the crowd, Annixter elbowed his way through, ran up the stairs two at a time, put a hand on the little man's shoulder.

'Just a minute,' Annixter said. 'I've been looking for you.'

The little man checked instantly, at the touch of Annixter's hand. Then he turned his head and looked at Annixter. His eyes were pale behind the hexagonal, rimless glasses—a pale grey. His mouth was a straight line, almost colourless.

Annixter loved the little man like a brother. Merely finding the little man was a relief so great that it was like the lifting of a black cloud from his spirits. He patted the little man's shoulder affectionately.

'I've got to talk to you,' said Annixter. 'It won't take a minute. Let's go somewhere.'

The little man said, 'I can't imagine what you want to talk to me about.'

He moved slightly to one side, to let a woman pass. The crowd from the train had thinned, but there were still people going up and down the stairs. The little man looked, politely inquiring, at Annixter.

Annixter said, 'Of course you can't, it's so damned silly! But it's about that play—'
'Play?'

Annixter felt a faint anxiety.

'Look,' he said, 'I was drunk that night—I was very, very drunk! But looking back, my impression is that you were dead sober. You were, weren't you?'

'I've never been drunk in my life.'

'Thank heaven for that!' said Annixter. 'Then you won't have any difficulty in remembering the little point I want you to remember.' He grinned, shook his head. 'You had me going there, for a minute. I thought—'

'I don't know what you thought,' the little man said. 'But I'm quite sure you're mistaking me for somebody else. I haven't any idea what you're talking about. I never saw you before in my life. I'm sorry. Good night.'

He turned and started up the stairs. Annixter stared after him. He couldn't believe his ears. He stared blankly after the little man for an instant, then a rush of anger and suspicion swept away his bewilderment. He raced up the stairs, caught the little man by the arm.

'Just a minute,' said Annixter. 'I may have been drunk, but—'

'That,' the little man said, 'seems evident. Do you mind taking your hand off me?'

Annixter controlled himself. 'I'm sorry,' he said. 'Let me get this right, though. You say you've never seen me before. Then you weren't at the Casa Havana on the 27th—somewhere between ten o'clock and midnight? You didn't have a drink or two with me, and listen to an idea for a play that had just come into my mind?'

The little man looked steadily at Annixter.

'I've told you,' the little man said. 'I've never set eyes on you before.'

'You didn't see me get hit by a taxi?' Annixter pursued, tensely. 'You didn't say to the hat-check girl, "He's not my friend. He's just someone I met"?'

'I don't know what you're talking about,' the little man said sharply.

He made to turn away, but Annixter gripped his arm again.

'I don't know,' Annixter said, between his teeth, 'anything about your private affairs, and I don't want to. You may have had some good reason for wanting to duck giving evidence as a witness of that taxi accident. You may have some good reason for this act you're pulling on me, now. I don't know and I don't care. But it is an act. You *are* the man I told my play to!

'I want you to tell that story back to me as I told it to you; I have my reasons— personal reasons, of concern to me and me only. I want you to tell the story back to me—that's all I want! I don't want to know who you are, or anything about you, *I just want you to tell me that story!'*

'You ask,' the little man said, 'an impossibility, since I never heard it.'

Annixter kept an iron hold on himself.

He said, 'Is it money? Is this some sort of a hold-up? Tell me what you want; I'll give it to you. Lord help me, I'd go so far as to give you a share in the play! That'll mean real money. I know, because I know my business. And maybe—maybe,' said Annixter, struck by a sudden thought, '*you* know it, too! Eh?'

'You're insane or drunk!' the little man said.

With a sudden movement, he jerked his arm free, raced up the stairs. A train was rumbling in, below. People were hurrying down. He weaved and dodged among them with extraordinary celerity.

He was a small man, light, and Annixter was heavy. By the time he reached the street, there was no sign of the little man. He was gone.

Was the idea, Annixter wondered, to steal his play? By some wild chance did the little man nurture a fantastic ambition to be a dramatist? Had he, perhaps, peddled his precious manuscripts in vain, for years, around the managements? Had Annixter's play appeared to him as a blinding flash of hope in the gathering darkness of frustration and failure: something he had imagined he could safely steal because it had seemed to him the random inspiration of a drunkard who by morning would have forgotten he had ever given birth to anything but a hangover?

That, Annixter thought, would be a laugh! That would be irony—

He took another drink. It was his fifteenth since the little man with the hexagonal glasses had given him the slip, and Annixter was beginning to reach the stage where he lost count of how many places he had had drinks in tonight. It was also the stage, though, where he was beginning to feel better, where his mind was beginning to work.

He could imagine just how the little man must have felt as the quality of the play he was being told, with hiccups, gradually had dawned upon him.

'This is mine!' the little man would have thought. 'I've got to have this. He's drunk, he's soused, he's bottled—he'll have forgotten every word of it by the morning! Go on! Go on, mister! Keep talking!'

That was a laugh, too—the idea that Annixter would have forgotten his play by the morning. Other things Annixter forgot, unimportant things; but never in his life had he forgotten the minutest detail that was to his purpose as a playwright. Never! Except once, because a taxi had knocked him down.

Annixter took another drink. He needed it. He was on his own now. There wasn't any little man with hexagonal glasses to fill that blind spot for him. The little man was gone. He was gone as though he'd never been. To hell with him! Annixter had to fill in that blind spot himself. He *had* to do it—somehow!

He had another drink. He had quite a lot more drinks. The bar was crowded and noisy, but he didn't notice the noise—till someone came up and slapped him on the shoulder. It was Ransome.

Annixter stood up, leaning with his knuckles on the table.

'Look, Bill,' Annixter said, 'how about this? Man forgets an idea, see? He wants to get it back—gotta get it back! Idea comes from inside, works outwards—right? So he starts on the outside, works back inward. How's that?'

He swayed, peering at Ransome.

'Better have a little drink,' said Ransome. 'I'd need to think that out.'

'I,' said Annixter, '*have* thought it out!' He crammed his hat shapelessly on to his head. 'Be seeing you, Bill. I got work to do!'

He started, on a slightly tacking course, for the door—and his apartment.

It was Joseph, his 'man,' who opened the door of his apartment to him, some twenty minutes later. Joseph opened the door while Annixter's latchkey was still describing vexed circles around the lock.

'Good evening, sir,' said Joseph.

Annixter stared at him. 'I didn't tell you to stay in tonight.'

'I hadn't any reason for going out, sir,' Joseph explained. He helped Annixter off with his coat. 'I rather enjoy a quiet evening in, once in a while.'

'You got to get out of here,' said Annixter.

'Thank you, sir,' said Joseph. 'I'll go and throw a few things into a bag.'

Annixter went into his big living-room-study, poured himself a drink.

The manuscript of his play lay on the desk. Annixter, swaying a little, glass in hand, stood frowning down at the untidy stack of yellow paper, but he didn't begin to read. He waited until he heard the outer door click shut behind Joseph, then he gathered up his manuscript, the decanter and a glass, and the cigarette box. Thus laden, he went into the hall, walked across it to the door of Joseph's room.

There was a bolt on the inside of this door, and the room was the only one in the apartment which had no window—both facts which made the room the only one suitable to Annixter's purpose.

With his free hand, he switched on the light.

It was a plain little room, but Annixter noticed, with a faint grin, that the bed-spread and the cushion in the worn basket-chair were both blue. Appropriate, he thought—a good omen. *Room Blue* by James Annixter—

Joseph had evidently been lying on the bed, reading the evening paper; the paper lay on the rumpled quilt, and the pillow was dented. Beside the head of the bed, opposite the door, was a small table littered with shoe-brushes and dusters.

Annixter swept this paraphernalia on to the floor. He put his stack of manuscript, the decanter and glass and cigarette box on the table, and went across and bolted the door. He pulled the basket-chair up to the table and sat down, lighted a cigarette.

He leaned back in the chair, smoking, letting his mind ease into the atmosphere he wanted—the mental atmosphere of Cynthia, the woman in his play, the woman who was afraid, so afraid that she had locked and bolted herself into a windowless room, a sealed room.

'This is how she sat,' Annixter told himself, 'just as I'm sitting now: in a room with no windows, the door locked and bolted. Yet he got at her. He got at her with a knife—in a room with no windows, the door remaining locked and bolted on the inside. *How was it done?*'

There was a way in which it could be done. He, Annixter, had thought of that way; he had conceived it, invented it—and forgotten it. His idea had produced the circumstances. Now, deliberately, he had reproduced the circumstances, that he might think back to the idea. He had put his person in the position of the victim, that his mind might grapple with the problem of the murderer.

It was very quiet: not a sound in the room, the whole apartment.

For a long time, Annixter sat unmoving. He sat unmoving until the intensity of his concentration began to waver. Then he relaxed. He pressed the palms of his hands to his forehead for a moment, then reached for the decanter. He splashed himself a strong drink. He had almost recovered what he sought; he had felt it close, had been on the very verge of it.

'Easy,' he warned himself, 'take it easy. Rest. Relax. Try again in a minute.'

He looked around for something to divert his mind, picked up the paper from Joseph's bed.

At the first words that caught his eye, his heart stopped.

The woman, in whose body were found three knife wounds, any of which might have been fatal, was in a windowless room, the only door to which was locked and bolted on the inside. These elaborate precautions appear to have been habitual with her, and no doubt she went in continual fear of her life, as the police know her to have been a persistent and pitiless blackmailer.

Apart from the unique problem set by the circumstance of the sealed room is the problem of how the crime could have gone undiscovered for so long a period, the doctor's estimate from the condition of the body as some twelve to fourteen days.

Twelve to fourteen days—

Annixter read back over the remainder of the story; then let the paper fall to the floor. The pulse was heavy in his head. His face was grey. Twelve to fourteen days? He could put it closer than that. *It was exactly thirteen nights ago that he had sat in the Casa Havana and told a little man with hexagonal glasses how to kill a woman in a sealed room!*

Annixter sat very still for a minute. Then he poured himself a drink. It was a big one, and he needed it. He felt a strange sense of wonder, of awe.

They had been in the same boat, he and the little man—thirteen nights ago. They had both been kicked in the face by a woman. One, as a result, had conceived a murder play. The other had made the play reality!

'And I actually, tonight, offered him a share!' Annixter thought. 'I talked about "real" money!'

That was a laugh. All the money in the universe wouldn't have made that little man admit that he had seen Annixter before—that Annixter had told him the plot of a play about how to kill a woman in a sealed room! Why, he, Annixter, was the one person in the world who could denounce that little man! Even if he couldn't tell them, because he had forgotten, just how he had told the little man the murder was to be committed, he could still put the police on the little man's track. He could describe him, so that they could trace him. And once on his track, the police would ferret out links, almost inevitably, with the dead woman.

A queer thought—that he, Annixter, was probably the only menace, the only danger, to the little prim, pale man with the hexagonal spectacles. The only menace—as, of course, the little man must know very well.

He must have been very frightened when he had read that the playwright who had been knocked down outside the Casa Havana had only received 'superficial injuries.' He must have been still more frightened when Annixter's advertisements had begun to appear. *What must he have felt tonight, when Annixter's hand had fallen on his shoulder?*

A curious idea occurred, now, to Annixter. It was from tonight, precisely from tonight, that he was a danger to that little man. He was, because of the inferences the little man must infallibly draw, a deadly danger as from the moment the discovery of the murder in the sealed room was published. The discovery had been published tonight and the little man had a paper under his arm—

Annixter's was a lively and resourceful imagination.

It was, of course, just in the cards that, when he'd lost the little man's trail at the subway station, the little man might have turned back, picked up *his*, Annixter's trail.

And Annixter had sent Joseph out. He was, it dawned slowly upon Annixter, alone in the apartment—alone in a windowless room, with the door locked and bolted on the inside, at his back.

Annixter felt a sudden, icy and wild panic.

He half rose, but it was too late.

It was too late, because at that moment the knife, slid, thin and keen and delicate, into his back, fatally, between the ribs.

Annixter's head bowed slowly forward until his cheek rested on the manuscript of his play. He made only one sound—a queer sound, indistinct, yet identifiable as a kind of laughter.

The fact was, Annixter had just remembered.

THE CATBIRD SEAT

JAMES THURBER
(1894–1961)

Although he was blind in one eye, with progressively diminishing vision in the other until he became legally blind, Thurber was a cartoonist of immense success and humor. He honed his writing skills until he preferred them to his talent as an artist, and his wickedly funny stories, many related to crime and mystery, show a deceptively simple style. The eerily weird character of many of his tales, much like this one, conceal terror behind his mirthful mask.

R. MARTIN BOUGHT THE PACK of Camels on Monday night in the most crowded cigar store on Broadway. It was theater time and seven or eight men were buying cigarettes. The clerk didn't even glance at Mr. Martin, who put the pack in his overcoat pocket and went out. If any of the staff at F & S had seen him buy the cigarettes, they would have been astonished, for it was generally known that Mr. Martin did not smoke, and never had. No one saw him.

It was just a week to the day since Mr. Martin had decided to rub out Mrs. Ulgine Barrows. The term "rub out" pleased him because it suggested nothing more than the correction of an error—in this case an error of Mr. Fitweiler. Mr. Martin had spent each night of the past week working over it again. For the hundredth time he resented the element of imprecision, the margin of guesswork that entered into the business. The project as he had worked it out was casual and bold, the risks were considerable. Something might go wrong anywhere along the line. And therein lay the cunning of his scheme. No one would ever see in it the cautious, painstaking hand of Erwin Martin, head of the filing department at F & S, of whom Mr. Fitweiler had once said, "Man is fallible but Martin isn't." No one would see his hand, that is, unless it were caught in the act.

Sitting in his apartment, drinking a glass of milk, Mr. Martin reviewed his case against Mrs. Ulgine Barrows, as he had every night for seven nights. He began at the beginning. Her quacking voice and braying laugh had first profaned the halls of F & S on March 7, 1941 (Mr. Martin had a head for dates). Old Roberts, the personnel chief, had introduced her as the newly appointed special adviser to the president of the firm, Mr. Fitweiler. The woman had appalled Mr. Martin instantly, but he hadn't shown it. He had given her his dry hand, a look of studious concentration, and a faint smile. "Well," she had said, looking at the papers on his desk, "are you lifting the oxcart out of the ditch?" As Mr. Martin recalled that moment, over his milk, he squirmed slightly. He must keep his mind on her crimes as a special adviser, not on her pecca-dillos as a personality. This he found difficult to do, in spite of entering an objection and sustaining it. The faults of the woman as a woman kept chattering on in his mind like an unruly witness. She had, for almost two years now, baited him. In the halls, in the elevator, even in his own office, into which she romped now and then like a cir-cus horse, she was constantly shouting these silly questions at him. "Are you lifting the oxcart out of the ditch? Are you tearing up the pea patch? Are you hollering down the rain barrel? Are you scraping the bottom of the pickle barrel? Are you sit-ting in the catbird seat?"

It was Joey Hart, one of Mr. Martin's two assistants, who had explained what the gibberish meant. "She must be a Dodger fan," he had said. "Red Barber announces the Dodger games over the radio and he uses those expressions—picked 'em up down South." Joey had gone on to explain one or two. "Tearing up the pea patch" meant going on a rampage; "sitting in the catbird seat" meant sitting pretty, like a batter with three balls and no strikes on him. Mr. Martin dismissed all this with an effort. It had been annoying, it had driven him near to distraction, but he was too solid a man to be moved to murder by anything so childish. It was fortunate, he reflected as he passed on to the important charges against Mrs. Barrows, that he had stood up under it so well. He had maintained always an outward appearance of polite tolerance. "Why, I even believe you like the woman," Miss Paird, his other assistant, had once said to him. He had simply smiled.

A gravel rapped in Mr. Martin's mind and the case proper was resumed. Mrs. Ulgine Barrows stood charged with willful, blatant, and persistent attempts to destroy the efficiency and system of F & S. It was competent, material, and relevant to review her advent and rise to power. Mr. Martin had got the story from Miss Paird, who seemed always to be able to find things out. According to her, Mrs. Barrows had met Mr. Fitweiler at a party, where she had rescued him from the embraces of a powerfully built drunken man who had mistaken the president of F & S for a famous retired Middle Western football coach. She had led him to a sofa and somehow worked upon him a monstrous magic. The aging gentleman had jumped to the con-clusion there and then that this was a woman of singular attainments, equipped to bring out the best in him and in the firm. A week later he had introduced her into F & S as his special adviser. On that day confusion got its foot in the door. After Miss Tyson, Mr. Brundage, and Mr. Bartlett had been fired and Mr. Munson had taken his hat and stalked out, mailing in his resignation later, old Roberts had been emboldened to speak to Mr. Fitweiler. He mentioned that Mr. Munson's department had been "a little disrupted" and hadn't they perhaps better resume the old system there? Mr. Fitweiler had said certainly not. He had the greatest faith in Mrs. Barrows's ideas. "They require a little seasoning, a little seasoning, is all," he had added. Mr. Roberts had given it up. Mr. Martin reviewed in detail all the changes wrought by Mrs. Barrows. She had begun chipping at the cornices of the firm's edifice and now she was swing-ing at the foundation stones with a pickaxe.

Mr. Martin came now, in his summing up, to the afternoon of Monday, November 2, 1942—just one week ago. On that day, at 3 P.M., Mrs. Barrows had bounced into his office. "Boo!" she had yelled. "Are you scraping around the bottom of the pickle barrel?" Mr. Martin had looked at her from under his green eyeshade, saying noth-ing. She had begun to wander about the office, taking it in with her great, popping eyes. "Do you really need *all* these filing cabinets?" she had demanded suddenly. Mr. Martin's heart had jumped. "Each of these files," he said, keeping his voice even, "plays an indispensable part in the system of F & S." She had brayed at him,

"Well, don't tear up the pea patch!" and gone to the door. From there she had bawled, "But you sure have got a lot of fine scrap in here!" Mr. Martin could no longer doubt that the finger was on his beloved department. Her pickaxe was on the upswing, poised for the first blow. It had not come yet; he had received no blue memo from the enchanted Mr. Fitweiler bearing nonsensical instructions deriving from the obscene woman. But there was no doubt in Mr. Martin's mind that one would be forthcoming. He must act quickly. Already a precious week had gone by. Mr. Martin stood up in his living room, still holding his milk glass. "Gentlemen of the jury," he said to himself, "I demand the death penalty for this horrible person."

The next day Mr. Martin followed his routine, as usual. He polished his glasses more often and once sharpened an already sharp pencil, but not even Miss Paird noticed. Only once did he catch sight of his victim; she swept past him in the hall with a patronizing, "Hi!" At five-thirty he walked home, as usual, and had a glass of milk, as usual. He had never drunk anything stronger in his life—unless you could count ginger ale. The late Sam Schlosser, the S of F & S, had praised Mr. Martin at a staff meeting several years before for his temperate habits. "Our most efficient worker neither drinks nor smokes," he had said. "The results speak for themselves." Mr. Fitweiler had sat by, nodding approval.

Mr. Martin was still thinking about that red-letter day as he walked over to the Schrafft's on Fifth Avenue near Forty-sixth Street. He got there, as he always did, at eight o'clock. He finished his dinner and the financial page of the *Sun* at a quarter to nine, as he always did. It was his custom after dinner to take a walk. This time he walked down Fifth Avenue at a casual pace. His gloved hands felt moist and warm, his forehead cold. He transferred the Camels from his overcoat to a jacket pocket. He wondered, as he did so, if they did not represent an unnecessary note of strain. Mrs. Barrows smoked only Luckies. It was his idea to puff a few puffs on a Camel (after the rubbing-out), stub it out in the ashtray holding her lipstick-stained Luckies, and thus drag a small red herring across the trail. Perhaps it was not a good idea. It would take time. He might even choke, too loudly.

Mr. Martin had never seen the house on West Twelfth Street where Mrs. Barrows lived, but he had a clear enough picture of it. Fortunately, she had bragged to everybody about her ducky first-floor apartment in the perfectly darling three-story redbrick. There would be no doorman or other attendants; just the tenants of the second and third floors. As he walked along, Mr. Martin realized that he would get there before nine-thirty. He had considered walking north on Fifth Avenue from Schrafft's to a point from which it would take him until ten o'clock to reach the house. At that hour people were less likely to be coming in or going out. But the procedure would have made an awkward loop in the straight thread of his casualness, and he had abandoned it. It was impossible to figure when people would be entering or leaving the house, anyway. There was a great risk at any hour. If he ran into anybody, he would simply have to place the rubbing-out of Ulgine Barrows in the inactive file forever. The same thing would hold true if there were someone in her apartment. In that case he would just say that he had been passing by, recognized her charming house and thought to drop in.

It was eighteen minutes after nine when Mr. Martin turned into Twelfth Street. A man passed him, and a man and a woman talking. There was no one within fifty paces when he came to the house, halfway down the block. He was up the steps and in the small vestibule in no time, pressing the bell under the card that said "Mrs. Ulgine Barrows." When the clicking in the lock started, he jumped forward against the door. He got inside fast, closing the door behind him. A bulb in a lantern hung from the hall ceiling on a chain seemed to give a monstrously bright light. He went toward it swiftly, on tiptoe.

"Well, for God's sake, look who's here!" bawled Mrs. Barrows, and her braying laugh rang out like the report of a shotgun. He rushed past her like a football tackle, bumping her. "Hey, quit shoving!" she said, closing the door behind them. They were in her living room, which seemed to Mr. Martin to be lighted by a hundred lamps. "What's after you?" she said. "You're as jumpy as a goat." He found he was unable to speak. His heart was wheezing in his throat. "I—yes," he finally brought out. She was jabbering and laughing as she started to help him off with his coat. "No, no," he said. "I'll put it here." He took it off and put it on a chair near the door. "Your hat and gloves, too," she said. "You're in a lady's house." He put his hat on top of the coat. Mrs. Barrows seemed larger than he had thought. He kept his gloves on. "I was passing by," he said. "I recognized—is there anyone here?" She laughed louder than ever. "No," she said, "we're all alone. You're as white as a sheet, you funny man. Whatever *has* come over you? I'll mix you a toddy." She started toward a door across the room. "Scotch-and-soda will be all right," he heard himself say. He could hear her laughing in the kitchen.

Mr. Martin looked quickly around the living room for the weapon. He had counted on finding one there. There were andirons and a poker and something in a corner that looked like an Indian club. None of them would do. It couldn't be that way. He began to pace around. He came to a desk. On it lay a metal paper knife with an ornate handle. Would it be sharp enough? He reached for it and knocked over a small brass jar. Stamps spilled out of it and it fell to the floor with a clatter. "Hey," Mrs. Barrows yelled from the kitchen, "are you tearing up the pea patch?" Mr. Martin gave a strange laugh. Picking up the knife, he tried its point against his left wrist. It was blunt. It wouldn't do.

When Mrs. Barrows reappeared, carrying two highballs, Mr. Martin, standing there with his gloves on, became acutely conscious of the fantasy he had wrought. Cigarettes in his pocket, a drink prepared for him—it was all too grossly improbable. It was more than that; it was impossible. Somewhere in the back of his mind a vague idea stirred, sprouted. "For heaven's sake, take off those gloves," said Mrs. Barrows. "I always wear them in the house," said Mr. Martin. The idea began to bloom, strange and wonderful. She put the glasses on a coffee table in front of a sofa and sat on the sofa. "Come over here, you odd little man," she said. Mr. Martin went over and sat beside her. It was difficult getting a cigarette out of the pack of Camels, but he managed it. She held a match for him, laughing. "Well," she said, handing him his drink, "this is perfectly marvelous. You with a drink and a cigarette."

Mr. Martin puffed, not too awkwardly, and took a gulp of the highball. "I drink and smoke all the time," he said. He clinked his glass against hers. "Here's nuts to that old windbag, Fitweiler," he said, and gulped again. The stuff tasted awful, but he made no grimace. "Really, Mr. Martin," she said, her voice and posture changing, "you're insulting our employer." Mrs. Barrows was now all special adviser to the president. "I am preparing a bomb," said Mr. Martin, "which will blow the old goat higher than hell." He had only had a little of the drink, which was not strong. It couldn't be that. "Do you take dope or something?" Mrs. Barrows asked coldly. "Heroin," said Mr. Martin. "I'll be coked to the gills when I bump that old buzzard off." "Mr. Martin!" she shouted, getting to her feet. "That will be all of that. You must go at once." Mr. Martin took another swallow of his drink. He tapped his cigarette out in the ashtray and put the pack of Camels on the coffee table. Then he got up. She stood glaring at him. He walked over and put on his hat and coat. "Not a word about this," he said, and laid an index finger against his lips. All Mrs. Barrows could bring out was "Really!" Mr. Martin put his hand on the doorknob. "I'm sitting in the catbird seat," he said. He stuck his tongue out at her and left. Nobody saw him go.

Mr. Martin got to his apartment, walking, well before eleven. No one saw him go in. He had two glasses of milk after brushing his teeth, and he felt elated. It wasn't tipsiness, because he hadn't been tipsy. Anyway, the walk had worn off all effects of the whiskey. He got in bed and read a magazine for a while. He was asleep before midnight.

Mr. Martin got to the office at eight-thirty the next morning, as usual. At a quarter to nine, Ulgine Barrows, who had never before arrived at work before ten, swept into his office. "I'm reporting to Mr. Fitweiler now!" she shouted. "If he turns you over to the police, it's no more than you deserve!" Mr. Martin gave her a look of shocked surprise. "I beg your pardon?" he said. Mrs. Barrows snorted and bounced out of the room, leaving Miss Paird and Joey Hart staring after her. "What's the matter with that old devil now?" asked Miss Paird. "I have no idea," said Mr. Martin, resuming his work. The other two looked at him and then at each other. Miss Paird got up and went out. She walked slowly past the closed door of Mr. Fitweiler's office. Mrs. Barrows was yelling inside, but she was not braying. Miss Paird could not hear what the woman was saying. She went back to her desk.

Forty-five minutes later, Mrs. Barrows left the president's office and went into her own, shutting the door. It wasn't until half an hour later that Mr. Fitweiler sent for Mr. Martin. The head of the filing department, neat, quiet, attentive, stood in front of the old man's desk. Mr. Fitweiler was pale and nervous. He took his glasses off and twiddled them. He made a small, bruffing sound in his throat. "Martin," he said, "you have been with us more than twenty years." "Twenty-two, sir," said Mr. Martin. "In that time," pursued the president, "your work and your—uh—manner have been exemplary." "I trust so, sir," said Mr. Martin. "I have understood, Martin," said Mr. Fitweiler, "that you have never taken a drink or smoked." "That is correct, sir," said Mr. Martin. "Ah, yes." Mr. Fitweiler polished his glasses. "You may describe what you did after leaving the office yesterday, Martin," he said. Mr. Martin allowed less than a second for his bewildered pause. "Certainly, sir," he said. "I walked home. Then I went to Schrafft's for dinner. Afterwards I walked home again. I went to bed early, sir, and read a magazine for a while. I was asleep before eleven." "Ah, yes," said Mr. Fitweiler again. He was silent for a moment, searching for the proper words to say to the head of the filing department. "Mrs. Barrows," he said finally, "Mrs. Barrows had worked hard, Martin, very hard. It grieves me to report that she has suffered a severe breakdown. It has taken the form of a persecution complex accompanied by distressing hallucinations." "I am very sorry, sir," said Mr. Martin. "Mrs. Barrows is under the delusion," continued Mr. Fitweiler, "that you visited her last evening and behaved yourself in an—uh—unseemly manner." He raised his hand to silence Mr. Martin's little pained outcry. "It is the nature of these psychological diseases," Mr. Fitweiler said, "to fix upon the least likely and most innocent party as the—uh—source of persecution. These matters are not for the lay mind to grasp, Martin. I've just had my psychiatrist, Dr. Fitch, on the phone. He would not, of course, commit himself, but he made enough generalizations to substantiate my suspicions. I suggested to Mrs. Barrows when she had completed her—uh—story to me this morning, that she visit Dr. Fitch, for I suspected a condition at once. She flew, I regret to say, into a rage, and demanded—uh—requested that I call you on the carpet. You may not know, Martin, but Mrs. Barrows had planned a reorganization of your department—subject to my approval, of course, subject to my approval. This brought you, rather than anyone else, to her mind—but again that is a phenomenon for Dr. Fitch and not for us. So, Martin, I am afraid Mrs. Barrows' usefulness here is at an end."

"I am dreadfully sorry, sir," said Mr. Martin.

It was at this point that the door to the office blew open with the suddenness of a gas-main explosion and Mrs. Barrows catapulted through it. "Is the little rat denying it?" she screamed. "He can't get away with that!" Mr. Martin got up and moved discreetly to a point beside Mr. Fitweiler's chair. "You drank and smoked at my apartment," she bawled at Mr. Martin, "and you know it! You called Mr. Fitweiler an old windbag and said you were going to blow him up when you got coked to the gills on your heroin!" She stopped yelling to catch her breath and a new glint came into her popping eyes. "If you weren't such a drab, ordinary little man," she said, "I'd think you'd planned it all. Sticking your tongue out, saying you were sitting in the catbird seat, because you thought no one would believe me when I told it! My God, it's really too perfect!" She brayed loudly and hysterically, and the fury was on her again. She glared at Mr. Fitweiler. "Can't you see how he has tricked us, you old fool? Can't you see his little game?" But Mr. Fitweiler had been surreptitiously pressing all the buttons under the top of his desk and employees of F & S began pouring into the room. "Stockton," said Mr. Fitweiler, "you and Fishbein will take Mrs. Barrows to her home. Mrs. Powell, you will go with them." Stockton, who had played a little football in high school, blocked Mrs. Barrows as she made for Mr. Martin. It took him and Fishbein together to force her out of the door into the hall, crowded with stenographers and office boys. She was still screaming imprecations at Mr. Martin, tangled and contradictory imprecations. The hubbub finally died out down the corridor.

"I regret that this has happened," said Mr. Fitweiler. "I shall ask you to dismiss it from your mind, Martin." "Yes, sir," said Mr. Martin, anticipating his chief's "That will be all" by moving to the door. "I will dismiss it." He went out and shut the door, and his step was light and quick in the hall. When he entered his department he had slowed down to his customary gait, and he walked quietly across the room to the W 20 file, wearing a look of studious concentration.

RECIPE FOR MURDER

C. P. DONNEL JR.
(1906–1977)

"And in each of these dishes I concealed a bit of—" . . .

Cornelius Philip Donnel was a professional writer who began his career as a police reporter. As was commonplace for working writers in another era, his range was wide enough to include light verse (published in the Saturday Evening Post*) as well as mystery fiction for* Black Mask *and* Argosy. *His only novel,* Murder-Go-Round, *was published in 1945 by David McKay.*

UST AS THE VILLA, CLAMorous with flowers, was not what he had expected, so was its owner a new quantity in his calculations. Madame Chalon, at forty, fitted no category of murderess; she was neither Cleopatra nor beldame. A Minerva of a woman, he told himself instantly, whose large liquid eyes were but a shade lighter than the cobalt blue of the Mediterranean twinkling outside the tall windows of the salon where they sat.

Not quite a Minerva, he decided on closer inspection. Her cheeks had the peach bloom of eighteen, and she was of a roundness, a smoothness, a desirability that rendered her, if less regal, infinitely more interesting. An ungraceful woman of her weight might be considered as journeying toward stoutness, but with Madame Chalon, he knew by instinct, the body was static with regard to weight and outline, and she would be at sixty what she was this day, neither more nor less.

"Dubonnet, Inspector Miron?" As he spoke she prepared to pour. His reflex of hesitation lit a dim glow of amusement in her eyes, which her manners prevented from straying to her lips.

"Thank you." Annoyed with himself, he spoke forcefully.

Madame Chalon made a small, barely perceptible point of drinking first, as though to say, *See, M. Miron, you are quite safe.* It was neat. Too neat?

With a tiny smile now: "You have called about my poisoning of my husbands," she stated flatly.

"Madame!" Again he hesitated, nonplused. "Madame, I . . ."

"You must already have visited the Prefecture. All Villefranche believes it," she said placidly.

He adjusted his composure to an official calm. "Madame, I come to ask your permission to disinter the body of M. Charles Wesser, deceased January 1939, and M. Etienne Chalon, deceased May 1946, for official analysis of certain organs. You have already refused Sergeant Luchaire of the local station this permission. Why?"

"Luchaire is a type without politeness. I found him repulsive. He is, unlike you, without finesse. I refused the attitude of the man, not the law." She raised the small glass to her full lips. "I shall not refuse you, Inspector Miron." Her eyes were almost admiring.

"You are most flattering."

"Because," she continued gently, "I am quite sure, knowing the methods of you Paris police, that the disinterment has already been conducted secretly." She waited for his color to deepen, affecting not to notice the change. "And the analyses," she went on, as though there had been no break, "completed. You are puzzled. You found nothing. So now you, new to the case, wish to estimate me, my character, my capacity for self-control—and incidentally your own chances for maneuvering me into talk that will guide you in the direction of my guilt."

So accurately did these darts strike home that it would be the ultimate stupidity to deny the wounds. Better a disarming frankness, Miron decided quickly. "Quite true, Madame Chalon. True to the letter. But"—he regarded her closely—"when one loses two husbands of some age—but not old—to a fairly violent gastric disturbance, each within two years of marriage, each of a substantial fortune and leaving all to the widow . . . You see . . .?"

"Of course." Madame Chalon went to the window, let her soft profile, the grand line of her bosom, be silhouetted against the blue water. "Would you care for a full confession, Inspector Miron?" She was very much woman, provocative woman, and her tone, just short of caressing, warned Miron to keep a grip on himself.

"If you would care to make one, Madame Chalon," he said, as casually as he could. A dangerous woman.

"Then I shall oblige." Madame Chalon was not smiling. Through the open window a vagrant whiff of air brought him the scent of her. Or was it the scent of the garden? Caution kept his hand from his notebook. Impossible that she would really talk so easily. And yet . . .

"You know something of the art of food, M. Miron?"

"I am from Paris, you remember."

"And love, too?"

"As I said, I am from Paris."

"Then"—the bosom swelled from her long breath—"I can tell you that I, Hortense Eugénie Villerois Wesser Chalon, did slowly and deliberately, with full purpose, kill and murder my first husband, M. Wesser, aged fifty-seven, and likewise my second, M. Chalon, aged sixty-five."

"For some reason, no doubt." Was this a dream? Or insanity?

"M. Wesser I married through persuasion of family. I was no longer a girl. M. Wesser, I learned within a fortnight, was a pig—a pig of insatiable appetites. A crude man, Inspector; a belcher, a braggart, cheater of the poor, deceiver of the innocent. A gobbler of food, an untidy man of unappetizing habits—in short, with all the revolting faults of advancing age and none of its tenderness or dignity. Also, because of these things, his stomach was no longer strong."

Having gone thoroughly into the matter of M. Wesser in Paris and obtained much the same picture, Inspector Miron nodded. "And M. Chalon?"

"Older—as I was older when I wed him."

With mild irony, "And also with a weak stomach?"

"No doubt. Say, rather, a weak will. Perhaps less brutish than Wesser. Perhaps, *au fond,* worse, for he knew too many among the Germans here. Why did they take pains to see that we had the very best, the most unobtainable of foods and wines, when, daily, children fainted in the street? Murderess I may be, Inspector, but also a French-woman. So I decided without remorse that Chalon should die, as Wesser died."

Very quietly, not to disturb the thread. "How, Madame Chalon?"

She turned, her face illumined by a smile. "You are familiar, perhaps, with such dishes as *Dindonneau Forci aux Marrons*? Or *Supremes de Volaille à l'Indienne*? Or *Tournedos Mascotte*? Or *Omelette en Surprise à la Napolitaine*? Or *Potage Bagration Gras, Aubergines à la Turcque, Chaud-Froid de Cailles en Belle Vue,* or . . .?"

"Stop, Madame Chalon! I am simultaneously ravenous and smothering in food. Such richness of food!"

"You asked my method, Inspector Miron. I used these dishes, and a hundred others. And in each of these dishes I concealed a bit of—" Her voice broke suddenly.

Inspector Miron, by a mighty effort, steadied his hand as he finished his Dubonnet. "You concealed a bit of what, Madame Chalon?"

"You have investigated me. You know who was my father."

"Jean-Marie Villerois, chef superb, matchless disciple of the matchless Escoffier. Once called Escoffier's sole worthy successor."

"Yes. And before I was twenty-two, my father—just before his death—admitted that outside of a certain negligible weakness in the matter of braising he would not be ashamed to own me as his equal."

"Most interesting. I bow to you." Miron's nerves tightened at this handsome woman's faculty for irrelevancy. "But you said you concealed in each of these dishes a bit of . . .?"

Madame Chalon turned her back to him. Fine shoulders, he noted; a waist not to be ignored; hips that delighted. She addressed the sea: "A bit of my art, and no more. That and no more, Inspector. The art of Escoffier, or Villerois. What man like Wesser or Chalon could resist? Three, four times a day I fed them rich food of the richest; varied, irresistible. I tempted them to gorge to bursting, sleep, gorge again; and drink too much wine that they might gorge still more. How could they, at their ages, live—even as long as they did?"

A silence like the ticking of a far-off clock. "And love, Madame Chalon? Forgive me, but it was you who mentioned it."

"Rich food breeds love—or the semblance of it. What they called love, Inspector. They had me. Nor did I discourage them having also some little friends. And so they died—M. Wesser, aged fifty-seven, M. Chalon, aged sixty-five. That is all."

Another silence, one that hummed. Inspector Miron stood up so abruptly that she started, whirled. She was paler.

"You will come with me to Nice this evening, Madame Chalon."

"To the police station, Inspector Miron?"

"To the Casino, Madame Chalon. For champagne and music. We shall talk some more."

"But Inspector Miron . . .!"

"Listen to me, Madame. I am a bachelor. Of forty-four. Not too bad to look at, I have been told. I have a sum put away. I am not a great catch, but still, not one to be despised." He looked into her eyes. "I wish to die."

He straightened his shoulders, set his figure at its best as Madame Chalon's eloquent eyes roamed over him in the frankest of frank appraisals.

"The diets," said Madame Chalon finally and thoughtfully, "if used in moderation, are not necessarily fatal. Would you care to kiss my hand, Inspector Miron?"

THE NINE MILE WALK

HARRY KEMELMAN
(1908–1996)

Kemelman's first Nicky Welt story, collected here, was selected as one of the best first mysteries of the year when it was published in Ellery Queen's Mystery Magazine, *but it is unlikely that the eight stories about the arrogant but seemingly infallible English professor would have been collected in book form if the author hadn't ultimately created Rabbi David Small, whose first book,* Friday the Rabbi Slept Late *(1964), became an instant best-seller.*

HAD MADE AN ASS OF MYSELF in a speech I had given at the Good Government Association dinner, and Nicky Welt had cornered me at breakfast at the Blue Moon, where we both ate occasionally, for the pleasure of rubbing it in. I had made the mistake of departing from my prepared speech to criticize a statement my predecessor in the office of county attorney had made to the press. I had drawn a number of inferences from his statement and had thus left myself open to a rebuttal, which he had promptly made and which had the effect of making me appear intellectually dishonest. I was new to this political game, having but a few months before left the law school faculty to become the Reform party candidate for county attorney. I said as much in extenuation, but Nicholas Welt, who could never drop his pedagogical manner (he was Snowdon Professor of English Language and Literature), replied in much the same tone that he would dismiss a request from a sophomore for an extension on a term paper, "That's no excuse."

Although he is only two or three years older than I, in his late forties, he always treats me like a schoolmaster hectoring a stupid pupil. And I, perhaps because he looks so much older with his white hair and lined, gnome-like face, suffer it.

"They were perfectly logical inferences," I pleaded.

"My dear boy," he purred, "although human intercourse is well-nigh impossible without inference, most inferences are usually wrong. The percentage of error is particularly high in the legal profession, where the intention is not to discover what the speaker wishes to convey, but rather what he wishes to conceal."

I picked up my check and eased out from behind the table.

"I suppose you are referring to cross-examination of witnesses in court. Well, there's always an opposing counsel who will object if the inference is illogical."

"Who said anything about logic?" he retorted. "An inference can be logical and still not be true."

He followed me down the aisle to the cashier's booth. I paid my check and waited impatiently while he searched in an old-fashioned change purse, fishing out coins one by one and placing them on the counter beside his check, only to discover that the total was insufficient. He slid them back into his purse and with a tiny sigh extracted a bill from another compartment of the purse and handed it to the cashier.

"Give me any sentence of ten or twelve words," he said, "and I'll build you a logical chain of inferences that you never dreamed of when you framed the sentence."

Other customers were coming in, and since the space in front of the cashier's booth was small, I decided to wait outside until Nicky completed his transaction with the cashier. I remember being mildly amused at the idea that he probably thought I was still at his elbow and was going right ahead with his discourse.

When he joined me on the sidewalk I said, "A nine mile walk is no joke, especially in the rain."

"No, I shouldn't think it would be," he agreed absently. Then he stopped in his stride and looked at me sharply. "What the devil are you talking about?"

"It's a sentence and it has eleven words," I insisted. And I repeated the sentence, ticking off the words on my fingers.

"What about it?"

"You said that given a sentence of ten or twelve words—"

"Oh, yes." He looked at me suspiciously. "Where did you get it?"

"It just popped into my head. Come on now, build your inferences."

"You're serious about this?" he asked, his little blue eyes glittering with amusement. "You really want me to?"

It was just like him to issue a challenge and then to appear amused when I accepted it. And it made me angry.

"Put up or shut up," I said.

"All right," he said mildly. "No need to be huffy. I'll play. Hm-m, let me see, how did the sentence go? 'A nine mile walk is no joke, especially in the rain.' Not much to go on there."

"It's more than ten words," I rejoined.

"Very well." His voice became crisp as he mentally squared off to the problem. "First inference: the speaker is aggrieved."

"I'll grant that," I said, "although it hardly seems to be an inference. It's really implicit in the statement."

He nodded impatiently. "Next inference: the rain was unforeseen, otherwise he would have said, 'A nine mile walk in the rain is no joke,' instead of using the 'especially' phrase as an afterthought."

"I'll allow that," I said, "although it's pretty obvious."

"First inferences should be obvious," said Nicky tartly.

I let it go at that. He seemed to be floundering and I didn't want to rub it in.

"Next inference: the speaker is not an athlete or an outdoorsman."

"You'll have to explain that one," I said.

"It's the 'especially' phrase again," he said. "The speaker does not say that a nine mile walk in the rain is no joke, but merely the walk—just the distance, mind you— is no joke. Now, nine miles is not such a terribly long distance. You walk more than half that in eighteen holes of golf—and golf is an old man's game," he added slyly. *I play golf.*

"Well, that would be all right under ordinary circumstances," I said, "but there are other possibilities. The speaker might be a soldier in the jungle, in which case nine miles would be a pretty good hike, rain or no rain."

"Yes," and Nicky was sarcastic, "and the speaker might be one-legged. For that matter, the speaker might be a graduate student writing a Ph.D. thesis on humor and starting by listing all the things that are not funny. See here, I'll have to make a couple of assumptions before I continue."

"How do you mean?" I asked, suspiciously.

"Remember, I'm taking this sentence *in vacuo,* as it were. I don't know who said it or what the occasion was. Normally a sentence belongs in the framework of a situation."

"I see. What assumptions do you want to make?"

"For one thing, I want to assume that the intention was not frivolous, that the speaker is referring to a walk that was actually taken, and that the purpose of the walk was not to win a bet or something of that sort."

"That seems reasonable enough," I said.

"And I also want to assume that the locale of the walk is here."

"You mean here in Fairfield?"

"Not necessarily. I mean in this general section of the country."

"Fair enough."

"Then, if you grant those assumptions, you'll have to accept my last inference that the speaker is no athlete or outdoorsman."

"Well, all right, go on."

"Then my next inference is that the walk was taken very late at night or very early in the morning—say, between midnight and five or six in the morning."

"How do you figure that one?" I asked.

"Consider the distance, nine miles. We're in a fairly well-populated section. Take any road and you'll find a community of some sort in less than nine miles. Hadley is five miles away, Hadley Falls is seven and a half, Goreton is eleven, but East Goreton is only eight and you strike East Goreton before you come to Goreton. There is a local train service along the Goreton road and bus service along the others. All the highways are pretty well traveled. Would anyone have to walk nine miles in a rain unless it were late at night when no buses or trains were running and when the few automobiles that were out would hesitate to pick up a stranger on the highway?"

"He might not have wanted to be seen," I suggested.

Nicky smiled pityingly. "You think he would be less noticeable trudging along the highway than he would be riding in a public conveyance where everyone is usually absorbed in his newspaper?"

"Well, I won't press the point," I said brusquely.

"Then try this one: he was walking toward a town rather than away from one."

I nodded. "It is more likely, I suppose. If he were in a town, he could probably arrange for some sort of transportation. Is that the basis for your inference?"

"Partly that," said Nicky, "but there is also an inference to be drawn from the distance. Remember, it's a *nine* mile walk and nine is one of the exact numbers."

"I'm afraid I don't understand."

That exasperated schoolteacher-look appeared on Nicky's face again. "Suppose you say, 'I took a ten mile walk' or 'a hundred mile drive'; I would assume that you actually walked anywhere from eight to a dozen miles, or that you rode between ninety and a hundred and ten miles. In other words, *ten* and *hundred* are round numbers. You might have walked *exactly* ten miles or just as likely you might have walked *approximately* ten miles. But when you speak of walking *nine* miles, I have a right to assume that you have named an exact figure. Now, we are far more likely to know the distance of the city from a given point than we are to know the distance of a given point from the city. That is, ask anyone in the city how far out Farmer Brown lives, and if he knows him, he will say, 'Three or four miles.' But ask Farmer Brown how far he lives from the city and he will tell you, 'Three and six-tenths miles—measured it on my speedometer many a time."

"It's weak, Nicky," I said.

"But in conjunction with your own suggestion that he could have arranged transportation if he had been in a city—"

"Yes, that would do it," I said. "I'll pass it. Any more?"

"I've just begun to hit my stride," he boasted. "My next inference is that he was going to a definite destination and that he had to be there at a particular time. It was not a case of going off to get help because his car broke down or his wife was going to have a baby or somebody was trying to break into his house."

"Oh, come now," I said, "the car breaking down is really the most likely situation. He could have known the exact distance from having checked the mileage just as he was leaving the town."

Nicky shook his head. "Rather than walk nine miles in the rain, he would have curled up on the backseat and gone to sleep, or at least stayed by his car and tried to flag another motorist. Remember, it's nine miles. What would be the least it would take him to hike it?"

"Four hours," I offered.

He nodded. "Certainly no less, considering the rain. We've agreed that it happened very late at night or very early in the morning. Suppose he had his breakdown at one o'clock in the morning. It would be five o'clock before he would arrive. That's daybreak. You begin to see a lot of cars on the road. The buses start just a little later. In fact, the first buses hit Fairfield around five-thirty. Besides, if he were going for help, he would not have to go all the way to town—only as far as the nearest telephone. No, he had a definite appointment, and it was in a town, and it was for some time before five-thirty."

"Then why couldn't he have got there earlier and waited?" I asked. "He could have taken the last bus, arrived around one o'clock, and waited until his appointment. He walks nine miles in the rain instead, and you said he was no athlete."

We had arrived at the Municipal Building, where my office is. Normally, any arguments begun at the Blue Moon ended at the entrance to the Municipal Building. But I was interested in Nicky's demonstration and I suggested that he come up for a few minutes.

When we were seated I said, "How about it, Nicky, why couldn't he have arrived early and waited?"

"He could have," Nicky retorted. "But since he did not, we must assume that he was either detained until after the last bus left, or that he had to wait where he was for a signal of some sort, perhaps a telephone call."

"Then according to you, he had an appointment some time between midnight and five-thirty—"

"We can draw it much finer than that. Remember, it takes him four hours to walk the distance. The last bus stops at twelve-thirty A.M. If he doesn't take that, but starts at the same time, he won't arrive at his destination until four-thirty. On the other hand, if he takes the first bus in the morning, he will arrive around five-thirty. That would mean that his appointment was for some time between four-thirty and five-thirty."

"You mean that if his appointment was earlier than four-thirty, he would have taken the last night bus, and if it was later than five-thirty, he would have taken the first morning bus?"

"Precisely. And another thing: if he was waiting for a signal or a phone call, it must have come not much later than one o'clock."

"Yes, I see that," I said. "If his appointment is around five o'clock and it takes him four hours to walk the distance, he'd have to start around one."

He nodded, silent and thoughtful. For some queer reason I could not explain, I did not feel like interrupting his thoughts. On the wall was a large map of the county and I walked over to it and began to study it.

"You're right, Nicky," I remarked over my shoulder, "there's no place as far as nine miles away from Fairfield that doesn't hit another town first. Fairfield is right in the middle of a bunch of smaller towns."

He joined me at the map. "It doesn't have to be Fairfield, you know," he said quietly. "It was probably one of the outlying towns he had to reach. Try Hadley."

"Why Hadley? What would anyone want in Hadley at five o'clock in the morning?"

"The Washington Flyer stops there to take on water about that time," he said quietly.

"That's right, too," I said. "I've heard that train many a night when I couldn't sleep. I'd hear it pulling in and then a minute or two later I'd hear the clock on the Methodist Church banging out five." I went back to my desk for a timetable. "The Flyer leaves Washington at twelve forty-seven A.M. and gets into Boston at eight A.M."

Nicky was still at the map measuring distances with a pencil.

"Exactly nine miles from Hadley is the Old Sumter Inn," he announced.

"Old Sumter Inn," I echoed. "But that upsets the whole theory. You can arrange for transportation there as easily as you can in a town."

He shook his head. "The cars are kept in an enclosure and you have to get an attendant to check you through the gate. The attendant would remember anyone taking out his car at a strange hour. It's a pretty conservative place. He could have waited in his room until he got a call from Washington about someone on the Flyer—maybe the number of the car and the berth. Then he could just slip out of the hotel and walk to Hadley."

I stared at him, hypnotized.

"It wouldn't be difficult to slip aboard while the train was taking on water, and then if he knew the car number and the berth—"

"Nicky," I said portentously, "as the Reform District Attorney who campaigned on an economy program, I am going to waste the taxpayers' money and call Boston long distance. It's ridiculous, it's insane—but I'm going to do it!"

His little blue eyes glittered and he moistened his lips with the tip of his tongue.

"Go ahead," he said hoarsely.

I replaced the telephone in its cradle.

"Nicky," I said, "this is probably the most remarkable coincidence in the history of criminal investigation: *a man was found murdered in his berth on last night's twelve-forty-seven from Washington!* He'd been dead about three hours, which would make it exactly right for Hadley."

"I thought it was something like that," said Nicky. "But you're wrong about its being a coincidence. It can't be. Where did you get that sentence?"

"It was just a sentence. It simply popped into my head."

"It couldn't have! It's not the sort of sentence that pops into one's head. If you had taught composition as long as I have, you'd know that when you ask someone for a sentence of ten words or so, you get an ordinary statement such as 'I like milk'—with the other words made up by a modifying clause like, 'because it is good for my health.' The sentence you offered related to a *particular situation.*"

"But I tell you I talked to no one this morning. And I was alone with you at the Blue Moon."

"You weren't with me all the time I paid my check," he said sharply. "Did you meet anyone while you were waiting on the sidewalk for me to come out of the Blue Moon?"

I shook my head. "I was outside for less than a minute before you joined me. You see, a couple of men came in while you were digging out your change and one of them bumped me, so I thought I'd wait—"

"Did you ever see them before?"

"Who?"

"The two men who came in," he said, the note of exasperation creeping into his voice again.

"Why no—they weren't anyone I knew."

"Were they talking?"

"I guess so. Yes, they were. Quite absorbed in their conversation, as a matter of fact—otherwise, they would have noticed me and I would not have been bumped."

"Not many strangers come into the Blue Moon," he remarked.

"Do you think it was they?" I asked eagerly. "I think I'd know them again if I saw them."

Nicky's eyes narrowed. "It's possible. There had to be two—one to trail the victim in Washington and ascertain his berth number, the other to wait here and do the job. The Washington man would be likely to come down here afterward. If there was theft as well as murder, it would be to divide the spoils. If it was just murder, he would probably have to come down to pay off his confederate."

I reached for the telephone.

"We've been gone less than half an hour," Nicky went on. "They were just coming in and service is slow at the Blue Moon. The one who walked all the way to Hadley must certainly be hungry and the other probably drove all night from Washington."

"Call me immediately if you make an arrest," I said into the phone and hung up.

Neither of us spoke a word while we waited. We paced the floor, avoiding each other almost as though we had done something we were ashamed of.

The telephone rang at last. I picked it up and listened. Then I said, "Okay," and turned to Nicky.

"One of them tried to escape through the kitchen but Winn had someone stationed at the back and they got him."

"That would seem to prove it," said Nicky with a frosty little smile.

I nodded agreement.

He glanced at his watch. "Gracious," he exclaimed, "I wanted to make an early start on my work this morning, and here I've already wasted all this time talking with you."

I let him get to the door. "Oh, Nicky," I called, "what was it you set out to prove?"

"That a chain of inferences could be logical and still not be true," he said.

"Oh."

"What are you laughing at?" he asked snappishly. And then he laughed too.

KILL OR BE KILLED

Brander Gillis had nothing to fear from man or devil . . .

OGDEN NASH
(1902–1971)

A author of unquestionably the funniest light verse produced in this century, Ogden Nash had a catholic range of interests which included Sherlock Holmes and all of mystery fiction. He fills a warm corner of many hearts for having written this assessment of one of the most popular detectives of another era: "Philo Vance/Needs a kick in the pance."

 ATURALLY IT NEVER OCCURRED to lawyer Brander Gillis that sudden death would be his either to give or to receive.

He was not a shyster, but a professional man of open mind who presumed his clients to be innocent until after the acquittal; not a usurer, but a friend of man, always willing to rent part of his hard-earned money to the needy for what it might be worth to them; not a blackmailer, but a discreet and reasonable trustee of distressing information. In his home he was neither a miser nor a tyrant, but an unswervable advocate of economy and discipline, two virtues the lack of which had deposited so many deplorable examples in the hard chair facing the light in his modest offices.

There was not an ounce of jealousy in his body—as indeed why should there be? The wistful light that glowed in the eyes of his wife when they dared glance at each other was easily extinguished by a mere twist of the wrist, the slightest pressure of the thumb on the nerve center.

And if his wife's sister occasionally gave him a look that no one could like, it did not affect her efficiency as cook-housekeeper or her devotion to that strange girl child of hers with the thick lenses and the thick speech, that child who, as he was careful to remark with commendable frankness when the roast beef was overdone, would perhaps be far better fed in an institution.

As for Burger—soft-footed Burger— butler, chauffeur, handyman, door mat, he knew which side his bread was buttered on, as well as which side of stone walls he wanted to eat it on. No, Brander Gillis had nothing to fear from man or devil, and his thoughts did not often turn to God.

Why, then, on one particular weekend did this good man with nothing to fear remove the bed of his unprotesting wife to a guest room and take pains to lock himself in alone each night? Why was he careful never to turn his back to her? Why did he wait, spoon poised, to taste his soup until his sister-in-law had first swallowed hers? Why

313

did he continually flick Burger into cringing hysteria with one sharp, almost inaudible phrase?

Perhaps the episode of the roller skate had disturbed him, though it was plainly attributable to the slovenliness of a backward child. But his fall after stepping on the skate at the top of the stairs had been a severe one, aggravating the pain he still felt from his previous fall in the bathtub, a mishap he could not understand. He, who was proud of the luxurious remnants of his hair, the plump resiliency of his beloved flesh, who used nothing but the whitest of Castile, had trod on a cake of pink soap nearly invisible against pink porcelain.

Still, if accidents really come in threes, he should have nothing more to worry about, and certainly there was nothing mysterious about the other misadventure. True, he could have sworn that the car was in the driveway when he dozed off after so skillfully guiding it home from the cozy apartment of a cherished client, and it had been a surprise to awake to find himself behind the wheel in the garage with the doors closed and the motor running—but a man gets used to these discrepancies when he likes a little drink once in a while.

Perhaps his apprehension had started with the book. It was called *How to Be a Mind Reader*. The dark, ungainly child had been absorbed in it for days, so the reasonable result of the rollerskate business was the book's confiscation. Unreasonably, she had not been upset. "I know everything in it," she declared with complacence, "I can read every mind in this house. A certain someone wants to kill you, Uncle Brander.

"Someone besides me," she added reflectively.

Gillis was a hardheaded man, but that was the night he banished his wife, and the first of the nights that found him hunched over *How to Be a Mind Reader*; scoffing, then comprehending, finally believing. It was at Sunday supper that he suddenly looked through the smooth, uncommunicative foreheads of his wife, of his sister-in-law, of Burger the butler—and Brander Gillis knew the identity of the certain someone.

He locked himself in his room early, and because his need for the book was past he did not miss it from the bedside table. Brander Gillis sat in his chair all night, not awake, not asleep, and dreamed a dream.

It's kill or be killed, dreamed Brander Gillis, *kill or be killed.* And being a hardheaded man, he forthwith dreamed the unsuspected, the undetected, the undetectable, the perfect murder.

He was smiling when he woke and glanced at the door, well bolted, honestly locked. *Let me just run over it once to make sure,* he thought. *I seem to forget some of the minor points. . . .*

"Never mind," said a hateful and familiar voice behind him. "I remember."

THE SPECIALTY
OF THE HOUSE

STANLEY ELLIN
(1916–1986)

In 1962, only fourteen years after the publication of this, the author's first short story, Anthony Boucher, the long-time mystery reviewer for The New York Times *and other publications, called him the most distinguished contemporary writer of short crime fiction in America. Another quarter century of productivity merely confirmed the statement. Based on an incident in which Ellin repeatedly ordered a steak that wasn't delivered until after his waiter vanished, this tale was wonderfully filmed for television by Alfred Hitchcock.*

ND THIS," SAID LAFFLER, "IS Sbirro's." Costain saw a square brownstone facade identical with the others that extended from either side into the clammy darkness of the deserted street. From the barred windows of the basement at his feet, a glimmer of light showed behind heavy curtains.

"Lord," he observed, "it's a dismal hole, isn't it?"

"I beg you to understand," said Laffler stiffly, "that Sbirro's is the restaurant without pretensions. Besieged by these ghastly, neurotic times, it has refused to compromise. It is perhaps the last important establishment in this city lit by gas jets. Here you will find the same honest furnishings, the same magnificent Sheffield service, and possibly, in a far corner, the very same spider webs that were remarked by the patrons of a half century ago!"

"A doubtful recommendation," said Costain, "and hardly sanitary."

"When you enter," Laffler continued, "you leave the insanity of this year, this day, and this hour, and you find yourself for a brief span restored in spirit, not by opulence, but by dignity, which is the lost quality of our time."

Costain laughed uncomfortably. "You make it sound more like a cathedral than a restaurant," he said.

In the pale reflection of the street lamp overhead, Laffler peered at his companion's face. "I wonder," he said abruptly, "whether I have not made a mistake in extending this invitation to you."

Costain was hurt. Despite an impressive title and large salary, he was no more than a clerk to this pompous little man, but he was impelled to make some display of his feelings. "If you wish," he said coldly, "I can make other plans for my evening with no trouble."

With his large, cowlike eyes turned up to Costain, the mist drifting into the ruddy, full moon of his face, Laffler seemed strangely ill at ease. Then "No, no," he said at last, "absolutely not. It's important that you dine at Sbirro's with me." He grasped Costain's arm firmly and led the way to the wrought-iron gate of the basement. "You see, you're the sole person in my office who seems to know anything at all about good food. And on my part, knowing about Sbirro's but not having some appreciative friend to share it is like having a unique piece of art locked in a room where no one else can enjoy it."

Costain was considerably mollified by this. "I understand there are a great many people who relish that situation."

"I'm not one of that kind!" Laffler said sharply. "And having the secret of Sbirro's locked in myself for years has finally become unendurable." He fumbled at the side of the gate and from within could be heard the small, discordant jangle of an ancient pull-bell. An interior door opened with a groan, and Costain found himself peering into a dark face whose only discernible feature was a row of gleaming teeth.

"Sair?" said the face.

"Mr. Laffler and a guest."

"Sair," the face said again, this time in what was clearly an invitation. It moved aside and Costain stumbled down a single step behind his host. The door and gate creaked behind him, and he stood blinking in a small foyer. It took him a moment to realize that the figure he now stared at was his own reflection in a gigantic pier glass that extended from floor to ceiling. "Atmosphere," he said under his breath and chuckled as he followed his guide to a seat.

He faced Laffler across a small table for two and peered curiously around the dining room. It was no size at all, but the half-dozen guttering gas jets which provided the only illumination threw such a deceptive light that the walls flickered and faded into uncertain distance.

There were no more than eight or ten tables about, arranged to insure the maximum privacy. All were occupied, and the few waiters serving them moved with quiet efficiency. In the air were a soft clash and scrape of cutlery and a soothing murmur of talk. Costain nodded appreciatively.

Laffler breathed an audible sigh of gratification. "I knew you would share my enthusiasm," he said. "Have you noticed, by the way, that there are no women present?"

Costain raised inquiring eyebrows.

"Sbirro," said Laffler, "does not encourage members of the fair sex to enter the premises. And, I can tell you, his method is decidedly effective. I had the experience of seeing a woman get a taste of it not long ago. She sat at a table for not less than an hour waiting for service which was never forthcoming."

"Didn't she make a scene?"

"She did." Laffler smiled at the recollection. "She succeeded in annoying the customers, embarrassing her partner, and nothing more."

"And what about Mr. Sbirro?"

"He did not make an appearance. Whether he directed affairs from behind the scenes, or was not even present during the episode, I don't know. Whichever it was, he won a complete victory. The woman never reappeared nor, for that matter, did the witless gentleman who by bringing her was really the cause of the entire contretemps."

"A fair warning to all present," laughed Costain.

A waiter now appeared at the table. The chocolate-dark skin, the thin, beautifully molded nose and lips, the large liquid eyes, heavily lashed, and the silver white hair so heavy and silken that it lay on the skull like a cap, all marked him definitely as an East Indian of some sort, Costain decided. The man arranged the stiff table linen, filled two tumblers from a huge, cut-glass pitcher, and set them in their proper places.

"Tell me," Laffler said eagerly, "is the special being served this evening?"

The waiter smiled regretfully and showed teeth as spectacular as those of the majordomo. "I am so sorry, sair. There is no special this evening."

Laffler's face fell into lines of heavy disappointment. "After waiting so long. It's been a month already, and I hoped to show my friend here . . ."

"You understand the difficulties, sair."

"Of course, of course." Laffler looked at Costain sadly and shrugged. "You see, I had in mind to introduce you to the greatest treat that Sbirro's offers, but unfortunately it isn't on the menu this evening."

The waiter said, "Do you wish to be served now, sair?" and Laffler nodded. To Costain's surprise the waiter made his way off without waiting for any instructions.

"Have you ordered in advance?" he asked.

"Ah," said Laffler, "I really should have explained. Sbirro's offers no choice whatsoever. You will eat the same meal as everyone else in this room. Tomorrow evening you would eat an entirely different meal, but again without designating a single preference."

"Very unusual," said Costain, "and certainly unsatisfactory at times. What if one doesn't have a taste for the particular dish set before him?"

"On that score," said Laffler solemnly, "you need have no fears. I give you my word that no matter how exacting your tastes, you will relish every mouthful you eat in Sbirro's."

Costain looked doubtful, and Laffler smiled. "And consider the subtle advantages of the system," he said. "When you pick up the menu of a popular restaurant, you find yourself confronted with innumerable choices. You are forced to weigh, to evaluate, to make uneasy decisions which you may instantly regret. The effect of all this is a tension which, however slight, must make for discomfort.

"And consider the mechanics of the process. Instead of a hurly-burly of sweating cooks rushing about a kitchen in a frenzy to prepare a hundred varying items, we have a chef who stands serenely alone, bringing all his talents to bear on one task, with all assurance of a complete triumph!"

"Then you have seen the kitchen?"

"Unfortunately, no," said Laffler sadly. "The picture I offer is hypothetical, made of conversational fragments I have pieced together over the years. I must admit, though, that my desire to see the functioning of the kitchen here comes very close to being my sole obsession nowadays."

"But have you mentioned this to Sbirro?"

"A dozen times. He shrugs the suggestion away."

"Isn't that a rather curious foible on his part?"

"No, no," Laffler said hastily, "a master artist is never under the compulsion of petty courtesies. Still," he sighed, "I have never given up hope."

The waiter now reappeared bearing two soup bowls which he set in place with mathematical exactitude and a small tureen from which he slowly ladled a measure of clear, thin broth. Costain dipped his spoon into the broth and tasted it with some curiosity. It was delicately flavored, bland to the verge of tastelessness. Costain frowned, tentatively reached for the salt and pepper cellars, and discovered there were none on the table. He looked up, saw Laffler's eyes on him, and although unwilling to compromise his own tastes, he hesitated to act as a damper on Laffler's enthusiasm. Therefore he smiled and indicated the broth.

"Excellent," he said.

Laffler returned his smile. "You do not find it excellent at all," he said coolly. "You find it flat and badly in need of condiments. I know this," he continued as Costain's eyebrows shot upward, "because it was my own reaction many years ago, and because like yourself I found myself reaching for salt and pepper after the first mouthful. I also learned with surprise that condiments are not available in Sbirro's."

Costain was shocked. "Not even salt!" he exclaimed.

"Not even salt. The very fact that you require it for your soup stands as evidence that your taste is unduly jaded. I am confident that you will now make the same discovery that I did: by the time you have nearly finished your soup, your desire for salt will be nonexistent."

Laffler was right; before Costain had reached the bottom of his plate, he was relishing the nuances of the broth with steadily increasing delight. Laffler thrust aside his own empty bowl and rested his elbows on the table. "Do you agree with me now?"

"To my surprise," said Costain, "I do."

As the waiter busied himself clearing the table, Laffler lowered his voice significantly. "You will find," he said, "that the absence of condiments is but one of several noteworthy characteristics which mark Sbirro's. I may as well prepare you for these. For example, no alcoholic beverages of any sort are served here, nor for that matter any beverage except clear, cold water, the first and only drink necessary for a human being."

"Outside of mother's milk," suggested Costain dryly.

"I can answer that in like vein by pointing out that the average patron of Sbirro's has passed that primal stage of his development."

Costain laughed. "Granted," he said.

"Very well. There is also a ban on the use of tobacco in any form."

"But, good heavens," said Costain, "doesn't that make Sbirro's more a teetotaler's retreat than a gourmet's sanctuary?"

"I fear," said Laffler solemnly, "that you confuse the words *gourmet* and *gourmand.* The gourmand, through glutting himself, requires a wider and wider latitude of experience to stir his surfeited senses, but the very nature of the gourmet is simplicity. The ancient Greek in his coarse chiton savoring the ripe olive; the Japanese in his bare room contemplating the curves of a single flower stem—these are the true gourmets."

"But an occasional drop of brandy or pipeful of tobacco," said Costain dubiously, "are hardly overindulgence."

"By alternating stimulant and narcotic," said Laffler, "you see-saw the delicate balance of your taste so violently that it loses its most precious quality: the appreciation of fine food. During my years as a patron of Sbirro's, I have proved this to my satisfaction."

"May I ask," said Costain, "why you regard the ban on these things as having such deep esthetic motives? What about such mundane reasons as the high cost of a liquor license, or the possibility that patrons would object to the smell of tobacco in such confined quarters?"

Laffler shook his head violently. "If and when you meet Sbirro," he said, "you will understand at once that he is not the man to make decisions on a mundane basis. As a matter of fact, it was Sbirro himself who first made me cognizant of what you call 'esthetic' motives."

"An amazing man," said Costain as the waiter prepared to serve the entree.

Laffler's next words were not spoken until he had savored and swallowed a large portion of meat. "I hesitate to use superlatives," he said, "but to my way of thinking, Sbirro represents man at the apex of his civilization!"

Costain cocked an eyebrow and applied himself to his roast which rested in a pool of stiff gravy ungarnished by green or vegetable. The thin steam rising from it carried to his nostrils a subtle, tantalizing odor which made his mouth water. He chewed a piece slowly and thoughtfully as if he were analyzing the intricacies of a Mozart symphony. The range of taste he discovered was really extraordinary, from the pungent nip of the crisp outer edge to the peculiarly flat, yet soul-satisfying ooze of blood which the pressure of his jaws forced from the half-raw interior.

Upon swallowing he found himself ferociously hungry for another piece, and then another, and it was only with an effort that he prevented himself from wolfing down all his share of the meat and gravy without waiting to get the full voluptuous satisfaction from each mouthful. When he had scraped his platter clean, he realized that both he and Laffler had completed the entire course without exchanging a single word. He commented on this, and Laffler said, "Can you see any need for words in the presence of such food?"

Costain looked around at the shabby, dimly lit room, the quiet diners, with a new perception. "No," he said humbly, "I cannot. For any doubts I had I apologize unreservedly. In all your praise of Sbirro's there was not a single word of exaggeration."

"Ah," said Laffler delightedly. "And that is only part of the story. You heard me mention the special which unfortunately was not on the menu tonight. What you have just eaten is as nothing when compared to the absolute delights of that special!"

"Good Lord!" cried Costain. "What is it? Nightingale's tongues? Filet of unicorn?"

"Neither," said Laffler. "It is lamb."

"Lamb?"

Laffler remained lost in thought for a minute. "If," he said at last, "I were to give you in my own unstinted words my opinion of this dish, you would judge me completely insane. That is how deeply the mere thought of it affects me. It is neither the fatty chop, nor the too solid leg; it is, instead, a select portion of the rarest sheep in existence and is named after the species—lamb Amirstan."

Costain knit his brow. "Amirstan?"

"A fragment of desolation almost lost on the border which separates Afghanistan and Russia. From chance remarks dropped by Sbirro, I gather it is no more than a plateau which grazes the pitiful remnants of a flock of superb sheep. Sbirro, through some means or other, obtained rights to the traffic in this flock and is, therefore, the sole restaurateur ever to have lamb Amirstan on his bill of fare. I can tell you that the appearance of this dish is a rare occurrence indeed, and luck is the only guide in determining for the clientele the exact date when it will be served."

"But surely," said Costain, "Sbirro could provide some advance knowledge of this event."

"The objection to that is simply stated," said Laffler. "There exists in this city a huge number of professional gluttons. Should advance information slip out, it is quite likely that they will, out of curiosity, become familiar with the dish and thenceforth supplant the regular patrons at these tables."

"But you don't mean to say," objected Costain, "that these few people present are the only ones in the entire city, or for that matter, in the whole wide world, who know of the existence of Sbirro's!"

"Very nearly. There may be one or two regular patrons who, for some reason, are not present at the moment."

"That's incredible."

"It is done," said Laffler, the slightest shade of menace in his voice, "by every patron making it his solemn obligation to keep the secret. By accepting my invitation this evening you automatically assume that obligation. I hope you can be trusted with it."

Costain flushed. "My position in your employ should vouch for me. I only question the wisdom of a policy which keeps such magnificent food away from so many who would enjoy it."

"Do you know the inevitable result of the policy *you* favor?" asked Laffler bitterly. "An influx of idiots who would nightly complain that they are never served roast duck with chocolate sauce. Is that picture tolerable to you?"

"No," admitted Costain, "I am forced to agree with you."

Laffler leaned back in his chair wearily and passed his hand over his eyes in an uncertain gesture. "I am a solitary man," he said quietly, "and not by choice alone. It may sound strange to you, it may border on eccentricity, but I feel to my depths that this restaurant, this warm haven in a coldly insane world, is both family and friend to me."

And Costain, who to this moment had never viewed his companion as other than tyrannical employer or officious host, now felt an overwhelming pity twist inside his comfortably expanded stomach.

By the end of two weeks the invitations to join Laffler at Sbirro's had become something of a ritual. Every day, at a few minutes after five, Costain would step out into the office corridor and lock his cubicle behind him; he would drape his overcoat neatly over his left arm, and peer into the glass of the door to make sure his Homburg was set at the proper angle. At one time he would have followed this by lighting a cigarette, but under Laffler's prodding he had decided to give abstinence a fair trial. Then he would start down the corridor, and Laffler would fall in step at his elbow, clearing his throat. "Ah, Costain. No plans for this evening, I hope."

"No," Costain would say, "I'm footloose and fancy-free," or "At your service," or something equally inane. He wondered at times whether it would not be more tactful to vary the ritual with an occasional refusal, but the glow with which Laffler received his answer, and the rough friendliness of Laffler's grip on his arm, forestalled him.

Among the treacherous crags of the business world, reflected Costain, what better way to secure your footing than friendship with one's employer. Already, a secretary close to the workings of the inner office had commented publicly on Laffler's highly favorable opinion of Costain. That was all to the good.

And the food! The incomparable food at Sbirro's! For the first time in his life, Costain, ordinarily a lean and bony man, noted with gratification that he was certainly gaining weight; within two weeks his bones had disappeared under a layer of sleek, firm flesh, and here and there were even signs of incipient plumpness. It struck Costain one night, while surveying himself in his bath, that the rotund Laffler, himself, might have been a spare and bony man before discovering Sbirro's.

So there was obviously everything to be gained and nothing to be lost by accepting Laffler's invitations. Perhaps after testing the heralded wonders of lamb Amirstan and meeting Sbirro, who thus far had not made an appearance, a refusal or two might be in order. But certainly not until then.

That evening, two weeks to a day after his first visit to Sbirro's, Costain had both desires fulfilled: he dined on lamb Amirstan and he met Sbirro. Both exceeded his expectations.

When the waiter leaned over their table immediately after seating them and gravely announced: "Tonight is special, sair," Costain was shocked to find his heart pounding with expectation. On the table before him he saw Laffler's hands trembling violently. But it isn't natural, he thought suddenly. Two full grown men, presumably intelligent and in the full possession of their senses, as jumpy as a pair of cats waiting to have their meal flung at them!

"This is it!" Laffler's voice startled him so that he almost leaped from his seat. "The culinary triumph of all times! And faced by it you are embarrassed by the very emotions it distills."

"How did you know that?" Costain asked faintly.

"How? Because a decade ago I underwent your embarrassment. Add to that your air of revulsion and it's easy to see how affronted you are by the knowledge that man has not yet forgotten how to slaver over his meat."

"And these others," whispered Costain, "do they all feel the same thing?"

"Judge for yourself."

Costain looked furtively around at the nearby tables. "You are right," he finally said. "At any rate, there's comfort in numbers."

Laffler inclined his head slightly to the side. "One of the numbers," he remarked, "appears to be in for a disappointment."

Costain followed the gesture. At the table indicated a gray-haired man sat conspicuously alone, and Costain frowned at the empty chair opposite him.

"Why, yes," he recalled, "that very stout, bald man, isn't it? I believe it's the first dinner he's missed here in two weeks."

"The entire decade more likely," said Laffler sympathetically. "Rain or shine, crisis or calamity, I don't think he's missed an evening at Sbirro's since the first time I dined here. Imagine his expression when he's told that, on his very first defection, lamb Amirstan was the *plat de jour*."

Costain looked at the empty chair again with a dim discomfort. "His very first?" he murmured.

"Mr. Laffler! And friend! I am so pleased. So very, very pleased. No, do not stand; I will have a place made." Miraculously a seat appeared under the figure standing there at the table. "The lamb Amirstan will be an unqualified success, hurr? I myself have been stewing in the miserable kitchen all the day, prodding the foolish chef to do everything just so. The just so is the important part, hurr? But I see your friend does not know me. An introduction, perhaps?"

The words ran in a smooth, fluid eddy. They rippled, they purred, they hypnotized Costain so that he could do no more than stare. The mouth that uncoiled this sinuous monologue was alarmingly wide, with thin mobile lips that curled and twisted with every syllable. There was a flat nose with a straggling line of hair under it; wide-set eyes, almost oriental in appearance, that glittered in the unsteady flare of gaslight; and the long, sleek hair that swept back from high on the unwrinkled forehead—hair so pale that it might have been bleached of all color. An amazing face surely, and the sight of it tortured Costain with the conviction that it was somehow familiar. His brain twitched and prodded but could not stir up any solid recollection.

Laffler's voice jerked Costain out of his study. "Mr. Sbirro. Mr. Costain, a good friend and associate." Costain rose and shook the proffered hand. It was warm and dry, flint-hard against his palm.

"I am so very pleased, Mr. Costain. So very, very pleased," purred the voice. "You like my little establishment, hurr? You have a great treat in store, I assure you."

Laffler chuckled. "Oh, Costain's been dining here regularly for two weeks," he said. "He's by way of becoming a great admirer of yours, Sbirro."

The eyes turned on Costain. "A very great compliment. You compliment me with your presence and I return same with my food, hurr? But the lamb Amirstan is far superior to anything of your past experience, I assure you. All the trouble of obtaining it, the difficulty of preparation, is truly merited."

Costain strove to put aside the exasperating problem of that face. "I have wondered," he said, "why with all these difficulties you mention, you even bother to present lamb Amirstan to the public. Surely your other dishes are excellent enough to uphold your reputation."

Sbirro smiled so broadly that his face became perfectly round. "Perhaps it is a matter of the psychology, hurr? Someone discovers a wonder and must share it with others. He must fill his cup to the brim, perhaps, by observing the so evident pleasure of those who explore it with him. Or," he shrugged, "perhaps it is just a matter of good business."

"Then in the light of all this," Costain persisted, "and considering all the conventions you have imposed on your customers, why do you open the restaurant to the public instead of operating it as a private club?"

The eyes abruptly glinted into Costain's, then turned away. "So perspicacious, hurr? Then I will tell you. Because there is more privacy in a public eating place than in the most exclusive club in existence! Here no one inquires of your affairs; no one desires to know the intimacies of your life. Here the business is eating. We are not curious about names and addresses or the reasons for the coming and going of our guests. We welcome you when you are here; we have no regrets when you are here no longer. That is the answer, hurr?"

Costain was startled by this vehemence. "I had no intention of prying," he stammered.

Sbirro ran the tip of his tongue over his thin lips. "No, no," he reassured, "you are not prying. Do not let me give you that impression. On the contrary, I invite your questions."

"Oh, come, Costain," said Laffler. "Don't let Sbirro intimidate you. I've known him for years and I guarantee that his bark is worse than his bite. Before you know it, he'll be showing you all the privileges of the house—outside of inviting you to visit his precious kitchen, of course."

"Ah," smiled Sbirro, "for that, Mr. Costain may have to wait a little while. For everything else I am at his beck and call."

Laffler slapped his hand jovially on the table. "What did I tell you!" he said. "Now let's have the truth, Sbirro. Has anyone, outside of your staff, ever stepped into the sanctum sanctorum?"

Sbirro looked up. "You see on the wall above you," he said earnestly, "the portrait of one to whom I did the honor. A very dear friend and a patron of most long standing, he is evidence that my kitchen is not inviolate."

Costain studied the picture and started with recognition. "Why," he said excitedly, "that's the famous writer—you know the one, Laffler—he used to do such wonderful short stories and cynical bits and then suddenly took himself off and disappeared in Mexico!"

"Of course!" cried Laffler, "and to think I've been sitting under his portrait for years without even realizing it!" He turned to Sbirro. "A dear friend, you say? His disappearance must have been a blow to you."

Sbirro's face lengthened. "It was, it was, I assure you. But think of it this way, gentlemen: he was probably greater in his death than in his life, hurr? A most tragic man, he often told me that his only happy hours were spent here at this very table. Pathetic, is it not? And to think the only favor I could ever show him was to let him witness the mysteries of my kitchen, which is, when all is said and done, no more than a plain, ordinary kitchen."

"You seem very certain of his death," commented Costain. "After all, no evidence has ever turned up to substantiate it."

Sbirro contemplated the picture. "None at all," he said softly. "Remarkable, hurr?"

With the arrival of the entree Sbirro leaped to his feet and set about serving them himself. With his eyes alight he lifted the casserole from the tray and sniffed at the fragrance from within with sensual relish. Then, taking great care not to lose a single drop of gravy, he filled two platters with chunks of dripping meat. As if exhausted by this task, he sat back in his chair, breathing heavily. "Gentlemen," he said, "to your good appetite."

Costain chewed his first mouthful with great deliberation and swallowed it. Then he looked at the empty lines of his fork with glazed eyes.

"Good God!" he breathed.

"It is good, hurr? Better than you imagined?"

Costain shook his head dazedly. "It is impossible," he said slowly, "for the uninitiated to conceive the delights of lamb Amirstan as for mortal man to look into his own soul."

"Perhaps—" Sbirro thrust his head so close that Costain could feel the warm, fetid breath tickle his nostrils—"perhaps you have just had a glimpse into your soul, hurr?"

Costain tried to draw back slightly without giving offense. "Perhaps." He laughed. "And a gratifying picture it made: all fang and claw. But without intending any disrespect, I should hardly like to build my church on *lamb en casserole*."

Sbirro rose and laid a hand gently on his shoulder. "So perspicacious," he said. "Sometimes when you have nothing to do, nothing, perhaps, but sit for a very little while in a dark room and think of this world—what it is and what it is going to be— then you must turn your thoughts a little to the significance of the Lamb in religion. It will be so interesting. And now—" he bowed deeply to both men—"I have held you long enough from your dinner. I was most happy," he said, nodding to Costain, "and I am sure we will meet again." The teeth gleamed, the eyes glittered, and Sbirro was gone down the aisle of tables.

Costain twisted around to stare after the retreating figure. "Have I offended him in some way?" he asked.

Laffler looked up from his plate. "Offended him? He loves that kind of talk. Lamb Amirstan is a ritual with him; get him started and he'll be back at you a dozen times worse than a priest making a conversion."

Costain turned to his meal with the face still hovering before him. "Interesting man," he reflected. "Very."

It took him a month to discover the tantalizing familiarity of that face, and when he did, he laughed aloud in his bed. Why, of course! Sbirro might have sat as the model for the Cheshire cat in *Alice*!

He passed this thought on to Laffler the very next evening as they pushed their way down the street to the restaurant against a chill, blustering wind. Laffler only looked blank.

"You may be right," he said, "but I'm not a fit judge. It's a far cry back to the days when I read the book. A far cry, indeed."

As if taking up his words, a piercing howl came ringing down the street and stopped both men short in their tracks. "Someone's in trouble there," said Laffler. "Look!"

Not far from the entrance to Sbirro's two figures could be seen struggling in the near darkness. They swayed back and forth and suddenly tumbled into a writhing heap on the sidewalk. The piteous howl went up again, and Laffler, despite his firth, ran toward it at a fair speed with Costain tagging cautiously behind.

Stretched out full-length on the pavement was a slender figure with the dusky complexion and white hair of one of Sbirro's servitors. His fingers futilely plucking at the huge hands which encircled his throat, and his knee pushed weakly up at the gigantic bulk of a man who brutally bore down with his full weight.

Laffler came up panting, "Stop this!" he shouted. "What's going on here?"

The pleading eyes almost bulging from their sockets turned toward Laffler. "Help, sair. This man—drunk—"

"Drunk am I, ya dirty—" Costain saw now that the man was a sailor in a badly soiled uniform. The air around him reeked with the stench of liquor. "Pick me pocket and then call me drunk, will ya!" He dug his fingers in harder, and his victim groaned.

Laffler seized the sailor's shoulder. "Let go of him, do you hear! Let go of him at once!" he cried, and the next instant was sent careening into Costain, who staggered back under the force of the blow.

The attack on his own person sent Laffler into immediate and berserk action. Without a sound he leaped at the sailor, striking and kicking furiously at the unprotected face and flanks. Stunned at first, the man came to his feet with a rush and turned on Laffler. For a moment they stood locked together, and then as Costain joined the attack, all three went sprawling to the ground. Slowly Laffler and Costain got to their feet and looked down at the body before them.

"He's either out cold from liquor," said Costain, "or he struck his head going down. In any case, it's a job for the police."

"No, no, sair!" The waiter crawled weakly to his feet, and stood swaying. "No police, sair. Mr. Sbirro do not want such. You understand, sair." He caught hold of Costain with a pleading hand, and Costain looked at Laffler.

"Of course not," said Laffler. "We won't have to bother with the police. They'll pick him up soon enough, the murderous sot. But what in the world started all this?"

"That man, sair. He make most erratic way while walking, and with no meaning I push against him. Then he attack me, accusing me to rob him."

"As I thought." Laffler pushed the waiter gently along. "Now go in and get yourself attended to."

The man seemed ready to burst into tears. "To you, sair, I owe my life. If there is anything I can do—"

Laffler turned into the areaway that led to Sbirro's door. "No, no, it was nothing. You go along, and if Sbirro has any questions send him to me. I'll straighten it out."

"My life, sair," were the last words they heard as the inner door closed behind them.

"There you are, Costain," said Laffler, as a few minutes later he drew his chair under the table, "civilized man in all his glory. Reeking with alcohol, strangling to death some miserable innocent who came too close."

Costain made an effort to gloss over the nerve-shattering memory of the episode. "It's the neurotic cat that takes to alcohol," he said. "Surely there's a reason for that sailor's condition."

"Reason? Of course there is. Plain atavistic savagery!" Laffler swept his arm in an all-embracing gesture. "Why do we all sit here at our meat? Not only to appease physical demands, but because our atavistic selves cry for release. Think back, Costain. Do you remember that I once described Sbirro as the epitome of civilization? Can you now see why? A brilliant man, he fully understands the nature of human beings. But unlike lesser men he bends all his efforts to the satisfaction of our innate nature without resultant harm to some innocent bystander."

"When I think back on the wonders of lamb Amirstan," said Costain, "I quite understand what you're driving at. And, by the way, isn't it nearly due to appear on the bill of fare? It must have been over a month ago that it was last served."

The waiter, filling the tumblers, hesitated. "I am so sorry, sair. No special this evening."

"There's your answer," Laffler grunted, "and probably just my luck to miss out on it altogether next time."

Costain stared at him. "Oh, come, that's impossible."

"No, blast it." Laffler drank off half his water at a gulp and the waiter immediately refilled the glass. "I'm off to South America for a surprise tour of inspection. One month, two months, Lord knows how long."

"Are things bad down there?"

"They could be better." Laffler suddenly grinned. "Mustn't forget it takes very mundane dollars and cents to pay the tariff at Sbirro's."

"I haven't heard a word of this around the office."

"Wouldn't be a surprise tour if you had. Nobody knows about this except myself—and now you. I want to walk in on them completely unexpected. Find out what flimflammery they're up to down there. As far as the office is concerned, I'm off on a jaunt somewhere. Maybe recuperating in some sanatorium from my hard work. Anyhow, the business will be in good hands. Yours, among them."

"Mine?" said Costain, surprised.

"When you go in tomorrow you'll find yourself in receipt of a promotion, even if I'm not there to hand it to you personally. Mind you, it has nothing to do with our friendship, either; you've done fine work, and I'm immensely grateful for it."

Costain reddened under the praise. "You don't expect to be in tomorrow. Then you're leaving tonight?"

Laffler nodded. "I've been trying to wangle some reservations. If they come through, well, this will be in the nature of a farewell celebration."

"You know," said Costain slowly, "I devoutly hope that your reservations don't come through. I believe our dinners here have come to mean more to me than I ever dared imagine."

The waiter's voice broke in. "Do you wish to be served now, sair?" and they both started.

"Of course, of course," said Laffler sharply, "I didn't realize you were waiting."

"What bothers me," he told Costain as the waiter turned away, "is the thought of the lamb Amirstan I'm bound to miss. To tell you the truth, I've already put off my departure a week, hoping to hit a lucky night, and now I simply can't delay any more. I do hope that when you're sitting over your share of lamb Amirstan, you'll think of me with suitable regrets."

Costain laughed, "I will indeed," he said as he turned to his dinner.

Hardly had he cleared the plate when a waiter silently reached for it. It was not their usual waiter, he observed; it was none other than the victim of the assault.

"Well," Costain said, "how do you feel now? Still under the weather?"

The waiter paid no attention to him. Instead, with the air of a man under great strain, he turned to Laffler. "Sair," he whispered. "My life. I owe it to you. I can repay you!"

Laffler looked up in amazement, then shook his head firmly. "No," he said. "I want nothing from you, understand? You have repaid me sufficiently with your thanks. Now get on with your work and let's hear no more about it."

The waiter did not stir an inch, but his voice rose slightly. "By the body and blood of your God, sair, I will help you even if you do not want! *Do not go into the kitchen, sair.* I trade you my life for yours, sair, when I speak this. Tonight or any night of your life, do not go into the kitchen at Sbirro's!"

Laffler sat back, completely dumbfounded. "Not go into the kitchen? Why shouldn't I go into the kitchen if Mr. Sbirro ever took it into his head to invite me there? What's this all about?"

A hard hand was laid on Costain's back, and another gripped the waiter's arm. The waiter remained frozen to the spot, his lips compressed, his eyes downcast.

"What is all *what* about, gentlemen?" purred the voice. "So opportune an arrival. In time as ever, I see, to answer all the questions, hurr?"

Laffler breathed a sigh of relief. "Ah, Sbirro, thank heaven you're here. This man is saying something about my not going into your kitchen. Do you know what he means?"

The teeth showed in a broad grin. "But of course. This good man was giving you advice in all amiability. It so happens that my emotional chef heard some rumor that I might have a guest into his precious kitchen, and he flew into a fearful rage. Such a rage, gentlemen! He even threatened to give notice on the spot, and you can understand what that would mean to Sbirro's, hurr? Fortunately, I succeeded in showing him what a signal honor it is to have an esteemed patron and true connoisseur observe him at his work firsthand, and now he is quite amenable. Quite, hurr?"

He released the waiter's arm. "You are at the wrong table," he said softly. "See that it does not happen again."

The waiter slipped off without daring to raise his eyes and Sbirro drew a chair to the table. He seated himself and brushed his hand lightly over his hair. "Now I am afraid that the cat is out of the bag, hurr? This invitation to you, Mr. Laffler, was to be a surprise; but the surprise is gone, and all that is left is the invitation."

Laffler mopped beads of perspiration from his forehead. "Are you serious?" he said huskily. "Do you mean that we are really to witness the preparation of your food tonight?"

Sbirro drew a sharp fingernail along the tablecloth, leaving a thin, straight line printed on the linen. "Ah," he said, "I am faced with a dilemma of great proportions." He studied the line soberly. "You, Mr. Laffler, have been my guest for ten long years. But our friend here—"

Costain raised his hand in protest. "I understand perfectly. This invitation is solely to Mr. Laffler, and naturally my presence is embarrassing. As it happens, I have an early engagement for this evening and must be on my way anyhow. So you see there's no dilemma at all, really."

"No," said Laffler, "absolutely not. That wouldn't be fair at all. We've been sharing this until now, Costain, and I won't enjoy the experience half as much if you're not along. Surely Sbirro can make his conditions flexible, this one occasion."

They both looked at Sbirro who shrugged his shoulders regretfully.

Costain rose abruptly. "I'm not going to sit here, Laffler, and spoil your great adventure. And then, too," he bantered, "think of that ferocious chef waiting to get his cleaver on you. I prefer not to be at the scene. I'll just say good-bye," he went on, to cover Laffler's guilty silence, "and leave you to Sbirro. I'm sure he'll take pains to give you a good show." He held out his hand and Laffler squeezed it painfully hard.

"You're being very decent, Costain," he said. "I hope you'll continue to dine here until we meet again. It shouldn't be too long."

Sbirro made way for Costain to pass. "I will expect you," he said. *"Au 'voir."*

NEARLY PERFECT

A. A. MILNE
(1882–1956)

The Winnie-the-Pooh books are A. A. Milne's chief claim to immortality, but he also made several significant contributions to the literature of crime. His only true detective novel, The Red House Mystery (1922), is one of the classics of the genre, bringing the "oh, what fun!" notion to the amateur sleuth in a sharply plotted traditional exercise in deductive reasoning. He also wrote a popular play, The Perfect Alibi (1928), at which the audience sees the crime committed and the Columbo-like way in which the murderer is caught.

INDNESS DOESN'T ALWAYS pay," said Coleby, "and I can tell you a very sad story that proves it."

"Kindness is its own reward," I said. I knew that somebody else would say it if I didn't.

"The reward in this case was the hangman's rope. Which is what I was saying."

"Is it a murder story?"

"Very much so."

"Good."

"What was the name of the kind gentleman?" asked Sylvia.

"Julian Crayne."

"And he was hanged?"

"Very unfairly, or so he thought. And if you will listen to the story instead of asking silly questions, you can say whether you agree with him."

"How old was he?"

"About thirty."

"Good-looking?"

"Not after he was hanged. Do you want to hear this story, or don't you?"

"Yes!" said everybody.

So Coleby told us the story.

Julian Crayne (he said) was an unpleasantly smooth young man who lived in the country with his Uncle Marius. He should have been working, but he disliked work. He disliked the country, too, but a suggestion that Julian should help the export drive in London—with the aid of a handsome allowance from Marius—met with an unenthusiastic response even when Julian threw in an offer to come down regularly for weekends and bring some of his friends with him. Marius didn't particularly like his nephew, but he liked having him about. Rich, elderly bachelors often become bores, and bores prefer to have somebody at hand who cannot escape. Marius did not intend to let Julian escape. To have nobody to talk to through the week, and then to have a houseful of rowdy young people at the weekend, none of whom wanted to listen to him, was not his idea of pleasure. He had the power over his nephew that money gives, and he preferred to use it.

"It will all come to you when I die,

my boy," he said, "and until then you won't grudge a sick old man the pleasure of your company."

"Of course not," said Julian. "It was only that I was afraid you were getting tired of me."

If Marius had really been a sick old man, any loving nephew such as Julian might have been content to wait. But Marius was a sound sixty-five, and in that very morning's newspaper there had been talk of somebody at Runcorn who had just celebrated his hundred-and-fifth birthday. Julian didn't know where Runcorn was, but he could add forty years to his own age, and ask himself what the devil would be the use of this money at seventy; whereas now, with £150,000 in the bank, and all life to come— Well, you can see for yourself how the thing would look to him.

I don't know if any of you have ever wondered about how to murder an uncle— an uncle whose heir and only relation you are. As we all know, the motives for murder are many. Revenge, passion, gain, fear, or simply the fact that you have seen the fellow's horrible face in the paper so often that you feel it to be almost a duty to eliminate it. The only person I ever wanted to murder is— Well, I won't mention names, because I may do it yet. But the point is that the police, in their stolid, unimaginative way, always look first for the money motive, and if the money motive is there, you are practically in the bag.

So you see the very difficult position in which Julian was placed. He lived alone with his uncle, he was his uncle's heir, and his uncle was a very rich man. However subtly he planned, the dead weight of that £150,000 was against him. Any other man might push Marius into the river, and confidently wait for a verdict of accidental death; but not Julian. Any other man might place a tablet of some untraceable poison in the soda-mint bottle, and look for a certificate of "Death from Natural Causes"; but not Julian. Any other man might tie a string across the top step of the attic stairs— But I need not go on. You see, as Julian saw, how terribly unfair it was. The thing really got into his mind. He used to lie awake night after night thinking how unfair it was, and how delightfully easy it would be if it weren't for that £150,000.

The trouble was that he had nobody in whom to confide. He wished now, and for the first time, that he were married. With a loving wife to help him, how blithely they could have pursued, hand in hand, the search for the foolproof plan. What a stimulant to his brain would have been some gentle, fair-haired creature of the intelligence of the average policeman, who would point out the flaws and voice the suspicions the plan might raise. In such a delicate matter as this, two heads were better than one, even if the other head did nothing but listen with its mouth slightly ajar. At least he would then have the plan out in the open and be able to take a more objective view of it.

Unfortunately, the only person available was his uncle.

What he had to find—alone, if so it must be—was an alternative suspect to himself; somebody, in the eyes of the police, with an equally good motive. But what other motive could there be for getting rid of such an estimable man as Marius Crayne? A bore, yes; but would the average Inspector recognize boredom as a reasonable motive? Even if he did, it would merely be an additional motive for Julian. There was, of course, the possibility of "framing" somebody, a thing they were always doing in detective stories. But the only person in a position to be framed was old John Coppard, the gardener, and the number of footprints, fingerprints, blunt instruments, and blood-stained handkerchiefs with the initials J. C. on them that would be necessary to offset the absence of motive was more than Julian cared to contemplate.

I have said that Uncle Marius was a bore. Bores can be divided into two classes: those who have their own particular subject, and those who don't need a subject. Marius was in the former, and less offensive class. Shortly before his retirement (he was in the tea business), he had brought off a remarkable double. He had filled in his first football-pool form "just to see how it went," distributing the numbers and the crosses in an impartial spirit, and had posted it "just for fun." He followed this up by taking over a lottery ticket from a temporarily embarrassed but rather intimidating gentleman whom he had met on a train. The result being what it was, Marius was convinced that he had a flair—as he put it, "a nose for things." So when he found that through the long winter evenings—and, indeed, during most of the day—there was nothing to do in the country but read detective stories, it soon became obvious to him that he had a nose for crime.

Well, it was this nose poor Julian had had to face. It was bad enough, whenever a real crime was being exploited in the papers, to listen to his uncle's assurance that once again Scotland Yard was at fault, as it was obviously the mother-in-law who had put the arsenic in the gooseberry tart; it was much more boring when the murder had taken place in the current detective story, and Marius was following up a confused synopsis of the first half with his own analysis of the clues.

"Oh, I forgot to tell you, this fellow—I forget his name for a moment—Carmichael, something like that—had met the girl, Doris—I mean Phyllis—had met Phyllis accidentally in Paris some years before—well, a year or two, the exact time doesn't matter—it was just that she and this fellow, what did I call him, Arbuthnot? . . ."

And it was at just such a moment as this that Julian was suddenly inspired.

"You know, Uncle Marius," he said, "*you* ought to write a detective story."

Marius laughed self-consciously, and said he didn't know about that.

"Of course you could! You're just the man. You've got a flair for that sort of thing, and you wouldn't make the silly mistakes all these other fellows make."

"Oh, I dare say I should be all right with the deduction and induction and so on—that's what I'm really interested in—but I've never thought of myself as a writer. There's a bit of a knack to it, you know. More in your line than mine, I should have thought."

"Uncle, you've said it!" cried Julian. "We'll write it together. Two heads are better than one. We can talk it over every evening and criticize each other's suggestions. What do you say?"

Marius was delighted with the idea. So, of course, was Julian. He had found his collaborator.

Give me a drink, somebody.

Yes (went on Coleby, wiping his mouth), I know what you are expecting. Half of you are telling yourselves that, ironically enough, it was Uncle who thought of the foolproof plan for murder that Nephew put into execution; and the rest of you are thinking what much more fun it would be if Nephew thought of the plan, and, somewhat to his surprise, Uncle put it into execution. Actually, it didn't happen quite like that.

Marius, when it came to the point, had nothing much to contribute. But he knew what he liked. For him, one murder in a book was no longer enough. There must be two, the first one preferably at a country house party, with plenty of suspects. Then, at a moment when he is temporarily baffled, the Inspector receives a letter inviting him to a secret *rendezvous* at midnight, where the writer will be waiting to give him important information. He arrives to find a dying man, who is just able to gasp out "Horace" (or was it Hoxton?) before expiring in his arms. The murderer has struck again!

"You see the idea, my boy? It removes any doubt in the reader's mind that the first death was accidental, and provides the detective with a second set of clues. By collating the two sets—"

"You mean," asked Julian, "that it would be taken for granted that the murderer was the same in the two cases?"

"Well, of course, my dear boy, of course!" said Marius, surprised at the question. "What else? The poacher, or whoever it was, had witnessed the first murder but had foolishly given some hint of his knowledge to others—possibly in the bar of the local public house. Naturally the murderer has to eliminate him before the information can be passed on to the police."

"Naturally," said Julian thoughtfully. "Yes. . . . Exactly. . . . You know"—and he smiled at his uncle—"I think something might be done on those lines."

For there, he told himself happily, was a foolproof plan. First, commit a completely motiveless murder, of which he could not possibly be suspected. Then, which would be easy, encourage Uncle Marius to poke his "nose for things" into the case, convince him that he and he alone had found the solution, and persuade him to make an appointment with the local inspector. And then, just before the Inspector arrives, "strike again." It was, as he was accustomed to say when passing as a Battle of Britain pilot in Piccadilly bars, a piece of cake.

It may seem to some of you that in taking on this second murder Julian was adding both to his difficulties and his moral responsibility. But you must remember that through all these months of doubt he had been obsessed by one thing only, the intolerable burden of motive, so that suddenly to be rid of it, and to be faced with a completely motiveless killing, gave him an exhilarating sense of freedom in which nothing could go wrong. He had long been feeling that such a murder would be easy. He was now persuaded that it would be blameless.

The victim practically selected himself, and artistically, Julian liked to think, was one of whom Uncle Marius would have approved. A mile or two away at Birch Hall lived an elderly gentleman by the name of Corphew. Not only was he surrounded by greedy relations of both sexes, but in his younger days he had lived a somewhat mysterious life in the East. It did not outrage credibility to suppose that, as an innocent young man, he might have been mixed up in some Secret Society, or, as a more experienced one, might have robbed some temple of its most precious jewel. Though no dark men had been seen loitering in the neighborhood lately, it was common knowledge that Sir George had a great deal of money to leave and was continually altering or threatening to alter his will. In short, his situation fulfilled the conditions Uncle Marius demanded of a good detective story.

At the moment Julian had no personal acquaintance with Sir George. Though, of course, they would have to be in some sort of touch with each other at the end, his first idea was to remain discreetly outside the family circle. Later reflection, however, told him that in this case he would qualify as one of those mysterious strangers who were occasionally an alternative object of suspicion for the police— quite effectively, because Julian was of a dark, even swarthy, complexion. It would be better, he felt, to be recognized as a friendly acquaintance; obviously harmless, obviously with nothing to gain, even something to lose, by Sir George's death.

In making this acquaintance with his victim, Julian was favored by fortune. Rejecting his usual method of approach to a stranger (an offer to sell him some shares in an oil well in British Columbia), he was presenting himself at the Hall as the special representative of a paper interested in Eastern affairs, when he heard a cry for help from a little coppice that bordered the drive. Sir George, it seemed, had tripped over a root and sprained his ankle. With the utmost good will, Julian carried him up to the house. When he left an hour later, it was with a promise to drop in on a bedridden Sir George the next day, and play a game of chess with him.

Julian was no great chess player, but he was sufficiently intimate with the pieces to allow Sir George the constant pleasure of beating him. Between games, he learned all he could of his host's habits and the family's members. There seemed to him to be several admirable candidates for chief suspect, particularly a younger brother of sinister aspect called Eustace, who had convinced himself that he was to be the principal legatee. Indeed, the possibility of framing Eustace did occur to him, but he remembered in time that a second framing for the murder of Marius would then be necessary, and might easily be impracticable. Let them sort it out. The more suspects the better.

Any morbid expectations you may now have of a detailed account of the murder of Sir George Corphew will not be satisfied. It is enough to say that it involved the conventional blunt instrument, and took place at a time when at least some of the family would not be likely to have an alibi. Julian was not at this time an experienced murderer, and he would have been the first to admit that he had been a little careless about footprints, fingerprints, and cigarette ashes. But as he would never be associated with murder, this did not matter.

All went as he had anticipated. A London solicitor had produced a will in which all the family was heavily involved, and the Inspector had busied himself with their alibis, making it clear that he regarded each one with the liveliest suspicion. Moreover, Uncle Marius was delighted to pursue his own line of investigation, which, after hovering for a moment round the Vicar, was now rapidly leading to a denunciation of an undergardener called Spratt.

"Don't put anything on paper," said Julian kindly. "It might be dangerous. Ring up the Inspector, and ask him to come in and see you tonight. Then you can tell him all about it."

"That's a good idea, my boy," said Marius. "That's what I'll do."

But, as it happened, the Inspector was already on his way. A local solicitor had turned up with a new will, made only a few days before. "In return for his kindness in playing chess with an old man," as he put it, Sir George had made Julian Crayne his sole legatee.

THE GETTYSBURG BUGLE

ELLERY QUEEN
(PSEUDONYM OF FREDERIC DANNAY, 1905–1982, AND MANFRED B. LEE, 1905–1971)

This prolific writing team of two Brooklyn-born cousins created the shrewd public relations notion of naming their detective and their pseudonym one and the same, reasoning that people often forget authors but not the names of favorite characters. Their early work was pure pastiche of the then immensely popular Philo Vance, but they eventually found their own voice and produced a character much loved in books, on radio and television, and in the movies.

HIS IS A VERY OLD STORY AS Queen stories go. It happened in Ellery's salad days, when he was tossing his talents about like a Sunday chef and a red-headed girl named Nikki Porter had just attached herself to his typewriter. But it was not staled, this story; it has an unwithering flavor which those who partook of it relish to this day.

There are gourmets in America whose taste buds leap at any concoction dated 1861–1865. To such, the mere recitation of ingredients like Bloody Angle, Minié balls, Little Mac, "Tenting Tonight," the brand of Ulyss Grant's whisky, not to mention Father Abraham, is sufficient to start the passionate flow of juices. These are the misty-hearted to whom the Civil War is "the War" and the blue-gray armies rather more than men. Romantics, if you will; garnishers of history. But it is they who pace the lonely sentrypost by the night Potomac, they who hear the creaking of the ammunition wagons, the snap of campfires, the scream of the thin gray line and the long groan of the battlefield. They personally flee the burning hell of the Wilderness as the dead rise and twist in the flames; under lanterns, in the flickering mud, they stoop compassionately with the surgeons over quivering heaps. It is they who keep the little flags flying and the ivy ever green on the graves of the old men.

Ellery is of this company, and that is why he regards the case of the old men of Jacksburg, Pennsylvania, with particular affection.

Ellery and Nikki came upon the village of Jacksburg as people often come upon the best things, unpropitiously. They had been driving back to New York from Washington, where Ellery had had some sleuthing to do among the stacks of the Library of Congress. Perhaps the Potomac, Arlington's eternal geometry, giant Lincoln frozen in sadness brought their weight to bear upon Ellery's decision to veer towards Gettysburg, where murder had been national. And

Nikki had never been there, and May was coming to its end. There was a climate of sentiment.

They crossed the Maryland-Pennsylvania line and spent timeless hours wandering over Culp's Hill and Seminary Ridge and Little Round Top and Spangler's Spring among the watchful monuments. It is a place of everlasting life, where Pickett and Jeb Stuart keep charging to the sight of those with eyes to see, where the blood spills fresh if colorlessly, and the high-pitched tones of a tall and ugly man still ring out over the graves. When they left, Ellery and Nikki were in a mood of wonder, unconscious of time or place, oblivious to the darkening sky and the direction in which the nose of the Duesenberg pointed. So in time they were disagreeably awakened by the alarm clock of nature. The sky had opened on their heads, drenching them to the skin instantly. From the horizon behind them Gettysburg was a battlefield again, sending great flashes of fire through the darkness to the din of celestial cannon. Ellery stopped the car and put the top up, but the mood was drowned when he discovered that something ultimate had happened to the ignition system. They were marooned in a faraway land, Nikki moaned; making Ellery angry, for it was true.

"We can't go in these wet clothes, Ellery!"

"Do you suggest that we stay here in them? I'll get this crackerbox started if . . ." But at that moment the watery lights of a house wavered on somewhere ahead, and Ellery became cheerful again.

"At least we'll find out where we are and how far it is to where we ought to be. Who knows? There may even be a garage."

It was a little white house on a little swampy road marked off by a little stone fence covered with rambler rose vines, and the man who opened the door to the dripping wayfarers was little, too, little and weatherskinned and gallused, with eyes that seemed to have roots in the stones and springs of the Pennsylvania countryside. He smiled hospitably, but the smile became concern when he saw how wet they were.

"Won't take no for an answer," he said in a remarkably deep voice, and he chuckled. "That's doctor's orders, though I expect you didn't see my shingle—mostly overgrown with ivy. Got a change of clothing in your car?"

"Oh, yes!" said Nikki abjectly.

Ellery, being a man, hesitated. The house looked neat and clean, there was an enticing fire, and the rain at their backs was coming down with a roar. "Well, thank you . . . but if I might use your phone to call a garage—"

"You just give me the keys to your car trunk."

"But we can't turn your home into a tourist house—"

"It's that, too, when the good Lord sends a wanderer my way. Now see here, this storm's going to keep up most of the night and the roads hereabout get mighty soupy." The little man was bustling into waterproof and overshoes. "I'll get Lew Bagley over at the garage to pick up your car, but for now let's have those keys."

So an hour later, while the elements warred outside, they were toasting safely in a pleasant little parlor, full of Dr. Martin Strong's homemade poppy-seed twists, scrapple, and coffee. The doctor, who lived alone, was his own cook. He was also, he said with a chuckle, mayor of the village of Jacksburg and its chief of police.

"Lot of us in the village run double harness. Bill Yoder of the hardware store's our undertaker. Lew Bagley's also the fire chief. Ed MacShane—"

"Jacksburger-of-all-trades you may be, Dr. Strong," said Ellery, "but to me you'll always be primarily the Good Samaritan."

"Hallelujah," said Nikki, piously wiggling her toes.

"And make it Doc," said their host. "Why, it's just selfishness on my part, Mr. Queen. We're off the beaten track here, and you do get a hankering for a new face. I guess I know every dimple and wen on the five hundred and thirty-four in Jacksburg."

"I don't suppose your police chiefship keeps you very busy."

Doc Strong laughed. "Not any. Though last year—" His eyes puckered and he got up to poke the fire. "Did you say, Miss Porter, that Mr. Queen is sort of a detective?"

"Sort of a!" began Nikki. "Why, Dr. Strong, he's solved some simply unbeliev—"

"My father is an inspector in the New York police department," interrupted Ellery, curbing his new secretary's enthusiasm with a glance. "I stick my nose into a case once in a while. What about last year, Doc?"

"What put me in mind of it," said Jacksburg's mayor thoughtfully, "was your saying you'd been to Gettysburg today. And also you being interested in crimes . . ." Dr. Strong said abruptly, "I'm a fool, but I'm worried."

"Worried about what?"

"Well . . . Memorial Day's tomorrow, and for the first time in my life I'm not looking forward to it. Jacksburg makes quite a fuss about Memorial Day. It's not every village can brag about three living veterans of the Civil War."

"Three?" exclaimed Nikki. "How thrilling."

"Gives you an idea what the Jacksburg doctoring business is like," grinned Doc Strong. "We run to pioneer-type women and longevity . . . I ought to have said we *had* three Civil War veterans—Caleb Atwell, ninety-seven, of the Atwell family, there are dozens of 'em in the county; Zach Bigelow, ninety-five, who lives with his grandson Andy and Andy's wife and seven kids; and Abner Chase, ninety-four, Cissy Chase's great-grandpa. This year we're down to two. Caleb Atwell died last Memorial Day."

"A, B, C," murmured Ellery.

"What's that?"

"I have a bookkeeper's mind, Doc. Atwell, Bigelow, and Chase. Call it a spur-of-the-moment mnemonic system. A died last Memorial Day. Is that why you're not looking forward to this one? B following A sort of thing?"

"Didn't it always?" said Doc Strong with defiance. "Though I'm afraid it ain't—isn't as simple as all that. Maybe I better tell you how Caleb Atwell died.

"Every year Caleb, Zach, and Abner have been the star performers of our Memorial Day exercises, which are held at the old burying ground on the Hookerstown road. The oldest of the three—"

"That would be A. Caleb Atwell."

"That's right. As the oldest, Caleb always blew taps on a cracked bugle that's 'most as old as he was. Caleb, Zach, and Abner were in the Pennsylvania Seventy-second of Hancock's Second Corps, Brigadier General Alexander S. Webb commanding. They covered themselves with immortal glory—the Seventy-second, I mean—at Gettysburg when they fought back Pickett's charge, and that bugle played a big part in their fighting. Ever since it's been known as the Gettysburg bugle—in Jacksburg, anyway."

The little mayor of Jacksburg looked softly down the years. "It's been a tradition, the oldest living vet tootling that bugle, far back as I remember. I recollect as a boy standing around with my mouth open watching the G.A.R.s—there were lots more then—take turns in front of Maroney Offcutt's general store . . . been dead thirty-eight years, old Offcutt . . . practicing on the bugle, so any one of 'em would be ready when his turn came." Doc Strong sighed. "And Zach Bigelow, as the next oldest to Caleb Atwell, he'd be standard bearer, and Ab Chase, as the next-next oldest, he'd lay the wreath on the memorial monument in the burying ground.

"Well, last Memorial Day, while Zach was holding the regimental colors and Ab the wreath, Caleb blew taps the way he'd done nigh onto twenty times before. All of a sudden, in the middle of a high note, Caleb keeled over. Dropped in his tracks deader than church on Monday."

"Strained himself," said Nikki sympathetically. "But what a poetic way for a Civil War veteran to die."

Doc Strong regarded her oddly. "Maybe," he said. "If you like that kind of poetry." He kicked a log, sending sparks flying up his chimney.

"But surely, Doc," said Ellery with a smile, for he was young in those days, "surely you can't have been suspicious about the death of a man of ninety-seven?"

"Maybe I was," muttered their host. "Maybe I was because it so happened I'd given old Caleb a thorough physical checkup only the day before he died. I'd have staked my medical license he'd live to break a hundred and then some. Healthiest old copperhead I ever knew. Copperhead! I'm blaspheming the dead. Caleb lost an eye on Cemetery Ridge . . . I know—I'm senile. That's what I've been telling myself for the past year."

"Just what was it you suspected, Doc?" Ellery forbore to smile now, but only because of Dr. Strong's evident distress.

"Didn't know what to suspect," said the country doctor shortly. "Fooled around with the notion of an autopsy, but the Atwells wouldn't hear of it. Said I was a blame jackass to think a man of ninety-seven would die of anything but old age. I found myself agreeing with 'em. The upshot was we buried Caleb whole."

"But, Doc, at that age the human economy can go to pieces without warning like the one-hoss shay. You must have had another reason for uneasiness. A motive you knew about?"

"Well . . . maybe."

"He was a rich man," said Nikki sagely.

"He didn't have a pot he could call his own," said Doc Strong. "But somebody stood to gain by his death just the same. That is, if the old yarn's true.

"You see, there's been kind of a legend in Jacksburg about those three old fellows, Mr. Queen. I first heard it when I was running around barefoot with my tail hanging out. Folks said then, and they're still saying it, that back in '65 Caleb and Zach and Ab, who were in the same company, found some sort of treasure."

"Treasure . . ." Nikki began to cough.

"Treasure," repeated Doc Strong doggedly. "Fetched it home to Jacksburg with them, the story goes, hid it, and swore they'd never tell a living soul where it was buried. Now there's lots of tales like that came out of the War"—he fixed Nikki with a stern and glittering eye—"and most folks either cough or go into hysterics, but there's something about this one I've always half-believed. So I'm senile on two counts. Just the same, I'll breathe a lot easier when tomorrow's ceremonies are over and Zach Bigelow lays Caleb Atwell's bugle away till next year. As the older survivor Zach does the tootling tomorrow."

"They hid the treasure and kept it hidden for considerably over half a century?" Ellery was smiling again. "Doesn't strike me as a very sensible thing to do with a treasure, Doc. It's only sensible if the treasure is imaginary. Then you don't have to produce it."

"The story goes," mumbled Jacksburg's mayor, "that they'd sworn an oath—"

"Not to touch any of it until they all died but one," said Ellery, laughing outright now. "Last-survivor-takes-all department. Doc, that's the way most of these fairy tales go." Ellery rose, yawning. "I think I hear the featherbed in that other guest room calling. Nikki, your eyeballs are hanging out. Take my advice, Doc, and follow suit. You haven't a thing to worry about but keeping the kids quiet tomorrow while you read the Gettysburg Address!"

As it turned out, the night shared prominently in Doc Martin Strong's Memorial Day responsibilities. Ellery and Nikki awakened to a splendid world, risen from its night's ablutions with a shining eye and a scrubbed look; and they went downstairs within seconds of each other to find the mayor of Jacksburg, galluses dangling on his pants bottom, pottering about the kitchen.

"Morning, morning," said Doc Strong, welcoming but abstracted. "Just fixing things for your breakfast before catching an hour's nap."

"You lamb," said Nikki. "But what a shame, Doctor. Didn't you sleep well last night?"

"Didn't sleep at all. Tossed around a bit and just as I was dropping off my phone rings and it's Cissy Chase. Emergency sick call. Hope it didn't disturb you."

"Cissy Chase." Ellery looked at their host. "Wasn't that the name you mentioned last night of—?"

"Of old Abner Chase's great-granddaughter. That's right, Mr. Queen. Cissy's an orphan and Ab's only kin. She's kept house for the old fellow and taken care of him since she was ten." Doc Strong's shoulders sloped.

Ellery said peculiarly: "It was old Abner . . .?"

"I was up with Ab all night. This morning, at six-thirty, he passed away."

"On Memorial Day!" Nikki sounded like a little girl in her first experience with a fact of life.

There was a silence, fretted by the sizzling of Doc Strong's bacon.

Ellery said at last, "What did Abner Chase die of?"

Doc Strong looked at him. He seemed angry. But then he shook his head. "I'm no Mayo brother, Mr. Queen, and I suppose there's a lot about the practice of medicine I'll never get to learn, but I do know a cerebral hemorrhage when I see one, and that's what Ab Chase died of. In a man of ninety-four, that's as close to natural death as you can come . . . No, there wasn't any funny business in this one."

"Except," mumbled Ellery, "that—again—it happened on Memorial Day."

"Man's a contrary animal. Tell him lies and he swallows 'em whole. Give him the truth and he gags on it. Maybe the Almighty gets tired of His thankless job every once in an eon and cuts loose with a little joke." But Doc Strong said it as if he were addressing, not them, but himself. "Any special way you like your eggs?"

"Leave the eggs to me, Doctor," Nikki said firmly. "You go on up those stairs and get some sleep."

"Reckon I better if I'm to do my usual dignified job today," said the mayor of Jacksburg with a sigh. "Though Abner Chase's death is going to make the proceedings solemner than ordinary. Bill Yoder says he's not going to be false to an ancient and honorable profession by doing a hurry-up job undertaking Ab, and maybe that's just as well. If we added the Chase funeral to today's program, even old Abe's immortal words would find it hard to compete! By the way, Mr. Queen, I talked to Lew Bagley this morning and he'll have your car ready in an hour. Special service, seeing you're guests of the mayor." Doc Strong chuckled. "When you planning to leave?"

"I *was* intending . . ." Ellery stopped with a frown. Nikki regarded him with a sniffy look. She had already learned to detect the significance of certain signs peculiar to the Queen physiognomy. "I wonder," murmured Ellery, "how Zach Bigelow's going to take the news."

"He's already taken it, Mr. Queen. Stopped in at Andy Bigelow's place on my way home. Kind of a detour, but I figured I'd better break the news to Zach early as possible."

"Poor thing," said Nikki. "I wonder how it feels to learn you're the only one left." She broke an egg viciously.

"Can't say Zach carried on about it," said Doc Strong dryly. "About all he said, as I recall, was: 'Doggone it, now who's goin' to lay the wreath after I toot the Gettysburg bugle!' I guess when you reach the age of ninety-five, death don't mean what it does to young squirts of sixty-three like me. What time'd you say you were leaving, Mr. Queen?"

"Nikki," muttered Ellery, "are we in any particular hurry?"

"I don't know. Are we?"

"Besides, it wouldn't be patriotic. Doc, do you suppose Jacksburg would mind if a couple of New York Yanks invited themselves to your Memorial Day exercises?"

The business district of Jacksburg consisted of a single paved street bounded at one end by the sightless eye of a broken traffic signal and at the other by the twin gas pumps before Lew Bagley's garage. In between, some stores in need of paint sunned themselves, enjoying the holiday. Red, white, and blue streamers crisscrossed the thoroughfare overhead. A few seedy frame houses, each decorated with an American flag, flanked the main street at both ends.

Ellery and Nikki found the Chase house exactly where Doc Strong had said it would be—just around the corner from Bagley's garage, between the ivy-hidden church and the firehouse of the Jacksburg Volunteer Pump and Hose Company No. 1. But the mayor's directions were a superfluity; it was the only house with a crowded porch.

A heavy-shouldered young girl in a black Sunday dress sat in a rocker, the center of the crowd. Her nose was as red as her big hands, but she was trying to smile at the cheerful words of sympathy winged at her from all sides.

"Thanks, Mis' Plum . . . That's right, Mr. Schmidt, I know . . . But he was such a spry old soul, Emerson, I can't believe . . ."

"Miss Cissy Chase?"

Had the voice been that of a Confederate spy, a deeper silence could not have drowned the noise. Jacksburg eyes examined Ellery and Nikki with cold curiosity, and feet shuffled.

"My name is Queen and this is Miss Porter. We're attending the Jacksburg Memorial Day exercises as guests of Mayor Strong"—a warming murmur, like a zephyr, passed over the porch—"and he asked us to wait here for him. I'm sorry about your great-grandfather, Miss Chase."

"You must have been very proud of him," said Nikki.

"Thank you, I was. It was so sudden—Won't you set? I mean—Do come into the house. Great-grandpa's not here . . . he's over at Bill Yoder's, on some ice . . ."

The girl was flustered and began to cry, and Nikki took her arm and led her into the house. Ellery lingered a moment to exchange appropriate remarks with the neighbors who, while no longer cold, were still curious; and then he followed. It was a dreary little house with a dark and damp parlor.

"Now, now, this is no time for fussing—may I call you Cissy?" Nikki was saying soothingly. "Besides, you're better off away from all those folks. Why, Ellery, she's only a child!"

And a very plain child, Ellery thought, with a pinched face and empty eyes; and he almost wished he had gone on past the broken traffic light and turned north.

"I understand the parade to the burying ground is going to form outside your house, Cissy," he said. "By the way, have Andrew Bigelow and his grandfather Zach arrived yet?"

"Oh, I don't know," said Cissy Chase dully. "It's all such a dream, seems like."

"Of course. And you're left alone. Haven't you any family at all, Cissy?"

"No."

"Isn't there some young man—?"

Cissy shook her head bitterly. "Who'd marry me? This is the only decent dress I got, and it's four years old. We lived on Great-grandpa's pension and what I could earn hiring out by the day. Which ain't much, nor often. Now . . ."

"I'm sure you'll find something to do," said Nikki, very heartily.

"In Jacksburg?"

Nikki was silent.

"Cissy." Ellery spoke casually, and she did not even look up. "Doc Strong mentioned something about a treasure. Do you know anything about it?"

"Oh, that." Cissy shrugged. "Just when Great-grandpa told me, and he hardly ever told the same story twice. But near as I was ever able to make out, one time during the War him and Caleb Atwell and Zach Bigelow got separated from the army—scouting, or foraging, or something. It was down South somewhere, and they spent the night in an old empty mansion that was half-burned down. Next morning they went through the ruins to see what they could pick up, and buried in the cellar they found the treasure. A big fortune in money, Great-grandpa said. They were afraid to take it with them, so they buried it in the same place in the cellar and made a map of the location and after the War they went back, the three of 'em, and dug it up again. Then they made the pact."

"Oh, yes," said Ellery. "The pact."

"Swore they'd hold onto the treasure till only one of them remained alive, I don't know why, then the last one was to get it all. Leastways, that's how Great-grandpa told it. That part he always told the same."

"Did he ever say how much of a fortune it was?"

Cissy laughed. "Couple of hundred thousand dollars. I ain't saying Great-grandpa was cracked, but you know how an old man gets."

"Did he ever give you a hint as to where he and Caleb and Zach hid the money after they got it back North?"

"No, he'd just slap his knee and wink at me."

"Maybe," said Ellery suddenly, "maybe there's something to that yarn after all."

Nikki stared. "But Ellery, you said—! Cissy, did you hear that?"

But Cissy only drooped. "If there is, it's all Zach Bigelow's now."

Then Doc Strong came in, fresh as a daisy in a pressed blue suit and a stiff collar and a bow tie, and a great many other people came in, too. Ellery and Nikki surrendered Cissy Chase to Jacksburg.

"If there's anything to the story," Nikki whispered to Ellery, "and if Mayor Strong is right, then that old scoundrel Bigelow's been murdering his friends to get the money!"

"After all these years, Nikki? At the age of ninety-five?" Ellery shook his head. "But then what—?"

"I don't know." But when the little mayor happened to look their way, Ellery caught his eye and took him aside and whispered in his ear.

The procession—near every car in Jacksburg, Doc Strong announced proudly, over a hundred of them—got under way at exactly two o'clock.

Nikki had been embarrassed but not surprised to find herself being handed into the leading car, an old but brightly polished touring job contributed for the occasion by Lew Bagley; for the moment Nikki spied the ancient, doddering head under the Union Army hat in the front seat she detected the fine Italian whisper of her employer. Zach Bigelow held his papery frame fiercely if shakily erect between the driver and a powerful red-necked man with a brutal face who, Nikki surmised, was the old man's grandson, Andy Bigelow. Nikki looked back, peering around the flapping folds of the flag stuck in the corner of the car. Cissy Chase was in the second car in a black veil, weeping on a stout woman's shoulder. So the female Yankee from New York sat back between Ellery and Mayor Strong, against the bank of flowers in which the flag was set, and glared at the necks of the two Bigelows, having long since taken sides in this matter. And when Doc Strong made the introductions, Nikki barely nodded to Jacksburg's sole survivor of the Grand Army of the Republic, and then only in acknowledgment of his historic importance.

Ellery, however, was all deference and cordiality, even to the brute grandson. He leaned forward, talking into the hairy ear.

"How do I address your grandfather, Mr. Bigelow? I don't want to make a mistake about his rank."

"Gramp's a general," said Andy Bigelow loudly. "Ain't you, Gramp?" He beamed at the ancient, but Zach Bigelow was staring proudly ahead, holding fast to something in a rotted musette bag on his lap. "Went through the War a private," the grandson confided, "but he don't like to talk about that."

"General Bigelow—" began Ellery.

"That's his deef ear," said the grandson. "Try the other one."

"General Bigelow!"

"Hey?" The old man turned his trembling head, glaring, "Speak up, bub. Ye're mumblin'."

"General Bigelow," shouted Ellery, "now that all the money is yours, what are you going to do with it?"

"Hey? Money?"

"The treasure, Gramp," roared Andy Bigelow. "They've even heard about it in New York. What are you goin' to do with it, he wants to know?"

"Does, does he?" Old Zach sounded grimly amused. "Can't talk, Andy. Hurts m'neck."

"How much does it amount to, General?" cried Ellery.

Old Zach eyed him. "Mighty nosy, ain't ye?" Then he cackled. "Last time we counted it—Caleb, Ab, and me—came to nigh on a million dollars. Yes, sir, one million dollars." The old man's left eye, startlingly, drooped. "Goin' to be a big surprise to the smart-alecks and the doubtin' Thomases. You wait an' see."

Andy Bigelow grinned, and Nikki murmured to Doc Strong, "Abner Chase said it was only two hundred thousand."

"Zach makes it more every time he talks about it," said the mayor unhappily.

"I heard ye, Martin Strong!" yelled Zach Bigelow, swiveling his twig of a neck so suddenly that Nikki winced, expecting it to snap. "You wait! I'll show ye, ye durn whippersnapper, who's a lot o' wind!"

"Now, Zach," said Doc Strong pacifyingly. "Save your wind for that bugle."

Zach Bigelow cackled and clutched the musette bag in his lap, glaring ahead in triumph, as if he had scored a great victory.

Ellery said no more. Oddly, he kept staring not at old Zach but at Andy Bigelow, who sat beside his grandfather grinning at invisible audiences along the empty countryside as if he, too, had won—or was on his way to winning—a triumph.

The sun was hot. Men shucked their coats and women fanned themselves with handkerchiefs and pocketbooks.

"It is for us the living, rather, to be dedicated . . ."

Children dodged among the graves, pursued by shushing mothers. On most of the graves there were fresh flowers.

"—that from these honored dead . . ."

Little American flags protruded from the graves, too.

" . . . gave the last full measure of devotion . . ."

Doc Martin Strong's voice was deep and sure, not at all like the voice of that tall ugly man, who had spoken the same words apologetically.

" . . . that these dead shall not have died in vain . . ."

Doc was standing on the pedestal of the Civil War Monument, which was decorated with flags and bunting and faced the weathered stone ranks like a commander in full-dress uniform.

"—that this nation, under God . . ."

A color guard of the American Legion, Jacksburg Post, stood at attention between the mayor and the people. A file of Legionnaires carrying old Sharps rifles faced the graves.

"—and that government of the people . . ."

Beside the mayor, disdaining the simian shoulder of his grandson, stood General Zach Bigelow. Straight as the barrel of a Sharps, musette bag held tightly to his blue tunic.

" . . . shall not perish from the earth."

The old man nodded impatiently. He began to fumble with the bag.

"Comp-'ny! Present—arms!"

"Go ahead, Gramp!" Andy Bigelow bellowed.

The old man muttered. He was having difficulty extricating the bugle from the bag.

"Here, lemme give ye a hand!"

"Let the old man alone, Andy," said the mayor of Jacksburg quietly. "We're in no hurry."

Finally the bugle was free. It was an old army bugle, as old as Zach Bigelow, dented and scarred in a hundred places.

The old man raised it to his earth-colored lips.

Now his hands were not shaking.

Now even the children were quiet.

Now the Legionnaires stood more rigidly.

And the old man began to play taps.

It could hardly have been called playing. He blew, and out of the bugle's bell came cracked sounds. And sometimes he blew and no sounds came out at all. Then the veins of his neck swelled and his face turned to burning bark. Or he sucked at the mouthpiece, in and out, to clear it of his spittle. But still he blew, and the trees in the burying ground nodded in the warm breeze, and the people stood at attention listening as if the butchery sound were sweet music.

And then, suddenly, the butchery faltered. Old Zach Bigelow stood with bulging eyes. The Gettysburg bugle fell to the pedestal with a tiny clatter.

For an instant everything seemed to stop—the slight movements of the children, the breathing of the people, even the rustling of the leaves.

Then into the vacuum rushed a murmur of horror, and Nikki unbelievingly opened the eyes which she had shut to glimpse the last of Jacksburg's G.A.R. veterans crumpling to the feet of Doc Strong and Andy Bigelow.

"You were right the first time, Doc," Ellery said.

They were in Andy Bigelow's house, where old Zach's body had been taken from the cemetery. The house was full of chittering women and scampering children, but in this room there were only a few, and they talked in low tones. The old man was laid out on a settee with a patchwork quilt over him. Doc Strong sat in a rocker beside the body, looking very old.

"It's my fault," he mumbled. "I didn't examine Caleb's mouth last year. I didn't examine the mouthpiece of that bugle. It's my fault, Mr. Queen."

Ellery soothed him. "It's not an easy poison to spot, Doc, as you know. And after all, the whole thing was so ludicrous. You'd have caught it in autopsy, but the Atwells laughed you out of it."

"They're all gone. All three." Doc Strong looked up fiercely. "Who poisoned their bugle?"

"God Almighty, don't look at me," said Andy Bigelow. "Anybody could of, Doc."

"Anybody, Andy?" the mayor cried. "When Caleb Atwell died, Zach took the bugle and it's been in this house for a year!"

"Anybody could of," said Bigelow stubbornly. "The bugle was hangin' over the fireplace and anybody could of snuck in durin' the night . . . Anyway, it wasn't here before old Caleb died; he had it up to last Memorial Day. Who poisoned it in *his* house?"

"We won't get anywhere on this tack, Doc," Ellery murmured. "Bigelow. Did your grandfather ever let on where that Civil War treasure is hidden?"

"Suppose he did." The man licked his lips, blinking, as if he had been surprised into the half-admission. "What's it to you?"

"That money is behind the murders, Bigelow."

"Don't know nothin' about that. Anyway, nobody's got no right to that money but me." Andy Bigelow spread his thick chest. "When Ab Chase died, Gramp was the last survivor. That money was Zach Bigelow's. I'm his next o' kin, so now it's mine!"

"You know where it's hid, Andy." Doc was on his feet, eyes glittering. "Where?"

"I ain't talkin'. Git outen my house!"

"I'm the law in Jacksburg, too, Andy," Doc said softly. "This is a murder case. Where's that money?"

Bigelow laughed.

"You didn't know, Bigelow, did you?" said Ellery.

"Course not." He laughed again. "See, Doc? He's on your side, and he says I don't know, too."

"That is," said Ellery, "until a few minutes ago."

Bigelow's grin faded. "What are ye talkin' about?"

"Zach Bigelow wrote a message this morning, immediately after Doc Strong told him about Abner Chase's death."

Bigelow's face went ashen.

"And your grandfather sealed the message in an envelope—"

"Who told ye that?" yelled Bigelow.

"One of your children. And the first thing you did when we got home from the burying ground with your grandfather's corpse was to sneak up to the old man's bedroom. Hand it over."

Bigelow made two fists. Then he laughed again. "All right, I'll let ye see it. Hell, I'll let ye dig the money up for me! Why not? It's mine by law. Here, read it. See? He wrote my name on the envelope!"

And so he had. And the message in the envelope was also written in ink, in the same wavering hand:

Dere Andy now that Ab Chase is ded to—if sumthin happins to me you wil find the money we been keepin all these long yeres in a iron box in the coffin *wich we beried Caleb Atwell in.* I leave it all to you my beluved grandson cuz you ben sech a good grandson to me. Yours truly Zach Bigelow.

"In Caleb's coffin," choked Doc Strong.

Ellery's face was impassive. "How soon can you get an exhumation order, Doc?"

"Right now," exclaimed Doc. "I'm also deputy coroner of this district!"

And they took some men and they went back to the old burying ground, and in the darkening day they dug up the remains of Caleb Atwell and they opened the casket and found, on the corpse's knees, a flattish box of iron with a hasp but no lock. And, while two strong men held Andy Bigelow to keep him from hurling himself at the crumbling coffin, Doctor-Mayor-Chief of Police-Deputy Coroner Martin Strong held his breath and raised the lid of the iron box.

And it was crammed to the brim with moldy bills of large denominations.

In Confederate money.

No one said anything for some time, not even Andy Bigelow.

Then Ellery said, "It stood to reason. They found it buried in the cellar of an old Southern mansion—would it be Northern greenbacks? When they dug it up again after the War and brought it up to Jacksburg they probably had some faint hope that it might have some value. When they realized it was worthless, they decided to have some fun with it. This had been a private joke of those three old rascals since, roughly, 1865. When Caleb died last Memorial Day, Abner and Zach probably decided that, as the first of the trio to go, Caleb ought to have the honor of being custodian of their Confederate treasure in perpetuity. So one of them managed to slip the iron box into the coffin before the lid was screwed on. Zach's note bequeathing his 'fortune' to his 'beloved grandson'—in view of what I've seen of his beloved grandson today—was the old fellow's final joke."

Everybody chuckled; but the corpse stared mirthlessly and the silence fell again, to be broken by a weak curse from Andy Bigelow and Doc Strong's puzzled: "But Mr. Queen, that doesn't explain the murders."

"Well, now, Doc, it does," said Ellery; and then he said in a very different tone: "Suppose we put old Caleb back the way we found him, for your re-exhumation later for autopsy, Doc—and then we'll close the book on your Memorial Day murders."

Ellery closed the book in town, in the dusk, on the porch of Cissy Chase's house, which was central and convenient for everybody. Ellery and Nikki and Doc Strong and Cissy and Andy Bigelow—still clutching the iron box dazedly—were on the porch, and Lew Bagley and Bill Yoder and everyone else in Jacksburg, it seemed, stood about on the lawn and sidewalk, listening. And there was a touch of sadness to the soft twilight air, for something vital and exciting in the life of the village had come to an end.

"There's no trick to this," began Ellery, "and no joke, either, even though the men who were murdered were so old that death had grown tired of waiting for them. The answer is simple as the initials of their last names. Who knew that the supposed fortune was in Confederate money and therefore worthless? Only the three old men. One or another of the three would hardly have planned the deaths of the other two for possession of some scraps of valueless paper. So the murderer has to be someone who believed the fortune was legitimate and who—since until today there was no clue to the money's hiding place—knew he could claim it legally.

"Now of course that last-survivor-take-all business was pure moonshine, invented by Caleb, Zach, and Abner for their own amusement and the mystification of the community. But the would-be murderer didn't know that. The would-be murderer went on the assumption that the *whole* story was true, or he wouldn't have planned murder in the first place.

"Who would be able to claim the fortune legally if the last of the three old men— the survivor who presumably came into possession of the fortune on the deaths of the other two—died in his turn?"

"Last survivor's heir," said Doc Strong, and he rose.

"And who is the last survivor's heir?"

"Zach Bigelow's grandson, Andy." And the little mayor of Jacksburg stared hard at Bigelow, and a grumbling sound came from the people below, and Bigelow shrank against the wall behind Cissy, as if to seek her protection. But Cissy only looked at him and moved away.

"You thought the fortune was real," Cissy said scornfully, "so you killed Caleb Atwell and my great-grandpa so your grandfather'd be the last survivor so you could kill him the way you did today and get the fortune."

"That's it Ellery," cried Nikki.

"Unfortunately, Nikki, that's not it at all. You all refer to Zach Bigelow as the last survivor—"

"Well, he was," said Nikki in amazement.

"How could he not be?" said Doc Strong. "Caleb and Abner died first—"

"Literally, that's true," said Ellery, "but what you've all forgotten is that Zach Bigelow was the last survivor *only by accident.* When Abner Chase died early this morning, was it through poisoning, or some other violent means? No, Doc, you were absolutely positive he'd died of a simple cerebral hemorrhage—not by violence, but a natural death. Don't you see that if Abner Chase hadn't died a natural death early this morning, *he'd still be alive this evening?* Zach Bigelow would have put the bugle to his lips this afternoon, just as he did, just as Caleb Atwell did a year ago . . . *and at this moment Abner Chase would have been the last survivor.*

"And who was Abner Chase's only living heir, the girl who would have fallen heir to Abner's 'fortune' when, in time, or through her assistance, he joined his cronies in the great bivouac on the other side?

"You lied to me, Cissy," said Ellery to the shrinking girl in his grip, as a horror very like the horror of the burying ground in the afternoon came over the crowd of mesmerized Jacksburgers. "You pretended you didn't believe the story of the fortune. But that was only after your great-grandfather had inconsiderately died of a stroke just a few hours before old Zach would have died of poisoning, and you couldn't inherit that great, great fortune, anyway!"

Nikki did not speak until they were twenty-five miles from Jacksburg. Then all she said was, "And now there's nobody left to blow the Gettysburg bugle," and she continued to stare into the darkness toward the south.

THE LAST SPIN

EVAN HUNTER
(1926–   )

Two incredibly successful careers have been fashioned by the same man. He published the best-selling The Blackboard Jungle *when he was still in his twenties and had several additional best-sellers under the Evan Hunter name. In 1956 he created the ground-breaking 87th Precinct series and added a pseudonym, Ed McBain, as which he has become one of the world's most loved and esteemed authors. On the side, he wrote the screenplay for Alfred Hitchcock's* The Birds.

HE BOY SITTING OPPOSITE HIM was his enemy.

The boy sitting opposite him was called Tigo, and he wore a green silk jacket with an orange stripe on each sleeve. The jacket told Danny that Tigo was his enemy. The jacket shrieked, "Enemy, enemy!"

"This is a good piece," Tigo said, indicating the gun on the table. "This runs you close to forty-five bucks, you try to buy it in a store. That's a lot of money."

The gun on the table was a Smith & Wesson .38 Police Special.

It rested exactly in the center of the table, its sawed-off, two-inch barrel abruptly terminating the otherwise lethal grace of the weapon. There was a checked walnut stock on the gun, and the gun was finished in a flat blue. Alongside the gun were three .38 Special cartridges.

Danny looked at the gun disinterestedly. He was nervous and apprehensive, but he kept tight control of his face. He could not show Tigo what he was feeling. Tigo was the enemy, and so he presented a mask to the enemy,

cocking one eyebrow and saying, "I seen pieces before. There's nothing special about this one."

"Except what we got to do with it," Tigo said. Tigo was studying him with large brown eyes. The eyes were moist-looking. He was not a bad-looking kid, Tigo, with thick black hair and maybe a nose that was too long, but his mouth and chin were good. You could usually tell a cat by his mouth and his chin. Tigo would not turkey out of this particular rumble. Of that, Danny was sure.

"Why don't we start?" Danny asked. He wet his lips and looked across at Tigo.

"You understand," Tigo said, "I got no bad blood for you."

"I understand."

"This is what the club said. This is how the club said we should settle it. Without a big street diddlebop, you dig? But I want you to know I don't know you from a hole in the wall—except you wear a blue and gold jacket."

"And you wear a green and orange one," Danny said, "and that's enough for me."

347

"Sure, but what I was trying to say . . ."

"We going to sit and talk all night, or we going to get this thing rolling?" Danny asked.

"What I'm trying to say," Tigo went on, "is that I just happened to be picked for this, you know? Like to settle this thing that's between the two clubs. I mean, you got to admit your boys shouldn't have come in our territory last night."

"I got to admit nothing," Danny said flatly.

"Well, anyway, they shot at the candy store. That wasn't right. There's supposed to be a truce on."

"Okay, okay," Danny said.

"So like . . . like this is the way we agreed to settle it. I mean, one of us and . . . and one of you. Fair and square. Without any street boppin', and without any law trouble."

"Let's get on with it," Danny said.

"I'm trying to say, I never even seen you on the street before this. So this ain't nothin' personal with me. Whichever way it turns out, like . . ."

"I never seen you neither," Danny said.

Tigo stared at him for a long time. "That's cause you're new around here. Where you from originally?"

"My people come down from the Bronx."

"You got a big family?"

"A sister and two brothers, that's all."

"Yeah, I only got a sister." Tigo shrugged. "Well." He sighed. "So." He sighed again. "Let's make it, huh?"

"I'm waitin'," Danny said.

Tigo picked up the gun, and then he took one of the cartridges from the table top. He broke open the gun, slid the cartridge into the cylinder, and then snapped the gun shut and twirled the cylinder. "Round and round she goes," he said, "and where she stops, nobody knows. There's six chambers in the cylinder and only one cartridge. That makes the odds five-to-one that the cartridge'll be in firing position when the cylinder stops whirling. You dig?"

"I dig."

"I'll go first," Tigo said.

Danny looked at him suspiciously. "Why?"

"You want to go first?"

"I don't know."

"I'm giving you a break." Tigo grinned. "I may blow my head off first time out."

"Why you giving me a break?" Danny asked.

Tigo shrugged. "What the hell's the difference?" He gave the cylinder a fast twirl.

"The Russians invented this, huh?" Danny asked.

"Yeah."

"I always said they was crazy bastards."

"Yeah, I always . . ." Tigo stopped talking. The cylinder was stopped now. He took a deep breath, put the barrel of the .38 to his temple, and then squeezed the trigger.

The firing pin clicked on an empty chamber.

"Well, that was easy, wasn't it?" he asked. He shoved the gun across the table, "Your turn, Danny."

Danny reached for the gun. It was cold in the basement room, but he was sweating now. He pulled the gun toward him, then left it on the table while he dried his palms on his trousers. He picked up the gun then and stared at it.

"It's a nifty piece," Tigo said. "I like a good piece."

"Yeah, I do too," Danny said. "You can tell a good piece just by the way it feels in your hand."

Tigo looked surprised. "I mentioned that to one of the guys yesterday, and he thought I was nuts."

"Lots of guys don't know about pieces," Danny said, shrugging.

"I was thinking," Tigo said, "when I get old enough, I'll join the Army, you know? I'd like to work around pieces."

"I thought of that, too. I'd join now only my old lady won't give me permission. She's got to sign if I join now."

"Yeah, they're all the same," Tigo said, smiling. "Your old lady born here or the old country?"

"The old country," Danny said.

"Yeah, well, you know they got these old-fashioned ideas."

"I better spin," Danny said.

"Yeah," Tigo agreed.

Danny slapped the cylinder with his left hand. The cylinder whirled, whirled, and then stopped. Slowly, Danny put the gun to his head. He wanted to close his eyes, but he didn't dare. Tigo, the enemy, was watching him. He returned Tigo's stare, and then he squeezed the trigger.

His heart skipped a beat, and then over the roar of his blood he heard the empty click. Hastily, he put the gun down on the table.

"Makes you sweat, don't it?" Tigo said.

Danny nodded, saying nothing. He watched Tigo. Tigo was looking at the gun.

"Me now, huh?" Tigo said. He took a deep breath, then picked up the .38. He twirled the cylinder, waited for it to stop, and then put the gun to his head.

"Bang!" Tigo said, and then he squeezed the trigger. Again the firing pin clicked on an empty chamber. Tigo let out his breath and put the gun down.

"I thought I was dead that time," he said.

"I could hear the harps," Danny said.

"This is a good way to lose weight, you know that?" Tigo laughed nervously, and then his laugh became honest when he saw Danny was laughing with him. "Ain't it the truth? You could lose ten pounds this way."

"My old lady's like a house," Danny said, laughing. "She ought to try this kind of diet." He laughed at his own humor, pleased when Tigo joined him.

"That's the trouble," Tigo said. "You see a nice deb in the street, you think it's crazy, you know? Then they get to be our people's age, and they turn to fat." He shook his head.

"You got a chick?" Danny asked.

"Yeah, I got one."

"What's her name?"

"Aw, you don't know her."

"Maybe I do," Danny said.

"Her name is Juana." Tigo watched him. "She's about five-two, got these brown eyes . . ."

"I think I know her," Danny said. He nodded. "Yeah, I think I know her."

"She's nice, ain't she?" Tigo asked. He leaned forward, as if Danny's answer was of great importance to him.

"Yeah, she's nice," Danny said.

"The guys rib me about her. You know, all they're after . . . well, you know . . . they don't understand something like Juana."

"I got a chick, too," Danny said.

"Yeah. Hey maybe sometime we could . . ." Tigo cut himself short. He looked down at the gun, and his sudden enthusiasm seemed to ebb completely. "It's your turn," he said.

"Here goes nothing," Danny said. He twirled the cylinder, sucked in his breath, and then fired.

The empty click was loud in the stillness of the room.

"Man!" Danny said.

"We're pretty lucky, you know?" Tigo said.

"So far."

"We better lower the odds. The boys won't like it if we . . ." He stopped himself again, and then reached for one of the cartridges on the table. He broke open the gun again, and slipped the second cartridge into the cylinder. "Now we got two cartridges in here," he said. "Two cartridges, six chambers. That's four-to-two. Divide it, and you get two-to-two." He paused. "You game?"

"That's . . . that's what we're here for, ain't it?"

"Sure."

"Okay then."

"Gone," Tigo said, nodding his head. "You got courage, Danny."

"You're the one needs the courage," Danny said gently. "It's your spin."

Tigo lifted the gun. Idly, he began spinning the cylinder.

"You live on the next block, don't you?" Danny asked.

"Yeah." Tigo kept slapping the cylinder. It spun with a gently whirring sound.

"That's how come we never crossed paths, I guess. Also, I'm new on the scene."

"Yeah, well you know, you get hooked up with one club, that's the way it is."

"You like the guys on your club?" Danny asked, wondering why he was asking such a stupid question, listening to the whirring of the cylinder at the same time.

"They're okay." Tigo shrugged. "None of them really send me, but that's the club on my block, so what're you gonna do, huh?" His hand left the cylinder. It stopped spinning. He put the gun to his head.

"Wait!" Danny said.

Tigo looked puzzled. "What's the matter?"

"Nothing. I just wanted to say . . . I mean . . ." Danny frowned. "I don't dig too many of the guys on my club, either."

Tigo nodded. For a moment, their eyes locked. Then Tigo shrugged, and fired.

The empty click filled the basement room.

"Phew," Tigo said.

"Man, you can say that again."

Tigo slid the gun across the table.

Danny hesitated an instant. He did not want to pick up the gun. He felt sure that this time the firing pin would strike the percussion cap of one of the cartridges. He was sure that this time he would shoot himself.

"Sometimes I think I'm turkey," he said to Tigo, surprised that his thoughts had found voice.

"I feel that way sometimes, too," Tigo said.

"I never told that to nobody," Danny said. "The guys on my club would laugh at me, I ever told them that."

"Some things you got to keep to yourself. There ain't nobody you can trust in this world."

"There should be somebody you can trust," Danny said. "Hell, you can't tell nothing to your people. They don't understand."

Tigo laughed. "That's an old story. But that's the way things are. What're you gonna do?"

"Yeah. Still, sometimes I think I'm turkey."

"Sure, sure," Tigo said. "It ain't only that, though. Like sometimes . . . well, don't you wonder what you're doing stomping some guy in the street? Like . . . you know what I mean? Like . . . who's the guy to you? What you got to beat him up for? 'Cause he messed with somebody else's girl?" Tigo shook his head. "It gets complicated sometimes."

"Yeah, but . . ." Danny frowned again. "You got to stick with the club. Don't you?"

"Sure, sure . . . hell yes." Again their eyes locked.

"Well, here goes," Danny said. He lifted the gun. "It's just . . ." He shook his head, and then twirled the cylinder. The cylinder spun, and then stopped. He studied the gun, wondering if one of the cartridges would roar from the barrel when he squeezed the trigger.

Then he fired.

Click.

"I didn't think you was going through with it," Tigo said.

"I didn't neither."

"You got heart, Danny," Tigo said. He looked at the gun. He picked it up and broke it open.

"What you doing?" Danny asked.

"Another cartridge," Tigo said. "Six chambers, three cartridges. That makes it even money. You game?"

"You?"

"The boys said . . ." Tigo stopped talking. "Yeah, I'm game," he added, his voice curiously low.

"It's your turn, you know."

"I know."

Danny watched as Tigo picked up the gun.

"You ever been rowboating on the lake?"

Tigo looked across the table at Danny, his eyes wide. "Once," he said. "I went with Juana."

"Is it . . . is it any kicks?"

"Yeah. Yeah, it's grand kicks. You mean you never been?"

"No," Danny said.

"Hey, you got to try it, man," Tigo said excitedly. "You'll like it. Hey, you try it."

"Yeah, I was thinking maybe this Sunday I'd . . ." He did not complete the sentence.

"My spin," Tigo said wearily. He twirled the cylinder. "Here goes a good man," he said, and he put the revolver to his head and squeezed the trigger.

Click.

Danny smiled nervously. "No rest for the weary," he said. "But Jesus you've got heart. I don't know if I can go through with it."

"Sure, you can," Tigo assured him. "Listen, what's there to be afraid of?" He slid the gun across the table.

"We keep this up all night?" Danny asked.

"They said . . . you know . . ."

"Well, it ain't so bad. I mean, hell, we didn't have this operation, we wouldn'ta got a chance to talk, huh?" He grinned feebly.

"Yeah," Tigo said, his face splitting in a wide grin. "It ain't been so bad, huh?"

"No, it's been . . . well, you know, these guys on the club, who can talk to them?" He picked up the gun.

"We could . . ." Tigo started.

"What?"

"We could say . . . well . . . like we kept shootin' an' nothing happened, so . . ." Tigo shrugged. "What the hell! We can't do this all night, can we?"

"I don't know."

"Let's make this the last spin. Listen, they don't like it, they can take a flying leap, you know?"

"I don't think they'll like it. We're supposed to settle this for the clubs."

"Screw the clubs!" Tigo said. "Can't we pick our own . . ." The word was hard coming. When it came, his eyes did not leave Danny's face. ". . . friends?"

"Sure we can," Danny said vehemently. "Sure we can! Why not?"

"The last spin," Tigo said. "Come on, the last spin."

"Gone," Danny said. "Hey, you know, I'm *glad* they got this idea. You know that? I'm actually glad!" He twirled the cylinder. "Look, you want to go on the lake this Sunday? I mean with your girl and mine? We could get two boats. Or even one if you want."

"Yeah, one boat," Tigo said. "Hey, your girl'll like Juana, I mean it. She's a swell chick."

The cylinder stopped. Danny put the gun to his head quickly.

"Here's to Sunday," he said. He grinned at Tigo, and Tigo grinned back, and then Danny fired.

The explosion rocked the small basement room, ripping away half of Danny's head, shattering his face. A small cry escaped Tigo's throat, and a look of incredulous shock knifed his eyes.

Then he put his head on the table and began weeping.

STAND UP AND DIE!

MICKEY SPILLANE
(1918–   )

By most methods of keeping score, Spillane is the most successful mystery writer America has produced, with more than 200 million books sold. At one point, he had penned seven of the top ten best-selling works of fiction in the history of America. Though for a long time regarded as a pariah by critics and those who produced conventional detective fiction, he was finally given a Grand Master award by the Mystery Writers of America for lifetime achievement—and about time, too, many thought, as he almost single-handedly kept alive mystery fiction in the 1950s.

LAY ON MY BACK IN THE brush and watched the three buzzards circle over the ridge. "They're the smart ones," I thought. "No matter who loses, they win."

The three of them circled on a thermal, catching the updraft to the top of the rock shelf, then sliding down in formation, picking up speed so they could buzz the kill area for a quick check before picking a landing spot. They saw me, and when I waved, rode the breeze out of range and orbited until Operation Downstairs was complete.

For a second I grinned at them and wondered who learned from who. A long time ago I maneuvered like that over a Pacific beachhead.

But then it was different. It was honorable and noble and young. It was war and killing was righteously explained away and sometimes it was even fun to pull the trigger. Then you bragged to your wingmates about the kills, glorying in the noise and fumes and sometimes it took a long while before you realized the complete waste and foolishness of it all.

Now dying was only a few trees or a couple rocks away—and upstairs the real winners watched and waited.

Left of me there was a metallic clang of a bolt-action rifle reloading. The shrill whistle of the tree bugs stopped abruptly and I turned over on my stomach, bellying down as close as I could get so I could see through the underside of the brush.

I knew they wouldn't give me credit for having any sense. To them outsiders and animals were classed together— fair game stupid enough to get themselves treed. It made me think of that classic line from a book, *Animal Farm* . . . "All men are created equal, but some are created more equal than others." Then I grinned again and wondered how they'd take to having the buzzards circle their side of the deal for a while.

The spot I had been watching for a few minutes moved and I knew it wasn't a tree fungus. It took a minute more, I could see the length of rifle barrel. It was angled off, so they hadn't located me fully yet. They needed a sound, or a movement, then all the guns I couldn't see would swivel and zero in. They knew I had the .45 and maybe I had the two boxes of shells. But it wouldn't matter. They had the rifles. They could stay out of range.

Trouble was, I thought, they didn't really know the range of a .45. They discounted trajectory. When you had to live off birds you shot with a .45 for three long weeks before they rescued you from that stupid little Pacific island, you didn't discount trajectory any more.

I leveled the gun in the crotch of the brush root and sighted it. The target was nice and white and unsuspecting. Then I squeezed the trigger and the whole mountainside blew up in noise and the target was a screaming, cursing joker yelling the hillbilly version of "medic!"

Old Man Hart's voice rolled up from the gully and said, "Who got hit?"

Then it was real funny because nobody wanted to talk and give away his position. But not Clemson. He found either a rock or a tree to hide behind and hollered out, "He done it to me, Paw. It's Clem! He done . . ."

"How bad he git you, son?"

"My hand, Paw. He's got him a rifle someplace. He's got . . ."

"He ain't got no rifle, son. He just got you. You come down here, Clemson."

It was quiet for a second while the horror of it went through Clemson's mind. Then he sobbed softly, "He'll get me sure, Paw. He's got a rifle."

"He ain't got no rifle, son," the old man repeated.

Clemson's voice had a wail in it. "He'll get me, Paw. I'm hurt."

My leg started to knot with a cramp and I eased my foot out. The slightest sound, the tiniest movement, and I'd have had it.

Upstairs the buzzards were at 3,000 again, circling for a complete reconnoiter.

The old man's rumbling voice said, "Mitch . . . you hear me, Mitch? You won't shoot my boy if he comes out to git fixed up, will you now?"

I thought, *Hart, old boy, you're a rotten one. I speak up like a sportsman, give the kid a chance and you zero in on me by sound.*

I didn't say a word. Down the hill, Clemson was still sobbing. Over thirty and crying like a baby. Maybe he knew what his Paw had in mind.

Hart said, "Okay, boy, you come down here right now and get yourself fixed up."

The sobbing was so jerky and unrestrained then. The old snake was ready to throw his son to the lions. So I wouldn't talk. Now I'd try for a kill shot and the others could zero in on that.

Clemson was hurting too hard to think. He was crying and thrashing around loud enough to cover any sound and when he broke for it and started down the slope I rolled out of my cover, skirted a pair of fallen trees and went under the brush to the spot he had left.

My shot had smashed his hand and taken a chunk out of the rifle stock besides. It lay there in a mess of blood on top of a dozen shells Clemson never got to use. While there was enough clatter to cover me, I propped the rifle in the general direction of the old man, lit a butt to use as a fuse, and with a thin strip of shirt I rigged up a Rube Goldberg crazy invention-type deal that would fire the gun when the cigarette burned through the cloth.

When it was set, I got out, held a position far to the south and waited. Clemson made the bottom of the gully and a hard smack stopped the yelling. It grew quiet again. Too quiet. The old man was thinking. Things weren't working out like he wanted them to. He had the wrong cat by the ears and the back feet scratched pretty deep. Of all six, the old one'd be the only one to see the picture clearly. He'd be the only one to know the shot wasn't an accident, the only one to know that the hunted could steer clear of the bait.

Those damned black buzzards dropped another thousand feet trying to determine if it was over yet or not.

Then suddenly the rifle spat out a roll of thunder and while the slug ricocheted off with a screaming whistle, every gun out there zeroed in on the spot and salvoed a full clip. A moment later it was a full barrage and nobody heard me getting out of there. Nobody at all.

They didn't even hear Old Man Hart yelling himself hoarse that it was a trick and I was laughing because the old fox had figured it right, but his line of communication had broken down.

He sat there in his wheelchair hating me with his whole face and just before I got to him he did something nobody knew or even thought he could do. He moved one hand and jerked an antique Colt revolver up and just as fast I shot it out of his fingers.

I said, "It's good you got no feeling in that hand, old man."

"I got feeling."

"Hurts?"

"It hurts," he said.

I turned and looked up the mountain. "I've seen better hill men in white shirts and ties."

"They'll git you," he told me.

When I shook my head, I was grinning. "Maybe. But I'll tell you something, old man. If I get took, I get most of them first. You too. I'm not worth fighting over."

"It's a long way out of these hills, Mitch. Long way. If I were younger, I'd git you myself."

"No you wouldn't. You'd be dead like the rest of your stupid breed will be if they get too close to me. Because an animal runs, don't figure it to be scared. Sometimes it's smart. Strategic."

"You won't get out, boy. You know it too." The old man's eyes were so blue and watery he looked dead. "Yer lost right now. Even if you got past my kin, you'd die on the hills. There ain't no way out, boy—for you. You'd better off shot fast and proper. Even a good hill man would have trouble gettin' out if they didn't take the pass and you can't find it. The kin is back there too. You . . ."

Then he stopped because he knew I figured it. He was stalling. Maybe I didn't even have a second left, but I took the time to do it anyway. *You're no good if you're not mean,* I thought. *You'll never get the time to squeeze out or even think unless they figure you to be as mean as they are.* I grabbed the side wheel of the chair, ripped it loose and the old man toppled out cursing.

I started to move then—and none too soon. What I expected came fast. Two of the shots kicked up dirt at my feet and another whistled right by my face. I made the rocks and the shade side of the mountain where I had at least a million-to-one chance of getting out alive and when I picked a decent defensive position I squatted and took a breather.

The wind carried their voices up to me now. Anger and chagrin pitched their tone high and over it all the old man was swearing at them. One of them, most likely Big George, would be trailing me, I knew. I sat, waited, and when I saw the swaying of the grass against the wind, picked up a fist-sized rock and underhanded it in a long arc.

Chance and circumstance play cute tricks. I didn't mean it to happen, but Big George was pulling himself up a shale face when that rock smashed his fingers to pulp and he made more racket than his kid brother when he scrambled back into the gully.

For maybe thirty seconds there was utter, complete silence. An absolute void of sound, but the wonder and awe in their minds was like an odor I could smell all the way up here. I sat back, felt the trickle of water coming out of the mountainside and decided that it wouldn't be too bad a place to die.

Luck only went so far. You were only so good . . . and others were good too.

Too bad. It was really too bad. I looked up the slope and knew I'd never make it after all.

With Caroline it could have been pretty nice. Beautiful even.

Now I'd never find out.

It was funny, how things worked out.

Some place in back of the ridge, she'd be tearing things up and throwing them around, wishing I was there to throw them at. She'd be hating me as hard as she could hate anything and even with all that primitive fury charging around inside her mind, she'd be lovely and beautiful. That crazy blonde hair would still be swirling soft and the grey-green of her eyes alive and hungry-looking. Because I did what I did to her she would cook a special supper tonight and for the one who fired the kill shot she'd make a special dish.

By then the three vultures would be exploring their main course—me.

Caroline. Lovely, wild Caroline.

She was looking up with wide eyes and that luscious mouth pulled tight when I came down out of the blue. She didn't see me until I called from twenty feet up and when she saw me twisting under the chute she froze.

"Hey kid . . . get outa the way! Beat it . . . get over, will you!" I yelled.

I yanked hard on the suspension lines and spilled enough air to come in at a gentle rake. But she didn't move. She just watched. It was bad enough trying to hit the only clearing within miles from 5,500 feet without having to clobber the only broad around doing it. I could see the ground breeze that shot up the gully and before it caught me, unhooked my chest and leg snaps as if for a water landing, came in with a *swoosh*, hit the dirt and ran with it ten feet or so—right into the dame. For some silly reason the wind stopped and the chute came down around us like a tent collapsing on its centerpole and I said, "Well, hello."

"Man, man," she said, "I never did see anything like that in all my whole life."

"Honey," I grinned, "you better remember this day because you'll never see another one like it again."

Slowly, her face untightened and I had to squint to make sure it was the same girl. She reached out and touched my arm. "Where'd you come from, man?"

"From a lobster pot, honey."

"Lobster?"

"They're like crawfish but with two great big claws so big." The corners of her mouth twitched. Her eyes went over my head and I saw the beauty in them. "From up there?"

"That's right. Up there."

"I know you're not lying, man. I saw you come. You real for sure?"

"Honey," I said, "I ought to ask *you* that. I've gone over the side before, but it was never like this."

"What?"

"When's the last time you've been kissed, honey?"

The eyes went real big and she showed white high on her cheeks. There was a strange rigidity in her body that outlined the flat of her stomach and swelled the gentle curves into taut, unbelievable contours. I took her arms, gently, pulled her to me easy, then kissed her. I did it softly, feeling that soft tension in her mouth, feeling the kiss go suddenly hot, though she barely touched me.

I should have known then. I should have been on the ball. I should have taken off like Moody's goose right then, only it was the kind of kiss I had never known before. It was all stupid and impossible. Who ever heard of bailing out to come down under the sheet with a strange blonde in never-never land?

She pushed me away and when she did, the fire burned out. Her face was cold and hard, her mouth trembling under an emotion I couldn't catch. "You want to go back, man. You go back where you came from."

Very softly I told her, "There's no going back, sugar."

Just as softly she said, "You in trouble now, man."

I flipped back the folds of the chute, threw it over our heads and rolled it up into a tight pack. There was a hollow in the side of the hill that took it nicely, then I stowed the .45 and the two boxes of shells in the knee pockets of the coveralls and turned back to the dame.

"Where to now, girl?" She frowned at my expression. "Where do we go from here?"

I explained.

"To home. No place else, is there? Not 'thout crossing the hills and we can't do that."

Out of curiosity I asked, "Why not?"

"You'd get killed."

"Oh." I grinned at her again. "What about you?"

"I could go. Not you, though."

My grin was getting hard to hold in place. "I'm important?"

She frowned again, but the meaning got through to her. "You kissed me," she said. "You kissed me a shooting kiss. You going to have to shoot for kissing me, man. I'm spoke up for. You going to have to shoot to keep me or shoot to get rid of me. You in trouble, man."

There wasn't anything I could say. Suddenly she came out with the screwiest-looking revolver I'd seen in a long time and let it dangle in her hand. "What you want to do, man?" she asked me.

I had to laugh. "Oh, hell, honey, I'm with you," I said.

She tucked the gun away in her patchwork shirt. "Then we go tell them, man. We go see Pap and the boys and tell them. You in real trouble, man, but I ain't scared." She looked up at the blue again, her eyes showing the puzzle behind them. "I used to think something like this would happen one day."

Then she looked at me and there wasn't any before or any afterward. There was only now and she was all soft and gone and in my hands she was mine and beautiful. Her mouth was a wet thing full of unexpected life that surprised even her.

It was me that pulled back and I said, "Was that a shooting kiss too?"

She nodded solemnly, strangely. "That was a killin' shootin' kiss."

"What's your name?"

"Caroline. What's yours?"

"Mitch."

She took my hand. "We go now," she said.

357

Up-hollow they called it. There was water and grass with a mountainside of grey chestnuts for firewood, fifty years dead from the blight. There were deer runs and ducks nested in the reeds on the far side of the pond. Fish were for pulling or netting in the stream that coursed through the hollow and you didn't need a license. The road was packed dirt and where a cart or wagon could bog down, the soft spot was filled with head-sized rocks.

It was lush with planted things, bearing fruit heavily though seeded with the abandon of the agriculturally-ignorant. It was a place time had overlooked.

The three stores we passed bore the earmarks of a civilization far off, express stickers on the sides of the barrels and cartons in the unloaded wagon, a small, limp mailsack . . . a window dressed with a rack of shotguns and rifles. The people outside looked our way with only passing curiosity, never thinking a newcomer could be here by design or desire.

The up-trail was serpentine and noisy with the sounds of wildlife in the trees. A mile off a pack of hounds blared a welcome at the sound of our cart and came rushing to meet it. All of them grinned a dog grin at her and let their bristles up when they caught my smell on her. But they didn't try for me. I said "Shut up," softly to the red one in the lead and we knew each other quick. His tail didn't wag or drop. But he looked and knew. I wasn't a patsy.

Then the cabin was there in the clearing with the six men standing on the porch watching. The old man in the wheelchair sat calmly, the cigar in his mouth drifting off lazy smoke. One of the men came down, flicked the ash off the stogie, then put it back in his mouth again.

Caroline said, "My papa. The other ones are my brothers."

The quiet came on again. "What's your last name, sugar?"

"Hart."

"Mine's Valler. In case you have to introduce me. What's wrong with the old man?"

"He got backbone shot by a Grady. That was ten years ago."

"What happened to Grady?"

"They ain't no more Gradys," she said.

The cart pulled up to the cabin, the mule nosing the rail familiarly. I jumped down, reached up for Caroline's arm and even though she pulled away, took it anyhow. She sprang off beside me and if I hadn't held her, would have gone ahead.

But not this time. I made sure of that. I walked up by myself and looked at the old guy in the wheelchair. I said, "My name is Mitch Valler, Mr. Hart." I didn't hold out my hand.

He nodded. "How come you here, man?"

Behind me Caroline said, "He come from the air, Pap. On a white sheet."

That struck the old man funny and he smiled. "You come outa the air?"

"That's right. From a lobster pot."

"From a lobster pot, Papa?" Caroline said. "Is there such?"

The smile stayed on. "There's such, girl." The smile changed. "But not upstairs. Not in the sky." He paused, then said, "You told my gal that?"

Caroline answered for me. "I seen him. It was for real, Papa. He came down from the sky."

"But not from a lobster pot, son," Old Man Hart said.

Now I smiled. "We call it that. *Lobster Pot* was her name, a C-47 by WW2 out of 13th AF. You catch, Papa?"

"I catch, son."

I let my shoulders relax. "Then get off my back."

"You nervous, son."

"No."

"I wasn't asking. I was telling."

"Still no, Papa."

"We don't like outsiders, son."

"Tough."

"We can make it that way."

This time I gave him my biggest smile. All the teeth. I looked up at the porch, at him, then at Caroline. "You ain't got enough men to even try, Pap," I said.

The bomb went off slow and easy. When it hit the old man all the way, the smile faded, but what he was waiting for didn't come soon enough. The first step on the porch steps took too long like somebody was saying, "*You* do it first . . ." and when it did come the lad who took it hadn't really got the meaning of what I'd said.

He came down and edged up to me slowly, trying hard to be sure.

This had to be the tough one, so I said, "You slob. You stinking, miserable, inhospitable slob."

All the eyes in his own world were on him, so he came in swinging.

I knocked him cold with one shot. My guts were all gone and churning and now I couldn't be still any more. I said, "I kissed the kid a shooting kiss, too. I did it twice and I'll do it again and if you want to start shooting, then go ahead."

Down in the dirt the big guy rolled up in a ball and groaned. The old man said, "We don't want to shoot, son. Not yet. We ain't got claim yet. She's spoke for by Billy Bussy and he'll be over soon enough. A few days and he'll be over." He rubbed his chin against his chest to wipe off the cigar spit. "If he didn't, then we would. But we won't have to. Billy Bussy'll shoot you."

"Meanwhile I'll stick around, Papa."

"Meanwhile you gotta, son." He turned his head and looked at Caroline. "Get the boy fixed up, Carrie. Give him a runnin' room where he has a chance to git from."

"I'll stay outside," I said.

"The bugs'll get you," he told me.

"So I'll take the runnin' room, Papa," I grinned.

At supper I was guested at the far end of the table. I had taken off the coveralls and my slacks and black sport shirt looked almost formal for the occasion. Conversation was built on silence, on underbrow glances and grimaces that had their beginning in suspicion and hatreds.

Caroline came in with a tray loaded with foods peculiar to the country, smoking an aroma rare and exotic. She put the tray down, then served food in gluttonous portions to the old man and her brothers.

When it came my turn, their faces fell in a screwy disbelief. I got the tenderloin. What was best went on my plate. I looked at her, threw a kiss and said, "Thanks, sugar."

Old Man Hart made a noise eating. "There's a saying . . ." he started.

I nodded. "The condemned man, and so on . . ."

"That's the one I was thinking of," he said.

Two words I gave him. They weren't "Good night."

Down next to the old man at the end, Big George managed to chew in spite of the bump on his jaw and tried to kill me with his eyes.

I said, "Mr. Hart . . ."

"Yes, son?"

"What's with these lumps you raised? Seems like you've been around."

He answered noncommittally, "Environment, son. Or maybe what a man likes to do. Me, I got a taste for reading and knowin' things. The boys here'll have none of it."

Evidently he caught my glance toward the kitchen. "Some of it rubbed off me onto Carrie, but she's as wild as the rest too."

"But you like to see a good shooting," I said.

"Not so much a shootin' as a good killin'."

"Why me?"

Big George had enough listening. "Ye outsiders need killin'," he said. "Ye gonna git it too. Ye dig holes and scare folks hereabouts with them things and take their land so don't ye complain none about gettin' dead."

He had something else to say, but Caroline came in again and stacked the old man's plate so he could eat just bending his head . . . and that ended the talking.

The boys all finished eating and went out to the porch where they lined up and smoked. In three hip pockets the butt-ends of single-action Colts lay at an angle.

The old man wiped his mouth against his shoulders before looking at me.

"It's the girl I care about, son," he told me. "Jest don't do my girl wrong. Y'hear? It's just an 'in case.' Billy Bussy'll kill you anyway, so it's just an 'in case.'" His eyes went real watery, then he turned his head and bellowed, "Carrie!"

She came out, barely glancing my way, then rolled the old man out of the room. I got up, walked outside, across the porch, then went down the steps. All six of them converged behind me. I swivelled fast with the .45 in my fist and said, "If any one of you got the guts of a snake, you'll draw and shoot. Go ahead. There's six of you. One's got to get me, but the rest are going to get their stomachs opened up."

Nobody moved. I let them see the hammer of the rod thumbed all the way back, then shoved it under my belt so it nestled against my navel. "You're a bunch of gutless pigs," I said. "Don't try for my back because I'll get at least one."

To make it real showy, I turned and started walking away. At ten feet I turned, dropped and shot the hat off Big George's head and the hand that was on the gun came back in front trembling a little and the expression on the faces of the rest was worth the dust I had to spit out of my mouth.

The rest of the way I didn't have to worry. I went down the road toward the stores and though they followed, it was out of range. It was a good three miles, but the walking was pleasant and the evening cool and comfortable. For a condemned man the freedom was great and I wondered how far I could go on the road.

When I turned the bend, I was smiling. Then I stopped.

Everybody was there. It wasn't Saturday night, but everybody was there.

A great telegraph system. Something like Chinese, I guessed. Nobody could figure out how, but it worked.

I turned in on the board sidewalks and let all the faces look at me. Sixty, I estimated. That would make the entire population. Sixty and most were interbred. Sixty toothy grins. Some maybe not so toothy.

At the far end of the road a wagon was drawn up and two men and a boy sat there with rifles crooked across their arms. The road didn't go very far at all.

It could have been rough then if it weren't for Caroline. She came in on the cart, nosed the mule onto the rail and jumped out. She came straight for me and stood there tall and blonde and different from all the rest with her mouth set and said, "What you aim to do?"

"Nothing, honey." I reached for her hand, but instead of taking it, just touched it. She had to live here. Not me.

She said, "They heard how you come to be here. The Cahill boy saw you. They figger for another trick. You in bad trouble, man."

"So will you be if you stick too close to me."

"Townfolk won't bother me none."

I reached out and touched her again. "No, but *I* will."

Things happened in her eyes again and she sucked her breath in deep. This was a real dame, I thought. One of the few. Her smile was big and moist-looking when it came, her tongue making a nervous flick across her lips.

"I'm gonna hate for Billy Bussy to have to kill you, Mitch."

I grinned and shook me head. "He won't."

She grinned back and nodded. "Yes he will."

Across the street an old man giggled. It was high and nervous and out of proportion to the situation. It wasn't good to be stationary. I took her arm and started down the walk.

The hostility in their faces was ridiculous. Softly, I said, "Honey, why they so riled up?"

She looked at me queerly. "They love their land, Mitch. For a long time they've been here and they don't want it stole."

"I don't get it. Who's stealing it?"

She shook her head and said nothing. We kept on walking.

The post office was one corner of a store that bore a faded "DRY GOODS" sign on the window. Behind the counter on the wall were rows of boxes, each meticulously marked with spit-wet indelible pencil. Only two had letters; a few others held scrawled and folded notes, a roll of yarn. In one, in the lower left-hand corner, was a gun.

"Howdy, son."

I looked around and nodded at the old man who came from the back of the room. Then I grinned and pointed to the gun. "Whose mail is that?"

"Reckon you'll find out soon enough, son." He lifted the hinged counter-top and squeezed inside.

"It's not with the B's, Pop. Isn't that where it belongs?"

"Shouldn't make fun of Billy Bussy, son."

"I can't help it. He sounds like somebody out of Treasure Island."

"He'll be in for that gun soon. By now he heard."

"If he keeps his ears open, he'll hear even more."

"Billy's been to war, son. He even killed a few hereabouts." He looked at me carefully. "You ever killed anybody, son?"

"Why you asking?"

"Kind of like you maybe."

I nodded, but I wasn't grinning anymore. "I've killed. I didn't like it any. Somebody forced it on me. Sometimes it was the one who forced it who got killed. If I have to, I'll do it again. But I don't figure on ever having to do it again. It makes me sick . . . you know why?"

"Don't get so wound-up, son. You're yelling."

I took a deep, slow breath. "Because I'm good at killing, Pop. Something inside me makes me an expert and I hate it. I'm like a damn snake when it comes to killing and I can do it fast and quiet and get out and only a long time later do I feel the hate at myself building up." I leaned over the counter with my hands all balled-up and said, "If I find anybody who makes me want to do those things again, I'll tear him apart."

"No call to get wound-up son."

I stared at him and stood up. "Sure, Pop, sure."

"What was it you wanted?"

"There a phone in this town?"

"No phone. T'aint decent anyway. You want to say something to a body you . . ."

"How do you get out of here?"

He fingered the counter uneasily and shrugged. "Used to be a road, but . . ."

"Pop," I said.

"Son?"

"The mail comes in. It goes out. How?"

"Chigger Bolidy takes it out by mule. Been doin' it ten years now. Same mule."

"Pop . . . they don't give post-office franchises to go every other week. This is the government."

". . . Goes over the mountain. Doesn't mean much 'cause there's never mail anyhow. Sometimes gov'ment stuff, sometimes a real letter. Gov'ment don't care much 'cause there ain't no other way. They got to go along. You know the gov'ment."

"Yeah," I said. "I know." I straightened up and tried again. "How does anybody get out at all?"

"To where, son? Who wants to go?"

He was starting to grate on me. "Anybody with sense."

"If you know what's outside, why go back? Hear tell there's nothing but trouble and taxes."

"Plus central heating, taxis, hotels . . ." I stopped, looked at him and grinned real big. "Pop, can you make a sucker out of me! A regular Groucho Marx, you are. Okay, I'll go along for the ride. I'll be the straight man. Now look . . . you have a handful of shops down the street out there. I saw some nice new guns, some modern hardware, household staples in pretty city-printed boxes and bags . . . well, hell, goodies I can pick up in any city. It all has to come in, Pop. Not by mule. By truck maybe. At the worst, by cart. But it comes in. How? We played our little game. Now how do things come in and go out?"

"Why so, son?"

"Because I want to leave."

"Why?"

I wiped my hand across my face. "Because I have an accident report to fill out for the Civil Aeronautics people. I have an insurance policy to collect on. I have some people to let know I am alive before they start collecting survivor's pay. Because the sky will be black with . . ."

This time I stopped cold and ran it down inside my head a bit. Then I said, "So how do those things come in, Pop?"

"Like you mentioned, son."

"What?"

"By cart. Billy Bussy brings 'em in. He got his own ways. But the only one who could ever do it is Billy Bussy."

"And Billy Bussy's going to shoot me."

He agreed. "So it shouldn't be no use trying to leave."

"The news passed fast, Pop."

Once more he nodded.

"Billy Bussy'll take me?"

"You're almost dead as of now, son. Billy likes to do it slow. He's real mean, he is."

"I can hardly wait."

"That's good, son, because he'll be in this afternoon. He's heard."

"And what will he do?"

The old man looked sad. "He'll get his gun. He'll hurt you first, then you'll get shot up."

"I will?"

"You will."

I looked up at the sign over his head that read, "U.S. POST OFFICE" and under it in smaller letters, hand printed, "Oliver Cooper, Postmaster." I asked. "No law . . .?"

"County seat's in Pawley. Deputy comes sometimes when there's need, but never before."

For some reason I grinned again. "Isn't there need now?"

"Sure," he nodded, "but there ain't that much time." He tightened his face and there was pity in his eyes. "Besides," he added, "the deputy is scared headless of Billy. You see, Billy killed his last boss."

"Oh." I frowned and said, "Why didn't somebody do something about it? You just don't shoot people."

"He didn't shoot him, Billy didn't. They was wrestling friendly-like, sort of showing off in front of Caroline Hart and Billy broke his neck sort of."

"I told you I was like a snake, Pop. Cold blood all through. Billy won't kill me."

"Oh, it's not just Billy."

I stared at him. "I had a feeling it was more than that."

The old man waved a thumb toward the street. "Almost anybody out there'd be more than glad to do it, son."

"Why? What the hell's wrong with this place?"

He shrugged and came out from behind the counter. "People like you. What you come for?"

I grabbed his arm and squeezed it until he winced. "I bailed out of a C-47 at five thousand feet. I never would have been over this section at all if a weather front hadn't moved in." I let his arm go and watched while he rubbed it. I could have picked one side of that damned mountain or the other and this time I sure goofed!

"You knew what you were doing, son."

"What?"

"It was one way of getting in."

"I want to get out."

"You'll have to ask Billy Bussy. It's his road."

I breathed in deeply. "Sure, Pop, sure. See you around."

She was waiting for me outside, standing with her back to the sun without knowing it was playing tricks with her hair. In silhouette she was a lithe thing, and with the breeze pressing her dress tight against her you knew that there was nothing dainty or soft about her. Her thighs would be smooth, taut flesh, firm and supple with youth, hardened by hill-running.

When I touched her arm, she tightened and flicked a glance toward the group down the street. "Scared?"

"No, but after Billy kills you he'll beat me. Bad."

"Then your tough brothers can work him over," I said.

"They scared, man. Besides, they don't want you around. They guess I need to be beat. I kissed you back, man."

"Everybody know that?"

She nodded. "The Cahill boy saw it."

I had to laugh at her. "But we were under the sheet, remember?"

"It figgered though," she said.

I stopped and looked at her a long time, drinking in the yellow of her hair that framed her face and the wet fullness of her mouth. There was a deep softness in her eyes, but they were unreadable. I said, "That's right, honey. It figured. There could have been no other answer."

She said, "What're you thinkin'?"

I shook my head. "I don't know. It has you in it, but I don't know." Before she could answer, I grabbed her arm and swung into a walk. We crossed the wheel-gouged street to the shady side and in the dusty face of the store windows I could count the hostile eyes behind us that counted each step we took.

A dirty little kid ran out from between the buildings, one arm pumping while the other held up his pants. He was laughing back over his shoulder at the pair chasing him and never saw us. The others did and kept straight on out into the street. He slammed head on into me, staggered back with his breath wooshing out of him and sat down.

I reached down and yanked him up. "Get hurt?"

His pants were halfway down his legs and he wasn't even trying to get them back up. He just stood there with his eyes big and round.

Caroline said, "That's the Cahill boy."

I let him go and half hissed between my teeth, *"Take me to your leader!"*

Nothing in the world ever jumped and ran so fast with half-hung pants as he did then.

"What'd you say to him, man?"

I squeezed her arm. "Science fiction joke, kitten. Never mind. Look . . . Do you know where I can find Chigger Bolidy?"

She squinted at me curiously. "Down by the old barn where he keeps his mule, maybe."

"Come on."

"Mitch, man . . ." She paused, frowning. "You might make trouble for him. You strictly trouble, man and Chigger . . . he's had plenty."

I said, "Don't be silly. I won't hurt him. Come on."

Up close you could see that at one time the barn had been red. One half the door was gone and the huge hand-wrought hinges had been wrenched loose by too many chinning contests. The air was tangy with the smell of manure and dried hay, and inside heavy hooves shuffled impatiently on the dirt floor.

We found him propped up against the back of the place asleep, his hat down over his face. He was small and dried out like an old pea, his hands rein-calloused and brown from the sun. I shoved his hat back with my toe and nudged him and when his eyes worked open they were hangover-red and watery.

He knew who I was. He got that tight, scared looked and struggled to his feet, his back pressed against the wall.

"Caroline Hart . . ." his voice had a wheeze to it, "what you . . . think you doin', girl!"

"Easy, Chigger. Relax."

He swallowed again. "What you want with me? You know what's goin' to happen to you?"

I nodded. "Yeah. Everybody's told me. I'm hep. Now you tell me something."

His face pulled so tight he had to talk between his teeth. "I ain't telling you nothin'! You dirty killin' . . ." He stopped suddenly. "What you want, mister?"

"You go over that mountain to the other side," I said. "I want to go along with you."

His teeth were chipped and worn close to the gums. They were brown with tobacco stain but he was real glad to let me see every one he had left inside his smile. "You goin' to stay here and get what's comin', mister."

"That could be a long time," I said.

"So."

364

"The mail franchise. You *have* to go out."

The smile stretched wider. "I don't have to do nothin'."

"The government . . ."

"You know what they can do," he finished. He shook his head before I could say it. "Nobody here writes hardly. If they do, nobody answers hardly. Post office won't miss my trip none. Not till after you're dead."

The whole thing started to scratch at me. "Old man, you had to leave a trail someplace."

He came away from the wall, still grinning, but sure of himself now. "I did? Find it, son. Go look for it. I go over the same trail twice it's something. Can't even find it myself half the time." He stopped and looked me up and down. "Don't figger you could find it if I painted it white." He craned his neck toward the mountain. "*She'd* kill you, she would. Ain't scarcely nobody who can get over her. Sure you won't."

"You'd be real happy to see me dead, wouldn't you, Pop?"

"Real happy."

"Why?"

The smile faded. "Murdering, stealing sons, all of you . . ." He stopped there, then shuffled off into the barn.

"Mitch . . ."

I swung around. "Okay, sugar, maybe you'll know the answer. Since I'm almost already dead it won't make much difference anyway. Chigger goes out by mule. So he's got his own trail. But how come he don't follow Billy Bussy's road out? The guy uses a cart and that's a trail nobody can hide—not even an Indian. How come?"

Her eyes showed the pity she felt. "Nobody has nothing much hereabouts. You have a farming patch, you keep it. You have a store, you keep that. What you got, you pass on. Nothing else to leave to kin 'cept what you got. Try to take it away and you got killin' talkin'. Chigger . . . he's got his mule and his trail. Billy got his cart and his road. Take it away and you got a killin' talkin'."

"*Damn!*"

"Mitch . . ."

"Aw, shut up." I turned and looked back at the row of buildings that lay dirty in the sun. "Is that all those slobs think of, what they got? Is this their whole damn world?"

Her hand touched my arm. "Ain't much, what they got, but everybody respects everybody else's. Chigger wouldn't go on Billy's trail."

"And if he did?" I turned and watched her. Very gently she bit on her lip.

"He'd never come back down off'n the mountain."

"And if Billy took Chigger's trail?"

Something happened in her eyes. She shrugged, not answering.

From the street back of us somebody shouted her name. We both looked and saw Big George standing there, his hands tight on his hips.

"I got to go. Pap and the boys are in."

"For the killin'?"

She sucked her breath in hard. "Maybe."

"Billy's due in soon?"

This time she looked at the sun first, then turned back to me and nodded. "Two more hours."

I glanced toward the buildings and she caught it.

"Pap and the boys like to get comfortable," she said.

"And you?"

Softly, she touched my hand.

I grinned, reached out and pulled her in close. Her body was warm and alive, pressing against me hard, searching to touch me all over. Her breathing was a quick sob—and then her mouth exploded into mine. For one brief second there was nobody in the world but us—then I pushed her away and looked into her eyes and saw what they said.

She ran then.

I said, "Hell, you can only get killed once."

From the doorway of the barn Chigger Bolidy grinned at me. "Once is enough, mister."

From the rise behind the buildings where the pines stood thick and tall I could see the mountain. From here she looked tall and soft, like the enveloping arms of some great mother.

Enveloping hell! Those same arms could smother you just as fast!

Height and distance were deceptive and you had the feeling that you were in the center of some natural coliseum. I grinned at the simile because in a way it was. This was the floor of an amphitheater and behind me were the cages of killers waiting for the right time to put on the show.

The sun had gone down far enough to put half the bowl in shadows, but across the way all was gold and fiery-looking.

Pretty, I thought, Real nice. It was a beautiful spot to die in.

I felt the motion behind me before I heard it. I turned around easily, as though still watching the rim of the mountain, then paused a few seconds. It come again and this time I jumped so fast the thing in the bushes didn't have time to scream before I had a hand across its mouth.

I took it back to the clearing and laughed at the great big eyeballs that quivered almost as much as its skin.

I said, "What's your first name?"

It took a long time coming out. "Trumble."

"Trumble Cahill," I said, and dropped the kid who had seen me come down out of the blue.

"You . . . gonna kill me?"

I didn't say anything.

He looked up at the sky. "You ain't agonna . . ." then the full horror of it struck him, ". . . take me . . . up there!"

I could have had some fun, but I took the curse off it by laughing and there's one thing a kid knows for real and that's a laugh. When you mean it, he knows it and that's a laugh. When you mean it, he knows it and this one knew it.

He let go his hands, his shoulders dropped and those big eyes went back to normal. A quick smile jerked at the corner of his mouth.

"I seen you when you come."

"I know."

"How'd you do that?" He squirmed and drew back, another thought coming to his mouth. "You a man, ain'tcha?"

"That's right."

He relaxed, then asked, "So how'd you do that?"

It took a while, but I got it across. I painted a big picture of the blue and the men who used it. He remembered the few times he had seen the growling birds glide past his part of the earth, and from the few magazines he had seen he recalled the puzzling machines that were so foreign to his mind.

But boys are boys and their imaginations can conjure up anything. It could have been no better had I come from the moon. There were lights in his eyes when I finished and I knew here I had a friend. He was a little one, but a friend.

When I finished, he was quiet a long while, then sadness touched him as it had Caroline and he said, "If it's like you said, it's real nice. It must be awful never to see them things no more."

"I'll see them again."

He stayed silent. Watching, saying nothing.

When he was ready again I asked, "What's the matter with Chigger?"

The Cahill kid wet his lips and plucked at the grass. "Men burned him out. Did him almost like the others."

"What men?"

"Like you."

"Trumble . . . all men are alike."

"You ain't. You like the others."

"How come?"

He picked at the grass again. "They had no-hole clothes. Big shoes. They had lots of *things,* too."

The way he said "things" was puzzling. "What things?"

"You know. Just *things.* They point one at you and you get killed."

I didn't get it. "Guns?"

"Not guns. *Things.* They made *that* noise and you got killed."

I leaned back against the tree. "You sure nobody around here has television?"

"What?"

"Just a thought. Skip it." I tried again. "About these men. How'd they get in here?"

His face went into a lopsided grin and he looked up at the mountainside. "See up there where the chunk is out?"

I followed his finger and nodded at the cleft in the almost smooth ridge.

"'Twas old Heller Beansy's Crotch, that's what. Tumble-ground set her up, Pap told me, way back fore Granny's time. Then tumble-ground closed her up after them men come through."

"What's this tumble-ground bit?"

"You kiddin'? Ground, she jump up and tumbles all round."

Earthquake.

"Boy . . . you should hear! Like a million guns all together. Shook old Heller Beansy right down the hill, it did. Can't nobody get through the crotch now."

"And all the men who came through first with the *things*?"

"Got killed in the tumble-ground where they chased Old Beansy. They ain't no more left of them, that's for sure."

I looked up at the niche in the rim of the bowl and tried to measure the distance. Twelve miles maybe. Could be fifteen. The dark side of the mountain was closer, at least no more than five miles.

I went out at 5,500 heading south. The *Lobster Pot* was trimmed back for a glide that should have dropped her in no more than a few miles from where I hit. But damn it, you can never figure out a C-47! They always gave it the old college try. She could be anyplace from here to Jax but if the law of aerodynamics and chance worked for a change, that wrecked had to be inside the bowl!

I said, "Trumble . . . you remember when you saw me?"

His head bobbed hard.

"About that time did you hear any big noises down there?" I waved my hand to the southern ridge of mountains. "Or see any fires?"

He followed the sweep of my hand, studied it, then shook his head. "Not *me.*"

"So not you. Who saw something?"

And the kid said, grinning, "Macbruder. He was up by the crotch when he sees this big thing and hears a awful noise and comes runnin' down. Figures it's a tumble-ground and gets out, but because he saw that thing he's scared to tell. Only me he told."

Maybe I was lucky, I thought. Maybe it was still there, intact. The ship didn't burn and if it hit on top of the trees, there might still be a chance I could get to the radio. If the main set was out I still had the Hallicrafters. The old S-38A receiver was there and the newer RD-56F transmitter and I could bring in the army with that if I had to.

Right then I remembered the Cargo had some kid's hobby gear in it—and I felt good.

I said, "Look, Trumble . . . You think you could get this kid."

"Macbruder?"

"Yeah. Can you get him to show you where he saw this business?"

"Sure, I can get him. Why?"

"Never mind why."

His eyes got wise then. "Won't do you no good," he said.

"No?"

He looked up at the waning sun. "Billy Bussy'll be in town 'bout now. He'll be looking for you."

"Find out anyway, okay?"

"Sure. Won't do you no good though." His tongue wet his mouth down again, leaving a cleaned oval in his face. "Carrie . . . she liked you pretty good, huh?"

"Could be."

He bobbed his head. "Kind of liked you myself," he said.

"And this Bussy character?"

"Mean. Real mean. Too bad he's goin' to kill you."

"Really think he will?"

"He *got* to. Everybody's waitin' for him to. He will, too. He don't, then he ain't no head man nohow never again."

I got up and dusted off my pants. He jumped up with me, all excited. "You going down and let Billy kill you now?"

I laughed and gave him a fake chop in the jowls. "Not yet, sunshine. We'll have to let Billy wait awhile."

"But Billy'll . . ."

"He won't do anything. Now you get back there and tell him I'm going to take him apart in little pieces. You got that?"

He stared at me like I was brand new to this world. Then those lights came back in his eyes and he said softly, believingly, "Sure, I'll tell him all right. I'll sure tell him."

I hoped I was up to what the kid thought.

When we got to Chigger Bolidy's he was leaving the yard on his mule. I took him by the arm and he put the animal back in the stall and locked the gate.

I said, "You didn't always run mail, Chigger."

When he didn't answer, I squeezed a little and he said, "I hill-farmed."

"How long ago?"

"Before they came in."

"What'd you grow?"

"I had apples." He was scared almost voiceless now. "Didn't want no silver. They didn't have to burn me out!"

"Who, Chigger?"

"From the other side. Like 'em all. I know 'em on the other side, always killin' and stealing! I got the mail. I see . . ."

"Why'd they burn you, Chigger?"

"Burned me out, they did. Blew up my whole place. Damn them! I didn't want no silver! Damn . . ."

"How many?"

"Ten! They come in, ten all. Damn 'em! Ten all and they go one by one to the hill farms and I'm the only one alive 'ceptin' the Harts and iff'n they weren't so many they'd be dead too! Tooken land and killed. *Them and their things!*" He spit the last words out.

I had two hands on him, dragging him so high his feet barely touched the floor. "Who else died, Chigger? Say their names."

He breathed in short gasps. "Brother Melse. Cooper. All the Belcheys."

"And their places?"

"Land all blowed up. Nothing but rocks. Can't grow nothing now. All rocks. Did it with their things. Want everybody's land, they did. Took it. Took all the sayings."

Under my hands he was coming apart. I put him down and he sunk to his haunches, squatting there and drooling on the floor. I walked out into the dusk and looked down the street.

This could be my dying night, I thought. I grinned, felt the safe bulge of the .45 under my belt and walked toward the lights. It wasn't far, but it gave me a chance to remember how people were. You could fight without wanting to fight, but it was hard to kill without wanting to kill. It took time to work up to that point. Oh, it was easy to do, all right, but it took time to do it. Some place Billy Bussy was working up to it and when he was ready, he'd try it.

But first he had to be ready. Some place he'd be going through his mental war dance and putting on his hypothetical paint. But it would keep.

I winked at the stars that were showing and they winked back. Then I walked down past the stores and maybe even past the place where the medicine dance was going on. I grunted a laugh and kept on.

When I got to where the wagon was that had "HART" burned on its transom with a hot iron, I turned, opened the door and stepped inside.

I was wrong about passing the place where the medicine dance was going on. I hadn't passed it. It was here. They were all there, the Hart clan with the boys standing around the wheelchair and Caroline beside them. But they weren't talking. They were listening to the biggest guy I ever saw with the nastiest face that ever happened to anybody.

They all looked at me and the big one grinned. Then George moved and I had the .45 out and the grin on the big one's face stopped and I said, "So you're Billy Bussy."

He looked at me the hard way and if I had anything other than that .45 he would have jumped and even then he was counting off the odds of a misfire, a jam or an off-target shot.

Old Man Hart rolled the chair forward a foot. "You thinking to shoot somebody, son?"

I didn't look at him. I didn't watch any of them but the big one in the middle. I said, "I could shoot six, Pappy."

369

"We're many, son. One would get you sure."

"That's right, Pappy. But don't forget that you'd go first. Right through the old beano you'd catch one. I'd get at least four confirmed and two probables before I went down. This big slob here would get it right in the beginning too." I stopped, then added, "Now what?"

"That's up to you, son."

"Yeah," I said, "I guess it is," I watched Billy's face when I said, "Come here, Caroline."

I saw her move, saw her body go tight and saw the furtive glance she threw at her father.

The old boy said, "She won't do you no good as a hostage, son. You can't get away."

The routine was getting stale. I was getting damn sick and tired of the treatment. I let them see my mouth twist into a screwy grin and I said, "You've overlooked something, Pap."

He waited before he answered. "I did? I don't think so."

I let him wait just so long and I said, "Maybe I didn't come here accidentally, Pap. Maybe I wanted in. Maybe I wanted to take care of something real bad."

Some place in the room somebody sucked their breath in hard. So they wouldn't take chances I turned the .45 a little bit sidewise so they could all see the hammer lying back, ready to start the first one on the long road to nowhere.

I said, "Come here, Caroline," and she came over, never looking back. I reached behind me and opened the door, then touched her so she went out through it.

Bill Bussy just stood there. His face was hard, immobile. Above the week-old stubble of a beard his eyes were tiny silted things, but they weren't quite expressionless. They were lying in wait, satisfied to take whatever time was necessary. There was a laugh in them too because no matter where he went he was always the biggest the strongest and the best. And now he was laughing at me, looking down across the room from his six-and-a-half feet—but not looking down too much because the .45 made me as big as he was.

Then he spoke. He sounded a little unreal because his voice wasn't as big as he was. He said, "I'm going to kill you, man."

I nodded. "Later I'll let you try. First I got business."

I started to back out the door but I couldn't make it without getting a hook in. I said, "Billy . . . you're bigger and stronger, but I'm something you're not."

His reedy voice was startling in the quiet. "What's that?"

I grinned real nasty-like. "You're going to have to find that out for yourself."

When I left, I closed the door, turned around and walked to where she waited. It was dark now, but I know she was smiling.

"They'll come after you," she said.

"Uh-uh. Not with the light at their backs and me with a .45. There's no back door to that store anyway. No, sugar, they'll wait some. But meantime we walk away nice and slow so everybody can see us and the word can go around that the fly boy's no patsy."

"Where are we going?"

"Post Office."

"Closed."

"The light's on."

"I know, but Mr. Cooper, he's gone. He never stays after dark."

"You have many Coopers here?"

"Only Mr. Cooper. The others are all dead now."

She didn't have to speak an answer. She dropped my hand and stood there in the dark, rigid. I said, "Caroline . . . would you believe me if I told you I had nothing to do at all with the things that happened?"

"Back there you told Pap . . ."

"I was feeling for things. I never knew this whole damn valley existed until I blew an engine over it. You understand that?"

Again, she didn't have to answer. Her hand slipped back into mine, and she was close again. "Mitch," she whispered, "don't fool me. Please don't fool me."

I found her mouth in the dark. "I'll never fool you, kitten."

The cabin was in a lonely place. It was too big for one man and showed it with many doors that led to long unused rooms and furniture used to many people.

He sat there rocking gently before a small hearth fire, the table beside him set with supper scarcely eaten.

Caroline said, "Mr. Cooper . . ."

"Come in, Carrie."

"I have a friend."

"Bring him in, Carrie. I've been expecting him."

He turned when I came in, smiled tiredly and nodded. "I thought you might be dead by now."

"Dying takes time, Pop. Billy get his mail?"

"He got it. First thing. He see you?"

"He saw me."

"Then how come you still alive, son?"

"I saw him first. Easy. Just like that. Didn't you kind of expect it to be that way?"

"Let's say I ain't exactly surprised none."

We all stared at the fire, watching it flicker and spark. When he was ready he said, "You didn't come to say hello."

"No, I came for information." When he didn't answer, i went on, "What's a *saying*?"

He swung around slowly, his face strained. "I was thinking you'd be asking something like that sooner or later."

"So?"

"Why'd you ask?"

"Because the government might be pretty stupid and usually is, but they have a line they won't cross. They won't hire a postmaster who can't read."

He looked up at me, saying nothing.

I said, "Caroline . . . who can read around here?"

She stepped forward. "He can."

"Who else?"

"Pap and Billy Bussy and Big George and, fore his eyes went, Mr. Dukes could." She stopped, then said, "I can read."

"That's all?"

"Nobody else."

I walked around in front of him and leaned against the fieldstone pillars of the fireplace. "What's a *saying*, Mr. Cooper?"

The fire coughed sparks almost to his feet but he never moved. When his was ready, he said, "Can't you guess?"

I nodded. "Sure. I think I even heard the expression once from a crew chief I had back when I was flying P-51s."

He glanced up, his hand rubbing his chin. "I guess there's no harm in my tellin' you. Seems like you sorta know already." He nodded thoughtfully.

"All the way, Pop."

"A *saying's* a . . . when you have land like . . . well . . ."

"You mean a deed?"

"Sort of. You write a person a chunk of property, you give it on paper and it's his."

"And you're the recorder," I said. "You hold the paper because you can read."

He reached to the table for his pipe, loaded and lit it, and in the smoke of the drawing said, "That's right, son."

I tried hard to play it as slowly as he had. "And how often do you record these . . . *sayings*?"

He sucked on the pipe, letting the smoke curl over his head. "Well . . . people 'round here been trusting me a long while now. A long while."

"When did you record the last . . . deed . . . with the county, Mr. Cooper? How long ago?"

"Couple years ago. My own property, matter of fact."

"One more question. How long you been postmaster?"

"Eight years, son. Long time. Why did you ask?"

"Because I'm burned up at everybody wanting me dead. Besides that, there's no TV in this little hamlet and I'm no jerk who believes in men from Mars. I'm thinking. I got here by accident, but it looks like I got to think my way out. Well, by damn, this laddie doesn't figure to get his neck twisted by this Bussy boy and I don't like getting shot up by the Harts. I'm sick of all these crazy hillbillies glaring at me like I was Typhoid Terry!"

I had to stop and take a breath. My mouth was tight and when I looked over at Caroline, she was holding the back of the chair, watching me with guarded eyes. I turned back to the old boy.

"What did you do before you were postmaster?"

"I thought you asked your last question?"

"I'm thinking again."

"I was a farmer."

"Of what?"

"Corn. Pumpkins."

"How'd you get it to market?"

"I didn't. We traded here in the valley."

This time I grinned at him. "Who made you postmaster?"

"Government man came through the Crotch in war time to get the boys. Only one he got was Billy Bussy. He done it then. Made my brother Donan postmaster. When Donan got—when he died I wrote a letter. They made me postmaster."

"And official recorder."

He leaned forward and stirred up the fire again. "And everything. Like Donan. Government needed somebody."

"Tell me," I said, "the Crotch was open from before the war until—until there was a tumble-ground."

His face showed that he had caught the meaning of that. "Go on, son."

"How long ago did it happen?"

He kicked at the fire. "Few years back."

Before I could answer, Caroline drifted into the light of the fire and said, "It was nine years ago, Mr. Cooper. It was before you were postmaster."

Then I said, "Now I'm going to ask you the big one. Answer me straight and I'll damn well know it if you lie. Look at me, Cooper!" His head came up until he was meeting my eyes. "Who killed Melse and the Belcheys and your family? Who, Cooper? What happened to them!"

"Damn you and your kind!" He was up in my hands trying to claw at me and I had to shove him down in the chair. "You know what happened. You killed them!"

"Why, Cooper, why?"

He sat there, his face contorted with rage.

I said quietly. "You don't really know, do you. You've been thinking on it a long time, but you don't really know." I let a few seconds go by. "Think on it some more, Mr. Cooper. I'll be back. Meantime, you think on it."

From outside came a long thin wail. Another one joined it, deeper in tone. The others joined it then, yapping and howling and coming closer all the while.

Caroline said, "He got the dogs back, man. They only minutes away."

I joined her at the door, looked back and said, "Remember, think on it," then slammed the door shut and pushed Caroline ahead of me into the darkness.

The dogs were all downhill, quartering the field to pick up our scent.

The scallion patches had them foxed and the two streams would stop them for a little while, but sooner or later they would find the perimeter of the false trails and close in on the true ones.

I took her hand and started running. Ahead the moon was blossoming over the mountain and the baleful light of it scoured a course through the fields. We followed the glow, running easily, and every once in a while I could hear her laugh. When we reached the trees, we stopped.

Below us the lights went on in the old man's cabin.

Caroline said, "They'll be coming up here."

"You want them to?"

"No. But they will. What can stop them?"

"Watch hard, honey. It won't be often that you get an answer to something like this, not when we're mixing getting killed and fun at the same time."

I pushed her away and took the matches from my pocket. You could see the flame from miles away, but before you could do anything about it, it was too late. The wind was at my back, blowing crossfield, and with half a dozen matches I had the entire damn field screaming in flames toward the cabin and down there the last sounds you could hear were the hate yells coming in over the hounds and one of the lasting ones was the reedy voice of Billy Bussy.

At our feet the flames toyed with the pine needles, barely enough to make her hair a shining gold. She was too pretty not to describe. She was something you wanted to tell everybody about. She stood there, tall and straight, always with that laugh trying hard not to show on her mouth. She was big in the shoulders and she breasted the downslope wind from the mountain with her legs spread wide under her dress, the taut lines of her thighs softening into the sweep of her hips. The wind in her hair was a caress that stirred it around her face; golden yellow, a rich, natural golden yellow. For a moment you could see the wet fullness of her mouth, eyes that had a touch of Hawaiian mischief, eyes that could love or kill, eyes not quite tamed yet.

I said, "They'll be expecting us to run. They'll search the flanks."

"And us, Mitch."

"Not *us*, sugar. Me. They're expecting me to run."

I swooped her up in my arms, kissed her face and her eyes, then lowered her gently to the soft pine needles.

Down where the fire raced you could see the tiny figures trying desperately to hold it back. If you listened hard, you could hear the dogs and almost sense their disappointment.

There was none of the burning in front of us any longer. The wind had whipped it all downhill and the only light came from the full risen moon. I stood watching the frantic commotion in front of the cabin, wondering what crazy streak of fate ever dropped me into the middle of such a situation.

The whole world is my oyster, I thought. I knew it intimately, every country, every city, every swamp.

Now I'm crowded again. The last time was in Stalag 4, but that was in '44. It happened again in Korea. Now I'm home and they're still crowding me. They're pushing hard to kill me. There's a home base, but it's sure getting hard to get to. It was like Ring-a-levio if you know what that means.

I let the mad eke out slowly, took a deep breath and watched the little people below me. I hardly heard the sounds behind me because they were so foreign to what I was watching.

When I turned around, Caroline was lying there, the only white thing in the moonlight, and white. There had never been anything more beautiful before. In the lights and shadows of that pale glow she was a Valkyrie, blonde, and ever so blonde. Big. The soft rises of her ever so big and so noticeable.

I stood over her, feeling the things crawl along my skin that you feel when you see a sight like that, a tightness that makes your voice sound strange and makes it hard to swallow.

"You're lovely, girl," I said.

She seemed to caress my name. "Mitch . . ."

My legs crossed under me and I sat down beside her. "Not yet, kitten." I let my hand pass over her, my fingertips barely touching. "It would be wonderful, but, for you, wonderful isn't enough."

"I never had a man, Mitch."

"I know."

"I want you, man."

"No. Not when we'd have to be watching the skyline for . . . them. Or be listening for dogs." I paused and found her hand.

She lay there quietly, her eyes studying my face. "That isn't the reason."

My hand tightened around hers and a small laugh got away from me. "I want it to be right, Sugar. I think from that first minute under the chute I knew that I wanted you. Not for one night and not because time could be running out fast for me."

"Tell it to me then."

"Billy's really going to have to fight for you, kitten," I said. "If he blows his chance, I'm taking you out of this place."

I kissed her, feeling the hunger that made her quiver and pushed her away gently while there was still time.

Above, the sky was ablaze with stars. I watched them awhile, then closed my eyes.

A strange sort of music brought me out of the blackness of sleep. There was a gentle warmth, a tangy freshness in the air, and, from what seemed far off, the chuckle of voices.

I squinted against the long reaches of sunlight that washed across my face and sat up. It was the time of morning when the whole mountain was alive with sound and color, smelling fresh with dew after a nighttime of rest.

When I heard the voices again, I swung around and saw Caroline, her hair wet and skin-tight against shoulders showing pink from an icy creek bath. The other one was Trumble Cahill and he had two loops of smoked sausage hung around his neck and a bag of biscuits in his hand.

He waved and said in a light tone, "You sure sleep late, mister."

I looked at my watch. It was 5:10.

Caroline slipped a sausage loose and tossed it to me, a grin making her face impish. "You fell asleep fast last night."

"I had a big day."

"I tried to wake you up."

After I bit into the sausage, I faked a swipe at her chin. I picked up a biscuit, bit into each and grunted with satisfaction. For some it might have been one hell of a breakfast, but right then nothing ever tasted better to me.

When I had the second biscuit I said, "How'd you find us?"

He grinned all the way across his face. "Saw the fire last night. Everybody had to fight it 'fore it reached the buildings and didn't think you'd be hanging around.

"Didn't guess you could go far at night. Guess you'd be hungry this morning, though. Swiped the sausage. Ma made the biscuits. She thunk I was takin' off for fishin. Gimme'em."

Minutes later, Trumble said, "Saw Macbruder last night."

"And—"

"Told me where it is, he did. He's scared to go up there, but not me."

My breath went out in a long sigh. "It didn't burn?"

"No fire. He said it's all busted up, but there weren't no fire."

"How long will it take to get there?"

His face screwed up and he bit his lip. He glanced up at the sun. "Go straight there in three hours maybe. Only we can't go straight. They'll be coming up searching, so we got to take the rocks around."

"So how long!"

"Come sundown we be there."

We had been taking a roundabout route up the mountain side for three hours, my watch told me. We stayed in the trees, keeping them between us and the plateaus below. When we could, we took to stone ridges where we left no tracks. Twice we followed streams to their sources in the face of the slope before we cut back to the grass.

When the wind was right, you could hear the shrill yips of the dogs, and everybody so often the crack of a gunshot would roll across the hills. We weren't in any danger yet. The hunt had just begun, and as long as we could keep from being seen, it would take its natural course.

Neither Caroline nor the Cahill kid seemed too concerned yet, figuring the shooting to be somebody knocking down a squirrel. I had told them nothing of my purposes, not did they ask them. It couldn't have been blind faith, I thought. More likely they were too sure of the outcome. Nobody was willing to give me any reasonable chance at all.

We broke out into a clearing around noon. It was too squared off to be natural formation and when I looked around I saw the charred remains of a building. In a half dozen places on the ten-acre spread the ground had been torn up through the scant topsoil exposing the jagged teeth of a shale formation.

Caroline said, "Brother Melse had the place."

I nodded toward the wreckage. "He die there?"

"No. Not there. They just found him dead one day."

Trumble had crowded over close to me, not liking it here at all. "Them things done it, that's what. Them men with their things."

I turned him around. "*What* things?"

He licked his mouth nervously. "They point 'em at you and they go *zip-zip-zip-zip* and you got dead. That's what they are!"

"Do you know what he means, Caroline?"

"No, but they sure had them. Everybody says."

"And Brother Melse. It left a hole in him too?"

Trumble shook his head and pointed to a ridge a quarter of a mile away. "No holes, man. He got his head broke instead. Like to tooken him right off that rim rock it did."

"He couldn't have fallen?"

"Nope. Landed too far out. He got *thinged* off it."

"The rest of the Coopers. The Belcheys. How did they die?"

"The Coopers were flung off their wagon in Silverman's ravine. Flung mule and all off the road," Caroline said.

"Where?"

Before she could answer, Trumble said, "We going to pass that place. You'll see. Somebody tooken the wheels off, but the rest of the wagon's still down there."

I said, "Okay, let's go," and followed him off. We went by two of the torn patches and when I paused to scratch up the dirt with my toe, the kid came back and watched me. I said, "How'd they do this?"

"Powder blowed it somehow. Done it out of pure meanness 'cause they wouldn't sell. Burned the shack. Killed everybody."

I grunted and waved them off. It would take some pretty fancy handling of explosives just to blow the topsoil off the ground. Not impossible, but pretty fancy. At the other end of the field I stopped out again and looked back. We were a lot higher now and the patch stood out clearly. Something about the layout bothered me and I stood there until I saw what it was.

The gouges blown into the ground weren't the result of any haphazard operation. They followed a rise that crossed the clearing and from any angle I could see where second-growth brush all but closed what could have once been a wide pathway.

By the time we reached the road, I was soaked wet with sweat and all three of us took a breather. The kid found a spring that gushed finger-thick from the sheer rock and it put us back on our feet again.

It was easier then, following the road. The surface was powdered rock and dirt worn smooth from years of use. The steel bands of wagon wheels had etched furrows in the softer sections and scarred the saplings on either side.

The road swung then, curving around an outcropping, then suddenly angled upward sharply. For a thousand feet we stayed at that twenty-degree climb, then we burst out into the open with sheer rock face on one side and a drop-off on the other. The wagon tracks blended into a single pair that patiently followed the dangerously narrow road until it disappeared again into the brush.

Nobody had to point out the accident site. You could see the wagon bed, bottom up, impaled on the rocks at the bottom of the precipice.

"Caroline, nobody would cross this point if somebody were coming the other way, would they?"

"No. I know what you mean. Nobody could run them off because there's not that much room."

"Did you see the tracks?"

She pointed to the kid and he bobbed his head. "I seen 'em. They just stopped like and went over the edge. Telling you . . . they got *thinged* off too."

"Suppose a man was waiting there?"

"Old mule they had wouldn't move for no man," Caroline said. "Fact is, nobody'd get in front of Blue but Bud Cooper without getting teethed." She shook her hair around her shoulders. "No, weren't a soul on that road."

"That could be too," I told her.

At the mid-point you could still see where the wagon had torn the leading edge off the lip. You could still follow the groove with your eyes until it ended at the wreckage. I turned and studied the wall at our backs. It went up a hundred feet or so then leveled off out of sight.

It didn't take long to find it. The vertical fault in the rock wall was a foot wide and not much more than four feet in. It was almost directly in line with the spot where the wagon went over and I didn't wonder about it any more. I reached in, rubbed my hand over the stone interior, working through surface dirt and grit to the stone itself. When I pulled my arm out, I showed it to Caroline. There was more on it than grit and natural dirt. My skin was carbon-black.

Her brow pulled together, puzzled. "What is it?"

"Booby trap."

She didn't get it.

I said, "Somebody laid a charge of powder in there and exploded it from up above. That mule who wouldn't move for any man did a quick leap when the blast hit him. A loud bang in the ear and over he leaped, cart, baggage and all."

Her face went cold then. "They were killed deliberate-like."

"Let's call it murder, kitten." I brushed at the grime on my arm. "Where does this road go to?"

"Forks up ahead. Takes off one way to some of the hill farms. Other fork goes to Billy Bussy's."

There didn't seem to be anything special about Billy Bussy's place. There were two buildings, one a house and the other obviously a barn. But at least they were painted. There was nothing ramshackle about either and, by comparison, every other place I had seen was a shack.

I left the two of them by the road and hustled across the yard to the house.

It looked better up close. There was a generator in the back with a portable windmill all together in what was supposed to be a woodbin. The house was locked tight and the shades drawn, but from the discard piles carelessly laid up, I could see Billy had more modern conveniences than anyone else in the valley.

The barn was locked too, an oversized hasp and padlock, quiet signs that the place was more than a stable. Caroline came over, the kid trailing behind.

I tapped Trumble's shoulder, "You ever follow Billy's road out?"

His negative was a quick jerk.

"Why not?"

"Billy Bussy . . . he got . . ." He stopped and squinted at Caroline and she nodded understandingly.

"Billy fixed it so you'd get blowed up good if you try to cross his land. Folks here-abouts don't like trespassers."

"Even your neighbors!"

"Nobody. That's why Billy fixed it."

"He's pretty clever at booby-trapping."

"Trumble." I waved my thumb at the barn. "You know what's inside?"

"Not me. Seen his cart and the mule once, but that's all."

"Big wagon."

"Small wagon."

"Big loads?"

"Never loaded high. Just what folks want down below."

"How many carts has he got?"

"Just one."

I pointed to the tracks leading away from the building to the hidden pass in the mountains. "He changes his wheels to go to town, sugar. Those tracks going that-away were made by automobile tires. Clever boy, this Billy."

"Why?"

"I don't know, honey. Not yet."

There was little else left to look at. I went back to the front of the house, stepped up on the porch and tried to peer in the window. I couldn't see past the shade so I stepped back and was coming down the single step when I saw the topographical map stuck in a handy place under the eaves.

I pulled it out, unfolded it all the way and saw the entire valley and mountain ridge laid out in detail. There were areas circled, some blocked out, while marginal notes ran down both sides of the sheet. On the reverse side a rubber stamp had imprinted NEWHOPE EXPLORATION CO.

My watch said 1:10. I folded the map, stuck it in my pocket and said, "We better roll if we're going to make it."

Trumble said, "We ain't going, mister."

I looked up fast, and saw Billy Bussy coming across the yard.

The shotgun in his hands was almost toylike. He walked light, and you knew he was a fast one and you could almost read what went on in his head.

He was still a hundred feet off when I stepped off the porch with the .45 in my fist and I said, "One step more, friend, just one, that's all, and you're dead."

He started to take it, so I shot one ear right off his head.

It shouldn't have hurt that fast, but he choked out a yell, grabbed at what was left and the shotgun fell at his feet.

Trumble whispered, "Glory be!"

You really had to be close up to see what he was like. Black and scowling, with blood smeared across one side of his face dripping through his beard. His whole face was pulled into a grimace that made tiny slits where his eyes were. His muscles were bunched into knotty mounds and I knew damn well that if I didn't get the bull on him fast I'd never get it at all.

I gave him the smile with all the teeth showing and let him look down the hole in the .45, then I said, "You don't get tough by getting big, you pig. I told you the first time that you had an item to remember. I'm something you're not."

His answer was the same as before. The crazy rage left his face and was replaced by a crafty smirk. "What?"

I tossed the .45 away. "I'm meaner," I said.

For one second he just stood there, then his hand came away from the remains of his ear and a kill-crazy lust hit his eyes like somebody pushed a button. With a silly, high-pitched bellow he did the wrong thing and ducked for the shotgun without going for me and while he was bent over I kicked every tooth out of his face and rocked him back on his neck.

He tried to scream when I put both feet in his mouth and what came out made all red bubbles. It didn't stop him. He rolled away, dazed, but with his arms sweeping out. He grabbed me then, tight around the hips, but it was what I wanted. My two hands dug into him and I squeezed harder than I had ever squeezed anything. I squeezed and twisted at the same time and the high shriek that tore out of the thing he had for a mouth reached a crescendo, stopped abruptly and Billy Bussy was totally unconscious from the kind of pain he had never even imagined before.

I stood up, booted him again for fun and said, "After that he's going to be a real soprano."

Trumble's breathing was almost a wheeze and when I looked at Caroline her hands were tight against her face. I pulled them down and she trembled hard against me. "Is he dead?"

"Nah. He'll maybe wish he was though."

"You didn't have to do . . . that to him."

"No? I got news for you sugar. I had to. I don't like the idea of getting killed . . . and since I'm not fond of murder either I learned that it's not a bad idea to put in people's minds what will happen if they play it hard. The next time that bastard even touches me I'll kill him sure. They get oversize big like that, then all of a sudden they get tough. Well, damn it, this one can look in the mirror or hum a tune, then he'll remember what tough is really like."

Before she could answer the kid turned away abruptly, listening. He ran to the road, sighted down it, then came tearing back. "Your Pap and the boys, Carrie! They comin'!"

I said, "How far?"

"Ten minutes they be here!"

"Mitch . . ." Her face was white and drawn. "You go."

"Not without you. Damn it, after they see . . ."

"No. It was only him . . ." she looked at Billy stretched out on the grass, ". . . who would beat on me. He won't now."

"Listen . . ."

"I'll stay, Mitch. The boys'll follow faster'n you can git, 'less I steer them off. Clemson, he'll smell you out. You go, Mitch."

I said, "You can tell 'em from me that if you get touched, that what happened to Billy boy will be nothing."

We left then, me and the kid, running like crazy across the grass and dirt to the trees, then reaching the road, going up it to the notch where Trumble stopped for the first breather.

Behind us there was no sound of the chase as yet. Billy was going to need taking care of for a while and after one look at him none of them were going to be too anxious to start up a blind alley. With Caroline playing it hill-smart, she could set the whole pack off on a phony trail without any trouble.

I winked at Trumble and he blinked back at me. "How much longer, son?"

He glanced at the sun and shrugged. "We'll hit the Crotch. Dunno if'n we'll get there all the way tonight."

"Okay, let's not fight it then. The morning's time enough."

The sun was behind the mountain again when we reached the Crotch. Or what was left of it. The slanting rays of deep red turned it into a jigsaw puzzle of light and shadow, but distinguishable enough for somebody who had seen it before to know what had happened.

I said, "This is the tumble-ground place?"

His nod was vigorous. "Kilt old Heller, wiped out his place. Kilt them others and their things too."

"You remember it?"

"No. Only hear tell. I was a mite then. Tooken plenty of looks around here, though. Tooken plenty."

"Never saw anything?"

He shivered and said no. "Saw bones," he added. "Saw bones only once. Me and Macbruder run like hell then. When we come back, they was gone. All et. Something scratched them up and et'em."

"Like what?"

"Pigs." He shivered again at the thought. "Plenty pigs around here. They eat anything. Crunch the bones even."

I started off through the split rocks and the ground that had been heaved up. I followed the pattern of light that was still left, poking into some of the depressions that showed shock wave formations. When I finished, I walked back to the kid and we skirted the entire Crotch to the tree line and found a small hollow that looked like a good place to stop for the night.

The kid started raking in pine needles with his feet and so did I. He had his bed pile formed and stopped to look at me because I was staring at a spot I had cleared. He looked down and almost choked on his breath. When he got it out again, it came spasmodically and he yelled, *"It's from the things! They were in the things!"* His finger was a rigid pointer.

I reached down and picked up the battery. *"Things* my foot," I said. "They're batteries from a Geiger counter." I looked around and nodded thoughtfully. "Somebody else has camped here before us. Maybe the same people who blew the Crotch to hell and back to close off an entry and make a good excuse for murder."

The Cahill kid just stared. His mouth was dry and his tongue didn't help any. "You ain't scairt none?"

"Not none," I told him.

I patted the tail of the *Lobster Pot* and kissed her gently on her busted fusilage. She had come down easy into the trees and hadn't scattered much. Most of the cargo was still alive, tumbled out into the wet mossy ground and it was going to be a sad animal who came on those big Maine jobs with unpegged claws.

The first time he saw one, the kid almost threw a fit, but when I explained what a Maine lobster was, he calmed down and almost believed me. But it took a fire, and one roasted the hard way before he got the point.

By noon I had broken through the wreck to the mid-section where the radio was and had it dragged out on the ground. Both receiver and transmitter were intact, nicely bundled in their wrappers without a scratch on them.

But it was a fumble. When I went back for the battery from the plane, all I found was a smashed, smelly compartment fuming gently from acid-eaten metal.

Sometimes you don't even have dirty words to fit the occasion. I just stood there and kicked at the radio cases, trying hard to keep from booting them all the way across the mountain.

The kid said, "It ain't no good?"

"No good."

Above us the sky went purple. In the trees the night things sang their songs and from a long way off a howl rose and fell. Life that had been dormant during the bright hours suddenly took form in noise and soft *swooshes* that glided by.

Trumble Cahill said, "Billy Bussy had one down the store."

For a minute it didn't sink in, then, "What?"

"Seen him spark it once. Was lookin' in window we was. Sparked it hard and we lit out."

I sat up slowly. "You know what I'm talking about?"

"Yup. Same thing. Thunk it over hard."

"He's got one . . . in a store?"

The kid grinned. "Same place you was where the Harts met Billy. Used to be a meetin' place only nobody ever met. Harts trade off stuff there. Billy keeps his stuff back there too."

"Yeah, it's beginning to figure."

His eyes questioned me.

"Forget it."

"Can't forget it. Keep thinkin' what you did to Billy. Things're different since you came."

"What do you mean?"

"Dunno. Everything's different. Like things'll change."

I grinned at him. "Optimist. But, by damn, that's all you have. It's about time something different happened around here." I looked down into the valley. "If there's a storage battery down there I can be sure. I know what the scoop is already, but then I can be sure and we can cream the bastards who have pulled all this crap. Maybe . . ."

"Mister?"

I stopped and breathed in hard.

"I don't even know what you're talking about," he said.

Very slowly, I let it ooze out, all the tight feeling in my chest. I inched off the box and lay out on the ground beside it. "I'll spell it out later in small letters, Trumble. Right now let's cork off. Tomorrow we go to town. I mean really go to town."

For a long time after the kid's light snoring told me he was asleep, I lay awake. It was getting clear now. All this business about "tumble-ground" and "things" and outsiders killing everyone could sound like something from the supernatural to the ignorant hill folks—but then they hadn't seen what I'd seen. I knew damn well no earthquake ever planted a man-made booby trap. And I knew that that tumble-ground earthquake wasn't even a natural quake, much less a supernatural phenomenon. And those "things" weren't out of Buck Rogers either. They were something anyone who went to the outside once in a while—like say Billy Bussy—could buy just about any place.

No, it wasn't really that much of a puzzle when you got to see all the pieces. Someone had started his own earthquake. Why? Easy. It was either to destroy something or hide something. I bet on the second choice. But what was it that was worth so much to hide? I was still wondering when another thought took hold of my mind.

All I knew wasn't going to do me any good, unless I found out the most important thing there was to know about this valley—how to get out of it alive. I was still thinking about that little matter when I conked off.

We roasted two more of the Maine cargo for breakfast before we started off downhill. I had the radios in a Jerry rig built from the spare chute harness on my back. The kid picked the way from long knowledge of the mountainside, staying close to water, but well out of sight of anyone who could be following the old trail.

Any party coming up behind us would be shortstopped by the wreckage of the plane and all the goodies that were there for the taking, so neither of us was worried about the rear.

Occasionally Trumble looked at me and grinned, his face splitting into a grimy smile. He was a funny little kid, a real wood's colt. But he was relaxed and happy and whatever I wanted to do was all right with him.

The snapping of a stick a little too close made his grin fade. He sat rigid, like a bird, listening hard. A funny little whistle came from the trees and he whistled back and nodded happily to me. When I looked over my shoulder, the other kid came out of the brush, skirted us until he was well-protected behind Trumble and rolled his eyes at me so that the white showed all the way around the irises.

My little buddy said, "He's Macbruder."

"Hi."

His head moved, but nothing came out of his mouth. He had to stare awhile, swallow, then with a tremendous effort, "People gonna hang you."

"Me, Macbruder?"

This time his eyes rolled from Trumble to me. "Both." He swallowed again. "Billy come to town. He all cut, he is. Old Man Hart, him mean mad. Boys even worse. Billy, he beat on all the boys up by his place. Him real mad at 'em for something. They 'low how they going to hang you both."

"Wait . . ." I hunched forward and scowled at him. "They're hanging who?"

His eyes rolled again. "Both you. Trumble, they gonna hang . . . *you*!"

I stood up and shrugged into the backpack. "In a pig's whozis they're going to hang anybody. Who says this?"

Trumble's face twisted into a grin. "Mister here did it to 'im. Mister here give it to him good."

"To Billy!"

"Sure," Trumble said. "Now let's go. Mister's ready."

I said, "Macbruder . . . how did you find us?"

He looked uphill. "Said you gonna look fer what's . . . up there. No place to go after that 'cept down this way."

"Okay," I said.

"But Billy . . ."

"He won't hang anybody. Come on."

Dusk was heavy in the air when we reached the outskirts of the single street that was the town. The sun paint was still on one side of the mountain, diminishing rapidly into the deep blue that was almost night.

Along the street the wagons and carts were nose-to-tail, the animals standing patiently in their harnesses. Lights showed in nearly all the buildings this time. The Dry Goods and Post Office was dark, the store marked with the weatherbeaten feed sign was empty, and the single blank space on the other side was the one Trumble mentioned as the old meeting place.

Down at the end a couple dozen kids milled around the hitch rail outside the hardware store. You could hear the rumble of voices from inside, some one single monotone leading them into impassioned yells, and whenever it happened the kids would all gather to one side, quiet and frightened.

When it was dark enough, I edged across to the other side, circled the buildings and came up behind the one I wanted. I let down my pack and shoved the harness at Trumble. "I'm going in there, kid. You stay here and don't show yourself, understand?"

"Yeah, but suppose . . ."

"Be still and it'll be all right." I tried the window and it slid up easily. When I went to climb in, the .45 came out of my waistband and fell to the ground. I threw the map down with it and called over quietly, "Hang on to this stuff too."

He picked them up, shuffled back to the pack and I slipped into the room. The darkness was thick, too thick to see in, so I felt my way along. My hand hit a box that rattled to the floor and spilled out its contents. I raked some of it over, felt the heads of stick matches and flicked one alive with my thumbnail.

For one moment the room flared yellow and I could see it all, the household items, the tightly nailed and steel strap bound boxes against the wall . . . and the two storage batteries. I blew out the match, hefted one of the batteries and eased back to the window. I balanced it on the sill while I climbed out, lifted it down and turned around.

The whole top of my head seemed to fly off then. There was that single wooden sound, an incredible flash of pain that raked across the inside of my skull and all my parts seemed to suddenly rot off and fall away. I knew when the ground hit my face, but that was all.

Daylight poured in a window high over my head and I tried to look at my watch. But I wasn't about to see it. There must have been fifty feet of quarter-inch hemp wound around me, strapping my hands tight to my sides, my legs together with the ends knotted together between my shoes.

A whole night. I had been unconscious a whole night. I tried to move and stopped with a quick intake of breath. My body was one giant bundle of pain and when I squeezed my face together I could feel the pull of dried blood that caked it. Somebody had really worked me over.

Outside, a door banged open and indistinct voices spoke across the room. Heavy feet walked across the floor, then another door slammed open behind me. The mangled face of Billy Bussy leered down at me and before he could kick me in the head, Big George Hart nudged him to quit and pointed outside. "He be kilt in here, it ain't no good. You do it like we said."

His split lips tried hard to laugh. "Sure," he said. Then he looked at me. "We're hanging you. Not later. Right now. You're going to be a good sight to see, hanging from a tree."

He reached down, grabbed a handful of rope and dragged me out into the other room and dumped me at the feet of the Harts. The old man smiled at me from his chair and shook his head in sympathy. "Too bad, son. Jest got to be, though, you know how it is."

I didn't bother to answer him.

"Before you die, you can satisfy an old man's curiosity." He sat back and sucked on his teeth. "How come you here? You told Caroline about the *Lobster Pot*. 'Twas a good story, son, but why you really here?"

I said, "I already told you. I *wanted* to come here."

"Why, son?"

I forced a grin and stayed quiet.

Old Man Hart leaned out in his chair. "I'd say it was an accident. Like you told Carrie. You die now, we tell folks you dies in the accident. We know about what's up there on the mountain side. All we do is put you back inside it, light a little fire and who can say different?"

He smiled sadly again and sat back. I said, "I could be with the New Hope Exploration outfit. I could've come looking to see how the others *really* died."

One of the boys cursed softly and the old man silenced him with a wave. "You talkin' big now, boy. Way over your head."

"I am?" I looked around and saw the tight faces above me, like a television scene of an operation from the patient's eyes. I said, "You're a bunch of amateurs at murder, you slobs. With me you're only feeling the beginning of the heat. There'll be more coming in."

"You're not saying much, son." The interest in his eyes was a deadly interest. "You got more to say?"

"Yeah. I'll give it to you all the way and you can start sweating. What I know others will know and one day you'll be swinging yourself. You left an easy trail to follow, but the picture is even easier to see. Right after the war the New Hope Company came in looking for uranium and found it."

I looked at the old man first. "You were the smart one. You knew what they were up to because you could read. You kept up with the events. You and Billy were the only ones who had any appreciation at all for the outside. You knew what money could buy and you wanted it all."

Billy's face was black with malice. I said to him, "You pulled some nice stunts with explosives. You caved in the Crotch, you blasted the Coopers off the road with a gimmick . . ."

Old Man Hart grunted and cursed the suddenly-astonished Billy. Then relaxed and smiled again. "You smart boy."

"I've been told," I said. "I even know how Melse got it." I looked at Billy again. "This big guy here picked him up and threw him off that ledge. Just like that."

From what happened to Billy's face, I knew that I was right. He bared his broken mouth and bent down to grab me when Hart cursed him again. He stopped, his eyes wild.

"Someplace," I said, "the Belcheys are waiting to be uncovered. I wonder what it was they found out?"

"Go on, son."

"And the suckers are the ones in the valley. The ones you kept closed off all these years. Ignorant slobs, they couldn't read, they had no desire to go outside this section and they listened to everything you set up. Billy would haul in supplies, but separately he'd haul in mining equipment. You're getting all ready for the big project, aren't you?"

"You're saying it."

Softly, I went on, "Somehow you faked it so the original uranium prospectors got negative reports through. But that wouldn't have been hard. Then you and your bunch here killed them off in one beautiful landslide. You convinced the people here it was an earthquake, so it wasn't hard to get it put down as an accident on the report that went into the New Hope Company. The bodies were buried under tons of rubble that nobody was about to disturb. To be on the safe side, you've waited until you were positive there would be no delayed-action investigation. And all this time you were making ready for the day when you could really start digging."

The old man's face was an impassive mask. For a moment he listened to the sounds from outside, the frantic sounds that precede a lynching.

I said, "It's great, the way you worked them up out there. The story about the *things* was a good one. A strange-looking box that made clicking noises could be turned into a pretty weird weapon, especially when a lot of bodies were around to see. They're so worked up at outsiders they're ready to kill the first new face they see, especially when it's been told that the new one is like 'the others.'"

From the wheelchair he gave me a smile that was almost benevolent. "That's a good story, son, but jest who'd ever believe it?"

The answer came quietly from the back of the room. "Guess I'd believe it, Paw."

They all swung around, went to move, then stopped short. Lovely, wild Caroline stood there with a shotgun in her hands and nobody had to be told that she'd use it as fast as she'd blink an eye.

"Carrie . . ."

"Jest stay still, Paw. Killin' you won't hurt me none. Better remind the boys to be quiet. Billy too."

"Your move, Pop," I grinned.

His eyes narrowed slightly and he nodded again. He looked toward Caroline and said, "He didn't tell it true, girl."

"I believe him, Paw. I love that man."

Her father shook his head gently. "He's one of the others, Carrie."

"He ain't."

"He brung in a *thing*. That's why he came. Like the others."

She looked straight at me, and said, "Don't believe it."

Very casually the old man rolled himself around in the chair, his hands well in sight. I craned my neck around and saw him attaching connectors to the battery. He turned, smiled at me and picked up the Hallifcrafters receiver, and with only me to see what he was doing, switched it on, flipped it to CW and turned it to the short-wave selector. With the first faint hum he found a station, held the volume down until he turned around, then ran the volume up and shouted, "Here's what he brung down from the hills. He brung a *thing* like the others!"

The noisy clicking of the high-speed radio transmission filled the room like a dozen Geiger counters working all at once and when he shut it off I could see the horror in Caroline's face tighten into absolute disgust at herself and me too. Then she sobbed once, dropped the shotgun and ran from the room.

"You made your point, old man," I said. "What now?"

"You're getting throwed to the dogs, son. We're going out there and open a barrel of corn likker for the folks, then coming back for you when things look ready."

He nodded to Big George and was wheeled out the door. The lock clicked shut and I tried to swallow but there wasn't even any saliva left.

From some place I heard the whispered call. I twisted hard to look back. The kid was there, shaking with nervous excitement.

"Trumble! Come here, damn it. Get me out of these ropes!"

Staying crouched down, he angled over to me.

"What happened to you, boy?"

"Last night . . . we seen Billy and the Harts come up. We had to run like hell, mister.

Billy, he hit you. Got you good. Old Man Hart, he said he guessed you'd come to here for something."

"Kid, untie these ropes, will you?"

Without answering he whipped out a clasp knife, felt its honed edge then drew it down my side. The ropes came apart like thread and so did I, lying there like a suddenly bloated balloon. It wasn't until the circulation was normal that I started to ache again.

But pain could be cured. Not hanging. I followed the kid out the back way, let him help me over the window and through the trash to the trees and the mule he had ready. Somehow I got on and collapsed over his neck.

When I woke up again, I was in a haypile on a floor heavy with animal smell and Trumble was holding water to my mouth.

I felt better then. The pain in my skull had dulled and I could move without being helped.

Dusk was coming on fast outside. I said to the kid, "Can you get to Cooper?"

"Guess so." He squinched around a bit. "What you want I should do?"

"Just bring him back here. Can do?"

"Sure. Take an hour. We ain't far off." He slid out of the hay and ducked out the door.

He wasn't gone quite an hour. He let me know he was coming with a piping whistle, stepped in the barn and waved in the old boy. I said, "Evening, Mr. Cooper."

At first he couldn't locate me, then his face turned in my direction. "You raising hell, youngster."

"Isn't it about time somebody did?"

"What you mean?"

I spelled it out for him nice and easy, giving him all the little details. I knew I got through to him and when I finished I asked him the final question. "The *sayings* we talked about. Who's been picking up land options?"

"Hart. He been gettin' 'em one way or another fer years. Ever since them men were here. Got 'em with whiskey, got 'em with guns. Folks, they don't care none. Half never owned the places anyway. Jest squatted. Hart, he took over."

"Okay, thanks."

"What should I do, son?"

"You take care of this kid here. Make sure nothing happens to him. I'll do the rest."

Cooper shook his head. "You can't do much. Harts all out looking for you. Them and Billy. They'll catch you."

"Not this time. They had their chance. I'm not looking any more. I'm moving. I've been through a rat-race like this before and the tricks are all still up here." I tapped my head and grinned at him. "You do what I told you."

Trumble edged forward. "You goin' out alone?"

"Soon's I get a gun."

"Heck, mister . . ." He walked forward, reached under the hay and came out with my .45 and the map. "Kept 'em like you said." He pulled the box of shells from his shirt and laid them in my lap.

"I'll be damned," I said. "What an orderly! Got a light?"

The kid didn't, but Cooper pulled out some stick matches and we stretched out the map. It didn't take long to spot the positions I asked for and mark out the directions

I needed. When it was done I put the map away, checked the load in the gun and walked to the door with Cooper and the kid.

"I'll be away for a while, but I'll be back, Trumble. I'm coming back and take you over the mountains with me. It won't be a long time to wait. You just be patient. Okay?"

For a moment I thought he'd cry, then his face grew serious and he nodded. "You sure 'nuff coming back?"

"Promise. Now you stay with Mr. Cooper here."

"All right. But you come back, hear?"

I winked at him, put him down and slipped his hand into Cooper's. They walked away and at the treeline Trumble looked back, waved and was gone into the night.

By morning I stood on the crest of the slope that overlooked the Hart place, watching carefully to make sure she was alone.

I had traveled fast to get here, bypassing the rest of the clan an hour earlier. The old man and his wheelchair governed their speed and it was unlikely any of them would go ahead.

She came out of the cabin below me, threw a bucket of water into the yard and went back inside. When she was out of sight, I walked in easily, not bothering the dogs or the chickens scratching around the house.

I opened the door, stepped in and said, "Hi, kitten."

Little muscles twitched in her back. She turned slowly, expressionless, big and blonde and beautiful, but with a deadness in her eyes that didn't belong there. Her breathing was shallow, controlled, her breasts straining against her blouse with the tension inside her. "Get out," she said.

"Not until I tell you something."

"No need."

"Your old man tricked you. The thing he had wasn't a . . . a *thing*, a Geiger counter. It was a short-wave radio. He put it on high-speed code and it sounded the same."

"I heard," she said stiffly.

"He told you wrong, Caroline."

"You sayin' Pap's a liar?"

"Uh-huh. Pap's a liar. A murderer, a thief and a liar." She didn't answer me so I went on. "I'm getting out of here, kitten."

She shook her head and the yellow of her hair shimmered in the light. "Nobody can get out."

I held up the map. "It's not so hard."

After a moment she said, "Then why don't you go?"

"Because I want to take you with me, kitten. I wouldn't be a damn bit good by myself."

It seemed that a sheen went over her eyes. "I'm spoke for by Billy."

"Nuts. That bastard wanted you for insurance. He wanted to marry into the family to solidify his position in the deal. The old man held all the property."

"You lie."

"I want you, kid."

"You want me to show you the way out, is all."

"I want you, kid. Here or anyplace else. Coming?"

She smiled a tiny smile and I thought she was coming into my arms. Her hands went out long enough to feint me off guard, then she spun, grabbed a shotgun from beside the closet, wheeled and fired and I thought my hand had been torn off. I smashed the gun out of her hand before she could fire the other barrel and knocked her on her tail.

There was still feeling in my hand so it was still on. I looked at it, opened the fingers and the scrap that was the remainder of the map fell out. The charge had ripped the rest of it out and blew the pieces all over the room. I'd have a sore hand from the concussion, but that was all.

Caroline come up into a sitting position, her hand touching her face. There were tears streaming down her cheeks, but she wasn't crying. I said, "Okay, honey, let it be." I kicked at the paper at my feet. "I guess now it's the way you like it."

I reached down, snatched her to her feet. She didn't get a chance to stop me before I kissed her quickly. I shoved her away, ran to the door and looked out.

The Hart clan had heard the shot and had scattered. The first section was coming in fast with Big George and Billy leading the pack. I said, "So long, kitten," and took off for the hills with the house screening my maneuver.

Inside Caroline was screaming for them to hurry . . . hurry . . .

The three bogies overhead wheeled in the updrafts, then spiraled down for a closer look. They come low enough so I could see the quick movement of their heads and the anticipation in their eyes. This was their death watch and they were ready to ply their trade.

There was quiet in the gully again. Now that I was on the other side of them they'd have to plan a new approach. From where I lay I could retreat across the mountainside and if I played it smart I wouldn't get where they could flank me. But they could afford to wait. Sooner or later sleep would catch me and that would be the end. The best I could do was play for that one chance in a million and maybe make a few good dead Harts out of bad live Harts.

I picked my way slowly around the ridge, flat against the ground. Twice I saw movement at the bottom of the hill, but it could have been deliberate carelessness to draw my fire.

After a half-hour, the wind came about slowly and I picked up traces of a whisper from my left before it stopped. I crawled toward it, waited, bellied down and inched some more. It took thirty minutes to go fifty feet. Then all I did was lie there and wait until the head poked around the rock. The butt end of the .45 smashed down and the head rammed the ground and never moved. I knew by the feel of it that this one was for the birds upstairs. I didn't even bother to see which one I got.

I found another spot that seemed to be good cover and sat waiting. The sun toured the sky and started to glow red with approaching sunset. It made the whole valley a beautiful place, alive with color, a place seemingly distant from death.

With Caroline it could have been nice. With Caroline anything could have been nice. Very softly I said, "Caroline . . ."

And she said, "Mitch . . ."

I flipped onto my stomach with the .45 out, pointing right at her head. She stood there, screened in the bushes, her face flushed and tear streaked, the blouse and skirt torn and grimy. But this time her hands were held out to me, pleadingly.

"I had to come, Mitch."

My hand waved her to silence, made her go flat on her face. I crawled up to her. "This could be a sweet trick, kitten."

The tears told me it wasn't. "Please, Mitch." She wiped her hand across her eyes. "When Pap chased you, he . . . he left it there. The *thing*. I turned the knobs. Pretty soon . . . music came out. Pap. . . was lying to me. It was like you said."

I patted her face gently. "I know, kid. Too bad it's so late."

No. It ain't late. I know how we can get away."

"And you're ready to go?"

She nodded. "I'll go anyplace with you, Mitch."

I kissed her, tasting the tears and the love she was asking for, all of a sudden alive again and happy. "Which way?"

"Billy Bussy's road. We run like hell when it gets dark. The boys know the way, but they won't want to get too close."

"When it gets dark," I said.

The sun still had a long way to go. Down below, there was no movement. No sound. They were playing it cute and waiting. I rolled over close to her, feeling the warmth of her body through my clothes. Her hand found mine and brought it to her mouth and we stayed like that for long minutes. Then she looked up and her face was close, her mouth full, and lushly-red, wet, and wanting hard to be kissed. Her body was a trembling thing screaming silently and when I touched her lips, she twitched against me spasmodically.

The sun swung through its oval and death stayed only yards away, but we hardly knew it at all.

This night was different from the others. There was a stillness that hadn't existed before as if the whole valley wanted to hear the hunt and the kill. The moon scoured the ground with a pale light, the shadows throwing mimic trails and obscuring the real one.

Caroline stayed in front, trotting steadily, never seeming to stray from the animal path she followed. No other sound seemed to reach us, but there was no doubt that they were back there. She knew it too, and turned off the trail to another one that led against the summit. It would be longer this way, she said, but she didn't want to tip off our destination. Otherwise they'd be there waiting.

From our new position we were able to see them as they passed the turnoff. Billy Bussy, the four boys, and on Big George's back like a leech was Old Man Hart. While we still had a lead, we ran because they wouldn't stay on that false trail long.

It was 12:10 when we intersected the road. We stopped, sprawled out on the wet ground, breathing harshly from the climb. I said, "How far?"

Caroline shook her head. "I . . . can't tell. Never been past here. We follow the road . . . that's all."

"Okay. We'll sit here an hour and rest up. We're going to need it. I haven't got enough left to go ten feet."

She sat up suddenly. "Better have, Mitch."

"Why?"

"Listen." She cocked her head. "I hear them coming. They found out and took the short way!"

We got up shakily and began to run again. It was a dream kind of a run, getting nowhere, having to force your way through the air. Our feet were too heavy, the road too steep and too long. For a second I thought that we should have fought it out back in the hills, then I put the thought away and plodded ahead.

Time lost its meaning and its sense of importance. Time was just something that swam around you. Time was something Old Man Hart's voice swam in and yelled, "Mitch, damn you. You stop, hear? You stop and maybe we'll let you go. I know who you got there!"

Caroline looked back tiredly and shook her head. "He don't want fer me to git killed. That'll make folks think. He don't want 'em to think."

I had nothing left to answer with, so I nodded.

"Mitch, damn you!"

We rounded a bend in the trees and came on a widening-out point. But it made the sweetest little trap you saw because on each side of the bulge was a twenty-foot high rock face and stretched across the road was a multi-strand barb-wire fence with a gate set right in the middle of it.

I said, "Hold it, kitten," and stopped her before she touched it. It only took about five seconds to find the wire and just as long to detach it. "Booby trap, sugar. He's got this place rigged to go off the minute anybody touches the gate. Ten-to-one the Belcheys got it here trying to get out of the valley."

When I shoved the gate open, I waved her through. Then with the gate swung halfway in I re-attached the gimmick.

There was no sound from the trail. They were waiting to see what would happen. They were waiting for the big boom.

The moon flooded the bottleneck now, showing every detail of it clearly. I walked out of its glow to the road and yelled, "All right, you stinking killers, come and get it! Come and get it!" Then I emptied the .45 at the sky.

It happened like I knew it would, when Billy Bussy yelled his weasel yell and came tearing around the corner knowing the rod was empty, ready to nail me or force me through the gate. The others were right behind him and when they saw the open gate all they could do was think that something went wrong with the trap and the chase was still going.

They came on, every one of them, swearing, yelling their crazy rage, and nobody at all heard the old man who was the only one who could read through the picture. I did. I heard him yell. "NO . . . NO . . . IT'S A TRAP! BILLY . . . GEORGE . . . BY DAMN . . ."

Then they pushed the gate open the rest of the way in their mad rush to get to us and the sky was split apart, and for the span of a full breath the valley below lay painted in the bright red and yellow of the blast.

We came away from the rocks that sheltered us and I looked at the girl I loved so much. I felt her face and there were no tears, no remorse. I kissed her gently and she kissed me back.

We stepped out on the road that we knew would take us out, then started up it hand in hand.

A NEW LEAF

JACK RITCHIE
(1922–1983)

A prolific short story writer (his only novel was published posthumously by a small press), Ritchie had only three books published in his lifetime but had works collected in anthologies of the year's best mystery stories twenty-one times between 1961 and 1983, a feat matched by no other author of his time. His most famous work, which follows, was filmed in 1970 starring Walter Matthau and Elaine May, who also directed and wrote the screenplay.

E HAD BEEN MARRIED THREE months and I rather thought it was time to get rid of my wife.

I searched the greenhouse and its shed, but they contained only such non-toxic items as grafting wax, powdered limestone, sphagnum moss, and the like.

I returned to the house. "Henrietta, where do you keep the poisons? I mean the sprays and things like that for the garden?"

"But, dear," my wife said. "We use the organic method. No sprays or chemicals of any kind. We enrich the soil nature's way with organic materials—leaves, grass clippings, and especially spoiled hay. A healthy soil produces healthy plants, and insects simply do not destroy healthy plants. What did you want the poison for, dear?"

"I saw a beetle on one of the shrubs."

She smiled mildly. "One mustn't kill beetles indiscriminately, William. So many of them are beneficial."

I studied her. "Henrietta, I've been meaning to ask you, just where do you buy those dresses you wear?" I had also

meant to ask, "And why?" but I did not.

She glanced briefly at a mirror. "Every month or so I just phone Elaine's shop and have her send over three or four dresses."

"Don't you ever try them on before you buy them?"

"There's no need to, dear, Elaine knows my size." She looked down at her dress. "Do you like it, William?"

"It fits perfectly. However, the next time you feel the inclination to buy another dress, I think that we'd both better go to Elaine's and look over her stock first."

When my father departed this world, he left me an inheritance that was just short of adequate. By that I mean that it was necessary for me to dip into my capital in order to exist in a civilized manner. During the course of fifteen years that capital, of course, diminished to nonexistence. In short, at the time I met Henrietta, I lived on credit.

I have never felt that work is a duty, a pleasure, or a challenge, and I have always suspected that those who enjoy it are basically masochistic.

I had existed forty-five years without the necessity of stooping to labor, and I felt that it was manifestly unfair to expect me to do so now.

There remained one last recourse. Marriage.

I have never been against that institution for others. I realize that the average mind must occupy itself with something, whether it be labor, comic books, or marriage. However, I have always cherished my position of independence, and the prospect of becoming a member of a "team"—even if that team consisted of only two people—was acutely depressing.

Yet I was penniless, and it was necessary for me to dip into marriage.

Once having arrived at that decision, I now attended the functions of my set with an appraising eye. Desperate though I was, I found myself rejecting one prospect after another. Eventually I extended my search to afternoon teas—and at one of them I first glimpsed Henrietta.

I was not impressed. Her clothes were not exactly out of fashion, but one had the impression that she had purchased them blindfolded. She was a small, fragile-appearing woman who sat alone in a corner, smiling faintly to herself, and one had the feeling that she had wandered in accidentally and now was not quite certain of how to get out.

I had been stifling a yawn when Henrietta spilled her cup of tea.

The hostess's eyes darted like arrows. "Really, Henrietta!"

She blushed scarlet. "I'm sorry, Clara. I was thinking of something else."

Clara's shoulders twitched. "Why can't you be more careful? I've just had the rug cleaned."

It occurred to me that a woman who dressed as Henrietta did, did so because she was either poor, or too rich to care. When the chattering resumed, I turned to Hawley Purvis, who was sitting at my right. "Henrietta? Would she be one of the Bartons? The ones who lost practically all their money last year?"

"Good heavens, no!" Purvis said. "She's a Lowell. Has that fabulous place on the Lakeview Road. Fifty acres or something like that and scores of servants."

"Married?"

"No. Never has been."

I stared across the room at Henrietta. A maid approached her with the teapot. Henrietta seemed alarmed at the prospect of again holding a full cup of tea. She was about to refuse, but she was too late. The maid poured.

Henrietta held the cup gingerly between the fingers of both hands.

I rubbed my jaw speculatively. Fifty acres? Scores of servants? I watched Henrietta covertly. She consumed half the cup of tea, and after five minutes her mind evidently wandered again. The cup slipped from her fingers and the contents spilled over the rug.

Clara's face turned livid and she shrieked, "Henrietta!"

This time Henrietta paled. If she could have fainted, I am positive she would have.

I rose and elaborately poured the contents of my own cup onto Clara's rug. "Madam," I said stiffly. "Take your damn rug to the cleaners and charge the bill to me." It was the moment for action.

I offered my arm to Henrietta and we left.

The greatest obstacle to my marriage plans did not come from Henrietta, but from her attorney, Adam McPherson.

I made his acquaintance one week after Henrietta and I announced our engagement. He came to my apartment, introduced himself, and then stared at me stonily. "How much do you want?"

"For what?"

"How much do you want to call off your marriage to Henrietta?"

I frowned. "Did she send you?"

"No. This is my own idea. I'm offering you ten thousand."

"If you will turn, you will find a door behind you. It is the way out."

He was not intimidated. "When I heard about you, I had you investigated. You are penniless and in debt to any number of establishments, including Curley's Rug Cleaning Service." His lips tightened. "You are marrying Henrietta for her money."

"Really? And what, besides the state of my finances, makes you so positive about that?"

"I have had your acquaintances polled. They unanimously agree that you are as capable of a tender emotion as a fish. A cold fish, they all specified." He reiterated his offer. "Ten thousand dollars."

What was a paltry ten thousand compared to Henrietta's millions? "Henrietta and I are deeply in love," I said firmly. "I would not part with her for less than . . . for *all* the money in the world."

"Twenty thousand."

"Never."

"Thirty. And that's absolutely final."

"So is my no. Is this *your* money you are offering?"

"Yes."

"And what is your motive?"

"I do not want Henrietta to make a mistake she will regret all her life."

I ventured a guess. "Have you ever asked her to marry you?"

He nodded glumly. "About four times a year for the last twelve years."

"And her sentiments?"

"She regards me as a dear trustworthy friend. Very depressing." A thought suddenly brightened his face. "Do you *really* love Henrietta?"

I used a word strange to me. "Passionately."

He rubbed his hands. "Then of course you would have no objection to signing a document disclaiming all rights to Henrietta's money?"

"Henrietta would never consent to anything like that."

"I'll ask her."

"I'll wring your neck." I regained control of myself. "If it is your interest to see that Henrietta is happy, undoubtedly you have noticed that she has achieved a certain euphoria since I met her."

He admitted it reluctantly. Then he sighed. "All right. I will not oppose the marriage further."

"How good of you."

He studied me a moment. "Henrietta needs to be protected."

I agreed. "She is rather simple."

He corrected me. "Ingenuous." He went to the door and then turned. "I suppose you know that she teaches at the university?"

I blinked. "Henrietta?"

"Yes. Associate professor. Botany. Donates her entire salary to charity."

So that was why she had never been home on weekdays, except for the evenings. "She never told me."

"Probably forgot," McPherson said. "She's absentminded about some things."

Henrietta and I were married three weeks later. It was a small private ceremony marred only by the fact that McPherson arrived drunk and burst into tears as I slipped the ring on Henrietta's finger. She was excited and cried.

We spent our honeymoon in the Bahamas, where Henrietta collected an incredible number of ferns and various tropical vegetations for further study at home.

When we returned to her estate, I endured a week of bad service and poor food while I occupied my time by checking the household accounts.

The day Henrietta returned to teaching at the university, I called the servants together. They regarded me with uniformly narrow eyes and a collective insolence.

I attacked the keystone first—the housekeeper. "Mrs. Tragger. Front and center."

She folded her arms. "What is it?"

I smiled with infinite sweetness. "There is something about you that puzzles me. Why do you go about with that perpetual frown upon your face?"

She frowned.

I spoke gently. "I should think that you would be bubblingly happy. Gay. Absolutely hilarious. Whistling day and night. After all, you have successfully managed to pad the household accounts to the sum of eighteen thousand dollars in the last six years."

Her face darkened. "Are you accusing me of—"

"Yes."

She glared. "I'll sue immediately."

"Please do. As soon as you are released from prison."

Uncertainty flickered in her eyes, but she said, "You can't prove a thing."

It would have been difficult. However, I showed my teeth. "Madam, I *can* prove it for the satisfaction of any judge or jury. Yet I am inclined to be generous. Do you have a suitcase?"

She blinked. "Yes."

"Splendid. Then pack it at once and leave. You are fired."

She seemed about to utter something profane and devastating, but perhaps the nature of my smile changed her mind. She licked her lips and glanced at her audience. Finally she harrumphed and stalked out of the room.

I turned next to the chauffeur, an unshaven creature who evidently slept in his uniform. "Simpson."

"Yeah?"

"Do you think that we ought to junk our cars?"

"Huh?"

"I really believe that in the interests of economy we ought to get rid of them— one and all. According to our records of gas consumption and mileage, I find that not one of them gives us more than one mile per gallon."

He shifted his feet. "Then figures are probably wrong somewhere."

"Possibly. But you need worry about them no longer. I presume that you too have a suitcase?"

He glowered. "Only Miss Lowell can fire me."

I smiled. "Miss Lowell is now Mrs. Graham, and if I find you on the grounds one hour from now, I shall regard you as a trespasser. I will not shoot you in the head. That is impenetrable. However, enough of you remains so that I cannot possibly miss."

I did not dismiss all of the servants—only seventy percent of them—and I had half of those replaced immediately by a reputable employment agency.

That evening dinner was on time, served flawlessly, and satisfying to the palate.

Henrietta did not notice the food—she seldom does—but toward the end of the meal she happened to glance at the serving maid and frowned thoughtfully. "Are you new here? I haven't seen you before."

"Yes, madam."

Henrietta turned to me. "What happened to Tessie?"

"I dismissed her. Also quite a few of the others. I replaced some, but only those necessary to the proper functioning of this house. Was it essential for you to have *three* personal inadequate maids?"

"Three? I'm sorry, William. I didn't know I had *any*. Mrs. Tragger does all the hiring. And besides, I've never seen any of them. I dress myself." She looked at me hopefully. "Did you fire Mrs. Tragger?"

"Yes."

"And the chauffeur?"

"Yes."

Her gaze was one of profound admiration. "I was always a little . . . *afraid* . . . of them. Especially the chauffeur. He always seemed so put out when I asked him to drive me anywhere. So I always took a bus."

After a month I had the immediate estate functioning with reasonable efficiency and honesty on the part of the servants.

And now, at breakfast, I pondered my next step—independence, with wealth. And that called for the quite permanent disposal of my wife.

Poison? Yes, an agreeable method, but could I purchase any without having to sign some sort of a register?

I had never killed anyone, yet I had the feeling that I could murder with a certain equanimity. Not that I would linger for the death agonies, of course. I would tactfully leave the room.

"Dear," Henrietta said. "Have you ever thought of teaching?"

"Teaching?"

"Yes, dear. There's an instructorship in history going to be open this fall, and there seems to be no prospect of filling it. So many teachers have majored in the sciences lately. They consider it more patriotic, I suppose."

Rat poison? Somehow the idea seemed too plebeian.

"All you would need is a B.A.," Henrietta said. "And you have that. And I think it would be so nice if you and I left together for the university each morning."

"I haven't the slightest inclination to teach. I much prefer to spend my time learning."

"But just learning is selfish."

"Me? *Selfish?*"

"I don't mean you specifically, dear," she said hastily. "I just meant that learning is *taking* and teaching is *giving*. And if you taught, you would feel useful."

"I dislike feeling useful. It is much too common." I suddenly remembered Ralph Winkler. Possibly he would have poison lying about his premises. He and I had been roommates in college, and he had majored in chemistry, or some such trade.

After breakfast I looked up Ralph's address in the phone book and arrived there forty-five minutes later. It was a painfully neat house set behind twenty-five feet of precise lawn.

Ralph poured coffee and settled back in his chair. "I haven't seen you at any of the alumni meetings."

"Ralph," I said. "I wonder if you might be able to lend me a little—"

His eyes clouded reminiscently. "Remember good old Gillie Stearns?"

"No. It doesn't necessarily have to be arsen—"

"He could wiggle his ears," Ralph said. "Became an anthropologist."

I glanced out the window at what appeared to be apple trees.

"He's the one who wrote that term paper on the appendix," Ralph said.

"Who did?"

"Stearns. Nobody knows what the function of the appendix really is, but it was Stearns's theory that the way to have a healthy appendix was to wiggle—"

"I see you're quite a gardener," I said.

"Orchardist. I have five apple trees, two peach, and one pecan." He frowned slightly. "The pecan doesn't seem to produce."

"Aren't you supposed to have *two* pecan trees?"

"I never thought of that."

"Ralph," I said. "Do you spray? I mean your fruit trees? Often?"

I had touched his subject. He rose enthusiastically. "William, follow me."

I took my cup along.

He led me through the house, into the backyard, and to the garage. He selected a key from an impressive ring and unlocked the door. "I keep the car parked on the street. Not enough room in here." He opened the door and stepped aside. "See for yourself, William."

I received the immediate impression that I had entered a combination garden shop and pharmacy. A riding mower, a tractor, and various accessory attachments occupied the floor space. The shelves lining one entire side were filled with bottles, jars, cans, and cartons. An assortment of manual spray guns hung on the walls. "How big is your place, Ralph?"

"A full quarter of an acre."

My eyes ran over the shelves and I made a random choice. "What's in that little red can in the corner?"

"Just about the strongest stuff I have," he said proudly. "It'll kill anything." He pointed to a gas mask and a rubber suit hanging on a peg. "I have to wear that when I spray. Can't leave an inch of skin exposed."

I stared at the can. "And you spray this poison on your apples?"

"You've never seen better ones in your life, William: Not a sign of sooty blotch, calyx end rot, or Brooks fruit spot."

"And you eat these apples?"

"Perfectly safe. The spray eventually washes off through wind and weather. Besides, I always peel the ones I eat."

I finished my coffee and handed him the cup. "Would I be imposing if I asked for a refill? I'll wait here and browse."

While he was gone, I pried open the red can with a screwdriver. The contents were a sickly yellow dust. I filled an envelope, gingerly licked the flap to seal it, and put it back into my pocket.

Ralph returned with my cup. "Remember good old Jimmy Haskins?"

"No." I took the cup. "What do you think about the organic method of raising apples?"

A chill descended. "Most unscientific."

"We have about forty apple trees on our place," I said. "We never spray."

His lips tightened. "There are all kinds of people in this world."

I had the impression that he regretted bringing me the coffee. There was no point in departing on such a frigid note. I searched my memory and then chuckled. "Remember good old Clarence? The one we all said could get his hair cut in a pencil sharpener?"

"Yes," Ralph said coldly. "He's my brother."

I did not, of course, intend to poison Henrietta in our own home. That would lead to the inevitable autopsy and the equally inevitable electric chair.

But an earlier conversation with Henrietta had given me a splendid idea.

"Dear," she had said. "Every summer I go on a field trip for a week or two. Would it be all right if I went this year?"

I had been about to tell her that I had no objections—providing that she did not expect me to go with her—but then a thought had occurred to me. "Where will you be going?"

"It would be a canoe trip, William," she had said. "The Minnesota woods."

"You've been taking trips like this alone?"

"Oh, no. I usually go with some of my students. But this year I was hoping that . . . that just you and I could go. We could hire a guide if you think we'd need one, but actually I don't think that would be necessary if we didn't wander from our camp."

The idea of battling mosquitoes was not inviting, but I smiled. "Of course I will go with you. And we will not require a guide."

My problem had been solved. We would be alone in the middle of nowhere. I would simply kill her and bury her.

Then I would inform the authorities that my wife had wandered away from our camp and been lost. There would be a search, of course, but Henrietta would not be found.

And the actual method of the murder itself? I had dallied with shooting, stabbing, strangling, and bludgeoning. I eventually ejected them all. They required a primitive violence that is foreign to my nature. This morning I finally decided that poisoning was the civilized procedure.

When I returned from Ralph Winkler's home, I put the poison under lock and key.

In the evening, as usual, Henrietta brought her notes and reference books into the living room and worked on her latest paper for the *Botany Journal*. I put a stack of records into the phonograph and settled under a lamp for another review of Henrietta's accounts.

After a while I turned in my chair. "Henrietta, there's one item that keeps recurring. Every month you withdraw two thousand dollars from one of your bank accounts. The money seems to disappear. At least I can't find my accounting for it."

Henrietta hesitated. "I'm afraid it's blackmail, dear."

"Blackmail?" Perhaps I had underestimated her. "What in the world have you done to be blackmailed for?"

"Nothing, dear. It's because of Professor Henrich. You see, he and his wife adopted a child. Only it wasn't through a regular agency. Black market, they call it. And they thought that everything was fine. But a year later a man came to them and claimed that he was the child's father. He seemed to have evidence to prove it, and he wanted the baby back unless . . ."

It was obvious. "Unless Professor Henrich paid?"

"Yes. First it was one hundred dollars a month, and then gradually he was paying five hundred. But the professor and his wife simply couldn't afford that for long. They had to dip into their savings, and when those were gone, Professor Henrich came to me to borrow money. He more or less broke down and told me the entire story. And so I took over the payments."

"*You* took over the payments? How could Henrich possibly *allow* you to do something like that?"

"But he doesn't really know what I'm doing, dear. I just told him that I'd talk to

Smith—that's the name of the blackmailer. And later I told the professor that I'd managed to frighten Smith away by threatening to go to the police."

"But obviously you didn't."

"No, I thought it over and realized that there wasn't any actual *proof* that Smith was a blackmailer. He always insisted on cash from the professor. And so if I failed to *prove* to the police that Smith was a blackmailer, he might become very angry with my interference and actually take the child back. I was in a dilemma and money seemed to be the only way out."

"Five hundred dollars at first? And then more and more? Until today is two thousand dollars a month?"

"Yes, dear."

I rubbed my forehead and eyes. "Don't you realize that eventually it will be three thousand? Four?"

She shook her head. "No. Two thousand is my absolute limit. I told him so when he asked for two thousand five hundred. He seemed disappointed, but he accepted the situation." She smiled. "I can be very firm when I want to."

I had difficulty speaking. "Just how much have you given this contemptible wretch?"

"I'm not positive. About fifty thousand dollars by now, I imagine."

"*Fifty thousand dollars* of my . . . of *our* money? To a man who neither sows nor reaps?"

She nodded. "That reminds me, William. You'd have only three classes a day. That's because instructorships are usually given to students who are also working for advanced degrees, and the university doesn't want to overload them. Would you like to work for your M.A. too?"

"When are you going to see Smith again?"

"He comes here the first Monday of each month. He's very prompt and he always phones me on the Sunday before to remind me to get to the bank for the cash Monday morning."

I went to the liquor cabinet and made myself a stiff drink. "When he phones next, let me talk to him."

The call came Sunday afternoon, and Henrietta handed the phone to me.

"Would you please leave the room, Henrietta," I said. "I am always a bit embarrassed when I reason with people."

When she was gone, I spoke into the mouthpiece. "You've received your last cent, you miserable parasite."

"Who the hell are you?"

I explained precisely and then added, "I control every penny that leaves this house and you are no longer included in our charities."

"In that case I'll take the kid away from the professor."

"I doubt very much if you can. Your references aren't exactly the best—as Professor Henrich and his wife, and I and mine, will gladly testify in any court."

"Look, mister, I can still make a lot of trouble. A lot of trouble."

"You are welcome to try." But then something occurred to me. A man deprived of a two-thousand-dollar-a-month income has a tendency to turn ugly. Undoubtedly he would keep an eye on us. And when Henrietta disappeared, would he put two and two together? Blackmailers are notoriously suspicious. Would he approach me and demand money for silence? And if I did not pay, would he see to it that I was caused considerable embarrassment with the police? Would he cause the authorities to resume the search for Henrietta a bit more diligently—with an eye directed toward the subsurface of our last encampment?

There is only one way to deal with a blackmailer—be he real or potential.

"Just one moment," I said. "Do you have proof that you are the father of the child? Real proof?"

"The professor saw the papers."

"But I haven't. I doubt if you have any proof at all. But if you do, bring it here Monday evening. No proof, no money." I hung up.

I explained to Henrietta that I wanted to see Smith alone when he came—to further reason with him—and on Monday evening she returned happily to the university to attend a lecture on the shallow root systems of the sequoias.

When she was gone, I saw to it that the servants retired to their quarters and then went to the liquor cabinet in the study.

I opened the envelope containing Winkler's yellow powder. How much of this stuff was sufficient to kill a human being? I didn't know. I solved the problem by pouring the entire contents into a bottle of Scotch.

Smith arrived at eight-thirty. He was a somewhat bulky man with long arms, and his hairline initiated approximately one inch from his eyebrows. He was expensively, if not tastefully, dressed.

I closed the door of the study behind us. "The proof, please."

He revealed marigold-yellow teeth and removed a revolver from his pocket. "This is just so that you don't get any funny ideas." Then he put the gun back into his pocket and handed me an envelope.

I examined the contents. The papers were originals, not photostats, and apparently authentic. I wandered over to the liquor cabinet as I studied a hospital birth record. I made myself a bourbon and soda and then looked up as though I'd suddenly remembered he was still there. "A drink?"

"What you got?"

"Scotch?"

"That's it."

I poured a generous glass and handed it to him. He drained the entire contents and smacked his lips. "Good stuff."

That confirmed a suspicion of mine. People who drink Scotch have no sense of taste.

He extended the glass. "How about making that wet again?"

"Gladly." His simian aspect reminded me of good old Gillie Stearns, and I asked a question. "Can you wiggle your ears?"

He seemed a bit saddened. "Used to be able to. But ever since my appendix got took out I lost the touch."

When I noticed that his coloring seemed to verge toward purple, I hastily put the papers back into the envelope and returned them. "These seem to be in order. And now if you'll excuse me, I'll get you the cash. I have it in the library safe." His color grew worse.

I went to the library and sat down. I finished a pipe and then returned to the study.

Smith lay on the floor, quite dead, and it appeared that his departure had not been a pleasant one.

I withdrew the envelope from his pocket and then slung him over my shoulder. I carried him through the French doors to the automobile he'd parked in the circular driveway.

I drove toward the outskirts of the city, following a bus line. When the area seemed relatively unpopulated, I turned off and parked the car.

I walked back half a dozen blocks before I boarded a bus.

Perhaps Smith's picture would appear in the newspapers when his body was found. If it did, and Henrietta noticed it, I would explain that a man like Smith undoubtedly had many enemies and that one of them had killed him. I felt confident that she would accept that explanation.

At Fremont Street, I left the bus and walked the two blocks to Ralph Winkler's home.

He opened the door and regarded me with distinct inhospitality. "Yes?"

"Ralph," I said. "We've been having a little trouble with field mice in our apple orchard."

His economic smile indicated vindication. "So organic gardeners have field mice problems?"

"I'm afraid so. I wonder whether you might have something potent—some chemical—that might enable us to get rid of them?"

I was welcome instantly. He stepped aside and we journeyed through the house and to his garage.

He surveyed his pharmacy. "What'll you have? I've got compounds here that will throw mice into convulsions."

I recalled the messy decline of Smith. "Basically I'm a humanitarian. Do you have something gentle, yet still lethal?"

He was disappointed in me. "Very well. I suppose I have something like that here . . . somewhere. But you really should try Cyclolodidan. I use it all the time."

"Do you have field mice?"

He nodded glumly. "Can't seem to get rid of them."

When Henrietta returned at eleven that night, I told her that Smith would never bother her or Professor Henrich again. "Threatened him with the police and twenty years in prison. He left here shaken, trembling, and penitent."

Henrietta gazed at me admiringly. "You seem to be able to get things done, William. I feel so safe with you."

During the week, Henrietta usually lunches at the university, but at twelve-thirty the next day she came home breathless and smiling like a child. She waved an envelope. "It's been accepted."

"What has?"

"Alsophilia grahamicus."

"Alsophilia grahamicus?"

"A tropical tree fern, William. I discovered it during our honeymoon, and when I couldn't classify it, I realized that it might be a true species. So I named it after you—that's the 'grahamicus' part—and sent it to the Society for verification."

I rolled the words on my tongue. *"Alsophilia grahamicus."* Rather pleasing. Perhaps I might yet become a footnote in some textbook—my bid toward immortality.

"Are you pleased, William?"

"That was very thoughtful of you."

"I'm having the tip of one frond put into a plastic token so that you can wear it always."

That evening Adam McPherson appeared for dinner. It had been his habit to do so the first Tuesday of every month for the past ten years, and after our marriage Henrietta had still chosen to honor the standing invitation.

I met him at the door. "McPherson, I want a word with you."

He regarded me for a moment. "Really? What a coincidence. It was my intention to speak to you too." He glanced about. "Where is Henrietta?"

"Upstairs grading some term papers."

I led him into the study and came directly to the point. "McPherson, you are

Henrietta's lawyer and comptroller. Surely you must have been aware that prior to my appearance this household was run in a most strange manner—padded pay-rolls, superfluous servants, astronomical household expenses."

He nodded. "Of course."

My eyes narrowed. "And yet you did nothing about it?"

"Why should I? After all, I am the one who was responsible for the entire glorious arrangement."

"You baldly *admit* that?"

"Certainly." McPherson went to the liquor cabinet and surveyed the contents. "It was quite a profitable arrangement for me. Kickbacks, you know." He looked back at me. "Henrietta is an excellent botanist, but she has no accounting ability what-soever. And she trusted me."

I felt the impulse to strangle. "I do not care how messy this is going to be, I intend to prosecute."

He was not perturbed. "If you do, I shall see that you join me in prison—or pos-sibly worse. For murder."

I was, of course, temporarily quieted.

He brought forth a bottle and a glass. "Several years ago I noticed that Henrietta regularly withdrew five hundred dollars from one of her bank accounts. It was a rel-atively insignificant sum, but she seldom uses cash, and I became curious. I asked her about it, and when she proved uncharacteristically evasive, I questioned the servants—who were under my command, so to speak—and eventually ascertained the existence of Mr. Smith. Further investigation on my part—if one may use that term for eavesdropping—established the reason for his monthly visits."

McPherson poured liquor into his glass. "Smith had a limited imagination. He was apparently satisfied with five hundred dollars. But I was not." He smiled. "Therefore I approached him with the proposal of prison or cooperation. Naturally he chose cooperation. Of the two thousand he eventually received monthly from Henrietta, one went to me."

I stared at the bottle he still held in his hand. It was the Scotch that had elimi-nated Smith. I had forgotten to dispose of it.

McPherson put the bottle back on the shelf. "When Smith informed me that *you* wanted to see him personally, I wondered what you were up to now—after all, you had already ruined one of my sources of income. And so I drove here last night, parked on the street, and waited for him to come out of your house. It was my intention to ques-tion him immediately about his meeting with you." He smiled. "His car came out of the driveway, but *you* were driving." He looked at his glass and then at me. "Can I make you a drink?"

"No, thank you," I said. "But by all means, please help yourself."

He savored and then finished the contents of his glass. He coughed apprecia-tively and reached for the bottle again. "I followed you. And when you walked away from Smith's car, I looked inside. Smith lay on the floor, obviously dead. I did not pry into the manner of his death and left immediately. How did you kill him?"

"I stabbed him in the back," I said.

He smiled. "Please do not attempt the same with me. I am wary and will remain at arm's length." He tried to stay alert.

And now *I* smiled. "I cannot expose you without being exposed myself? And so it is your intention to resume bilking Henrietta's estate? With my passive cooperation?"

He nodded. "Exactly."

I noticed that his complexion was changing to a more colorful hue. "We will discuss this further after dinner," I said pleasantly. "And now I shall see if Henrietta is ready."

I retired to the library, smoked a pipe, and returned to the study.

McPherson was dead.

I removed his car keys from his pocket and carried his body to his car outside. I deposited him in the trunk compartment and parked the car on the street.

I returned to the house just as Henrietta came down the stairs. "Is Adam here yet?"

"No, my dear."

She smiled. "He's rather fond of me. It was very thoughtful of him to cry at our wedding."

We delayed dinner half an hour and then sat down without him.

At ten that evening when I went out for a walk, I disposed of McPherson's car in the same manner I had used for Smith and returned by bus.

Henrietta was considerably shocked when she read of McPherson's death and the police were puzzled. Henrietta recovered, but the police remained puzzled and the days passed.

At the end of the semester, Henrietta and I packed and drove north to the Minnesota lake country. We rented a canoe, purchased supplies, and bravely proceeded into the wilderness on a warm Saturday afternoon.

Since we proceeded downstream, the paddling was not particularly tedious and the first hour passed pleasantly.

However, as we approached the first white water, I realized, a bit too late, that the occupation of running rapids is a bit specialized.

I would gladly have paddled to shore and portaged, but I found that we were in the grip of the current. We had no choice but to hold on and attempt to steer.

We safely rode two-thirds of the rapids, and I had reached a faint optimism, when suddenly a jagged rock appeared directly ahead. I endeavored frantically to avoid it. However, the after end of the canoe smashed into the obstruction and we turned over.

I found myself tumbling in the rushing water, grasping wildly for some handhold, but my fingers merely slipped off the wet rocks. Suddenly I found myself falling. I plunged deep into the water. When I fought my way to the surface, I discovered that I had successfully passed all obstacles and now floated in a relatively quiet pool at their base. Then I relaxed.

I swam to shore, climbed the bank, and looked back upstream.

Henrietta clung to an outcropping of rock just before the drop into the pool. She was pale and her eyes looked toward me for help.

I shouted, "Henrietta, let go of that rock. You'll be carried into the pool below. It's perfectly safe."

She looked down and then at me. "But I can't swim."

I blinked. *She couldn't swim?*

I felt my heart beating. This was the opportunity! There would be no need for poison. There had been a canoe accident and she had drowned. It was as simple as that. And I would walk back to the nearest habitation and tell the story.

I raised my voice again. "Hold your breath and let go of that rock. I'll be waiting down below and I'll bring you to shore."

I took off my soaking shoes, my trousers, and my shirt. Then I smiled at her and waved my hand. "All right. Let go."

She did not hesitate.

The current caught her and she plunged over and down into the pool.

I turned my back toward the water. All I would have to do now was wait. How long? Five minutes? Ten?

I looked down at my clothes. The round plastic token containing the tip of frond had fallen out of my pocket and lay on the grass. *Alsophilia grahamicus.*

I found myself trembling.

I had killed Smith and McPherson and they had deserved to die. But does one kill a child?

A child? Yes, a child-woman, and she loved me. And in my own way I had grown rather . . .

I cursed savagely and plunged into the water.

I found Henrietta immediately and brought her to the surface. She was still obeying my injunction to hold her breath, though rather desperately.

I grasped her and began backstroking toward the shore. "You may breathe now, Henrietta. But only through your mouth. Not your nose. Taste the air, and if it has water in it, spit it out and try again."

When we reached shore, we sat in the sun. But it was still a bit cool and so I held her.

She looked up at me. "I'll always be able to depend on you, won't I, William? All the rest of my life?"

I almost sighed. "I'm afraid so."

And in September I would probably be teaching at the university.

Suddenly I looked forward to it.

THE SNAIL-WATCHER

Patricia Highsmith
(1921–1995)

Highsmith's first novel was published when she was twenty-nine years old. It was nothing less than Strangers on a Train, *so memorably filmed by Alfred Hitchcock. As with her other work, it is dark and exists without compassion or any hint of human decency or justice. Even her series character, Tom Ripley, is entirely amoral. As in the following story, her characters are largely psychological cripples who become entangled in unpleasant events from which they cannot escape.*

HEN MR. PETER KNOPPERT began to make a hobby of snail-watching, he had no idea that his handful of specimens would become hundreds in no time. Only two months after the original snails were carried up to the Knoppert study, some thirty glass tanks and bowls, all teeming with snails, lined the walls, rested on the desk and windowsills, and were beginning even to cover the floor. Mrs. Knoppert disapproved strongly, and would no longer enter the room. It smelled, she said, and besides she had once stepped on a snail by accident, a horrible sensation she would never forget. But the more his wife and friends deplored his unusual and vaguely repellent pastime, the more pleasure Mr. Knoppert seemed to find in it.

"I never cared for nature before in my life," Mr. Knoppert often remarked— he was a partner in a brokerage firm, a man who had devoted all his life to the science of finance—"but snails have opened my eyes to the beauty of the animal world."

If his friends commented that snails were not really animals, and their slimy habitats hardly the best example of the beauty of nature, Mr. Knoppert would tell them with a superior smile that they simply didn't know all that he knew about snails.

And it was true. Mr. Knoppert had witnessed an exhibition that was not described, certainly not adequately described, in any encyclopedia or zoology book that he had been able to find. Mr. Knoppert had wandered into the kitchen one evening for a bite of something before dinner, and had happened to notice that a couple of snails in the china bowl on the drainboard were behaving very oddly. Standing more or less on their tails, they were weaving before each other for all the world like a pair of snakes hypnotized by a flute player. A moment later, their faces came together in a kiss of voluptuous intensity. Mr. Knoppert bent closer and studied them from all angles. Something else was happening: a protuberance like an ear was appearing on the right side of the head of both snails. His instinct told him that he was watching a sexual activity of some sort.

The cook came in and said something to him, but Mr. Knoppert silenced her with an impatient wave of his hand. He couldn't take his eyes from the enchanted little creatures in the bowl.

When the earlike excrescences were precisely together rim to rim, a whitish rod like another small tentacle shot out from one ear and arched over toward the ear of the other snail. Mr. Knoppert's first surmise was dashed when a tentacle sallied from the other snail, too. Most peculiar, he thought. The two tentacles withdrew, then came forth again, and as if they had found some invisible mark, remained fixed in either snail. Mr. Knoppert peered intently closer. So did the cook.

"Did you ever see anything like this?" Mr. Knoppert asked.

"No. They must be fighting," the cook said indifferently and went away. That was a sample of the ignorance on the subject of snails that he was later to discover everywhere.

Mr. Knoppert continued to observe the pair of snails off and on for more than an hour, until first the ears, then the rods, withdrew, and the snails themselves relaxed their attitudes and paid no further attention to each other. But by that time, a different pair of snails had begun a flirtation, and were slowly rearing themselves to get into position for kissing. Mr. Knoppert told the cook that the snails were not to be served that evening. He took the bowl of them up to his study. And snails were never again served in the Knoppert household.

That night, he searched his encyclopedias and a few general science books he happened to possess, but there was absolutely nothing on snails' breeding habits, though the oyster's dull reproductive cycle was described in detail. Perhaps it hadn't been a mating he had seen after all, Mr. Knoppert decided after a day or two. His wife Edna told him either to eat the snails or get rid of them—it was at this time that she stepped upon a snail that had crawled out onto the floor—and Mr. Knoppert might have, if he hadn't come across a sentence in Darwin's *Origin of Species* on a page given to gastropoda. The sentence was in French, a language Mr. Knoppert did not know, but the word *sensualité* made him tense like a bloodhound that has suddenly found the scent. He was in the public library at the time, and laboriously he translated the sentence with the aid of a French-English dictionary. It was a statement of less than a hundred words, saying that snails manifested a sensuality in their mating that was not to be found elsewhere in the animal kingdom. That was all. It was from the notebooks of Henri Fabre. Obviously Darwin had decided not to translate it for the average reader, but to leave it in its original language for the scholarly few who really cared. Mr. Knoppert considered himself one of the scholarly few now, and his round, pink face beamed with self-esteem.

He had learned that his snails were the fresh water type that laid their eggs in sand or earth, so he put moist earth and a little saucer of water into a big washbowl and transferred his snails into it. Then he waited for something to happen. Not even another mating happened. He picked up the snails one by one and looked at them, without seeing anything suggestive of pregnancy. But one snail he couldn't pick up. The shell might have been glued to the earth. Mr. Knoppert suspected the snail had buried its head in the ground to die. Two more days went by, and on the morning of the third, Mr. Knoppert found a spot of crumbly earth where the snail had been. Curious, he investigated the crumbles with a match stem, and to his delight discovered a pit full of shiny new eggs. Snail eggs! He hadn't been wrong. Mr. Knoppert called his wife and the cook to look at them. The eggs looked very much like big caviar, only they were white instead of black or red.

"Well, naturally they have to breed some way," was his wife's comment. Mr. Knoppert couldn't understand her lack of interest. He had to go and look at the eggs every hour that he was at home. He looked at them every morning to see if any change had taken place, and the eggs were his last thought every night before he went to bed. Moreover, another snail was now digging a pit. And another pair of snails was mating! The first batch of eggs turned a grayish color, and minuscule spirals of shells became discernible on one side of each egg. Mr. Knoppert's anticipation rose to a higher pitch. At last a morning arrived—the eighteenth after laying, according to Mr. Knoppert's careful count—when he looked down into the egg pit and saw the first tiny moving head, the first stubby little antennae uncertainly exploring the nest. Mr. Knoppert was as happy as the father of a new child. Every one of the seventy or more eggs in the pit came miraculously to life. He had seen the entire reproductive cycle evolve to a successful conclusion. And the fact that no one, at least no one that he knew of, was acquainted with a fraction of what he knew, lent his knowledge a thrill of discovery, the piquancy of the esoteric. Mr. Knoppert made notes on successive matings and egg hatchings. He narrated snail biology to fascinated, more often shocked friends and guests, until his wife squirmed with embarrassment.

"But where is it going to stop, Peter? If they keep on reproducing at this rate, they'll take over the house!" his wife told him after fifteen or twenty pits had hatched.

"There's no stopping nature," he replied good-humoredly. "They've only taken over the study. There's plenty of room there."

So more and more glass tanks and bowls were moved in. Mr. Knoppert went to the market and chose several of the more lively looking snails, and also a pair he found mating, unobserved by the rest of the world. More and more egg pits appeared in the dirt floors of the tanks, and out of each pit crept finally from seventy to ninety baby snails, transparent as dewdrops, gliding up rather than down the strips of fresh lettuce that Mr. Knoppert was quick to give all the pits as edible ladders for the climb. Matings went on so often that he no longer bothered to watch them. A mating could last twenty-four hours. But the thrill of seeing the white caviar become shells and start to move—that never diminished however often he witnessed it.

His colleagues in the brokerage office noticed a new zest for life in Peter Knoppert. He became more daring in his moves, more brilliant in his calculations, became in fact a little vicious in his schemes, but he brought money in for his company. By unanimous vote, his basic salary was raised from forty to sixty thousand dollars per year. When anyone congratulated him on his achievements, Mr. Knoppert gave all the credit to his snails and the beneficial relaxation he derived from watching them.

He spent all his evenings with his snails in the room that was no longer a study but a kind of aquarium. He loved to strew the tanks with fresh lettuce and pieces of boiled potato and beet, then turn on the sprinkler system that he had installed in the tanks to simulate natural rainfall. Then all the snails would liven up and begin eating, mating, or merely gliding through the shallow water with obvious pleasure. Mr. Knoppert often let a snail crawl onto his forefinger—he fancied his snails enjoyed this human contact—and he would feed it a piece of lettuce by hand, would observe the snail from all sides, finding as much aesthetic satisfaction as another man might from contemplating a Japanese print.

By now, Mr. Knoppert did not allow anyone to set foot in his study. Too many snails had the habit of crawling around on the floor, of going to sleep glued to chair bottoms and to the backs of books on the shelves. Snails spent much of their time sleeping, especially the older snails. But there were enough less indolent snails who preferred love-making. Mr. Knoppert estimated that about a dozen pairs of snails must be kissing all the time. And certainly there was a multitude of baby and adolescent snails. They were impossible to count. But Mr. Knoppert did count the snails sleeping and creeping on the ceiling alone, and arrived at something between eleven and twelve hundred. The tanks, the bowls, the underside of his desk and the bookshelves must surely have held fifty times that number. Mr. Knoppert meant to scrape the snails off the ceiling one day soon. Some of them had been up there for weeks, and he was afraid they were not taking in enough nourishment. But of late he had been a little too busy, and too much in need of the tranquility that he got simply from sitting in the study in his favorite chair.

During the month of June he was so busy he often worked late into the evening at his office. Reports were piling in for the end of the fiscal year. He made calculations, spotted a half-dozen possibilities of gain, and reserved the most daring, the least obvious moves for his private operations. By this time next year, he thought, he should be three or four times as well off as now. He saw his bank account multiplying as easily and rapidly as his snails. He told his wife this, and she was overjoyed. She even forgave him the ruination of the study, and the stale, fishy smell that was spreading throughout the whole upstairs.

"Still, I do wish you'd take a look just to see if anything's happening, Peter," she said to him rather anxiously one morning. "A tank might have overturned or something, and I wouldn't want the rug to be spoiled. You haven't been in the study for nearly a week, have you?"

Mr. Knoppert hadn't been in for nearly two weeks. He didn't tell his wife that the rug was pretty much gone already. "I'll go up tonight," he said.

But it was three more days before he found time. He went in one evening just before bedtime and was surprised to find the floor quite covered with snails, with three or four layers of snails. He had difficulty closing the door without mashing any. The dense clusters of snails in the corners made the room look positively round, as if he stood inside some huge, conglomerate stone. Mr. Knoppert cracked his knuckles and gazed around him in astonishment. They had not only covered every surface, but thousands of snails hung down into the room from the chandelier in a grotesque clump.

Mr. Knoppert felt for the back of a chair to steady himself. He felt only a lot of shells under his hand. He had to smile a little: there were snails in the chair seat, piled up on one another, like a lumpy cushion. He really must do something about the ceiling, and immediately. He took an umbrella from the corner, brushed some of the snails off it, and cleared a place on his desk to stand. The umbrella point tore the wallpaper, and then the weight of the snails pulled down a long strip that hung almost to the floor. Mr. Knoppert felt frustrated and angry. The sprinklers would make them move. He pulled the lever.

The sprinklers came on in all the tanks, and the seething activity of the entire room increased at once. Mr. Knoppert slid his feet along the floor, through tumbling snail shells that made a sound like pebbles on a beach, and directed a couple of the sprinklers at the ceiling. This was a mistake, he saw at once. The softened paper began to tear, and he dodged one slowly falling mass only to be hit by a swinging festoon of snails, really hit quite a stunning blow on the side of the head. He went down on one knee, dazed. He should open a window, he thought, the air was stifling. And there were snails crawling over his shoes and up his trouser legs. He shook his feet irritably. He was just going to the door, intending to call for one of the servants to help him, when the chandelier fell on him. Mr. Knoppert sat down heavily on the floor. He saw now that he couldn't possibly get a window open, because the snails were fastened thick and deep over the windowsills. For a moment, he felt he couldn't get up, felt as if he were suffocating. It was not only the musty smell of the room, but everywhere he looked long wallpaper strips covered with snails blocked his vision as if he were in a prison.

"Edna!" he called, and was amazed at the muffled, ineffectual sound of his voice. The room might have been soundproof.

He crawled to the door, heedless of the sea of snails he crushed under hands and knees. He could not get the door open. There were so many snails on it, crossing and recrossing the crack of the door on all four sides, they actually resisted his strength.

"Edna!" A snail crawled into his mouth. He spat it out in disgust. Mr. Knoppert tried to brush the snails off his arms. But for every hundred he dislodged, four hundred seemed to slide upon him and fasten to him again, as if they deliberately sought him out as the only comparatively snailfree surface in the room. There were snails crawling over his eyes. Then just as he staggered to his feet, something else hit him—Mr. Knoppert couldn't even see what. He was fainting! At any rate, he was on the floor. His arms felt like leaden weights as he tried to reach his nostrils, his eyes, to free them from the sealing, murderous snail bodies.

"Help!" He swallowed a snail. Choking, he widened his mouth for air and felt a snail crawl over his lips onto his tongue. He was in hell! He could feel them gliding over his legs like a glutinous river, pinning his legs to the floor. "Ugh!" Mr. Knoppert's breath came in feeble gasps. His vision grew black, a horrible, undulating black. He could not breathe at all, because he could not reach his nostrils, could not move his hands. Then through the slit of one eye, he saw directly in front of him, only inches away, what had been, he knew, the rubber plant that stood in its pot near the door. A pair of snails were quietly making love in it. And right beside them, tiny snails as pure as dewdrops were emerging from a pit like an infinite army into their widening world.

THE LONG WAY DOWN

EDWARD D. HOCH
(1930–)

The most inventive mind in the mystery world belongs to Hoch, who has written about eight hundred short stories and may be the only writer since the pulps died to earn his entire living from the short form. Several of his stories have been filmed, including the following one, which appeared as a two-hour made-for-television movie in the McMillan and Wife *series. The former president of the Mystery Writers of America was awarded an Edgar by that organization for his 1968 story, "The Oblong Room."*

ANY MEN HAVE DISAPPEARED under unusual circumstances, but perhaps none more unusual than those that befell Billy Calm.

The day began in a routine way for McLove. He left his apartment in midtown Manhattan and walked through the foggy March morning, just as he did on every working day of the year. When he was still several blocks away he could make out the bottom floors of the great glass slab that was the home office of the Jupiter Steel & Brass Corporation. But above the tenth floor the fog had taken over, shrouding everything in a dense coat of moisture that could have been the roof of the world.

Underfoot, the going was slushy. The same warm air mass that had caused the fog was making short work of the previous day's two-inch snowfall. McLove, who didn't really mind Manhattan winters, was thankful that spring was only days away. Finally he turned into the massive marble lobby of the Jupiter Steel Building, thinking for the hundredth time that only the garish little newsstand in one corner kept it from being an exact replica of the interior of an Egyptian tomb. Anyway, it was dry inside, without slush underfoot.

McLove's office on the twenty-first floor had been a point of creeping controversy from the very beginning. It was the executive floor, bulging with the vice-presidents and others who formed the inner core of Billy Calm's little family. The very idea of sharing this exclusive office space with the firm's security chief had repelled many of them, but when Billy Calm spoke there were few who openly dared challenge his mandates.

McLove had moved to the executive floor soon after the forty-year-old genius of Wall Street had seized control of Jupiter Steel in a proxy battle that had split stockholders into armed camps. On the day Billy Calm first walked through the marble lobby to take command of his newest acquisition, a disgruntled shareholder named Raimey had shot his hat off, and actually managed to get off a second shot before being overpowered. From that day on, Billy Calm used the private elevator at the rear of the building, and McLove supervised security from the twenty-first floor.

It was a thankless task that amounted to little more than being a sometime body-guard for Calm. His duties, in the main, consisted of keeping Calm's private elevator in working order, attending directors' meetings with the air of a reluctant outsider, supervising the security forces at the far-flung Jupiter mills, and helping with arrangements for Calm's numerous public appearances. For this he was paid fifteen thousand dollars a year, which was the principal reason he did it.

On the twenty-first floor, this morning, Margaret Mason was already at her desk outside the directors' room. She looked up as McLove stepped into the office, and flashed him their private smile. "How are you, McLove?"

"Morning, Margaret. Billy in yet?"

"Mr. Calm? Not yet. He's flying in from Pittsburgh. Should be here any time now."

McLove glanced at his watch. He knew the directors' meeting was scheduled for ten, and that was only twenty minutes away. "Heard anything?" he asked, knowing that Margaret Mason was the best source of information on the entire floor. She knew everything and would tell you most of it, provided it didn't concern herself.

Now she nodded, and bent forward a bit across the desk. "Mr. Calm phoned from his plane and talked with Jason Greene. The merger is going through. He'll announce it officially at the meeting this morning."

"That'll make some people around here mighty sad." McLove was thinking of W. T. Knox and Sam Hamilton, two directors who had opposed the merger talk from the very beginning. Only twenty-four hours earlier, before Billy Calm's rush flight to Pittsburgh in his private plane, it had appeared that their efforts would be successful.

"They should know better than to buck Mr. Calm," Margaret said.

"I suppose so." McLove glanced at his watch again. For some reason he was get-ting nervous. "Say, how about lunch, if we get out of the meeting in time?"

"Fine." She gave him the small smile again. "You're the only one I feel safe drinking with at noon."

"Be back in a few minutes."

"I'll buzz you if Mr. Calm gets in."

He glanced at the closed doors of the private elevator and nodded. Then he walked down the hall to his own office once more. He got a pack of cigarettes from his desk and went across the hall to W. T. Knox's office.

"Morning, W. T. What's new?"

The tall man looked up from a file folder he'd been studying. Thirty-seven, a man who had retained most of his youthful good looks and all his charm, Knox was popu-lar with the girls on twenty-one. He'd probably have been more popular if he hadn't had a pregnant wife and five children of varying ages.

"McLove, look at this weather!" He gestured toward the window, where a curtain of fog still hung. "Every winter I say I'll move to Florida and every winter the wife talks me into staying."

Jason Greene, balding and ultraefficient, joined them with a sheaf of reports. "Billy should be in at any moment. He phoned me to say the merger had gone through."

Knox dropped his eyes. "I heard."

"When the word gets out, Jupiter stock will jump another ten points."

McLove could almost feel the tension between the two men; one gloating, and the other bitter. He walked to the window and stared out at the fog, trying to see the invis-ible building across the street. Below, he could not even make out the setback of their own building, though it was only two floors lower. Fog . . . well, at least it meant that spring was on the way.

Then there was a third voice behind him, and he knew without turning that it belonged to Shirley Taggert, the president's personal secretary. "It's almost time for the board meeting," she said, with that hint of a southern drawl that either attracted or repelled but left no middle ground. "You people ready?"

Shirley was grim-faced but far from ugly. She was a bit younger than Margaret Mason's mid-thirties, a bit sharper of dress and mind. But she paid the penalty for being Billy Calm's secretary every time she walked down the halls. Conversations ceased, suspicious glances followed her, and there was always a half-hidden air of tension at her arrival. She ate lunch alone, and one or two fellows who had been brave enough to ask her for a date hadn't bothered to ask a second time.

"We're ready," Jason Greene told her. "Is he here yet?"

She shook her head and glanced at the clock. "He should be in any minute."

McLove left them grouped around Knox's desk and walked back down the hall. Sam Hamilton, the joker, passed him on the way and stopped to tell him a quick gag. He, at least, didn't seem awfully upset about the impending merger, even though he had opposed it. McLove liked Sam better than any of the other directors, probably because at the age of fifty he was still a big kid at heart. You could meet him on even ground, and, at times, feel he was letting you outdo him.

"Anything yet?" McLove asked Margaret, returning to her desk outside the directors' room.

"No sign of Mr. Calm, but he shouldn't be long now. It's just about ten."

McLove glanced at the closed door of Billy Calm's office, next to the directors' room, and then entered the latter. The room was quite plain, with only the one door through which he had entered, and unbroken walls of dull oak paneling on either wall. The far end of the room, with two wide windows looking out at the fog, was only twenty feet away, and the conference table that was the room's only piece of furniture had just the eight necessary chairs grouped around it. Some had been heard to complain that the room lacked the stature of Jupiter Steel, but Billy Calm contended he liked the forced intimacy of it.

Now, as McLove stood looking out the windows, the whole place seemed to reflect the cold mechanization of the modern office building. The windows could not be opened. Even their cleaning had to be done from the outside, on a gondola-like platform that climbed up and down the sheer glass walls. There were no windowsills; and McLove's fingers ran unconsciously along the bottom of the window frame as he stood staring out. The fog might be lifting a little, but he couldn't be certain.

McLove went out to Margaret Mason's desk, saw that she was gathering together her copybooks and pencils for the meeting, and decided to take a glance into Billy Calm's office. It was the same size as the directors' room, and almost as plain in its furnishings. Only the desk, cluttered with the trivia of a businessman's lifetime, gave proof of human occupancy. On the left wall still hung the faded portrait of the firm's founder, and on the right, a more recent photograph of Israel Black, former president of Jupiter, and still a director, though he never came to the meetings. This was Billy Calm's domain. From here he ruled a vast empire of holdings, and a word from him could send men to their financial ruin.

McLove straightened suddenly on hearing a man's muffled voice at Margaret's desk outside. He heard her ask, "What's the matter?" and then heard the door of the directors' room open. Hurrying back to her desk, he was just in time to see the door closing again.

"Is he finally here?"

Margaret, unaccountably white-faced, opened her mouth to answer, just as there came the tinkling crash of a breaking window from the inner room. They both heard it clearly, and she dropped the cigarette she'd been in the act of lighting. "Billy!" she screamed out. "No, Billy!"

They were at the door together after only an instant's hesitation, pushing it open before them, hurrying into the directors' room. "No," McLove said softly, staring straight ahead at the empty room and the long table and the shattered window in the opposite wall. "He jumped." Already the fog seemed to be filling the room with its damp mists as they hurried to the window and peered out at nothing.

"Billy jumped," Margaret said dully, as if unable to comprehend the fact. "He killed himself."

McLove turned and saw Knox standing in the doorway. Behind him, Greene and Hamilton and Shirley Taggert were coming up fast. "Billy Calm just jumped out of the window," McLove told them.

"No," Margaret Mason said, turning from the window. "No, no, no, no . . ." Then, suddenly, overcome with the shock of it, she tumbled to the floor in a dead faint.

"Take care of her," McLove shouted to the others. "I've got to get downstairs."

Knox bent to lift the girl in his arms, while Sam Hamilton hurried to the telephone. Shirley had settled into one of the padded directors' chairs, her face devoid of all expression. And Jason Greene, loyal to the end, actually seemed to be crying.

In the hallway, McLove pushed the button of Billy Calm's private elevator and waited for it to rise from the depths of the building. The little man would have no further use for it now. He rode down alone, leaning against its padded walls, listening to, but hardly hearing, the dreary hum of its descent. In another two minutes he was on the street, looking for the crowd that would surely be gathered, listening for the sounds of rising sirens.

But there was nothing. Nothing but the usual midmorning traffic. Nothing but hurrying pedestrians and a gang of workmen drilling at the concrete and a policeman dully directing traffic.

There was no body.

McLove hurried over to the police officer. "A man just jumped out of the Jupiter Steel Building," he said. "What happened to him?"

The policeman wrinkled his brow. "Jumped? From where?"

"Twenty-first floor. Right above us."

They both gazed upward into the gradually lifting fog. The police officer shrugged his shoulders. "Mister, I been standing in this very spot for more than an hour. Nobody jumped from up there."

"But . . ." McLove continued staring into the fog. "But he *did* jump. I practically saw him do it. And if he's not down here, where *is* he?"

Back on twenty-one, McLove found the place in a state somewhere between sheer shock and calm confusion. People were hurrying without purpose in every direction, bent on their own little useless errands. Sam Hamilton was on the phone to his broker's, trying to get the latest quotation on Jupiter stock. "The bottom'll drop out of it when this news hits," he confided to McLove. "With Bill gone, the merger won't go through."

McLove lit a cigarette. "Billy Calm is gone, all right, but he's not down there. He vanished somewhere between the twenty-first floor and the street."

"What?"

W. T. Knox joined them, helping a pale but steady Margaret Mason by the arm. "She'll be all right," he said. "It was the shock."

McLove reached out his hand to her. "Tell us exactly what happened. Every word of it."

"Well . . ." She hesitated and then sat down. Behind her, Hamilton and Shirley Taggert were deep in animated conversation, and Jason Greene had appeared from somewhere with a policeman in tow.

"You were at the desk," McLove began, helping her. "And I came out of the directors' room and went into Billy's office. Then what?"

"Well, Mr. Calm came in, and as he passed my desk he mumbled something. I didn't catch it, and I asked him what was the matter. He seemed awfully upset about something. Anyway, he passed my desk and went into the directors' room. He was just closing the door when you came out, and you know the rest."

McLove nodded. He knew the rest, which was nothing but the shattered window and the vanished man. "Well, the body's not down there," he told them again. "It's not anywhere. Billy Calm dived through that window and flew away."

Shirley passed Hamilton a telephone she had just answered. "Yes?" He listened a moment and then hung up. "The news about Billy went out over the stock ticker. Jupiter Steel is selling off fast. It's already down three points."

"Goodby merger," Knox said, and though his face was grim his voice was not.

A detective arrived on the scene to join the police officer. Quickly summoned workmen were tacking cardboard over the smashed window, carefully removing some of the jagged splinters of glass from the bottom of the frame. Things were settling down a little, and the police were starting to ask questions.

"Mr. McLove, you're in charge of security for the company?"

"That's right."

"Why was it necessary to have a security man sit in on directors' meetings?"

"Some nut tried to kill Billy Calm a while back. He was still nervous. Private elevator and all."

"What was the nut's name?"

"Raimey, I think. Something like that. Don't know where he is now."

"And who was usually present at these meetings? I see eight chairs in there."

"Calm, and three vice presidents; Greene, Knox, and Hamilton. Also Calm's secretary, Miss Taggert, and Miss Mason, who kept the minutes of the meeting. The seventh chair is mine, and the eighth one is kept for Mr. Black, who never comes down for the meetings any more."

"There was resentment between Calm and Black?"

"A bit. You trying to make a mystery out of this?"

The detective shrugged. "Looks like pretty much of a mystery already."

And McLove had to admit that it did.

He spent an hour with the police, both upstairs and down in the street. When they finally left just before noon, he went looking for Margaret Mason. She was back at her desk, surprisingly, looking as if nothing in the world had happened.

"How about lunch?" he said. "Maybe a martini would calm your nerves."

"I'm all right now, thanks. The offer sounds good, but you've got a date." She passed him an interoffice memo. It was signed by William T. Knox, and it requested McLove's presence in his office at noon.

"I suppose I have to tell them what I know."

"Which is?"

"Nothing. Absolutely nothing. All I know is a dozen different things that couldn't have happened to Calm. I'll try to get out of there as soon as I can. Will you wait for me? Till one, anyway?" he asked.

"Sure. Good luck."

He returned her smile, then went down the long hallway to Knox's office. It wasn't surprising to find Hamilton and Greene already there, and he settled down in the remaining chair feeling himself the center of attraction.

"Well?" Knox asked. "Where is he?"

"Gentlemen, I haven't the faintest idea."

"He's dead, of course," Jason Greene spoke up.

"Probably," McLove agreed. "But where's the body?"

Hamilton rubbed his fingers together in a nervous gesture. "That's what we have to find out. My phone has been ringing for an hour. The brokers are going wild, to say nothing of Pittsburgh!"

McLove nodded. "I gather the merger stands or falls on Billy Calm."

"Right! If he's dead, it's dead."

Jason Greene spoke again. "Billy Calm was a great man, and I'd be the last person in the world to try to sink the merger for which he worked so hard. But he's dead, all right. And there's just one place the body could have gone."

"Where's that?" Knox asked.

"It landed on a passing truck or something like that, of course."

Hamilton's eyes widened. "Sure!" he remarked sarcastically.

But McLove reluctantly shook his head. "That was the first thought the police had. We checked it out and it couldn't have happened. This building is set back from the street; it has to be, on account of this sheer glass wall. I doubt if a falling body could hit the street, and even if it did, the traffic lane on this side is torn up for repairs. And there's been a policeman on duty there all morning. The body didn't land on the sidewalk or the street, and no truck or car passed anywhere near enough."

W. T. Knox blinked and ran a hand through his thinning but still wavy hair. "If he didn't go down, where did he go? Up?"

"Maybe he never jumped," Hamilton suggested. "Maybe Margaret made the whole thing up."

McLove wondered at his words, wondered if Margaret had been objecting to some of his jokes again. "You forget that I was there with her. I saw her face when that window smashed. The best actress in the world couldn't have faked that expression. Besides, I saw him go in—or at least I saw the door closing after him. It couldn't close by itself."

"And the room was empty when you two entered it a moment later," Knox said. "Therefore Billy must have gone through the window. We have to face the fact. He couldn't have been hiding under the table."

"If he didn't go down," Sam Hamilton said, "he went up! By a rope to the roof or another window."

But once more McLove shook his head. "You're forgetting that none of the windows can be opened. And it's a long way up to the roof. The police checked it, though. They found nothing but an unmarked sea of melting snow and slush. Not a footprint, just a few pigeon tracks."

Jason Greene frowned across the desk. "But he didn't go down, up, or sideways, and he didn't stay in the room."

McLove wondered if he should tell them his idea, or wait until later. He decided now was as good a time as any. "Suppose he did jump, and something caught him on the way down. Suppose he's hanging there now, hidden by the fog."

"A flagpole? Something like that?"

"But there aren't any," Knox protested. "There's nothing but a smooth glass wall."

"There's one thing," McLove reminded them, looking around the desk at their expectant faces. "The thing they use to wash the windows."

Jason Greene walked to the window. "We can find out easily enough. The sun has just about burned the fog away."

They couldn't see from that side of the building, so they rode down in the elevator to the street. As quickly as it had come, the fog seemed to have vanished, leaving a clear and sparkling sky with a brilliant sun seeking out the last remnants of the previous day's snow. The four of them stood in the street, in the midst of digging equipment abandoned for the lunch hour, and stared up at the great glass side of the Jupiter Street Building.

There was nothing to see. No body dangling in space, no window-washing scaffold. Nothing.

"Maybe he took it back up to the roof," Knox suggested.

"No footprints, remember?" McLove tried to cover his disappointment. "It was a long shot, anyway. The police checked the tenants for several floors beneath the broken window, and none of them saw anything. If Calm had landed on a scaffold, someone would have noticed it."

For a while longer they continued staring up at the building, each of them drawn to the tiny speck on the twenty-first floor where cardboard temporarily covered the shattered glass. "Why," Jason Greene asked suddenly, "didn't the cop down here see the falling glass when it hit? Was the window broken from the outside?"

McLove smiled. "No, the glass all went out, and down. It was the drilling again; the sound covered the glass hitting. And that section of sidewalk was blocked off. The policeman didn't hear it hit, but we were able to find pieces of it. You can see where they were swept up."

W. T. Knox sighed deeply. "I don't know. I guess I'll go to lunch. Maybe we can all think better on a full stomach."

They separated a few moments after that, and McLove went back up to twenty-one for Margaret Mason. He found her in Billy Calm's office with Shirley Taggert. They were on their knees, running their hands over the oak-paneled wall.

"What's all this?" he asked.

"Just playing detective," Margaret said. "It was Shirley's idea. She mentioned about how Mr. Calm always wanted the office left exactly as it was, and with the directors' room right next door, even though both rooms were really too small. She thought of a secret panel of some sort."

"Margaret!" Shirley got reluctantly to her feet. "You make it sound like something out of a dime novel. Really, though, it was a possibility. It would explain how he left the room without jumping from the window."

"Don't keep me in suspense," McLove said. "Did you find anything?"

"Nothing. And we've been over both sides of the wall."

"They don't build them like they used to in merry old England. Let's forget it and have lunch."

Shirley Taggert smoothed the wrinkles from her skirt. "You two go ahead. You don't want me along."

She was gone before they could protest, and McLove wasn't about to protest too loudly anyway. He didn't mind Shirley as a co-worker but, like everyone else, he was acutely conscious of her position in the office scheme of things. Even now, with

Billy Calm vanished into the blue, she was still a dangerous force not to be shared at social hours.

He went downstairs with Margaret, and they found an empty booth at the basement restaurant across the street. It was a place they often went after work for a drink, though lately he'd seen less of her outside office hours. Thinking back to the first time he'd become aware of Margaret, he had only fuzzy memories of the tricks Sam Hamilton used to play. He loved to walk up behind the secretaries and tickle them—or occasionally even unzip their dresses—and he had quickly discovered that Margaret Mason was a likely candidate for his attentions. She always rewarded his efforts with a lively scream, without ever really getting upset.

It had been a rainy autumn evening some months back that McLove's path crossed hers most violently, linking them with a secret that made them drinking companions if nothing more. He'd been at loose ends that evening, and wandered into a little restaurant over by the East River. Surprisingly enough, Margaret Mason had been there, defending her honor in a back booth against a very drunk escort. McLove had moved in, flattened him with one punch, and they left him collapsed against a booth.

After that, on different drinking occasions, she had poured out the sort of lonely story he might have expected. And he's listened and lingered, and sometimes fruitlessly imagined that he might become one of the men in her life. He knew there was no one for a long time after the bar incident, just as he knew now, by her infrequent free evenings, that there was someone again. Their drinking dates were more often being confined to lunch hours, when even two martinis were risky, and she never talked about being lonely or bored.

This day, over the first drink, she said, "It was terrible, really terrible."

"I know. It's going to get worse, I'm afraid. He's got to turn up somewhere."

"Dead or alive?"

"I wish I knew."

She lit a cigaret. "Will you be blamed for it?"

"I couldn't be expected to guard him from himself. Besides, I wasn't hired as a personal bodyguard. I'm chief of security, and that's all. I'm not a bodyguard or a detective. I don't know the first thing about fingerprints or clues. All I know about is people."

"What do you know about the Jupiter people?"

McLove finished his drink before answering. "Very little, really. Except for you, Hamilton and Knox and Greene and the rest of them are nothing more than names and faces. I've never even had a drink with any of them. I sit around at those meetings, and frankly, I'm bored stiff. If anybody tries to blame me for this thing, they'll be looking for a new security chief."

Margaret's glass was empty too, and he signaled the waiter for two more. It was that sort of a day. When they came, he noticed that her usually relaxed face was a bit tense, and the familiar sparkle of her blue eyes was no longer in evidence. She'd been through a lot that morning, and even the drinks were failing to relax her.

"Maybe I'll quit with you," she said.

"It's been a long time since we've talked. How have things been?"

"All right." She said it with a little shrug.

"The new boy friend?"

"Don't call him that, please."

"I hope he's an improvement over the last one."

"So do I. At my age you get involved with some strange ones."

"Do you love him?"

She thought a moment and then answered, "I guess I do."

He lit another cigaret. "When Billy Calm passed your desk this morning, did he seem . . .?" The sentence stopped in the middle, cut short by a sudden scream from the street. McLove stood up and looked toward the door, where a waiter was already running outside to see what had happened.

"What is it?" Margaret asked.

"I don't know, but there seems to be a crowd gathering. Come on!"

Outside, they crossed the busy street and joined the crowd on the sidewalk of the Jupiter Building. "What happened?" Margaret asked somebody.

"Guy jumped, I guess."

They fought their way through now, and McLove's heart was pounding with the anticipation of what they would see. It was Billy Calm, all right, crushed and dead and looking very small. But there was no doubt it was he.

A policeman arrived from somewhere with a blanket and threw it over the thing on the sidewalk. McLove saw Sam Hamilton fighting his way through the crowd to their side. "Who is it?" Hamilton asked, but he too must have known.

"Billy," McLove told him. "It's Billy Calm."

Hamilton stared at the blanket for a moment and then looked at his watch. "Three hours and forty-five minutes since he jumped. I guess he must have taken the long way down."

W. T. Knox was pacing the floor like a caged animal, and Shirley Taggert was sobbing silently in a corner chair. It was over. Billy Calm had been found. The reaction was only beginning to set in. The worst, they all realized, was still ahead.

Jason Greene glared at Hamilton as he came into the office. "Well, the market's closed. Maybe you can stay off that phone for a while now."

Sam Hamilton didn't lose his grim smile. "Right now the price of Jupiter stock happens to be something that's important to all of us. You may be interested to know that it fell fourteen more points before they had to suspend trading in it for the rest of the session. They still don't have a closing price on it."

Knox held up both hands. "All right, all right! Let's everybody calm down and try to think. What do the police say, McLove?"

Feeling as if he were only a messenger boy between the two camps, McLove replied, "Billy was killed by the fall, and he'd been dead only a few minutes when they examined him. Body injuries would indicate that he fell from this height."

"But where was he for nearly four hours?" Greene wanted to know. "Hanging there, invisible, outside the window?"

Shirley Taggert collected herself enough to join in the conversation. "He got out of that room somehow, and then came back and jumped later," she said. "That's how it must have been."

But McLove shook his head. "I hate to throw cold water on logical explanations, but that's how it *couldn't* have been. Remember, the windows in this building can't be opened. No other window has been broken, and the one on this floor is still covered by cardboard."

"The roof!" Knox suggested.

"No. There still aren't any footprints on the roof. We checked."

"Didn't anybody see him falling?"

"Apparently not till just before he hit."

"The thing's impossible," Knox said.

"No."

They were all looking at McLove. "Then what happened?" Greene asked.

"I don't know what happened, except for one thing. Billy Calm didn't hang in space for four hours. He didn't fall off the roof, or out of any other window, which means he could only have fallen from the window in the directors' room."

"But the cardboard—"

"Somebody replaced it afterwards. And that means . . ."

"It means Billy was murdered," Knox breathed. "It means he didn't commit suicide."

McLove nodded. "He was murdered, and by somebody on this floor. Probably by somebody in this room." He glanced around.

Night settled cautiously over the city, with a scarlet sunset to the west that clung inordinately long to its reign over the skies. The police had returned, and the questioning went on, concurrently with long-distance calls to Pittsburgh and five other cities where Jupiter had mills. There was confusion, somehow more so with the coming of darkness to the outer world. Secretaries and workers from the other floors gradually drifted home, but on twenty-one life went on.

"All right," Knox breathed finally, as it was nearing eight o'clock. "We'll call a directors' meeting for Monday morning, to elect a new president. That should give the market time to settle down, and let us know just how bad things really are. At the same time we'll issue a statement about the proposed merger. I gather we're in agreement that it's a dead issue for the time being."

Sam Hamilton nodded, and Jason Greene reluctantly shrugged his assent. Shirley Taggert looked up from her pad. "What about old Israel Black? With Mr. Calm dead, he'll be back in the picture."

Jason Greene shrugged. "Let him come. We can keep him in line. I never thought the old guy was so bad anyway, not really."

It went on like this, the talk, the bickering, the occasional flare of temper, until nearly midnight. Finally, McLove felt he could excuse himself and head for home. In the outer office, Margaret was straightening her desk, and he was surprised to realize that she was still around. He hadn't seen her in the past few hours.

"I thought you went home," he said.

"They might have needed me."

"They'll be going all night at this rate. How about a drink?"

"I should get home."

"All right. Let me take you, then. The subways aren't safe at this hour."

She turned her face up to smile at him. "Thanks, McLove. I can use someone like you tonight."

They went down together in the elevator, and out into a night turned decidedly coolish. He skipped the subway and hailed a cab. Settled back on the red leather seat, he asked, "Do you want to tell me about it, Margaret?"

He couldn't see her face in the dark, but after a moment she asked, "Tell you what?"

"What really happened. I've got part of it doped out already, so you might as well tell me the whole thing."

"I don't know what you mean, McLove. Really," she protested.

"All right," he said, and was silent for twenty blocks. Then, as they stopped for a traffic light, he added, "This is murder, you know. This isn't a kid's game or a simple love affair."

"There are some things you can't talk over with anyone. I'm sorry. Here's my place. You can drop me at the corner."

He got out with her and paid the cab driver. "I think I'd like to come up," he said quietly.

"I'm sorry, McLove. I'm awfully tired."

"Want me to wait for him down here?"

She sighed and led the way inside, keeping silent until they were in the little three-room apartment he'd visited only once before. Then she shrugged off her raincoat and asked, "How much do you know?"

"I know he'll come here tonight, of all nights."

"What was it? What told you?"

"A lot of things. The elevator, for one."

She sat down. "What about the elevator?"

"Right after Billy Calm's supposed arrival, and suicide, I ran to his private elevator. It wasn't on twenty-one. It had to come up from below. He never rode any other elevator. When I finally remembered it, I realized he hadn't come up on that one, or it would still have been there."

Margaret sat frozen in the chair, her head cocked a little to one side as if listening. "What does it matter to you? You told me just this noon that none of them meant anything to you."

"They didn't, they don't. But I guess you do, Margaret. I can see what he's doing to you, and I've got to stop it before you get in too deep."

"I'm in about as deep as I can ever be, right now."

"Maybe not."

"You said you believed me. You told them all that I couldn't have been acting when I screamed out his name."

He closed his eyes for a moment, thinking that he'd heard something in the hallway. Then he said: "I did believe you. But then after the elevator bit, I realized that you never called Calm by his first name. It was always Mr. Calm, not Billy, and it would have been the same even in a moment of panic. Because he was still the president of the company. The elevator and the name—I put them together, and I knew it wasn't Billy Calm who had walked into that directors' room."

There was a noise at the door, the sound a familiar key turning in the lock. "No," she whispered, almost to herself. "No, no, no . . ."

"And that should be our murderer now," McLove said, leaping to his feet.

"Billy!" she screamed. "Billy, run! It's a trap!"

But McLove was already to the door, yanking it open, staring into the startled, frightened face of W. T. Knox.

Sometimes it ends with a flourish, and sometimes only with the dull thud of a collapsing dream. For Knox, the whole thing had been only an extension of some sixteen hours in his life span. The fantastic plot, which had been set in motion by his attempt at suicide that morning at the Jupiter Steel Building, came to an end when he succeeded in leaping to his death from the bathroom window of Margaret's apartment, while they sat waiting for the police to come.

The following morning, with only two hours' sleep behind him, McLove found himself facing Greene and Hamilton and Shirley Taggert once more, telling them the story of how it had been. There was an empty chair in the office too, and he wondered vaguely whether it had been meant for Knox or Margaret.

"He was just a poor guy at the end of his rope," McLove told them. "He was deeply involved in an affair with Margaret Mason, and he'd sunk all his money into a desperate gamble that the merger wouldn't go through. He sold a lot of Jupiter stock short, figuring that when the merger talks collapsed the price would fall sharply. Only Billy Calm called from his plane yesterday morning and said the merger was on. Knox thought about it for an hour or so, and did some figuring. When he realized he'd be wiped out, he went into the directors' room to commit suicide."

"Why?" Shirley Taggert interrupted. "Why couldn't he jump out his own window?"

"Because there's a setback two stories down on his side. He couldn't have cleared it. He wanted a smooth drop to the sidewalk. Billy Calm could hardly have taken a running jump through the window. It was far off the floor even for a tall man, and Billy was short. And remember the slivers of glass at the bottom of the pane? When I remembered them, and remembered the height of the bottom sill from the floor, I knew that no one—especially a short man—could have gone through that window without knocking them out. No, Knox passed Margaret's desk, muttered some sort of farewell, and entered the room just as I came out of Calm's office. He smashed the window with a chair so he wouldn't have to try a dive through the thick glass, head first. And then he got ready to jump."

"Why didn't he?"

"Because he heard Margaret shout his name from the outer office. And with the shouted word *Billy,* a sudden plan came to him in that split second. He recrossed the small office quickly, and stood behind the door as we entered, knowing that I would think it was Billy Calm who had jumped. As soon as we were in the room, he simply stepped out and stood there. I thought he had arrived with the rest of you, and you, of course, thought he had entered the room with Margaret and me. I never gave it a second thought, because I was looking for Calm. But Margaret fainted when she saw he was still alive."

"But she said it was Billy Calm who entered the office," Greene protested.

"Not until later. She was starting to deny it, in fact, when she saw Knox and fainted. Remember, he carried her into the next room, and he was alone with her when she came to. He told her his money would be safe if only people thought Calm dead for a few hours. So she went along with her lover; I needn't remind you he was a handsome fellow, even though he was married. She went along with what we all thought happened, not realizing it would lead to murder."

Sam Hamilton lit a cigar. "The stock did go down."

"But not enough. And Knox knew Calm's arrival would reactivate the merger and ruin everything. I don't think he planned to kill Calm in the beginning, but as the morning wore on it became the only way out. He waited in the private elevator when he knew Billy was due to arrive, slugged him, carried his small body to that window while we were all out to lunch, and threw him out, replacing the cardboard afterwards."

"And the stock went down some more," Hamilton said.

"That's right."

"She called him Billy," Shirley reminded them.

"It was his name. We all called him W. T., but he signed his memo to me *William T. Knox.* I suppose the two of them thought it was a great joke, her calling him Billy when they were together."

"Where is she now?" someone asked.

"The police are still questioning her. I'm going down there now, to be with her. She's been through a lot." He thought probably this would be his final day at Jupiter Steel. Somehow *he* was tired of these faces and their questions.

But as he got to his feet, Sam Hamilton asked, "Why wasn't Billy here for the meeting at ten? Where was he for those missing hours? And how did Knox know when he would really arrive?"

"Knox knew because Billy phoned him, as he had earlier in the morning."

"Phoned him? From where?"

McLove turned to stare out the window, at the clear blue of the morning sky. "From his private plane. Billy Calm was circling the city for nearly three hours. He couldn't land because of the fog."

THE MAN WHO NEVER
TOLD A LIE

ISAAC ASIMOV
(1920–1992)

It is impossible to think of Asimov without noting his varied and prolific output—the product of a prodigious mind and an extraordinary work ethic. After declaring that his favorite thing in the world was writing, he was challenged: "If you had only six months left to live, what would you do?" He replied: "Type faster." Though mostly famous for his science fiction and nonfiction works, Asimov wrote several mystery novels and numerous short stories, most popularly his series about the Black Widowers.

HEN ROGER HALSTED MADE his appearance at the head of the stairs on the day of the monthly meeting of the Black Widowers, the only others yet present were Avalon, the patent-attorney, and Rubin, the writer. They greeted him with jubilation.

Emmanuel Rubin said, "Well, you've finally managed to stir yourself up to the point of meeting your old friends, have you?' He trotted over and held out both his hands, his straggly beard stretching to match his grin. "Where've you been the last two meetings?"

"Hello, Roger," said Geoffrey Avalon, smiling from his stiff height.

Halsted shucked his coat. "Damned cold outside. Henry, bring—"

Henry, the only waiter the Black Widowers ever had or ever would have, already had the drink waiting. "I'm glad to see you again, sir."

Halsted took it with a nod of thanks. "Twice running something came up— Say, you know what I've decided to do?"

"Give up mathematics and make an honest living?" asked Rubin,

Halsted sighed. "Teaching math at a junior high school is as honest a living as one can find. That's why it pays so little."

"In that case," said Avalon, swirling his drink gently, "why is free-lance writing so dishonest a racket?"

"Free-lance writing is *not* dishonest," said free-lance Rubin, rising to the bait at once.

"What have you decided to do, Roger?" asked Avalon.

"It's this project I've dreamed up," said Halsted. His forehead rose white and high, showing no signs of the hairline that had been there perhaps ten years ago, though the hair was still copious enough around the sides and in the back. "I'm going to rewrite the *Iliad* and the *Odyssey* in limericks, one for each of the forty-eight books they contain."

Avalon nodded. "Any of it written?"

"I've got the first book of the *Iliad* taken care of. It goes like this:

"Agamemnon, the top-ranking Greek,
To Achilles in anger did speak. They
    argued a lot, Then Achilles grew hot,
And went stamping away in a pique."

"Not bad," said Avalon. "In fact, quite good. It gets across the essence of the first book in full. Of course, the proper name of the hero of the *Iliad* is Achilleus, with the 'ch' sound as in—"

"That would throw off the meter," said Halsted.

"Besides," said Rubin, "everyone would think the 'u' was a typographical error and that's all they'd see in the limerick."

Mario Gonzalo, the artist, came racing up the stairs. He was host for this session and he said, "Anyone else here?"

"Nobody here but us old folks," said Avalon.

"My guest is on his way up. Real interesting guy. Henry will like him because he never tells a lie."

Henry lifted an eyebrow as he produced Mario's drink.

"Don't tell me you're bringing the ghost of George Washington!" said Halsted.

"Roger! A pleasure to see you again.—By the way, Jim Drake won't be here with us today. He sent back the card saying there was some family shindig he had to attend. The guest I'm bringing is a fellow named Sand—John Sand. I've known him on and off for years. Real crazy guy. Horserace buff who never tells a lie. I've heard him *not* telling lies. It's about the only virtue he has." And Gonzalo winked.

Avalon nodded. "Good for those who can. As one grows older, however—"

"And I think it will be an interesting session," added Gonzalo hurriedly, visibly avoiding one of Avalon's long-winded confidences. "I was telling him about the Black Widowers Club and how the last two times we had mysteries on our hands—"

"Mysteries?" said Halsted, with sudden interest.

Gonzalo said, "You're a member of the club in good standing. So we can tell you. But get Henry to do it. He was a principal both times."

"Henry?" Halsted looked over his shoulder in mild surprise "Are they getting you involved in their idiocies?"

"I assure you, Mr. Halsted. I tried not to be," said Henry.

"Tried not to be!" exclaimed Rubin. "Listen, Henry was the Sherlock of the session last time. He—"

"The point is," said Avalon, "that you may have talked too much, Mario. What did you tell your friend about us?"

"What do you mean, talked too much? I'm not Mannie Rubin, you know. I carefully told Sand that we were priests at the confessional, one and all, as far as anything in this room is concerned, and he said he wished he were a member because he has a difficulty that's been driving him wild, and I said he could come the next time because it was my turn to be host and he could be my guest and—here he is!"

A slim man, his neck swathed in a thick scarf, was mounting the stairs. The slimness was emphasized when he took off his coat. Under the scarf his tie gleamed blood-red and seemed to lend color to a thin and pallid face. He was thirtyish.

"John Sand," said Mario, introducing him all round in a pageant that was interrupted by Thomas Trumbull's heavy tread on the steps and the code expert's loud cry of "Henry, a Scotch and soda for a dying man!"

Rubin said, "Tom, you could be here early if only you'd relax and stop trying so hard to be late."

"The later I come," said Trumbull, "the less I have to hear of your stupid remarks. Ever think of that?" Then he was introduced too, and they all sat down.

Since the menu for that meeting had been so incautiously planned as to begin with artichokes, Rubin launched into a dissertation on the preparation of the only proper sauce. Then, when Trumbull said disgustedly that the only proper preparation for artichokes involved a large garbage can, Rubin said, "Sure, *if* you don't have exactly the right sauce."

Sand ate uneasily and left at least one-third of his excellent steak untouched. Halsted, who had a tendency to plumpness, eyed the remains enviously. His own plate was the first one to be cleaned. Only a scraped bone and some fat were left.

Sand seemed to grow aware of Halsted's eyes and said, "Frankly, I'm too worried to have much appetite. Would you care for the rest of my steak?"

"Me? No, thank you," said Halsted glumly.

Sand smiled. "May I be frank?"

"Of course. If you've been listening to the conversation around the table, you'll realize frankness is the order of the day."

"Good, because I would be anyway. It's my—fetish. You're lying, Mr. Halsted. Of course you want the rest of my steak, and you'd eat it, too, if you thought no one would notice. That's perfectly obvious, but social convention requires you to lie. You don't want to seem greedy and you don't want to seem to ignore the elements of hygiene by eating something possibly contaminated by the saliva of a stranger."

Halsted frowned. "And what if the situation were reversed?"

"And I was hungry for more steak?"

"Yes."

"Well, I might not want to eat yours for hygienic reasons, but I would admit I wanted it. Almost all lying is the result of a desire for self-protection or out of respect for social conventions. To me, however, a lie is rarely a useful defense and I am not at all interested in social conventions."

Rubin said, "Actually, a lie is a useful defense if it is a thoroughgoing one. The trouble with most lies is that they don't go far enough."

"Been reading *Mein Kampf* lately?" said Gonzalo.

Rubin's eyebrows went up. "You think *Hitler* was the first to use the technique of the big lie? You can go back to Napoleon III; you can go back to Julius Caesar. Have you ever read his *Commentaries*?"

Henry was bringing the baba au rhum and pouring the coffee delicately when Avalon said, "Let's get to our honored guest."

Gonzalo said, "As host and chairman of this session I'm going to cancel the grilling. Our guest has a problem and I direct him to favor us with its details." He was drawing a quick caricature of Sand on the back of the menu card, with a thin sad face accentuated into the face of a distorted bloodhound.

Sand cleared his throat. "I understand everything said in this room is in the strictest confidence. But—"

Trumbull followed Sand's glance, then growled, "Don't worry about Henry. He is the best of us all. If you want to doubt someone's discretion, doubt someone else."

"Thank you, sir," murmured Henry, setting up the brandy glasses on the sideboard.

Sand said, "The trouble, gentlemen, is that I am suspected of a crime."

"What kind of crime?" demanded Trumbull. It was his duty, ordinarily, to grill the guests and the look in his eye was that of a person who had no intention of missing his opportunity.

"Theft," said Sand. "There is a sum of money and a wad of negotiable bonds missing from a safe in my company. I'm one of those who know the combination, and I've had a chance to open the safe unobserved. I also have a motive—I've had bad luck at the races and needed cash urgently. So it doesn't look good for me."

Gonzalo said eagerly, "But he didn't do it. That's the point. He didn't do it."

Avalon twirled the half drink he was not going to finish and said, "I think in the interest of coherence we ought to allow Mr. Sand to tell his story."

"Yes," said Trumbull, "How do *you* know he didn't do it, Mario?"

"That's the whole point, damn it. He *says* he didn't do it," replied Gonzalo, "and if he says so, that's good enough for me. Maybe not for a court, but it's good enough for anyone who knows him. I've heard him admit enough rotten things that other people wouldn't—"

"Suppose I ask him myself, okay?" said Trumbull. "*Did* you take the stuff, Mr. Sand?"

Sand paused. His blue eyes flicked from face to face, then he said, "Gentlemen, I am telling the absolute truth. I did not take the cash or the bonds."

Halsted passed his hand upward over his forehead, as though trying to clear away doubts.

"Mr. Sand," he said, "you seem to have a position of some trust. You can get into a safe with negotiable assets in it. Yet you play the horses."

"Lots of people do."

"And lose."

"I didn't quite plan it that way."

"But don't you risk losing your job?"

"My advantage, sir, is that I am employed by my uncle, who is aware of my weakness, but who also knows I don't lie. He knew I had the means and the opportunity to steal, and he knew I had debts. He also knew I had recently paid off my gambling debts. I told him so. Yet the circumstantial evidence against me looked bad. But then he asked me directly if I was responsible for the loss and I told him exactly what I told you: I did not take the cash or the bonds. Since he knows me well, he believes me."

"How were you able to pay off your gambling debts?" said Avalon.

"Because a long shot came through. That happens, too, sometimes. It happened shortly before the theft was discovered and I paid off the bookies."

"But then you didn't have a motive," said Gonzalo.

"I can't say that. The theft may have been committed as long as two weeks before its discovery. No one looked in that particular drawer in the safe for that period of time—except the thief, of course. It could be argued that after I took the cash and bonds, the horse came through and made the theft unnecessary—too late."

"It might also be argued," said Halsted, "that you took the money in order to place a large bet on the horse."

"The bet wasn't that large, and I had other sources. But, yes, it could also be argued that way."

Trumbull broke in, "But if you still have your job, as I suppose you do, and if your uncle isn't prosecuting you, as I assume he isn't—Has he notified the police at all?"

"No, he can absorb the loss and he feels the police will only try to pin it on me. He knows that what I have told him is true."

"Then what's the problem, for God's sake?"

"There's simply no one else who could have done it. My uncle can't think of any other way of accounting for the theft. Nor, for that matter, can I. And as long as he can't see any alternative, there will always be a residuum of uneasiness, of suspicion, in his mind. He will always keep his eye on me. He will always be reluctant to trust me. I'll keep my job, but I'll never be promoted; and I may be made uncomfortable enough to be forced to resign. If I do, I can't count on a wholehearted recommendation, and from an uncle, a half-hearted one would be ruinous."

Rubin was frowning. "So you came here, Mr. Sand, because Gonzalo said we solve mysteries. You want us to tell you who really took the stuff."

Sand shrugged. "Maybe not. I don't even know if I can give you enough information. It's not as though you're detectives who can go to the scene of the crime and make inquiries. If you could just tell me how it *might* have been done—even if it's farfetched, that would help. If I could go to my uncle and say, 'Uncle, it might have been done this way, mightn't it?' Even if he couldn't be sure, even if he couldn't ever get the money and bonds back, it would at least spread the suspicion. He wouldn't have the eternal nagging thought that I was the *only possible* thief."

"Well," said Avalon, "we can try to be logical, I suppose. How about the other people who work with you and your uncle? Would any of them need money badly?"

Sand shook his head "Enough to risk the possible consequences of being caught? I don't know. One of them might be in debt, or one might be paying blackmail, or one might be greedy, or just had the opportunity and acted on impulse. If I were a detective I could go about asking questions, or I could track down documents, or whatever it is they do. As it is—"

"Of course," said Avalon, "we can't do that either.—Now you say you had both means and opportunity. Did anyone else have them?"

"At least three people could have got into the safe more easily than I and got away with it more easily, but not one of them knew the combination, and the safe wasn't broken into; that is certain. There are two people besides my uncle and myself who know the combination, but one has been hospitalized over the entire period in question and the other is such an old and reliable member of the firm that to suspect him seems unthinkable."

"Aha," said Mario Gonzalo, "there's our man right there."

"You've been reading too many Agatha Christies," said Rubin. "The fact of the matter is that in almost every crime on record, the most suspicious person turns out to be the criminal."

"That's beside the point," said Halsted, "and too dull besides. What we have here is a pure exercise in logic. Let's have Mr. Sand tell us everything he knows about every member of the firm, and we can all try to see if there's any way in which we can work out motive, means, and opportunity for some other person."

"Oh, hell," said Trumbull, "who says it has to be *one* person? So someone's in a hospital. Big deal. The telephone exists. He phones the combination to a confederate."

"All right, all right," said Halsted hastily, "we're bound to think up all sorts of possibilities and some may be more plausible than others. After we've thrashed them out, Mr. Sand can choose the most plausible and tell it to his uncle."

"May I speak, sir?" Henry spoke so quickly, and at a sound level so much higher than his usual murmur that everyone turned to face him.

Henry said, this time softly, "Although I'm not a Black Widower—"

"Not so," said Rubin. "You know you're a Black Widower. In fact, you're the only one who's never missed a single meeting."

"Then may I point out, gentlemen, that if Mr. Sand carries your conclusion, whatever it may be, to his uncle, he will be carrying the proceedings of this meeting beyond the walls of this room."

There was an uncomfortable silence. Halsted said, "In the interest of saving an innocent person's reputation, surely—"

Henry shook his head gently. "But it would be at the cost of spreading suspicion to one or more other people, who might also be innocent."

Avalon said, "Henry's got something there. We seem to be stymied."

"Unless," said Henry, "we can come to a definite conclusion that will satisfy the club and will not involve the outside world."

"What do you have in mind, Henry?" asked Trumbull.

"If I may explain—I was, as Mr. Gonzalo said before dinner, interested to meet someone who never tells a lie."

"Now come, Henry," said Rubin, "you're pathologically honest yourself. You know you are. That's been established more than once."

"That may be so," said Henry, "but I *do* tell lies."

"Do you doubt Sand? Do you think he's lying?" said Rubin.

"I assure you—" began Sand, almost in anguish.

"No," said Henry, "I believe that every word Mr. Sand has said is true. He didn't take the money or the bonds. He is the logical one at whom suspicion points. His career may be ruined. His career, on the other hand, may not be ruined if some reasonable alternative explanation can be found, even if that does not actually lead to a solution. And, since he can think of no reasonable alternative himself, he wants us to help find one for him. I am convinced, gentlemen, that all this is true."

Sand nodded. "Well, thank you."

"And yet," said Henry, "what is truth? For instance, Mr. Trumbull, I think that your habit of perpetually arriving late with a cry of 'Scotch and soda for a dying man' is rude, unnecessary, and, worse yet, has grown boring. I suspect others here feel the same."

Trumbull flushed, but Henry went on firmly, "Yet if, under ordinary circumstances, I were asked whether I disapproved of it, I would say I did not. Strictly speaking, that would be a lie, but I like you for other reasons, Mr. Trumbull, that far outweigh this verbal trick of yours; so telling the strict truth, which would imply a dislike for you, would end up being a greater lie. Therefore I lie to express a truth—my liking for you."

Trumbull muttered, "I'm not sure I like your way of liking, Henry."

Henry said, "Or consider Mr. Halsted's limerick on the first book of the *Iliad*. Mr. Avalon quite rightly said that Achilleus is the correct name of the hero, or even Akhilleus with a 'k,' I suppose, to suggest the correct sound. But then Mr. Rubin pointed out that the truth would seem like a typographical error and spoil the effect of the limerick. Again, literal truth creates a problem.

"Mr. Sand said that all lies arise out of a desire for self-protection or out of respect for social conventions. But we cannot always ignore self-protection and social conventions. If we cannot lie, we must make the truth lie for us."

Gonzalo said, "You're not making sense, Henry."

"I think I am, Mr. Gonzalo. Few people listen to exact words, and many a literal truth tells a lie by implication. Who should know that better than a person who always tells the literal truth?"

Sand's pale cheeks were less pale, or his red tie was reflecting more color upward. He said, "What the hell are you implying?"

"I would like to ask you just one question, Mr. Sand? If the members of the club are willing, of course."

"I don't care if they are or not," said Sand, glowering at Henry. "If you take that tone I might not choose to answer."

"You may not have to," said Henry. "The point is that each time you deny having committed the crime, you deny it in precisely the same words. I couldn't help but notice since I made up my mind to listen to your exact words as soon as I heard that you never lied. Each time, you said, 'I did not take the cash or the bonds.'"

"And that is perfectly true," said Sand loudly.

"I'm sure it is, or you wouldn't have said so," said Henry. "Now this is the question I would like to ask you. Did you, by any chance, take the cash *and* the bonds?"

There was a short silence. Then Sand rose and said, "I'll get my coat now. Goodbye. I remind you all that nothing said here can be repeated outside."

When Sand was gone, Trumbull said, "Well, I'll be damned."

To which Henry replied, "Perhaps not, Mr. Trumbull. Don't despair."

I HAVE

JOHN GARDNER
(1926–   )

One of the brightest lights in the world of the British spy novel, Gardner was chosen by the estate of Ian Fleming to continue the James Bond saga. When he finally decided to stop writing them, he had produced sixteen books—three more than Fleming. The books did nothing to help his reputation, though his banker could not have been more pleased. His finest work is about big Herbie Kruger, notably The Garden of Weapons, *which may be the best espionage novel ever written.*

T HAPPENED TOWARDS THE end of the war. Somewhere around the winter of 1944. Anyway, I was stationed just outside some unpronounceable Welsh village, and remember the nearest thing to civilisation was Aberystwyth. The boys used to go over there on a Saturday night, but there were only a couple of hotels 'in-bounds' for officers, so it was hardly worth the effort.

In any case all that is really begging the question because I was returning from leave when the thing occurred. It had been a hectic six months and the moment pressure slackened I took the opportunity to grab seven days, due to me from my last leave period, and go down to Berkshire to see my parents.

I recall it took the best part of a Saturday to travel from Wales to the market town in which they were then living. The curses came on the Tuesday, about noon, when the telegram arrived. In those days telegrams were dreaded things; rarely did they bring good news. More often than not the little form began with the words *Deeply Regret to*

Inform You. In my case the telegram said *Leave Cancelled Prior Drafting to Holding Unit and Posting Overseas.* I rang the Unit Adjutant to find that I was to join the Brigade in the Middle East. The only consolation was that I would have two weeks' embarkation leave. In the meantime my presence was requested back in Welsh Wales by 09:00 hours the following morning.

At that time you could never be quite certain about trains. On any long journey there were delays, late arrivals and, worst of all, sudden unannounced changes of schedule. I checked on the alternative methods of getting back to my base and finally plumped for a bus to Oxford around six, followed by a lengthy wait on Oxford station to catch a train to Shrewsbury at 10:30. Once in Shrewsbury there would be a milk train, or something, to my destination.

It was a clear night, very cold but with a full moon—a bombers' moon they used to call it. Once in Oxford I sloped off to a pub near the station, rationed myself to four single Scotches before closing time, then tried to make the best of it. Needless to say the Shrewsbury train was late, an hour late. Then we waited for what seemed to be at least another hour before pulling out. Actually, if my memory is correct, we left Oxford just before midnight. The train was practically empty and I had a compartment to myself. No heating, of course, but that was pretty standard in those days. I wrapped my greatcoat round me, huddled myself into a corner and tried to stare out of the window. The train was unlit, but the moon still shone outside so there was a certain amount of visibility. I remember feeling dozy and going through that rather pleasant sensation of surrendering the body to the rhythm of the train.

The next thing I knew was a feeling of intense cold. My neck was stiff, as I had fallen asleep in the usual awkward angle. It was nearly ten to two and we were not moving. I stretched and rubbed my eyes, though it was a moment or so before I became aware that someone else had joined me in the compartment. For some reason which I still cannot explain, there was a fair amount of light in the carriage and I could see with moderate clarity throughout the events which followed. My companion was slumped in the seat opposite, his chin resting in the fork of his right hand between the thumb and index finger. He was a thin man, quite tall, I imagined, though it was difficult to tell from his sitting position. He wore a threadbare lightweight overcoat which had originally been a fawn check of some kind. It was a long garment which reached, even sitting down, to mid-calf, while around his neck the man had wound a thick, dirty, multi-coloured scarf. His face was abnormally pale and drawn, the eyes staring with a half-unreal filmy look. He was either a very worried or very sick man, and I began to feel a little apprehensive, uncomfortable.

The train started to move again and my fellow traveller shifted his position. By this time I was feeling for the battered blue paper packet of wartime Players cigarettes in my greatcoat pocket. I found them, and the matches, then reached out to offer the fellow a smoke. He looked at the proffered cigarettes, then slowly nodded.

"Might as well, I suppose." The voice was low and husky as though drained of life, and I noticed how badly his hand shook as he pulled one of the cigarettes from the torn paper.

"You all right?" It was a stupid question but I had to say something. He did not reply until I had lighted the cigarettes, then he fell back into his seat as though utterly exhausted.

"Be OK in a minute," he wheezed, a smile wry on his lips. "Funny business life. Funny." His eyes flickered and for a moment I thought he was going to faint. But he revived quickly and looked straight at me. For the first time there was a spark of life behind the eyes. "Sorry. Must look terrible. Had a bit of a shock."

"I can see," I said. "If you don't mind me saying so, you look all in."

"Wonder how you'd feel. You're an officer, must be used to hearing other people's troubles."

"Yes," I nodded my head affirmatively. "You want to talk about it?"

"Wouldn't do any harm."

"OK."

My companion puffed inexpertly at his cigarette. I was very much aware of the train's noise, the dirt on the floor, and the unique smell which one always used to associate with the Great Western Railway. When he spoke I had to concentrate hard, for his voice never remained completely audible. It rose to a moderate husky level, then sank to a whisper which I could barely hear. Memory may well have played tricks, but I am pretty certain that what followed is a reasonably accurate account.

"I suppose," he began, "it started with Dunkirk."

"You were at Dunkirk?"

"Yes, I was there. In good shape too, when I arrived. Then one moment I was just lying on the beach, and the next it was all blood and pain. Messerschmidt, I think they said it was. Got me in the guts. Anyhow I woke up in hospital in England with my wife looking all worried. A year I had in hospital, then they invalided me out of the service and gave me a pension." He gave a rough, bitter laugh. "Man-power. Shouting out for man-power and nobody seems to want a fellow with half his guts blown away. Would you believe me if I told you I've spent the last three years going from job to job, searching for work?"

"Yes." I had come up against this sort of thing many times before. There was plenty of sympathy around, but, in spite of the need for man-power throughout the country, people could not be bothered to saddle themselves with ex-servicemen already on pension and likely to become liabilities. I could well picture this tall bag of bones traipsing from temporary job to temporary job.

"You've had some?" he asked.

"Not personally, but I know others who have had a difficult time."

He nodded again. "Hasn't been too bad, really, I suppose," he continued. "Not until about three weeks ago, that is. Really hit me, then. The lot. How much can one man take?" His voice trailed off and the eyes slowly turned towards the window. It was almost as though he had forgotten that I was there. Then he began to speak again. "Yes, three weeks ago. I'd been havin' these pains down in me stomach. Not the side where I was shot up. The other side. The left side. That laid me off work and the old doc fixed up for me to have these tests done in Oxford. Radcliffe Hospital. Took a whole day, then things really started when I got back." He stopped again as though trying to get his breath. I waited patiently, willing a look of sympathy onto my face, vaguely wondering if I was being taken for a ride and the story would end up with a touch. He began to talk again.

"I've got two kids. Funny, you don't notice them growing up. Bobby, he's fourteen, and Beryl, she's the eldest, sixteen. Sixteen last August. They always seemed all right to me, but I was probably too wrapped up in myself. Really I've got to take the blame, haven't I?"

"That depends. They go off the rails?"

"One way of putting it. Off the rails." Again the bitter laugh. "It was Bobby first. About half-ten I got home but it was all over by then. They'd already had him down at the police station and charged him. Four of them there were, all about his age. Breaking and entering. Petty larceny. We had to go up the juvenile the following week. Magistrates were quite nice about it, but they said he needed specialised treatment. A year they gave him. A year in an Approved School."

"Rough."

"Pha." He made a noise like spitting. "That wasn't enough. We get back from the magistrates' court and there's Beryl sitting at home sniffing and all puffy round the eyes. Two months' gone. An American Top Sergeant, and she didn't even know his name."

"Oh, Lord." I had quite made up my mind that it was some kind of confidence trick. "That's really grim. Both children."

"There's more yet. A lot more." He had settled back, looking paler than ever but very relaxed. "Today I went back to the hospital. Results of the tests."

"Bad?" It was not worth the word, of course the results would be bad.

"The worst. Said they'd have to open me up to be sure, but they're certain I've got cancer of the stomach. What's left of it, that is."

"You mean . . .?" This was no ordinary con. The chap was really laying it on hard. Son in Borstal, daughter in the family way. Any minute now he would tell me he had only six months to live. As if reading my thoughts he said.

"The quack only gives me about six months. Asked him to tell me straight."

"I'm terribly sorry." I said it quietly, as though in the presence of a corpse.

"No need for you to feel sorry. It was when I got home it knocked me. For six it knocked me. Knocked me for six."

"I bet."

"Not the cancer, chief, not that. The wife. Never thought she was like that. No hint. Nothing." He was rummaging through the pockets of his long coat. Finally he drew out a crumpled piece of paper which he held towards me without leaning forward. I took the paper, torn, it seemed, from a child's exercise book. It was a letter written in a bold, heavy hand.

"Joe's a mate of mine," he said, by way of explanation.

I held the paper at an angle so that I could read it more clearly. If it was genuine, the very simplicity of the wording made it a tragic little document.

Dear Bert,

This will come as a shock I know because I do not think you have any idea of what has been going on. I am sorry because I know you are ill but there will be good people at the hospital to look after you. I cannot take any more and Joe and me have been friendly for a long time what with the kids and everything it is all too much and we are going up north to make a fresh start. We are taking Beryl with us and I will write to Bobby so you will not have to trouble with that. Truly I am sorry to leave you this way but what else can I do.

Your loving wife,
Judy.

It was the *Your Loving Wife Judy* bit that got me. If it was all true what would a man do? I heard myself murmuring, "Good God, if it was me, I'd cut my throat."

There was a movement. I looked up. The man was slowly unwinding the scarf from his neck. The dirty, multi-coloured grey was giving way to a darkish shade. With a final snatch he pulled it off displaying the hideous ripped and jagged gap trickling heavy with blood.

"I have." He breathed.

The thin man moved seats shortly after Dymore had finished talking. They were once more crossing the English coastline. Another twenty minutes and he would be home, dry and powdered. Then, it happened.

The whole explosion could not have taken more than a fraction of a second, but Dymore saw its beginnings up at the front—a quick lick of flame. One is always told that a dying man relives his life in the moment of death. In that fragment of time, Dymore did not go back through a flickering biography. Instead, fictional figures and fantasies were clear and colourful in his brain. The man in the railway compartment with blood dripping from the gashed throat; Boysie Oakes surrounded by explosions in the New Territories; the Auburn motor car disintegrating; a picture of Big Jim Sales' front door; Cecil cleaning his gun; the insignificant Jumplin walking with precision to his train; the girl looking from her window at the parting mock-lover; and, last of all, Boysie Oakes spinning away on his parachute jump, this time into eternal darkness.

"Poor old Dymore getting caught like that." Collingwood was talking to his second-in-command. "In the clear, too. Funny how these things happen."

"I'm not so worried about Dymore," said the second-in-command, looking grim over the evening paper strung with banner headlines proclaiming the air disaster above southern England. "It's all the other people who were on board. Dymore always knew what risks he was taking. What I'd like to know is, did he fall or was he pushed?"

QUITTERS, INC.

STEPHEN KING
(1947–   )

As the most popular horror writer of all time, King has surpassed Poe and Lovecraft, Shelley and Stoker, as the name most identified with tales of dark fantasy. With book sales in the hundreds of millions, King has demonstrated an uncanny (forgive the pun) inventiveness that extends to his short fiction and, especially in his earlier works, a meticulous craftsmanship usually associated with authors who are far less prolific. The following story is one of the rare King tales that does not rely on the supernatural—or does it?

ORRISON WAS WAITING FOR someone who was hung up in the air traffic jam over Kennedy International when he saw a familiar face at the end of the bar and walked down.

"Jimmy? Jimmy McCann?"

It was. A little heavier than when Morrison had seen him at the Atlanta Exhibition the year before, but otherwise he looked awesomely fit. In college he had been a little thin, pallid chain smoker buried behind huge horn-rimmed glasses. He had apparently switched to contact lenses.

"Dick Morrison?"

"Yeah. You look great." He extended his hand and they shook.

"So do you," McCann said, but Morrison knew it was a lie. He had been overworking, overeating, and smoking too much. "What are you drinking?"

"Bourbon and bitters," Morrison said. He hooked his feet around a bar stool and lighted a cigarette. "Meeting someone, Jimmy?"

"No. Going to Miami for a conference. A heavy client. Bills six million. I'm supposed to hold his hand because we lost out on a big special next spring."

"Are you still with Crager and Barton?"

"Executive veep now."

"Fantastic! Congratulations! When did all this happen?" He tried to tell himself that the little worm of jealousy in his stomach was just acid indigestion. He pulled out a roll of antacid pills and crunched one in his mouth.

"Last August. Something happened that changed my life." He looked speculatively at Morrison and sipped his drink. "You might be interested."

My God, Morrison thought with an inner wince. Jimmy McCann's got religion.

"Sure," he said, and gulped at his drink when it came.

"I wasn't in very good shape," McCann said. "Personal problems with Sharon, my dad died—heart attack— and I'd developed this hacking cough. Bobby Crager dropped by my office one day and gave me a fatherly little pep talk. Do you remember what those are like?"

"Yeah." He had worked at Crager and Barton for eighteen months before joining the Morton Agency. "Get your butt in gear or get your butt out."

McCann laughed. "You know it. Well, to put the capper on it, the doc told me I had an incipient ulcer. He told me to quit smoking." McCann grimaced. "Might as well tell me to quit breathing."

Morrison nodded in perfect understanding. Nonsmokers could afford to be smug. He looked at his own cigarette with distaste and stubbed it out, knowing he would be lighting another in five minutes.

"Did you quit?" he asked.

"Yes, I did. At first I didn't think I'd be able to—I was cheating like hell. Then I met a guy who told me about an outfit over on Forty-sixth Street. Specialists. I said what do I have to lose and went over. I haven't smoked since."

Morrison's eyes widened. "What did they do? Fill you full of some drug?"

"No." He had taken out his wallet and was rummaging through it. "Here it is. I knew I had one kicking around." He laid a plain white business card on the bar between them.

QUITTERS, INC.
Stop Going Up in Smoke!
237 East 46th Street
Treatments by Appointment

"Keep it, if you want," McCann said. "They'll cure you. Guaranteed."

"How?"

"I can't tell you," McCann said.

"Huh? Why not?"

"It's part of the contract they make you sign. Anyway, they tell you how it works when they interview you."

"You signed a *contract*?"

McCann nodded.

"And on the basis of that—"

"Yep." He smiled at Morrison, who thought: Well, it's happened. Jim McCann has joined the smug bastards.

"Why the great secrecy if this outfit is so fantastic? How come I've never seen any spots on TV, billboards, magazine ads—"

"They get all the clients they can handle by word of mouth."

"You're an advertising man, Jimmy. You can't believe that."

"I do," McCann said. "They have a ninety-eight percent cure rate."

"Wait a second," Morrison said. He motioned for another drink and lit a cigarette. "Do these guys strap you down and make you smoke until you throw up?"

"No."

"Give you something so that you get sick every time you light—"

"No, it's nothing like that. Go and see for yourself." He gestured at Morrison's cigarette. "You don't really like that, do you?"

"Nooo, but—"

"Stopping really changed things for me," McCann said. "I don't suppose it's the same for everyone, but with me it was just like dominoes falling over. I felt better and my relationship with Sharon improved. I had more energy, and my job performance picked up."

"Look, you've got my curiosity aroused. Can't you just—"

"I'm sorry, Dick. I really can't talk about it." His voice was firm.

"Did you put on any weight?"

For a moment he thought Jimmy McCann looked almost grim. "Yes. A little too much, in fact. But I took it off again. I'm about right now. I was skinny before."

"Flight 206 now boarding at Gate 9," the loudspeaker announced.

"That's me," McCann said, getting up. He tossed a five on the bar. "Have another, if you like. And think about what I said, Dick. Really." And then he was gone, making his way through the crowd to the escalators. Morrison picked up the card, looked at it thoughtfully, then tucked it away in his wallet and forgot it.

The card fell out of his wallet and onto another bar a month later. He had left the office early and had come here to drink the afternoon away. Things had not been going well at the Morton Agency. In fact, things were bloody horrible.

He gave Henry a ten to pay for his drink, then picked up the small card and reread it—237 East Forty-sixth Street was only two blocks over; it was a cool, sunny October day outside, and maybe, just for chuckles—

When Henry brought his change, he finished his drink and then went for a walk.

Quitters, Inc., was in a new building where the monthly rent on the office space was probably close to Morrison's yearly salary. From the directory in the lobby, it looked to him like their offices took up one whole floor, and that spelled money. Lots of it.

He took the elevator up and stepped off into a lushly carpeted foyer and from there into a gracefully appointed reception room with a wide window that looked out on the scurrying bugs below. Three men and one woman sat in the chairs along the walls, reading magazines. Business types, all of them. Morrison went to the desk.

"A friend gave me this," he said, passing the card to the receptionist. "I guess you'd say he's an alumnus."

She smiled and rolled a form into her typewriter. "What is your name, sir?"

"Richard Morrison."

Clack-clackety-clack. But very muted clacks; the typewriter was an IBM.

"Your address?"

"Twenty-nine Maple Lane, Clinton, New York."

"Married?"

"Yes."

"Children?"

"One." He thought of Alvin and frowned slightly. "One" was the wrong word. "A half" might be better. His son was mentally retarded and lived at a special school in New Jersey.

"Who recommended us to you, Mr. Morrison?"

"An old school friend. James McCann."

"Very good. Will you have a seat? It's been a very busy day."

"All right."

He sat between the woman, who was wearing a severe blue suit, and a young executive type wearing a herringbone jacket and modish sideburns. He took out his pack of cigarettes, looked around, and saw there were no ashtrays.

He put the pack away again. That was all right. He would see this little game through and then light up while he was leaving. He might even tap some ashes on their maroon shag rug if they made him wait long enough. He picked up a copy of *Time* and began to leaf through it.

He was called a quarter of an hour later, after the woman in the blue suit. His nicotine center was speaking quite loudly now. A man who had come in after him took out a cigarette case, snapped it open, saw there were no ashtrays, and put it away—looking a little guilty, Morrison thought. It made him feel better.

At last the receptionist gave him a sunny smile and said, "Go right in, Mr. Morrison."

Morrison walked through the door beyond her desk and found himself in an indirectly lit hallway. A heavyset man with white hair that looked phony shook his hand, smiled affably, and said, "Follow me, Mr. Morrison."

He led Morrison past a number of closed, unmarked doors and then opened one of them about halfway down the hall with a key. Beyond the door was an austere little room walled with drilled white cork panels. The only furnishings were a desk with a chair on either side. There was what appeared to be a small oblong window in the wall behind the desk, but it was covered with a short green curtain. There was a picture on the wall to Morrison's left—a tall man with iron-gray hair. He was holding a sheet of paper in one hand. He looked vaguely familiar.

"I'm Vic Donatti," the heavyset man said. "If you decide to go ahead with our program, I'll be in charge of your case."

"Pleased to know you," Morrison said. He wanted a cigarette very badly.

"Have a seat."

Donatti put the receptionist's form on the desk, and then drew another form from the desk drawer. He looked directly into Morrison's eyes. "Do you want to quit smoking?"

Morrison cleared his throat, crossed his legs, and tried to think of a way to equivocate. He couldn't. "Yes," he said.

"Will you sign this?" He gave Morrison the form. He scanned it quickly. The undersigned agrees not to divulge the methods or techniques or et cetera, et cetera.

"Sure," he said, and Donatti put a pen in his hand. He scratched his name, and Donatti signed below it. A moment later the paper disappeared back into the desk drawer. Well, he thought ironically, I've taken the pledge. He had taken it before. Once it had lasted for two whole days.

"Good," Donatti said. "We don't bother with propaganda here, Mr. Morrison. Questions of health or expense or social grace. We have no interest in why you want to stop smoking. We are pragmatists."

"Good," Morrison said blankly.

"We employ no drugs. We employ no Dale Carnegie people to sermonize you. We recommend no special diet. And we accept no payment until you have stopped smoking for one year."

"My God," Morrison said.

"Mr. McCann didn't tell you that?"

"No."

"How is Mr. McCann, by the way? Is he well?"

"He's fine."

"Wonderful. Excellent. Now . . . just a few questions, Mr. Morrison. These are somewhat personal, but I assure you that your answers will be held in strictest confidence."

"Yes?" Morrison asked noncommittally.

"What is your wife's name?"

"Lucinda Morrison. Her maiden name was Ramsey."

"Do you love her?"

Morrison looked up sharply, but Donatti was looking at him blandly. "Yes, of course," he said.

"Have you ever had marital problems? A separation, perhaps?"

"What has that got to do with kicking the habit?" Morrison asked. He sounded a little angrier than he had intended, but he wanted—hell, he *needed*—a cigarette.

"A great deal," Donatti said. "Just bear with me."

"No. Nothing like that." Although things *had* been a little tense just lately.

"You just have the one child?"

"Yes. Alvin. He's in a private school."

"And which school is it?"

"That," Morrison said grimly, "I'm not going to tell you."

"All right," Donatti said agreeably. He smiled disarmingly at Morrison. "All your questions will be answered tomorrow at your first treatment."

"How nice," Morrison said, and stood.

"One final question," Donatti said. "You haven't had a cigarette for over an hour. How do you feel?"

"Fine," Morrison lied. "Just fine."

"Good for you!" Donatti exclaimed. He stepped around the desk and opened the door. "Enjoy them tonight. After tomorrow, you'll never smoke again."

"Is that right?"

"Mr. Morrison," Donatti said solemnly, "we guarantee it."

He was sitting in the outer office of Quitters, Inc., the next day promptly at three. He had spent most of the day swinging between skipping the appointment the receptionist had made for him on the way out and going in a spirit of mulish cooperation—*Throw your best pitch at me, buster.*

In the end, something Jimmy McCann had said convinced him to keep the appointment—*It changed my whole life.* God knew his own life could do with some changing. And then there was his own curiosity. Before going up in the elevator, he smoked a cigarette down to the filter. Too damn bad if it's the last one, he thought. It tasted horrible.

The wait in the outer office was shorter this time. When the receptionist told him to go in, Donatti was waiting. He offered his hand and smiled, and to Morrison the smile looked almost predatory. He began to feel a little tense, and that made him want a cigarette.

"Come with me," Donatti said, and led the way down to the small room. He sat behind the desk again, and Morrison took the other chair.

"I'm very glad you came," Donatti said. "A great many prospective clients never show up again after the initial interview. They discover they don't want to quit as badly as they thought. It's going to be a pleasure to work with you on this."

"When does the treatment start?" Hypnosis, he was thinking. It must be hypnosis.

"Oh, it already has. It started when we shook hands in the hall. Do you have cigarettes with you, Mr. Morrison?"

"Yes."

"May I have them, please?"

Shrugging, Morrison handed Donatti his pack. There were only two or three left in it, anyway.

Donatti put the pack on the desk. Then, smiling into Morrison's eyes, he curled his right hand into a fist and began to hammer it down on the pack of cigarettes, which twisted and flattened. A broken cigarette end flew out. Tobacco crumbs spilled. The sound of Donatti's fist was very loud in the closed room. The smile remained on his face in spite of the force of the blows, and Morrison was chilled by it. Probably just the effect they want to inspire, he thought.

At last Donatti ceased pounding. He picked up the pack, a twisted and battered ruin. "You wouldn't believe the pleasure that gives me," he said, and dropped the pack into the wastebasket. "Even after three years in the business, it still pleases me."

"As a treatment, it leaves something to be desired," Morrison said mildly. "There's a newsstand in the lobby of this very building. And they sell all brands."

"As you say," Donatti said. He folded his hands. "Your son, Alvin Dawes Morrison, is in the Paterson School for Handicapped Children. Born with cranial brain damage. Tested IQ of 46. Not quite in the educable retarded category. Your wife—"

"How did you find that out?" Morrison barked. He was startled and angry. "You've got no goddamn right to go poking around my—"

"We know a lot about you," Donatti said smoothly. "But, as I said, it will all be held in strictest confidence."

"I'm getting out of here," Morrison said thinly. He stood up.

"Stay a bit longer."

Morrison looked at him closely. Donatti wasn't upset. In fact, he looked a little amused. The face of a man who has seen this reaction scores of times—maybe hundreds.

"All right. But it better be good."

"Oh, it is." Donatti leaned back. "I told you we were pragmatists here. As pragmatists, we have to start by realizing how difficult it is to cure an addiction to tobacco. The relapse rate is almost eighty-five percent. The relapse rate for heroin addicts is lower than that. It is an extraordinary problem. *Extraordinary.*"

Morrison glanced into the wastebasket. One of the cigarettes, although twisted, still looked smokeable. Donatti laughed good-naturedly, reached into the wastebasket, and broke it between his fingers.

"State legislatures sometimes hear a request that the prison systems do away with the weekly cigarette ration. Such proposals are invariably defeated. In a few cases where they have passed, there have been fierce prison riots. *Riots,* Mr. Morrison. Imagine it."

"I," Morrison said, "am not surprised."

"But consider the implications. When you put a man in prison you take away any normal sex life, you take away his liquor, his politics, his freedom of movement. No riots—or few in comparison to the number of prisons. But when you take away his *cigarettes*—wham! bam!" He slammed his fist on the desk for emphasis.

"During World War I, when no one on the German home front could get cigarettes, the sight of German aristocrats picking butts out of the gutter was a common one. During World War II, many American women turned to pipes when they were unable to obtain cigarettes. A fascinating problem for the true pragmatist, Mr. Morrison."

"Could we get to the treatment?"

"Momentarily. Step over here, please." Donatti had risen and was standing by the green curtains Morrison had noticed yesterday. Donatti drew the curtains, discovering a rectangular window that looked into a bare room. No, not quite bare. There was a rabbit on the floor, eating pellets out of a dish.

"Pretty bunny," Morrison commented.

"Indeed. Watch him." Donatti pressed a button by the windowsill. The rabbit stopped eating and began to hop about crazily. It seemed to leap higher each time its feet struck the floor. Its fur stood out spikily in all directions. Its eyes were wild.

"Stop that! You're electrocuting him!"

Donatti released the button. "Far from it. There's a very low-yield charge in the floor. Watch the rabbit, Mr. Morrison!"

The rabbit was crouched about ten feet away from the dish of pellets. His nose wriggled. All at once he hopped away into a corner.

"If the rabbit gets a jolt often enough while he's eating," Donatti said, "he makes the association very quickly. Eating causes pain. Therefore, he won't eat. A few more shocks, and the rabbit will starve to death in front of his food. It's called aversion training."

Light dawned in Morrison's head.

"No, thanks." He started for the door.

"Wait, please, Mr. Morrison."

Morrison didn't pause. He grasped the doorknob . . . and felt it slip solidly through his hand. "Unlock this."

"Mr. Morrison, if you'll just sit down—"

"Unlock this door or I'll have the cops on you before you can say Marlboro Man."

"Sit down." The voice was cold as shaved ice.

Morrison looked at Donatti. His brown eyes were muddy and frightening. My God, he thought, I'm locked in here with a psycho. He licked his lips. He wanted a cigarette more than he ever had in his life.

"Let me explain the treatment in more detail," Donatti said.

"You don't understand," Morrison said with counterfeit patience. "I don't want the treatment. I've decided against it."

"No, Mr. Morrison. *You're* the one who doesn't understand. You don't have any choice. When I told you the treatment had already begun, I was speaking the literal truth. I would have thought you'd tipped to that by now."

"You're crazy," Morrison said wonderingly.

"No. Only a pragmatist. Let me tell you all about the treatment."

"Sure," Morrison said. "As long as you understand that as soon as I get out of here I'm going to buy five packs of cigarettes and smoke them all the way to the police station." He suddenly realized he was biting his thumbnail, sucking on it, and made himself stop.

"As you wish. But I think you'll change your mind when you see the whole picture."

Morrison said nothing. He sat down again and folded his hands.

"For the first month of the treatment, our operatives will have you under constant supervision," Donatti said. "You'll be able to spot some of them. Not all. But they'll always be with you. *Always.* If they see you smoke a cigarette, I get a call."

"And I suppose you bring me here and do the old rabbit trick," Morrison said. He tried to sound cold and sarcastic, but he suddenly felt horribly frightened. This was a nightmare.

"Oh, no," Donatti said. "Your wife gets the rabbit trick, not you."

Morrison looked at him dumbly.

Donatti smiled. "You," he said, "get to watch."

After Donatti let him out, Morrison walked for over two hours in a complete daze. It was another fine day, but he didn't notice. The monstrousness of Donatti's smiling face blotted out all else.

"You see," he had said, "a pragmatic problem demands pragmatic solutions. You must realize we have your best interests at heart."

Quitters, Inc., according to Donatti, was a sort of foundation—a nonprofit organization begun by the man in the wall portrait. The gentleman had been extremely successful in several family businesses—including slot machines, massage parlors, numbers, and a brisk (although clandestine) trade between New York and Turkey. Mort "Three-Fingers" Minelli had been a heavy smoker—up in the three-pack-a-day range. The paper he was holding in the picture was a doctor's diagnosis: lung cancer. Mort had died in 1970, after endowing Quitters, Inc., with family funds.

"We try to keep as close to breaking even as possible," Donatti had said. "But we're more interested in helping our fellow man. And of course, it's a great tax angle."

The treatment was chillingly simple. A first offense and Cindy would be brought to what Donatti called "the rabbit room." A second offense, and Morrison would get the dose. On a third offense, both of them would be brought in together. A fourth offense would show grave cooperation problems and would require sterner measures. An operative would be sent to Alvin's school to work the boy over.

"Imagine," Donatti said, smiling, "how horrible it will be for the boy. He wouldn't understand it even if someone explained. He'll only know someone is hurting him because Daddy was bad. He'll be very frightened."

"You bastard," Morrison said helplessly. He felt close to tears. "You dirty, filthy bastard."

"Don't misunderstand," Donatti said. He was smiling sympathetically. "I'm sure it won't happen. Forty percent of our clients never have more than three falls from grace. Those are reassuring figures, aren't they?"

Morrison didn't find them reassuring. He found them terrifying.

"Of course, if you transgress a *fifth* time—"

"What do you mean?"

Donatti beamed. "The room for you and your wife, a second beating for your son, and a beating for your wife."

Morrison, driven beyond the point of rational consideration, lunged over the desk at Donatti. Donatti moved with amazing speed for a man who had apparently been completely relaxed. He shoved the chair backward and drove both of his feet over the desk and into Morrison's belly. Gagging and coughing, Morrison staggered backward.

"Sit down, Mr. Morrison," Donatti said benignly. "Let's talk this over like rational men."

When he could catch his breath, Morrison did as he was told. Nightmares had to end sometime, didn't they?

Quitters, Inc., Donatti had explained further, operated on a ten-step punishment scale. Steps six, seven, and eight consisted of further trips to the rabbit room (and increased voltage) and more serious beating. The ninth step would be the breaking of his son's arms.

"And the tenth?" Morrison asked, his mouth dry.

Donatti shook his head sadly. "Then we give up, Mr. Morrison. You become part of the unregenerate two percent."

"You really give up?"

"In a manner of speaking." He opened one of the desk drawers and laid a silenced .45 on the desk. He smiled into Morrison's eyes. "But even the unregenerate two percent never smoke again. We guarantee it."

The Friday Night Movie was *Bullitt,* one of Cindy's favorites, but after an hour of Morrison's mutterings and fidgetings, her concentration was broken.

"What's the matter with you?" she asked during station identification.

"Nothing . . . everything," he growled. "I'm giving up smoking."

She laughed. "Since when? Five minutes ago?"

"Since three o'clock this afternoon."

"You really haven't had a cigarette since then?"

"No," he said, and began to gnaw his thumbnail. It was ragged, down to the quick.

"That's wonderful! What ever made you decide to quit?"

"You," he said. "And . . . and Alvin."

Her eyes widened, and when the movie came back on, she didn't notice. Dick rarely mentioned their retarded son. She came over, looked at the empty ashtray by his right hand, and then into his eyes. "Are you really trying to quit, Dick?"

"Really." And if I go to the cops, he added mentally, the local goon squad will be around to rearrange your face, Cindy.

"I'm glad. Even if you don't make it, we both thank you for the thought, Dick."

"Oh, I think I'll make it," he said, thinking of the muddy, homicidal look that had come into Donatti's eyes when he kicked him in the stomach.

He slept badly that night, dozing in and out of sleep. Around three o'clock he woke up completely. His craving for a cigarette was like a low-grade fever. He went downstairs and to his study. The room was in the middle of the house. No windows. He slid open the top drawer of his desk and looked in, fascinated by the cigarette box. He looked around and licked his lips.

Constant supervision during the first month, Donatti had said. Eighteen hours a day during the next two—but he would never know *which* eighteen. During the fourth month, the month when most clients backslid, the "service" would return to twenty-four hours a day. Then twelve hours of broken surveillance each day for the rest of the year. After that? Random surveillance for the rest of the client's life. *For the rest of his life.*

"We may audit you every other month," Donatti said. "Or every other day. Or constantly for one week two years from now. The point is, *you won't know.* If you smoke, you'll be gambling with loaded dice. Are they watching? Are they picking up my wife or sending a man after my son right now? Beautiful, isn't it? And if you do sneak a smoke, it'll taste awful. It will taste like your son's blood."

But they couldn't be watching now, in the dead of night, in his own study. The house was grave-quiet.

He looked at the cigarettes in the box for almost two minutes, unable to tear his gaze away. Then he went to the study door, peered out into the empty hall, and went back to look at the cigarettes some more. A horrible picture came: his life stretching before him and not a cigarette to be found. How in the name of God was he ever going to be able to make another tough presentation to a wary client, without that cigarette burning nonchalantly between his fingers as he approached the charts and layouts? How would he be able to endure Cindy's endless garden shows without a cigarette? How could he even get up in the morning and face the day without a cigarette to smoke as he drank his coffee and read the paper?

He cursed himself for getting into this. He cursed Donatti. And most of all, he cursed Jimmy McCann. How could he have done it? The son of a bitch had *known*. His hands trembled in their desire to get hold of Jimmy Judas McCann.

Stealthily, he glanced around the study again. He reached into the drawer and brought out a cigarette. He caressed it, fondled it. What was the old slogan? *So round, so firm, so fully packed.* Truer words had never been spoken. He put the cigarette in his mouth and then paused, cocking his head.

Had there been the slightest noise from the closet? A faint shifting? Surely not. But—

Another mental image—that rabbit hopping crazily in the grip of electricity. The thought of Cindy in that room—

He listened desperately and heard nothing. He told himself that all he had to do was to go to the closet door and yank it open. But he was too afraid of what he might find. He went back to bed but didn't sleep for a long time.

In spite of how lousy he felt in the morning, breakfast tasted good. After a moment's hesitation, he followed his customary bowl of cornflakes with scrambled eggs. He was grumpily washing out the pan when Cindy came downstairs in her robe.

"Richard Morrison! You haven't eaten an egg for breakfast since Hector was a pup."

Morrison grunted. He considered *since Hector was a pup* to be one of Cindy's stupider sayings, on a par with *I should smile and kiss a pig.*

"Have you smoked yet?" she asked, pouring orange juice.

"No."

"You'll be back on them by noon," she proclaimed airily.

"Lot of goddamn help you are!" he rasped, rounding on her. "You and anyone else who doesn't smoke, you all think . . . ah, never mind."

He expected her to be angry, but she was looking at him with something like wonder. "You're really serious," she said. "You really are."

"You bet I am." *You'll never know* how *serious. I hope.*

"Poor baby," she said, going to him. "You look like death warmed over. But I'm very proud."

Morrison held her tightly.

Scenes from the life of Richard Morrison, October-November:

Morrison and a crony from Larkin Studios at Jack Dempsey's bar. Crony offers a cigarette. Morrison grips his glass a little more tightly and says: *I'm quitting.* Crony laughs and says: *I give you a week.*

Morrison waiting for the morning train, looking over the top of the *Times* at a young man in a blue suit. He sees the young man almost every morning now, and sometimes at other places. At Onde's, where he is meeting a client. Looking at 45s in

Sam Goody's, where Morrison is looking for a Sam Cooke album. Once in a foursome behind Morrison's group at the local golf course.

Morrison getting drunk at a party, wanting a cigarette—but not quite drunk enough to take one.

Morrison visiting his son, bringing him a large ball that squeaked when you squeezed it. His son's slobbering, delighted kiss. Somehow not as repulsive as before. Hugging his son tightly, realizing what Donatti and his colleagues had so cynically realized before him: love is the most pernicious drug of all. Let the romantics debate its existence. Pragmatists accept it and use it.

Morrison losing the physical compulsion to smoke little by little, but never quite losing the psychological craving, or the need to have something in his mouth—cough drops, Life Savers, a toothpick. Poor substitutes, all of them.

And finally, Morrison hung up in a colossal traffic jam in the Midtown Tunnel. Darkness. Horns blaring. Air stinking. Traffic hopelessly snarled. And suddenly, thumbing open the glove compartment and seeing the half-open pack of cigarettes in there. He looked at them for a moment, then snatched one and lit it with the dashboard lighter. If anything happens, it's Cindy's fault, he told himself defiantly. I told her to get rid of all the damn cigarettes.

The first drag made him cough smoke out furiously. The second made his eyes water. The third made him feel lightheaded and swoony. It tastes awful, he thought.

And on the heels of that: My God, what am I doing?

Horns blatted impatiently behind him. Ahead, the traffic had begun to move again. He stubbed the cigarette out in the ashtray, opened both front windows, opened the vents, and then fanned the air helplessly like a kid who had just flushed his first butt down the john.

He joined the traffic flow jerkily and drove home.

"Cindy?" he called. "I'm home."

No answer.

"Cindy? Where are you, hon?"

The phone rang, and he pounced on it. "Hello? Cindy?"

"Hello, Mr. Morrison," Donatti said. He sounded pleasantly brisk and businesslike. "It seems we have a small business matter to attend to. Would five o'clock be convenient?"

"Have you got my wife?"

"Yes, indeed." Donatti chuckled indulgently.

"Look, let her go," Morrison babbled. "It won't happen again. It was a slip, just a slip, that's all. I only had three drags and for God's sake *it didn't even taste good!*"

"That's a shame. I'll count on you for five then, shall I?"

"Please," Morrison said, close to tears. "Please—"

He was speaking to a dead line.

At 5 P.M. the reception room was empty except for the secretary, who gave him a twinkly smile that ignored Morrison's pallor and disheveled appearance. "Mr. Donatti?" she said into the intercom. "Mr. Morrison to see you." She nodded to Morrison. "Go right in."

Donatti was waiting outside the unmarked room with a man who was wearing a SMILE sweatshirt and carrying a .38. He was built like an ape.

"Listen," Morrison said to Donatti. "We can work something out, can't we? I'll pay you. I'll—"

"Shaddap," the man in the SMILE sweatshirt said.

"It's good to see you," Donatti said. "Sorry it has to be under such adverse circumstances. Will you come with me? We'll make this as brief as possible. I can assure you your wife won't be hurt . . . this time."

Morrison tensed himself to leap at Donatti.

"Come, come," Donatti said, looking annoyed. "If you do that, Junk here is going to pistol-whip you and your wife is still going to get it. Now where's the percentage in that?"

"I hope you rot in hell," he told Donatti.

Donatti sighed. "If I had a nickel for every time someone expressed a similar sentiment, I could retire. Let it be a lesson to you, Mr. Morrison. When a romantic tries to do a good thing and fails they give him a medal. When a pragmatist succeeds, they wish him in hell. Shall we go?"

Junk motioned with the pistol.

Morrison preceded them into the room. He felt numb. The small green curtain had been pulled. Junk prodded him with the gun. This is what being a witness at the gas chamber must have been like, he thought.

He looked in. Cindy was there, looking around bewilderedly.

"Cindy!" Morrison called miserably. "Cindy, they—"

"She can't hear or see you," Donatti said. "One-way glass. Well, let's get it over with. It really was a very small slip. I believe thirty seconds should be enough. Junk?"

Junk pressed the button with one hand and kept the pistol jammed firmly into Morrison's back with the other.

It was the longest thirty seconds of his life.

When it was over, Donatti put a hand on Morrison's shoulder and said, "Are you going to throw up?"

"No," Morrison said weakly. His forehead was against the glass. His legs were jelly. "I don't think so." He turned around and saw that Junk was gone.

"Come with me," Donatti said.

"Where?" Morrison asked apathetically.

"I think you have a few things to explain, don't you?"

"How can I face her? How can I tell her that I . . . I . . ."

"I think you're going to be surprised," Donatti said.

The room was empty except for a sofa. Cindy was on it, sobbing helplessly.

"Cindy?" he said gently.

She looked up, her eyes magnified by tears. "Dick?" she whispered. "Dick? Oh . . . Oh God . . ." He held her tightly. "Two men," she said against his chest. "In the house and at first I thought they were burglars and then I thought they were going to rape me and then they took me someplace with a blindfold over my eyes and . . . and . . . oh it was *h-horrible*—"

"Shhh," he said. "Shhh."

"But why?" she asked, looking up at him. "Why would they—"

"Because of me," he said. "I have to tell you a story, Cindy—"

When he had finished he was silent a moment and then said, "I suppose you hate me. I wouldn't blame you."

He was looking at the floor, and she took his face in both hands and turned it to hers. "No," she said. "I don't hate you."

He looked at her in mute surprise.

"It was worth it," she said. "God bless these people. They've let you out of prison."

"Do you mean that?"

"Yes," she said, and kissed him. "Can we go home now? I feel much better. Ever so much."

The phone rang one evening a week later, and when Morrison recognized Donatti's voice, he said, "Your boys have got it wrong. I haven't even been near a cigarette."

"We know that. We have a final matter to talk over. Can you stop by tomorrow afternoon?"

"Is it—"

"No, nothing serious. Bookkeeping really. By the way, congratulations on your promotion."

"How did you know about that?"

"We're keeping tabs," Donatti said noncommittally, and hung up.

When they entered the small room, Donatti said, "Don't look so nervous. No one's going to bite you. Step over here, please."

Morrison saw an ordinary bathroom scale. "Listen, I've gained a little weight, but—"

"Yes, seventy-three percent of our clients do. Step up, please."

Morrison did, and tipped the scales at one-seventy-four.

"Okay, fine. You can step off. How tall are you, Mr. Morrison?"

"Five-eleven."

"Okay, let's see." He pulled a small card laminated in plastic from his breast pocket. "Well, that's not too bad. I'm going to write you a prescrip for some highly illegal diet pills. Use them sparingly and according to directions. And I'm going to set your maximum weight at . . . let's see . . ." He consulted the card again. "One eighty-two, how does that sound? And since this is December first, I'll expect you the first of every month for a weigh-in. No problem if you can't make it, as long as you call in advance."

"And what happens if I go over one-eighty-two?"

Donatti smiled. "We'll send someone out to your house to cut off your wife's little finger," he said. "You can leave through this door, Mr. Morrison. Have a nice day."

Eight months later:

Morrison runs into the crony from the Larkin Studios at Dempsey's bar. Morrison is down to what Cindy proudly calls his fighting weight: one-sixty-seven. He works out three times a week and looks as fit as whipcord. The crony from Larkin, by comparison, looks like something the cat dragged in.

Crony: Lord, how'd you ever stop? I'm locked into this damn habit tighter than Tillie. The crony stubs his cigarette out with real revulsion and drains his scotch.

Morrison looks at him speculatively and then takes a small white business card out of his wallet. He puts it on the bar between them. You know, he says, these guys changed my life.

Twelve months later:

Morrison receives a bill in the mail. The bill says:

QUITTERS, INC.

237 East 46th Street
New York, N.Y. 10017

1 Treatment	$ 2500.00
Counselor (Victor Donatti)	$ 2500.00
Electricity	$ .50
total (Please pay this amount)	$ 5000.50

Those sons of bitches! he explodes. They charged me for the electricity they used to . . . to . . .

Just pay it, she says, and kisses him.

Twenty months later:

Quite by accident, Morrison and his wife meet the Jimmy McCanns at the Helen Hayes Theatre. Introductions are made all around. Jimmy looks as good, if not better, than he did on that day in the airport terminal so long ago. Morrison has never met his wife. She is pretty in the radiant way plain girls sometimes have when they are very, very happy.

She offers her hand and Morrison shakes it. There is something odd about her grip, and halfway through the second act, he realizes what it was. The little finger on her right hand is missing.

HORN MAN

CLARK HOWARD
(1934–   )

Although best-known for his true crime books, notably the Edgar-nominated Six Against the Rock, *about Alcatraz, and* Zebra, *also nominated, which examined the infamous San Francisco murders of the early 1970s, Howard has developed a great following for his short stories, four of which have been nominated for Edgar Allan Poe Awards by the Mystery Writers of America; the following story was picked as the best of the year for 1980.*

HEN DIX STEPPED OFF THE Greyhound bus in New Orleans, old Rainey was waiting for him near the terminal entrance. He looked just the same as Dix remembered him. Old Rainey had always looked old, since Dix had known him, ever since Dix had been a little boy. He had skin like black saddle leather and patches of cotton-white hair, and his shoulders were round and stooped. When he was contemplating something, he chewed on the inside of his cheeks, pushing his pursed lips in and out as if he were revving up for speech. He was doing that when Dix walked up to him.

"Hey, Rainey."

Rainey blinked surprise and then his face split into a wide smile of perfect, gleaming teeth. "Well, now. Well, well, well, now." He looked Dix up and down. "They give you that there suit of clothes?"

Dix nodded. "Everyone gets a suit of clothes if they done more than a year." Dix's eyes, the lightest blue possible without being gray, hardened just enough for Rainey to notice. "And I sure done more than a year," he added.

"That's the truth," Rainey said. He kept the smile on his face and changed the subject as quickly as possible. "I got you a room in the Quarter. Figured that's where you'd want to stay."

Dix shrugged. "It don't matter no more."

"It will," Rainey said with the confidence of years. "It will when you hear the music again."

Dix did not argue the point. He was confident that none of it mattered. Not the music, not the French Quarter, none of it. Only one thing mattered to Dix.

"Where is she, Rainey?" he asked. "Where's Madge?"

"I don't rightly know," Rainey said.

Dix studied him for a moment. He was sure Rainey was lying. But it didn't matter. There were others who would tell him.

They walked out of the terminal, the stooped old black man and the tall, prison-hard white man with a set to his mouth and a canvas zip-bag containing all his worldly possessions. It was late afternoon: the sun was almost gone and the evening coolness was coming in. They walked toward the Quarter, Dix keeping his long-legged pace slow to accommodate old Rainey.

Rainey glanced at Dix several times as they walked, chewing inside his mouth and working up to something. Finally he said, "You been playing at all while you was in?"

Dix shook his head. "Not for a long time. I did a little the first year. Used to dry play, just with my mouthpiece. After a while, though, I gave it up. They got a different kind of music over there in Texas. Stompin' music. Not my style." Dix forced a grin at old Rainey. "I ever kill a man again, I'll be sure I'm on *this* side of the Louisiana line."

Rainey scowled. "You know you ain't never killed nobody, boy," he said harshly. "You know it wudn't you that done it. It was *her*."

Dix stopped walking and locked eyes with old Rainey. "How long have you knowed me?" he asked.

"Since you was eight months old," Rainey said. "You know that. Me and my sistuh, we worked for your grandmamma, Miz Jessie DuChatelier. She had the finest gentlemen's house in the Quarter. Me and my sistuh, we cleaned and cooked for Miz Jessie. And took care of you after your own poor mamma took sick with the consumption and died—"

"Anyway, you've knowed me since I was less than one, and now I'm *forty*-one."

Rainey's eyes widened. "Naw," he said, grinning again, "you ain't that old. Naw."

"Forty-one, Rainey. I been gone sixteen years. I got twenty-five, remember? And I done sixteen."

Sudden worry erased Rainey's grin. "Well, if you forty-one how old that make *me*?"

"About two hundred. I don't know. You must be seventy or eighty. Anyway, listen to me now. In all the time you've knowed me, have I ever let anybody make a fool out of me?"

Rainey shook his head. "Never. No way."

"That's right. And I'm not about to start now. But if word got around that I done sixteen years for a killing that was somebody else's, I'd look like the biggest fool that ever walked the levee, wouldn't I?"

"I reckon so," Rainey allowed.

"Then don't ever say again that I didn't do it. Only one person alive knows for certain positive that I didn't do it. And I'll attend to her myself. Understand?"

Rainey chewed the inside of his cheeks for a moment, then asked, "What you fixin' to do about her?"

Dix's light-blue eyes hardened again. "Whatever I have to do, Rainey," he replied.

Rainey shook his head in slow motion. "Lord, Lord, Lord," he whispered.

Old Rainey went to see Gaston that evening at Tradition Hall, the jazz emporium and restaurant that Gaston owned in the Quarter. Gaston was slick and dapper. For him, time had stopped in 1938. He still wore spats.

"How does he look?" Gaston asked old Rainey.

"He *look* good," Rainey said. "He *talk* bad." Rainey leaned close to the white club-owner. "He fixin' to kill that woman. Sure as God made sundown."

Gaston stuck a sterling-silver toothpick in his mouth. "He know where she is?"

"I don't think so," said Rainey. "Not yet."

"*You* know where she is?"

"Latest I heard, she was living over on Burgundy Street with some doper."

Gaston nodded his immaculately shaved and lotioned chin. "Correct. The doper's name is LeBeau. He's young. I think he keeps her around to take care of him when he's sick." Gaston examined his beautifully manicured nails. "Does Dix have a lip?"

Rainey shook his head. "He said he ain't played in a while. But a natural like him, he can get his lip back in no time a'tall."

"Maybe," said Gaston.

"He can," Rainey insisted.

"Has he got a horn?"

"Naw. I watched him unpack his bag and I didn't see no horn. So I axed him about it. He said after a few years of not playing, he just give it away. To some cowboy he was in the Texas pen with."

Gaston sighed. "He should have killed that fellow on this side of the state line. If he'd done the killing in Louisiana, he would have went to the pen at Angola. They play good jazz at Angola. Eddie Lumm is up there. You remember Eddie Lumm? Clarinetist. Learned to play from Frank Teschemacher and Jimmie Noone. Eddie killed his old lady. So now he blows at Angola. They play good jazz at Angola."

Rainey didn't say anything. He wasn't sure if Gaston thought Dix had really done the killing or not. Sometimes Gaston *played* like he didn't know a thing, just to see if somebody *else* knew it. Gaston was smart. Smart enough to help keep Dix out of trouble if he was a mind. Which was what old Rainey was hoping for.

Gaston drummed his fingertips silently on the table where they sat. "So. You think Dix can get his lip back with no problem, is that right?"

"Tha's right. He can."

"He's planning to come around and see me?"

"I don't know. He probably set on finding that woman first. Then he might not be *able* to come see you."

"Well, see if you can get him to come see me first. Tell him I've got something for him. Something I've been saving for him. Will you do that?"

"You bet." Rainey got up from the table. "I'll go do it right now."

George Tennell was big and beefy and mean. Rumor had it that he had once killed two men by smashing their heads together with such force that he literally knocked their brains out. He had been a policeman for thirty years, first in the colored section, which was the only place he could work in the old days, and now in the *Vieux Carré,* the Quarter, where he was detailed to keep the peace to whatever extent it was possible. He had no family, claimed no friends. The Quarter was his home as well as his job. The only thing in the world he admitted to loving was jazz.

That was why, every night at seven, he sat at a small corner table in Tradition Hall and ate dinner while he listened to the band tune their instruments and warm up. Most nights, Gaston joined him later for a liqueur. Tonight he joined him before dinner.

"Dix got back today," he told the policeman. "Remember Dix?"

Tennell nodded. "Horn man. Killed a fellow in a motel room just across the Texas line. Over a woman named Madge Noble."

"That's the one. Only there's some around don't think he did it. There's some around think *she* did it."

"Too bad he couldn't have found twelve of those people for his jury."

"He didn't have no jury, George. Quit laying back on me. You remember it as well as I do. One thing you'd *never* forget is a good horn man."

Tennell's jaw shifted to the right a quarter of an inch, making his mouth go crooked. The band members were coming out of the back now and moving around on the bandstand, unsnapping instrument cases, inserting mouthpieces, straightening chairs. They were a mixed lot—black, white, and combinations; clean-shaven and goateed; balding and not; clear-eyed and strung out. None of them was under fifty— the oldest was the trumpet player, Luther Dodd, who was eighty-six. Like Louis Armstrong, he had learned to blow at the elbow of Joe "King" Oliver, the great cornetist. His Creole-style trumpet playing was unmatched in New Orleans. Watching him near the age when he would surely die was agony for the jazz purists who frequented Tradition Hall.

Gaston studied George Tennell as the policeman watched Luther Dodd blow out the spit plug of his gleaming Balfour trumpet and loosen up his stick-brittle fingers on the valves. Gaston saw in Tennell's eyes that odd look of a man who truly worshipped traditional jazz music, who felt it down to the pit of himself just like the old men who played it, but who had never learned to play himself. It was a look that had the mix of love and sadness and years gone by. It was the only look that ever turned Tennell's eyes soft.

"You know how long I been looking for a horn man to take Luther's place?" Gaston asked. "A straight year. I've listened to a couple dozen guys from all over. Not a one of them could play traditional. Not a one." He bobbed his chin at Luther Dodd. "His fingers are like old wood, and so's his heart. He could go on me any night. And if he does, I'll have to shut down. Without a horn man, there's no Creole sound, no tradition at all. Without a horn, this place of mine, which is the last of the great jazz emporiums, will just give way to"—Gaston shrugged helplessly, "—whatever. Disco music, I suppose."

A shudder circuited George Tennell's spine, but he gave no outward sign of it. His body was absolutely still, his hands resting motionlessly on the snow-white tablecloth, eyes steadily fixed on Luther Dodd. Momentarily the band went into its first number, *Lafayette,* played Kansas City style after the way of Bennie Moten. The music pulsed out like spurts of water, each burst overlapping the one before it to create an even wave of sound that flooded the big room. Because Kansas City style was so rhythmic and highly danceable, some of the early diners immediately moved onto the dance floor and fell in with the music.

Ordinarily, Tennell liked to watch people dance while he ate; the moving bodies lent emphasis to the music he loved so much, music he had first heard from the window of the St. Pierre Colored Orphanage on Decatur Street when he had been a boy; music he had grown up with and would have made his life a part of if he had not been so completely talentless, so inept that he could not even read sharps and flats. But tonight he paid no attention to the couples out in front of the bandstand. He concentrated only on Luther Dodd and the old horn man's breath intake as he played. It was clear to Tennell that Luther was struggling for breath, fighting for every note he blew, utilizing every cubic inch of lung power that his old body could marshal.

After watching Luther all the way through *Lafayette,* and halfway through *Davenport Blues,* Tennell looked across the table at Gaston and nodded.

"All right," he said simply. "All right."

For the first time ever Tennell left the club without eating dinner.

As Dix walked along with old Rainey toward Gaston's club, Rainey kept pointing out places to him that he had not exactly forgotten, but had not remembered in a long time.

"That house there," Rainey said, "was where Paul Mares was born back in nineteen-and-oh-one. He's the one formed the original New Orleans Rhythm Kings. He only lived to be forty-eight but he was one of the best horn men of all time."

Dix would remember, not necessarily the person himself but the house and the story of the person and how good he was. He had grown up on those stories, gone to sleep by them as a boy, lived the lives of the men in them many times over as he himself was being taught to blow trumpet by Rozell "The Lip" Page when Page was already past sixty and he, Dix was only eight. Later, when Page died, Dix's education was taken over by Shepherd Norden and Blue Johnny Meadows, the two alternating as his teacher between their respective road tours. With Page, Norden, and Meadows in his background, it was no wonder that Dix could blow traditional.

"Right up the street there," Rainey said as they walked, "is where Wingy Manone was born in nineteen-and-oh-four. His given name was Joseph, but after his accident ever'body taken to calling him 'Wingy.' The accident was, he fell under a street car and lost his right arm. But that boy didn't let a little thing like that worry him none, no sir. He learned to play trumpet *left-handed,* and *one-handed.* And he was *good.* Lord, he was good."

They walked along Dauphin and Chartres and Royal. All around them were the French architecture and grillework and statuary and vines and moss that made the *Vieux Carré* a world unto itself, a place of subtle sights, sounds, and smells—black and white and fish and age—that no New Orleans tourist, no Superdome visitor, no casual observer, could ever experience, because to experience was to understand, and understanding of the Quarter could not be acquired, it had to be lived.

"Tommy Ladnier, he use to live right over there," Rainey said, "right up on the second floor. He lived there when he came here from his hometown of Mandeville, Loozey-ana. Poor Tommy, he had a short life too, only thirty-nine years. But it was a good life. He played with King Oliver and Fletcher Henderson and Sidney Bechet. Yessir, he got in some good licks."

When they got close enough to Tradition Hall to hear the music, at first faintly, then louder, clearer, Rainey stopped talking. He wanted Dix to hear the music, to *feel* the sound of it as it wafted out over Pirate's Alley and the Café du Monde and Congo Square (they called it Beauregard Square now, but Rainey refused to recognize the new name). Instinctively, Rainey knew that it was important for the music to get back into Dix, to saturate his mind and catch in his chest and tickle his stomach. There were some things in Dix that needed to be washed out, some bad things, and Rainey was certain that the music would help. A good purge was always healthy.

Rainey was grateful, as they got near enough to define melody, that *Sweet Georgia Brown* was being played. It was a good melody to come home to.

They walked on, listening, and after a while Dix asked, "Who's on horn?"

"Luther Dodd."

"Don't sound like Luther. What's the matter with him?"

Rainey waved one hand resignedly. "Old. Dying, I'spect."

They arrived at the Hall and went inside. Gaston met them with a smile. "Dix," he said, genuinely pleased, "it's good to see you." His eyes flicked over Dix. "The years have been good to you. Trim. Lean. No gray hair. How's your lip?"

"I don't have a lip no more, Mr. Gaston," said Dix. "Haven't had for years."

"But he can get it back quick enough," Rainey put in. "He gots a natural lip."

"I don't play no more, Mr. Gaston," Dix told the club owner.

"That's too bad," Gaston said. He bobbed his head toward the stairs. "Come with me. I want to show you something."

Dix and Rainey followed Gaston upstairs to his private office. The office was furnished the way Gaston dressed—old-style, roaring Twenties. There was even a wind-up Victrola in the corner.

Gaston worked the combination of a large, ornate floor vault and pulled its big-tiered door open. From somewhere in its dark recess he withdrew a battered trumpet case, one of the very old kind with heavy brass fittings on the corners and, one knew, real velvet, not felt, for a lining. Placing it gently in the center of his desk, Gaston carefully opened the snaplocks and lifted the top. Inside, indeed on real velvet, deep-purple real velvet, was a gleaming, silver, hand-etched trumpet. Dix and Rainey stared at it in unabashed awe.

"Know who it once belonged to?" Gaston asked.

Neither Dix nor Rainey replied. They were mesmerized by the instrument. Rainey had not seen one like it in fifty years. Dix had *never* seen one like it; he had only heard stories about the magnificent silver horns that the quadroons made of contraband silver carefully hidden away after the War Between the States. Because the silver cache had not, as it was supposed to, been given over to the Federal army as part of the reparations levied against the city, the quadroons, during the Union occupation, had to be very careful what they did with it. Selling it for value was out of the question. Using it for silver service, candlesticks, walking canes, or any other of the more obvious uses would have attracted the notice of a Union informer. But letting it lie dormant, even though it was safer as such, was intolerable to the quads, who refused to let a day go by without circumventing one law or another.

So they used the silver to plate trumpets and cornets and slide trombones that belonged to the tabernacle musicians who were just then beginning to experiment with the old *Sammsamounn* tribal music that would eventually mate with work songs and prison songs and gospels, and evolve into traditional blues, which would evolve into traditional, or Dixie-style, jazz.

"Look at the initials," Gaston said, pointing to the top of the bell. Dix and Rainey peered down at three initials etched in the silver: BRB.

"Lord have mercy," Rainey whispered. Dix's lips parted as if he too intended to speak, but no words sounded.

"That's right," Gaston said. "Blind Ray Blount. The first, the best, the *only*. Nobody has ever touched the sounds he created. That man hit notes nobody ever heard before—or since. He was the master."

"Amen," Rainey said. He nodded his head toward Dix. "Can he touch it?"

"Go ahead," Gaston said to Dix.

Like a pilgrim to Mecca touching the holy shroud, Dix ever so lightly placed the tips of three fingers on the silver horn. As he did, he imagined he could feel the touch left there by the hands of the amazing blind horn man who had started the great blues evolution in a patch of town that later became Storyville. He imagined that—

"It's yours if you want it," Gaston said. "All you have to do is pick it up and go downstairs and start blowing."

Dix wet his suddenly dry lips. "Tomorrow I—"

"Not tomorrow," Gaston said. "Tonight. Now."

"Take it boy," Rainey said urgently.

Dix frowned deeply, his eyes narrowing as if he felt physical pain. He swallowed, trying to push an image out of his mind; an image he had clung to for sixteen years. "I can't tonight—"

"Tonight or never," Gaston said firmly.

"For God's sake, boy, take it!" said old Rainey.

But Dix could not. The image of Madge would not let him.

Dix shook his head violently, as if to rid himself of devils, and hurried from the room.

Rainey ran after him and caught up with him a block from the Hall. "Don't do it," he pleaded. "Hear me now. I'm an old man and I know I ain't worth nothin' to nobody, but I'm begging you, boy, please, please, please don't do it. I ain't never axed you for nothing in my whole life, but I'm axing you for this: *please* don't do it."

"I got to," Dix said quietly. "It ain't that I want to; I *got* to."

"But why, boy? *Why?*"

"Because we made a promise to each other," Dix said. "That night in that Texas motel room, the man Madge was with told her he was going to marry her. He'd been telling her that for a long time. But he was already married and kept putting off leaving his wife. Finally Madge had enough of it. She asked me to come to her room between sets. I knew she was doing it to make him jealous, but it didn't matter none to me. I'd been crazy about her for so long that I'd do anything she asked me to, and she knew it.

"So between sets I slipped across the highway to where she had her room. But he was already there. I could hear through the transom that he was roughing her up some, but the door was locked and I couldn't get in. Then I heard a shot and everything got quiet. A minute later Madge opened the door and let me in. The man was laying across the bed dying. Madge started bawling and saying how they would put her in the pen and how she wouldn't be able to stand it, she'd go crazy and kill herself.

"It was then I asked her if she'd wait for me if I took the blame for her. She promised me she would. And I promised her I'd come back to her." Dix sighed quietly. "That's what I'm doing, Rainey—keeping my promise."

"And what going to happen if she ain't kept *hers*?" Rainey asked.

"Mamma Rulat asked me the same thing this afternoon when I asked her where Madge was at." Mamma Rulat was an octoroon fortuneteller who always knew where everyone in the Quarter lived.

"What did you tell her?"

"I told her I'd do what I had to do. That's all a man *can* do, Rainey."

Dix walked away, up a dark side street. Rainey, watching him go, shook his head in the anguish of the aged and helpless.

"Lord, Lord, Lord—"

The house on Burgundy Street had once been a grand mansion with thirty rooms and a tiled French courtyard with a marble fountain in its center. It had seen nobility and aristocracy and great generals come and go with elegant, genteel ladies on their arms. Now the thirty rooms were rented individually with hotplate burners for light cooking, and the only ladies who crossed the courtyard were those of the New Orleans night.

A red light was flashing atop a police car when Dix got there, and uniformed policemen were blocking the gate into the courtyard. There was a small curious crowd talking about what happened.

"A doper named LeBeau," someone said. "He's been shot."

"I heared it," an old man announced. "I heared the shot."

"There's where it happened, that window right up there—"

Dix looked up, but as he did another voice said, "They're bringing him out now!"

Two morgue attendants wheeled a sheet-covered gurney across the courtyard and lifted it into the back of a black panel truck. Several policemen, led by big beefy George Tennell, brought a woman out and escorted her to the car with the flashing red light. Dix squinted, focusing on her in the inadequate courtyard light. He frowned. Madge's mother, he thought, his mind going back two decades. What's Madge's mother got to do with this?

Then he remembered. Madge's mother was dead. She had died five years after he had gone to the pen.

Then who—?

Madge?

Yes, it *was* her. It was Madge. Older, as he was. Not a girl any more, as he was not a boy any more. For a moment he found it difficult to equate the woman in the courtyard with the memory in his mind. But it was Madge, all right.

Dix tried to push forward, to get past the gate into the courtyard, but two policemen held him back. George Tennell saw the altercation and came over.

"She's under arrest, mister," Tennell told Dix. "Can't nobody talk to her but a lawyer right now."

"What's she done anyhow?" Dix asked.

"Killed her boyfriend," said Tennell. "Shot him with this."

He showed Dix a pearl-handled over-and-under Derringer two-shot.

"Her boyfriend?"

Tennell nodded. "Young feller. 'Bout twenty-five. Neighbors say she was partial to young fellers. Some women are like that."

"Who says she shot him?"

"I do. I was in the building at the time, on another matter. I heard the shot. Matter of fact, I was the first one to reach the body. Few minutes later she come waltzing in. Oh, she put on a good act, all right, like she didn't even know what happened. But I found the gun in her purse myself."

By now the other officers had Madge Noble in the police car and were waiting for Tennell. He slipped the Derringer into his coat pocket and hitched up his trousers. Jutting his big jaw out an inch, he fixed Dix in a steady gaze.

"If she's a friend of yours, don't count on her being around for a spell. She'll do a long time for this."

Tennell walked away, leaving Dix still outside the gate. Dix waited there, watching, as the police car came through to the street. He tried to catch a glimpse of Madge as it passed, but there was not enough light in the back seat where they had her. As soon as the car left, the people who had gathered around began to leave too.

Soon Dix was the only one standing there.

At midnight, George Tennell was back at his usual table in Tradition Hall for the dinner he had missed earlier. Gaston came over and joined him. For a few minutes they sat in silence, watching Dix up on the bandstand. He was blowing the silver trumpet that had once belonged to Blind Ray Blount; sitting next to the aging Luther Dodd; jumping in whenever he could as they played *Tailspin Blues,* then *Tank Town Bump,* then *Everybody Loves My Baby.*

"Sounds like he'll be able to get his lip back pretty quick," Tennell observed.

"Sure," said Gaston. "He's a natural. Rozell Page was his first teacher, you know."

"No, I didn't know that."

"Sure." Gaston adjusted the celluloid collar he wore, and turned the diamond stickpin in his tie. "What about the woman?" he asked.

Tennell shrugged. "She'll get twenty years. Probably do ten or eleven."

Gaston thought for a moment, then said, "That should be time enough. After ten or eleven years nothing will matter to him except the music. Don't you think?"

"It won't even take that long," Tennell guessed. "Not for him."

Up on the bandstand the men who played traditional went into *Just a Closer Walk with Thee*.

And sitting on the sawdust floor behind the bandstand, old Rainey listened with happy tears in his eyes.

THE NEW GIRL FRIEND

RUTH RENDELL
(1930–   )

Perhaps the most distinguished mystery writer working today, Rendell was given the Grand Master Award for lifetime achievement by the Mystery Writers of America. Her versatility has produced brilliant short stories as well as some of the greatest psychological suspense novels ever written, both under her own name and as Barbara Vine. Her series character, Inspector Reg Wexford, is beloved and fascinating for his interaction with his family on the one hand and his associate Mike Burden on the other. The following story won an Edgar as the best of 1983.

OU KNOW WHAT WE DID LAST time?' he said.

She had waited for this for weeks. 'Yes?'

'I wondered if you'd like to do it again.'

She longed to but she didn't want to sound too keen. 'Why not?'

'How about Friday afternoon, then? I've got the day off and Angie always goes to her sister's on Friday.'

'Not *always*, David.' She giggled.

He also laughed a little. 'She will this week. Do you think we could use your car? Angie'll take ours.'

'Of course. I'll come for you about two, shall I?'

'I'll open the garage doors and you can drive straight in. Oh, and Chris, could you fix it to get back a bit later? I'd love it if we could have the whole evening together.'

'I'll try,' she said, and then, 'I'm sure I can fix it. I'll tell Graham I'm going out with my new girl friend.'

He said goodbye and that he would see her on Friday. Christine put the receiver back. She had almost given up expecting a call from him. But there must have been a grain of hope still, for she had never left the receiver off the way she used to.

The last time she had done that was on a Thursday three weeks before, the day she had gone round to Angie's and found David there alone. Christine had got into the habit of taking the phone off the hook during the middle part of the day to avoid getting calls for the Midland Bank. Her number and the Midland Bank's differed by only one digit. Most days she took the receiver off at nine-thirty and put it back at three-thirty. On Thursday afternoons she nearly always went round to see Angie and never bothered to phone first.

Christine knew Angie's husband quite well. If she stayed a bit later on Thursdays she saw him when he came home from work. Sometimes she and Graham and Angie and David went out together as a foursome. She knew that David, like Graham, was a salesman or sales executive, as Graham always described himself, and she guessed from her friend's life style that David was rather more successful at it. She had never found him particularly attractive, for, although he was quite tall, he had something of a girlish look and very fair wavy hair.

Graham was a heavily built, very dark man with a swarthy skin. He had to shave twice a day. Christine had started going out with him when she was fifteen and they had got married on her eighteenth birthday. She had never really known any other men at all intimately and now if she ever found herself alone with a man she felt awkward and apprehensive. The truth was that she was afraid a man might make an advance to her and the thought of that frightened her very much. For a long while she carried a penknife in her handbag in case she should need to defend herself. One evening, after they had been out with a colleague of Graham's and had had a few drinks, she told Graham about this fear of hers.

He said she was silly but he seemed rather pleased.

'When you went off to talk to those people and I was left with John I felt like that. I felt terribly nervous. I didn't know how to talk to him.'

Graham roared with laughter. 'You don't mean you thought old John was going to make a pass at you in the middle of a crowded restaurant?'

'I don't know,' Christine said. 'I never know what they'll do.'

'So long as you're not afraid of what I'll do,' said Graham, beginning to kiss her, 'that's all that matters.' There was no point in telling him now, ten years too late, that she was afraid of what he did and always had been. Of course she had got used to it, she wasn't actually terrified, she was resigned and sometimes even quite cheerful about it. David was the only man she had ever been alone with when it felt all right.

That first time, that Thursday when Angie had gone to her sister's and hadn't been able to get through on the phone and tell Christine not to come, that time it had been fine. And afterwards she had felt happy and carefree, though what had happened with David took on the colouring of a dream next day. It wasn't really believable. Early on he had said: 'Will you tell Angie?'

'Not if you don't want me to.'

'I think it would upset her, Chris. It might even wreck our marriage. You see . . .' He had hesitated. 'You see, that was the first time I—I mean, anyone ever . . .' And he had looked into her eyes. 'Thank God it was you.'

The following Thursday she had gone round to see Angie as usual. In the meantime there had been no word from David. She stayed late in order to see him, beginning to feel a little sick with apprehension, her heart beating hard when he came in.

He looked quite different from how he had when she had found him sitting at the table reading, the radio on. He was wearing a grey flannel suit and a grey striped tie. When Angie went out of the room and for a minute she was alone with him, she felt a flicker of that old wariness that was the forerunner of her fear. He was getting her a drink. She looked up and met his eyes and it was all right again. He gave her a conspiratorial smile, laying a finger on his lips.

'I'll give you a ring,' he had whispered.

She had to wait two more weeks. During that time she went twice to Angie's and twice Angie came to her. She and Graham and Angie and David went out as a foursome and while Graham was fetching drinks and Angie was in the Ladies, David looked at her and smiled and lightly touched her foot with his foot under the table.

'I'll phone you. I haven't forgotten.'

It was a Wednesday when he finally did phone. Next day Christine told Graham she had made a new friend, a girl she had met at work. She would be going out somewhere with this new friend on Friday and she wouldn't be back till eleven. She was desperately afraid he would want the car—it was *his* car or his firm's—but it so happened he would be in the office that day and would go by train. Telling him these lies didn't make her feel guilty. It wasn't as if this were some sordid affair, it was quite different.

When Friday came she dressed with great care. Normally, to go round to Angie's, she would have worn jeans and a tee shirt with a sweater over it. That was what she had on the first time she found herself alone with David. She put on a skirt and blouse and her black velvet jacket. She took the heated rollers out of her hair and brushed it into curls down on her shoulders. There was never much money to spend on clothes. The mortgage on the house took up a third of what Graham earned and half what she earned at her part-time job. But she could run to a pair of sheer black tights to go with the highest heeled shoes she'd got, her black pumps.

The doors of Angie and David's garage were wide open and their car was gone. Christine turned into their driveway, drove into the garage and closed the doors behind her. A door at the back of the garage led into the yard and garden. The kitchen door was unlocked as it had been that Thursday three weeks before and always was on Thursday afternoons. She opened the door and walked in.

'Is that you, Chris?'

The voice sounded very male. She needed to be reassured by the sight of him. She went into the hall as he came down the stairs.

'You look lovely,' he said.

'So do you.'

He was wearing a suit. It was of navy silk with a pattern of pink and white flowers. The skirt was very short, the jacket clinched into his waist with a navy patent belt. The long golden hair fell to his shoulders, he was heavily made-up and this time he had painted his fingernails. He looked far more beautiful than he had that first time.

Then, three weeks before, the sound of her entry drowned in loud music from the radio, she had come upon this girl sitting at the table reading *Vogue*. For a moment she had thought it must be David's sister. She had forgotten Angie had said David was an only child. The girl had long fair hair and was wearing a red summer dress with white spots on it, white sandals and around her neck a string of white beads. When Christine saw that it was not a girl but David himself she didn't know what to do.

He stared at her in silence and without moving and then he switched off the radio. Christine said the silliest and least relevant thing.

'What are you doing home at this time?'

That made him smile. 'I'd finished so I took the rest of the day off. I should have locked the back door. Now you're here you may as well sit down.'

She sat down. She couldn't take her eyes off him. He didn't look like a man dressed up as a girl, he looked like a girl and a much prettier one than she or Angie. 'Does Angie know?'

He shook his head.

'But why do you do it?' she burst out and she looked about the room, Angie's small, rather untidy living room, at the radio, the *Vogue* magazine. 'What do you get out of it?' Something came back to her from an article she had read. 'Did your mother dress you as a girl when you were little?'

'I don't know,' he said. 'Maybe. I don't remember. I don't want to *be* a girl. I just want to dress up as one sometimes.'

The first shock of it was past and she began to feel easier with him. It wasn't as if there was anything grotesque about the way he looked. The very last thing he reminded her of was one of those female impersonators. A curious thought came into her head, that it was *nicer,* somehow more civilized, to be a woman and that if only all men were more like women . . . That was silly, of course, it couldn't be.

'And it's enough for you just to dress up and be here on your own?'

He was silent for a moment. Then, 'Since you ask, what I'd really like would be to go out like this and . . .' He paused, looking at her, 'and be seen by lots of people, that's what I'd like. I've never had the nerve for that.'

The bold idea expressed itself without her having to give it a moment's thought. She wanted to do it. She was beginning to tremble with excitement.

'Let's go out then, you and I. Let's go out now. I'll put my car in your garage and you can get into it so the people next door don't see and then we'll go somewhere. Let's do that, David, shall we?'

She wondered afterwards why she had enjoyed it so much. What had it been, after all, as far as anyone else knew but two girls walking on Hampstead Heath? If Angie had suggested that the two of them do it she would have thought it a poor way of spending the afternoon. But with David . . . She hadn't even minded that of the two of them he was infinitely the better dressed, taller, better-looking, more graceful. She didn't mind now as he came down the stairs and stood in front of her.

'Where shall we go?'

'Not the Heath this time,' he said. 'Let's go shopping.' He bought a blouse in one of the big stores. Christine went into the changing room with him when he tried it on. They walked about in Hyde Park. Later on they had dinner and Christine noted that they were the only two women in the restaurant dining together.

'I'm grateful to you,' David said. He put his hand over hers on the table.

'I enjoy it,' she said. 'It's so—crazy. I really love it. You'd better not do that, had you? There's a man over there giving us a funny look.'

'Women hold hands,' he said.

'Only *those* sort of women. David, we could do this every Friday you don't have to work.'

'Why not?' he said.

There was nothing to feel guilty about. She wasn't harming Angie and she wasn't being disloyal to Graham. All she was doing was going on innocent outings with another girl. Graham wasn't interested in her new friend, he didn't even ask her name. Christine came to long for Fridays, especially for the moment when she let herself into Angie's house and saw David coming down the stairs and for the moment when they stepped of the car in some public place and the first eyes turned on him. They went to Holland Park, they went to the zoo, to Kew Gardens. They went to the cinema and a man sitting next to David put his hand on his knee. David loved that, it was a triumph for him, but Christine whispered they must change their seats and they did.

When they parted at the end of an evening he kissed her gently on the lips. He smelled of Alliage or Je Reviens or Opium. During the afternoon they usually went into one of the big stores and sprayed themselves out of the tester bottles.

Angie's mother lived in the north of England. When she had to convalesce after an operation Angie went up there to look after her. She expected to be away two weeks and the second weekend of her absence Graham had to go to Brussels with the sales manager.

'We could go away somewhere for the weekend,' David said.

'Graham's sure to phone,' Christine said.

'One night then. Just for the Saturday night. You can tell him you're going out with your new girl friend and you're going to be late.'

'All right.'

It worried her that she had no nice clothes to wear. David had a small but exquisite wardrobe of suits and dresses, shoes and scarves and beautiful underclothes. He kept them in a cupboard in his office to which only he had a key and he secreted items home and back again in his briefcase. Christine hated the idea of going away for the night in her grey flannel skirt and white silk blouse and that velvet jacket while David wore his Zandra Rhodes dress. In a burst of recklessness she spent all of two weeks' wages on a linen suit.

They went in David's car. He had made the arrangements and Christine had expected that they would be going to a motel twenty miles outside London. She hadn't thought it would matter much to David where they went. But he surprised her by his choice of an hotel that was a three-hundred-year-old house on the Suffolk coast.

'If we're going to do it,' he said, 'we may as well do it in style.'

She felt very comfortable with him, very happy. She tried to imagine what it would have felt like going to spend a night in an hotel with a man, a lover. If the person sitting next to her were dressed, not in a black and white printed silk dress and scarlet jacket but in a man's suit with shirt and tie. If the face it gave her so much pleasure to look at were not powdered and rouged and mascara'd but rough and already showing beard growth. She couldn't imagine it. Or, rather, she could only think how in that case she would have jumped out of the car at the first red traffic lights.

They had single rooms next door to each other. The rooms were very small but Christine could see that a double might have been awkward for David who must at some point—though she didn't care to think of this—have to shave and strip down to being what he really was.

He came in and sat on her bed while she unpacked her nightdress and spare pair of shoes.

'This is fun, isn't it?'

She nodded, squinting into the mirror, working on her eyelids with a little brush. David always did his eyes beautifully. She turned round and smiled at him.

'Let's go down and have a drink.'

The dining room, the bar, the lounge were all low-ceilinged timbered rooms with carved wood on the walls David said was called linenfold panelling. There were old maps and pictures of men hunting in gilt frames and copper bowls full of roses. Long windows were thrown open on to a terrace. The sun was still high in the sky and it was very warm. While Christine sat on the terrace in the sunshine David went off to get their drinks. When he came back to their table he had a man with him, a thickset paunchy man of about forty who was carrying a tray with four glasses on it.

'This is Ted,' David said.

'Delighted to meet you,' Ted said. 'I've asked my friend to join us. I hope you don't mind.'

She had to say she didn't. David looked at her and from his look she could tell he had deliberately picked Ted up.

'But why did you?' she said to him afterwards. 'Why did you want to? You told me you didn't really like it when that man put his hand on you in the cinema.'

'That was so physical. This is just a laugh. You don't suppose I'd let them touch me, do you?'

Ted and Peter had the next table to theirs at dinner. Christine was silent and stand-offish but David flirted with them. Ted kept leaning across and whispering to him and David giggled and smiled. You could see he was enjoying himself tremendously. Christine knew they would ask her and David to go out with them after dinner and she began to be afraid. Suppose David got carried away by the excitement of it, the 'fun,' and went off somewhere with Ted, leaving her and Peter alone together? Peter had a red face and a black moustache and beard and a wart with black hairs growing out of it on his left cheek. She and David were eating steak and the waiter had brought them sharp pointed steak knives. She hadn't used hers. The steak was very tender. When no one was looking she slipped the steak knife into her bag.

Ted and Peter were still drinking coffee and brandies when David got up quite abruptly and said, 'Coming?' to Christine.

'I suppose you've arranged to meet them later?' Christine said as soon as they were out of the dining room.

David looked at her. His scarlet-painted lips parted into a wide smile. He laughed. 'I turned them down.'

'Did you *really*?'

'I could tell you hated the idea. Besides, we want to be alone, don't we? I know I want to be alone with you.'

She nearly shouted his name so that everyone could hear, the relief was so great. She controlled herself but she was trembling. 'Of course I want to be alone with you,' she said.

She put her arm in his. It wasn't uncommon, after all, for girls to walk along with linked arms. Men turned to look at David and one of them whistled. She knew it must be David the whistle was directed at because he looked so beautiful with his long golden hair and high-heeled red sandals. They walked along the sea front, along the little low promenade. It was too warm even at eight-thirty to wear a coat. There were a lot of people about but not crowds for the place was too select to attract crowds. They walked to the end of the pier. They had a drink in the Ship Inn and another in the Fishermen's Arms. A man tried to pick David up in the Fisher-men's Arms but this time he was cold and distant.

'I'd like to put my arm round you,' he said as they were walking back, 'but I sup-pose that wouldn't do, though it is dark.'

'Better not,' said Christine. She said suddenly, 'This has been the best evening of my life.'

He looked at her. 'You really mean that?'

They came into the hotel. 'I'm going to get them to send us up a couple of drinks. To my room. Is that OK?'

She sat on the bed. David went into the bathroom. To do his face, she thought, maybe to shave before he let the man with the drinks see him. There was a knock at the door and a waiter came in with a tray on which were two long glasses of something or other with fruit and leaves floating in it, two pink table napkins, two olives on sticks and two peppermint creams wrapped in green paper.

Christine tasted one of the drinks. She ate an olive. She opened her handbag and took out a mirror and a lipstick and painted her lips. David came out of the bathroom. He had taken off the golden wig and washed his face. He hadn't shaved, there was a pale stub-ble showing on his chin and cheeks. His legs and feet were bare and he was wearing a very masculine robe made of navy blue towelling. She tried to hide her disappointment.

'You've changed,' she said brightly.

He shrugged. 'There are limits.'

He raised his glass and she raised her glass and he said: 'To us!'

The beginnings of a feeling of panic came over her. Suddenly he was so evidently a man. She edged a little way along the mattress.

'I wish we had the whole weekend.'

She nodded nervously. She was aware her body had started a faint trembling. He had noticed it too. Sometimes before he had noticed how emotion made her tremble.

'Chris,' he said.

She sat passive and afraid.

'I'm not really like a woman, Chris. I just play at that sometimes for fun. You know that, don't you?' The hand that touched her smelt of nail varnish remover. There were hairs on the wrist she had never noticed before. 'I'm falling in love with you,' he said. 'And you feel the same, don't you?'

She couldn't speak. He took her by the shoulders. He brought his mouth up to hers and put his arms round her and began kissing her. His skin felt abrasive and a smell as male as Graham's came off his body. She shook and shuddered. He pushed her down on the bed and his hands began undressing her, his mouth still on hers and his body heavy on top of her.

She felt behind her, put her hand into the open handbag and pulled out the knife. Because she could feel his heart beating steadily against her right breast she knew where to stab and she stabbed again and again. The bright red heart's blood spurted over her clothes and the bed and the two peppermint creams on the tray.

BY THE DAWN'S EARLY LIGHT

LAWRENCE BLOCK
(1938–   )

Some years ago, when Bob Randisi first proposed my writing a story about Scudder for a collection, it seemed safe enough to agree. The collection was as yet unsold, the Private Eye Writers of America not yet so much as a gleam in Randisi's eye. By the time both became realities, I had written two more novels about my detective. In the last of them, Eight Million Ways to Die, *he underwent a catharsis. It made for a book I'm very happy with, but it also constituted a hard act to follow. I spent much of a year trying to write a sixth Scudder novel and concluded that, at least for the time being, it was something I couldn't comfortably do.*

How then could I sit down and write a short story? I told Bob I didn't think I could. I passed the same word to Otto Penzler. Then, relieved of my responsibilities, I went home and saw how to manage it. I thought of the opening line and after that everything was easy.

I hope you enjoy the result.

—L.B.

When the notion of successful versatility is raised in the world of mystery fiction, Donald E. Westlake and Lawrence Block stand alone. Block's work includes the humorous escapades of Bernie Rhodenbarr, the bibliophilic burglar; Evan Tanner's adventures as a spy who never sleeps; dark novels under the pseudonym Paul Kavanagh; escapades of the sex-crazed Chip Harrison's gripping suspense without series characters; and mainly the brilliant chronicles of Matt Scudder, the alcoholic ex-cop who accidentally killed a child and is haunted by the memory.

—O.P.

ALL THIS HAPPENED A LONG time ago.

Abe Beame was living in Gracie Mansion, although even he seemed to have trouble believing he was really the Mayor of the City of New York. Ali was in his prime, and the Knicks still had a year or so left in Bradley and DeBusschere. I was still drinking in those days, of course, and at the time it seemed to be doing more for me than it was doing to me.

I had already left my wife and kids, my home in Syosset, and the NYPD. I was living in the hotel on West Fifty-seventh Street where I still live, and I was doing most of my drinking around the corner in Jimmy Armstrong's saloon. Billie was the nighttime bartender, his own best customer for the twelve-year-old Jameson. A Filipino youth named Dennis was behind the stick most days.

And Tommy Tillary was one of the regulars.

He was big, probably six-two, full in the chest, big in the belly, too. He rarely showed up in a suit but always wore a jacket and tie, usually a navy and burgundy blazer with gray flannel slacks, or white duck pants in warmer weather. He had a loud voice that boomed from his barrel chest, and a big cleanshaven face that was innocent around the pouting mouth and knowing around the eyes. He was somewhere in his late forties, and he drank a lot of top-shelf Scotch. Chivas, as I remember it, but it could have been Johnny Black. Whatever it was, his face was beginning to show it, with patches of permanent flush at the cheekbones and a tracery of broken capillaries across the bridge of the nose.

We were saloon friends. We didn't speak every time we ran into each other, but at least we always acknowledged one another with a nod or a wave. He told a lot of dialect jokes and told them reasonably well, and I laughed at my share of them. Sometimes I was in a mood to reminisce about my days on the force, and when my stories were funny his laugh was as loud as anyone's.

Sometimes he showed up alone, sometimes with male friends. About a third of the time he was in the company of a short and curvy blonde name Carolyn. "Caro-lyn from the Caro-line," was the way he occasionally introduced her, and she did have a faint southern accent that became more pronounced as the drink got to her. Generally they came in together, but sometimes he got there first and she joined him later.

Then one morning I picked up the *Daily News* and read that burglars had broken into a house on Colonial Road, in the Bay Ridge section of Brooklyn. They had stabbed to death the only occupant present, one Margaret Tillary. Her husband, Thomas J. Tillary, a salesman, was not at home at the time.

It's an uncommon name. There's a Tillary Street in Brooklyn, not far from the entrance to the Brooklyn Bridge, but I've no idea what war hero or war heeler they named it after, or if he's a relative of Tommy's. I hadn't known Tommy was a salesman, or that he'd had a wife. He did wear a wide yellow gold band on the appropriate finger, and it was clear that he wasn't married to Carolyn from the Caroline, and it now looked as though he was a widower. I felt vaguely sorry for him, vaguely sorry for the wife I'd never even known of, but that was the extent of it. I drank enough back then to avoid feeling any emotion very strongly.

And then, two or three nights later, I walked into Armstrong's and there was Carolyn. She didn't look to be waiting for him or anyone else, nor did she look as though she'd just breezed in a few minutes ago. She had a stool by herself at the bar and she was drinking something dark from a lowball glass.

I took a seat a few stools down from her. I ordered two double shots of bourbon, drank one, and poured the other into the cup of black coffee Billie brought me. I was sipping the coffee when a voice with a Piedmont softness to it said, "I forget your name."

I looked up.

"I believe we were introduced," she said, "but I don't recall your name."

"It's Matt," I said, "and you're right, Tommy introduced us. You're Carolyn."

"Carolyn Cheatham. Have you seen him?"

"Tommy? Not since it happened."

"Neither have I. Were you-all at the funeral?"

"No. When was it?"

"This afternoon. Neither was I. There. Matt. Whyn't you buy me a drink? Or I'll buy you one, but come sit next to me so's I don't have to shout. Please?"

She was drinking Amaretto, sweet almond liqueur that she took on the rocks. It tastes like dessert but it's as strong as whiskey.

"He told me not to come," she said. "To the funeral. It was someplace in Brooklyn, that's a whole foreign nation to me, Brooklyn, but a lot of people went from the office. I could have had a ride, I could have been part of the office crowd, come to pay our respects. But he said not to, he said it wouldn't look right."

"Because—"

"He said it was a matter of respect for the dead." She picked up her glass and stared into it. I've never known what people hope to see there, although it's a gesture I've performed often enough myself.

"Respect," she said. "What's he care about respect? I would have just been part of the office crowd, we both work at Tannahill, far as anyone there knows we're just friends. And all we ever were is friends, you know."

"Whatever you say."

"Oh, *shit*," she said. "Ah don't mean Ah wasn't fucking him, for the Lord's sake. Ah mean it was just laughs and good times. He was married and he went home to Mama every night and that was jes fine, because who in her right mind'd want Tommy Tillary around by the dawn's early light? Christ in the foothills, did Ah spill this or drink it?"

We agreed that she was drinking them a little too fast. Sweet drinks, we told each other, had a way of sneaking up on a person. It was this fancy New York Amaretto shit, she maintained, not like the bourbon she'd grown up on. You knew where you stood with bourbon.

I told her I was a bourbon drinker myself, and it pleased her to learn this. Alliances have been forged on thinner bonds than that, and ours served to propel us out of Armstrong's, with a stop down the block for a fifth of Maker's Mark—her choice—and a four-block walk to her apartment. There were exposed brick walls, I remember, and candles stuck in straw-wrapped bottles, and several travel posters from Sabena, the Belgian airline.

We did what grownups do when they find themselves alone together. We drank our fair share of the Maker's Mark and went to bed. She made a lot of enthusiastic noises and more than a few skillful moves, and afterward she cried some.

A little later she dropped off to sleep. I was tired myself, but I put on my clothes and sent myself home. Because who in her right mind'd want Matt Scudder around by the dawn's early light?

Over the next couple of days, I wondered every time I entered Armstrong's if I'd run into her, and each time I was more relieved than disappointed when I didn't. I didn't encounter Tommy either, and that too was a relief, and in no sense disappointing.

Then one morning I picked up the *News* and read that they'd arrested a pair of young Hispanics from Sunset Park for the Tillary burglary and homicide. The paper ran the usual photo—two skinny kids, their hair unruly, one of them trying to hide his face from the camera, the other smirking defiantly, and each of them handcuffed to a broadshouldered grimfaced Irishman in a suit. You didn't need the careful caption to tell the good guys from the bad guys.

Sometime in the middle of the afternoon I went over to Armstrong's for a hamburger and drank a beer with it, then got the day going with a round or two of laced coffee. The phone behind the bar rang and Dennis put down the glass he was wiping and answered it. "He was here a minute ago," he said. "I'll see if he stepped out." He covered the mouthpiece with his hand and looked quizzically at me. "Are you still here?" he asked. "Or did you slip away while my attention was somehow diverted?"

"Who wants to know?"

"Tommy Tillary."

You never know what a woman will decide to tell a man, or how a man will react to it. I didn't want to find out, but I was better off learning over the phone than face to face. I nodded and took the phone from Dennis.

I said, "Matt Scudder, Tommy. I was sorry to hear about your wife."

"Thanks, Matt. Jesus, it feels like it happened a year ago. It was what, a week?"

"At least they got the bastards."

There was a pause. Then he said, "Jesus. You haven't seen a paper, huh?"

"That's where I read about it. Two. Spanish kids."

"You read the *News* this morning."

"I generally do. Why?"

"You didn't happen to see this afternoon's *Post*."

"No. Why, what happened? They turn out to be clean?"

Another pause. Then he said, "I figured you'd know. The cops were over early this morning, even before I saw the story in the *News*. It'd be easier if you already knew."

"I'm not following you, Tommy."

"The two Spics. Clean? Shit, they're about as clean as the men's room in the Times Square subway station. The cops hit their place and found stuff from my house everywhere they looked. Jewelry they had descriptions of, a stereo that I gave them the serial number, everything. Monogrammed shit. I mean that's how clean they were, for Christ's sake."

"So?"

"They admitted the burglary but not the murder."

"That's common, Tommy."

"Lemme finish, huh? They admitted the burglary, but according to them it was a put-up job. According to them I hired them to hit my place. They could keep whatever they got and I'd have everything out and arranged for them, and in return I got to clean up on the insurance by over-reporting the loss."

"What did the loss amount to?"

"Shit, *I* don't know. There were twice as many things turned up in their apartment as I ever listed when I made out a report. There's things I missed a few days after I filed the report and others I didn't know were gone until the cops found them. You don't notice everything right away, at least I don't, and on top of it how could I think straight with Peg dead? You know?"

"It hardly sounds like an insurance set-up."

"No, of course it wasn't. How the hell could it be? All I had was a standard homeowner's policy. It covered maybe a third of what I lost. According to them, the place was empty when they hit it. Peg was out."

"And?"

"And I set them up. They hit the place, they carted everything away, and I came home with Peg and stabbed her six, eight times, whatever it was, and left her there so it'd look like it happened in a burglary."

"How could the burglars testify that you stabbed your wife?"

"They couldn't. All they said was they didn't and she wasn't home when they were there, and that I hired them to do the burglary. The cops pieced the rest of it together."

"What did they do, arrest you?"

"No. They came over to the house, it was early, I don't know what time. It was the first I knew that the Spics were arrested, let alone that they were trying to do a job on me. They just wanted to talk, the cops, and at first I talked to them, and then I started to get the drift of what they were trying to put onto me. So I wasn't saying anything more without my lawyer present, and I called him, and he left half his breakfast on the table and came over in a hurry, and he wouldn't let me say a word."

"And the cops didn't take you in or book you?"

"No."

"Did they buy your story?"

"No way. I didn't really tell 'em a story because Kaplan wouldn't let me say anything. They didn't drag me in because they don't have a case yet, but Kaplan says they're gonna be building one if they can. They told me not to leave town. You believe it? My wife's dead, the *Post* headline says *Quiz Husband in Burglary Murder,* and what the hell do they think I'm gonna do? Am I going fishing for fucking trout in Montana? 'Don't leave town.' You see this shit on television, you think nobody in real life talks this way. Maybe television's where they get it from."

I waited for him to tell me what he wanted from me. I didn't have long to wait.

"Why I called," he said, "is Kaplan wants to hire a detective. He figured maybe these guys talked around the neighborhood, maybe they bragged to their friends, maybe there's a way to prove they did the killing. He says the cops won't concentrate on that end if they're too busy nailing the lid shut on me."

I explained that I didn't have any official standing, that I had no license and filed no reports.

"That's okay," he insisted. "I told Kaplan what I want is somebody I can trust, and somebody who'll do the job for me. I don't think they're gonna have any kind of a case at all, Matt, but the longer this drags on the worse it is for me. I want it cleared up, I want it in the papers that these Spanish assholes did it all and I had nothing to do with anything. You name a fair fee and I'll pay it, me to you, and it can be cash in your hand if you don't like checks. What do you say?"

He wanted somebody he could trust. Had Carolyn from the Caroline told him how trustworthy I was?

What did I say? I said yes.

I met Tommy Tillary and his lawyer in Drew Kaplan's office on Court Street a few blocks from Brooklyn's Borough Hall. There was a Syrian restaurant next door, and at the corner a grocery store specializing in Middle Eastern imports stood next to an antique shop overflowing with stripped oak furniture and brass lamps and bedsteads. Kaplan's office ran to wood paneling and leather chairs and oak file cabinets. His name and the names of two partners were painted on the frosted glass door in old-fashioned gold and black lettering. Kaplan himself looked conservatively up-to-date, with a three-piece striped suit that was better cut than mine. Tommy wore his burgundy blazer and gray flannel trousers and loafers. Strain showed at the corners of his blue eyes and around his mouth. His complexion was off, too, as if anxiety had drawn the blood inward, leaving the skin sallow.

"All we want you to do," Drew Kaplan said, "is find a key in one of their pants pockets, Herrera's or Cruz's, and trace it to a locker in Penn Station, and in the locker there's a footlong knife with their prints and her blood on it."

"Is that what it's going to take?"

He smiled. "It wouldn't hurt. No, actually we're not in such bad shape. They got some shaky testimony from a pair of Latins who've been in and out of trouble since they got weaned to Tropicana. They got what looks to them like a good motive on Tommy's part."

"Which is?"

I was looking at Tommy when I talked. His eyes slipped away from mine. Kaplan said, "A marital triangle, a case of the shorts, and a strong money motive. Margaret Tillary inherited a little over a quarter of a million dollars six or eight months ago. An aunt left a million two and it got cut four ways. What they don't bother to notice is he loved his wife, and how many husbands cheat? What is it they say? Ninety percent cheat and ten percent lie?"

"That's good odds."

"One of the killers, Angel Herrera, did some odd jobs at the Tillary house last March or April. Spring cleaning, he hauled stuff out of the basement and attic, a little donkey work for hourly wages. According to common sense, that's how Herrera and his buddy Cruz knew the house and what was in it and how to gain access."

"The case against Tommy sounds pretty thin."

"It is," Kaplan said. "The thing is, you go to court with something like this and you lose even if you win. For the rest of your life everybody remembers you stood trial for murdering your wife, never mind that you won an acquittal. All that means, some Jew lawyer bought a judge or tricked a jury."

"So I'll get a guinea lawyer," Tommy said. "And they'll think he threatened the judge and beat up the jury."

"Besides," the lawyer said, "you never know which way a jury's going to jump. Tommy's alibi is he was with another lady at the time of the burglary. The woman's a colleague, they could see it as completely above-board, but who says they're going to? What they sometimes do, they decide they don't believe the alibi because it's his girlfriend lying for him, and at the same time they label him a scumbag for screwing around while his wife's getting killed."

"You keep it up," Tommy said, "I'll find myself guilty, the way you make it sound."

"Plus he's hard to get a sympathetic jury for. He's a big handsome guy, a sharp dresser, and you'd love him in a gin joint but how much do you love him in a courtroom? He's a telephone securities salesman, he's beautiful on the phone, and that means every clown whoever lost a hundred dollars on a stock tip or bought magazine subscriptions over the phone is going to walk into the courtroom with a hard-on for him. I'm telling you, I want to stay the hell *out* of court. I'll *win* in court, I know that, or the worst that'll happen is I'll win on appeal, but who needs it? This is a case that shouldn't be in the first place, and I'd love to clear it up before they even go so far as presenting a bill to the Grand Jury."

"So from me you want—"

"Whatever you can find, Matt. Whatever discredits Cruz and Herrera. I don't know what's there to be found, but you were a cop and now you're a private, and you can get down in the streets and nose around."

I nodded. I could do that. "One thing," I said. "Wouldn't you be better off with a Spanish-speaking detective? I know enough to buy a beer in a bodega, but I'm a long ways from fluent."

Kaplan shook his head. "Tommy says he wants somebody he can trust," he said. "I think he's right. A personal relationship's worth more than a dime's worth of 'Me llamo Matteo y como está usted?'"

"That's the truth," Tommy Tillary said. "Matt, I know I can count on you."

I wanted to tell him all he could count on was his fingers. I didn't really see what I could expect to uncover that wouldn't turn up in a regular police investigation. But I'd spent enough time carrying a shield to know not to push away money when somebody wants to give it to you. I felt comfortable taking a fee. The man was inheriting a quarter of a million dollars, plus whatever insurance she carried. If he was willing to spread some of it around, I was willing to take it.

So I went to Sunset Park and spent some time in the streets and some more time in the bars. Sunset Park is in Brooklyn, of course, on the borough's western edge above Bay Ridge and south and west of Greenwood Cemetery. These days there's a lot of brownstoning going on there, with young urban professionals renovating the old houses and gentrifying the neighborhood. Back then the upwardly mobile young had not yet discovered Sunset Park, and the area was a mix of Latins and Scandinavians, most of the former Puerto Ricans, most of the latter Norwegians. The balance was gradually shifting from Europe to the islands, from light to dark, but this was a process that had been going on for ages and there was nothing hurried about it.

I talked to Herrera's landlord and Cruz's former employer and one of his recent girlfriends. I drank beer in bars and the back rooms of bodegas. I went to the local stationhouse—they hadn't caught the Margaret Tillary murder case, that had been a matter for the local precinct in Bay Ridge and some detectives from Brooklyn Homicide. I read the sheets on both of the burglars and drank coffee with the cops and picked up some of the stuff that doesn't get on the yellow sheets.

I found out that Miguelito Cruz once killed a man in a tavern brawl over a woman. There were no charges pressed; a dozen witnesses reported the dead man had gone after Cruz first with a broken bottle. Cruz had most likely been carrying the knife, but several witnesses insisted it had been tossed to him by an anonymous benefactor, and there hadn't been enough evidence to make a case of weapons possession, let alone homicide.

I learned that Herrera had three children living with their mother in Puerto Rico. He was divorced, but wouldn't marry his current girlfriend because he regarded himself as still married to his ex-wife in the eyes of God. He sent money to his children, when he had any to send.

I learned other things. They didn't seem terribly consequential then and they've faded from memory altogether by now, but I wrote them down in my pocket notebook as I learned them, and every day or so I duly reported my findings to Drew Kaplan. He always seemed pleased with what I told him.

Some nights I stayed fairly late in Sunset Park. There was a dark beery tavern called The Fjord that served as a comfortable enough harbor after I tired of playing Sam Spade. But I almost invariably managed a stop at Armstrong's before I called it a night. Billie would lock the door around two, but he'd keep serving until four and he'd let you in if he knew you.

One night she was there, Carolyn Cheatham, drinking bourbon this time instead of Amaretto, her face frozen with stubborn old pain. It took her a blink or two to recognize me. Then tears started to form in the corners of her eyes, and she used the back of one hand to wipe them away.

I didn't approach her until she beckoned. She patted the stool beside hers and I eased myself onto it. I had coffee with bourbon in it, and bought a refill for her. She was pretty drunk already, but that's never been enough reason to turn down a drink.

She talked about Tommy. He was being nice to her, she said. Calling up, sending flowers. Because he might need to testify that he'd been with her when his wife was killed, and he'd need her to back him up.

But he wouldn't see her because it wouldn't look right, not for a new widower, not for a man who'd been publicly accused of murder.

"He sends flowers with no card enclosed," she said. "He calls me from pay phones. The son of a bitch."

Billie called me aside. "I didn't want to put her out," he said, "a nice woman like that, shitfaced as she is. But I thought I was gonna have to. You'll see she gets home?"

I said I would.

First I had to let her buy us another round. She insisted. Then I got her out of there and a cab came along and saved us the walk. At her place, I took the keys from her and unlocked the door. She half sat, half sprawled on the couch. I had to use the bathroom, and when I came back her eyes were closed and she was snoring lightly.

I got her coat and shoes off, put her to bed, loosened her clothing and covered her with a blanket. I was tired from all that and sat down on the couch for a minute, and I almost dozed off myself. Then I snapped awake and let myself out. Her door had a spring lock. All I had to do was close it and it was locked.

Much of the walk back to my hotel disappeared in blackout. I was crossing Fifty-seventh Street, and then it was morning and I was stretched out in my own bed, my clothes a tangle on the straight-backed chair. That happened a lot in those days, that kind of before-bed blackout, and I used to insist it didn't bother me. What ever happened on the way home? Why waste brain cells remembering the final fifteen minutes of the day?

I went back to Sunset Park the next day. I learned that Cruz had been in trouble as a youth. With a gang of neighborhood kids, he used to go into the city and cruise Greenwich Village, looking for homosexuals to beat up. He'd had a dread of homosexuality, probably flowing as it generally does out of a fear of a part of himself, and he stifled that dread by fag-bashing.

"He still doan like them," a woman told me. She had glossy black hair and opaque eyes, and she was letting me pay for her rum and orange juice. "He's pretty, you know, and they come on to him, an' he doan like it."

I called that item in, along with a few others equally earth-shaking. I bought myself a steak dinner at the Slate over on Tenth Avenue that night, then finished up at Armstrong's, not drinking very hard, just coasting along on bourbon and coffee.

Twice, the phone rang for me. Once it was Tommy Tillary, telling me how much he appreciated what I was doing for him. It seemed to me that all I was doing was taking his money, but he had me believing that my loyalty and invaluable assistance were all he had to cling to.

The second call was from Carolyn. More praise. I was a gentleman, she assured me, and a hell of a fellow all around. And I should forget that she'd been bad-mouthing Tommy. Everything was going to be fine with them.

I told her I'd never doubted it for a minute, and that I couldn't really remember what she'd said anyway.

I took the next day off. I think I went to a movie, and it may have been *The Sting*, with Newman and Redford achieving vengeance through swindling.

The day after that I did another tour of duty over in Brooklyn. And the day after that I picked up the *News* first thing in the morning. The headline was nonspecific, something like *Kill Suspect Hangs Self in Cell*, but I knew it was my case before I turned to the story on Page Three.

Miguelito Cruz had torn his clothing into strips, knotted the strips together, stood his iron bedstead on its side, climbed onto it, looped his homemade rope around an overhead pipe, and jumped off the upended bedstead and into the next world.

That evening's six o'clock TV news had the rest of the story. Informed of his friend's death, Angel Herrera had recanted his original story and admitted that he and Cruz had conceived and executed the Tillary burglary on their own. It had been Miguelito who had stabbed the Tillary woman when she walked in on them. He'd picked up a kitchen knife while Herrera watched in horror. Miguelito always had a short temper, Herrera said, but they were friends, even cousins, and they had hatched their story to protect Miguelito. But now that he was dead, Herrera could admit what had really happened.

I was in Armstrong's that night, which was not remarkable. I had it in mind to get drunk, though I could not have told you why, and that was remarkable, if not unheard of. I got drunk a lot those days, but I rarely set out with that intention. I just wanted to feel a little better, a little more mellow, and somewhere along the way I'd wind up waxed.

I wasn't drinking particularly hard or fast, but I was working at it, and then somewhere around ten or eleven the door opened and I knew who it was before I turned around. Tommy Tillary, well dressed and freshly barbered, making his first appearance in Jimmy's place since his wife was killed.

"Hey, look who's here!" he called out, and grinned that big grin. People rushed over to shake his hand. Billie was behind the stick, and he'd no sooner set one up on the house for our hero than Tommy insisted on buying a round for the bar. It was an expensive gesture, there must have been thirty or forty people in there, but I don't think he cared if there were three or four hundred.

I stayed where I was, letting the others mob him, but he worked his way over to me and got an arm around my shoulders. "This is the man," he announced. "Best fucking detective ever wore out a pair of shoes. This man's money—" he told Billie "—is no good at all tonight. He can't buy a drink, he can't buy a cup of coffee, if you went and put in pay toilets since I was last here, he can't use his own dime."

"The john's still free," Billie said, "but don't give the boss any ideas."

"Oh, don't tell me he didn't already think of it," Tommy said. "Matt, my boy, I love you. I was in a tight spot, I didn't want to walk out of my house, and you came through for me."

What the hell had I done? I hadn't hanged Miguelito Cruz or coaxed a confession out of Angel Herrera. I hadn't even set eyes on either man. But he was buying the drinks, and I had a thirst, so who was I to argue?

I don't know how long we stayed there. Curiously, my drinking slowed down even as Tommy's picked up speed. Carolyn, I noticed, was not present, nor did her name find its way into the conversation. I wondered if she would walk in—it was, after all, her neighborhood bar, and she was apt to drop in on her own. I wondered what would happen if she did.

I guess there were a lot of things I wondered about, and perhaps that's what put the brakes on my own drinking. I didn't want any gaps in my memory, any gray patches in my awareness.

After a while Tommy was hustling me out of Armstrong's. "This is celebration time," he told me. "We don't want to sit in one place till we grow roots. We want to bop a little."

He had a car, and I just went along with him without paying too much attention to exactly where we were. We went to a noisy Greek club on the East Side, I think, where the waiters looked like mob hitmen. We went to a couple of trendy singles joints. We wound up somewhere in the Village, in a dark beery cave that reminded me, I realized after a while, of the Norwegian joint in Sunset Park. The Fjord? Right.

It was quiet there, and conversation was possible, and I found myself asking him what I'd done that was so praiseworthy. One man had killed himself and another had confessed, and where was my role in either incident?

"The stuff you came up with," he said.

"What stuff? I should have brought back fingernail parings, you could have had someone work voodoo on them."

"About Cruz and the fairies."

"He was up for murder. He didn't kill himself because he was afraid they'd get him for fag-bashing when he was a juvenile offender."

Tommy took a sip of Scotch. He said, "Couple days ago, black guy comes up to Cruz in the chow line. Huge spade, built like the Seagram's Building. 'Wait'll you get up to Green Haven,' he tells him. 'Every blood there's gonna have you for a girlfriend. Doctor gonna have to cut you a brand-new asshole, time you get outta there.'"

I didn't say anything.

"Kaplan," he said. "Drew talked to somebody who talked to somebody, and that did it. Cruz took a good look at the idea of playin' Drop the Soap for half the jigs in captivity, and the next thing you know the murderous little bastard was dancing on air. And good riddance to him."

I couldn't seem to catch my breath. I worked on it while Tommy went to the bar for another round. I hadn't touched the drink in front of me but I let him buy for both of us.

When he got back I said, "Herrera."

"Changed his story. Made a full confession."

"And pinned the killing on Cruz."

"Why not? Cruz wasn't around to complain. Who knows which one of 'em did it, and for that matter who cares? The thing is, you gave us the lever."

"For Cruz," I said. "To get him to kill himself."

"And for Herrera. Those kids of his in Santurce. Drew spoke to Herrera's lawyer and Herrera's lawyer spoke to Herrera, and the message was, look, you're going up for burglary whatever you do, and probably for murder, but if you tell the right story you'll draw shorter time and on top of that, that nice Mr. Tillary's gonna let bygones be bygones and every month there's a nice check for your wife and kiddies back home in Puerto Rico."

At the bar, a couple of old men were reliving the Louis–Schmeling fight, the second one, where Louis punished the German champion. One of the old fellows was throwing roundhouse punches in the air, demonstrating.

I said, "Who killed your wife?"

"One or the other of them. If I had to bet I'd say Cruz. He had those little beady eyes, you looked at him up close and you got that he was a killer."

"When did you look at him up close?"

"When they came and cleaned the house, the basement and the attic. Not when they came and cleaned me out, that was the second time."

He smiled, but I kept looking at him until the smile lost its certainty. "That was Herrera who helped around the house," I said. "You never met Cruz."

"Cruz came along, gave him a hand."

"You never mentioned that before."

"Oh, sure I did, Matt. What difference does it make, anyway?"

"Who killed her, Tommy?"

"Hey, let it alone, huh?"

"Answer the question."

"I already answered it."

"You killed her, didn't you?"

"What are you, crazy? Cruz killed her and Herrera swore to it, isn't that enough for you?"

"Tell me you didn't kill her."

"I didn't kill her."

"Tell me again."

"I didn't fucking kill her. What's the matter with you?"

"I don't believe you."

"Oh, Jesus," he said. He closed his eyes, put his head in his hands. He sighed and looked up and said, "You know, it's a funny thing with me. Over the telephone, I'm the best salesman you could ever imagine. I swear I could sell sand to the Arabs, I could sell ice in the winter, but face to face I'm no good at all. Why do you figure that is?"

"You tell me."

"I don't know. I used to think it was my face, the eyes and the mouth, I don't know. It's easy over the phone. I'm talking to a stranger, I don't know who he is or what he looks like, and he's not lookin' at me, and it's a cinch. Face to face, especially with someone I know, it's a different story." He looked at me. "If we were doin' this over the phone, you'd buy the whole thing."

"It's possible."

"It's fucking certain. Word for word, you'd buy the package. Suppose I was to tell you I did kill her, Matt. You couldn't prove anything. Look, the both of us walked in there, the place was a mess from the burglary, we got in an argument, tempers flared, something happened."

"You set up the burglary. You planned the whole thing, just the way Cruz and Herrera accused you of doing. And now you wriggled out of it."

"And you helped me, don't forget that part of it."

"I won't."

"And I wouldn't have gone away for it anyway, Matt. Not a chance. I'da beat it in court, only this way I don't have to go to court. Look, this is just the booze talkin', and we can both forget it in the morning, right? I didn't kill her, you didn't accuse me, we're still buddies, everything's fine. Right?"

Blackouts are never there when you want them. I woke up the next day and remembered all of it, and I found myself wishing I didn't. He'd killed his wife and he was getting away with it. And I'd helped him. I'd taken his money, and in return I'd shown him how to set one man up for suicide and pressure another into making a false confession.

And what was I going to do about it?

I couldn't think of a thing. Any story I carried to the police would speedily be denied by Tommy and his lawyer, and all I had was the thinnest of hearsay evidence, my own client's own words when he and I both had a skinful of booze. I went over it for a few days, looking for ways to shake something loose, and there was nothing. I could maybe interest a newspaper reporter, maybe get Tommy some press coverage that wouldn't make him happy, but why? And to what purpose?

It rankled. But I would just have a couple of drinks, and then it wouldn't rankle so much.

Angel Herrera pleaded to burglary, and in return the Brooklyn D.A.'s office dropped all homicide charges. He went upstate to serve five-to-ten.

And then I got a call in the middle of the night. I'd been sleeping a couple of hours but the phone woke me and I groped for it. It took me a minute to recognize the voice on the other end.

It was Carolyn Cheatham.

"I had to call you," she said, "on account of you're a bourbon man and a gentleman. I owed it to you to call you."

"What's the matter?"

"He ditched me," she said, "and he got fired out of Tannahill & Co. so he won't have to look at me around the office. Once he didn't need me he let go of me, and do you know he did it over the phone?"

"Carolyn—"

"It's all in the note," she said. "I'm leaving a note."

"Look, don't do anything yet," I said. I was out of bed, fumbling for my clothes. "I'll be right over. We'll talk about it."

"You can't stop me, Matt."

"I won't try to stop you. We'll talk first, and then you can do anything you want."

The phone clicked in my ear.

I threw my clothes on, rushed over there, hoping it would be pills, something that took its time. I broke a small pane of glass in the downstairs door and let myself in, then used an old credit card to slip the bolt of her spring lock. If she had engaged the dead bolt lock I would have had to kick the door in.

The room smelled of cordite. She was on the couch she'd passed out on the last time I saw her. The gun was still in her hand, limp at her side, and there was a black-rimmed hole in her temple.

There was a note, too. An empty bottle of Maker's Mark stood on the coffee table, an empty glass beside it. The booze showed in her handwriting, and in the sullen phrasing of the suicide note.

I read the note. I stood there for a few minutes, not for very long, and then I got a dish towel from the pullman kitchen and wiped the bottle and the glass. I took another matching glass, rinsed it out and wiped it, and put it in the drainboard of the sink.

I stuffed the note in my pocket. I took the gun from her fingers, checked routinely for a pulse, then wrapped a sofa pillow around the gun to muffle its report. I fired one round into her chest, another into her open mouth.

I dropped the gun into a pocket and left.

They found the gun in Tommy Tillary's house, stuffed between the cushions of the living room sofa, clean of prints inside and out. Ballistics got a perfect match. I'd aimed for soft tissue with the round shot into her chest because bullets can fragment on impact with bone. That was one reason I'd fired the extra shots. The other was to rule out the possibility of suicide.

After the story made the papers, I picked up the phone and called Drew Kaplan. "I don't understand it," I said. "He was free and clear, why the hell did he kill the girl?"

"Ask him yourself," Kaplan said. He did not sound happy. "You want my opinion, he's a lunatic. I honestly didn't think he was. I figured maybe he killed his wife, maybe he didn't. Not my job to try him. But I didn't figure he was a homicidal maniac."

"It's certain he killed the girl?"

"Not much question. The gun's pretty strong evidence. Talk about finding somebody with the smoking pistol in his hand, here it was in Tommy's couch. The idiot."

"Funny he kept it."

"Maybe he had other people he wanted to shoot. Go figure a crazy man. No, the gun's evidence, and there was a phone tip, a man called in the shooting, reported a man running out of there and gave a description that fitted Tommy pretty well. Even had him wearing that red blazer he wears, tacky thing makes him look like an usher at the Paramount."

"It sounds tough to square."

"Well, somebody else'll have to try to do it," Kaplan said. "I told him I can't defend him this time. What it amounts to, I wash my hands of him."

I thought of this when I read that Angel Herrera got out just the other day. He served all ten years because he was as good at getting into trouble inside the walls as he'd been on the outside.

Somebody killed Tommy Tillary with a homemade knife after he'd served two years and three months of a manslaughter stretch. I wondered at the time if that was Herrera getting even, and I don't suppose I'll ever know. Maybe the checks stopped going to Santurce and Herrera took it the wrong way. Or maybe Tommy said the wrong thing to somebody else, and said it face to face instead of over the phone.

I don't think I'd do it that way now. I don't drink any more, and the impulse to play God seems to have evaporated with the booze.

But then a lot of things have changed. Billie left Armstrong's not long after that, left New York too; the last I heard he was off drink himself, living in Sausalito and making candles.

I ran into Dennis the other day in a bookstore on lower Fifth Avenue, full of odd volumes on yoga and spiritualism and holistic healing. And Armstrong's is scheduled to close the end of next month. The lease is up for renewal, and I suppose the next you know the old joint'll be another Korean fruit market.

I still light a candle now and then for Carolyn Cheatham and Miguelito Cruz. Not very often. Just every once in a while.

IRIS

STEPHEN GREENLEAF
(1942–   )

Just as Ross McDonald consciously emulated Raymond Chandler when he began his private eye series, so did Greenleaf attempt to pastiche the style (and even the structure) of Macdonald's Lew Archer series. Also like Macdonald, Greenleaf has evolved into a first-rate novelist whose own voice can now be clearly discerned. His ten novels about John Marshall Tanner are among the finest private eye series ever written, with a grace of style and overwhelming decency too rare in contemporary fiction.

HE BUICK TRUDGED TOWARD the summit, each step slower than the last, the automatic gearing slipping ever-lower as the air thinned and the grade steepened and the trucks were rendered snails. At the top the road leveled, and the Buick spent a brief sigh of relief before coasting thankfully down the other side, atop the stiff gray strap that was Interstate 5. As it passed from Oregon to California the car seemed cheered. Its driver shared the mood, though only momentarily.

He blinked his eyes and shrugged his shoulders and twisted his head. He straightened his leg and shook it. He turned up the volume of the radio, causing a song to be sung more loudly than it merited. But the acid fog lay still behind his eyes, eating at them. As he approached a roadside rest area he decided to give both the Buick and himself a break.

During the previous week he had chased a wild goose in the shape of a rumor all the way to Seattle, with tantalizing stops in Eugene and Portland along the way. Eight hours earlier, when he had finally recognized the goose for what it was, he had headed home, hoping to make it in one day but realizing as he slowed for the rest area that he couldn't reach San Francisco that evening without risking more than was sensible in the way of vehicular manslaughter.

He took the exit, dropped swiftly to the bank of the Klamath River and pulled into a parking slot in the Randolph Collier safety rest area. After making use of the facilities, he pulled out his map and considered where to spend the night. Redding looked like the logical place, out of the mountains, at the head of the soporific valley that separated him from home. He was reviewing what he knew about Redding when a voice, aggressively gay and musical greeted him from somewhere near the car. He glanced to his side, sat up straight and rolled down the window. "Hi," the thin voice said again.

"Hi."

She was blond, her long straight tresses misbehaving in the wind that tumbled through the river canyon. Her narrow face was white and seamless, as though it lacked flesh, was only skull. Her eyes were blue and tardy. She wore a loose green blouse gathered at the neck and wrists and a long skirt of faded calico, fringed in white ruffles. Her boots were leather and well-worn, their tops disappearing under her skirt the way the tops of the mountains at her back disappeared into a disc of cloud.

He pegged her for a hitchhiker, one who perpetually roams the roads and provokes either pity or disapproval in those who pass her by. He glanced around to see if she was fronting for a partner, but the only thing he saw besides the picnic and toilet facilities and travelers like himself was a large bundle resting atop a picnic table at the far end of the parking lot. Her worldly possessions, he guessed; her only aids to life. He looked at her again and considered whether he wanted to share some driving time and possibly a motel room with a girl who looked a little spacy and a little sexy and a lot heedless of the world that delivered him his living.

"My name's Iris," she said, wrapping her arms across her chest, shifting her weight from foot to foot, shivering in the autumn chill.

"Mine's Marsh."

"You look tired." Her concern seemed genuine, his common symptoms for some reason alarming to her.

"I am," he admitted.

"Been on the road long?"

"From Seattle."

"How far is that about?" The question came immediately, as though she habitually erased her ignorance.

"Four hundred miles. Maybe a little more."

She nodded as though the numbers made him wise. "I've been to Seattle."

"Good."

"I've been lots of places."

"Good."

She unwrapped her arms and placed them on the door and leaned toward him. Her musk was unadulterated. Her blouse dropped open to reveal breasts sharpened to twin points by the mountain air. "Where you headed, Marsh?"

"South."

"L.A.?"

He shook his head. "San Francisco."

"Good. Perfect."

He expected it right then, the flirting pitch for a lift, but her request was slightly different. "Could you take something down there for me?"

He frowned and thought of the package on the picnic table. Drugs? "What?" he asked.

"I'll show you in a sec. Do you think you could, though?"

He shook his head. "I don't think so. I mean, I'm kind of on a tight schedule, and . . ."

She wasn't listening. "It goes to . . ." She pulled a scrap of paper from the pocket of her skirt and uncrumpled it. "It goes to 95 Albosa Drive, in Hurley City. That's near Frisco, isn't it? Marvin said it was."

He nodded. "But I don't . . ."

She put up a hand. "Hold still. I'll be right back."

She skipped twice, her long skirt hopping high above her boots to show a shaft of gypsum thigh, then trotted to the picnic table and picked up the bundle. Halfway back to the car she proffered it like a prize soufflé.

"Is this what you want me to take?" he asked as she approached.

She nodded, then looked down at the package and frowned. "I don't like this one," she said, her voice dropping to a dismissive rasp.

"Why not?"

"Because it isn't happy. It's from the B Box, so it can't help it, I guess, but all the same it should go back, I don't care *what* Marvin says."

"What is it? A puppy?"

She thrust the package through the window. He grasped it reflexively, to keep it from dropping to his lap. As he secured his grip the girl ran off. "Hey! Wait a minute," he called after her. "I can't take this thing. You'll have to . . ."

He thought the package moved. He slid one hand beneath it and with the other peeled back the cotton strips that swaddled it. A baby—not canine but human—glared at him and screamed. He looked frantically for the girl and saw her climbing into a gray Volkswagen bug that was soon scooting out of the rest area and climbing toward the freeway.

He swore, then rocked the baby awkwardly for an instant, trying to quiet the screams it formed with every muscle. When that didn't work, he placed the child on the seat beside him, started the car and backed out. As he started forward he had to stop to avoid another car, and then to reach out wildly to keep the child from rolling off the seat.

He moved the gear to park and gathered the seat belt on the passenger side and tried to wrap it around the baby in a way that would be more safe than throttling. The result was not reassuring. He unhooked the belt and put the baby on the floor beneath his legs, put the car in gear and set out after the little gray VW that had disappeared with the child's presumptive mother. He caught it only after several frantic miles, when he reached the final slope that descended to the grassy plain that separated the Siskiyou range from the lordly aspect of Mt. Shasta.

The VW buzzed toward the mammoth mountain like a mad mouse assaulting an elephant. He considered overtaking the car, forcing Iris to stop, returning the baby, then getting the hell away from her as fast as the Buick would take him. But something in his memory of her look and words made him keep his distance, made him keep Iris in sight while he waited for her to make a turn toward home.

The highway flattened, then crossed the high meadow that nurtured sheep and cattle and horses below the lumps of the southern Cascades and the Trinity Alps. Traffic was light, the sun low above the western peaks, the air a steady splash of autumn. He checked his gas gauge. If Iris didn't turn off in the next fifty miles he would either have to force her to stop or let her go. The piercing baby sounds that rose from beneath his knees made the latter choice impossible.

They reached Yreka, and he closed to within a hundred yards of the bug, but Iris ignored his plea that the little city be her goal. Thirty minutes later, after he had decided she was nowhere near her destination, Iris abruptly left the interstate, at the first exit to a village that was hand-maiden to the mountain, a town reputed to house an odd collection of spiritual seekers and religious zealots.

The mountain itself, volcanic, abrupt, spectacular, had been held by the Indians to be holy, and the area surrounding it was replete with hot springs and mud baths and other prehistoric marvels. Modern mystics had accepted the mantle of the mountain, and the crazy girl and her silly bug fit with what he knew about the place and those who gathered there. What didn't fit was the baby she had foisted on him.

He slowed and glanced at his charge once again and failed to receive anything resembling contentment in return. Fat little arms escaped the blanket and pulled the air like taffy. Spittle dribbled down its chin. A translucent bubble appeared at a tiny nostril, then broke silently and vanished.

The bug darted through the north end of town, left, then right, then left again, quickly, as though it sensed pursuit. He lagged behind, hoping Iris was confident she had ditched him. He looked at the baby again, marveling that it could cry so loud, could for so long expend the major portion of its strength in unrequited pleas. When he looked at the road again the bug had disappeared.

He swore and slowed and looked at driveways, then began to plan what to do if he had lost her. Houses dwindled, the street became dirt, then flanked the log decks and lumber stacks and wigwam burners of a sawmill. A road sign declared it unlawful to sleigh, toboggan or ski on a county road. He had gasped the first breaths of panic when he saw the VW nestled next to a ramshackle cabin on the back edge of town, empty, as though it had been there always.

A pair of firs sheltered the cabin and the car, made the dwindling day seem night. The driveway was mud, the yard bordered by a falling wormwood fence. He drove to the next block and stopped his car, the cabin now invisible.

He knew he couldn't keep the baby much longer. He had no idea what to do, for it or with it, had no idea what it wanted, no idea what awaited it in Hurley City, had only a sense that the girl, Iris, was goofy, perhaps pathologically so, and that he should not abet her plan.

Impossibly, the child cried louder. He had some snacks in the car—crackers, cookies, some cheese—but he was afraid the baby was too young for solids. He considered buying milk, and a bottle, and playing parent. The baby cried again, gasped and sputtered, then repeated its protest.

He reached down and picked it up. The little red face inflated, contorted, mimicked a steam machine that continuously whistled. The puffy cheeks, the tiny blue eyes, the round pug nose, all were engorged in scarlet fury. He cradled the baby in his arms as best he could and rocked it. The crying dimmed momentarily, then began again.

His mind ran the gauntlet of childhood scares—diphtheria, smallpox, measles, mumps, croup, even a pressing need to burp. God knew what ailed it. He patted its forehead and felt the sticky heat of fever.

Shifting position, he felt something hard within the blanket, felt for it, finally drew it out. A nippled baby bottle, half-filled, body-warm. He shook it and presented the nipple to the baby, who sucked it as its due. Giddy at his feat, he unwrapped his package further, enough to tell him he was holding a little girl and that she seemed whole and healthy except for her rage and fever. When she was feeding steadily he put her back on the floor and got out of the car.

The stream of smoke it emitted into the evening dusk made the cabin seem dangled from a string. Beneath the firs the ground was moist, a spongy mat of rotting twigs and needles. The air was cold and damp and smelled of burning wood. He walked slowly up the drive, courting silence, alert for the menace implied by the hand-lettered sign, nailed to the nearest tree, that ordered him to KEEP OUT.

The cabin was dark but for the variable light at a single window. The porch was piled high with firewood, both logs and kindling. A maul and wedge leaned against a stack of fruitwood piled next to the door. He walked to the far side of the cabin and looked beyond it for signs of Marvin.

A tool shed and a broken-down school bus filled the rear yard. Between the two a tethered nanny goat grazed beneath a line of drying clothes, silent but for her neck bell, the swollen udder oscillating easily beneath her, the teats extended like accusing fingers. Beyond the yard a thicket of berry bushes served as fence, and beyond the bushes a stand of pines blocked further vision. He felt alien, isolated, exposed, threatened, as Marvin doubtlessly hoped all strangers would.

He thought about the baby, wondered if it was all right, wondered if babies could drink so much they got sick or even choked. A twinge of fear sent him trotting back to the car. The baby was fine, the bottle empty on the floor beside it, its noises not wails but only muffled whimpers. He returned to the cabin and went onto the porch and knocked at the door and waited.

Iris wore the same blouse and skirt and boots, the same eyes too shallow to hold her soul. She didn't recognize him; her face pinched only with uncertainty.

He stepped toward her and she backed away and asked him what he wanted. The room behind her was a warren of vague shapes, the only source of light far in the back by a curtain that spanned the room.

"I want to give you your baby back," he said.

She looked at him more closely, then opened her mouth in silent exclamation, then slowly smiled. "How'd you know where I lived?"

"I followed you."

"Why? Did something happen to it already?"

"No, but I don't want to take it with me."

She seemed truly puzzled. "Why not? It's on your way, isn't it? Almost?"

He ignored the question. "I want to know some more about the baby."

"Like what?"

"Like whose is it? Yours?"

Iris frowned and nibbled her lower lip. "Sort of."

"What do you mean, 'sort of?' Did you give birth to it?"

"Not exactly." Iris combed her hair with her fingers, then shook it off her face with an irritated twitch. "What are you asking all these questions for?"

"Because you asked me to do you a favor and I think I have the right to know what I'm getting into. That's only fair, isn't it?"

She paused. Her pout was dubious. "I guess."

"So where did you get the baby?" he asked again.

"Marvin got it."

"From whom?"

"Those people in Hurley City. So I don't know why you won't take it back, seeing as how it's theirs and all."

"But why . . ."

His question was obliterated by a high glissando, brief and piercing. He looked at Iris, then at the shadowy interior of the cabin.

There was no sign of life, no sign of anything but the leavings of neglect and a spartan bent. A fat gray cat hopped off a shelf and sauntered toward the back of the cabin and disappeared behind the blanket that was draped on the rope that spanned the rear of the room. The cry echoed once again. "What's that?" he asked her.

Iris giggled. "What does it sound like?"

"Another baby?"

Iris nodded.

"Can I see it?"

"Why?"

"Because I like babies."

"If you like them, why won't you take the one I gave you down to Hurley City?"

"Maybe I'm changing my mind. Can I see this one?"

"I'm not supposed to let anyone in here."

"It'll be okay. Really. Marvin isn't here, is he?"

She shook her head. "But he'll be back any time. He just went to town."

He summoned reasonableness and geniality. "Just let me see your baby for a second, Iris. Please? Then I'll go. And take the other baby with me. I promise."

She pursed her lips, then nodded and stepped back. "I got more than one," she suddenly bragged. "Let me show you." She turned and walked quickly toward the rear of the cabin and disappeared behind the blanket.

When he followed he found himself in a space that was half-kitchen and half-nursery. Opposite the electric stove and Frigidaire, along the wall between the wood stove and the rear door, was a row of wooden boxes, seven of them, old orange crates, dividers removed, painted different colors and labeled A to G. Faint names of orchards and renderings of fruits rose through the paint on the stub ends of the crates. Inside boxes C through G were babies, buried deep in nests of rags and scraps of blanket. One of them was crying. The others slept soundly, warm and toasty, healthy and happy from all the evidence he had.

"My God," he said.

"Aren't they beautiful? They're just the best little things in the whole world. Yes they are. Just the best little babies in the whole wide world. And Iris loves them all a bunch. Yes, she does. Doesn't she?"

Beaming, Iris cooed to the babies for another moment, then her face darkened. "The one I gave you, she wasn't happy here. That's because she was a B Box baby. My B babies are always sad, I don't know why. I treat them all the same, but the B babies are just contrary. That's why the one I gave you should go back. Where is it, anyway?"

"In the car."

"By itself?"

He nodded.

"You shouldn't leave her there like that," Iris chided. "She's pouty enough already."

"What about these others?" he asked, looking at the boxes. "Do they stay here forever?"

Her whole aspect solidified. "They stay till Marvin needs them. Till he does, I give them everything they want. Everything they need. No one could be nicer to my babies than me. *No* one."

The fire in the stove lit her eyes like ice in sunlight. She gazed raptly at the boxes, one by one, and received something he sensed was sexual in return. Her breaths were rapid and shallow, her fists clenched at her sides. "Where'd you get these babies?" he asked softly.

"Marvin gets them." She was only half-listening.

"Where?"

"All over. We had one from Nevada one time, and two from Idaho I think. Most are from California, though. And Oregon. I think that C Box baby's from Spokane. That's Oregon, isn't it?"

He didn't correct her. "Have there been more besides these?"

"Some."

"How many?"

"Oh, maybe ten. No, more than that. I've had three of all the babies except G babies."

"And Marvin got them all for you?"

She nodded and went to the stove and turned on a burner. "You want some tea? It's herbal. Peppermint."

He shook his head. "What happened to the other babies? The ones that aren't here any more?"

"Marvin took them." Iris sipped her tea.

"Where?"

"To someone that wanted to love them." The declaration was as close as she would come to gospel.

The air in the cabin seemed suddenly befouled, not breathable. "Is that what this is all about, Iris? Giving babies to people that want them?"

"That want them and will *love* them. See, Marvin gets these babies from people that *don't* want them, and gives them to people that *do*. It's his business."

"Does he get paid for it?"

She shrugged absently. "A little, I think."

"Do you go with Marvin when he picks them up?"

"Sometimes. When it's far."

"And where does he take them? To Idaho and Nevada, or just around here?"

She shrugged again. "He doesn't tell me where they go. He says he doesn't want me to try and get them back." She smiled peacefully. "He knows how I am about my babies."

"How long have you and Marvin been doing this?"

"I been with Marvin about three years."

"And you've been trading in babies all that time?"

"Just about."

She poured some more tea into a ceramic cup and sipped it. She gave no sign of guile or guilt, no sign that what he suspected could possibly be true.

"Do you have any children of your own, Iris?"

Her hand shook enough to spill her tea. "I *almost* had one once."

"What do you mean?"

She made a face. "I got pregnant, but nobody wanted me to keep it so I didn't."

"Did you put it up for adoption?"

She shook her head.

"Abortion?"

Iris nodded, apparently in pain, and mumbled something. He asked her what she'd said. "I did it myself," she repeated. "That's what I can't live with. I scraped it out of there myself. I passed out. I . . ."

She fell silent. He looked back at the row of boxes that held her penance. When she saw him look she began to sing a song. "Aren't they just perfect?" she said when she was through. "Aren't they all just perfect?"

"How do you know where the baby you gave me belongs?" he asked quietly.

"Marvin's got a book that keeps track. I sneaked a look at it one time when he was stoned."

"Where's he keep it?"

"In the van. At least that's where I found it." Iris put her hands on his chest and pushed. "You better go before Marvin gets back. You'll take the baby, won't you? It just don't belong here with the others. It fusses all the time and I can't love it like I should."

He looked at Iris's face, at the firelight washing across it, making it alive. "Where are you from, Iris?"

"Me? Minnesota."

"Did you come to California with Marvin?"

She shook her head. "I come with another guy. I was tricking for him when I got knocked up. After the abortion I told him I wouldn't trick no more so he ditched me. Then I did a lot of drugs for a while, till I met Marvin at a commune down by Mendocino."

"What's Marvin's last name?"

"Hessel. Now you got to go. Really. Marvin's liable to do something crazy if he finds you here." She walked toward him and he retreated.

"Okay, Iris. Just one thing. Could you give me something for the baby to eat? She's real hungry."

Iris frowned. "She only likes goat's milk, is the problem, and I haven't milked today." She walked to the Frigidaire and returned with a bottle. "This is all I got. Now, git."

He nodded, took the bottle from her, then retreated to his car.

He opened the door on the stinging smell of ammonia. The baby greeted him with screams. He picked it up, rocked it, talked to it, hummed a tune, finally gave it the second bottle, which was the only thing it wanted.

As it sucked its sustenance he started the car and let the engine warm, and a minute later flipped the heater switch. When it seemed prudent, he unwrapped the child and unpinned her soggy diaper and patted her dumplinged bottom dry with a tissue from the glove compartment. After covering her with her blanket he got out of the car, pulled his suitcase from the trunk and took out his last clean T-shirt, then returned to the car and fashioned a bulky diaper out of the cotton shirt and affixed it to the child, pricking his finger in the process, spotting both the garment and the baby with his blood. Then he sat for a time, considering his obligations to the children that had suddenly littered his life.

He should go to the police, but Marvin might return before they responded and might learn of Iris' deed and harm the children or flee with them. He could call the police and wait in place for them to come, but he doubted his ability to convey his precise suspicions over the phone. As he searched for other options, headlights ricocheted off his mirror and into his eyes, then veered off. When his vision was re-established he reached into the glove compartment for his revolver. Shoving it into his pocket, he got out of the car and walked back to the driveway and disobeyed the sign again.

A new shape had joined the scene, rectangular and dark. Marvin's van, creaking as it cooled. He waited, listened, and when he sensed no other presence he approached it. A converted bread truck, painted Navy blue, with sliding doors into the driver's cabin and hinged doors at the back. The right fender was dented, the rear bumper wired in place. A knobby-tired motorcycle was strapped to a rack on the top. The door on the driver's side was open, so he climbed in.

The high seat was rotted through, its stuffing erupting like white weeds through the dirty vinyl. The floorboards were littered with food wrappers and beer cans and cigarette butts. He activated his pencil flash and pawed through the refuse, pausing at the only pristine object in the van—a business card, white with black engraving, taped to a corner of the dash: 'J. Arnold Rasker, Attorney at Law. Practice in all Courts. Initial Consultation Free. Phone day or night.'

He looked through the cab for another minute, found nothing resembling Marvin's notebook and nothing else of interest. After listening for Marvin's return and hearing nothing he went through the narrow doorway behind the driver's seat into the cargo area in the rear, the yellow ball that dangled from his flash bouncing playfully before him.

The entire area had been carpeted, ceiling included, in a matted pink plush that was stained in unlikely places and coming unglued in others. A roundish window had been cut into one wall by hand, then covered with plasticine kept in place with tape. Two upholstered chairs were bolted to the floor on one side of the van, and an Army cot stretched out along the other. Two orange crates similar to those in the cabin, though empty, lay between the chairs. Above the cot a picture of John Lennon was tacked to the carpeted wall with a rusty nail. A small propane bottle was strapped into one corner, an Igloo cooler in another. Next to the Lennon poster a lever-action rifle rested in two leather slings. The smells were of gasoline and marijuana and unwashed flesh. Again he found no notebook.

He switched off his light and backed out of the van and walked to the cabin, pausing on the porch. Music pulsed from the interior, heavy metal, obliterating all noises including his own. He walked to the window and peered inside.

Iris, carrying and feeding a baby, paced the room, eyes closed, mumbling, seemingly deranged. Alone momentarily, she was soon joined by a wide and woolly man, wearing cowboy boots and Levi's, a plaid shirt, full beard, hair to his shoulders. A light film of grease coated flesh and clothes alike, as though he had just been dipped. Marvin strode through the room without speaking, his black eyes angry, his shoulders tipping to the frenetic music as he sucked the final puffs of a joint held in an oddly dainty clip.

Both Marvin and Iris were lost in their tasks. When their paths crossed they backed away as though they feared each other. He watched them for five long minutes. When they disappeared behind the curtain in the back he hurried to the door and went inside the cabin.

The music paused, then began again, the new piece indistinguishable from the old. The heavy fog of dope washed into his lungs and lightened his head and braked his brain. Murmurs from behind the curtain erupted into a swift male curse. A pan clattered on the stove; wood scraped against wood. He drew his gun and moved to the edge of the room and sidled toward the curtain and peered around its edge.

Marvin sat in a chair at a small table, gripping a bottle of beer. Iris was at the stove, her back to Marvin, opening a can of soup. Marvin guzzled half the bottle, banged it on the table, and swore again. "How could you be so fucking stupid?"

"Don't, Marvin. Please?"

"Just tell me who you gave it to. That's all I want to know. It was your buddy Gretel, wasn't it? Had to be, she's the only one around here as loony as you."

"It wasn't anyone you know. Really. It was just a guy."

"What guy?"

"Just *a guy.* I went out to a rest area way up by Oregon, and I talked to him and he said he was going to Frisco so I gave it to him and told him where to take it. You *know* it didn't belong here, Marvin. You know how puny it was."

Marvin stood up, knocking his chair to the floor. "You stupid bitch." His hand raised high, Marvin advanced on Iris with beer dribbling from his chin. "I'll break your jaw, woman. I swear I will."

"Don't hit me, Marvin. Please don't hit me again."

"Who was it? I want a name."

"I don't *know,* I told you. Just some guy going to Frisco. His name was Mark, I think."

"And he took the kid?"

Iris nodded. "He was real nice."

"You bring him here? Huh? Did you bring the son-of-a-bitch to the cabin? Did you tell him about the others?"

"No, Marvin. No. I swear. You know I'd never do that."

"Lying bitch."

Marvin grabbed Iris by the hair and dragged her away from the stove and slapped her across the face. She screamed and cowered. Marvin raised his hand to strike again.

Sucking a breath, he raised his gun and stepped from behind the curtain. "Hold it," he told Marvin. "Don't move."

Marvin froze, twisted his head, took in the gun and released his grip on Iris and backed away from her, his black eyes glistening. A slow smile exposed dark and crooked teeth. "Well, now," Marvin drawled. "Just who might you be besides a fucking trespasser? Don't tell me; let me guess. You're the nice man Iris gave a baby to. The one she swore she didn't bring out here. Right?"

"She didn't bring me. I followed her."

Both men glanced at Iris. Her hand was at her mouth and she was nibbling a knuckle. "I thought you went to Frisco," was all she said.

"Not yet."

"What do you want?" Her question assumed a fearsome answer.

Marvin laughed. "You stupid bitch. He wants the *rest* of them. Then he wants to throw us in jail. He wants to be a hero, Iris. And to be a hero he has to put you and me behind bars for the rest of our fucking lives." Marvin took a step forward.

"Don't be dumb." He raised the gun to Marvin's eyes.

Marvin stopped, frowned, then grinned again. "You look like you used that piece before."

"Once or twice."

"What's your gig?"

"Detective. Private."

Marvin's lips parted around his crusted teeth. "You must be kidding. Iris flags down some bastard on the freeway and he turns out to be a private cop?"

"That's about it."

Marvin shook his head. "Judas H. Priest. And here you are. A professional hero, just like I said."

He captured Marvin's eyes. "I want the book."

"What book?" Marvin burlesqued ignorance.

"The book with the list of babies and where you got them and where you took them."

Marvin looked at Iris, stuck her with his stare. "You're dead meat, you know that? You bring the bastard here and tell him all about it and expect him to just take off and not try to *stop* us? You're too fucking dumb to breathe, Iris. I got to put you out of your misery."

"I'm sorry, Marvin."

"He's going to take them *back*, Iris. Get it? He's going to take those sweet babies away from you and give them back to the assholes that don't want them. And then he's going to the cops and they're going to say you *kidnapped* those babies, Iris, and that you were bad to them and should go to jail because of what you did. Don't you see that, you brain-fried bitch? *Don't you see what he's going to do?*"

"I . . ." Iris stopped, overwhelmed by Marvin's incantation. "Are you?" she asked, finally looking away from Marvin.

"I'm going to do what's best for the babies, Iris. That's all."

"What's best for them is with me and Marvin."

"Not any more," he told her. "Marvin's been shucking you, Iris. He steals those babies. Takes them from their parents, parents who love them. He roams up and down the coast stealing children and then he sells them, Iris. Either back to the people he took them from or to people desperate to adopt. I think he's hooked up with a lawyer named Rasker, who arranges private adoptions for big money and splits the take with Marvin. He's not interested in who loves those kids, Iris. He's only interested in how much he can sell them for."

Something had finally activated Iris' eyes. "Marvin? Is that true?"

"No, baby. The guy's blowing smoke. He's trying to take the babies away from you and then get people to believe you did something bad, just like that time with the abortion. He's trying to say you did bad things to babies again, Iris. We can't let him do that."

He spoke quickly, to erase Marvin's words. "People don't give away babies, Iris. Not to guys like Marvin. There are agencies that arrange that kind of thing, that check to make sure the new home is in the best interests of the child. Marvin just swipes them and sells them to the highest bidder, Iris. That's all he's in it for."

"I don't believe you."

"It doesn't matter. Just give me Marvin's notebook and we can check it out, contact the parents and see what they say about their kids. Ask if they wanted to be rid of them. That's fair, isn't it?"

"I don't know. I guess."

"Iris?"

"What, Marvin?"

"I want you to pick up that pan and knock this guy on the head. Hard. Go on, Iris. He won't shoot you, you know that. Hit him on the head so he can't put us in jail."

He glanced at Iris, then as quickly to Marvin and to Iris once again. "Don't do it, Iris. Marvin's trouble. I think you know that now." He looked away from Iris and gestured at her partner. "Where's the book?"

"Iris?"

Iris began to cry. "I can't, Marvin. I can't do that."

"The book," he said to Marvin again. "Where is it?"

Marvin laughed. "You'll never know, detective."

"Okay. We'll do it your way. On the floor. Hands behind your head. Legs spread. Now."

Marvin didn't move. When he spoke the words were languid. "You don't look much like a killer, detective, and I've known a few, believe me. So I figure if you're not gonna shoot me I don't got to do what you say. I figure I'll just take that piece away from you and feed it to you inch by inch. Huh? Why don't I do just that?"

He took two quick steps to Marvin's side and sliced open Marvin's cheek with a quick swipe of the gun barrel. "Want some more?"

Marvin pawed at his cheek with a grimy hand, then examined his bloody fingers. "You bastard. Okay. I'll get the book. It's under here."

Marvin bent toward the floor, twisting away from him, sliding his hands toward the darkness below the stove. He couldn't tell what Marvin was doing, so he squinted, then moved closer. When Marvin began to stand he jumped back, but Marvin wasn't attacking, Marvin was holding a baby, not a book, holding a baby by the throat.

"Okay, pal," Marvin said through his grin. "Now, you want to see this kid die before your eyes, you just keep hold of that gun. You want to see it breathe some more, you drop it."

He froze, his eyes on Marvin's fingers, which inched further around the baby's neck and began to squeeze.

The baby gurgled, gasped, twitched, was silent. Its face reddened; its eyes bulged. The tendons in Marvin's hand stretched taut. Between grimy gritted teeth, Marvin wheezed in rapid streams of glee.

He dropped his gun. Marvin told Iris to pick it up. She did, and exchanged the gun for the child. Her eyes lapped Marvin's face, as though to renew its acquaintance. Abruptly, she turned and ran around the curtain and disappeared.

"Well, now." Marvin's words slid easily. "Looks like the worm has turned, detective. What's your name, anyhow?"

"Tanner."

"Well, Tanner, your ass is mine. No more John Wayne stunts for you. You can kiss this world good-bye."

Marvin fished in the pocket of his jeans, then drew out a small spiral notebook and flashed it. "It's all in here, Tanner. Where they came from; where they went. Now watch."

Gun in one hand, notebook in the other, Marvin went to the wood stove and flipped open the heavy door. The fire made shadows dance.

"Don't."

"Watch, bastard."

Marvin tossed the notebook into the glowing coals, fished in the box beside the stove for a stick of kindling, then tossed it in after the notebook and closed the iron door. "Bye-bye babies." Marvin's laugh was quick and cruel. "Now turn around. We're going out back."

He did as he was told, walking toward the door, hearing only a silent shuffle at his back. As he passed her he glanced at Iris. She hugged the baby Marvin had threatened, crying, not looking at him. "Remember the one in my car," he said to her. She nodded silently, then turned away.

Marvin prodded him in the back and he moved to the door. Hand on the knob, he paused, hoping for a magical deliverance, but none came. Marvin prodded him again and he moved outside, onto the porch then into the yard. "Around back," Marvin ordered. "Get in the bus."

He staggered, tripping over weeds, stumbling over rocks, until he reached the rusting bus. The moon and stars had disappeared; the night was black and still but for the whistling wind, clearly Marvin's ally. The nanny goat laughed at them, then trotted out of reach. He glanced back at Marvin. In one hand was a pistol, in the other a blanket. "Go on in. Just pry the door open."

He fit his finger between the rubber edges of the bus door and opened it. The first step was higher than he thought, and he tripped and almost fell. "Watch it. I almost blasted you right then."

He couldn't suppress a giggle. For reasons of his own, Marvin matched his laugh. "Head on back, Tanner. Pretend you're on a field trip to the zoo."

He walked down the aisle between the broken seats, smelling rot and rust and the lingering scent of skunk. "Why here?" he asked as he reached the rear.

"Because you'll keep in here just fine till I get time to dig a hole out back and open that emergency door and dump you in. Plus it's quiet. I figure with the bus and the blanket no one will hear a thing. Sit."

He sat. Marvin draped the blanket across the arm that held the gun, then extended the shrouded weapon toward his chest. He had no doubt that Marvin would shoot without a thought or fear. "Any last words, Tanner? Any parting thoughts?"

"Just that you forgot something."

"What?"

"You left the door open."

Marvin glanced quickly toward the door in the front of the bus. He dove for Marvin's legs, sweeping at the gun with his left hand as he did so, hoping to dislodge it into the folds of the blanket where it would lie useless and unattainable.

"Cocksucker."

Marvin wrested the gun from his grasp and raised it high, tossing off the blanket in the process. He twisted frantically to protect against the blow he knew was coming, but Marvin was too heavy and strong, retained the upper hand by kneeling on his chest. The revolver glinted in the darkness, a missile poised to descend.

Sound split the air, a piercing scream of agony from the cabin or somewhere near it. "What the hell?" Marvin swore, started to retreat, then almost thoughtlessly clubbed him with the gun, once, then again. After a flash of pain a broad black creature held him down for a length of time he couldn't calculate.

When he was aware again he was alone in the bus, lying in the aisle. His head felt crushed to pulp. He put a hand to his temple and felt blood. Midst throbbing pain he struggled to his feet and made his way outside and stood leaning against the bus while the night air struggled to clear his head.

He took a step, staggered, took another and gained an equilibrium, then lost it and sat down. Back on his feet, he trudged toward the porch and opened the door. Behind him, the nanny laughed again.

The cabin was dark, the only light the faint flicker from the stove behind the curtain. He walked carefully, trying to avoid the litter on the floor, the shapes in the room. Halfway to the back his foot struck something soft. As he bent to shove it out of his way it made a human sound. He knelt, saw that it was Iris, then found a lamp and turned it on.

She was crumpled, face down, in the center of the room, arms and legs folded under her, her body curled to avoid assault. He knelt again, heard her groan once more, and saw that what he'd thought was a piece of skirt was in fact a pool of blood and what he'd thought was shadow was a broad wet trail of the selfsame substance leading toward the rear of the cabin.

He ran his hands down her body, feeling for wounds. Finding none, he rolled Iris to her side, then to her back. Blood bubbled from a point beneath her sternum. Her eyelids fluttered, open, closed, then open again. "He shot me," she said. "It hurt so bad I couldn't stop crying so he shot me."

"I know. Don't try to talk."

"Did he shoot the babies, too? I thought I heard . . ."

"I don't know."

"Would you look? Please?"

He nodded, stood up, fought a siege of vertigo, then went behind the curtain, then returned to Iris. "They're all right."

She tried to smile her thanks. "Something scared him off. I think some people were walking by outside and heard the shot and went for help. I heard them yelling."

"Where would he go, Iris?"

"Up in the woods. On his dirt bike. He knows lots of people up there. They grow dope, live off the land. The cops'll never find him." Iris moaned again. "I'm dying, aren't I?"

"I don't know. Is there a phone here?"

She shook her head. "Down at the end of the street. By the market."

"I'm going down and call an ambulance. And the cops. How long ago did Marvin leave?"

She closed her eyes. "I blacked out. Oh, God. It's real bad now, Mr. Tanner. Real bad."

"I know, Iris. You hang on. I'll be back in a second. Try to hold this in place." He took out his handkerchief and folded it into a square and placed it on her wound.

"Press as hard as you can." He took her left hand and placed it on the compress, then stood up.

"Wait. I have to . . ."

He spoke above her words. "You have to get to a hospital. I'll be back in a minute and we can talk some more."

"But . . ."

"Hang on."

He ran from the cabin and down the drive, spotted the lights of the convenience market down the street and ran to the phone booth and placed his calls. The police said they'd already been notified and a car was on the way. The ambulance said it would be six minutes. As fast as he could he ran back to the cabin, hoping it would be fast enough.

Iris had moved. Her body was straightened, her right arm outstretched toward the door, the gesture of a supplicant. The sleeve of her blouse was tattered, burned to a ragged edge above her elbow. Below the sleeve her arm was red in spots, blistered in others, dappled like burned food. The hand at its end was charred and curled into a crusty fist that was dusted with gray ash. Within the fingers was an object, blackened, burned, and treasured.

He pried it from her grasp. The cover was burned away, and the edges of the pages were curled and singed, but they remained decipherable, the written scrawl preserved. The list of names and places was organized to match the gaily painted boxes in the back. Carson City. Boise. Grant's Pass. San Bernardino. Modesto. On and on, a gazetteer of crime.

"I saved it," Iris mumbled. "I saved it for my babies."

He raised her head to his lap and held it till she died. Then he went to his car and retrieved his B Box baby and placed her in her appointed crib. For the first time since he'd known her the baby made only happy sounds, an irony that was lost on the five dead children at her flank and on the just dead woman who had feared it all.

HIGH DARKTOWN

JAMES ELLROY
(1948–   )

*The story has been told often of the eleven-year-old Ellroy coming home after a weekend
with his father to find the police at his house and the strangled body of his mother in the
bushes outside it. Ellroy's descent into alcoholism, drug abuse, and crime turned around
by his sheer strength of will when he taught himself to write novels. Now, he is an international best-seller with a goal: to be recognized as the greatest crime writer of his era.*

ROM MY OFFICE WINDOWS I
watched L.A. celebrate
the end of World War II.
Central Division Warrants took up the
entire north side of City Hall's eleventh
floor, so my vantage point was high
and wide. I saw clerks drinking straight
from the bottle in the Hall of Records
parking lot across the street and harness bulls forming a riot squad and
heading for little Tokyo a few blocks
away, bent on holding back a conga
line of youths with 2 by 4s who looked
bent on going the atom bomb one better. Craning my neck, I glimpsed tall
black plumes of smoke on Bunker
Hill—a sure sign that patriotic Belmont
High students were stripping cars and
setting the tires on fire. Over on Sunset
and Figueroa, knots of zooters were
assembling in violation of the Zoot Suit
Ordinance, no doubt figuring that
today it was anything goes.

The tiny window above my desk
had an eastern exposure, and it offered
up nothing but smog and a giant traffic
jam inching toward Boyle Heights. I
stared into the brown haze, imagining
shitloads of code 2s and 3s thwarted

by noxious fumes and bumper-to-
bumper revelry. My daydreams got
more and more vivid, and when I had a
whole skyful of A-bombs descending
on the offices of the L.A.P.D. Detective
Bureau, I slammed my desk and picked
up the two pieces of paper I had been
avoiding all morning.

The first sheet was a scrawled
memo from the Daywatch Robbery
boss down the hall: "Lee—Wallace
Simpkins paroled from Quentin last
week—to our jurisdiction. Thought
you should know. Be careful. G.C."

Cheery V-J Day tidings.

The second page was an interde-
partmental teletype issued from University Division, and, when combined
with Georgie Caulkins's warning, it
spelled out the beginning of a new one-
front war.

Over the past five days there had
been four heavy-muscled stickups in
the West Adams district, perpetrated
by a two-man heist team, one white,
one negro. The MO was identical in all
four cases: liquor stores catering to
upper-crust negroes were hit at night,
half an hour before closing, when the

cash registers were full. A well-dressed male Caucasian would walk in and beat the clerk to the floor with the barrel of a .45 automatic, while the negro heister stuffed the till cash into a paper bag. Twice customers had been present when the robberies occurred; they had also been beaten senseless—one elderly woman was still in critical condition at Queen of Angels.

It was as simple and straightforward as a neon sign. I picked up the phone and called Al Van Patten's personal number at the County Parole Bureau.

"Speak, it's your nickel."

"Lee Blanchard, Al."

"Big Lee! You working today? The war's over!"

"No, it's not. Listen, I need the disposition on a parolee. Came out of Quentin last week. If he reported in, I need an address; if he hasn't, just tell me."

"Name? Charge?"

"Wallace Simpkins, 655 PC. I sent him up myself in '39."

Al whistled. "Light jolt. He got juice?"

"Probably kept his nose clean and worked a war industries job inside; his partner got released to the army after Pearl Harbor. Hurry it up, will you?"

"Off and running."

Al dropped the receiver to his desk, and I suffered through long minutes of static-filtered party noise—male and female giggles, bottles clinking together, happy county flunkies turning radio dials trying to find dance music but getting only jubilant accounts of the big news. Through Edward R. Murrow's uncharacteristically cheerful drone I pictured Wild Wally Simpkins, flush with cash and armed for bear, looking for me. I was shivering when Al came back on the line and said, "He's hot, Lee."

"Bench warrant issued?"

"Not yet."

"Then don't waste your time."

"What are you talking about?"

"Small potatoes. Call Lieutenant Holland at University dicks and tell him Simpkins is half of the heist team he's looking for. Tell him to put out an APB and add, 'armed and extremely dangerous' and 'apprehend with all force deemed necessary.'"

Al whistled again. "That bad?"

I said, "Yeah," and hung up. "Apprehend with all force deemed necessary" was the L.A.P.D. euphemism for "shoot on sight." I felt my fear decelerate just a notch. Finding fugitive felons was my job. Slipping an extra piece into my back waistband, I set out to find the man who had vowed to kill me.

After picking up standing mugs of Simpkins and a carbon of the robbery report from Georgie Caulkins, I drove toward the West Adams district. The day was hot and humid, and sidewalk mobs spilled into the street, passing victory bottles to horn-honking motorists. Traffic was bottlenecked at every stoplight, and paper debris floated down from office windows—a makeshift ticker-tape parade. The scene made me itchy, so I attached the roof light and hit my siren, weaving around stalled cars until downtown was a blur in my rearview mirror. When I slowed, I was all the way to Alvarado and the city I had sworn to protect looked normal again. Slowing to a crawl in the right-hand lane, I thought of Wallace Simpkins and knew the itch wouldn't stop until the bastard was bought and paid for.

We went back six years, to the fall of '39, when I was a vice officer in University Division and a regular light-heavyweight attraction at the Hollywood-Legion Stadium. A black-white stickup gang had been clouting markets and juke joints on West Adams, the white guy passing himself off as a member of Mickey Cohen's mob, coercing the proprietor into opening up the safe for the monthly protection pay-ment while the negro guy looked around innocently, then hit the cash registers. When the white guy got to the safe, he took all the money, then pistol-whipped the proprietor senseless. The heisters would then drive slowly north into the respectable Wilshire district, the white guy at the wheel, the negro guy huddled down in the back seat.

I got involved in the investigation on a fluke.

After the fifth job, the gang stopped cold. A stoolie of mine told me that Mickey Cohen found out that the white muscle was an ex-enforcer of his and had him snuffed. Rumor had it that the colored guy—a cowboy known only as Wild Wallace—was looking for a new partner and a new territory. I passed the information along to the dicks and thought nothing more of it. Then, a week later, it all hit the fan.

As a reward for my tip, I got a choice moonlight assignment: bodyguarding a high-stakes poker game frequented by L.A.P.D. brass and navy bigwigs up from San Diego. The game was held in the back room at Minnie Roberts's Casbah, the swanki-est police-sanctioned whorehouse on the south side. All I had to do was look big, mean, and servile and be willing to share boxing anecdotes. It was a major step toward sergeant's stripes and a transfer to the Detective Division.

It went well—all smiles and backslaps and recountings of my split-decision loss to Jimmy Bivins—until a negro guy in a chauffeur's outfit and an olive-skinned youth in a navy officer's uniform walked in the door. I saw a gun bulge under the chauf-feur's left arm, and chandelier light fluttering over the navy man's face revealed pale negro skin and processed hair.

And I knew.

I walked up to Wallace Simpkins, my right hand extended. When he grasped it, I sent a knee into his balls and a hard left hook at his neck. When he hit the floor, I pinned him there with a foot on his gun bulge, drew my own piece, and leveled it at his part-ner. "Bon voyage, Admiral," I said.

The admiral was named William Boyle, an apprentice armed robber from a black bourgeois family fallen on hard times. He turned state's evidence on Wild Wallace, drew a reduced three-to-five jolt at Chino as part of the deal, and was paroled to the war effort early in '42. Simpkins was convicted of five counts of robbery one with aggravated assault, got five-to-life at Big Q, and voodoo-hexed Billy Boyle and me at his trial, vowing on the soul of Baron Samedi to kill both of us, chop us into stew meat, and feed it to his dog. I more than half believed his vow, and for the first few years he was away, every time I got an unexplainable ache or pain I thought of him in his cell, sticking pins into a blue-suited Lee Blanchard voodoo doll.

I checked the robbery report lying on the seat beside me. The addresses of the four new black-white stickups covered 26th and Gramercy to La Brea and Adams. Hitting the racial demarcation line, I watched the topography change from negligent middle-class white to proud colored. East of St. Andrews, the houses were unkempt, with peeling paint and ratty front lawns. On the west the homes took on an air of elegance: small dwellings were encircled by stone fencing and well-tended green-ery; the mansions that had earned West Adams the sobriquet High Darktown put Beverly Hills pads to shame—they were older, larger, and less architecturally pre-tentious, as if the owners knew that the only way to be rich and black was to down-play the performance with the quiet noblesse oblige of old white money.

I knew High Darktown only from the scores of conflicting legends about it. When I worked University Division, it was never on my beat. It was the lowest per capita crime area in L.A. The University brass followed an implicit edict of letting rich black police rich black, as if they figured blue suits couldn't speak the language there at all. And the High Darktown citizens did a good job. Burglars foolish enough to trek across giant front lawns and punch in Tiffany windows were dispatched by volleys from thousand-dollar skeet guns held by negro financiers with an aristo-cratic panache to rival that of *anyone* white and big-moneyed. High Darktown did a damn good job of being inviolate.

But the legends were something else, and when I worked University, I wondered if they had been started and repeatedly embellished only because square-john white cops couldn't take the fact that there were "niggers," "shines," "spooks," and "jigs" who were capable of buying their low-rent lives outright. The stories ran from the relatively prosaic: negro boot-leggers with mob connections taking their loot and buying liquor stores in Watts and wetback-staffed garment mills in San Pedro, to exotic: the same thugs flooding low darktowns with cut-rate heroin and pimping out their most beautiful high-yellow sweethearts to L.A.'s powers-that-be in order to circumvent licensing and real estate statutes enforcing racial exclusivity. There was only one common denominator to all the legends: it was agreed that although High Darktown money started out dirty, it was now squeaky clean and snow white.

Pulling up in front of the liquor store on Gramercy, I quickly scanned the dick's report on the robbery there, learning that the clerk was alone when it went down and saw both robbers up close before the white man pistol-whipped him uncon-scious. Wanting an eyeball witness to back up Lieutenant Holland's APB, I entered the immaculate little shop and walked up to the counter.

A negro man with his head swathed in bandages walked in from the back. Eyeing me top to bottom, he said, "Yes, officer?"

I liked his brevity and reciprocated it. Holding up the mug shot of Wallace Simpkins, I said, "Is this one of the guys?"

Flinching backward, he said, "Yes. Get him."

"Bought and paid for," I said.

An hour later I had three more eyeball confirmations and turned my mind to strat-egy. With the all-points out on Simpkins, he'd probably get juked by the first blue suit who crossed his path, a thought only partly comforting. Artie Holland probably had stake-out teams stationed in the back rooms of other liquor stores in the area, and a prowl of Simpkins's known haunts was a ridiculous play for a solo white man. Parking on an elm-lined street, I watched Japanese gardeners tend football field–sized lawns and started to sense that Wild Wallace's affinity for High Darktown and white partners was the lever I needed. I set out to trawl for pale-skinned intruders like myself.

South on La Brea to Jefferson, then up to Western and back over to Adams. Runs down 1st Avenue, 2nd Avenue, 3rd, 4th, and 5th. The only white men I saw were other cops, mailmen, store owners, and poontang prowlers. A circuit of the bars on Washington yielded no white faces and no known criminal types I could shake down for information.

Dusk found me hungry, angry, and still itchy, imagining Simpkins poking pins in a brand-new, plainclothes Blanchard doll. I stopped at a barbecue joint and wolfed down a beef sandwich, slaw, and fries. I was on my second cup of coffee when the mixed couple came in.

The girl was a pretty high yellow—soft angularity in a pink summer dress that tried to downplay her curves, and failed. The man was squat and muscular, wearing a rumpled Hawaiian shirt and pressed khaki trousers that looked like army issue. From my table I heard them place their order: jumbo chicken dinners for six with extra gravy and biscuits. "Lots of big appetites," the guy said to the counterman. When the line got him a deadpan, he goosed the girl with his knee. She moved away, clenching her fists and twisting her head as if trying to avoid an unwanted kiss. Catching her face full view, I saw loathing etched into every feature.

They registered as trouble, and I walked out to my car in order to tail them when they left the restaurant. Five minutes later they appeared, the girl walking ahead, the man a few paces behind her, tracing hourglass figures in the air and flicking his tongue like a lizard. They got into a prewar Packard sedan parked in front of me, Lizard Man taking the wheel. When they accelerated, I counted to ten and pursued.

The Packard was an easy surveillance. It had a long radio antenna topped with a foxtail, so I was able to remain several car lengths in back and use the tail as a sighting device. We moved out of High Darktown on Western, and within minutes mansions and proudly tended homes were replaced by tenements and tar-paper shacks encircled by chicken wire. The farther south we drove the worse it got; when the Packard hung a left on 94th and headed east, past auto graveyards, storefront voodoo mosques and hair-straightening parlors, it felt like entering White Man's Hell.

At 94th and Normandie, the Packard pulled to the curb and parked; I continued on to the corner. From my rearview I watched Lizard Man and the girl cross the street and enter the only decent-looking house on the block, a whitewashed adobe job shaped like a miniature Alamo. Parking myself, I grabbed a flashlight from under the seat and walked over.

Right away I could tell the scene was way off. The block was nothing but welfare cribs, vacant lots, and gutted jalopies, but six beautiful '40–'41 vintage cars were stationed at curbside. Hunkering down, I flashed my light at their license plates, memorized the numbers, and ran back to my unmarked cruiser. Whispering hoarsely into the two-way, I gave R&I the figures and settled back to await the readout.

I got the kickback ten minutes later, and the scene went from way off to way, *way* off.

Cupping the radio mike to my ear and clamping my spare hand over it to hold the noise down, I took in the clerk's spiel. The Packard was registered to Leotis McCarver, male negro, age 41, of 1348 West 94th Street, L.A.—which had to be the cut-rate Alamo. His occupation was on file as union officer in the Brotherhood of Sleeping Car Porters. The other vehicles were registered to negro and white thugs with strong-arm convictions dating back to 1922. When the clerk read off the last name—Ralph "Big Tuna" De Santis, a known Mickey Cohen trigger—I decided to give the Alamo a thorough crawling.

Armed with my flashlight and two pieces, I cut diagonally across vacant lots toward my target's back yard. In the far distance I could see fireworks lighting up the sky, but down here no one seemed to be celebrating—their war of just plain living was still dragging on. When I got to the Alamo's yard wall, I took it at a run and kneed and elbowed my way over the top, coming down onto soft grass.

The back of the house was dark and quiet, so I risked flashing my light. Seeing a service porch fronted by a flimsy wooden door, I tiptoed over and tried it—and found it unlocked.

I walked in flashlight first, my beam picking up dusty walls and floors, discarded lounge chairs, and a broom-closet door standing half open. Opening it all the way, I saw army officers' uniforms on hangers, replete with campaign ribbons and embroidered insignias.

Shouted voices jerked my attention toward the house proper. Straining my ears, I discerned both white- and negro-accented insults being hurled. There was a connecting door in front of me, with darkness beyond it. The shouting had to be issuing from a front room, so I nudged the door open a crack, then squatted down to listen as best I could.

". . . and I'm just tellin' you we gots to find a place and get us off the streets," a negro voice was yelling, "'cause even if we splits up, colored with colored and whites with the whites, there is still gonna be roadblocks!"

A babble rose in response, then a shrill whistle silenced it, and a white voice dominated: "We'll be stopping the train way out in the country. Farmland. We'll destroy the signaling gear, and if the passengers take off looking for help, the nearest farmhouse is ten fucking miles away—and those dogfaces are gonna be on foot."

A black voice tittered, "They gonna be mad, them soldiers."

Another black voice: "They gonna fought the whole fucking war for free."

Laughter, then a powerful negro baritone took over: "Enough clowning around, this is money we're talking about and nothing else!"

"'Cepting revenge, mister union big shot. Don't forget I got me other business on that train."

I knew that voice by heart—it had voodoo-cursed my soul in court. I was on my way out the back for reinforcements when my legs went out from under me and I fell head first into darkness.

The darkness was soft and rippling, and I felt like I was swimming in a velvet ocean. Angry shouts reverberated far away, but I knew they were harmless; they were coming from another planet. Every so often I felt little stabs in my arms and saw pinpoints of light that made the voices louder, but then everything would go even softer, the velvet waves caressing me, smothering all my hurt.

Until the velvet turned to ice and the friendly little stabs became wrenching thuds up and down my back. I tried to draw myself into a ball, but an angry voice from this planet wouldn't let me. "Wake up, shitbird! We ain't wastin' no more pharmacy morph on you! Wake up! Wake up, goddamnit!"

Dimly I remembered that I was a police officer and went for the .38 on my hip. My arms and hands wouldn't move, and when I tried to lurch my whole body, I knew they were tied to my sides and that the thuds were kicks to my legs and rib cage. Trying to move away, I felt head-to-toe muscle cramps and opened my eyes. Walls and a ceiling came into hazy focus, and it all came back. I screamed something that was drowned out by laughter, and the Lizard Man's face hovered only inches above mine. "Lee Blanchard," he said, waving my badge and ID holder in front of my eyes. "You got sucker-punched again, shitbird. I saw Jimmy Bivins put you down at the Legion. Left hook outta nowhere, and you hit your knees, then worthless-shine muscle puts you down on your face. I got no respect for a man who gets sucker-punched by niggers."

At "niggers" I heard a gasp and twisted around to see the negro girl in the pink dress sitting in a chair a few feet away. Listening for background noises and hearing nothing, I knew the three of us were alone in the house. My eyes cleared a little more, and I saw that the velvet ocean was a plushy furnished living room. Feeling started to return to my limbs, sharp pain that cleared my fuzzy head. When I felt a grinding in my lower back, I winced; the extra .38 snub I had tucked into my waistband at City

Hall was still there, slipped down into my skivvies. Reassured by it, I looked up at Lizard Face and said, "Robbed any liquor stores lately?"

He laughed. "A few. Chump change compared to the big one this after—"

The girl shrieked, "Don't tell him nothin'!"

Lizard Man flicked his tongue. "He's dead meat, so who cares. It's a train hijack, canvasback. Some army brass chartered the Super Chief, L.A. to Frisco. Poker games, hookers in the sleeping cars, smut movies in the lounge. Ain't you heard? The war's over, time to celebrate. We got hardware on board—shines playing porters, white guys in army suits. They all got scatter-guns, and sweetie pie's boyfriend Voodoo, he's got himself a tommy. They're gonna take the train down tonight, around Salinas, when the brass is smashed to the gills, just achin' to throw away all that good separation pay. Then Voodoo's gonna come back here and per-form some religious rites on you. He told me about it, said he's got this mean old pit bull named Revenge. A friend kept him while he was in Quentin. The buddy was white, and he tormented the dog so he hates white men worse than poison. The dog only gets fed about twice a week, and you can just bet he'd love a nice big bowl of canvasback stew. Which is you, white boy. Voodoo's gonna cut you up alive, turn you into dog food out of the can. Wanna take a bet on what he cuts off first?"

"That's not true! That's not what—"

"Shut up, Cora!"

Twisting on my side to see the girl better, I played a wild hunch. "Are you Cora Downey?"

Cora's jaw dropped, but Lizard spoke first. "Smart boy. Billy Boyle's ex, Voodoo's current. These high-yellow coozes get around. You know canvasback here, don't you, sweet? He sent both your boyfriends up, and if you're real nice, maybe Voodoo'll let you do some cutting on him."

Cora walked over and spat in my face. She hissed, "Mother" and kicked me with a spiked toe. I tried to roll away, and she sent another kick at my back.

Then my ace in the hole hit me right between the eyes, harder than any of the blows I had absorbed so far. Last night I had heard Wallace Simpkins's voice through the door: "'Cepting revenge, mister union big shot. I got me other business on that train." In my mind that "business" buzzed as snuffing Lieutenant Billy Boyle, and I was laying five-to-one that Cora wouldn't like the idea.

Lizard took Cora by the arm and led her to the couch, then squatted next to me. "You're a sucker for a spitball," he said.

I smiled at him. "Your mother bats cleanup at a two-dollar whorehouse."

He slapped my face. I spat blood at him and said, "And you're ugly."

He slapped me again; when his arm followed through I saw the handle of an auto-matic sticking out of his right pants pocket. I made my voice drip with contempt: "You hit like a girl. Cora could take you easy."

His next shot was full force. I sneered through bloody lips and said, "You queer? Only nancy boys slap like that."

A one-two set hit me in the jaw and neck, and I knew it was now or never. Slur-ring my words like a punch-drunk pug, I said, "Let me up. Let me up and I'll fight you man-to-man. Let me up."

Lizard took a penknife from his pocket and cut the rope that bound my arms to my sides. I tried to move my hands, but they were jelly. My battered legs had some feeling in them, so I rolled over and up onto my knees. Lizard had backed off into a chump's idea of a boxing stance and was firing roundhouse lefts and rights at the living room air. Cora was sitting on the couch, wiping angry tears from her cheeks.

Deep breathing and lolling my torso like a hophead, I stalled for time, waiting for feeling to return to my hands.

"Get up, shitbird!"

My fingers still wouldn't move.

"I said get up!"

Still no movement.

Lizard came forward on the balls of his feet, feinting and shadowboxing. My wrists started to buzz with blood, and I began to get unprofessionally angry, like I was a rookie heavy, not a thirty-one-year-old cop. Lizard hit me twice, left, right, open-handed. In a split second he became Jimmy Bivins, and I zoomed back to the ninth round at the Legion in '37. Dropping my left shoulder, I sent out a right lead, then pulled it and left-hooked him to the breadbasket. Bivins gasped and bent forward; I stepped backward for swinging room. Then Bivins was Lizard going for his piece, and I snapped to where I really was.

We drew at the same time. Lizard's first shot went above my head, shattering a window behind me; mine, slowed by my awkward rear pull, slammed into the far wall. Recoil spun us both around and before Lizard had time to aim I threw myself to the floor and rolled to the side like a carpet-eating dervish. Three shots cut the air where I had been standing a second before, and I extended my gun arm upward, braced my wrist, and emptied my snub-nose at Lizard's chest. He was blasted backward, and through the shots' echoes I heard Cora scream long and shrill.

I stumbled over to Lizard. He was on his way out, bleeding from three holes, unable to work the trigger of the .45. He got up the juice to give me a feeble middle-finger farewell, and when the bird was in midair I stepped on his heart and pushed down, squeezing the rest of his life out in a big arterial burst. When he finished twitching, I turned my attention to Cora, who was standing by the couch, putting out another shriek.

I stifled the noise by pinning her neck to the wall and hissing, "Questions and answers. Tell me what I want to know and you walk, fuck with me and I find dope in your purse and tell the DA you've been selling it to white nursery-school kids." I let up on my grip. "First question. Where's my car?"

Cora rubbed her neck. I could feel the obscenities stacking up on her tongue, itching to be hurled. All her rage went into her eyes as she said, "Out back. The garage."

"Have Simpkins and the stiff been clouting the liquor stores in West Adams?"

Cora stared at the floor and nodded, "Yes." Looking up, her eyes were filled with the self-disgust of the freshly turned stoolie. I said, "McCarver the union guy thought up the train heist?"

Another affirmative nod.

Deciding not to mention Billy Boyle's probable presence on the train, I said, "Who's bankrolling? Buying the guns and uniforms?"

"The liquor store money was for that, and there was this rich guy fronting the money."

Now the big question. "When does the train leave Union Station?"

Cora looked at her watch. "In half an hour."

I found a phone in the hallway and called the Central Division squadroom, telling Georgie Caulkins to send all his available plainclothes and uniformed officers to Union Station, that an army-chartered Super Chief about to leave for 'Frisco was going to be hit by a white-negro gang in army and porter outfits. Lowering my voice so Cora wouldn't hear, I told him to detain a negro quartermaster lieutenant named

William Boyle as a material witness, then hung up before he could say anything but "Jesus Christ."

Cora was smoking a cigarette when I reentered the living room. I picked my badge holder up off the floor and heard sirens approaching. "Come on," I said. "You don't want to get stuck here when the bulls show up."

Cora flipped her cigarette at the stiff, then kicked him one for good measure. We took off.

I ran code three all the way downtown. Adrenaline smothered the dregs of the morph still in my system, and anger held down the lid on the aches all over my body. Cora sat as far away from me as she could without hanging out the window and never blinked at the siren noise. I started to like her and decided to doctor my arresting officer's report to keep her out of the shithouse.

Nearing Union Station, I said, "Want to sulk or want to survive?"

Cora spat out the window and balled her fists.

"Want to get skin searched by some dyke matrons over at city jail or you want to go home?"

Cora's fist balls tightened up; the knuckles were as white as my skin.

"Want Voodoo to snuff Billy Boyle?"

That got her attention. "What!"

I looked sidelong at Cora's face gone pale. "He's on the train. You think about that when we get to the station and a lot of cops start asking you to snitch off your pals."

Pulling herself in from the window, Cora asked me the question that hoods have been asking cops since they patrolled on dinosaurs: "Why you do this shitty kind of work?"

I ignored it and said, "Snitch. It's in your best interest."

"That's for me to decide. Tell me."

"Tell you what?"

"Why you do—"

I interrupted, "You've got it all figured out, you tell me."

Cora started ticking off points on her fingers, leaning toward me so I could hear her over the siren. "One, you yourself figured your boxin' days would be over when you was thirty, so you got yourself a nice civil service pension job; two, the bigwig cops loves to have ball players and fighters around to suck up to them—so's you gets the first crack at the cushy 'signments. Three, you likes to hit people, and *po*-lice work be full of that; four, your ID card said Warrants Division, and I knows that warrants cops all serves process and does repos on the side, so I knows you pickin' up lots of extra change. Five—"

I held up my hands in mock surrender, feeling like I had just taken four hard jabs from Billy Conn and didn't want to go for sloppy fifths. "Smart girl, but you forgot to mention that I work goon squad for Firestone Tire and get a kickback for finger-ing wetbacks to the Border Patrol."

Cora straightened the knot in my disreputable necktie. "Hey, baby, a gig's a gig, you gots to take it where you finds it. I done things I ain't particularly proud of, and I—"

I shouted, "That's not it!"

Cora moved back to the window and smiled. "It certainly is, Mr. *Po*-liceman."

Angry now, angry at losing, I did what I always did when I smelled defeat: attack. "Shitcan it. Shitcan it now, before I forget I was starting to like you."

Cora gripped the dashboard with two white-knuckled hands and stared through the windshield. Union Station came into view, and pulling into the parking lot I saw a dozen black-and-whites and unmarked cruisers near the front entrance. Bullhorn-barked commands echoed unintelligibly as I killed my siren, and behind the police cars I glimpsed plainclothesmen aiming riot guns at the ground.

I pinned my badge to my jacket front and said, "Out." Cora stumbled from the car and stood rubber-kneed on the pavement. I got out, grabbed her arm, and shoved-pulled her all the way over to the pandemonium. As we approached, a harness bull leveled his .38 at us, then hesitated and said, "Sergeant Blanchard?"

I said "Yeah" and handed Cora over to him, adding, "She's a material witness, be nice to her." The youth nodded, and I walked past two bumper-to-bumper black-and-whites into the most incredible shakedown scene I had ever witnessed:

Negro men in porter uniforms and white men in army khakis were lying face-down on the pavement, their jackets and shirts pulled up to their shoulders, their trousers and undershorts pulled down to their knees. Uniformed cops were spread searching them while plainclothesmen held the muzzles of .12 gauge pumps to their heads. A pile of confiscated pistols and sawed-off shotguns lay a safe distance away. The men on the ground were all babbling their innocence or shouting epithets, and every cop trigger finger looked itchy.

Voodoo Simpkins and Billy Boyle were not among the six suspects. I looked around for familiar cop faces and saw Georgie Caulkins by the station's front entrance, standing over a sheet-covered stretcher. I ran up to him and said, "What have you got, Skipper?"

Caulkins toed the sheet aside, revealing the remains of a fortyish negro man. "The shine's Leotis McCarver," Georgie said. "Upstanding colored citizen, Brotherhood of Sleeping Car Porters big shot, a credit to his race. Put a .38 to his head and blew his brains out when the black-and-whites showed up."

Catching a twinkle in the old lieutenant's eyes, I said, "Really?"

Georgie smiled. "I can't shit a shitter. McCarver came out waving a white handkerchief, and some punk kid rookie canceled his ticket. Deserves a commendation, don't you think?"

I looked down at the stiff and saw that the entry wound was right between the eyes. "Give him a sharpshooter's medal and a desk job before he plugs some innocent civilian. What about Simpkins and Boyle?"

"Gone," Georgie said. "When we first got here, we didn't know the real soldiers and porters from the heisters, so we threw a net over the whole place and shook everybody down. We held every legit shine lieutenant, which was two guys, then cut them loose when they weren't your boy. Simpkins and Boyle probably got away in the shuffle. A car got stolen from the other end of the lot—citizen said she saw a nigger in a porter's suit breaking the window. That was probably Simpkins. The license number's on the air along with an all points. That shine is dead meat."

I thought of Simpkins invoking protective voodoo gods and said, "I'm going after him myself."

"You owe me a report on this thing!"

"Later."

"Now!"

I said, "Later, *sir*," and ran back to Cora, Georgie's "now" echoing behind me. When I got to where I had left her, she was gone. Looking around, I saw her a few yards away on her knees, handcuffed to the bumper of a black-and-white. A cluster of blue suits were hooting at her, and I got very angry.

I walked over. A particularly callow-looking rookie was regaling the others with his account of Leotis McCarver's demise. All four snapped to when they saw me coming. I grabbed the storyteller by his necktie and yanked him toward the back of the car. "Uncuff her," I said.

The rookie tried to pull away. I yanked at his tie until we were face-to-face and I could smell Sen-Sen on his breath. "And apologize."

The kid flushed, and I walked back to my unmarked cruiser. I heard muttering behind me, and then I felt a tap on my shoulder. Cora was there, smiling. "I owe you one," she said.

I pointed to the passenger seat. "Get in. I'm collecting."

The ride back to West Adams was fueled by equal parts of my nervous energy and Cora's nonstop spiel on her loves and criminal escapades. I had seen it dozens of times before. A cop stands up for a prisoner against another cop, on general principles or because the other cop is a turd, and the prisoner takes it as a sign of affection and respect and proceeds to lay out a road map of their life, justifying every wrong turn because he wants to be the cop's moral equal. Cora's tale of her love for Billy Boyle back in his heister days, her slide into call-house service when he went to prison, and her lingering crush on Wallace Simpkins was predictable and mawkishly rendered. I got more and more embarrassed by her "you dig?" punctuations and taps on the arm, and if I didn't need her as a High Darktown tour guide I would have kicked her out of the car and back to her old life. But then the monologue got interesting.

When Billy Boyle was cut loose from Chino, he had a free week in L.A. before his army induction and went looking for Cora. He found her hooked on ether at Minnie Roberts's Casbah, seeing voodoo visions, servicing customers as Coroloa, the African Slave Queen. He got her out of there, eased her off the dope with steambaths and vitamin B-12 shots, then ditched her to fight for Uncle Sam. Something snapped in her brain when Billy left, and, still vamped on Wallace Simpkins, she started writing him at Quentin. Knowing his affinity for voodoo, she smuggled in some slave-queen smut pictures taken of her at the Casbah, and they got a juicy correspondence going. Meanwhile, Cora went to work at Mickey Cohen's southside numbers mill, and everything looked peachy. Then Simpkins came out of Big Q, the voodoo sex fantasy stuff became tepid reality, and the Voodoo Man himself went back to stickups, exploiting her connections to the white criminal world.

When Cora finished her story, we were skirting the edge of High Darktown. It was dusk; the temperature was easing off; the neon signs of the Western Avenue juke joints had just started flashing. Cora lit a cigarette and said, "All Billy's people is from around here. If he's lookin' for a hideout or a travelin' stake, he'd hit the clubs on West Jeff. Wallace wouldn't show his evil face around here, 'less he's lookin' for Billy, which I figure he undoubtedly is. I—"

I interrupted, "I thought Billy came from a square-john family. Wouldn't he go to them?"

Cora's look said I was a lily-white fool. "Ain't no square-john families around here, 'ceptin those who work domestic. West Adams was built on bootlegging, sweetie. Black sellin' white lightnin' to black, gettin' fat, then investin' white. Billy's folks was runnin' shine when I was in pigtails. They're respectable now, and they hates him for takin' a jolt. He'll be callin' in favors at the clubs, don't you worry."

I hung a left on Western, heading for Jefferson Boulevard. "How do you know all this?"

"I am from High, *High* Darktown, sweet."

"Then why do you hold on to that Aunt Jemima accent?"

Cora laughed. "And I thought I sounded like Lena Horne. Here's why, sweetcakes. Black woman with a law degree they call 'nigger.' Black girl with three-inch heels and a shiv in her purse they call 'baby.' You dig?"

"I dig."

"No, you don't. Stop the car, Tommy Tucker's club is on the next block."

I said, "Yes, ma'am," and pulled to the curb. Cora got out ahead of me and swayed around the corner on her three-inch heels, calling, "I'll go in," over her shoulder. I waited underneath a purple neon sign heralding "Tommy Tucker's Playroom." Cora came out five minutes later, saying, "Billy was in here 'bout half an hour ago. Touched the barman for a double saw."

"Simpkins?"

Cora shook her head. "Ain't been seen."

I hooked a finger in the direction of the car. "Let's catch him."

For the next two hours we followed Billy Boyle's trail through High Darktown's nightspots. Cora went in and got the information, while I stood outside like a white wallflower, my gun unholstered and pressed to my leg, waiting for a voodoo killer with a tommy gun to aim and fire. Her info was always the same: Boyle had been in, had made a quick impression with his army threads, had gotten a quick touch based on his rep, and had practically run out the door. And no one had seen Wallace Simpkins.

11 P.M. found me standing under the awning of Hanks' Swank Spot, feeling pinpricks all over my exhausted body. Square-john negro kids cruised by waving little American flags out of backseat windows, still hopped up that the war was over. Male and female, they all had mug-shot faces that kept my trigger finger at half-pull even though I knew damn well they couldn't be *him.* Cora's sojourn inside was running three times as long as her previous ones, and when a car backfired and I aimed at the old lady behind the wheel, I figured High Darktown was safer with me off the street and went to see what was keeping Cora.

The Swank Spot's interior was Egyptian: silk wallpaper embossed with pharaohs and mummies, paper-mache pyramids surrounding the dance floor, and a long bar shaped like a crypt lying sideways. The patrons were more contemporary: negro men in double-breasted suits and women in evening gowns who looked disapprovingly at my rumpled clothes and two-and-a-half-day beard.

Ignoring them, I eyeballed in vain for Cora. Her soiled pink dress would have stood out like a beacon amid the surrounding hauteur, but all the women were dressed in pale white and sequined black. Panic was rising inside me when I heard her voice, distorted by bebop, pleading behind the dance floor.

I pushed my way through minglers, dancers, and three pyramids to get to her. She was standing next to a phonograph setup, gesturing at a black man in slacks and a camel-hair jacket. The man was sitting in a folding chair, alternately admiring his manicure and looking at Cora like she was dirt.

The music was reaching a crescendo; the man smiled at me; Cora's pleas were engulfed by saxes, horns, and drums going wild. I flashed back to my Legion days— rabbit punches and elbows and scrubbing my laces into cuts during clinches. The past two days went topsy-turvy, and I kicked over the phonograph. The Benny Goodman sextet exploded into silence, and I aimed my piece at the man and said, *"Tell me now."*

Shouts rose from the dance floor, and Cora pressed herself into a toppled pyramid. The man smoothed the pleats in his trousers and said, "Cora's old flame was in about half an hour ago, begging. I turned him down, because I respect my origins and hate snitches. But I told him about an old mutual friend—a soft touch. Another Cora flame was in about ten minutes ago, asking after flame number one. Seems he has a grudge against him. I sent him the same place."

I croaked, "Where?" and my voice sounded disembodied to my own ears. The man said, "No. You can apologize now, officer. Do it, and I won't tell my good friends Mickey Cohen and Inspector Waters about your behavior."

I stuck my gun in my waistband and pulled out an old Zippo I used to light suspects' cigarettes. Sparking a flame, I held it inches from a stack of brocade curtains. "Remember the Coconut Grove?"

The man said, "You wouldn't," and I touched the flame to the fabric. It ignited immediately, and smoke rose to the ceiling. Patrons were screaming "Fire!" in the club proper. The brocade was fried to a crisp when the man shrieked, "John Downey," ripped off his camel hair and flung it at the flames. I grabbed Cora and pulled her through the club, elbowing and rabbit punching panicky revelers to clear a path. When we hit the sidewalk, I saw that Cora was sobbing. Smoothing her hair, I whispered hoarsely, "What, babe, what?"

It took a moment for Cora to find a voice, but when she spoke, she sounded like a college professor. "John Downey's my father. He's very big around here, and he hates Billy because he thinks Billy made me a whore."

"Where does he li—"

"Arlington and Country Club."

We were there within five minutes. This was High, *High* Darktown—Tudor estates, French chateaus, and Moorish villas with terraced front lawns. Cora pointed out a plantation-style mansion and said, "Go to the side door. Thursday's the maid's night off, and nobody'll hear you if you knock at the front."

I stopped the car across the street and looked for other out-of-place vehicles. Seeing nothing but Packards, Caddys, and Lincolns nestled in driveways, I said, "Stay put. Don't move, no matter what you see or hear."

Cora nodded mutely. I got out and ran over to the plantation, hurdling a low iron fence guarded by a white iron jockey, then treading down a long driveway. Laughter and applause issued from the adjoining mansion, separated from the Downey place by a high hedgerow. The happy sounds covered my approach, and I started looking in windows.

Standing on my toes and moving slowly toward the back of the house, I saw rooms festooned with crewelwork wall hangings and hunting prints. Holding my face up to within a few inches of the glass, I looked for shadow movement and listened for voices, wondering why all the lights were on at close to midnight.

Then faceless voices assailed me from the next window down. Pressing my back to the wall, I saw that the window was cracked for air. Cocking an ear toward the open space, I listened.

". . . and after all the setup money I put in, you still had to knock down those liquor stores?"

The tone reminded me of a mildly outraged negro minister rebuking his flock, and I braced myself for the voice that I knew would reply.

"I got cowboy blood, Mister Downey, like you musta had when you was a young man runnin' shine. That cop musta got loose, got Cora and Whitey to snitch. Blew a sweet piece of work, but we can still get off clean. McCarver was the only one 'sides me knew you was bankrollin', and he be dead. Billy be the one *you* wants dead, and he be showin' up soon. Then I cuts him and dumps him somewhere, and nobody knows he was even here."

"You want money, don't you?"

"Five big get me lost somewheres nice, then maybe when he starts feelin' safe again, I comes back and cuts that cop. That sound about—"

Applause from the big house next door cut Simpkins off. I pulled out my piece and got up some guts, knowing my only safe bet was to backshoot the son of a bitch right where he was. I heard more clapping and joyous shouts that Mayor Bowron's reign was over, and then John Downey's preacher baritone was back in force: "I want him dead. My daughter is a white-trash consort and a whore, and he's—"

A scream went off behind me, and I hit the ground just as machine-gun fire blew the window to bits. Another burst took out the hedgerow and the next-door window. I pinned myself back first to the wall and drew myself upright as the snout of a tommy gun was rested against the ledge a few inches away. When muzzle flame and another volley exploded from it, I stuck my .38 in blind and fired six times at stomach level. The tommy strafed a reflex burst upward, and when I hit the ground again, the only sound was chaotic shrieks from the other house.

I reloaded from a crouch, then stood up and surveyed the carnage through both mansion windows. Wallace Simpkins lay dead on John Downey's Persian carpet, and across the way I saw a banner for the West Adams Democratic Club streaked with blood. When I saw a dead woman spread-eagled on top of an antique table, I screamed myself, elbowed my way into Downey's den, and picked up the machine gun. The grips burned my hands, but I didn't care; I saw the faces of every boxer who had ever defeated me and didn't care; I heard grenades going off in my brain and was glad they were there to kill all the innocent screaming. With the tommy's muzzle as my directional device, I walked through the house.

All my senses went into my eyes and trigger finger. Wind ruffled a window curtain, and I blew the wall apart; I caught my own image in a gilt-edged mirror and blasted myself into glass shrapnel. Then I heard a woman moaning, "Daddy, Daddy, Daddy," dropped the tommy, and ran to her.

Cora was on her knees on the entry hall floor, plunging a shiv into a man who had to be her father. The man moaned baritone low and tried to reach up, almost as if to embrace her. Cora's "Daddy's" got lower and lower, until the two seemed to be working toward harmony. When she let the dying man hold her, I gave them a moment together, then pulled Cora off of him and dragged her outside. She went limp in my arms, and with lights going on everywhere and sirens converging from all directions, I carried her to my car.

THE PIETRO ANDROMACHE

SARA PARETSKY
(1947–   )

When Paretsky brought her private detective, V. I. Warshawski, to life in 1982, she began one of the most successful careers in contemporary crime fiction. The Chicago-based P.I. is a vocal feminist whose cases are generally political, taking on such enormous villain-ous entities as the police department, the medical community, and, mainly, large corpo-rations, all of which are portrayed as victimizers of ordinary citizens. Paretsky herself was victimized by the movie V. I. Warshawski, universally acknowledged to be among the ten worst films of 1991.

I

OU ONLY AGREED TO HIRE HIM because of his art collec-tion. Of that I'm sure." Lotty Herschel bent down to adjust her stockings. "And don't waggle your eye-brows like that—it makes you look like an adolescent Groucho Marx."

Max Loewenthal obediently smoothed his eyebrows, but said, "It's your legs, Lotty; they remind me of my youth. You know, going into the Underground to wait out the air raids, looking at the ladies as they came down the escalators. The updraft always made their skirts billow."

"You're making this up, Max. I was in those Underground stations, too, and as I remember the ladies were always bundled in coats and children."

Max moved from the doorway to put an arm around Lotty. "That's what keeps us together, *Lottchen*: I am a romantic and you are severely logical. And you know we didn't hire Caudwell because of his collection. Although I

admit I am eager to see it. The board wants Beth Israel to develop a trans-plant program. It's the only way we're going to become competitive—"

"Don't deliver your publicity lecture to me," Lotty snapped. Her thick brows contracted to a solid black line across her forehead. "As far as I am concerned he is a cretin with the hands of a Caliban and the personality of Attila."

Lotty's intense commitment to med-icine left no room for the mundane consideration of money. But as the hospital's executive director, Max was on the spot with the trustees to see that Beth Israel ran at a profit. Or at least at a smaller loss than they'd achieved in recent years. They'd brought Caudwell in in part to attract more paying patients—and to help screen out some of the indigent who made up 12 percent of Beth Israel's patient load. Max won-dered how long the hospital could afford to support personalities as divergent as Lotty and Caudwell with their radically differing approaches to medicine.

He dropped his arm and smiled quizzically at her. "Why do you hate him so much, Lotty?"

"I am the person who has to justify the patients I admit to this—this troglodyte. Do you realize he tried to keep Mrs. Mendes from the operating room when he learned she had AIDS? He wasn't even being asked to sully his hands with her blood and he didn't want me performing surgery on her."

Lotty drew back from Max and pointed an accusing finger at him. "You may tell the board that if he keeps questioning my judgment they will find themselves looking for a new perinatologist. I am serious about this. You listen this afternoon, Max, you hear whether or not he calls me 'our little baby doctor.' I am fifty-eight years old, I am a Fellow of the Royal College of Surgeons besides having enough credentials in this country to support a whole hospital, and to him I am a 'little baby doctor.'"

Max sat on the daybed and pulled Lotty down next to him.

"No, no, *Lottchen*: don't fight. Listen to me. Why haven't you told me any of this before?"

"Don't be an idiot, Max: you are the director of the hospital. I cannot use our special relationship to deal with problems I have with the staff. I said my piece when Caudwell came for his final interview. A number of the other physicians were not happy with his attitude. If you remember, we asked the board to bring him in as a cardiac surgeon first and promote him to chief of staff after a year if everyone was satisfied with his performance."

"We talked about doing it that way," Max admitted. "But he wouldn't take the appointment except as chief of staff. That was the only way we could offer him the kind of money he could get at one of the university hospitals or Humana. And, Lotty, even if you don't like his personality you must agree that he is a first-class surgeon."

"I agree to nothing." Red lights danced in her black eyes. "If he patronizes me, a fellow physician, how do you imagine he treats his patients? You cannot practice medicine if—"

"Now it's my turn to ask to be spared a lecture," Max interrupted gently. "But if you feel so strongly about him, maybe you shouldn't go to his party this afternoon."

"And admit that he can beat me? Never."

"Very well then." Max got up and placed a heavily brocaded wool shawl over Lotty's shoulders. "But you must promise me to behave. This is a social function we are going to, remember, not a gladiator contest. Caudwell is trying to repay some hospitality this afternoon, not to belittle you."

"I don't need lessons in conduct from you: Herschels were attending the emperors of Austria while the Loewenthals were operating vegetable stalls on the Ring," Lotty said haughtily.

Max laughed and kissed her hand. "Then remember these regal Herschels and act like them, *Eure Hoheit*."

II

Caudwell had bought an apartment sight unseen when he moved to Chicago. A divorced man whose children are in college only has to consult with his own taste in these matters. He asked the Beth Israel board to recommend a realtor, sent his requirements to them—twenties construction, near Lake Michigan, good security, modern plumbing—and dropped seven hundred and fifty thousand for an eight-room condo facing the lake at Scott Street.

Since Beth Israel paid handsomely for the privilege of retaining Dr. Charlotte Herschel as their perinatologist, nothing required her to live in a five-room walk-up on the fringes of Uptown, so it was a bit unfair of her to mutter "Parvenu" to Max when they walked into the lobby.

Max relinquished Lotty gratefully when they got off the elevator. Being her lover was like trying to be companion to a Bengal tiger: you never knew when she'd take a lethal swipe at you. Still, if Caudwell was insulting her—and her judgment—maybe he needed to talk to the surgeon, explain how important Lotty was for the reputation of Beth Israel.

Caudwell's two children were making the obligatory Christmas visit. They were a boy and a girl, Deborah and Steve, within a year of the same age, both tall, both blond and poised, with a hearty sophistication born of a childhood spent on expensive ski slopes. Max wasn't very big, and as one took his coat and the other performed brisk introductions, he felt himself shrinking, losing in self-assurance. He accepted a glass of special *cuvée* from one of them—was it the boy or the girl, he wondered in confusion—and fled into the melee.

He landed next to one of Beth Israel's trustees, a woman in her sixties wearing a gray textured minidress whose black stripes were constructed of feathers. She commented brightly on Caudwell's art collection, but Max sensed an undercurrent of hostility: wealthy trustees don't like the idea that they can't out buy the staff.

While he was frowning and nodding at appropriate intervals, it dawned on Max that Caudwell did know how much the hospital needed Lotty. Heart surgeons do not have the world's smallest egos: when you ask them to name the world's three leading practitioners, they never can remember the names of the other two. Lotty was at the top of her field, and she, too, was used to having things her way. Since her confrontational style was reminiscent more of the Battle of the Bulge than the Imperial Court of Vienna, he didn't blame Caudwell for trying to force her out of the hospital.

Max moved away from Martha Gildersleeve to admire some of the paintings and figurines she'd been discussing. A collector himself of Chinese porcelains, Max raised his eyebrows and mouthed a soundless whistle at the pieces on display. A small Watteau and a Charles Demuth watercolor were worth as much as Beth Israel paid Caudwell in a year. No wonder Mrs. Gildersleeve had been so annoyed.

"Impressive, isn't it."

Max turned to see Arthur Gioia looming over him. Max was shorter than most of the Beth Israel staff, shorter than everyone but Lotty. But Gioia, a tall muscular immunologist, loomed over everyone. He had gone to the University of Arkansas on a football scholarship and had even spent a season playing tackle for Houston before starting medical school. It had been twenty years since he last lifted weights, but his neck still looked like a redwood stump.

Gioia had led the opposition to Caudwell's appointment. Max had suspected at the time that it was due more to a medicine man's not wanting a surgeon as his nominal boss than from any other cause, but after Lotty's outburst he wasn't so sure. He was debating whether to ask the doctor how he felt about Caudwell now that he'd worked with him for six months when their host surged over to him and shook his hand.

"Sorry I didn't see you when you came in, Loewenthal. You like the Watteau? It's one of my favorite pieces. Although a collector shouldn't play favorites any more than a father should, eh, sweetheart?" The last remark was addressed to the daughter, Deborah, who had come up behind Caudwell and slipped an arm around him.

Caudwell looked more like a Victorian sea dog than a surgeon. He had a round red face under a shock of yellow-white hair, a hearty Santa Claus laugh, and a bluff, direct manner. Despite Lotty's vituperations, he was immensely popular with his patients. In the short time he'd been at the hospital, referrals to cardiac surgery had increased 15 percent.

His daughter squeezed his shoulder playfully. "I know you don't play favorites with us, Dad, but you're lying to Mr. Loewenthal about your collection; come on, you know you are."

She turned to Max. "He has a piece he's so proud of he doesn't like to show it to people—he doesn't want them to see he's got vulnerable spots. But it's Christmas, Dad, relax, let people see how you feel for a change."

Max looked curiously at the surgeon, but Caudwell seemed pleased with his daughter's familiarity. The son came up and added his own jocular cajoling.

"This really is Dad's pride and joy. He stole it from Uncle Griffen when Grandfather died and kept Mother from getting her mitts on it when they split up."

Caudwell did bark out a mild reproof at that. "You'll be giving my colleagues the wrong impression of me, Steve. I didn't steal it from Grif. Told him he could have the rest of the estate if he'd leave me the Watteau and the Pietro."

"Of course he could've bought ten estates with what those two would fetch," Steve muttered to his sister over Max's head.

Deborah relinquished her father's arm to lean over Max and whisper back, "Mom could've used them, too."

Max moved away from the alarming pair to say to Caudwell, "A Pietro? You mean Pietro d'Alessandro? You have a model or an actual sculpture?"

Caudwell gave his staccato admiral's laugh. "The real McCoy, Loewenthal. The real McCoy. An alabaster."

"An alabaster?" Max raised his eyebrows. "Surely not. I thought Pietro worked only in bronze and marble."

"Yes, yes," chuckled Caudwell, rubbing his hands together. "Everyone thinks so, but there were a few alabasters in private collections. I've had this one authenticated by experts. Come take a look at it—it'll knock your breath away. You come, too, Gioia," he barked at the immunologist. "You're Italian, you'll like to see what your ancestors were up to."

"A Pietro alabaster?" Lotty's clipped tones made Max start—he hadn't noticed her joining the little group. "I would very much like to see this piece."

"Then come along, Dr. Herschel, come along." Caudwell led them to a small hallway, exchanging genial greetings with his guests as he passed, pointing out a John William Hill miniature they might not have seen, picking up a few other people who for various reasons wanted to see his prize.

"By the way, Gioia, I was in New York last week, you know. Met an old friend of yours from Arkansas. Paul Nierman."

"Nierman?" Gioia seemed to be at a loss. "I'm afraid I don't remember him."

"Well, he remembered you pretty well. Sent you all kinds of messages—you'll have to stop by my office on Monday and get the full strength."

Caudwell opened a door on the right side of the hall and let them into his study. It was an octagonal room carved out of the corner of the building. Windows on two sides looked out on Lake Michigan. Caudwell drew salmon drapes as he talked about the room, why he'd chosen it for his study even though the view kept his mind from his work.

Lotty ignored him and walked over to a small pedestal which stood alone against the paneling on one of the far walls. Max followed her and gazed respectfully at the statue. He had seldom seen so fine a piece outside a museum. About a foot high, it depicted a woman in classical draperies hovering in anguish over the dead body of a soldier lying at her feet. The grief in her beautiful face was so poignant that it reminded you of every sorrow you had ever faced.

"Who is it meant to be?" Max asked curiously.

"Andromache," Lotty said in a strangled voice. "Andromache mourning Hector."

Max stared at Lotty, astonished equally by her emotion and her knowledge of the figure—Lotty was totally uninterested in sculpture.

Caudwell couldn't restrain the smug smile of a collector with a true coup. "Beautiful, isn't it? How do you know the subject?"

"I should know it." Lotty's voice was husky with emotion. "My grandmother had such a Pietro. An alabaster given her great-grandfather by the Emperor Joseph the Second himself for his help in consolidating imperial ties with Poland."

She swept the statue from its stand, ignoring a gasp from Max, and turned it over. "You can see the traces of the imperial stamp here still. And the chip on Hector's foot which made the Hapsburg wish to give the statue away to begin with. How came you to have this piece? Where did you find it?"

The small group that had joined Caudwell stood silent by the entrance, shocked at Lotty's outburst. Gioia looked more horrified than any of them, but he found Lotty overwhelming at the best of times—an elephant confronted by a hostile mouse.

"I think you're allowing your emotions to carry you away, Doctor." Caudwell kept his tone light, making Lotty seem more gauche by contrast. "I inherited this piece from my father, who bought it—legitimately—in Europe. Perhaps from your—grandmother, was it? But I suspect you are confused about something you may have seen in a museum as a child."

Deborah gave a high-pitched laugh and called loudly to her brother, "Dad may have stolen it from Uncle Grif, but it looks like Grandfather snatched it to begin with anyway."

"Be quiet, Deborah," Caudwell barked sternly.

His daughter paid no attention to him. She laughed again and joined her brother to look at the imperial seal on the bottom of the statue.

Lotty brushed them aside. "*I* am confused about the seal of Joseph the Second?" she hissed at Caudwell. "Or about this chip on Hector's foot? You can see the line where some philistine filled in the missing piece. Some person who thought his touch would add value to Pietro's work. Was that you, *Doctor*? Or your father?"

"Lotty." Max was at her side, gently prising the statue from her shaking hands to restore it to its pedestal. "Lotty, this is not the place or the manner to discuss such things."

Angry tears sparkled in her black eyes. "Are you doubting my word?"

Max shook his head. "I'm not doubting you. But I'm also not supporting you. I'm asking you not to talk about this matter in this way at this gathering."

"But, Max: either this man or his father is a thief!"

Caudwell strolled up to Lotty and pinched her chin. "You're working too hard, Dr. Herschel. You have too many things on your mind these days. I think the board would like to see you take a leave of absence for a few weeks, go someplace warm, get yourself relaxed. When you're this tense, you're no good to your patients. What do you say, Loewenthal?"

Max didn't say any of the things he wanted to—that Lotty was insufferable and

Caudwell intolerable. He believed Lotty, believed that the piece had been her grandmother's. She knew too much about it, for one thing. And for another, a lot of artworks belonging to European Jews were now in museums or private collections around the world. It was only the most god-awful coincidence that the Pietro had ended up with Caudwell's father.

But how dare she raise the matter in the way most likely to alienate everyone present? He couldn't possibly support her in such a situation. And at the same time, Caudwell's pinching her chin in that condescending way made him wish he were not chained to a courtesy that would have kept him from knocking the surgeon out even if he'd been ten years younger and ten inches taller.

"I don't think this is the place or the time to discuss such matters," he reiterated as calmly as he could. "Why don't we all cool down and get back together on Monday, eh?"

Lotty gasped involuntarily, then swept from the room without a backward glance.

Max refused to follow her. He was too angry with her to want to see her again that afternoon. When he got ready to leave the party an hour or so later, after a long conversation with Caudwell that taxed his sophisticated urbanity to the utmost, he heard with relief that Lotty was long gone. The tale of her outburst had of course spread through the gathering at something faster than the speed of sound; he wasn't up to defending her to Martha Gildersleeve, who demanded an explanation of him in the elevator going down.

He went home for a solitary evening in his house in Evanston. Normally such time brought him pleasure, listening to music in his study, lying on the couch with his shoes off, reading history, letting the sounds of the lake wash over him.

Tonight, though, he could get no relief. Fury with Lotty merged into images of horror, the memories of his own disintegrated family, his search through Europe for his mother. He had never found anyone who was quite certain what became of her, although several people told him definitely of his father's suicide. And stamped over these wisps in his brain was the disturbing picture of Caudwell's children, their blond heads leaning backward at identical angles as they gleefully chanted, "Grandpa was a thief, Grandpa was a thief," while Caudwell edged his visitors out of the study.

By morning he would somehow have to reconstruct himself enough to face Lotty, to respond to the inevitable flood of calls from outraged trustees. He'd have to figure out a way of soothing Caudwell's vanity, bruised more by his children's behavior than anything Lotty had said. And find a way to keep both important doctors at Beth Israel.

Max rubbed his gray hair. Every week this job brought him less joy and more pain. Maybe it was time to step down, to let the board bring in a young MBA who would turn Beth Israel's finances around. Lotty would resign then, and it would be an end to the tension between her and Caudwell.

Max fell asleep on the couch. He awoke around five muttering, "By morning, by morning." His joints were stiff from cold, his eyes sticky with tears he'd shed unknowingly in his sleep.

But in the morning things changed. When Max got to his office he found the place buzzing, not with news of Lotty's outburst but word that Caudwell had missed his early morning surgery. Work came almost completely to a halt at noon when his children phoned to say they'd found the surgeon strangled in his own study and the Pietro Andromache missing. And on Tuesday, the police arrested Dr. Charlotte Herschel for Lewis Caudwell's murder.

III

Lotty would not speak to anyone. She was out on two hundred fifty thousand dollars' bail, the money raised by Max, but she had gone directly to her apartment on Sheffield after two nights in County Jail without stopping to thank him. She would not talk to reporters, she remained silent during all conversations with the police, and she emphatically refused to speak to the private investigator who had been her close friend for many years.

Max, too, stayed behind an impregnable shield of silence. While Lotty went on indefinite leave, turning her practice over to a series of colleagues, Max continued to go to the hospital every day. But he, too, would not speak to reporters: he wouldn't even say "No comment." He talked to the police only after they threatened to lock him up as a material witness, and then every word had to be pried from him as if his mouth were stone and speech Excalibur. For three days V. I. Warshawski left messages which he refused to return.

On Friday, when no word came from the detective, when no reporter popped up from a nearby urinal in the men's room to try to trick him into speaking, when no more calls came from the state's attorney, Max felt a measure of relaxation as he drove home. As soon as the trial was over he would resign, retire to London. If he could only keep going until then, everything would be—not all right, but bearable.

He used the remote release for the garage door and eased his car into the small space. As he got out he realized bitterly he'd been too optimistic in thinking he'd be left in peace. He hadn't seen the woman sitting on the stoop leading from the garage to the kitchen when he drove in, only as she uncoiled herself at his approach.

"I'm glad you're home—I was beginning to freeze out here."

"How did you get into the garage, Victoria?"

The detective grinned in a way he usually found engaging. Now it seemed merely predatory. "Trade secret, Max. I know you don't want to see me, but I need to talk to you."

He unlocked the door into the kitchen. "Why not just let yourself into the house if you were cold? If your scruples permit you into the garage, why not into the house?"

She bit her lip in momentary discomfort but said lightly, "I couldn't manage my picklocks with my fingers this cold."

The detective followed him into the house. Another tall monster; five foot eight, athletic, light on her feet behind him. Maybe American mothers put growth hormones or steroids in their children's cornflakes. He'd have to ask Lotty. His mind winced at the thought.

"I've talked to the police, of course," the light alto continued behind him steadily, oblivious to his studied rudeness as he poured himself a cognac, took his shoes off, found his waiting slippers, and padded down the hall to the front door for his mail.

"I understand why they arrested Lotty—Caudwell had been doped with a whole bunch of Xanax and then strangled while he was sleeping it off. And, of course, she was back at the building Sunday night. She won't say why, but one of the tenants I.D.'d her as the woman who showed up around ten at the service entrance when he was walking his dog. She won't say if she talked to Caudwell, if he let her in, if he was still alive."

Max tried to ignore her clear voice. When that proved impossible he tried to read a journal which had come in the mail.

"And those kids, they're marvelous, aren't they? Like something out of the *Fabulous Furry Freak Brothers*. They won't talk to me but they gave a long interview to Murray Ryerson over at the *Star*.

"After Caudwell's guests left, they went to a flick at the Chestnut Street Station, had a pizza afterwards, then took themselves dancing on Division Street. So they strolled in around two in the morning—confirmed by the doorman—saw the light on in the old man's study. But they were feeling no pain and he kind of overreacted—their term—if they were buzzed, so they didn't stop in to say goodnight. It was only when they got up around noon and went in that they found him."

V. I. had followed Max from the front hallway to the door of his study as she spoke. He stood there irresolutely, not wanting his private place desecrated with her insistent, air-hammer speech, and finally went on down the hall to a little-used living room. He sat stiffly on one of the brocade armchairs and looked at her remotely when she perched on the edge of its companion.

"The weak piece in the police story is the statue," V. I. continued.

She eyed the Persian rug doubtfully and unzipped her boots, sticking them on the bricks in front of the fireplace.

"Everyone who was at the party agrees that Lotty was beside herself. By now the story has spread so far that people who weren't even in the apartment when she looked at the statue swear they heard her threaten to kill him. But if that's the case, what happened to the statue?"

Max gave a slight shrug to indicate total lack of interest in the topic.

V. I. plowed on doggedly. "Now some people think she might have given it to a friend or a relation to keep for her until her name is cleared at the trial. And these people think it would be either her Uncle Stefan here in Chicago, her brother Hugo in Montreal, or you. So the Mounties searched Hugo's place and are keeping an eye on his mail. And the Chicago cops are doing the same for Stefan. And I presume someone got a warrant and went through here, right?"

Max said nothing, but he felt his heart beating faster. Police in his house, searching his things? But wouldn't they have to get his permission to enter? Or would they? Victoria would know, but he couldn't bring himself to ask. She waited for a few minutes, but when he still wouldn't speak, she plunged on. He could see it was becoming an effort for her to talk, but he wouldn't help her.

"But I don't agree with those people. Because I know that Lotty is innocent. And that's why I'm here. Not like a bird of prey, as you think, using your misery for carrion. But to get you to help me. Lotty won't speak to me, and if she's that miserable I won't force her to. But surely, Max, you won't sit idly by and let her be railroaded for something she never did."

Max looked away from her. He was surprised to find himself holding the brandy snifter and set it carefully on a table beside him.

"Max!" Her voice was shot with astonishment. "I don't believe this. You actually think she killed Caudwell."

Max flushed a little, but she'd finally stung him into a response. "And you are God who sees all and knows she didn't?"

"I see more than you do," V. I. snapped. "I haven't known Lotty as long as you have, but I know when she's telling the truth."

"So you are God." Max bowed in heavy irony. "You see beyond the facts to the innermost souls of men and women."

He expected another outburst from the young woman, but she gazed at him steadily without speaking. It was a look sympathetic enough that Max felt embarrassed by his sarcasm and burst out with what was on his mind.

"What else am I to think? She hasn't said anything, but there's no doubt that she returned to his apartment Sunday night."

It was V. I.'s turn for sarcasm. "With a little vial of Xanax that she somehow induced him to swallow? And then strangled him for good measure? Come on, Max, you know Lotty: honesty follows her around like a cloud. If she'd killed Caudwell, she'd say something like, 'Yes, I bashed the little vermin's brains in.' Instead she's not speaking at all."

Suddenly the detective's eyes widened with incredulity. "Of course. She thinks you killed Caudwell. You're doing the only thing you can to protect her—standing mute. And she's doing the same thing. What an admirable pair of archaic knights."

"No!" Max said sharply. "It's not possible. How could she think such a thing? She carried on so wildly that it was embarrassing to be near her. I didn't want to see her or talk to her. That's why I've felt so terrible. If only I hadn't been so obstinate, if only I'd called her Sunday night. How could she think I would kill someone on her behalf when I was so angry with her?"

"Why else isn't she saying anything to anyone?" Warshawski demanded.

"Shame, maybe," Max offered. "You didn't see her on Sunday. I did. That is why I think she killed him, not because some man let her into the building."

His brown eyes screwed shut at the memory. "I have seen Lotty in the grip of anger many times, more than is pleasant to remember, really. But never, never have I seen her in this kind of—uncontrolled rage. You could not talk to her. It was impossible."

The detective didn't respond to that. Instead she said, "Tell me about the statue. I heard a couple of garbled versions from people who were at the party, but I haven't found anyone yet who was in the study when Caudwell showed it to you. Was it really her grandmother's, do you think? And how did Caudwell come to have it if it was?"

Max nodded mournfully. "Oh, yes. It was really her family's, I'm convinced of that. She could not have known in advance about the details, the flaw in the foot, the imperial seal on the bottom. As to how Caudwell got it, I did a little looking into that myself yesterday. His father was with the Army of Occupation in Germany after the war. A surgeon attached to Patton's staff. Men in such positions had endless opportunities to acquire artworks after the war."

V. I. shook her head questioningly.

"You must know something of this, Victoria. Well, maybe not. You know the Nazis helped themselves liberally to artwork belonging to Jews everywhere they occupied Europe. And not just to Jews—they plundered Eastern Europe on a grand scale. The best guess is that they stole sixteen million pieces—statues, paintings, altarpieces, tapestries, rare books. The list is beyond reckoning, really."

The detective gave a little gasp. "Sixteen million! You're joking."

"Not a joke, Victoria. I wish it were so, but it is not. The U.S. Army of Occupation took charge of as many works of art as they found in the occupied territories. In theory, they were to find the rightful owners and try to restore them. But in practice few pieces were ever traced, and many of them ended up on the black market.

"You only had to say that such-and-such a piece was worth less than five thousand dollars and you were allowed to buy it. For an officer on Patton's staff, the opportunities for fabulous acquisitions would have been endless. Caudwell said he had the statue authenticated, but of course he never bothered to establish its provenance. Anyway, how could he?" Max finished bitterly. "Lotty's family had a deed of gift from the emperor, but that would have disappeared long since with the dispersal of their possessions."

"And you really think Lotty would have killed a man just to get this statue back? She couldn't have expected to keep it. Not if she'd killed someone to get it, I mean."

"You are so practical, Victoria. You are too analytical, sometimes, to understand why people do what they do. That was not just a statue. True, it is a priceless art-work, but you know Lotty, you know she places no value on such possessions. No, it meant her family to her, her past, her history, everything that the war destroyed forever for her. You must not imagine that because she never discusses such matters that they do not weigh on her."

V. I. flushed at Max's accusation. "You should be glad I'm analytical. It convinces me that Lotty is innocent. And whether you believe it or not I'm going to prove it."

Max lifted his shoulders slightly in a manner wholly European. "We each support Lotty according to our lights. I saw that she met her bail, and I will see that she gets expert counsel. I am not convinced that she needs you making her innermost secrets public."

V. I.'s gray eyes turned dark with a sudden flash of temper. "You're dead wrong about Lotty. I'm sure the memory of the war is a pain that can never be cured, but Lotty lives in the present, she works in hope for the future. The past does not obsess and consume her as, perhaps, it does you."

Max said nothing. His wide mouth turned in on itself in a narrow line. The detective laid a contrite hand on his arm.

"I'm sorry, Max. That was below the belt."

He forced the ghost of a smile to his mouth.

"Perhaps it's true. Perhaps it's why I love these ancient things so much. I wish I could believe you about Lotty. Ask me what you want to know. If you promise to leave as soon as I've answered and not to bother me again, I'll answer your questions."

IV

Max put in a dutiful appearance at the Michigan Avenue Presbyterian Church Monday afternoon for Lewis Caudwell's funeral. The surgeon's former wife came, flanked by her children and her husband's brother Griffen. Even after three decades in America Max found himself puzzled sometimes by the natives' behavior: since she and Caudwell were divorced, why had his ex-wife draped herself in black? She was even wearing a veiled hat reminiscent of Queen Victoria.

The children behaved in a moderately subdued fashion, but the girl was wearing a white dress shot with black lightning forks which looked as though it belonged at a disco or a resort. Maybe it was her only dress or her only dress with black in it, Max thought, trying hard to look charitably at the blond Amazon—after all, she had been suddenly and horribly orphaned.

Even though she was a stranger both in the city and the church, Deborah had hired one of the church parlors and managed to find someone to cater coffee and light snacks. Max joined the rest of the congregation there after the service.

He felt absurd as he offered condolences to the divorced widow: did she really miss the dead man so much? She accepted his conventional words with graceful melancholy and leaned slightly against her son and daughter. They hovered near her with what struck Max as a stagey solicitude. Seen next to her daughter, Mrs. Caudwell looked so frail and undernourished that she seemed like a ghost. Or maybe it was just that her children had a hearty vitality that even a funeral couldn't quench.

Caudwell's brother Griffen stayed as close to the widow as the children would permit. The man was totally unlike the hearty sea dog surgeon. Max thought if he'd met the brothers standing side by side he would never have guessed their relationship. He was tall, like his niece and nephew, but without their robustness. Caudwell had had a thick mop of yellow-white hair; Griffen's domed head was covered by thin wisps of gray. He seemed weak and nervous, and lacked Caudwell's outgoing bonhomie; no wonder the surgeon had found it easy to decide the disposition of their father's estate in his favor. Max wondered what Griffen had gotten in return.

Mrs. Caudwell's vague, disoriented conversation indicated that she was heavily sedated. That, too, seemed strange. A man she hadn't lived with for four years and she was so upset at his death that she could only manage the funeral on drugs? Or maybe it was the shame of coming as the divorced woman, not a true widow? But then why come at all?

To his annoyance, Max found himself wishing he could ask Victoria about it. She would have some cynical explanation—Caudwell's death meant the end of the widow's alimony and she knew she wasn't remembered in the will. Or she was having an affair with Griffen and was afraid she would betray herself without tranquilizers. Although it was hard to imagine the uncertain Griffen as the object of a strong passion.

Since he had told Victoria he didn't want to see her again when she left on Friday, it was ridiculous of him to wonder what she was doing, whether she was really uncovering evidence that would clear Lotty. Ever since she had gone he had felt a little flicker of hope in the bottom of his stomach. He kept trying to drown it, but it wouldn't quite go away.

Lotty, of course, had not come to the funeral, but most of the rest of the Beth Israel staff was there, along with the trustees. Arthur Gioia, his giant body filling the small parlor to the bursting point, tried finding a tactful balance between honesty and courtesy with the bereaved family; he made heavy going of it.

A sable-clad Martha Gildersleeve appeared under Gioia's elbow, rather like a furry football he might have tucked away. She made bright, unseemly remarks to the bereaved family about the disposal of Caudwell's artworks.

"Of course, the famous statue is gone now. What a pity. You could have endowed a chair in his honor with the proceeds from that piece alone." She gave a high, meaningless laugh.

Max sneaked a glance at his watch, wondering how long he had to stay before leaving would be rude. His sixth sense, the perfect courtesy that governed his movements, had deserted him, leaving him subject to the gaucheries of ordinary mortals. He never peeked at his watch at functions, and at any prior funeral he would have deftly pried Martha Gildersleeve from her victim. Instead he stood helplessly by while she tortured Mrs. Caudwell and other bystanders alike.

He glanced at his watch again. Only two minutes had passed since his last look. No wonder people kept their eyes on their watches at dull meetings: they couldn't believe the clock could move so slowly.

He inched stealthily toward the door, exchanging empty remarks with the staff members and trustees he passed. Nothing negative was said about Lotty to his face, but the comments cut off at his approach added to his misery.

He was almost at the exit when two newcomers appeared. Most of the group looked at them with indifferent curiosity, but Max suddenly felt an absurd stir of happiness. Victoria, looking sane and modern in a navy suit, stood in the doorway, eyebrows raised, scanning the room. At her elbow was a police sergeant Max had met with her a few times. The man was in charge of Caudwell's death, too: it was that unpleasant association that kept the name momentarily from his mind.

V. I. finally spotted Max near the door and gave him a discreet sign. He went to her at once.

"I think we may have the goods," she murmured. "Can you get everyone to go? We just want the family, Mrs. Gildersleeve, and Gioia."

"*You* may have the goods," the police sergeant growled. "I'm here unofficially and reluctantly."

"But you're here." Warshawski grinned, and Max wondered how he ever could have found the look predatory. His own spirits rose enormously at her smile. "You know in your heart of hearts that arresting Lotty was just plain dumb. And now I'm going to make you look real smart. In public, too."

Max felt his suave sophistication return with the rush of elation that an ailing diva must have when she finds her voice again. A touch here, a word there, and the guests disappeared like the hosts of Sennacherib. Meanwhile he solicitously escorted first Martha Gildersleeve, then Mrs. Caudwell to adjacent armchairs, got the brother to fetch coffee for Mrs. Gildersleeve, the daughter and son to look after the widow.

With Gioia he could be a bit more ruthless, telling him to wait because the police had something important to ask him. When the last guest had melted away, the immunologist stood nervously at the window rattling his change over and over in his pockets. The jingling suddenly was the only sound in the room. Gioia reddened and clasped his hands behind his back.

Victoria came into the room beaming like a governess with a delightful treat in store for her charges. She introduced herself to the Caudwells.

"You know Sergeant McGonnigal, I'm sure, after this last week. I'm a private investigator. Since I don't have any legal standing, you're not required to answer any questions I have. So I'm not going to ask you any questions. I'm just going to treat you to a travelogue. I wish I had slides, but you'll have to imagine the visuals while the audio track moves along."

"A private investigator!" Steve's mouth formed an exaggerated "O"; his eyes widened in amazement. "Just like Bogie."

He was speaking, as usual, to his sister. She gave her high-pitched laugh and said, "We'll win first prize in the 'How I Spent My Winter Vacation' contests. Our daddy was murdered. Zowie. Then his most valuable possession was snatched. Powie. But he'd already stolen it from the Jewish doctor who killed him. Yowie! And then a P.I. to wrap it all up. Yowie! Zowie! Powie!"

"Deborah, please," Mrs. Caudwell sighed. "I know you're excited, sweetie, but not right now, okay?"

"Your children keep you young, don't they, ma'am?" Victoria said. "How can you ever feel old when your kids stay seven all their lives?"

"Oo, ow, she bites, Debbie, watch out, she bites!" Steve cried.

McGonnigal made an involuntary movement, as though restraining himself from smacking the younger man. "Ms. Warshawski is right: you are under no obligation to answer any of her questions. But you're bright people, all of you: you know I wouldn't be here if the police didn't take her ideas very seriously. So let's have a little quiet and listen to what she's got on her mind."

Victoria seated herself in an armchair near Mrs. Caudwell's. McGonnigal moved to the door and leaned against the jamb. Deborah and Steve whispered and poked each other until one or both of them shrieked. They then made their faces prim and sat with their hands folded on their laps, looking like bright-eyed choirboys.

Griffen hovered near Mrs. Caudwell. "You know you don't have to say anything,

Vivian. In fact, I think you should return to your hotel and lie down. The stress of the funeral—then these strangers—"

Mrs. Caudwell's lips curled bravely below the bottom of her veil. "It's all right, Grif; if I managed to survive everything else, one more thing isn't going to do me in."

"Great." Victoria accepted a cup of coffee from Max. "Let me just sketch events for you as I saw them last week. Like everyone else in Chicago, I read about Dr. Caudwell's murder and saw it on television. Since I know a number of people attached to Beth Israel, I may have paid more attention to it than the average viewer, but I didn't get personally involved until Dr. Herschel's arrest on Tuesday."

She swallowed some coffee and set the cup on the table next to her with a small snap. "I have known Dr. Herschel for close to twenty years. It is inconceivable that she would commit such a murder, as those who know her well should have realized at once. I don't fault the police, but others should have known better: she is hot tempered. I'm not saying killing is beyond her—I don't think it's beyond any of us. She might have taken the statue and smashed Dr. Caudwell's head in in the heat of rage. But it beggars belief to think she went home, brooded over her injustices, packed a dose of prescription tranquilizer, and headed back to the Gold Coast with murder in mind."

Max felt his cheeks turn hot at her words. He started to interject a protest but bit it back.

"Dr. Herschel refused to make a statement all week, but this afternoon, when I got back from my travels, she finally agreed to talk to me. Sergeant McGonnigal was with me. She doesn't deny that she returned to Dr. Caudwell's apartment at ten that night—she went back to apologize for her outburst and to try to plead with him to return the statue. He didn't answer when the doorman called up, and on impulse she went around to the back of the building, got in through the service entrance, and waited for some time outside the apartment door. When he neither answered the doorbell nor returned home himself, she finally went away around eleven o'clock. The children, of course, were having a night on the town."

"*She* says," Gioia interjected.

"Agreed." V. I. smiled. "I make no bones about being a partisan: I accept her version. The more so because the only reason she didn't give it a week ago was that she herself was protecting an old friend. She thought perhaps this friend had bestirred himself on her behalf and killed Caudwell to avenge deadly insults against her. It was only when I persuaded her that these suspicions were as unmerited as—well, as accusations against herself—that she agreed to talk."

Max bit his lip and busied himself with getting more coffee for the three women. Victoria waited for him to finish before continuing.

"When I finally got a detailed account of what took place at Caudwell's party, I heard about three people with an ax to grind. One always has to ask, what ax and how big a grindstone? That's what I've spent the weekend finding out. You might as well know that I've been to Little Rock and to Havelock, North Carolina."

Gioia began jingling the coins in his pockets again. Mrs. Caudwell said softly, "Grif, I am feeling a little faint. Perhaps—"

"Home you go, Mom," Steve cried out with alacrity.

"In a few minutes, Mrs. Caudwell," the sergeant said from the doorway. "Get her feet up, Warshawski."

For a moment Max was afraid that Steve or Deborah was going to attack Victoria, but McGonnigal moved over to the widow's chair and the children sat down again.

Little drops of sweat dotted Griffen's balding head; Gioia's face had a greenish sheen, foliage on top of his redwood neck.

"The thing that leapt out at me," Victoria continued calmly, as though there had been no interruption, "was Caudwell's remark to Dr. Gioia. The doctor was clearly upset, but people were so focused on Lotty and the statue that they didn't pay any attention to that.

"So I went to Little Rock, Arkansas, on Saturday and found the Paul Nierman whose name Caudwell had mentioned to Gioia. Nierman lived in the same fraternity with Gioia when they were undergraduates together twenty-five years ago. And he took Dr. Gioia's anatomy and physiology exams his junior year when Gioia was in danger of academic probation, so he could stay on the football team.

"Well, that seemed unpleasant, perhaps disgraceful. But there's no question that Gioia did all his own work in medical school, passed his boards, and so on. So I didn't think the board would demand a resignation for this youthful indiscretion. The question was whether Gioia thought they would, and if he would have killed to prevent Caudwell making it public."

She paused, and the immunologist blurted out, "No. No. But Caudwell—Caudwell knew I'd opposed his appointment. He and I—our approaches to medicine were very opposite. And as soon as he said Nierman's name to me, I knew he'd found out and that he'd torment me with it forever. I—I went back to his place Sunday night to have it out with him. I was more determined than Dr. Herschel and got into his unit through the kitchen entrance; he hadn't locked that.

"I went to his study, but he was already dead. I couldn't believe it. It absolutely terrified me. I could see he'd been strangled and—well, it's no secret that I'm strong enough to have done it. I wasn't thinking straight. I just got clean away from there— I think I've been running ever since."

"You!" McGonnigal shouted. "How come we haven't heard about this before?"

"Because you insisted on focusing on Dr. Herschel," V. I. said nastily. "I knew he'd been there because the doorman told me. He would have told you if you'd asked."

"This is terrible," Mrs. Gildersleeve interjected. "I am going to talk to the board tomorrow and demand the resignations of Dr. Gioia and Dr. Herschel."

"Do," Victoria agreed cordially. "You could also tell them the reason you got to stay for this discussion was because Murray Ryerson at the *Herald-Star* was doing a little checking for me here in Chicago. He found out that part of the reason you were so jealous of Caudwell's collection is that you're living terribly in debt. I won't humiliate you in public by telling people what your money has gone to, but you've had to sell your husband's art collection and you have a third mortgage on your house. A valuable statue with no documented history would have taken care of everything."

Martha Gildersleeve shrank inside her sable. "You don't know anything about this."

"Well, Murray talked to Pablo and Eduardo. . . . Yes, I won't say anything else. So anyway, Murray checked whether either Gioia or Mrs. Gildersleeve had the statue. They didn't, so—"

"You've been in my house?" Mrs. Gildersleeve shrieked.

V. I. shook her head. "Not me. Murray Ryerson." She looked apologetically at the sergeant. "I knew you'd never get a warrant for me, since you'd made an arrest. And you'd never have got it in time, anyway."

She looked at her coffee cup, saw it was empty and put it down again. Max took it from the table and filled it for her a third time. His fingertips were itching with nervous irritation; some of the coffee landed on his trouser leg.

"I talked to Murray Saturday night from Little Rock. When he came up empty here,

I headed for North Carolina. To Havelock, where Griffen and Lewis Caudwell grew up and where Mrs. Caudwell still lives. And I saw the house where Griffen lives, and talked to the doctor who treats Mrs. Caudwell, and—"

"You really are a pooper snooper, aren't you," Steve said.

"Pooper snooper, pooper snooper," Deborah chanted. "Don't get enough thrills of your own so you have to live on other people's shit."

"Yeah, the neighbors talked to me about you two." Victoria looked at them with contemptuous indulgence. "You've been a two-person wolf pack terrifying most of the people around you since you were three. But the folks in Havelock admired how you always stuck up for your mother. You thought your father got her addicted to tranquilizers and then left her high and dry. So you brought her newest version with you and were all set—you just needed to decide when to give it to him. Dr. Herschel's outburst over the statue played right into your hands. You figured your father had stolen it from your uncle to begin with—why not send it back to him and let Dr. Herschel take the rap?"

"It wasn't like that," Steve said, red spots burning in his cheeks.

"What was it like, son?" McGonnigal had moved next to him.

"Don't talk to them—they're tricking you," Deborah shrieked. "The pooper snooper and her gopher gooper."

"She—Mommy used to love us before Daddy made her take all this shit. Then she went away. We just wanted him to see what it was like. We started putting Xanax in his coffee and stuff; we wanted to see if he'd fuck up during surgery, let his life get ruined. But then he was sleeping there in the study after his stupid-ass party, and we thought we'd just let him sleep through his morning surgery. Sleep forever, you know, it was so easy, we used his own Harvard necktie. I was so fucking sick of hearing 'Early to bed, early to rise' from him. And we sent the statue to Uncle Grif. I suppose the pooper snooper found it there. He can sell it and Mother can be all right again."

"Grandpa stole it from Jews and Daddy stole it from Grif, so we thought it worked out perfectly if we stole it from Daddy," Deborah cried. She leaned her blond head next to her brother's and shrieked with laughter.

V

Max watched the line of Lotty's legs change as she stood on tiptoe to reach a brandy snifter. Short, muscular from years of racing at top speed from one point to the next, maybe they weren't as svelte as the long legs of modern American girls, but he preferred them. He waited until her feet were securely planted before making his announcement.

"The board is bringing in Justin Hardwick for a final interview for chief of staff."

"Max!" She whirled, the Bengal fire sparkling in her eyes. "I know this Hardwick and he is another like Caudwell, looking for cost-cutting and no poverty patients. I won't have it."

"We've got you and Gioia and a dozen others bringing in so many nonpaying patients that we're not going to survive another five years at the present rate. I figure it's a balancing act. We need someone who can see that the hospital survives so that you and Art can practice medicine the way you want to. And when he knows what happened to his predecessor, he'll be very careful not to stir up our resident tigress."

"Max," She was hurt and astonished at the same time. "Oh. You're joking, I see. It's not very funny to me, you know."

"My dear, we've got to learn to laugh about it: it's the only way we'll ever be able to forgive ourselves for our terrible misjudgments." He stepped over to put an arm around her. "Now where is this remarkable surprise you promised to show me."

She shot him a look of pure mischief, Lotty on a dare as he first remembered meeting her at eighteen. His hold on her tightened and he followed her to her bedroom. In a glass case in the corner, complete with a humidity-control system, stood the Pietro Andromache.

Max looked at the beautiful, anguished face. I understand your sorrows, she seemed to say to him. I understand your grief for your mother, your family, your history, but it's all right to let go of them, to live in the present and hope for the future. It's not a betrayal.

Tears pricked his eyelids, but he demanded, "How did you get this? I was told the police had it under lock and key until lawyers decided on the disposition of Caudwell's estate."

"Victoria," Lotty said shortly. "I told her the problem and she got it for me. On the condition that I not ask how she did it. And Max, you know—*damned* well—that it was not Caudwell's to dispose of."

It was Lotty's. Of course it was. Max wondered briefly how Joseph the Second had come by it to begin with. For that matter, what had Lotty's great-great-grandfather done to earn it from the emperor? Max looked into Lotty's tiger eyes and kept such reflections to himself. Instead he inspected Hector's foot where the filler had been carefully scraped away to reveal the old chip.

SOFT MONKEY

HARLAN ELLISON
(1934–   )

One of the most honored and lavishly praised writers in the fantasy and science fiction world, Ellison has only occasionally ventured into the arena of mystery fiction. As might be expected, those brief forays have produced remarkable results, including Edgar Allan Poe Awards from the Mystery Writers of America for "The Whimper of Whipped Dogs," based on the real-life murder of Kitty Genovese, in 1974, and the present story.

T TWENTY-FIVE MINUTES past midnight on 51st Street, the wind-chill factor was so sharp it could carve you a new asshole.

Annie lay huddled in the tiny space formed by the wedge of locked revolving door that was open to the street when the document copying service had closed for the night. She had pulled the shopping cart from the Food Emporium at 1st Avenue near 57th into the mouth of the revolving door, had carefully tipped it onto its side, making certain her goods were jammed tightly in the cart, making certain nothing spilled into her sleeping space. She had pulled out half a dozen cardboard flats— broken-down sections of big Kotex cartons from the Food Emporium, the half dozen she had not sold to the junkman that afternoon—and she had fronted the shopping cart with two of them, making it appear the doorway was blocked by the management. She had wedged the others around the edges of the space, cutting the wind, and placed the two rotting sofa pillows behind and under her.

She had settled down, bundled in her three topcoats, the thick woolen merchant marine stocking cap rolled down to cover her ears, almost to the bridge of her broken nose. It wasn't bad in the doorway, quite cozy, really. The wind shrieked past and occasionally touched her, but mostly was deflected. She lay huddled in the tiny space, pulled out the filthy remnants of a stuffed baby doll, cradled it under her chin, and closed her eyes.

She slipped into a wary sleep, half in reverie and yet alert to the sounds of the street. She tried to dream of the child again. Alan. In the waking dream she held him as she held the baby doll, close under her chin, her eyes closed, feeling the warmth of his body. That was important: his body was warm, his little brown hand against her cheek, his warm, warm breath drifting up with the dear smell of baby.

Was that just today or some other day? Annie swayed in reverie, kissing the broken face of the baby doll. It was nice in the doorway; it was warm.

The normal street sounds lulled her for another moment, and then were shattered as two cars careened around the corner off Park Avenue, racing toward Madison. Even asleep, Annie sensed when the street wasn't right. It was a sixth sense she had learned to trust after the first time she had been mugged for her shoes and the small change in her snap-purse. Now she came fully awake as the sounds of trouble rushed toward her doorway. She hid the baby doll inside her coat.

The stretch limo sideswiped the Caddy as they came abreast of the closed repro center. The Brougham ran up over the curb and hit the light stanchion full in the grille. The door on the passenger side fell open and a man scrabbled across the front seat, dropped to all fours on the sidewalk, and tried to crawl away. The stretch limo, angled in toward the curb, slammed to a stop in front of the Brougham, and three doors opened before the tires stopped rolling.

They grabbed him as he tried to stand, and forced him back to his knees. One of the limo's occupants wore a fine navy blue cashmere overcoat; he pulled it open and reached to his hip. His hand came out holding a revolver. With a smooth stroke he laid it across the kneeling man's forehead, opening him to the bone.

Annie saw it all. With poisonous clarity, back in the V of the revolving door, cuddled in darkness, she saw it all. Saw a second man kick out and break the kneeling victim's nose. The sound of it cut against the night's sudden silence. Saw the third man look toward the stretch limo as a black glass window slid down and a hand emerged from the back seat. The electric hum of opening. Saw the third man go to the stretch and take from the extended hand a metal can. A siren screamed down Park Avenue, and kept going. Saw him return to the group and heard him say, "Hold the motherfucker. Pull his head back!" Saw the other two wrench the victim's head back, gleaming white and pumping red from the broken nose, clear in the sulfurous light from the stanchion overhead. The man's shoes scraped and scraped the sidewalk. Saw the third man reach into an outer coat pocket and pull out a pint of scotch. Saw him unscrew the cap and begin to pour booze into the face of the victim. "Hold his mouth open!" Saw the man in the cashmere topcoat spike his thumb and index fingers into the hinges of the victim's jaws, forcing his mouth open. The sound of gagging, the glow of spittle. Saw the scotch spilling down the man's front. Saw the third man toss the pint bottle into the gutter where it shattered; and saw his thumb press the center of the plastic cap of the metal can; and saw him make the cringing, crying, wailing victim drink the Drano. Annie saw and heard it all.

The cashmere topcoat forced the victim's mouth closed, massaged his throat, made him swallow the Drano. The dying took a lot longer than expected. And it was a lot noisier.

The victim's mouth was glowing a strange blue in the calcium light from overhead. He tried spitting, and a gobbet hit the navy blue cashmere sleeve. Had the natty dresser from the stretch limo been a dunky slob uncaring of what *GQ* commanded, what happened next would not have gone down.

Cashmere cursed, swiped at the slimed sleeve, let go of the victim; the man with the glowing blue mouth and the gut being boiled away wrenched free of the other two, and threw himself forward. Straight toward the locked revolving door blocked by Annie's shopping cart and cardboard flats.

He came at her in fumbling, hurtling steps, arms wide and eyes rolling, throwing spittle like a racehorse; Annie realized he'd fall across the cart and smash her flat in another two steps.

She stood up, backing to the side of the V. She stood up: into the tunnel of light from the Caddy's headlights.

"The nigger saw it all!" yelled the cashmere.

"Fuckin' bag lady!" yelled the one with the can of Drano.

"He's still moving!" yelled the third man, reaching inside his topcoat and coming out of his armpit with a blued steel thing that seemed to extrude to a length more aptly suited to Paul Bunyan's armpit.

Foaming at the mouth, hands clawing at his throat, the driver of the Brougham came at Annie as if he were spring-loaded.

He hit the shopping cart with his thighs just as the man with the long armpit squeezed off his first shot. The sound of the .45 magnum tore a chunk out of 51st Street, blew through the running man like a crowd roar, took off his face and spattered bone and blood across the panes of the revolving door. It sparkled in the tunnel of light from the Caddy's headlights.

And somehow he kept coming. He hit the cart, rose as if trying to get a first down against a solid defense line, and came apart as the shooter hit him with a second round.

There wasn't enough solid matter to stop the bullet and it exploded through the revolving door, shattering it open as the body crashed through and hit Annie.

She was thrown backward, through the broken glass, and onto the floor of the document copying center. And through it all, Annie heard a fourth voice, clearly a fourth voice, screaming from the stretch limo, "Get the old lady! Get her, she saw everything!"

Men in topcoats rushed through the tunnel of light.

Annie rolled over, and her hand touched something soft. It was the ruined baby doll. It had been knocked loose from her bundled clothing. *Are you cold, Alan?*

She scooped up the doll and crawled away, into the shadows of the reproduction center. Behind her, crashing through the frame of the revolving door, she heard men coming. And the sound of a burglar alarm. Soon police would be here.

All she could think about was that they would throw away her goods. They would waste her good cardboard, they would take back her shopping cart, they would toss her pillows and the hankies and the green cardigan into some trashcan; and she would be empty on the street again. As she had been when they made her move out of the room at 101st and First Avenue. After they took Alan from her . . .

A blast of sound, as the shot shattered a glass-framed citation on the wall near her. They had fanned out inside the office space, letting the headlight illumination shine through. Clutching the baby doll, she hustled down a hallway toward the rear of the copy center. Doors on both sides, all of them closed and locked. Annie could hear them coming.

A pair of metal doors stood open on the right. It was dark in there. She slipped inside, and in an instant her eyes had grown acclimated. There were computers here, big crackle-gray-finish machines that lined three walls. Nowhere to hide.

She rushed around the room, looking for a closet, a cubbyhole, anything. Then she stumbled over something and sprawled across the cold floor. Her face hung over into emptiness, and the very faintest of cool breezes struck her cheeks. The floor was composed of large removable squares. One of them had been lifted and replaced, but not flush. It had not been locked down; an edge had been left ajar; she had kicked it open.

She reached down. There was a crawlspace under the floor.

Pulling the metal-rimmed vinyl plate, she slid into the empty square. Lying face-up, she pulled the square over the aperture, and nudged it gently till it dropped onto its tracks. It sat flush. She could see nothing where, a moment before, there had been the faintest scintilla of filtered light from the hallway. Annie lay very quietly, emptying her mind as she did when she slept in the doorways, making herself invisible. A mound of rags. A pile of refuse. Gone. Only the warmth of the baby doll in that empty place with her.

She heard the men crashing down the corridor, trying doors. *I wrapped you in blankets, Alan. You must be warm.* They came into the computer room. The room was empty, they could see that.

"She *has* to be here, dammit!"

"There's gotta be a way out we didn't see."

"Maybe she locked herself in one of those rooms. Should we try? Break 'em open?"

"Don't be a bigger asshole than usual. Can't you hear that alarm? We gotta get out of here!"

"He'll break our balls."

"Like hell. Would he do anything else than we've done? He's sittin' on the street in front of what's left of Beaddie. You think he's happy about it?"

There was a new sound to match the alarm. The honking of a horn from the street. It went on and on, hysterically.

"We'll find her."

Then the sound of footsteps. Then running.

Annie lay empty and silent, holding the doll.

It was warm, as warm as she had been all November. She slept there through the night.

The next day, in the last Automat in New York with the wonderful little windows through which one could get food by insertion of a token, Annie learned of the two deaths.

Not the death of the man in the revolving door; the deaths of two black women. Beaddie, who had vomited up most of his internal organs, boiled like Chesapeake Bay lobsters, was all over the front of the *Post* that Annie now wore as insulation against the biting November wind. The two women had been found in midtown alleys, their faces blown off by heavy caliber ordnance. Annie had known one of them; her name had been Sooky and Annie got the word from a good Thunderbird worshipper who stopped by her table and gave her the skinny as she carefully ate her fish cakes and tea.

She knew who they had been seeking. And she knew why they had killed Sooky and the other street person: to white men who ride in stretch limos, all old nigger bag ladies look the same. She took a slow bite of fish cake and stared out at 42nd Street, watching the world swirl past; what was she going to do about this?

They would kill and kill till there was no safe place left to sleep in midtown. She knew it. This was mob business, the *Post* inside her coats said so. And it wouldn't make any difference trying to warn the women. Where would they go? Where would they *want* to go? Not even she, knowing what it was all about . . . not even she would leave the area: this was where she roamed, this was her territorial imperative. And they would find her soon enough.

She nodded to the croaker who had given her the word, and after he'd hobbled away to get a cup of coffee from the spigot on the wall, she hurriedly finished her fish cake and slipped out of the Automat as easily as she had the document copying center this morning.

Being careful to keep out of sight, she returned to 51st Street. The area had been roped off, with sawhorses and green tape that said *Police Investigation—Keep Off.* But there were crowds. The streets were jammed, not only with office workers coming and going, but with loiterers who were fascinated by the scene. It took very little to gather a crowd in New York. The falling of a cornice could produce a *minyan.*

Annie could not believe her luck. She realized the police were unaware of a witness: when the men had charged the doorway, they had thrown aside her cart and goods, had spilled them back onto the sidewalk to gain entrance; and the cops had thought it was all refuse, as one with the huge brown plastic bags of trash at the curb. Her cart and the good sofa pillows, the cardboard flats and her sweaters . . . all of it was in the area. Some in trash cans, some amid the piles of bagged rubbish, some just lying in the gutter.

That meant she didn't need to worry about being sought from two directions. One way was bad enough.

And all the aluminum cans she had salvaged to sell, they were still in the big Bloomingdale's bag right against the wall of the building. There would be money for dinner.

She was edging out of the doorway to collect her goods when she saw the one in navy blue cashmere who had held Beaddie while they fed him Drano. He was standing three stores away, on Annie's side, watching the police lines, watching the copy center, watching the crowd. Watching for her. Picking at an ingrown hair on his chin.

She stepped back into the doorway. Behind her a voice said, "C'mon, lady, get the hell outta here, this's a place uhbizness." Then she felt a sharp poke in her spine.

She looked behind her, terrified. The owner of the haberdashery, a man wearing a bizarrely-cut gray pinstripe worsted with lapels that matched his ears, and a passion flame silk hankie spilling out of his breast pocket like a crimson afflatus, was jabbing her in the back with a wooden coat hanger. "Move it on, get moving," he said, in a tone that would have gotten his face slapped had he used it on a customer.

Annie said nothing. She *never* spoke to anyone on the street. Silence on the street. *We'll go; Alan; we're okay by ourselves. Don't cry, my baby.*

She stepped out of the doorway, trying to edge away. She heard a sharp, piercing whistle. The man in the cashmere topcoat had seen her; he was whistling and signalling up 51st Street to someone. As Annie hurried away, looking over her shoulder, she saw a dark blue Oldsmobile that had been double-parked pull forward. The cashmere topcoat was shoving through the pedestrians, coming for her like the number 5 uptown Lexington express.

Annie moved quickly, without thinking about it. Being poked in the back, and someone speaking directly to her . . . that was frightening: it meant coming out to respond to another human being. But moving down her streets, moving quickly, and being part of the flow, that was comfortable. She knew how to do that. It was just the way she was.

Instinctively, Annie made herself larger, more expansive, her raggedy arms away from her body, the dirty overcoats billowing, her gait more erratic: opening the way for her flight. Fastidious shoppers and suited businessmen shied away, gave a start as the dirty old black bag lady bore down on them, turned sidewise praying she would not brush a recently Martinized shoulder. The Red Sea parted miraculously permitting flight, then closed over instantly to impede navy blue cashmere. But the Olds came on quickly.

Annie turned left onto Madison, heading downtown. There was construction around 48th. There were good alleys on 46th. She knew a basement entrance just three doors off Madison on 47th. But the Olds came on quickly.

Behind her, the light changed. The Olds tried to rush the intersection, but this was Madison. Crowds were already crossing. The Olds stopped, the driver's window rolled down and a face peered out. Eyes tracked Annie's progress.

Then it began to rain.

Like black mushrooms sprouting instantly from concrete, Totes blossomed on the sidewalk. The speed of the flowing river of pedestrians increased; and in an instant Annie was gone. Cashmere rounded the corner, looked at the Olds, a frantic arm motioned to the left, and the man pulled up his collar and elbowed his way through the crowd, rushing down Madison.

Low places in the sidewalk had already filled with water. His wing-tip cordovans were quickly soaked.

He saw her turn into the alley behind the novelty sales shop (*Nothing over $1.10!!!*); he *saw* her; turned right and ducked in fast; *saw* her, even through the rain and the crowd and half a block between them; *saw* it!

So where was she?

The alley was empty.

It was a short space, all brick, only deep enough for a big Dempsey Dumpster and a couple of dozen trash cans; the usual mounds of rubbish in the corners; no fire escape ladders low enough for an old bag lady to grab; no loading docks, no doorways that looked even remotely accessible, everything cemented over or faced with sheet steel; no basement entrances with concrete steps leading down; no manholes in the middle of the passage; no open windows or even broken windows at jumping height; no stacks of crates to hide behind.

The alley was empty.

Saw her come in here. *Knew* she had come in here, and couldn't get out. He'd been watching closely as he ran to the mouth of the alley. She was in here somewhere. Not too hard figuring out where. He took out the .38 Police Positive he liked to carry because he lived with the delusion that if he had to dump it, if it were used in the commission of a sort of kind of felony he couldn't get snowed on, and if it were traced, it would trace back to the cop in Teaneck, New Jersey, from whom it had been lifted as he lay drunk in the back room of a Polish social club three years earlier.

He swore he would take his time with her, this filthy old porch monkey. His navy blue cashmere already smelled like soaked dog. And the rain was not about to let up; it now came sheeting down, traveling in a curtain through the alley.

He moved deeper into the darkness, kicking the piles of trash, making sure the refuse bins were full. She was in here somewhere. Not too hard figuring out where.

Warm. Annie felt warm. With the ruined baby doll under her chin, and her eyes closed, it was almost like the apartment at 101st and First Avenue, when the Human Resources lady came and tried to tell her strange things about Alan. Annie had not understood what the woman meant when she kept repeating *soft monkey, soft monkey,* a thing some scientist knew. It had made no sense to Annie, and she had continued rocking the baby.

Annie remained very still where she had hidden. Basking in the warmth. *Is it nice,*

Alan? Are we toasty; yes, we are. Will we be very still and the lady from the City will go away? Yes, we will. She heard the crash of a garbage can being kicked over. *No one will find us. Shh, my baby.*

There was a pile of wooden slats that had been leaned against a wall. As he approached, the gun leveled, he realized they obscured a doorway. She was back in there, he knew it. Had to be. Not too hard figuring that out. It was the only place she could have hidden.

He moved in quickly, slammed the boards aside, and threw down on the dark opening. It was empty. Steel-plate door, locked.

Rain ran down his face, plastering his hair to his forehead. He could smell his coat, and his shoes, oh god, don't ask. He turned and looked. All that remained was the huge dumpster.

He approached it carefully, and noticed: the lid was still dry near the back side closest to the wall. The lid had been open just a short time ago. Someone had just lowered it.

He pocketed the gun, dragged two crates from the heap thrown down beside the Dempsey, and crawled up onto them. Now he stood above the dumpster, balancing on the crates with his knees at the level of the lid. With both hands bracing him, he leaned over to get his fingertips under the heavy lid. He flung the lid open, yanked out the gun, and leaned over. The dumpster was nearly full. Rain had turned the muck and garbage into a swimming porridge. He leaned over precariously to see what floated there in the murk. He leaned in to see. *Fuckin' porch monk—*

As a pair of redolent, dripping arms came up out of the muck, grasped his navy blue cashmere lapels, and dragged him head-first into the metal bin. He went down, into the slime, the gun going off, the shot spanging off the raised metal lid. The coat filled with garbage and water.

Annie felt him struggling beneath her. She held him down, her feet on his neck and back, pressing him face-first deeper into the goo that filled the bin. She could hear him breathing garbage and fetid water. He thrashed, a big man, struggling to get out from under. She slipped, and braced herself against the side of the dumpster, regained her footing, and drove him deeper. A hand clawed out of the refuse, dripping lettuce and black slime. The hand was empty. The gun lay at the bottom of the bin. The thrashing intensified, his feet hitting the metal side of the container. Annie rose up and dropped her feet heavily on the back of his neck. He went flat beneath her, trying to swim up, unable to find purchase.

He grabbed her foot as an explosion of breath from down below forced a bubble of air to break on the surface. Annie stomped as hard as she could. Something snapped beneath her shoe, but she heard nothing.

It went on for a long time, for a time longer than Annie could think about. The rain filled the bin to overflowing. Movement under her feet lessened, then there was hysterical movement for an instant, then it was calm. She stood there for an even longer time, trembling and trying to remember other, warmer times.

Finally, she closed herself off, buttoned up tightly, climbed out dripping and went away from there, thinking of Alan, thinking of a time after this was done. After that long time standing there, no movement, no movement at all in the bog beneath her waist. She did not close the lid.

When she emerged from the alley, after hiding in the shadows and watching, the Oldsmobile was nowhere in sight. The foot traffic parted for her. The smell, the dripping filth, the frightened face, the ruined thing she held close to her.

She stumbled out onto the sidewalk, lost for a moment, then turned the right way and shuffled off.

The rain continued its march across the city.

No one tried to stop her as she gathered her goods on 51st Street. The police thought she was a scavenger, the gawkers tried to avoid being brushed by her, the owner of the document copying center was relieved to see the filth cleaned up. Annie rescued everything she could, and hobbled away, hoping to be able to sell her aluminum for a place to dry out. It was not true that she was dirty; she had always been fastidious, even in the streets. A certain level of dishevelment was acceptable, but this was unclean.

And the blasted baby doll needed to be dried and brushed clean. There was a woman on East 60th, near Second Avenue; a vegetarian who spoke with an accent; a white lady who sometimes let Annie sleep in the basement. She would ask her for a favor.

It was not a very big favor, but the white woman was not home; and that night Annie slept in the construction of the new Zeckendorf Towers, where S. Klein-On-The-Square used to be, down on 14th and Broadway.

The men from the stretch limo didn't find her again for almost a week.

She was salvaging newspapers from a wire basket on Madison near 44th when he grabbed her from behind. It was the one who had poured the liquor into Beaddie, and then made him drink the Drano. He threw an arm around her, pulled her around to face him, and she reacted instantly, the way she did when the kids tried to take her snap-purse.

She butted him full in the face with the top of her head, and drove him backward with both filthy hands. He stumbled into the street, and a cab swerved at the last instant to avoid running him down. He stood in the street, shaking his head, as Annie careened down 44th, looking for a place to hide. She was sorry she had left her cart again. This time, she knew, her goods weren't going to be there.

It was the day before Thanksgiving.

Four more black women had been found dead in midtown doorways.

Annie ran, the only way she knew how, into stores that had exits on other streets. Somewhere behind her, though she could not figure it out properly, there was trouble coming for her and the baby. It was so cold in the apartment. It was always so cold. The landlord cut off the heat, he always did it in early November, till the snow came. And she sat with the child, rocking him, trying to comfort him, trying to keep him warm. And when they came from Human Resources, from the City, to evict her, they found her still holding the child. When they took it away from her, so still and blue, Annie ran from them, into the streets; and she ran, she knew how to run, to keep running so she could live out here where they couldn't reach her and Alan. But she knew there was trouble behind her.

Now she came to an open place. She knew this. It was a new building they had put up, a new skyscraper, where there used to be shops that had good throwaway things in the cans and sometimes on the loading docks. It was Citicorp Mall and she ran inside. It was the day before Thanksgiving and there were many decorations. Annie rushed through into the central atrium, and looked around. There were escalators, and she dashed for one, climbing to a second storey, and then a third. She kept moving. They would arrest her or throw her out if she slowed down.

At the railing, looking over, she saw the man in the court below. He didn't see her. He was standing, looking around.

Stories of mothers who lift wrecked cars off their children are legion.

When the police arrived, eyewitnesses swore it had been a stout, old black woman who had lifted the heavy potted tree in its terracotta urn, who had manhandled it up onto the railing and slid it along till she was standing above the poor dead man, and who had dropped it three storeys to crush his skull. They swore it was true, but beyond a vague description of old, and black, and dissolute looking, they could not be of assistance. Annie was gone.

On the front page of the *Post* she wore as lining in her right shoe, was a photo of four men who had been arraigned for the senseless murders of more than a dozen bag ladies over a period of several months. Annie did not read the article.

It was close to Christmas, and the weather had turned bitter, too bitter to believe. She lay propped in the doorway alcove of the Post Office on 43rd and Lexington. Her rug was drawn around her, the stocking cap pulled down to the bridge of her nose, the goods in the string bags around and under her. Snow was just beginning to come down.

A man in a Burberry and an elegant woman in a mink approached from 42nd Street, on their way to dinner. They were staying at the New York Helmsley. They were from Connecticut, in for three days to catch the shows and to celebrate their eleventh wedding anniversary.

As they came abreast of her, the man stopped and stared down into the doorway. "Oh, Christ, that's awful," he said to his wife. "On a night like this, Christ, that's just awful."

"Dennis, *please!*" the woman said.

"I can't just pass her by," he said. He pulled off a kid glove and reached into his pocket for his money clip.

"Dennis, they don't like to be bothered," the woman said, trying to pull him away. "They're very self-sufficient. Don't you remember that piece in the *Times*?"

"It's damned near Christmas, Lori," he said, taking a twenty dollar bill from the folded sheaf held by its clip. "It'll get her a bed for the night, at least. They can't make it out here by themselves. God knows, it's little enough to do." He pulled free of his wife's grasp and walked to the alcove.

He looked down at the woman swathed in the rug, and he could not see her face. Small puffs of breath were all that told him she was alive. "Ma'am, please take this." He held out the twenty.

Annie did not move. She never spoke on the street.

"Ma'am, please, let me do this. Go somewhere warm for the night, won't you . . . please?"

He stood for another minute, seeking to rouse her, at least for a *go away* that would free him, but the old woman did not move. Finally, he placed the twenty on what he presumed to be her lap, there in that shapeless mass, and allowed himself to be dragged away by his wife.

Three hours later, having completed a lovely dinner, and having decided it would be romantic to walk back to the Helmsley through the six inches of snow that had fallen, they passed the Post Office and saw the old woman had not moved. Nor had she taken the twenty dollars. He could not bring himself to look beneath the wrappings to see if she had frozen to death, and he had no intention of taking back the money. They walked on.

In her warm place, Annie held Alan close up under her chin, stroking him and feeling his tiny black fingers warm at her throat and cheeks. *It's all right, baby; it's all right. We're safe. Shhh, my baby. No one can hurt you.*

THE HAND OF CARLOS

CHARLES MCCARRY
(1930–   )

The greatest writer of espionage fiction that America has produced (Ross Thomas, his only peer, wrote in so many different forms that he is not regarded as a spy novelist), McCarry brings a sophistication and intelligence to his work that remains unmatched to this day. The undertone of reality and credibility is doubtless enhanced by the fact that he was a member of the Central Intelligence Agency for a decade until 1967 when he turned to writing full time.

HE TERRORIST'S ARABIC WAS poor and his Farsi was nonexistent, but he had a quick ear for hidden meanings. That was why he was still alive. That was why he was alone with this mad old man, speaking French, waiting to hear the name of his target.

He inclined his head and waited for the holy man to speak again. They were seated on the floor of a plain small room in a simple house in the holy city of Qum. The holy man, squatting on the coarse wool blanket that was his bed by night and his throne by day, smelled of dust. Beside him lay the bowl from which he had eaten his lunch of rice and yoghurt; the terrorist, whose taste ran to steak *au poivre,* had been unable to eat the food. Now, smelling it on the old man's sour breath, he wished that he had.

The holy man was the most successful revolutionary in the world. The richest and most ancient kingdom in the Near East lay at his feet. He imagined that he had conquered Iran by the power of his faith and the strength of

his voice. But the terrorist knew that he had had help; the militant youth who were the cutting edge of the holy man's revolution had been trained and armed in the camps of the Palestinian terror front. The terrorist himself had learned to use his workmanlike Soviet weapons—the 9mm Makarov pistol, the Skorpion machine pistol, the AK47 assault rifle—in those camps.

In the name of the Palestinian struggle, which was the personal cause of every progressive revolutionary in the world, the terrorist had shot an old Jew in London. He had bombed innocent people in Paris, kidnapped the head of the Iranian secret police, killed two French counter-intelligence men and a traitor, shot an Arab by mistake. He was not even an Arab: he had spilled all that blood out of idealism.

The holy man understood. It meant little to him. He was the spiritual leader of the Shi'a Moslems. To him, there was no blood except the blood spilled on the 19th of Ramadan, A.H. 40 (655 A.D.), when Ali, the son-in-law, cousin, and chosen heir of the Prophet Mohammed, was assassinated as he prayed in Mosque of Kufa.

The Shi'a believed that Islam had been led ever since by usurpers, for none but a descendant of Ali and of Mohammed's daughter Fatima could be the true successor to the Prophet. The holy man wore the black turban of a descendant of Mohammed; he slept always on his right side, as Ali had commanded the imams to do.

The terrorist was in the presence of the holy man because he was a famous assassin. But the Shi'a had given the world the very word "assassin." From the ranks of this sect, 800 years ago, came the Order of Assassins, the hashikin, takers of hashish, who set out systematically to murder the usurpers.

The enemies of Ali's younger son, Hussein, had refused him water when they slew him in the desert. The Shi'a had never forgotten or forgiven this bitter act of cruelty. It was a rite of remembrance to Hussein, and to the justice of the Shi'a cause, that no pious Shi'a ever put any creature to death—not a sheep on a feast day, not a chicken bought in the bazaar, not the most hated human enemy—without first offering it a drink of water.

The holy man, at last, opened his dry lips. The terrorist leaned closer.

"The shah," said the holy man, "must be offered a cup of water."

The terrorist handed him a slip of paper on which a dollar sign followed by six digits had been written. The holy man nodded, wearily, in agreement.

"Shah mat," the terrorist said. It was the only Persian he knew. It meant "the king is dead."

For this operation, the terrorist took the name Paco, and he traveled out of Tehran like any ordinary person in a first-class airline seat. In his attache case, in addition to the bottle of gasoline that he could sprinkle over a stewardess in an emergency, he carried an excellent Mexican passport, forged by East German experts working with the Libyan intelligence service.

Paco was enjoying himself thoroughly. The stewardesses had that wonderful silken skin that only German girls had, and those slender long legs that bourgeois German girls were so willing to spread for the revolution. He put his hand on the waist of one of the stewardesses and smiled at her and asked for another Martell brandy.

"Only Martell," he said. "No substitutes."

The stewardess smiled at him and he thought that he saw the beginning of something in her eyes. Even before his plastic surgery he had always had all the girls he wanted. Now he had even more. The East German doctors had given him a better face, thinning the lips that once had looked like blue slugs, taking the flab out of the cheeks and the chin.

Paco turned back to the American professor who was his seat mate. It pleased Paco, who loved to talk and loved to lie, to tell this man that he, Paco, was an important figure in the Popular Front for the liberation of Palestine.

"The PFLP is the terrorist arm of the PLO, isn't it?" the American asked. There was respect in his voice. Not for a moment did he doubt that Paco, who spoke English with a heavy latinate accent and drank enough cognac to kill a horse, was an Arab and a devout Moslem.

"You disapprove of terror?" Paco asked.

The professor lifted a soft bourgeois hand—who could imagine a gun or a woman's breast in such a hand?—to protest. "I sympathize," he said, "but . . ."

"There can be no 'buts,'" said Paco, scowling, making this sympathizer squirm. "Did you sympathize before the terror started? We were invisible to you. We are doctors of philosophy. George Habash, our chief terrorist, is a children's doctor. But you forced us to kill before you would see our suffering, before you would sympathize. That shows how sick you and your capitalist society are!"

The American professor gave him a look filled with shame. "I hate it as much as you do," he said. "More, because all the heroes are on your side."

Paco felt a rush of pleasure. How these pretenders, these toy store revolutionaries loved to be insulted, whipped, blamed! They hated their country, their parents, their species, because they hated themselves. They were doomed.

The stewardess came back with the Martell brandy, a whole bottle, and Paco put a forefinger on the back of her hand as she poured, pressing down so that she had to fill the glass to the rim. If she knew who he really was, he could have her in the lavatory. Watching her legs as she walked away, he was tempted to follow and tell her. Showing them a gun made them hot, he knew that from experience.

"It is not possible," said the sweating major. "It is not possible to go out to the camps without the personal permission of Colonel Kaddafi."

Paco stared through his sunglasses at the sweating German. How was it that a country which produced such perfect women as the stewardess on the Lufthansa flight could also produce such pigs for men? The major was past his youth, the desert sun had reddened his skin, and there was a great wrinkle of fat on the back of his thick neck. Also, like all the East Germans who sat in every office of Libyan intelligence, he was a racist, filled with contempt for Arabs. Paco himself was exasperated by Arabs. They were undependable, inefficient, maddening in their bloodymindedness. But they were, to Paco, the symbol of the cause. To this German, they were a subject race: beaky and circumcised.

"Kaddafi refuses me nothing," Paco said.

"That's your story," the German major said. But he lifted the telephone and ordered the transport that Paco had requested.

For a rarity, it was quite true, what Paco had said: Colonel Muammar Kaddafi, dictator of Libya, financier and keeper of the weapons warehouse of international terrorism, refused this peacock of a Latin-American nothing. It was even said, and the major believed it, that Kaddafi had given Paco ten million dollars in payment for kidnapping the oil minister of Saudi Arabia and the head of Savak, the shah's secret police. It was also said that the Saudis and the shah had put $50 million in ransom into Paco's Swiss bank account. Anyway, he had let his prisoners go without harming a hair of their heads.

The major didn't like him. He didn't care if the KGB had recruited and trained him. He didn't care about his exploits. He was a romantic, a weakling who liked women and food and liquor—and, above all, money—too much. Paco was a showoff. If he couldn't be bought, he could be out-witted. Paco was smoking a stinking Gauloise; he chain-smoked the things.

The Bedouin band moved across the desert floor—black figures trudging along beside a file of camels and a horse or two. A few miles ahead of the main body, a

Land Rover bucked through the rough country, stirring up a plume of dust that could be seen for miles.

Through the Perspex window of the small plane, Paco could see the weapons in the hands of the three men who rode with the headman in the Land Rover. He focused the plane's binoculars on the vehicle. Two of the men were equipped with Czech VZ-58s, a version of the AK-47 that had a nasty tendency to climb when fired on full automatic. The other carried a Dragunov sniper's rifle, a heavy, clumsy Soviet weapon that could put a heavy slug through a vest button at 900 meters. These desert tramps were coming up in the world.

On the horizon, an hour's drive for the Land Rover and four hours' march for the camels, Paco could see the Bedouins' objective, a well among the scrub. He had the Palestinian pilot make a long circle to the south, then come in low, below the crest of the hills and out of sight of the Bedouins, and land. "Fly out low, circle, and pass over the column again," Paco said. "Don't let them know you've landed."

The plane, an American Bonanza (Paco didn't trust Russian aircraft engines over the desert), churned away, creating a stinging sandstorm. Paco found a hiding place on a knoll overlooking the camp ground and settled down in the shade of a rubbery anemic bush that probably had roots 50 meters deep. If you cut it down, it would reach into the soil and find moisture and grow again. Like the revolution.

In the distance Paco could see the column of dust raised by the Land Rover. He opened his pack and checked it contents. First, he checked the two 9mm. Makarov pistols, oiled and loaded and stored in Ziploc plastic bags, another marvelous contribution to civilization by the Americans. He worked the bolt on his Skorpion, only 10.6 inches long with the butt folded, but capable of spewing 7.65mm. rounds at a rate of 14 rounds a second. Four RGD-5 anti-personnel grenades, painted cheap Russian green, nestled like eggs at the bottom of the sack. They weighed only a little over half a pound, about half as much as the far more powerful U.S. Army M-52 fragmentation grenades stolen from a U.S. base in West Germany by the Baader-Meinhoff Gang. Paco waited, watching the dust of the Land Rover. When he could hear its gearbox howling he took off his sunglasses so that the mirrors would not flash in the sun and give away his position.

It was dusk before Paco moved again. The crew of the Land Rover had searched the perimeter of the camp, studying the tracks of the light plane on the floor of the wadi. At last the camels came, the tents sprang up, and the cooking fires were lighted. Paco, crawling over the flinty ground, took up a position near the latrine, some 50 meters from the black tents.

The leader had been haranguing his men. Now he slung his assault rifle across his back and headed for the latrine. Paco, who knew his habits, waited. The leader hiked up his robes, swirling the layers of cloth around his body, holding up the robes with both hands and both elbows. Straddling the ditch, he was absolutely helpless. Paco smiled at the man's buttocks, fish-white, and fired all eight rounds from the Makarov between his legs. The slugs, traveling at the tremendous velocity of 1,023 feet per second, zipped into the earth. Paco had known there was no chance of a ricochet with this weapon.

The leader fell over sideways, more afraid of the filth in the ditch than of death, clawing for his slung weapon, swaddled and tripped by his robes. Paco put another clip into his Makarov, just in case, and began to laugh uproariously. The fallen man, tearing at his VZ-58, now looked up at Paco. Paco put on his mirror sunglasses.

"It's you," said the Bedouin leader, "you turd conceived by a jackal on a syphilitic whore rutting on a dung heap."

The other members of the band were running toward them, assault rifles and machine pistols at the ready. Paco pulled the leader to his feet.

"You'd better tell them who I am," said Paco. The leader gave a hand signal and the advancing tribesmen halted.

The leader introduced Paco, never mentioning the name by which the world knew him. He spoke first in Arabic, for he was a Palestinian from Jerusalem, and then in English, German, and French, for the tribesmen were men and women, all in their early twenties, who had come from the cities of Europe to learn how to do all the things that Paco already did so well. They knew perfectly well who their visitor was; Paco could see it in their eyes.

Paco ate the spartan dinner, almost as bad as the rice and yoghurt he had been given in Qum, and kept an aloof silence. The young terrorists, apprentices, watched his every move. It was hard to tell what the girls looked like under these robes, but he sat next to the one with the prettiest face. When she put down her plate, he tossed his dirty Makarov into her lap. "Clean this," he said.

Of the dozen bands of terrorists, disguised as Bedouins, that were now training in the Libyan desert, Paco had chosen this one because he knew that his old friend would have trained its members well in the use of weapons and in the making of bombs, and trained them even better in the most indispensable weapon of all, blind obedience. Paco, speaking to them, a legend speaking in the desert with the firelight flickering in the mirrors of his sunglasses, did not tell them that.

"Some of you have been chosen for a historic job," Paco told them. "I am leading. I expect we will all die, but before we do, we will accomplish our objective. I need two Germans, four Italians, two Spanish-speakers, two explosives experts from the IRA Provos, one American. Amir will tell you which of you is chosen. That's all."

Later, lying beside the girl who had cleaned his pistol, Paco advised her, as a sign of his satisfaction with her, never to carry any pistol other than the Makarov. "I shot a Jew in London with a Browning," he said, "and the bullet was stopped by his teeth. Not enough muzzle velocity. In Paris, a round from the Makarov went through a French DST man, through the floor, through a table in the room below, and then into the floor boards under the table. Or so the newspapers said."

Paco placed the cold gun on the girl's flat stomach. She put her hand over the gun. That was all the invitation he needed. While he had her, she shuddered and said wonderful things in Spanish.

"I thought you were the prize American," he said to her afterward. "How do you speak such . . . learned Spanish?"

The girl explained. She had gone to Cuba to work with the Venceremos Brigades, cutting sugar cane for Castro. The DGI, the Cuban intelligence service, had picked her up. She'd been trained in one of the camps outside Havana before she was chosen for Libya.

"What's your name?"

"Layal."

"Not your gamename. Your name."

"My name is Rosemary Kadowaki."

"Rosemary?"

"I was born in Los Angeles. Are you really who the others say you are? They said you were dead, that you had disappeared, that you had left the movement."

"They say what they like. I act," said Paco.

Paco loved to talk; he had always loved to talk. He lifted the girl's hair, it was damp with sweat, and whispered into her ear. "Shah mat," he whispered. "Do you know what that means?"

The girl looked up at him with adoring eyes. He had only been in bed with her for an hour—less—and she was willing to die for him. Paco knew from experience that this was so.

The Israeli whose workname was Eleazar closed the file and looked across the desk at his control.

"Carlos is going to kill the shah?" he said.

"Someone who is perhaps Carlos has been hired to kill the shah," said the control. "There is a report that the holy man personally gave him the contract."

"Do we have a description of this Carlos?"

"He's using the name Paco. The story is that his appearance has been altered by plastic surgery. He has all of Carlos' behavior patterns—ego, lust, recklessness, loquacity, contempt for women and the opposition."

"Fingerprints? Did they blood-type him when he entered Libya?"

Each terrorist who entered Libya for training gave up a smear of blood; other smears were taken at every subsequent meeting and the DNA was compared. It was an ingenious, foolproof method of identification: the East German touch.

"What good are fingerprints?" asked the control. "The fingerprints Carlos left in Paris and the fingerprints he left on the plane after the OPEC kidnapping were not the same."

"Do you think he was bought on that plane?" asked Eleazar. "Did the Saudis and the shah buy him with $50 million in a Swiss account?"

"Anything is possible. Hans Joachim Klein, the German terrorist who was wounded with Carlos in Vienna, swears that he was bought."

"So," said Eleazar, "maybe it's Carlos and maybe it isn't, but they are going to kill the shah."

"They are going to try. Do you think we should let fools murder a friend of Israel?"

"What about the Americans?"

A droplet of contemptuous silence formed in the stale air of the windowless room. "The Americans," said the control. "Impotent."

Then he said, "Eleazar, I want you to get your team together again."

Eleazar's Wrath of God team, Israelis trained as commandos, had reached into the rat holes of Europe—Germany, Scandinavia, even Poland—to liquidate, in a cold fury of revenge, the Palestinians who had murdered the Israeli athletes at the Munich Olympics, and all who had helped them.

Eleazar picked up his medical bag. "I'll contact the team," he said.

With Paco at his side, Colonel Muammar al-Kaddafi watched impassively as Amir's team carried out an exercise. They handled all the weapons of the Soviet arsenal, up to the RPG-7 portable rocket launcher and the shoulder-fired SAM 7 Strela anti-aircraft missile, with consummate skill. Paco did not like these heavy weapons: he had tried to rocket an Israeli airliner at Orly Airport in Paris, and later had attempted to bring down a passenger jet with the Strela. Neither operation had gone right. These clumsy battlefield devices were not for terrorists. They gave too much warning.

Kaddafi wore his usual outfit: starched safari suit, British-style officer's cap, burnished buckled shoes without socks. He was always ready to dart, barefoot, into the mosque to pray. He carried a swagger stick.

Revolution makes strange bedfellows, thought Paco. Here he was, an atheist whose millionaire father, a cafe Communist from Venezuela, had named his three sons Vladimir, Ilich, and Lenin, after the first Soviet saint, standing on a dune with a fanatical Moslem who had gone to Sandhurst, watching a crowd of children from good bourgeois Christian homes shoot up the landscape with guns made in Russia and Czechoslovakia.

Paco followed Kaddafi down the ranks of terrorists. The colonel asked each where he, or she, had come from. "Red Brigades, Milano!" they replied. Or "Red Army Faction, Hamburg!" Or "Euskadi to Askatunsa, Bilbao!" Or "Provisional IRA, Belfast!"

To Layal, standing at attention with her assault rifle across her chest, Kaddafi said, in English, "And you are from the heroic Japanese Red Army."

"No, Brother Colonel," said Layal. "I was born in California. In 1942, because we were Japanese, my family was robbed of its little farm and put into a concentration camp by the two-faced U.S. liberal imperialists. I have come here to help build the people's prisons where the American oppressors will pay for their crimes against humanity."

"Good," said Kaddafi. "Very good."

Kaddafi led Paco to his helicopter. The interior, like every interior belonging to Kaddafi, was decorated in shades of Islamic green: green bulkheads, green upholstery, green Perspex; the Brother Colonel drank tea from a green glass. He had left the machine guns blue-black. Kaddafi was in the middle of one of his long philosophical soliloquies. Paco sipped his tea, sickly sweet and minted. He liked the sweetness but hated the tea itself. It was hard enough following Kaddafi's ravings when you hadn't drunk a liter of tea. With your bladder bursting, it was next to impossible.

"You can do this?" Kaddafi asked.

"Yes. The plan is good. We have the people. Now we have your blessing, Brother Colonel, so we have everything."

"One thing only I demand," said Kaddafi.

Merde, thought Paco.

"The shah has one friend in the world, this swine Sadat," Kaddafi said. "In the end, he must run to Sadat, in Egypt. Kill him there. Kill him before Sadat's eyes. Humiliate Sadat. Let him see how long my arm is, that it can reach into his very house and kill a king."

"At your orders, Brother Colonel," said Paco. And again he thought, *merde.* How am I going to get around this piece of madness?

After fleeing from Iran on January 16, 1979, the shah had gone to Egypt, then to Morocco, then to the Bahamas. Now word came to Paco that the shah had rented a villa in the Mexican city of Cuernavaca, Mexico.

The word came at night. It was June, and cold in the desert. Layal woke and listened in her silent way as Paco talked to the courier. He and the courier, and officer of the Cuban Directorate General of Intelligence, spoke in Spanish. It did not matter if she understood, here in the middle of nowhere.

"It's a tough target," said the Cuban. "We have a man inside the shah's household, a survivor of the Communist League 23rd of September movement."

"Training?"

"He took our course in Havana, then the GRU picked him up and shipped him to Doupov."

Trained in Czechoslovakia by Soviet military intelligence, and smart enough to survive the brutal Mexican search for the Communist League 23rd of September after it had massacred 40 Mexican policemen, kidnapped the daughter of the Belgian ambassador and killed the son of the Mexican ambassador to the United States. A light came into Paco's eyes. He could use such a man.

"No," said the Cuban, who had been reading Paco's eyes since Paris days. "He's our last operative in Mexico who isn't scared shitless. You can't have him."

The Cuban told Paco about "La Villa," the shah's rented house in Cuernavaca. It was located at 100 del Rio Street, on a steep hill near the river, screened by trees. "No chance of using rockets, of course, because of the trees," said the Cuban. "There is a watchtower, ramproof steel gates, the usual electronic stuff—infra-red intruder detectors, temblor alarms to pick up footsteps."

"How many guards?"

"Twenty Americans, 34 Mexicans, six Iranians. Very well armed, very well paid. Oil company thugs."

"You're telling me nothing cheerful."

The Cuban grinned. "I saved the best for last. There is a tunnel, dug just before the shah arrived, that leads from La Villa to another house."

"Good. We can mine it."

"That's not all. The shah's men buy books about Trotsky at the local bookstores. He's fascinated with the details of how Stalin had Trotsky killed in Mexico. Second, a green station wagon brings in supplies twice a week and is not challenged at the gates. Third, the shah has been talking about going out to dinner."

"Going out to dinner?"

"To show he's got balls. He hears that Las Manitas is a good restaurant. Peacocks stroll in the grounds. He'll like that—the Peacock Throne."

Paco was in command now. He had separated the team into national groups, forbidding them to associate with each other or to speak each other's languages. The kids, thirsty for their chance to be a symbol of the revolution like Paco, gladly put up with this pointless bullying.

He routed out the two Germans. Klaus (Paco had stripped the band, except for Layal, of their Arab gamenames) was a typical Baader-Meinhoff type: sullen, fanatical, intellectual, the son of a man who manufactured cars that he sold to Americans for $50,000 apiece, dressed his wife in sable and his teenage mistresses in Wehrmacht uniforms (black lace underneath), and was now as good a democrat as he had once been a Nazi. Which was to say, in both cases, not awfully good, because money was what he was interested in and there was very little money in ideals unless, like Paco, you provided certain unique services idealists could not do without.

His son Klaus wanted to believe in something, he wanted to live like a soldier, sleeping rough and eating frugally, he wanted to die for a cause. His friend, Bernhild, was just as sullen, but simpler: she just wanted to kill. Anyone would do. Gabriele Krocher-Tiedemann, Paco's teammate in Vienna, had been like that. "Are you a policeman?" she had asked an old man during their raid on OPEC headquarters. "Yes," the old man replied. She shot him in the back of the neck and sent him down an elevator. Later, she shot another security guard, and wanted to shoot more.

In Paco's experience, Germans were useful people. So operatic in their love of themselves and in their love of death. They'd kill themselves if there was no one else around to murder.

Klaus and Bernhild, trying not to shiver in the frigid desert air, awaited their orders. Paco, as he spoke to them, faced the dawn, and they saw the big yellow Saharan sun come up in his sunglasses.

"I have a very important job for you," Paco said. "Everything, I mean everything, depends on your success."

"We will die for the revolution," said Klaus.

"Probably. But first you will help others to do so," said Paco.

Two weeks later, a man and a woman, posing as German tourists, were arrested in Cuernavaca. They had been observed loitering near La Villa. When the Mexican police followed them home, they found grenades and automatic weapons.

There were rumors that the Germans had in their possession a list of prominent Mexican citizens who were going to be assassinated if the shah was not thrown out of the country. It was said that under questioning by Mexico Federal Security the Germans had told everything about a plot to murder the shah.

No one asked the Germans, because they disappeared.

Miguel Nazar Haro, director of Mexico Federal Security, would not confirm that the Germans had ever existed. "We do not deal lightly with terrorists in Mexico," said Nazar. "That is why we have none." He added that the shah would always be safe in Mexico, and that his agency was on the lookout for German and Japanese terrorists especially. He smiled a confident smile.

When the green station wagon came through the gates of La Villa, after the Germans had disappeared, it carried, among the groceries, a copy of a book about Trotsky. One of the security men picked it up.

"I thought we had a copy of this one," he said.

The book exploded, taking off both his hands and most of his face.

This was Paco's way of saying, "Time to move."

Paco, lunching in Las Manitas, watched the man beside the shah taste his master's food before it was chewed by the royal teeth and swallowed by the royal esophagus. The shah drank vodka on the rocks and ate a steak.

There were thugs with walkie-talkies all over the place. "Someone could kill him," said the woman with Carlos. She trembled at being so close to a king, never knowing how close she was to the Makarov strapped to Paco's right leg.

Paco could have killed him then and there—and died romantically a moment afterward. At home, the shah was always accompanied by two Dobermans and a huge wolfhound. No man trained, like Paco, in the KGB technique (press the gun against the flesh before firing, no cowboy stuff) could have got close enough to shoot him. Here there were no dogs.

I am the dog, thought Paco, the wolf, in sheepdog's clothing, herding this royal sheep to Egypt.

He giggled. The woman gave him a puzzled look. Had he no regard for royalty?

Paco looked down on the snarled, braying traffic on Sixth Avenue. The big cars and the yellow taxis glittered in the unswept street—New York was having one of its garbagemen's strikes—like gems in the feces of a capitalist trying to escape from a revolution. Carlos drank what was left of the Lafite-Rothschild 1962 he had had with lunch, and padded in his bare feet across the living room of his suite at the Hilton. He loved Hiltons: the shrimp cocktails, the steaks you didn't have to chew, the jolly bars, filled with girls.

He slapped the sleeping girl in the bed on the buttocks. She woke with a snarl. Carlos undid the belt of his Sulka dressing gown and started to turn her over. The girl put a cold hand on his hairless chest.

"This is New York, killer," she said. "It's a hundred dollars a pop."

Paco threw her clothes at her. He got a handful of hundreds out of his shoulder bag and waved them at her, to show she wasn't worth it to him. "Out," he said, "before I flush your nose down the toilet."

When Flaherty came into the room a half-hour later, he stopped dead in his tracks and stared long and hard at Paco.

"It can't be you," said Flaherty. "No, it's a prank the lads are playing on me."

"It's the plastic surgery," said Paco.

"You mean to say you let the Arabs go at you with a scalpel and this handsome matinee idol is the result?"

Paco lifted his chin, turned his head.

"Even your voice is different," said Flaherty. "Less of a whinny, more of a baritone."

"They fixed my vocal chords too."

"Did they now? And what else? Can you fuck the way you used to?" The KGB had castrated more than one great agent, the better to control him. The odd thing was, it made men more loyal to their mutilators, even grateful.

These were friendly insults. Paco and Flaherty, who was one of the truly great bombers of the Provisional IRA, the Provos, went back a long way. They had met in the KGB school for terrorists at Karlovy Vary, in Czechoslovakia, and had ever since done each other favors. Paco had bought some dynamite in Zurich for Flaherty, who had used it to blow up a British politician in a London street. Flaherty had drilled a hole in the kneecap of a Swede Paco had suspected of being an informer; he'd used an electric drill, Provo style. Paco hadn't been quite suspicious enough to kill the man, who was a world-class sniper and might, if he proved to be innocent, turn out useful.

"So what is it this time?" asked Flaherty.

Paco told him. The shah was in a New York hospital, the Cornell Medical Center.

"If it's the shah you're after, it's no more trouble to blow up the hospital where he's recuperating from his dreadful surgical ordeal," said Flaherty. "There must be a good reliable lad who drives an ambulance or something, or a lonely nurse, or one of the oppressed who needs a few quid to put the kiddies through college. We'd wheel in, say 20 kilos of plastic, nicely molded to the underside of one of them rolling stretchers they use. It would go off in the room below the shah's bed and blow his majesty and most of the bloody hospital into the East River. Or is that too gruesome for a squeamish lad like you?"

"Can you use a time fuse?"

"Sure, I can do much fancier stuff than that book in Mexico."

"Call me here and give me the exact time it's set to go. I need at least an hour's notice," said Paco.

"What're you going to do, warn 'em?" asked Flaherty, and they both laughed and had more of the Old Bushmill out of Paco's bottle.

When Paco called, from a pay phone outside the men's room on the hotel mezzanine, to warn the shah's security about Flaherty's bomb, a voice said, "We have already taken care of that. Who's calling, please?"

Later, Flaherty came by for some more whiskey. "How could they have known?" asked Paco.

"My lad inside says the Israelis called up. They're still very thick with the shah; it was them that trained the Savak, you know, not the silly bloody CIA like everyone says."

"The Israelis?" Paco said. He didn't like their being after him, so close, so early in the game.

Captain Shariar Mustapha Chafik of the Royal Iranian Navy was walking down the Rue Villa Dupont, in the 16th arrondissement of Paris on the afternoon of December 7, 1979. He was on his way to a nearby apartment owned by his mother, Princess Ashraf, twin sister to the shah.

A young man in a plastic motorcyclist's helmet walked up behind Captain Chafik and, placing the muzzle of a Makarov pistol within an inch of his skull, fired two shots. The killer escaped.

Next day, in the windowless room in Jerusalem, Eleazar and his control discussed this event.

"Carlos wanted to kill Chafik himself," said the control. "Kaddafi's East Germans told him he had to let the Iranians do something. It's obvious from the close-in technique, pure KGB-Palestinian, who trained the assassin."

"But why? Why Chafik? Why Paris? It's a sideshow."

"It's all a sideshow. The Germans in Mexico, the bomb in New York. Carlos, if he is Carlos, could have killed the shah in either place."

"Then what is he waiting for?"

"To kill him in a particular place, for a particular reason."

A silence fell. It was stifling in the room despite the air conditioning, and notwithstanding thick sealed walls the peculiar noise of the Near East, a surf of voices breaking on the bleak shore of the jumbled city, came to their ears.

"Your team is ready?" asked the control, knowing that it was. Each member could speak Arabic and at least one other language, each could kill—kill with an Uzi machine pistol, kill with a knife, kill in ingenious ways. ("Is this really you?" one member had asked over a telephone. "Yes," replied his target, a Palestinian terrorist who happened to be in bed with a woman at the other end. The phone exploded in the terrorist's hand. They found the girl, quite mad, with her lover's severed head in her lap.)

"I'd like you to take your team to Cairo," said Eleazar's control. He handed him six British passports, six driver's licenses, six sets of credit cards, a few letters, stamped, postmarked, and opened, addressed to the fictitious names on the forged documents.

Their weapons would be waiting in Egypt.

In Havana, Paco woke up to find Layal's black eyes fixed on his face. They were strange eyes, all one glassy dark color, lacking pupils, absent light. It was disconcerting to wake up every day to find this flat, utterly expressionless, but beautiful face staring into his own.

"Why don't you learn to sleep?" Paco asked.

"I already know how to sleep," Layal said. "I need to learn how to stay awake."

"We have pills for that."

Something happened behind Layal's unrippled face that might have been a smile. She had no physical shame: clothed or unclothed, her behavior was the same. Her body, smooth as a court kimono, was as lithe and hard as the body of a gymnast. She had amazing muscular control.

Just before dark, the telephone rang—the first time since they had arrived in Cuba. Paco spoke a code phrase and listened to another. Then he got out his leather bag, unlocked it, and removed one of his Makarovs. He took five extra clips.

"Stay with the bag. Don't let anyone touch it," he said to Layal. "Not even your Cuban friends, not even Kotchergine if he stops by."

Colonel Vadim Kotchergine of the KGB had established the camps in Cuba that had trained the first pioneering terrorists from the Americas and Europe. Not many people knew that. Paco liked to show his women that the revolution kept no secrets from him.

Night fell. Paco departed. "I know you want to come with me," he said to Layal, "but this is not the operation for you. I'm saving you for the real work."

It was always a relief to Paco to speak Spanish. But Spanish is not a good language to speak in a boat, because voices carry over the water, and Latin Americans only speak softly when they are in brothel or in a church. Paco made his joke not to calm the men he was sending to attack Contadora Island off the coast of Panama, the shah's last refuge, but because he was, in some ways, weak. He wanted men he was sending to their deaths to think he was a good fellow.

There were two men from the desert band, a pair of Basques who had been sent to Libya by ETA to learn how to kill Spanish policemen. One of them was very good with explosives: it was the ETA that had tunneled under a Madrid street and planted a hundred kilos of dynamite in the hole, and blown a Dodge Dart carrying Admiral Luis Carrero Blanco, the premier of Spain, over a five-story building. Paco had given them the dynamite.

The two Basques laughed at Paco's joke. The third man did not. He was a Montonero, which is like saying that he was a tyrannosaur—terrifying, but thought to be extinct. The Montoneros, originally the secret bullies of the Peronist movement in Argentina, had turned sharply left and been crushed, 9,000 of them killed by the police and the army in a single year. Some had escaped and taken refuge with cells of the Red Brigades in Italy. They were rich fugitives: in just one operation, the Montoneros had extorted $60 million in kidnap ransom from one of Argentina's richest families.

Like all Montoneros, this one, Raul by gamename, thought that he was an aristo-crat. Paco had wanted to use M-19 people for this operation—a nifty outfit of doctors, lawyers, architects from Colombia—but they had just had a disaster when they released, rather than killed, the 14 foreign ambassadors they had seized as hostages in the Dominican Embassy at Bogota. The media could only cover one embassy full of hostages at a time, and they had a big investment in the Americans in Iran. Now M-19, to redeem itself, was planning to liquidate Anastasio Somoza Debayle, the for-mer dictator of Nicaragua. Their best men were in Paraguay, stalking Somoza.

Raul stepped into the boat. It was the best money could buy, but old—one of the many inflatable Zodiacs with powerful engines that the Cubans had captured from CIA teams 20 years before during the Kennedys' secret war against Castro.

"Come back," said Paco. Raul got out of the boat, wetting his shoes and trousers in the surf. "Remember, follow the plan of the mission," Paco said. "You're not shooting to kill. We just want two rounds from the bazooka to land near the house, not hit it." Raul looked with contempt at the RPG-7 rocket launcher lying in the bot-tom of the boat. It had a range of 500 meters and its projectile could, in theory, pierce 12 inches of armor. "If we hit the fucking island of Contadora from a moving boat, we'll be lucky," he said. "And why two rounds? So they'll see the flame from the backblast and have time to blow us out of the water?" Paco smiled. "After you fire, dive. The Basques will show you how," he said. All three men wore wet suits. Tanks and respirators lay beside the Russian bazookas in the bottom of the Zodiac.

This operation meant nothing. It was just a little something extra to let the shah and the Americans know it was time to move again, that there was danger that the sick monarch might yet be killed before he died of cancer. The Americans around President Carter were terrified that this might happen. Then they would lose their hostages, lose the election. Somebody from the White House was talking at this very moment to Ghotbzadeh, the Iranian foreign minister, about ways to betray the shah. The man from the White House was wearing a false beard.

Paco didn't bother to wait on the beach for Raul and the Basques to come back from Contadora. He just left an observer with a good pair of binoculars looking out over the Pacific. The observer saw, reflected from the low cloud over the choppy sea, two small red flashes, as from the backblast of a bazooka. Moments later he saw a helicopter hovering with tracer rounds falling lazily into the sea from its guns, and then the much larger flash, as from a boat loaded with gasoline going up.

He sent Paco the prearranged message: "The sheep is running."

At last the shah was on his way to Egypt. Outside Cairo, in a house directly under the glide path to the airport, Eleazar watched through the big glasses as the two men came out on the roof in Heliopolis. An American M-1 rifle, fitted with a tele-scope and certain other refinements, lay on the rug in which he had carried it through the streets. The men were wearing caftans, long roughspun gowns that reached to their ankles. Jets, approaching Cairo Airport, screamed overhead. The airport was almost two miles away. The men on the rooftop, though their faces were young in the bright circle of the powerful optic, moved stiffly, as if they had some crippling disease of the spine. Such things were not unusual in Egyptians, but the faces Eleazar saw were not Egyptians, but European. Italian? Yes, Italian.

The Italians lay down on the rooftop. From beneath their caftans one man drew a long tube, the other a missile with fins. The chartered jet carrying the shah was due in half an hour. The Italians were fitting the missile, a Strela SAM 7 infra-red projectile that could nose into the hot orifice of a jet engine at an altitude of 2,000 meters. There was no time to call the Egyptians: 30 minutes was not enough for them. Eleazar sighed. He picked up the rifle and gazed through the scope. He shot the first Italian in the spine and the second through the head. Then he put two rounds through the launcher, in case there was a backup team, abandoned his equipment, and went out into the teeming street.

"What was that noise?" asked an old fruit peddler.

"The world is nothing but noise." Eleazar said in his flawless Arabic. "What great price are you asking a thirsty man for one of those oranges?"

Paco closed his eyes and listened to the sound of the straight razor on his cheek. What a sensuous thing it was to be shaved by a woman. No female had taken such care of him before Layal. She massaged his body with oils, she gave him baths, scrubbing him down with a rough sponge, she even cleaned the wax from his ears. Without opening his eyes, Paco put his hand between Layal's thighs. He knew how much she enjoyed that, but she gave no sign: the razor kept moving in small, precise strokes over his face and throat. It was the sharpest instrument Paco had ever seen; Layal stropped it every day. She carried it always, in a little chamois sheath at the small of her back.

"Now we know for sure that the Israelis are after us," said Paco. "It's probably one of their Wrath of God teams. The Mossad wouldn't risk blowing their own people."

"But you lost two men. They were found with a Strela missile and launcher beside them. They were identified as Italians."

The speaker was an emissary from George Habash's PFLP Headquarters in Aden. Because Habash's people had trained a lot of European terrorists, they thought they were in charge of every operation. But they were just Palestinians. Everything they had, someone had given them: money from Kaddafi, arms from the GRU and the KGB, terrorists from the romantic upper middle class of the Free World. Even Paco himself was a gift. He controlled this operation.

"I have four Italians left," said Paco. "That should be enough."

"You have also the two Iranians," said the emissary. "They must be used."

"They're so good."

"Your employer insists. A Shi'a must offer the shah water before he is killed."

"I know more about the requirements than you do," Paco said. Layal took the hot towel off his face and rubbed his skin with an astringent. Paco opened his eyes for the first time and stared at the emissary. A television set flickered behind him, the sound turned up loud to muffle their conversation.

"We all wonder what private understanding you might have with the holy man," said the emissary.

There it was again: the suggestion that he, Paco, was stealing from the revolution, that he was risking everything for pay, that he was a mercenary and worse than a mercenary.

"Get out!" Paco shouted. "I don't like your manners!"

The emissary gave a sardonic smile. Layal whipped the barber's sheet off Paco, snapping it in the air. The emissary saw the Makarov, fitted with a long silencer, lying on Paco's lap, and stopped smiling.

"We would like to have the details of your plan," the emissary said.

"I'm sure you would," said Paco. "Now get out."

Layal was incredibly useful. Among the band in the desert, she had been the best shot with every kind of weapon. She spoke perfect Arabic in several regional variations. She even wrote Arabic: her only pastime was practicing Arabic script and Japanese calligraphy. She was strong: in the desert, in a training exercise at night, she had taken a loaded Skorpion—a loaded hair-trigger Skorpion!—away from one of the Germans who had come up behind her, and broken the man's arm. She was adept at Akihido, a kind of martial art Paco had not encountered before. She had the calm fearlessness of the true professional killer.

Also, she had type B-negative blood. This was going to get her into Maadi Military Hospital, where a team of American surgeons was preparing to remove the shah's cancerous spleen. The shah had B-negative blood, a rare type. So rare that donors would be let into the hospital through the crowd of Elite Guards and police who had kept out even the wailing relatives of other patients.

"Get dressed and go," Paco said.

Layal did as she was told. She did not nod, she did not say yes, nothing happened in her eyes. Unless Paco had her on the bed, she was a stone.

In the garage in Helwan, a village south of Cairo, Paco inspected the van while the Italians from the Red Brigades and the Iranians from the Islamic Revolutionary Youth, or whatever they called themselves, watched nervously. The team leader, gamename Bruno, showed Paco how it would work. It was one of those camper vans; the roof could be cranked open, to give headroom and air. Open, it looked like a lean-to, with mosquito netting over the opening. They had sanded the paint off the van, which was new and in perfect mechanical condition, in order to make it look old; the Italians were proud of the dents they had put in the van, using an old truck, not hammers.

"Very realistic," said Paco.

Inside the roof the Italians had fitted a device called "Stalin's organ." It was a rack holding 12 RPG-7 rocket launchers. Bruno cranked up the roof. The muzzles of the launchers were hidden by the mosquito netting.

"The weight won't be too much for the roof?" asked Paco. "You'll have to drive to the hospital with it open."

"No, we strengthened it," said Bruno. "The circuits are wired together, so all the rockets fire at the same instant. When they hit the hospital, they'll tear a hole the size of the van right through the side. We'll go in shooting."

"Good," said Paco. "Remember one thing: the timing. You fire your rockets from the corniche road at exactly 0852. You must be inside the building, shooting and throwing grenades, at 0857. I want noise, noise, noise."

Paco turned to the two Iranians. They actually came to attention when he looked in their direction, like Gungha Din in his rags, ready to die for the regiment.

"I will be in the operating room in the basement," Paco said. He pointed to the plan of the hospital taped to the side of the van. "What's your name?" he said to the less intelligent of the Iranians.

"Espendiar."

"Okay, Espendiar. You come straight to the operating room. You'll have a Skorpion. Use it. Kill everyone in your way. I want you rolling grenades into every room as you

Layal began, methodically, to fill the holes in the wall with plastic explosive. She inserted the detonators and strung the wire. When the plastic blew, it would open a hole three feet in diameter. Paco would duck through, shooting as he went. He smiled in pleasure. In his mind's eye he could see the profile of the shah, like the head of a dead chicken, lying on the table. And, already, he could hear the shrieks of panic—he had heard the shrieks so often before.

Eleazar and his team were waiting on the corniche, dressed as Elite Guards. They wore big, inefficient Tokagypt automatics, relics of Egypt's arms deal with the U.S.S.R., in holsters on their belts, and concealed small 9-mm. automatics in the palms of their hands. Inside their truck were more useful weapons.

They stopped the Volkswagen van. Eleazar had not shaved, and he had washed out his mouth with raki. Bruno, at the wheel of the van, noticed these signs of corruption. His papers were perfectly in order. In the back of the van, dressed as Arabs, were the other Italians and the two Iranians. Eleazar saw the beret on Espendiar's head, as Paco had meant him to do.

At this moment, one of Eleazar's team, dressed as a sergeant in the Elite Guard, said something to Eleazar. Eleazar flew into a rage. He screamed at the sergeant in Arabic, he stood him at attention. Finally, in a gesture of discipline that has all but disappeared from the Egyptian army, he commanded the sergeant to open his mouth. Eleazar spit into the sergeant's mouth, to show him that he could do anything he liked to him.

Eleazar waved the Volkswagen van by. In the mirror, Bruno could see this mad Egyptian, still shouting at his sergeant. It was the last thing he saw. Just as the island that splits the Nile opposite Maadi Military Hospital came into sight, the magnetic radio-controlled bomb that another of Eleazar's men had fastened to the gas tank of the van exploded. The Volkswagen vanished as the combined force of the Israeli bomb, the gas in the tank, the ammunition in the interior, and 12 RPG-7 rocket grenades produced an explosion that looked, just for an instant, like the sun reddened by a sandstorm, only brighter. The air over the Nile was filled with the smoky trails of exploding rounds.

Paco heard the racket through his earphones, strangely muffled. He heard the soldiers shouting, the beat of their running feet, and a burst or two of small arms fire. He ripped off the headset. It was only 0846.

"They're early, the fools," he said to Layal. "Blow it now!"

Layal ran backwards—he had to admire her physical capabilities even in such a moment—playing out the detonator wire from a spool. Paco followed her, a Makarov in his right hand.

Outside the door, they met a man. He held an Uzi submachine gun, an Israeli weapon, in his hands, and he had the look of a Jew: something about the mouth and eyes, the contempt, the intelligence; Paco could always tell.

Paco lifted the Makarov, clumsy as it was with the long silencer attached to the end of the barrel, and squeezed the trigger. The pistol exploded in his hand. In the same microsecond, Paco looked at his mangled hand, and also saw Layal shoot the intruder in the exact center of the forehead with her own Makarov. The intruder was Espendiar, without the black beret Paco had given him. Fool.

Paco was whimpering. He had no right hand. He couldn't look at it. Blood spurted from the shredded crimson thing at the end of his arm.

"Layal," he said, in a voice that sounded to him as thin as a thread. "What happened?"

"Special ammunition," she replied. Then, for the first time ever, she smiled. "Special for you, comrade."

Layal held her razor in her square small hand. Ah, Paco thought, she is going to save me, she is probably a surgeon too. Then he remembered! "Special ammunition."

Layal had loaded his Makarov. She had booby-trapped it. He tried to seize her weapon with the hand he had left. She stepped easily out of his reach.

He could feel, actually feel, his heart emptying through his wrist. "Not me," he said, in a strong voice, his last words.

Layal watched him die. Then she picked up his left hand and bent it backward at the wrist. As if she were disjointing a chicken, she cut off the hand with the razor.

She pinned a note, written in her beautiful Arabic script, to Paco's shirt. It read: "Islamic justice has cut off the hand of a thief who stole from the revolution."

The woman Paco had known as Layal drank an ice-cold Coca-Cola straight from the can while her American case officer, working cheerfully, fingerprinted the severed hand.

"Was he Carlos or was he not?" asked the case officer.

"He never actually claimed to be," Layal said. "He had all the mannerisms, all the skills, all the ego. All the vices, too. I can't get the taste of Martell brandy out of my mouth or the smell of Gauloise Disques Bleus out of my hair."

The case officer examined the card smudged with the fingerprints. "If these don't belong to the Carlos of Paris or the Carlos of Vienna, we may have to believe that the KGB or George Habash are outwitting us," he said. "Or somebody."

"Outwitting us was his thing. Paco thought it was easy."

"Is that what he said about us?"

"That's what they all say about us."

"What good news."

The case officer had a charming smile. "I can hardly believe the things they will believe."

He shook his head. The Japanese girl who was such a perfect American type smiled back at him, her eyes alive with humor and affection and a touch of mockery. She liked this outrageous Wasp with his St. Grottlesex accent and his sense of fun. The worst part of being out in the desert with crazed louts like the Bedouin band was their solemnity. The case officer dropped Paco's hand into a Ziploc plastic bag.

"But then again," he said, dropping the hand into his out basket, "where would we be, love, if strangers, men we'll never know, didn't give us a hand now and then?"

KAREN MAKES OUT

ELMORE LEONARD
(1925–   )

Arguably America's greatest living crime writer, Leonard has clearly been influenced by Hemingway and Cain, his efficient language depicting characters and scenes in fast but vivid line drawings rather than textured oil paintings. His rhythms are jazz, not symphonies. "I try to leave out the parts that readers skip," he says. It has worked wonderfully as success in two genres, the western and the crime novel, has demonstrated. Often filmed, his work has had mixed cinematic results, from the excellent Hombre *and* Get Shorty *to the lesser* Stick *and* Cat Chaser.

THEY DANCED UNTIL KAREN said she had to be up early tomorrow. No argument, he walked with her through the crowd outside Monaco, then along Ocean Drive in the dark to her car. He said, "Lady, you wore me out." He was in his forties, weathered but young-acting, natural, didn't come on with any singles-bar bullshit buying her a drink, or comment when she said thank you, she'd have Jim Beam on the rocks. They had cooled off by the time they reached her Honda and he took her hand and gave her a peck on the cheek saying he hoped to see her again. In no hurry to make something happen. That was fine with Karen. He said "Ciao," and walked off.

Two nights later they left Monaco, came out of that pounding sound to a sidewalk café and drinks and he became Carl Tillman, skipper of a charter deep-sea fishing boat out of American Marina, Bahia Mar. He was single, married seven years and divorced, no children; he lived in a ground-floor two-bedroom apartment in North Miami—one of the bedrooms full of fishing gear he didn't know where else to store. Carl said his boat was out of the water, getting ready to move it to Haulover Dock, closer to where he lived.

Karen liked his weathered, kind of shaggy look, the crow's-feet when he smiled. She liked his soft brown eyes that looked right at her talking about making his living on the ocean, about hurricanes, the trendy scene here on South Beach, movies. He went to the movies every week and told Karen—raising his eyebrows in a vague, kind of stoned way—his favorite actor was Jack Nicholson. Karen asked him if that was his Nicholson impression or was he doing Christian Slater doing Nicholson? He told her she had a keen eye; but couldn't understand why she thought Dennis Quaid was a hunk. That was okay.

He said, "You're a social worker."

Karen said, "A *social* worker—"

"A teacher."

"What kind of teacher?"

"You teach Psychology. College level."

She shook her head.

"English Lit."

"I'm not a teacher."

"Then why'd you ask what kind I thought you were?"

She said, "You want me to tell you what I do?"

"You're a lawyer. Wait. The Honda—you're a public defender." Karen shook her head and he said, "Don't tell me, I want to guess, even if it takes a while." He said, "If that's okay with you."

Fine. Some guys, she'd tell them what she did and they were turned off by it. Or they'd act surprised and then self-conscious and start asking dumb questions. "But how can a girl do that?" Assholes.

That night in the bathroom brushing her teeth Karen stared at her reflection. She liked to look at herself in mirrors: touch her short blond hair, check out her fanny in profile, long legs in a straight skirt above her knees, Karen still a size six approaching thirty. She didn't think she looked like a social worker or a school-teacher, even college level. A lawyer maybe, but not a public defender. Karen was low-key high style. She could wear her favorite Calvin Klein suit, the black one her dad had given her for Christmas, her Sig Sauer .38 for evening wear snug against the small of her back, and no one would think for a moment she was packing.

Her new boyfriend called and stopped by her house in Coral Gables Friday evening in a white BMW convertible. They went to a movie and had supper and when he brought her home they kissed in the doorway, arms slipping around each other, holding, Karen thanking God he was a good kisser, comfortable with him, but not quite ready to take her clothes off. When she turned to the door he said, "I can wait. You think it'll be long?"

Karen said, "What're you doing Sunday?"

They kissed the moment he walked in and made love in the afternoon, sunlight flat on the window shades, the bed stripped down to a fresh white sheet. They made love in a hurry because they couldn't wait, had at each other and lay per-spiring after. When they made love again, Karen holding his lean body between her legs and not wanting to let go, it lasted and lasted and got them smiling at each other, saying things like "Wow," and "Oh, my God," it was so good, serious business but really fun. They went out for a while, came back to her yellow stucco bungalow in Coral Gables and made love on the living room floor.

Carl said, "We could try it again in the morning."

"I have to be dressed and out of here by six."

"You're a flight attendant."

She said, "Keep guessing."

Monday morning Karen Sisco was outside the federal courthouse in Miami with a pump-action shotgun on her hip. Karen's right hand gripped the neck of the stock, the barrel extending above her head. Several more U.S. deputy marshals were out here with her; while inside, three Colombian nationals were being charged in District Court with the possession of cocaine in excess of five hundred kilograms. One of the marshals said he hoped the scudders like Atlanta as they'd be doing thirty to life there pretty soon. He said, "Hey, Karen, you want to go with me, drop 'em off? I know a nice ho-tel we could stay at."

She looked over at the good-ole-boy marshals grinning, shuffling their feet, waiting for her reply. Karen said, "Gary, I'd go with you in a minute if it wasn't a mortal sin." They liked that. It was funny, she'd been standing there thinking she'd gone to bed with four different boyfriends in her life: an Eric at Florida Atlantic, a Bill right after she graduated, then a Greg, three years of going to bed with Greg, and now Carl. Only four in her whole life, but two more than the national average for women in the U.S. according to *Time* magazine, their report of a recent sex survey. The average woman had two partners in her lifetime, the average man, six. Karen had thought everybody was getting laid with a lot more different ones than that.

She saw her boss now, Milt Dancey, an old-time marshal in charge of court support, come out of the building to stand looking around, a pack of cigarettes in his hand. Milt looked this way and gave Karen a nod, but paused to light a cigarette before coming over. A guy from the Miami FBI office was with him.

Milt said, "Karen, you know Daniel Burdon?"

Not Dan, not Danny, Daniel. Karen knew him, one of the younger black guys over there, tall and good looking, confident, known to brag about how many women he'd had of all kinds and color. He'd flashed his smile at Karen one time, hitting on her. Karen turned him down saying, "You have two reasons you want to go out with me." Daniel, smiling, said he knew of one reason, what was the other one? Karen said, "So you can tell your buddies you banged a marshal." Daniel said, "Yeah, but you could use it, too, girl. Brag on getting me in the sack." See? That's the kind of guy he was.

Milt said, "He wants to ask you about a Carl Tillman."

No flashing smile this time, Daniel Burdon had a serious, sort of innocent expression, saying to her, "You know the man, Karen? Guy in his forties, sandy hair, goes about five-ten, one-sixty?"

Karen said, "What's this, a test? Do I *know* him?"

Milt reached for her shotgun. "Here, Karen, lemme take that while you're talking."

She turned a shoulder saying, "It's okay, I'm not gonna shoot him," her fist tight on the neck of the twelve-gauge. She said to Daniel, "You have Carl under surveillance?"

"Since last Monday."

"You've seen us together—so what's this do-I-know-him shit? You playing a game with me?"

"What I meant to ask, Karen, was how long have you known him?"

"We met last week, Tuesday."

"And you saw him Thursday, Friday, spent Sunday with him, went to the beach, came back to your place . . . What's he think about you being with the marshals' service?"

"I haven't told him."

"How come?"

"He wants to guess what I do."

"Still working on it, huh? What you think, he a nice guy? Has a sporty car, has money, huh? He a pretty big spender?"

"Look," Karen said, "why don't you quit dickin' around and tell me what this is about, okay?"

"See, Karen, the situation's so unusual," Daniel said, still with the innocent expression, "I don't know how to put it, you know, delicately. Find out a U.S. marshal's fucking a bank robber."

Milt Dancey thought Karen was going to swing at Daniel with the shotgun. He took it from her this time and told the Bureau man to behave himself, watch his mouth if he wanted cooperation here. Stick to the facts. This Carl Tillman was a *suspect* in a bank robbery, a possible suspect in a half dozen more, all the robberies, judging from the bank videos, committed by the same guy. The FBI referred to him as "Slick," having nicknames for all their perps. They had prints off a teller's counter might be the guy's, but no match in their files and not enough evidence on Carl Edward Tillman—the name on his driver's license and car registration—to bring him in. He appeared to be most recently cherry, just getting into a career of crime. His motivation, pissed off at banks because Florida Southern foreclosed on his note and sold his forty-eight-foot Hatteras for nonpayment.

It stopped Karen for a moment. He might've lied about his boat, telling her he was moving it to Haulover; but that didn't make him a bank robber. She said, "What've you got, a video picture, a teller identified him?"

Daniel said, "Since you mentioned it," taking a Bureau wanted flyer from his inside coat pocket, the sheet folded once down the middle. He opened it and Karen was looking at four photos taken from bank video cameras of robberies in progress, the bandits framed in teller windows, three black guys, one white.

Karen said, "Which one?" and Daniel gave her a look before pointing to the white guy: a man with slicked-back hair, an earring, a full mustache, and dark sunglasses. She said, "That's not Carl Tillman," and felt instant relief. There was no resemblance.

"Look at it good."

"What can I tell you? It's not him."

"Look at the nose."

"You serious?"

"That's your friend Carl's nose."

It was. Carl's slender, rather elegant nose. Or like his. Karen said, "You're going with a nose ID, that's all you've got?"

"A witness," Daniel said, "believes she saw this man—right after what would be the first robbery he pulled—run from the bank to a strip mall up the street and drive off in a white BMW convertible. The witness got a partial on the license number and that brought us to your friend Carl."

Karen said, "You ran his name and date of birth . . ."

"Looked him up in NCIC, FCIC, and Warrant Information, drew a blank. That's why I think he's getting his feet wet. Managed to pull off a few, two three grand each, and found himself a new profession."

"What do you want me to do," Karen said, "get his prints on a beer can?"

Daniel raised his eyebrows. "That would be a start. Might even be all we need. What I'd like you to do, Karen, is snuggle up to the man and find out his secrets. You know what I'm saying—intimate things, like did he ever use another name. . . ."

"Be your snitch," Karen said, knowing it was a mistake as soon as the words were out of her mouth.

It got Daniel's eyebrows raised again. He said, "That what it sounds like to you? I thought you were a federal agent, Karen. Maybe you're too close to him—is that it? Don't want the man to think ill of you?"

Milt said, "That's enough of that shit," standing up for Karen as he would any of his people, not because she was a woman; he had learned not to open doors for her. The only time she wanted to be first through the door was on a fugitive warrant, this girl who scored higher with a handgun, more times than not, than any marshal in the Southern District of Florida.

Daniel was saying, "Man, I need to use her. Is she on our side or not?"

Milt handed Karen her shotgun. "Here, you want to shoot him, go ahead."

"Look," Daniel said, "Karen can get me a close read on the man, where he's lived before, if he ever went by any other names, if he has any identifying marks on his body, scars, maybe a gunshot wound, tattoos, things only lovely Karen would see when the man has his clothes off."

Karen took a moment. She said, "There is one thing I noticed."

"Yeah? What's that?"

"He's got the letters f-u-o-n tattooed on his penis."

Daniel frowned at her. "Foo-on?"

"That's when it's, you might say, limp. When he has a hard-on it says Fuck the Federal Bureau of Investigation."

Daniel Burdon grinned at Karen. He said, "Girl, you and I have to get together. I mean it."

Karen could handle "girl." Go either way. Girl, looking at herself in a mirror applying blush-on. Woman, well, that's what she was. Though until just a few years ago she only thought of women old enough to be her mother as women. Women getting together to form organizations of women, saying, Look, we're different from men. Isolating themselves in these groups instead of mixing it up with men and beating them at their own men's games. Men in general were stronger physically than women. Some men were stronger than other men and Karen was stronger than some too; so what did that prove? If she had to put a man on the ground, no matter how big or strong he was, she'd do it. One way or another. Up front, in his face. What she couldn't see herself playing was this sneaky role. Trying to get the stuff on Carl, a guy she liked, a lot, would think of with tender feelings and miss him during the day and want to be with him. Shit. . . . Okay, she'd play the game, but not undercover. She'd first let him know she was a federal officer and see what he thought about it.

Could Carl be a bank robber?

She'd reserve judgment. Assume almost anyone could at one time or another and go from there.

What Karen did, she came home and put a pot roast in the oven and left her bag on the kitchen table, open, the grip of a Beretta nine sticking out in plain sight.

Carl arrived, they kissed in the living room, Karen feeling it but barely looking at him. When he smelled the pot roast cooking Karen said, "Come on, you can make the drinks while I put the potatoes on." In the kitchen, then, she stood with the refrigerator door open, her back to Carl, giving him time to notice the pistol. Finally he said, "Jesus, you're a cop."

She had rehearsed this moment. The idea: turn saying, "You guessed," sounding surprised; then look at the pistol and say something like "Nuts, I gave it away." But she didn't. He said, "Jesus, you're a cop," and she turned from the refrigerator with an ice tray and said, "Federal. I'm a U.S. marshal."

"I would've never guessed," Carl said, "not in a million years."

Thinking about it before, she didn't know if he'd wig out or what. She looked at him now, and he seemed to be taking it okay, smiling a little.

He said, "But why?"

"Why what?"

"Are you a marshal?"

"Well, first of all, my dad has a company, Marshall Sisco Investigations. . . ."

"You mean because of his name, Marshall?"

"What I am—they're not spelled the same. No, but as soon as I learned to drive I started doing surveillance jobs for him. Like following some guy who was trying to screw his insurance company, a phony claim. I got the idea of going into law enforcement. So after a couple of years at Miami I transferred to Florida Atlantic and got in their Criminal Justice program."

"I mean why not FBI, if you're gonna do it, or DEA?"

"Well, for one thing, I liked to smoke grass when I was younger, so DEA didn't appeal to me at all. Secret Service guys I met were so fucking secretive, you ask them a question, they'd go, 'You'll have to check with Washington on that.' See, different federal agents would come to school to give talks. I got to know a couple of marshals—we'd go out after, have a few beers, and I liked them. They're nice guys, condescending at first, naturally; but after a few years they got over it."

Carl was making drinks now, Early Times for Karen, Dewar's in his glass, both with a splash. Standing at the sink, letting the faucet run, he said, "What do you do?"

"I'm on court security this week. My regular assignment is warrants. We go after fugitives, most of them parole violators."

Carl handed her a drink. "Murderers?"

"If they were involved in a federal crime when they did it. Usually drugs."

"Bank robbery, that's federal, isn't it?"

"Yeah, some guys come out of corrections and go right back to work."

"You catch many?"

"Bank robbers?" Karen said, "Nine out of ten," looking right at him.

Carl raised his glass. "Cheers."

While they were having dinner at the kitchen table he said, "You're quiet this evening."

"I'm tired, I was on my feet all day, with a shotgun."

"I can't picture that," Carl said. "You don't look like a U.S. marshal, or any kind of cop."

"What do I look like?"

"A knockout. You're the best-looking girl I've ever been this close to. I got a pretty close look at Mary Elizabeth Mastrantonio, when they were shooting *Scarface*? But you're a lot better looking. I like your freckles."

"I used to be loaded with them."

"You have some gravy on your chin. Right here."

Karen touched it with her napkin. She said, "I'd like to see your boat."

He was chewing pot roast and had to wait before saying, "I told you it was out of the water?"

"Yeah?"

"I don't have the boat anymore. It was repossessed when I fell behind in my payments."

"The bank sold it?"

"Yeah, Florida Southern. I didn't want to tell you when we first met. Get off to a shaky start."

"But now that you can tell me I've got gravy on my chin . . ."

"I didn't want you to think I was some kind of loser."

"What've you been doing since?"

"Working as a mate, up at Haulover."

"You still have your place, your apartment?"

"Yeah, I get paid, I can swing that, no problem."

"I have a friend in the marshals lives in North Miami, on Alamanda off a Hundred and twenty-fifth."

Carl nodded. "That's not far from me."

"You want to go out after?"

"I thought you were tired."

"I am."

"Then why don't we stay home?" Carl smiled. "What do you think?"

"Fine."

They made love in the dark. He wanted to turn the lamp on, but Karen said no, leave it off.

Geraldine Regal, the first teller at Sun Federal on Kendall Drive, watched a man with slicked-back hair and sunglasses fishing in his inside coat pocket as he approached her window. It was 9:40, Tuesday morning. At first she thought the guy was Latin. Kind of cool, except that up close his hair looked shellacked, almost metallic. She wanted to ask him if it hurt. He brought papers, deposit slips, and a blank check from the pocket saying, "I'm gonna make this out for four thousand." Began filling out the check and said, "You hear about the woman trapeze artist, her husband's divorcing her?"

Geraldine said she didn't think so, smiling, because it was a little weird, a customer she'd never seen before telling her a joke.

"They're in court. The husband's lawyer asks her, 'Isn't it true that on Monday, March the fifth, hanging from the trapeze upside down, without a net, you had sex with the ringmaster, the lion tamer, two clowns, and a dwarf?'"

Geraldine waited. The man paused, head down as he finished making out the check. Now he looked up.

"The woman trapeze artist thinks for a minute and says, 'What was that date again?'"

Geraldine was laughing as he handed her the check, smiling as she saw it was a note written on a blank check, neatly printed in block letters, that said:

THIS IS NO JOKE
IT'S A STICKUP!
I WANT $4000 *NOW*!

Geraldine stopped smiling. The guy with the metallic hair was telling her he wanted it in hundreds, fifties, and twenties, loose, no bank straps or rubber bands, no bait money, no dye packs, no bills off the bottom of the drawer, and he wanted his note back. Now.

"The teller didn't have four grand in her drawer," Daniel Burdon said, "so the guy settled for twenty-eight hundred and was out of there. Slick changing his style—we *know* it's the same guy, with the shiny hair? Only now he's the Joker. The trouble is, see, I ain't Batman."

Daniel and Karen Sisco were in the hallway outside the central courtroom on the second floor, Daniel resting his long frame against the railing, where you could look below at the atrium with its fountain and potted palms.

"No witness to see him hop in his BMW this time. The man coming to realize that was dumb, using his own car."

Karen said, "Or it's not Carl Tillman."

"You see him last night?"

"He came over."

"Yeah, how was it?"

Karen looked up at Daniel's deadpan expression. "I told him I was a federal agent and he didn't freak."

"So he's cool, huh?"

"He's a nice guy."

"Cordial. Tells jokes robbing banks. I talked to the people at Florida Southern, where he had his boat loan? Found out he was seeing one of the tellers. Not at the main office, one of their branches, girl named Kathy Lopez. Big brown eyes, cute as a puppy, just started working there. She's out with Tillman she tells him about her job, what she does, how she's counting money all day. I asked was Tillman interested, want to know anything in particular? Oh, yeah, he wanted to know what she was supposed to do if the bank ever got robbed. So she tells him about dye packs, how they work, how she gets a two-hundred-dollar bonus if she's ever robbed and can slip one in with the loot. The next time he's in, cute little Kathy Lopez shows him one, explains how you walk out the door with a pack of fake twenties? A half minute later the tear gas blows and you have that red shit all over you and the money you stole. I checked the reports on the other robberies he pulled? Every one of them he said to the teller, no dye packs or that bait money with the registered serial numbers."

"Making conversation," Karen said, trying hard to maintain her composure. "People like to talk about what they do."

Daniel smiled.

And Karen said, "Carl's not your man."

"Tell me why you're so sure."

"I know him. He's a good guy."

"Karen, you hear yourself? You're telling me what you feel, not what you know. Tell me about *him*—you like the way he dances, what?"

Karen didn't answer that one. She wanted Daniel to leave her alone.

He said, "Okay, you want to put a wager on it, you say Tillman's clean?"

That brought her back, hooked her, and she said, "How much?"

"You lose, you go out dancing with me."

"Great. And if I'm right, what do I get?"

"My undying respect," Daniel said.

As soon as Karen got home she called her dad at Marshall Sisco Investigations and told him about Carl Tillman, the robbery suspect in her life, and about Daniel Burdon's confident, condescending, smart-ass, irritating attitude.

Her dad said, "Is this guy colored?"

"Daniel?"

"I *know* he is. Friends of mine at Metro-Dade call him the white man's Burdon, on account of he gets on their nerves always being right. I mean your guy. There's a running back in the NFL named Tillman. I forget who he's with."

Karen said, "You're not helping any."

"The Tillman in the pros is colored—the reason I asked. I think he's with the Bears."

"Carl's white."

"Okay, and you say you're crazy about him?"

"I like him, a lot."

"But you aren't sure he isn't doing the banks."

"I said I can't believe he is."

"Why don't you ask him?"

"Come on—if he is he's not gonna tell me."

"How do you know?"

She didn't say anything and after a few moments her dad asked if she was still there.

"He's coming over tonight," Karen said.

"You want me to talk to him?"

"You're not serious."

"Then what'd you call me for?"

"I'm not sure what to do."

"Let the FBI work it."

"I'm supposed to be helping them."

"Yeah, but what good are you? You want to believe the guy's clean. Honey, the only way to find out if he is, you have to assume he isn't. You know what I'm saying? Why does a person rob banks? For money, yeah. But you have to be dumb, too, considering the odds against you, the security, cameras taking your picture. . . . So another reason could be the risk involved, it turns him on. The same reason he's playing around with you. . . ."

"He isn't playing around."

"I'm glad I didn't say, 'Sucking up to get information, see what you know.'"

"He's never mentioned banks." Karen paused. "Well, he might've once."

"You could bring it up, see how he reacts. He gets sweaty, call for backup. Look, whether he's playing around or loves you with all his heart, he's still risking twenty years. He doesn't know if you're on to him or not and that heightens the risk. It's like he thinks he's Cary Grant stealing jewels from the broad's home where he's having dinner, in his tux. But your guy's still dumb if he robs banks. You know all that. Your frame of mind, you just don't want to accept it."

"You think I should draw him out. See if I can set him up."

"Actually," her dad said, "I think you should find another boyfriend."

Karen remembered Christopher Walken in *The Dogs of War* placing his gun on a table in the front hall—the doorbell ringing—and laying a newspaper over the gun before he opened the door. She remembered it because at one time she was in love with Christopher Walken, not even caring that he wore his pants so high.

Carl reminded her some of Christopher Walken, the way he smiled with his eyes. He came a little after seven. Karen had on khaki shorts and a T-shirt, tennis shoes without socks.

"I thought we were going out."

They kissed and she touched his face, moving her hand lightly over his skin, smelling his after-shave, feeling the spot where his right earlobe was pierced.

"I'm making drinks," Karen said. "Let's have one and then I'll get ready." She started for the kitchen.

"Can I help?"

"You've been working all day. Sit down, relax."

It took her a couple of minutes. Karen returned to the living room with a drink in each hand, her leather bag hanging from her shoulder. "This one's yours." Carl took it and she dipped her shoulder to let the bag slip off and drop to the coffee table. Carl grinned.

"What've you got in there, a gun?"

"Two pounds of heavy metal. How was your day?"

They sat on the sofa and he told her how it took almost four hours to land an eight-foot marlin, the leader wound around its bill. Carl said he worked his tail off hauling the fish aboard and the guy decided he didn't want it.

Karen said, "After you got back from Kendall?"

It gave him pause.

"Why do you think I was in Kendall?"

Carl had to wait while she sipped her drink.

"Didn't you stop by Florida Southern and withdraw twenty-eight hundred?"

That got him staring at her, but with no expression to speak of. Karen thinking, Tell me you were somewhere else and can prove it.

But he didn't; he kept staring.

"No dye packs, no bait money. Are you still seeing Kathy Lopez?"

Carl hunched over to put his drink on the coffee table and sat like that, leaning on his thighs, not looking at her now as Karen studied his profile, his elegant nose. She looked at his glass, his prints all over it, and felt sorry for him.

"Carl, you blew it."

He turned his head to look at her past his shoulder. He said, "I'm leaving," pushed up from the sofa and said, "If this is what you think of me . . ."

Karen said, "Carl, cut the shit," and put her drink down. Now, if he picked up her bag, that would cancel out any remaining doubts. She watched him pick up her bag. He got the Beretta out and let the bag drop.

"Carl, sit down. Will you, please?"

"I'm leaving. I'm walking out and you'll never see me again. But first . . ." He made her get a knife from the kitchen and cut the phone line in there and in the bedroom.

He *was* pretty dumb. In the living room again he said, "You know something? We could've made it."

Jesus. And he had seemed like such a cool guy. Karen watched him go to the front door and open it before turning to her again.

"How about letting me have five minutes? For old times' sake."

It was becoming embarrassing, sad. She said, "Carl, don't you understand? You're under arrest."

He said, "I don't want to hurt you, Karen, so don't try to stop me." He went out the door.

Karen walked over to the chest where she dropped her car keys and mail coming in the house: a bombé chest by the front door, the door still open. She laid the folded copy of the *Herald* she'd placed there, over her Sig Sauer .38, picked up the pistol, and went out to the front stoop, into the yellow glow of the porch light. She saw Carl at his car now, its white shape pale against the dark street, only about forty feet away.

"Carl, don't make it hard, okay?"

He had the car door open and half turned to look back. "I said I don't want to hurt you."

Karen said, "Yeah, well . . ." raised the pistol to rack the slide and cupped her left hand under the grip. She said, "You move to get in the car, I'll shoot."

Carl turned his head again with a sad, wistful expression. "No, you won't, sweetheart."

Don't say ciao, Karen thought. Please.

Carl said, "Ciao," turned to get in the car, and she shot him. Fired a single round at his left thigh and hit him where she'd aimed, in the fleshy part just below his butt. Carl howled and slumped inside against the seat and the steering wheel, his leg extended straight out, his hand gripping it, his eyes raised with a bewildered frown as Karen approached. The poor dumb guy looking at twenty years, and maybe a limp.

Karen felt she should say something. After all, for a few days there they were as intimate as two people can get. She thought about it for several moments, Carl staring up at her with rheumy eyes. Finally Karen said, "Carl, I want you to know I had a pretty good time, considering."

It was the best she could do.